W9-BZP-803

HOUSE OF SHADOWS

HOUSE OF SHADOWS

Iris Gower

severn House

HARRISON COUNTY
PUBLIC LIBRARY
105 North Capitol Ave.
Corydon, IN 47112

This first world edition published 2010
in Great Britain and in the USA by
SEVERN HOUSE PUBLISHERS LTD of
9–15 High Street, Sutton, Surrey, England, SM1 1DF.
Trade paperback edition published
in Great Britain and the USA 2010 by
SEVERN HOUSE PUBLISHERS LTD

Copyright © 2010 by Iris Gower.

All rights reserved.
The moral right of the author has been asserted.

British Library Cataloguing in Publication Data

Gower, Iris.
  House of Shadows.
  1. Women artists – Fiction. 2. Women household employees –
  Crimes against – Fiction. 3. Suicide victims – Fiction.
  4. Wales – Fiction. 5. Suspense fiction.
  I. Title
  823.9'14-dc22

ISBN-13: 978-0-7278-6907-4   (cased)
ISBN-13: 978-1-84751-250-5   (trade paper)

Except where actual historical events and characters are being
described for the storyline of this novel, all situations in this
publication are fictitious and any resemblance to living persons
is purely coincidental.

All Severn House titles are printed on acid-free paper.

Severn House Publishers support The Forest Stewardship Council [FSC],
the leading international forest certification organisation. All our titles that
are printed on Greenpeace-approved FSC-certified paper carry the FSC logo.

Mixed Sources
Product group from well-managed
forests and other controlled sources
www.fsc.org Cert no. SA-COC-1565
© 1996 Forest Stewardship Council

FSC

Typeset by Palimpsest Book Production Ltd.,
Grangemouth, Stirlingshire, Scotland.
Printed and bound in Great Britain by
MPG Books Ltd., Bodmin, Cornwall.

ONE

The house should have had a haunted air, but on this fine late-spring day the stonework radiated warmth, the glass in the windows seemed to reflect golden light and there was no mist hanging over the chimney pots. It seemed a fine, normal country mansion, and it was one I coveted. One day I would take out my paints and make a picture of it – my very own Aberglasney. It had an air of peace about it, and I could have hugged it to me – my very own house.

And yet five young girls had died in this house more than twenty years ago, killed, though whether accidentally or intentionally no one knew, for the mystery of their deaths had never been really solved.

Murder was one theory, lead poisoning another, but Edwin Mansel-Atherton, the accused, had killed himself before the trial, so nothing was ever proved one way or another.

I walked in through the open door and stood in the large dusty hall and stared around, wondering where I was supposed to meet Mrs Mansel-Atherton.

And then, drawing me from my reverie, she was there standing before me.

'Are you sure you want to take the old house on, dear Miss Evans?' she said without preamble.

The old lady was odd, dressed in what looked like Victorian-style clothing, with a little lace cap hanging from the back of her head like pictures of Queen Victoria, and she was wearing a warm woollen shawl because, I suspected, the house was so cold. It was hard to believe she was only about seventy years old.

'I'll show you around, shall I?' She was clearly eccentric, but lovely in an old-fashioned way. She smiled sweetly and waved her delicate, ladylike fingers towards the interior of the house.

She took me on a tour of the house. 'This,' she said with a hint of bitterness, 'is the room where the supposed murders took place.'

I looked round the huge bedroom, painted blue halfway up the wall, the top part whitewashed with cracking paint. It was sparsely furnished with a bed and a plain wardrobe and a wash stand – although the room was big enough to fit three or four times as much furniture, I thought – and it was cold. It wasn't a very prepossessing start to my tour of the house, but a sense of excitement washed through me. I wanted Aberglasney.

'I'm sure I want the house, Mrs Mansel-Atherton –' my tone was positive – 'and call me Riana. I'd much prefer it.' I gazed around, imagining it as it would be: a grand house, refurbished, parts of it rebuilt, restored. The grounds were huge, so a nature park, a flower garden, a hotel with swimming pool . . . the possibilities were endless.

'How much do you want for it?' I asked at last, my throat dry. I had very little money; enough, perhaps, for a deposit. The rest would have to come from loans and, hopefully, investments by patrons who liked my rather florid painting style. But I would have it. Aberglasney.

'Well, Mrs Mansel-Atherton?'

She turned her head on one side, peering at me almost coquettishly. 'Beatrice, please. To you, dear Miss Evans, the sum will be what they call derisory, providing I can be here as often as I want.' She showed me a bill of sale – what some people would call a contract – and I gasped at the cheapness of the price of the house.

'"Be here." What do you mean by that?' I asked.

'Just to visit, dear, that's all. I know this will be a good buy for you, but there's a great deal of restoration needed. I want the old place looked after by someone who cares. I have no living relatives, you see, dear; no heirs to take over from me. And remember the American servicemen are still here, which makes selling difficult, but I'm sure they'll soon go home now the war is over. Until those men go away and take their Nissan huts with them the house is not very saleable, you understand?'

I stared at this frail old lady, her skin soft as a rose petal but her eyes shadowed. She had her sad memories; I could see it in those expressive eyes.

'But Mrs Mansel— Beatrice, the price is ridiculously cheap, even so.'

She held up her hand. 'No buts. I know what I want. My solicitor drew up the deeds some time ago. All we have to do is get you to sign them.' The paper was on the desk; she gestured to me to look at it. 'It's all in order, legal and binding. Once you sign it, Aberglasney is yours. Can you live with the ghosts, dear?'

I smiled, humouring the old lady. 'Oh, I can live with ghosts. Don't you worry about me.'

'Then all we need is your signature.'

I took up the pen she offered me, dipped it into the ink pot and signed quickly in case she changed her mind. I could afford the old ruin, but the restoration . . . well, that would be a problem, but one I was sure I could overcome.

Mrs Mansel-Atherton had already signed the bill of sale, even before I had agreed to her conditions. Her signature was bold and flourishing, as if she was young and strong.

'See you soon, dear,' she said cheerily, handing me the paperwork. 'Take it to my solicitor and the house will be legally yours.'

I left Aberglasney reluctantly and climbed into my waiting van – an old ambulance, battered but sound and strong – and as I drove away from my house I wondered if I'd been taken for a fool. The hall, run down though it might be, was such a bargain . . . perhaps too much of a bargain to be true.

And the eccentric old lady wanted to visit when she liked. But still, there was no harm in that. She probably loved the old place, but found it was crumbling away around her. I'd do anything to keep the hall, and I would soon find out if the bill of sale was legally binding when I went to see the solicitor in town later on today.

The solicitor, Mr Jeremy of Jeremy Bevan and Brown, wore a long coat and small glasses. He peered at me, and then at the paper, suspiciously. 'You are rather young, Miss . . .?'

'Evans,' I prompted.

'Ah yes, Miss Evans.' His tone suggested I needed confirmation of who I was. 'Mrs Mansel-Atherton signed this document in my presence,' he said, 'and now you must do the same if this –' he waved the document – 'is to be legally binding.'

'Of course.' I signed again where he indicated and sat back in my chair.

'Right, Miss Evans,' he said. 'You are now the owner of the Mansel-Athertons' house.'

I left the small dusty offices on a cloud and stood in the street watching, without seeing, the big dray horse plod past, the load of beer barrels on the cart rattling ominously.

I put the crisp deeds into my bag and snapped the clasp shut with a firm click; I was now the proud owner of a ruin called Aberglasney and, I giggled to myself, the ghosts of the past.

TWO

The builders were taking over my house; plaster-boards, white-overalled men and ladders seemed to proliferate in the large rooms. Summer had arrived: the sun was shining, the birds were singing in the over-grown gardens and my heart was light.

I was now in debt, it was true, and Mrs Mansel-Atherton – who insisted I called her Beatrice – showed no signs of leaving. When I broached the subject she laughed a deli-cate laugh with her tiny hand over her mouth. I said no more. Perhaps she thought it was part of the deal that she stayed, but she was quiet, unobtrusive, and I never saw her unless I wondered into the blue room. It wasn't her room, but she seemed drawn to it by some mysterious bond, though it was empty and cheerless at the moment. 'But not for long,' I said aloud. It would be decorated and furnished, and one day it would make a lovely guest room.

Occasionally, I saw lights flickering across the landings, and I wondered in amusement if the ghosts of the five maids were at their nightly haunting. Heavens! If I turned the place into a hotel, what a draw the 'ghosts' would be. I'd never seen any maids flitting around in voluminous nightgowns, but then I was a sceptic and didn't expect to see anything of the sort.

Gradually, I learned the story of Beatrice's life. She had married her husband when she was only twenty-one. She had one son who had gone to war and never returned, killed in action. 'So you see, my dear –' she never called me by name – 'I'm just a lost old widow without a soul in the world to care if I'm alive or dead.'

I changed the subject. 'What about the five maids who died, Mrs . . . Beatrice?'

Her small white hands fluttered. 'Oh dear, I thought you might ask about that.' She bent her head and her veil hid her face.

'The story was they were murdered by my husband, Edwin.' She paused. 'It's a lie, of course. Edwin never went near the maids, and to kill all five of them in one night would have taken a more cunning man than my Edwin.' She twisted her fingers together. 'He was to be hanged, you know. So unjust, an innocent man to be hanged for a murder that wasn't even proved to be a murder, but unable to bear the disgrace and the injustice, he shot himself. I'll never rest until his innocence is proved. I always insisted the maids died because of the paint.'

'The paint? Surely that was just a rumour?'

'So they say, but the paint, it always smelled funny to me.' She looked up at me, her eyes brimming with tears. 'I'm sure a smart girl like you could find out for me . . . find out about paint and fumes and things.'

'I don't—' I stopped speaking when I saw the pleading look in Beatrice's eyes. 'Perhaps I could go to the library in Swansea or something,' I said lamely.

She stood up. 'I realize petrol is still in short supply,' she said, 'but there's a good train, you know, into Swansea.' She stood up. 'I think I'll take a turn in the garden, stroll under the yews, sit down for a while and take the air.' She smiled her charming smile. 'I might go away for a few days, dear, so don't worry if you don't see me for a while.'

Strangely enough, I missed her. Not that she ever intruded into my life in any way, but she was always there – sitting in her room or in the blue room where the maids had died.

Curiosity drove me to the library later that week. I'd been to the bank and convinced my manager that I had another sale: one of my paintings was wanted by a rich family in the area. It was only half true; the lady in question had shown an interest in a half-finished painting of Aberglasney. Mr Pruedone, the under manager, sorted out more money, though his mouth was pinched and disapproving of 'lady artists' – who, to his mind, were no better than dilettantes in a man's world – and then, with a sigh of relief, I went out into the noisy street and then into the library.

In the welcome silence of the reading room, I took off my hat and settled to leaf through old newspapers. I was getting bored, until I found the story of the death of the five young girls.

The evidence against Mr Mansel-Atherton was circumstantial. The housekeeper, a Mrs Ward, had seen him outside the blue room that night with something, she knew not what, in his hand. She went on to the landing later and heard gasping and groaning noises. Later still she went into the bedroom to find the maids all dead. Each one of them had their hands against their breasts, nightgowns awry, hair loose and tangled.

Mrs Ward was found to be a woman of impeccable honesty, an ardent churchgoing Christian who would never swear an oath on the Holy Bible unless it was the truth. On this fragile evidence Mr Mansel-Atherton was arrested – and then released on bail because Beatrice Mansel-Atherton had sworn he'd never left her bed that night.

Questions buzzed in my mind, such as: was a doctor called to investigate the scene? Was there medical evidence that the girls had been interfered with? I determined to broach the subject with Beatrice, even though intimacy was a very sensitive issue.

I made some notes and then left the library. Outside, the streets were busy and sunny, and the black thought of murder drifted from my mind as I strolled around Swansea, looking into shops for fabrics for curtains and cushion covers. Gradually, I forgot the ghosts of my house and concentrated on the thrill of plans to restore my mansion.

It was late in the evening when I arrived home. The train journey from Swansea had been a swift one, but the station was a long way from Aberglasney. I had arranged for a car to pick me up, but the road outside the station was empty.

I waited a while and then began to walk, because there was nothing else I could do.

A car passed me, stopped, and then backed rapidly towards me. I thought at first that the car I'd ordered had caught up with me, and I sighed in gratitude. Already, my feet were aching in my new shoes that pinched like the devil.

The dark shape of the car screeched towards me at an

alarming speed, the black heavy wheels bearing down at me, the car bonnet – shiny and black in the rain – looking large and menacing as it hurtled towards me. Whoever was driving the car was trying to hit me!

I took a flying leap and landed in the ditch at the side of the road. Another car was coming towards me, its headlights picking out my startled face in the gloom. The black car zoomed away into the distance, gears grating, wheels spinning.

'Sorry I'm late, madam –' the driver leaned forward from his seat – 'but I seem to have arrived in the nick of time.'

His voice was strangely accented: a trace of American, or Canadian perhaps. Not what I was expecting from a driver of a hired cab. I tried to dust down my skirt; a button had come off my coat and the front bagged out unbecomingly. I'd lost my hat, and I was horrified and puzzled by what had happened.

'Who are you?' I asked suspiciously.

'You hired the car service from the Frazer Car Firm for six thirty outside the station. They phoned the office where I work and said they couldn't make it, so I came instead.'

'And who are you and . . .?'

'I'm Tom Maybury, and I'm working at the air force camp stationed at Aberglasney.'

'Show me some identification,' I demanded, still suspicious.

'Here are my dog tags, miss.'

'My name and destination?'

'Miss Evans, and your address is Aberglasney mansion. Do you want me to open the door for you or not?'

I jerked the door open myself, climbed into the car and sank back thankfully on the creaking leather seat. I was shaken. Who on earth would want to harm me? I had no enemies in the small village; no one knew I was here except for the Americans who were stationed near the perimeter of the grounds.

I breathed a sigh of relief as the car pulled to a halt outside my front door. The thought of the attack still gave me a thrill.

The driver opened the door for me, and I realized I had lost my bag. 'If you'll wait here, I'll go and get some money to pay you.' I realized I was still shaking.

He stood. He was tall and handsome; his hair was unfashionably cut; his clothes, casual as they were, suited him. He seemed to be wearing a worn flying jacket and a scarf.

He smiled. 'It's all right. Just ask for Tom when you next want a ride.' He didn't wait, just added, 'Be safe.' His voice sounded caring, warm and somehow familiar, though where would I have met an American serviceman before?

I sighed and went inside my house. The gas lamps shimmered and popped; the first thing I must do, I thought, is to install electricity. I smiled as the warmth of my house closed around me. I was home and safe.

THREE

Beatrice was still away or I would have talked to her about my mystery attacker. She might have some answers for me. Did someone else want Aberglasney? It hit me then like a deluge of cold water: I'd lost my bag and the deeds were inside. What would be my rights now? Would I still be the owner of the mansion? There had to be a copy at the solicitor's office, I realized. Reassured, I made some tea and sat in the only comfortable room in the house, my bedroom.

As I sat in front of the mirror tying up my hair, I heard strange sounds coming from the blue room. Putting on my dressing gown, I went to find out what it was.

I heard muffled gasps and small cries – the sounds of rape or murder? Trembling, I flung open the door. The room was empty. The window banged open and shut, and intermittently the branches of the just-blossoming cherry tree outside scratched the glass.

I gave a shaky laugh and closed the window. I was beginning to imagine things; I was being foolish, hysterical. I didn't believe in ghosts, did I? I had read the papers in the library, but I'd lost my notes along with my bag and my precious documents when I fell into the ditch. Still, I remembered the account of the five maids being killed, and I shivered.

I went back to bed and closed my ears to any strange sounds I heard, telling myself it was only the wind in the branches.

The next day I walked back to the ditch where I'd fallen. It was a long walk, and I was hot and panting by the time I got there. It took a while to find the spot where I'd dived from the road, and miraculously my bag was there – stuck in the muddy bed of the ditch.

The papers inside were wet but intact, although the

signatures had run. Still, my deeds were safe, and I clutched them to me as I made my way back home.

She was there, Beatrice, sitting in the blue room with the door open, her small hands holding a piece of delicate lace she seemed to be fashioning into a collar. 'They won't bother you now, dear,' she said with a smile. 'I'm back. They always keep away when I'm here.'

I didn't take much notice of what she said. My thoughts were too full of the things that had happened since I'd arrived, and anyway, I didn't really know what she was talking about.

'I went to the library in Swansea the other day,' I said without preliminary. 'I read some of the old newspapers.'

'Not very a convincing story, was it?'

'No.' I knew she was talking about the evidence against her husband. 'It was all circumstantial; not a shred of proof.'

'Except for the bodies, dear. There were the bodies of the five young girls who died.' She looked up at me briefly. 'Go about your business, now; put your plans into action. I can't wait to see what you're going to do to the old place.'

'I'll install electricity next.' I spoke eagerly. 'These gas lights are eerie and inefficient.'

'I'd have the chimneys swept if I were you.' Her voice was mild. 'Clear the house of smells.' Her eyes met mine briefly. 'We don't want you dying off with poisoning, do we?'

She had a point, in view of her suspicions about the paint, by which she probably meant fumes. Sweeping the chimneys should be a priority, but that small item would have to wait until vital changes had been made. I meant to install proper heating and not rely on messy coal. So in the end I just had the main chimney swept – for effect, more than anything – so that the hall, library and sitting room could be used.

I slept well that night: no sounds from the blue room, no branches tapping on the windowpanes. Probably, there was no wind; it was a calm moonlit night. In the early dawn I woke abruptly. There was no sound, and when I drew the curtains the dawn was shedding a rosy light on the untamed gardens.

Dimly, a figure of a man became visible. He was staring up at the house – at my window! – and I drew back quickly. Who was he? Why was he spying on me? I hid behind the curtain, but when I cautiously looked out again the overgrown lawn was empty.

Perhaps I was imagining things. The dawn light was still full of grey shadows, the trees only now beginning to be washed with colour.

I dressed and then went to see Beatrice. She was up already. It was as though she never moved from her chair and never put down her lacework. There was an antiquated bathroom nearby and a tiny staff kitchen, both of which I assume she used though I never ever saw her walking about.

'I'm going to Swansea again,' I said. 'I want to look up some reference books, see what else I can find out about the murders.'

'Not murders, dear,' Beatrice said firmly, 'just deaths by mysterious causes. Please look up the construction of the paint.'

It irritated me the way she went on about the paint. No one died a sudden death because of paint!

'I will,' I said, more to please her than anything.

As I left the grounds I saw one of the American officers smiling at me. I recognized him at once. 'Tom, you're being an officer today then, not a driver?'

He put his finger to his lips. 'That's hush hush. The driving, I mean.' He smiled, and his teeth looked very white against his tanned skin. Tom, I decided, was a very handsome man. 'How are the ghosts behaving?' He winked.

'How do you know about them?'

'Everyone knows about the poor maids who died all on the same night, and everyone knows about the old lady who keeps them in order.'

I shrugged. 'I don't believe in any of it myself. Don't say you do?'

'What was it that Shakespeare guy said about more things in heaven and earth than this world knows of?'

'Not quite correctly quoted, but I get the gist.'

'And?'

'And I've got a train to catch.'

'Going to Swansea? I'll give you a ride if you like.'

I hesitated and then shook my head. 'Thank you, Tom, but I can't afford to pay for a car. That's why I'm walking to the station.'

'Who's talking about paying? I'm going that way so jump in. It's gratis. Free. I'll be glad of the company, for Swansea's a good way off.'

Thankfully, I climbed into the big jeep. What a treat, being driven all the way to Swansea. The rough road to the station was bad enough to manoeuvre, especially with the danger of erratic car drivers on the lanes.

'Were you looking up at the house in the early light, Tom?' I asked as he did some trick with the clutch and the gears and set off through the lanes at an alarming speed.

'Now, why would I want to do that?'

'Any of your soldiers interested in ghosts then? Because some man was standing in the garden staring up at my window, just at dawn it was.'

'I'll check on that,' he said, 'but you know my soldiers are dark skinned Americans. Was this man dark skinned?'

I was confused for a moment. 'No, definitely not. His face was illuminated by the dawn. He was fair, just like you.' I heard the accusing note in my voice and instantly regretted it. 'I'm sorry, I wasn't implying—' I stopped speaking, not knowing how to go on.

'That I was a sort of peeping Tom?' He grinned. 'Excuse the levity.'

'Tom, forget I said anything. It was too dark to see, really. I was probably imagining things.'

'Like ghostly figures carrying lights along the landing in the middle of the night?'

'You've seen them?' I stared at him, and he took my hand. It felt warm and strong and very nice.

'There aren't any ghosts if you don't believe in them.' He lifted my hand to his lips and kissed it, and a shiver ran through me.

I drew my hand away. 'Concentrate on your driving,' I chided, but I was somehow touched by his gesture.

The sun came out, and I relaxed and secretly watched Tom – his foot deftly double-declutching the gears, his strong hands steering the car – and I felt happy and safe. I was quite sorry when at last the jeep stopped outside the library in Swansea.

I found myself longing to kiss Tom on the cheek, but familiarities that had been acceptable during the war were not acceptable now. I jumped out of the jeep, waved an airy hand and quickly walked up the steps into the solemn silence of the library.

FOUR

I was engrossed in my painting of the mansion when I felt a touch on my arm. I had a thrill of excitement and a smile grew on my face, as I thought it must be Tom. Distantly, I'd heard the sounds of shouted orders and the heavy roll of vehicles, and I'd wondered if the troops were moving out. The thought somehow disturbed me.

I turned slowly, my paintbrush arched in my hand . . . the garden around me was empty. I was frightened and shivery for a moment, but then I shrugged. I must have imagined it.

I gazed up at the sun, and a cloud seemed to obscure my vision. I felt my hand move into the paint and on to the canvas in swift, sure strokes. It was like a dream. I painted swiftly, my brush strokes sure, and yet my mind seemed blank, as if I were asleep. And then Tom was there, shaking me.

'Riana, are you all right? Speak to me, honey, speak to me, it's Tom. Are you dreaming? I wanted to tell you I'm going to stay here for a few weeks, although most of my troops are pulling out.'

I came awake and blinked at Tom, seeing the concern in his face. He touched my cheek briefly, and I remembered he'd called me 'honey', but then didn't Americans call everyone honey?

'You were in a dream,' he said, drawing me to a garden bench warmed by the sun. I sat beside him, and he held my hand. I didn't draw away. I felt strange, as though I *had* been asleep.

'Is that what an artist does when they paint?' His voice was gently teasing. 'Have I disturbed some creative mood?'

'No, not at all.' I shook my head. I looked at him and he was so familiar somehow, so warm, so concerned. 'I don't know what came over me. It was as if I'd fallen asleep

HARRISON COUNTY
PUBLIC LiBRARY
105 North Capitol Ave.
Corydon, IN 47112

or something.' I didn't mention the touch on my arm; I must have been too occupied with my work.

'Come to my hut and have a nice hot cup of coffee,' Tom said. 'I've got the pot on the stove.' He smiled as I hesitated. 'I promise not to ravish you.'

'I'm not coming for coffee then,' I said and laughed. Now, what on earth had possessed me to say such a thing? 'I'm joking, of course,' I added hastily.

'Of course.'

I'd never been as far at the huts before. They stood on the perimeter of the gardens, the grass cut now by the soldiers. Great mounds of dug-over earth formed a sort of street between the buildings.

Tom took me into his office, which was in the same makeshift sort of transient building the other huts were.

'No special luxury for the officers then?' I made an effort to laugh. 'Rough it like the privates – is that what Americans believe in?'

'I'm afraid not. We were billeted in the house until it was claimed back. We're not here for long now. As you can see, most of the men have moved out. There are only two left: Flight Officer Dave Smith and Airman Carl Jenkins. They'll stay until I am ready to leave.'

'And when will that be?' I was aware my voice was shaking. I sat in one of the comfortable armchairs in the room and watched Tom pour coffee into enamel mugs.

'I can't be sure. The three of us will pack up any left-over documents, any stray personal belongings, that sort of thing. We'll probably continue to fly on a few missions, but you could say our work here is almost done.'

I tried to think practically. 'And when will the huts be taken away?'

Tom shrugged. 'Don't know that either, sorry. Why? Are they a nuisance to you?'

'I want to begin on the gardens. Would you like to come and see the cloisters? I've made a start there myself.'

'Drink your coffee first and talk to me. Tell me about yourself, Riana Evans, I want to know all about you.'

I felt a warm glow. 'I'd like to know about you too, Tom,'

I said, trying not to sound wistful, 'but soon you'll be going away, remember?'

'Go on,' he said, 'you begin.'

'I'm an only child. My mum is very old and lives in a nursing home now.' I was sad thinking of my mother; she didn't even know me now. 'My father died in the war. He was a doctor. A bomb hit the hospital where he was working and that was it.' I felt tears blur my eyes.

'I was an art student. I loved it all: the big room, the paints, the linseed oil, the seats we used, each with an easel attached – we students called them donkeys. I loved it all. The war changed everything for me, Tom, did you know that?'

'Go on,' he said gently. 'What made you want Aberglasney?'

'I don't really know.' I was thoughtful. 'When I saw the house it felt like coming home. I sold up the family house; it's never been the same without my mother. With the money from the sale of the house, my savings, and the little money I made from my paintings, I had enough to buy me Aberglasney.'

I wondered why I was telling him all my business. I looked up at him. 'I will make a go of it, you know.'

'I believe you.' Tom touched my hand briefly. 'I've seen your work, remember. You're very good, very original. I'm not surprised folk want to buy from such a gifted artist.'

He moved about the small room. He was slim, lithe and very handsome in his officer's uniform. He turned and looked at me, and I wanted him so badly I felt almost ill.

I got up abruptly. 'Come and see the start I've made on the gardens,' I said softly.

Tom followed me from the hut and across the stretch of overgrown gardens to where the cloisters stood out from the surrounding greenery.

'See the arches?' I said. 'Aren't they graceful? They were built in Jacobean times. Isn't that incredible? And there's a walkway above them from where you can see the rest of the grounds.' I walked towards the cloisters and impotently tried to push aside a strong leafed bush. 'These are too difficult for me to cut,' I said, 'but one day I'll be able to afford a gardener, or at least a handyman, and then the arches will be cleared.'

Tom smiled and took my hand. 'I'm quite handy.' He looked down into my eyes; he was very tall.

'I couldn't impose.' He was kissing my hand again. I resisted the urge to rest my hand on his cheek. I wished he would call me honey again because I loved the way he said it, soft and warm and golden like honey itself.

The next morning I heard a noise in the garden, and when I went out I saw that Tom was there with the men left behind from the exodus and they were cutting a swathe through the bushes covering the cloisters.

'Gosh, you've been busy.' I knew I sounded full of admiration, and it was genuine.

'Surprising what a good team of men can do in a few hours.' He winked at me, and I felt a warm silly glow as I watched his strong, bare arms wield the saw.

'You left your painting out all night,' he remarked. 'Lucky it didn't rain, though I think the morning dew has affected the oils a little bit.'

I put my hand over my mouth to stifle the not-too-ladylike expletive I'd been about to give voice to. 'I'd best go and see.'

I hurried through the grass to where I'd left my easel, and at first the painting looked jumbled. In among the windows I could see figures, young girls in mob caps and ribbon-trimmed linen gowns. Behind them was an older figure wearing a blouse with overblown sleeves, such as Beatrice wore. Carefully, I counted the figures: five girls and an older woman. Ghosts?

'Don't be stupid,' I said to myself out loud. I sat down on a tree stump and closed my eyes, but when I opened them the painting was just the same: the figures were still there. I remembered then how vague I'd been for a time when I was painting. It was almost as though I'd drifted off to sleep or gone into a trance. I must have been daydreaming, drawing unconsciously, I decided.

The sun was hot above my head. I looked up at the windows of my house, my beloved mansion. The windows were blank. No one was there, no shadows, no strange lights.

I felt a touch on my arm and was almost afraid to turn round, but this time Tom was bending over me. 'Daydreaming again?' he asked.

'Yes, that's exactly what I've been doing.' I smiled. 'Daydreaming.'

FIVE

I sold my painting, including ghosts, to a London gallery, and as I walked out into the war-torn streets of the big city I felt a glow of achievement. This was the first time I'd had a painting taken by anyone other than a provincial gallery.

The owner, Mr Readings, had a buyer who liked old mansions and also liked the idea of hauntings, and the painting was just what he was looking for.

It was Aberglasney, it was bringing me luck. No, it was bringing out my real creativity, I told myself sensibly. Everyone made their *own* luck. As for the ghosts, they existed only in my imagination.

As I was in London, I took the opportunity to go to the library and look through the old newspapers. The mystery had made the London papers, and I found several articles on Aberglasney, on the deaths of the five maids who slept in the blue room. Most stories took the line that the girls were murdered; only one cast doubt on the story, citing the evidence as 'circumstantial', lacking in substance, and without a shred of proof to verify the police findings. It made no difference in the end. Beatrice's husband had been blamed for the deaths and had killed himself before he could be charged – all on the evidence of Mrs Ward.

I wanted to know more about this Mrs Ward – upholder of the truth, a paragon of virtue – was anyone that holy and good? I knew there would be very little about her in London, though. My search would have to be carried out in the little village where my house was built. Eventually, I grew tired of the big city and caught a train home.

To my surprise, Tom was waiting for me at Swansea Station. He smiled, and I felt a sharp tug at my heart. I smiled back at him, and he took my hand and led me to the staff car, equipped with a driver.

'Congratulations!' he said as he helped me into the car.

'How did you know I sold a painting?' I settled myself against the warm leather with a sigh of content. Tom sat close to me as the car pulled away along High Street.

'What makes you think I'm talking about a painting?' He was teasing.

'Come on, tell me.'

'I've bought it,' he said softly. 'A piece of you.'

I didn't know what to say. I studied his face, wondering exactly what he meant. He was such a handsome man, a lovely man. Did he like me, desire me, what? I didn't dare ask. In his flying jacket and thick boots, he seemed very official.

I was very aware of his arm close to mine. 'How could you afford to buy my painting? It was very expensive, judging by the money I received from the gallery owner.'

'As an officer in the United States Army Air Forces, I'm well paid. I have no wife, no family to keep, and I wanted the picture.' He touched my hair briefly. 'I saw your painting before it went away to be sold, remember?'

I looked down at my hands, aware of the intimacy of the car. We were close together, and for the first time in my life I felt desire for a man, real desire that burned in me. What was wrong with me? I hardly knew Tom, he was from America, and soon he would return home and I would be alone again. Best not to become too involved. In any case, I had Aberglasney to think about and, of course, the ghosts.

'Thank you for buying my painting,' I said primly and moved slightly away from him. 'The money will be a great help.'

'What's wrong?' Tom asked. 'Didn't you want me to have the painting?'

He seemed to look right into my head. I shrugged.

'I know the gallery wants more of them,' he said. 'I spoke to the owner. I'd like more myself, but the one I already have is wonderful.'

'I'm flattered you like it, but I didn't know you had any interest in the mansion except as a stopover while you did your service in the forces.'

'Some of my folks are from this area.' Tom's voice was cool. 'I'm interested in finding out about them, but if I'm presuming too much, intruding into your life, I can only apologize.'

'No, no.' I sounded weak. I shut up and sank back into the seat. It seemed *I* was presuming too much; Tom wasn't interested in me, just in his Welsh heritage. He only wanted the painting because it was a bit of background for him. I'd been flattering myself that he liked me.

'What's wrong, honey?' His gentle voice penetrated my thoughts. 'You've gone away from me. Now you're some-where I can't reach.'

'It's nothing. I was just wondering where your family were from.'

'Around here somewhere,' he said. 'I asked to be posted here when I knew I was coming abroad on service.' He sighed. 'I love this old house. It seems familiar to me now, as if I've always known it.' I could hear the smile in his voice when he spoke again. 'We officers were billeted here before you bought the house.'

'And Beatrice, was she here too?'

'Beatrice? No one was here – except the ghosts, of course.'

'You believe in ghosts?' I was surprised and it showed.

'Oh yes, I believe in ghosts . . . if it's only the ghosts from our past. Ghosts of people we've loved, lived with or never known. A bit of our past is always with us in the colour of our hair, the way we walk, or the turn of the head or the way we talk. Oh yes, the past lives on in all of us, so yes, we live with the ghosts of memory every day.'

'I didn't quite mean anything so profound by my painting, so why did I paint those figures in when I didn't actually see them?'

'I suppose they call that creativity.' His voice was smooth, golden, and I knew I would miss the sound of his voice when he went away.

'When will you be leaving here?' My question was blunt, but suddenly the answer was very important to me.

'Are you that anxious to get rid of me?' His voice was teasing.

I smiled. 'Not at all. I'll miss you when you go, that's all.' I turned to look at him, and then his lips were on mine, briefly but so sweetly. I hid my surprise very well, but I was warm and full of emotion. I was acting like a girl, a girl kissed for the very first time, and that's exactly how I felt.

The car pulled up outside the mansion and Tom hurried round to open the car door for me.

'Tom, would you like to come up this evening for a drink and perhaps look at some of my other paintings?' It sounded like an old line from a film actress, *come up and see me sometime*. I waved my hand. 'I'm sure you're far too busy.'

'I am, I'm sorry. An air force briefing, that sort of thing.'

I felt silly, then, and inept; too anxious for his company. 'Of course. Another time then.' I hurried indoors and closed myself inside the hall. My face was burning.

'My dear, what on earth is wrong?' Beatrice was coming towards me. Her clothes, as usual, were immaculately pressed and starched. How on earth did she manage it?

'Nothing, I've just made an ass of myself.'

'My dear, what an inelegant expression. I suppose you are talking about making a fool of yourself over a man?'

'I just offered an invitation, and I was turned down.'

'Come and tell me all about it, Riana.' Beatrice floated up the stairs, and I followed her, knowing she was only comfortable in her own room. She settled into her chair, as dainty as a butterfly landing on a flower. 'Now, talk to Beatrice,' she coaxed. 'Perhaps I can be of some help.'

'It's the American officer Tom. I clumsily invited him in, and he said he was busy. I've really shown myself to be too eager, haven't I?'

'Tom,' Beatrice said softly. 'Tom. I've seen him around, haven't I? He helped clear the area round the cloisters.'

'That's right, but I thought you were away then.'

'I'm never far from Aberglasney, my dear. Look, this Tom, he's a colonial, not of our race, dear. You'll meet some fine gentleman who will be a worthy master of Aberglasney, I'm sure of it.'

I swallowed my anger. I didn't want a 'master'. I was 'mistress' of the mansion, it was mine, and I didn't want to share it with any man. Except, perhaps, Tom, a little voice said inside my head. I brushed the thought away.

'I've decided,' I said abruptly, 'that I'll take some paintings up to London tomorrow. Just one or two small ones I can carry on the train, and if the gallery is interested they can send someone down to see the bigger pieces.'

'But, my dear, why rely on that sort of difficult venture? You are a clever, modern educated lady. Think of some sound business venture that will raise money. I know you can do it, otherwise I wouldn't have let you have the house.'

I nodded thoughtfully. Beatrice was right. Painting was slow and chancy work. It did bring in good money when a work sold, but it wasn't a solid income. I would have to think of something else.

'I'll go away and think,' I said. 'I had imagined making it into a superior country hotel.' At the door, I turned to look at the tiny lady sitting calmly in her chair.

'What about ghost weekends?' She smiled wickedly. 'I'm sure I could persuade some ghosts to show themselves.'

'That's a very good idea, Beatrice. Or perhaps I could teach painting and drawing,' I said, 'but that's not really art, is it?'

'Children are too messy, and there are all sorts of rules and regulations regarding housing children, aren't there?'

'I suppose so. I'll think about it, the ghost idea, Beatrice. It would be good to have adult company, more amusing and more stimulating. I would have to make the bedrooms liveable in first though.'

I went downstairs to the kitchen and put the kettle on the stove. I could really do with a cup of tea, I thought, and a chance to sit down and work out some figures. Perhaps I could do up some of the bedrooms with the money from my paintings? So far I'd only concentrated on the downstairs rooms.

I drunk the hot tea gratefully and sat at the scrubbed

wooden table to make some notes. People were short of money in these difficult times, food was still rationed and Beatrice was right; her ghost idea was beginning to grow on me. I dipped my pen into the ink and began to write.

SIX

London was bustling as usual, with rag and bone carts mingled with army vehicles and the latest sleek modern cars. There was money about, I decided, but how to attract the well-off to Aberglasney was the problem.

The gallery was busy, and I stood awkwardly with my canvases waiting for Mr Readings to come to speak to me. At last, he did. He smiled and took my painting with an apology for the delay. He placed my paintings on an easel and stood back, his fingers stroking his chin.

Meanwhile, I spotted all the faults I should have seen before: the angle of the roof, the colour of the grass.

Mr Readings spoke. 'Not bad, dear Miss Evans, but I think there's something lacking. Ah –!' he clicked his fingers – 'the ghostliness is missing, the mysterious figures wrapped in mist. That was what made your other painting special.'

'But a friend bought my other painting. He knew Aberglasney, knew about the ghosts, knew about everything.'

'Ghosts! We must have them, dear. Come back to me with ghosts and we'll talk.' He turned away to another customer.

Disappointed, I took my paintings back on the train with me. It had been a fruitless journey. I'd just wasted money going to London, and now I had nothing to help my plans along: no ideas, no money and two useless paintings.

At home, I lit the fire in the little sitting room and sat there alone, trying to think. After a while, my thoughts became jumbled. I realized I was hungry and made some tea and toast, which made me feel a little less lethargic.

Later, I wandered into my studio – an airy room, half walls and half glass – and stared at my pictures helplessly. I had no idea how to change them.

There was a knock on the front door, and my heart began

to beat faster. It surely must be Tom. No one else knew or cared that I now lived in Aberglasney. To my disappointment, the caller was one of Tom's men. He was very handsome, with dark skin and curly hair, and had the same soft American accent as Tom. Though the weather was mild, he wore a stout pilot's jacket of leather and fur.

He handed me a bottle covered in dust. 'My senior officer sent this for you, Miss Evans.' He bowed politely.

I took the bottle and saw it was a fifty-year-old brandy. 'Thank you, and please thank . . . your officer.' I realized I didn't know Tom's surname. 'Is he calling on me tonight?'

The pilot raised his cap. 'That I don't know, ma'am. Goodnight to you.'

I felt embarrassed as I closed the door. How cheap I must seem, hopeful, almost desperate. I decided I'd go to bed early and take a tot of the brandy with me.

It was cosy in bed with the oil light flickering and the thick quilt pulled up to my shoulders. I sipped the brandy, sweetened with honey, and consoled myself with the knowledge that Tom had at least thought of me.

Eventually, I put out the lamp and settled down to sleep, feeling light-headed and warmed by the liquor, but much as I wrestled with the problems of money and the paintings during the night, I didn't come up with any answers. And all night the ghosts plagued me.

The sounds from the blue room were abominable: strangled cries, bangs, thumps, and the opening and shutting of doors. In the end, I jumped out of bed and went to the bedroom. There was no sign of Beatrice; goodness knows where she'd gone.

'Will you shut up and be quiet!' I shouted in exasperation. 'If you don't keep quiet, I'll call in an exorcist!'

The noise subsided.

'That's it!' I said out loud, excitement bubbling inside me. 'That's it, Beatrice was right! I'll organize ghost hunts. Put people up for the night and charge them exorbitant fees.' I smiled round the room. 'Thanks, girls.'

I thought I heard a giggle as I closed the door and went to my studio. My poor old imagination had gone into overdrive.

I squeezed out some oils and began to paint in the shadowy figures: five girls in simple cotton nightgowns, with floating hair. I brushed in a mist behind them that blotted out part of the house, but the haze of greyish fog surrounding them was somehow effective.

At last, without bothering to clear up, I went back to bed, but I couldn't sleep. I kept thinking of the farms I could visit to buy eggs and butter and chickens and potatoes, and perhaps I could name the whole thing a 'ghost-hunting' or even a 'ghost-haunting' weekend. I was jubilant, and I didn't fall asleep until dawn was poking rosy fingers through the curtains.

The painting sold the next day. Mr Readings of the London gallery was greatly impressed.

'My dear Miss Evans, this is your signature. Your ghostly paintings give you an individuality other artists do not have.' He paused, examining the painting in the light from the window. 'Your strength is the spirit world, my dear. Did you know that?'

I didn't mention that the 'spirit world' had kept me awake all night – or was it the brandy?

I smiled. 'I'm so glad you like the work. Shall I paint some more?'

'Larger, my dear, you must have a larger canvas. Go inside the house. Paint the landings, flickering lights, that sort of thing. Be more . . . what shall we say? Misty, that's the word! Chilling. You are the artist; use your wonderful imagination.'

He came with me to the door.

'I shall expect another canvas in a week or two, Miss Evans.'

With money in my hand, quite a large sum of money, I went to a coffee house. I was lucky to find one that wasn't flattened to the ground by the war, and I sat alone with thoughts racing through my head. A few more paintings and I could refurbish some of the bedrooms, put in another bathroom on the second landing. Soon, very soon, I could begin to really work at my plans.

I would have to advertise my weekends in the local

newspapers at first and then further afield – Cardiff, Bristol, even London. I drank my coffee; there was no sugar and the milk was slightly tangy, but it tasted like nectar to me as I played happily with my ideas.

After coffee, I walked back along the street, past the gallery, and to my surprise my painting was already in the window. The price made me gasp; it was about time I negotiated a better payment from Mr Readings for my work.

I went home on the train, and when I arrived at Swansea I felt disappointed that Tom wasn't there to meet me. But why should he be? He didn't even know I'd been to London.

All at once my elation vanished. Tom was keeping away from me and it hurt.

SEVEN

I tried all week to paint the blue room, but somehow the essence of it escaped me. Beatrice fluttered around the landings like a ghost herself, scarcely making any noise but grumping as she looked at my futile attempts at painting.

At last I put down my brush in exasperation. 'What on earth is it, Beatrice? You sound like one of the bulls in the farmer's field! What are you hanging around me for?'

'You're not doing it right,' she said, her hands on her tiny hips, her chin lifted and her ballooning sleeves making patterns against the light from the windows.

Seized by a sudden inspiration I began to paint Beatrice. Her outline against the light was hazy, her lifted chin a proud silhouette. I etched her face like a cameo, the only distinct feature in the painting. Behind her I painted in a misty, indistinct room with blue walls and the outline of five beds with wraithlike figures sitting, standing and reclining on them.

I don't know how long I stood painting, but at last, with the daylight fading, I dropped my brush. 'Oh, dear lord Beatrice, have you put a spell on me?'

'You've forgotten the pot-bellied stove,' she said, her voice weak, and I realized she, too, must be very tired.

'Stove?' I looked into the blue room, trying to imagine how it must have been years ago. I picked up my brush and dipped it into the paint and picked up grey, white and deep blue oils. I drew a faint outline of a stove in the corner of the room. I stood back then. 'You're a genius, Beatrice! It's just what the painting needed.'

But Beatrice was at the door of the blue room, and I could see it as it really was: refurbished, bright but still blue, with only one bed in the room now, and old but smart Regency striped curtains and covers. The door to the blue room closed, and I carefully carried my canvas to the studio and set it against the wall to dry.

That night when I walked in the garden I smiled. Tom
and his men had made a good job of clearing the long
grass and bushes under the cloisters.

In the shadow of one of the cloister arches I found a
bench smelling of newly carved pine and guessed that one
of Tom's men had made it for me. I sat down, and then I
saw his familiar figure walking towards me, illuminated
now by a bright moon. My pulse quickened.

Tom sat beside me, and it was thrilling and comforting
to have his arm next to mine.

'Evening, Tom.' My voice was low, throaty.

'Tired, honey? Been working hard?'

'I finished work about an hour ago.'

'Just as well my men made you a seat then.'

'It's lovely,' I said, feeling the warmth of him next to me
and revelling in it. Tom had such a lovely voice, a golden
syrup sort of voice, smooth and devastating.

'This work you spoke of. Does it involve painting?' He
sat beside me, still and quiet, his voice lowered, blending
in with the subdued sounds of the night.

'It does, as it happens,' I said equally softly.

'What is it about?'

'Would you like to come and see?' I offered the invitation and immediately regretted it; now he'd think me fast.

'I'd love to.' He stood up and held his hand out to me.
I let him lead me to the house, wondering how I could tell
him that the invitation was simply that – a few minutes to
view my latest work. 'I'd like your opinion,' I said breathlessly. 'The gallery man suggested an indoor painting on
a large canvas. I wasn't sure at first and then—'

He stopped my nervous flow. 'It's all right,' he said. 'I'd
love to see the painting. I won't stay long. I don't want
to . . . What is the word you English use? "Compromise"
you, that's it. I wouldn't sully your reputation, not for
anything.'

I felt myself blush, and I left the front door open as I
went into the house. My studio was at the top of the building.
As we passed the blue room all was silent; I guessed Beatrice
had gone to bed. I was relieved, for I didn't know what

she'd make of me leading a man upstairs in the dead of night, like some wanton hussy.

Tom stood in silence staring at my painting, and even I was amazed and moved by the power in what I had done. The figure of Beatrice seemed to move against the backdrop of hazy light. Behind her, the stove, softly sketched in, threw out a remarkable glow of light, and the ghostly figures merged like real ghosts into the darkness at the rear of the blue room.

Tom took a sharp breath. 'That's brilliant, Riana.' It was the first time he'd been so familiar. 'You're really talented.'

I was flushed and happy with his praise. 'I think it's the house,' I said. 'Aberglasney has done something to me, given me peace, I don't know what it is.'

He took me in his arms then and kissed me, a real kiss, his mouth lingering on mine. I stood there like a lifeless doll. I'd never been in love. I'd never really kissed any man except my father. I'd played 'kiss chase' when we were children and when kissing the boys had been more of a laugh than anything, but this was different. It was as if I'd been brought alight; a glow filled me, colouring the world just like the flames from the imagined stove coloured my painting. *My painting*. Had *I* really done that?

I stood in the shelter of Tom's arms, and we both stared at the painting and then at each other.

'I think I'm falling in love with you, Riana,' he said softly.

'I hardly dare believe you.'

He sighed heavily. 'I really mean it, honey.'

I sensed a hesitation in his voice. 'Then what's wrong?'

'It can't come to anything.'

He released me, and I stood back away from him. 'Did you lie to me, Tom? Are you married after all?'

He shook his head, and a shock of hair fell over his forehead. 'It's not that . . . but you have a bright future here in England, while I . . . Well, I have my life in America and I'll have to go home soon, we both know that.'

His reference to America as 'home' upset me, but he was right – there was no future for us together. He was a pilot, he had his career to think of, and I . . . Well, I had Aberglasney. It would take all my strength and ingenuity to bring it back to its former glory.

I wanted the house and I wanted to succeed at my painting. There was no way I could abandon everything and go away with Tom, even if he asked me to – and he hadn't.

I led the way down the stairs and into the vast, half restored kitchen, gestured for Tom to sit down, and then made us both a cup of coffee. I made it hot and strong and black, just as I knew Tom liked it.

'You are so talented, Riana.' Tom smiled and my heart melted. I wanted to fling myself at him, tell him to love me, make love to me, but young ladies didn't do anything as forward as throw themselves at a man. The war was over; those days when young people grasped at life in case there was no tomorrow had gone. Times had changed now, and women were more circumspect.

I had seen the sad results of abandoned love affairs. Men gone back to their respectable lives after the danger of war was over. Weeping British girls left behind, sometimes with child, when their American and Canadian lovers went home.

'Drink up,' I said, unintentionally brisk. 'It's about time I got myself to bed. I've got a long day tomorrow.'

Tom stood. 'Going to London?'

'I might,' I prevaricated. 'I'll have to do a small study of the painting to show the gallery owner, I suppose. I can hardly transport a large canvas all that way without the certainty of a sale.' I led the way to the door. 'Night, Tom.'

I stood watching his tall figure stride away along the drive towards the barracks, and then I slowly climbed the stairs with tears running down my face, not knowing what I was crying for.

EIGHT

The morning sun slanted across the gallery from the big window; the light was why I'd chosen this room for my studio. A sheet hung across the large canvas, and I frowned when I noticed it. I didn't remember putting it there; for all I knew the paint was still tacky.

Carefully, I lifted the cloth and stood back with a cry of dismay. The canvas had been slashed from edge to edge so that a gaping hole hung in the middle of the painting, completely destroying the ghostly mist and the faint image of the dead girls.

I sat on my little stool near the window and stared out at the garden without seeing the cloisters, cleared now of bushes, or the garden, made neat by the Americans, or the clear sky. All I felt was despair and the pain of loss.

I had put my heart into that painting. I could almost say I'd been inspired. I could try to paint it again for I had the little study I'd done, but I knew it would never be the same work; it would never have the same ghostly atmosphere of the original.

I went to look for Tom. It seemed the natural thing to do because Tom would know a little of how I was feeling.

Tom wasn't there, he was flying, and my heart missed a beat. I knew Tom was still a working American airman, but I'd never thought of him facing danger – not now the war was over.

'It's only a training mission,' his second in command, Carl Jenkins, assured me. Disconsolately, I walked back to the mansion. *I must get to work*, I thought. *I need paintings to make more money if I intend to get my ghost weekends under way.*

I squeezed out the paints on to the palette, but for once I had no idea what to paint. The sunlight streamed into the room, hurting my eyes. I looked at the unused mounds of oil and knew they would dry and harden and be wasted and I couldn't afford to waste anything.

I began to paint, but nothing was going right. In my frustration, I threw down my brush. I wandered out into the garden again and sat in the shadow of the cloisters. I closed my eyes, dazzled by the sunlight that suddenly burst into my little nest beneath the arch. I think I slept, because next thing I knew Tom was sitting at my side.

'You were looking for me?' His honey-sweet voice washed over me like a balm. He was safely home from flying, and suddenly I wanted to hug him. Instead, I told him about the painting.

'Show me,' he said. He took my hand and led me upstairs; he knew the house as well as I did. It was shady now in the gallery, the sun slanting away to the west where it would sink behind the hills and illuminate them with brushes of gold.

I lifted the cloth over the canvas and stared in disbelief. The painting was intact, no terrible slashes, no holes in the fabric . . . Was I dreaming?

'What's this, Riana?' Tom asked. 'If you're trying to lure me upstairs there's no need for dramas.'

'The painting was cut to pieces!' I was indignant, chagrin making me blush to the roots of my hair.

'A trick of the light,' Tom said soothingly, but I could see he didn't believe me. I didn't blame him. I couldn't believe the evidence of my own eyes. Wonderingly, I touched the painting. It was nearly dry.

'It's one of your best,' Tom said. 'You were sleeping in the garden there; it must have all been a dream, the cuts in the canvas. A horrible dream, that's all.'

'No, Tom, I could feel the slashes in the painting. I touched it, it wasn't a dream.'

'A nightmare then.' Tom smiled. 'A daytime nightmare, that's all it was, Riana. Who is here to do such a thing? Who would *want* to destroy your work?'

'Someone who doesn't want the house done up,' I suggested.

'That would hold water if the painting was really

damaged, but it's not, Riana. The whole thing doesn't make any sense.'

I capitulated. 'I know. Let's go and get a drink. A stiff gin or something.'

We took our drinks out into the garden while I tried to fathom the whole thing out. The work on the easel was mine all right, so the cut-up canvas was a fake. But who would go to all that trouble and why? I wished now I'd looked closer at the destroyed canvas, but I'd been too horrified and baffled to examine it properly.

'Penny for them? Isn't that what you British folk say?'

I shook my head, not wanting to seem more foolish than I was. 'My thoughts are just a jumble, Tom. Someone tried to run me off the road when I first came here, and now this. What am I supposed to make of it all – except that someone doesn't want me here?'

'The ghosts?'

'Are you mocking me?'

'Trying to lighten the gloom a bit, Riana. Forget all this. Enjoy the warmth and the drink and, hopefully, the company.'

I looked at him as I sipped my drink. Could he be doing all this to get me out? Was he my enemy, not my friend? But why would he do such a thing? What could he hope to gain?

It was as if he read my thoughts. 'I wouldn't hurt you for the world, Riana. I hope you know that, honey.'

He took my glass out of my hand and put it on the floor, then he deliberately kissed me. My arms crept around him, my dear safe Tom. He was the one who had rescued me on the roadway; what was I thinking of being suspicious of the only friend I had in the world?

I pulled away just before I became swamped with passion, for I didn't want a lover, not just now. In any case, Tom's life was in America. What was the point in getting involved with him?

'I'll going indoors now, it's getting dark –' I shivered – 'and chilly. Goodnight, Tom, and thanks for being a friend.'

He stood up straight away and strode into the darkness.

I supposed I'd offended him, but that was just too bad. I could do without an involvement of any kind I had a living to make and a career to forge and a grand scheme to work out. My house would be ready for visitors any day now.

NINE

It was the end of July, and it was my opening night in more ways than one. My paintings had gone on display in the London gallery – just a small selection – and my house was open for the first 'ghost-haunting' night.

The local newspaper reporter had turned up with a camera and with an assistant who impressed me by writing shorthand when she interviewed me. 'This story will be circulated around the press all over Britain,' the assistant said proudly.

Granger, the chief reporter, pushed his way towards me. 'You have a good crowd, Miss Evans. About forty, would you say?'

I nodded, pleased and yet alarmed at the crowd of noisy people sitting round the big dining table in the newly refurbished dining room. Still, I didn't have to do all the work myself. I'd brought Rosie and her mother, Mrs Ward – the same Mrs Ward who had spoken up against Mr Edwin at the time of the murder. But she was the only one who would agree to work for me. The rest of the villagers were too superstitious about the ghosts.

Mrs Ward turned out to be a first-class cook, and she and Rosie would serve and wait on table and I had to be very grateful to them both. Supper and breakfast was all a part of the ghost night, and already on this first event I could tell the weekend was going to not only pay for itself but also make me a good profit.

The female guests were to stay in the bedrooms I'd already turned into dormitories. I could fit the sixteen women of various ages in three of the dorms. I expected the men, being men, wouldn't mind roughing it a bit and would prefer to ghost hunt all night rather than sleep. Indeed, even as they filed out of the dining room they looked around as if expecting to see apparitions floating around the house.

I had my sketch book at the ready and unobtrusively began to draw. One gentleman was an old army man, Colonel Fred, and he hugged his bottle of brandy close to him like a baby. He was affable and keen, with shrewd eyes and a sun-wrinkled face, and I liked him on sight.

'I mean to spend the whole night in the house,' he said. 'I'll sleep in the hall if I have to.'

'So will I,' Jim from Aberdeen said firmly. 'I'm determined to see this ghost of yours.'

'That won't be necessary,' I said, quickly amending my plan. 'You men can have the rooms at the back of the house on the ground floor.'

Tom appeared at my side. Startled, I stared at him. 'I didn't hear you coming in,' I whispered.

'Perhaps I'm a ghost too!' He put his arm around my shoulders and hugged me, and I laughed at him.

'You're a bit solid to be a ghost.' I had my arm around his slim waist, and I could feel the rough material of his uniform under my hand. 'Thank goodness,' I added with a mischievous wink.

'Hey, don't get fast with me, honey.' He playfully kissed my cheek, and then I noticed the guests were spreading out examining the rooms, some carrying glasses of wine or spirits they'd brought along to the 'party' themselves. Next time I would include the drinks in the price, I decided. A little 'cheer' would help things along nicely.

Later, as Tom and I walked in the garden, we could hear the ghost hunters singing some sort of chant which they all seemed to know. I smiled up at Tom. 'Something's keeping them happy.'

'It's the spirits,' Tom said, laughing. 'The ones in the bottles.'

I leaned against him, weak with laughter, and then I froze as I heard a blood-curdling scream from the hallway of the house.

I was running then, across the lawn with Tom just ahead of me. In the hall, everyone was on their feet, their white faces turned up to the top of the stairs. One of the younger girls was pointing, her hand shaking.

'Betty –' I touched her shoulder – 'don't be scared. It's only—' I broke off as Tom caught my arm and made a shushing noise.

'Young lady –' his voice was stern – 'pull yourself together. It's exactly what you came to see, wasn't it? A ghost from the past.'

Betty nodded her blonde head. 'I know, but this is the first time I've seen anything supernatural at one of these weekends! Usually, it's just a laugh and a drink and the chance to meet—' She stopped and looked around at the faces of the other guests.

'Come along now, dearie.' Colonel Fred shook his head reprovingly. 'This is not a dating club. This is a serious ghost hunt. She's gone now, frightened off by all that screaming. You've spoilt the night for us all, so please don't come here again.'

I started up the stairs. *Beatrice must be frightened and confused by all the noise*, I thought. *I must reassure her*. I got almost to the top before I realized the ghost hunters were following me.

One young gent stopped me and held out his hand. 'I'm William,' he said. 'And I'd like to use the description of your ghost in my report to *Spirit News*, the magazine for believers, if that's all right.' He shook my nerveless hand. 'This is the first time the whole thing hasn't been a charade, a set up, an act! Your ghost is real enough, for my sensors picked up something strange, some unfamiliar vibrations, and I will certainly book your next weekend of ghost hunting,' he said, gesturing to the other silent guests, 'and so will most of the people here, I feel sure.'

The others surged around me, and then I felt a push and I was falling downwards, hitting stair after stair, landing in a heap in the hall. My head narrowly missed hitting the huge sideboard that stood near the foot of the stairs.

Tom picked me up and held me gently in his arms. 'Riana, are you all right?' His face was pale, anxious.

I puffed out my breath and rested against him for a minute. 'I'm just winded that's all.' I tried to smile though I knew I'd have some bruises in the morning.

Betty brought me a cup of tea and, though she was fluffy and flirtatious, she was very concerned and very kind.

Young William, his camera swinging around his neck, enquired anxiously after my health, and when he had assured himself I wasn't really hurt he smiled. 'Dear Miss Evans, you will have to furnish other rooms because your fame will grow once this news gets out.' He leaned closer, smelling of brandy. 'Your ghost must have become irritated with the disturbance and used her force to project you back down the stairs. Tell me, Miss Evans, what do you call her? Your ghost, I mean.'

Weak and wanting to laugh hysterically, but restrained by Tom's warning hand on my shoulder, I told him, 'Well, we just call her Beatrice.'

'And,' Tom added, 'you are privileged to see her. She rarely comes out of her room. It is the blue room, the one that's haunted.'

I dug him in the side with my elbow.

'And are we likely to see the five maidens who died there so mysteriously?' the colonel asked.

I had no time to reply, which was just as well.

A young business-suited man stood in front of me. 'Jack Winford.' He held out his hand and I took it. Suddenly, I was surrounded by enthusiastic ghost hunters, each determined to ask questions concerning the murder story and the haunting and how often the ghosts were seen and my head was filled with the babble of voices.

Tom rescued me, taking me outside into the cool air of the cloisters. 'I don't think I can stand too much of this,' I said, sitting down abruptly in the shadows.

Tom sat beside me, his body warm as he rested his arm around my shoulder. 'You can and will put up with it until you make enough money to refurbish the entire house,' he said firmly, 'and then you can bring in a manager to run the ghost hunts and hide yourself away and do your wonderful painting.'

I remembered then how my painting, or what I thought was my painting, was slashed to shreds, and as I listened to the voices of my guests from inside the house I shivered.

What was I doing having strangers in my house, and who had pushed me down the stairs? Because I had been pushed by a human hand, not moved by some supernatural force. I shivered, suddenly scared.

'Can you sleep with me?' I asked before I realized what I'd said.

Tom understood me, however and kissed me lightly on the cheek. 'Yes, if that's what you want. I'll come and stay in your house. There are plenty of rooms and several comfortable sofas.'

'Thank you, Tom.' I felt myself blush, and I bent so that my hair covered my face.

Tom took my arm and led me inside to the comparative quiet of the library. The ghost hunters were all in the hall, watching the stairs, with Brownie cameras at the ready and flashlight and sensors and all sorts of equipment I didn't begin to understand.

Tom and I drank some wine and then fell asleep alongside each other on the sofa. I woke to find his arms around me. He had taken off his jacket and my face was against the smooth material of his shirt. I pretended to sleep a little while longer enjoying the closeness and warmth of him, but at last he stirred, and I sat up, rubbing my eyes.

There was a bustling noise in the hallway and the ghost hunters were coming back to life. I heard Mrs Ward in the kitchen, the smell of bacon permeated the air and I breathed a sigh of relief; after breakfast I would have the place to myself again. I could start to paint more pictures, work on the sketches I'd drawn last night.

William – 'young William' as the other guests called him – seemed to have formed a truce with Betty, who in spite of her plumpness was very pretty, and together they went outside to wait for the taxi taking them into town.

'Perhaps I should arrange a bus,' I murmured, and Tom, who had come outside after me, rested a friendly arm on my shoulder.

'I think that would be a very good idea. It would mean the visitors would have to keep to a time schedule and leave promptly at whatever time you decided.'

'I'd have to charge a small fee, or put up the price of the visit by a few shillings, otherwise I'd lose out,' I said and burst out laughing. 'I'm becoming quite mercenary, aren't I?'

'Businesslike, that's what you are becoming, and just as well if you mean to turn this old heap back into a liveable, pleasurable house with a show garden.'

'Oh, I never thought of showing the gardens.' I hesitated. 'I suppose the cloisters are worth seeing, and the yew-tree arch, and even the entrance flooring is as old as . . . well, very old.' I decided that I would have to research the history of Aberglasney very thoroughly. I would ask Beatrice where the original plans were and see if I could find out anything more about the house at the library in town.

At last, all the visitors had departed, and Mrs Ward was kind enough to provide us all with a roast for lunch. We sat down together: me and Tom, Mrs Ward and her daughter.

'Thank you so much, Mrs Ward.' I cut a juicy piece of beef and popped it into my mouth.

Rosie smirked. 'It was me who cooked the dinner, Miss Evans,' she said. 'My mam taught me. I've known how to cook since I was a little girl.'

'The gravy is a delight,' I said, feeling slightly reproved.

'Mam made that, miss. She's good at gravy is our mam.'

'Well, you are both invaluable to me.' I hoped I was being tactful. 'Perhaps we can make this a regular arrangement. Do you both think you can bear to come and work for me, say once a month?'

Mrs Ward nodded, her mouth full, and it was Rosie who spoke up. 'That would be very handy, miss, what with Dad lost in the war, but all this screaming about ghost shakes me up, mind.'

'This ghost business is a lot of nonsense.' Mrs Ward tightened the knot on her wraparound apron and adjusted her turban, tucking in a stray curl of permed hair. 'Hysterical people see what they want to see.'

'There's a lot of truth in that, Mrs Ward, but it seems to be paying, and if I earn money I can put the old house right and afford full-time help before too long.'

Mrs Ward brightened up. 'Well, as long as I don't have to speak to them townies. I'll stay in the kitchen and mind my own, and you, Rosie, will do the same thing.'

'I will that, Mam,' Rosie said meekly, but her eyes were on Tom. 'Mr Tom, sir, I hear the soldiers are having another party tonight with some of the village girls. Can I come along, sir?'

Mrs Ward bristled. 'Don't be so forward! In any case, remember that those soldiers are . . . are not from this country,' she added, looking flustered.

'They are black Americans, Mrs Ward. They are getting together from all over Wales,' Tom said easily, though I could tell he was offended. 'They are good brave men, and if the enemy had come here they would have defended the people of this village – including you and Rosie – with their lives.'

Mrs Ward lowered her eyes. 'I got to agree with that, sir,' she mumbled. 'I suppose you can go, Rosie, so long as you keep yourself tidy.'

We all knew what she meant, and I met Tom's eyes, trying not to laugh. Rosie was ecstatic.

'You'd be welcome,' Tom said. 'And perhaps Miss Evans would kindly come along as well?'

I could hardly say no in the circumstances. 'That would be very nice,' I mumbled.

At last I was alone in the house. Tom had gone, and there wasn't even a sign of Beatrice; she must have been frightened off by the crowds. The quiet was a little unnerving after all the excitement, but I looked forward to seeing Tom at the social evening he'd arranged for the remaining black airmen.

For the rest of the afternoon I painted as if I was possessed. I was so involved in my colours and what was appearing on the canvas I forgot to eat the sandwiches Mrs Ward had left for me for my supper; I only remembered them when I realized I badly needed a drink.

I sat outside, fed the sandwiches to one of the feral cats that wandered the estate looking for mice, and drank a hot cup of tea. Then I went back to the studio to catch the last of the light.

The painting was of the house; the weather-worn exterior was a lovely mellow golden, heavy with shadows where the light didn't touch it. In one window was a dim figure that I didn't even remember painting, but it looked good, very good, and my heart lightened. I felt in my bones that the canvas would be bought and put in the London gallery.

It was only when I heard music and laughter from the perimeter of the gardens that I remembered the party. Hastily, I washed and dressed in a clean full skirt and a white collared blouse. I couldn't find suitable shoes so I walked across the grounds barefoot, enjoying the cool feel of the grass.

Tom's men had cleared the lecture room, moving the tables to one side and leaving a good space for dancing. Rosie was looking very pretty in a demure blue dress and blue sandals, her hair loose around her flushed face. I hoped she wasn't drinking too much.

One of the Americans bowed and asked me to dance. I took his hand and he held me at a discreet distance, holding me lightly around the waist. 'I'm Billie,' he said in his soft drawl, 'but the men, they call me the black bomber, miss, because of the colour of my skin and—' He hesitated, and Tom appeared at my side.

'And because this man is a wonderful bomb-aimer,' he said. 'Now, may I cut in here and dance with Miss Evans?'

Before I knew it I had been swept into Tom's arms and we were whirling around the floor to the tunes of the Glen Miller orchestra. I felt my hair fly around my face and my cheeks flush with pleasure as we danced and laughed. After a while, breathless, I begged for a drink, and Tom brought me a glass full of amber liquid.

'Here's a scotch and rye, Riana. Drink it up! It will do you good.'

The liquor wove its way in a spiral of fire down my throat and into my bloodstream, and instantly I felt light headed. The music changed to a slow waltz, and Tom took my hand and led me to the dance floor. He drew me close, and – almost without thinking – I put my head on his shoulder. Gently, he rested his cheek against my hair, and

I'd never felt more happy and more comfortable with a man in my life.

I reminded myself that he would have to leave for America before long; I didn't really know when the last of the airmen would go. I supposed it would be wise to ask Tom rather than go on wondering when I would be alone again.

We had the last dance together, and then Tom took my arm. 'I'll walk you to the door, honey,' he said softly. He took my hand, and we left the heat and the cigarette smoke of the mess room and went out into the night.

The moon was full casting an eerie light over Aberglasney. As we drew nearer the doorway I thought I could hear voices. 'Tom, have the visitors made a mistake and come back to the house, do you think?'

'What do you mean, honey?' He sounded puzzled.

'Don't you hear the voices?'

'All I can hear is the pounding of my heart when I feel your hand in mine, honey.' He turned me to him and kissed me, a real kiss, deep and passionate. I warmed against him, the alcohol dancing in my blood, and the sounds of voices faded. I was drunk on Tom's Scotch – and what's more, I at last admitted it to myself, I was intoxicated with Tom. His hands gently moved over my shoulders, down my arms and on to my waist as he pulled me closer.

To my great disappointment, Tom released me at the door. 'See you tomorrow, Riana,' he said softly, and then he was gone into the shadows.

Being alone was such an anticlimax. I didn't know what I imagined would have happened if Tom had come in with me. Would I have allowed him into my bedroom, into my bed? On the other hand, how could he have walked away from me? I was his for the taking, wasn't I?

I sat at the kitchen table and rubbed my eyes wearily. I had been saved from making a fool of myself by Tom's good sense; he was an American officer and he would never take advantage of a drunken friend.

When I opened my eyes again, Beatrice was sitting opposite me. 'What were all those strange people doing here?' she asked.

'Oh –' I pulled my senses together as much as I could after drinking all evening – 'they were visitors, looking for ghosts. Remember your suggestion? Well, I thought about it and decided ghost hunting was a very good idea.'

'I presume they were paying good money to stay here then?'

'Yes, I suppose they were, but they all enjoyed themselves and intend to come again.' I was a little on the defensive.

'Well, don't let the old house down, and don't forget your vow to solve the murders, my dear. I would like my late husband's name cleared.'

'I didn't know I had actually *made* a vow,' I said, puzzled.

'Well, you did.' She smiled a beautiful and somehow old-fashioned smile. 'In spirit, anyway.'

I began to laugh. Everything seemed so funny suddenly: Tom, me, my ghost nights, and my struggle to build up a crumbling old house. I was a painter – what was I doing trying to be a businesswoman?

'Go to bed, dear,' Beatrice said reprovingly. 'You're a little bit the worse for wear, I believe.'

Like a child, I obeyed and went meekly to bed.

TEN

I didn't see Tom the next day. I deliberately stayed in my bright studio, working on my painting of Aberglasney. At one point I stood back a little way and thought that the light and shade I had added worked well and that the shadowy figure in an upper window looked rather like Beatrice. I smiled fondly. She was becoming a good friend, a companion, soothing me when my nerves were frayed.

Mrs Ward called early afternoon and I beckoned her into the kitchen. I lit the stove and set out two cups. 'Do you take milk Mrs Ward?' I asked cheerfully.

She nodded and put a basket on the table. 'I've brought you some eggs, Miss Evans.' Her voice was hoarse from her continuous smoking, and as she sat down she lit up another Woodbine. 'My Rosie didn't come home last night, Miss Evans. She told me she stayed with you.' She was narrowing her eyes against the smoke and scrutinizing my face.

I poured the tea to give myself time to think. The last I'd seen of Rosie was her dancing with a handsome American airman. 'Well, there's plenty of room here,' I prevaricated. 'And I was a little bit . . . tired myself, so everything is a bit blurred, but I'm sure if that's what Rosie says that's what she did.'

'I see, miss.'

I was sure she did: right through me. I hadn't the heart to let Rosie down, but I meant to have a word with her when I next saw her. How dare she use me as an alibi when she had obviously been up to no good?

'When will you want me and Rosie again, miss?' Mrs Ward's voice broke into my thoughts. I looked at her and saw her brows were drawn into a frown. She knew I was lying, and she was displeased with me.

'In a month's time, Mrs Ward,' I said flatly. She was

being paid to help me, not to question me. 'If you have the time to come and work for me at Aberglasney, that is.'

'Yes, I want to come. I need the money, and anyway, I like cooking and waiting on town folks and foreign folks alike. But –' her eyes narrowed – 'I don't like them dark-skinned airmen down at the barracks. Up to no good, they are. Chasing after respectable girls like my daughter.'

'Thank you for the eggs, Mrs Ward,' I said, hastily changing the subject. 'How much do I owe you?'

She told me, and I counted out a shilling and then took the eggs from the basket to put on the cold slab in the pantry. They were brown and fresh with bits of feather sticking to the shells, and my mouth watered. I realized I hadn't had anything to eat that morning, and it was well past lunchtime.

When Mrs Ward had gone, I made some poached eggs on toast and ate hungrily. When I had finished, I glanced out of the kitchen window and decided I'd do another hour or so's painting while there was still plenty of light.

I worked until my back was aching and it was almost dark, but finally the painting was finished and all I needed to do was to let it dry. I opened the big widow in the gallery – and then, on second thoughts, shut it again. I didn't want anything happening to this painting. I'd worked too long and hard on it.

I put on the gas lights and heard the pop and saw the widening of the light. One day I would be able to afford electricity in more of the rooms, but for now, the gas worked very well – at least it was most atmospheric for my guests on the ghost nights.

I helped myself to a glass of sherry and then, just when I felt relaxed and sleepy, there was a knock on the front door. My heart almost stopped as I imagined Tom's big figure waiting for me outside, but when I opened the door it was Rosie who was waiting for me.

'Just the person I wanted to see,' I said in a hard voice. 'Will you please keep me out of your private life in future? I won't be your alibi again.'

'I'm sorry, but it wasn't what you think,' Rosie said quickly.

'I was helping Carl with a letter he was writing home to his mother, that's all.'

'And for that you had to stay out all night, is that it?' My tone was steeped in sarcasm, which Rosie missed completely.

'Well, no, not *all* night, but then I fell asleep on the sofa – in the communal sitting room, mind – and Carl left me there while he went to the barracks' dorm, as he calls it.'

'I'll believe you, though not many would,' I said. 'Just don't tell your mother you stayed with me again, hear me?'

'I hear you, miss,' Rosie said meekly and made a quick exit.

Alone again, I tried to fall back into the relaxed state I had been in before she'd come, but somehow the mood was gone. I wanted to be with Tom. Almost without thinking, I went outside and stood in the garden and saw my seat, a patch of light wood, under the arches of the cloisters. I walked towards the seat, and as I came close I heard a scraping sound above my head.

I glanced up in time to see a huge stone object falling towards my head. I darted under the cloister just in time as the stone crashed down, throwing up dust and fragments that shot like bullets towards me.

When I caught my breath, I saw one of the stone dragons had fallen – or been *pushed* – from the walkway above the cloister. It now lay shattered and broken at my feet.

One huge wing stuck up from the ground – embedded in the earth like a giant, curving scythe. If the statue had fallen on me I'd have had very little chance of survival.

I scrambled up the steps, too incensed to be frightened. Someone was trying to kill me, or to destroy my mind! I stood there in the darkness . . . and, of course, I was alone. I stared out at the shadowed land around me. Why would anyone want to hurt me? Was it because I was trying, in a feeble way, to solve the deaths of the five young maids? Or was it because I was the new owner of Aberglasney?

Shivering, suddenly apprehensive, I returned to the house, curled up in my chair and helped myself to another glass

of sherry. Soon I felt more relaxed. It had all been an unfortunate accident, I told myself, but before I went to bed I
switched on some lights and made sure all the doors and
windows were locked against the outside world.

ELEVEN

In the morning, my painting of Aberglasney was almost dry. The colours seemed to blend in harmony, and the whole house had the mysterious air I'd been trying for. The figure, who looked a little like Beatrice with a dim glow of warmth behind her, gave the painting a piquancy that took it from a cold stone building to a lived-in house.

It was a great pity the ornate portico was missing from round the front door, I thought. It had been sold some time before I'd bought Aberglasney, but I vowed that one day, when I had enough money, I would get it back.

There was no sign of Tom, and feeling restless, I decided to take a train into town. I would go to the library, read up on the house and delve more into local reports of the deaths of the young maids.

The train journey was enlivened by the antics of a young girl and her brother, who were shut in the same small carriage as myself. At last, tired of the exuberance of the children, I wandered into the corridor for a little respite. Enclosed in the carriage behind me I could hear them play and fight, and then the girl began to cry, and by the time I arrived in Swansea I had a thumping headache.

Miss Grist, the woman behind the counter, helped another librarian carry the huge book of newspapers without so much as a smile and placed it on the table for me.

'Be careful with the papers, Miss Evans,' she said. 'You know how careless some folk are. They lick fingers and touch the old newspaper, and it doesn't do it any good at all.' She suddenly sat down beside me. She wasn't the typical type of librarian you see on the stage in a theatre: no glasses, no bun, but heavy lidded eyes and a full, drooping mouth.

True, her eyes had lines around them and the skin of her jaw was rather loose, but she would be a very good subject for a painting. I could see her in a Pre-Raphaelite gown of bright gold with her hair hanging loose against the silk. I realized I was staring and picked up my pencil.

'You are the lady who bought the old house, Aberglasney, aren't you?'

'That's right.' I carefully opened a newspaper, aware of her watching eyes.

'I hear there was quite a stir there last weekend. The ghost hunters actually found a ghost, I believe?'

'It seems so.' I tried to keep my voice steady and I took a deep breath. This was the sort of publicity I wanted, needed . . . so why did I feel such a cheat? 'Of course, I didn't see a ghost myself,' I added, absolving myself of some responsibility.

'And you living there. Isn't that strange?' She watched me with shrewd eyes. 'But there are some eerie goings-on there, I know that.'

My attention was caught; I turned to look at Miss Grist. 'How do you know?' I spoke gently, not wanting to frighten her away.

'I did some collating of books for the owners some time ago,' she volunteered. 'The library was extensive in those days, so I was told. I don't know what it's like now, of course.'

'Did you know Mr Mansel-Atherton?'

'Not personally. I'm a little too young for that.' Her tone was sharp, and I tried not to giggle. 'It's all very suspicious, if you ask me.'

'You think the maids were murdered then?'

'All I know is that they died in strange circumstances,' Miss Grist said briskly, as if *I* was prying into the past when it was *she* who had brought it up.

'Why are you so interested?' I looked at her suspiciously. She had sensible black shoes and even black thick stockings, like a nurse, perhaps . . . or a policeman.

'Just a feeling,' she snapped. Evidently, talking about Mr Mansel-Atherton was touching a raw nerve for Miss Grist. 'So, what have you found out about the strange things that happened *before* the girls died?' Miss Grist said after a moment's silence. She asked with more interest than a mere librarian would, I thought.

'Accidents,' I said. 'I read there were strange accidents, but not since Mr Mansel-Atherton died.' Just then someone came to hover at Miss Grist's side, and with an apologetic look at me she departed to help the other librarian.

I tried to concentrate on the papers and made notes about Aberglasney, the maids, and the accusations against poor Edwin. There were brief reports in most papers, and one lurid headline in a Sunday paper about 'Murder at the Manor'. No new details, though – just the suggestion of sexual misdemeanours, written for sensationalism.

I found nothing new or helpful in any of the reports. I would have to talk to the locals and read church records to try to find the background to it all. But I decided, as I hauled the book of papers back to the desk, that I would certainly talk to Miss Grist again when I had the opportunity.

It came sooner than I expected. I was sitting in a small tea room just minutes after I had left the library, admiring the pristine white tablecloths and the aprons of the waitresses, when a shadow fell over me.

'Could I join you, Miss Evans? I feel the need of a cup of tea.' She had a hat squashed over her hair and a black sober coat, straight-hemmed and with huge buttons.

'Please.' I indicated the chair beside me. 'I would love some company.'

I waved to one of the waitresses, and she came and took our order for a new pot of tea and some scones with jam and cream – a real treat after the wartime shortages. The cream was synthetic, but the jam was home-made and tasty. Miss Grist looked doubtful when they arrived.

'My treat,' I said breezily. 'Have you got the afternoon off, Miss Grist?'

'No, this is just my lunch hour, but I had to talk to you.' She leaned forward. 'I have to advise you to vacate that house before harm comes to you.'

'Do you mean the malign spirits, Miss Grist?' I hoped my scepticism didn't show in my voice.

'The threat is real enough,' Miss Grist said. 'I don't know who or why, but you are in danger from something – or someone – if you go prying into the past.'

'Were you in danger when you were collating the books at the house?' I heard the scepticism in my voice – but Miss Grist, apparently, didn't.

'A few nasty accidents happened.' She didn't look at me. 'A huge stone statue from the roof fell and nearly killed me.'

'Was it a dragon?' I asked suspiciously. She seemed to be echoing my own experiences, not her own.

'And then there were other things,' she said, as if I hadn't spoken. 'Someone came into my room in the night. I could hear footsteps, stealthy movements, but I never saw anything. Except, that is, an eccentric old lady.'

'Ah, Beatrice.'

'She was all right until Edwin had an illegitimate son,' Miss Grist said, almost absently, 'and then she became strange, almost – one would say – possessed.'

I hid my surprise. Beatrice was the most sane, practical woman I'd ever met. I didn't know anything about her having a child – only the grown-up son who was killed in the war.

'What child?'

'Edwin had a child, it wasn't Beatrice's. The child disappeared one night, never to be seen again. Apparently, he was the child of one of the five maids who died, you see.'

The news was a shock to me. I'd not heard of another child – not even from Beatrice. She'd talked about her lost son, of course, but nothing about the other boy. She must have been cut to the quick at her husband's infidelity. 'The child, he would be a man – grown, by now, of course. I wonder what happened to him.'

'Unless he was killed as well.' Miss Grist's tone was sombre.

'Why do you say that?'

'Because there's been no sign of the child for years.'

'He couldn't have just vanished. Wasn't there talk at the time? A search, police enquiries, something?'

Miss Grist looked at me thoughtfully. 'Why are you probing into the past, if I might ask?'

'You started all this, remember? Anyway, I'm curious because I own the mansion now. The house is mine, and I want to know all about it. Do you disapprove?'

'I disapprove of a lot of things, Miss Evans, but mostly I feel it best to let sleeping dogs lie, as they say.'

I took a deep breath to argue and then thought better of it. 'Well, I'd better be getting back,' I said instead. 'I have to pick up some brown paper and string first though. I have paintings to pack up, ready for London.'

Miss Grist brightened. 'Going to London? How exciting! Will you go on the train?'

'I can't travel by train tomorrow, not really. I'll have to take my old van to carry the paintings. I hate driving all that way, but I have no choice.'

Miss Grist wiped her chin with a nice blue-edged handkerchief, and I thought again what a strange woman she was. She must have been a voluptuous beauty once – still was in a mature way – but her ways were those of a spinster lady with nothing but dry books to keep her occupied.

I left her at the door of the little tea shop and walked along the High Street to the ironmongers. I made my way past zinc buckets and boxes of nails to the counter and bought my string and brown paper. Paper was still in short supply, but the owner of the shop knew me by now and sold me what he had in his cellar.

A few minutes later, I climbed into an empty carriage on the train and sank back appreciatively, hearing the *puff puff* of the steam and the clank of the wheels against the rails. I was on my way home from Swansea to Aberglasney.

TWELVE

One night, several weeks later, Tom invited me to supper in his billet, and I cursed myself as a fool for being at his beck and call. I saw him when *he* wanted it not when I wanted to, and yet I found myself enjoying the atmosphere and the company.

The food was plentiful; the Americans didn't know what rationing was all about. There was a dance that evening in the village hall, and after we'd eaten Tom invited me to go with him as his guest. 'My men will expect me to put in an appearance,' he explained as we walked the short distance to the village hall. 'And what lovelier lady could I have on my arm than my Miss Evans?'

I took in the 'my' with a sense of belonging. I felt suddenly happy.

It was a lovely evening, the last of the summer, with just a tinge of autumn about the air. Inside the hall it was hot, and the heavy scent of American cigarettes hung in the room like a haze.

Bright-eyed girls danced and laughed, and I caught sight of Mrs Ward's daughter with her soldier: a very handsome man, his skin dark as night and shining almost blue in the dimmed lights. How Mrs Ward would disapprove!

Tom had followed my gaze. 'I do believe that young lady is asking for trouble. Airman Jenkins is married with three children.' Tom didn't seem to make anything troubling from the colour of his corporal's skin. But then he wouldn't; he had no prejudice. To him, the man was brave and clever and a good aircraft officer – and that was all Tom required of his men. But I knew Mrs Ward would treat the men as 'foreigners' out to exploit the untried young ladies of the village.

'He's married?' I felt a pang of anxiety. 'Do you think Rosie knows that?'

'I doubt it. Most men are tight-lipped about marriage when they have a pretty girl in their arms.'

I looked up at him as he took me in his arms and swept me on to the dance floor. 'And you . . . are you being tight-lipped, Tom?' I heard the anxiety in my voice, and Tom did too.

'I have no wife, no child, no girlfriend – not at home, anyway,' he said, his eyes twinkling. 'I've been too busy fighting a war for any of that. Though I have plenty of time for flirting now, if I can find anyone to flirt with.'

Was that what I was to Tom – a flirtation?

'Excuse me.' I left him on the floor and made my way out of the crowded hall and into the night air. What a fool I was thinking I was special to him. To Tom I was just a girl to eat with, dance with, fall into his arms and give him her all while he looked on her as just a flirtation. Well, I'd been warned now, and I knew my place.

I left the dance and made my way back home alone. I saw the flickering lights on the top landing, the lights the locals insisted were carried by the ghosts of the dead maids, but I knew they were caused by just the clouds and the moonlight playing tricks against the glass. Besides, I was too wrapped up in my anger and humiliation to think too much about ghosts.

I went to my studio and spent some time wrapping the painting ready for carrying to the gallery in London. I resolved just to carry on with my life and concentrate on my business, my paintings, my house, my ghost parties and to forget Tom Maybury and the few remaining Americans. Soon they would go home. They would leave my property, and I could have the huts taken down. I could extend the garden – perhaps have a rose arbour, some wooden benches, and a water fountain with a chained cup on it like in the parks. Somewhere my guests could sit and write and discuss the ghosts.

The next day I went to London, and I was warmly welcomed at the gallery. Now I had enough paintings to make a proper exhibition! Mr Readings was delighted and made a fuss of each painting, admiring what he called the 'misty excellence' of each one. 'Same talented hand, same brush strokes, but each painting standing alone. I do so like your work, dear Miss Evans.'

For the first time, he led me into his small sitting room at the back of the gallery and poured me a glass of sherry. 'We shall have an opening event! Champagne, some good cheese and biscuits, and publicity in the London art magazines. My dear girl, you are a precious find for me. We shall make each other very rich and famous.'

I drank his excellent sherry and took his words with a pinch of salt. Still, it felt good to have such enthusiasm shown over my work. I didn't think I was that talented, just inspired by my house to make some paintings Mr Readings thought 'different' enough to attract buyers.

We arranged the opening for the next month – the first of September – and I wondered if Tom and the few men he had left would be gone back to America by then. The thought make me unhappy, and I pushed it out of my mind.

I drove back to Aberglasney with a mixture of elation and disquiet, wondering if any of my paintings would sell. Would I let Mr Readings and the audience down? Would they be disappointed with my mythical type of pictures? On the other hand, it was an opportunity to advertise my 'ghost-haunting' nights at the mansion. I had two strings to my bow now, two means of making funds to restore the old house, so I might as well make full use of both of them.

As I drew my rattling old van up at the back of the house I saw a figure lurking in the shadows. I felt a stark fear for a moment, and then I realized it was only the slight figure of a girl coming towards me, a handkerchief held to her streaming eyes. 'Rosie what is it?'

'Can I talk to you, miss?'

I led her to the bench in the vegetable garden, where we would be hidden by trees from the kitchen window. 'What is it, Rosie? You're not . . .?' I gestured to her tummy, not knowing how to frame the words for the disaster I thought was about to happen.

Her drooping head and renewed sobs told me my guess was correct.

'Oh, Rosie!' I put my arm around her. How could she give herself to an American serviceman who would fly away out of her life? But then hadn't I almost given myself to Tom, so how could I judge her?

'I love him, miss. He promised to take me to America, give me a new life away from my mother, but now he's finished with me, he doesn't want me, he says he's leaving at the end of the month. How can I bear the shame of having a child with no father?'

'You'll have to tell your mother,' I said at once. I didn't know how to deal with this situation. I was only a young woman myself.

Rosie sobbed louder.

'Look,' I said. 'You and the baby can stay at the house. The talk will die down after a while, and we can all help you bring the little one up.'

'I can't *have* it.' She looked up at me in alarm. 'You'll have to find me a doctor, or a midwife. Somebody to get me out of this mess.'

I was startled. 'What do you mean to do? Kill your baby?'

'I know, I know, but what if its skin is dark like its father? I'd never live down the shame! No, I can't let it ruin my life.'

I felt like telling her she should have thought of that before, but that wouldn't have been very kind or helpful. 'Look, I'll talk to Tom. He's the boss, he'll know what can be done.'

For the first time, Rosie looked hopeful. 'Perhaps he'll insist that Carl takes me back to America with him and at least settles me there, even if he doesn't want to marry me.'

Some hope when he had a wife and children, I thought, but then it wasn't for me to break the bad news of her boyfriend's treachery to Rosie.

'Go to bed now, Rosie,' I said soothingly. 'It can all be sorted out in the morning, I'm sure.' I wasn't sure at all, but what else could I say? Selfishly, I was cheerful as I undressed, for I had an excuse to go and see Tom in the morning.

I was to be disappointed and so was Rosie – for when I tried, the next morning, the men had gone out on a training exercise and no one knew where. The only man left on duty was the cook, and he told me in no uncertain terms that officers did not consult him when they were on manoeuvres.

Rosie burst into tears when I told her, and again I had the job of comforting her.

I didn't have a chance to see Tom over the weekend because I had my ghost guests there again, and the house was full of excited, chattering 'hunters' with lighting equipment and cameras and all sort of items I couldn't even begin to understand.

I hoped something would happen to please my guests and take my mind off Rosie's troubles, and it did in a most spectacular way. As Mrs Ward and Rosie served the soup, the dining room door opened and a chill wind blew through the room. The sound of moaning and crying could be heard clearly from upstairs!

Dinner forgotten, everyone rushed up the elegant staircase and along the landing to where the mysterious lights were flickering. Beatrice appeared briefly in her doorway, but retreated as soon as she saw the hoards of wild-eyed guests with cameras running towards her.

'Did you see that, the Victorian lady? Anyone catch a picture of her?' The old colonel was back, and he boasted this was the second time he'd seen the ghost. 'She's called Beatrice,' he explained all-knowingly.

I kept quiet as the guests moved more cautiously now along the landing. Lights still flickered. Even I could see them, and as there was no moon I was at a loss to explain them. I felt I had to say something dramatic, though, and give the guests something for their money. 'Here, on this landing, the five murdered maids are alleged to seek release from their chains of death.' I spoke in a sepulchral voice that suddenly silenced all the talking.

One lady, obviously of a nervous disposition, screamed and ran back down the stairs – but at the same time everything abruptly became silent and the eerie lights vanished.

'It's a hoax,' one of the men declared bravely. 'I shall search the rooms for trickery.'

'Please,' I said. 'Mr Bravage, all of you, search, and if you find anything rigged or to be a hoax I will refund your money.' I couldn't explain any more than they could what had taken place. I felt a little unnerved myself, but I led the way along the landing and into the rooms. When we walked back towards the stairs I hesitated outside Beatrice's room.

'Go on then!' Mr Bravage shouted. 'Let's see the lady ghost, find out if she's alive and kicking.'

Reluctantly, I opened Beatrice's door, worried about invading her privacy, but there was no one in the room – it was silent and empty. Relieved, I stepped back and let the other people in, led by Mr Bravage.

'I feel a distinct chill in here.' Mr Bravage spoke in hushed tones and looked around, evidently seeking an open window or two.

'I do feel a presence,' the colonel chimed in, his pipe suddenly smouldering into extinction as if it had been blown out by a ghostly breath. He took it out of his mouth and looked at it in disbelief. 'It's never done that before.' He sniffed. 'This room hasn't been occupied by anyone alive, not for a very long time. You can smell the scent of decay.'

That was going a bit far, but I closed my lips firmly. Dear Beatrice used an ancient violet perfume that *did* smell a bit musty. I wondered where she'd gone, but Beatrice knew every nook and cranny of the creaking old house. She was probably keeping out of the way until the nosy, camera-laden guests had gone.

We all returned to the dining room. The soup had gone cold, and Mrs Ward and Rosie, dressed in maid uniforms now – a new idea of mine – removed the plates. Mrs Ward had sniffed at the notion of a starched white apron instead of her wraparound floral pinny, but when I'd promised her a little bonus she had complied with my craven request for her to fit in with the mood of the night.

'Perhaps Your Ladyship should bring in a butler as well?' Her acid remark had left little circles running round in my head. I knew she had been joking, but would my budget stretch to a butler? It would be an added authentic touch!

The meal comprised of roast lamb, cooked and seasoned beautifully by Mrs Ward, with devilled slices of lamb's liver, mint, baby roast potatoes and several dishes of vegetables. Not from the garden, alas, but from a market gardener who'd sold me them fresh at a premium price. We had dishes of steaming suet pudding and custard after the main course.

My guests ate well – and they paid well for the privilege.

Tonight, the conversation was noisy and elated; the sounds and the noises and the ghostly scents of my dear, conspiring old house pleased the ghost hunters, as did the timely appearance of Beatrice – dressed, as always, as if she'd stepped out of a picture book of the past century.

'My dear Miss Evans.' The colonel swept off his glasses. 'I think your house is one that is truly possessed by spirits of the past. So many of these so called "haunted" houses are nothing but fakes, fooling gullible tourists into a cheap thrill, but this house, Aberglasney, is the real thing, and I will be a guest any time you have your weekend conferences.' He leaned over me, wiping the custard from his mouth with a pristine napkin. It was lucky Mrs Ward could still persuade the few Americans remaining in the huts to help her work the laundry.

'You know, Miss Evans, you should put out leaflets, advertise in the newspapers more. You would have waiting lists, you would need ghost weekends more frequently, and then you could repair more of the rooms. My dear young lady, you have a gold mine here. Not looking for a partner, are you, by any chance?'

I shook my head as if in regret. 'I like it as it is, Colonel. My regulars have become friends to me. What I hope to do is restore as many rooms as possible as bedrooms, and then the weekends might be able to accommodate a few more guests. What do you think?'

'Ah, I know I speak to my own disadvantage here, but I think you should charge more for the weekends. The hospitality is very good. I personally feel so much at home that

I could get up in the night and make myself a drink.' He dabbed his moustache again. 'I like the stone floors of the kitchen, the old wooden cupboards, the china cups hanging on hooks, the kettle singing on the hob. It is a lovely house, my dear, and you are so fortunate to own it.'

'I know I am,' I agreed.

After the meal, I suggested a 'candlelit' search of the house. 'But be careful, don't disturb anything, and please don't be careless with the candles. We don't want the house to be on fire, do we?'

I left the guests to their search of the house and grounds and helped Mrs Ward and Rosie to wash up the dishes. Mrs Ward took an enamel jug, filled it with boiling water from the kettle, and I watched as she sluiced the cutlery and then put it in the jug of steaming water. All except the bone-handled cheese knives.

'Why do you leave the cheese knives out, Mrs Ward?' I was silly enough to ask and was subjected to a lecture about bone and ivory handles coming apart and falling off and of silver blades needing gentle washing and cleaning.

I could see Rosie hovering wanting to talk to me, but what could I say to her? I couldn't condone the operation she planned, and yet I could see her position was intolerable.

When Mrs Ward had left, shopping bag of leftover food on her arm, Rosie made a beeline for me. The guests were silently searching the upper floors, and now everything was cleared up, and the dining table laid for breakfast, there was nothing more for me to busy myself with. I sat down with Rosie, wondering what I could advise.

'Please, Miss Riana, you will have to help me.' She bit her full lip, and I could see she was at the end of her tether.

Suddenly, anger washed through me: anger at Tom for allowing his men such freedom, and anger at Pilot Jenkins for taking advantage of a young girl like Rosie. Granted, her reputation wasn't spotless, but at least the man could have been careful. 'I'll see Tom in the morning.' My voice carried conviction. 'It is up to the Americans to sort out all this, not me or you, Rosie.'

Her young face was awash with gratitude. 'Thank you, Miss Riana. Perhaps some hospital visit can be arranged and paid for, and then my troubles will be over.'

I didn't reply. I was thinking about a new unborn infant, a real child who had a right to life. But then who was I to make such decisions? Tomorrow it would all be taken out of my hands. I was determined on that.

My guests departed the next day, full of a good breakfast and tales of ghosts and noises and 'paranormal research', having booked again for another weekend in a month's time. I had planned on having them less frequently, but the events were so successful that I couldn't turn down the opportunity to make more of the weekends and to make money enough to restore my house.

Later I walked down to the barracks, my heart in my mouth, ready to confront Tom. His smile when he saw me made my heart beat more quickly, and my resolve to be firm wavered slightly.

'You look lovely and summery,' he said, his eyes warm and admiring. It was a warm day, without the autumnal chill that had seemed to pervade the house and gardens over the weekend. It almost seemed that the house, the weather, and everything else was colluding to make my 'ghost hunts' a success.

I plucked up my courage. 'Can we talk privately? There's a serious matter I have to discuss with you.'

'Please come into my office.'

Tom, I felt, already knew what the problem was. He poured me coffee from one of his electric contraptions brought from America, and we sat down at his desk, Tom facing me almost as if I was being interviewed. I felt suddenly as though he was an officer – a leader of men – not the friend I'd become fond of.

'It's about Pilot Officer Jenkins and Rosie Ward.' I spoke softly, willing Tom to help me.

He didn't.

'They seem to have a very big problem,' I said.

'And, as far as I'm concerned, a very private problem.' Tom spoke evenly.

'Rosie has told me she is expecting a child.' I knew I was being abrupt, but Tom's attitude was making me angry. 'I think you and your officers should be the ones to deal with it.'

'Surely it's more women's work?' He wasn't being actually hostile – more obstructive.

'I know he can't make an honest woman of Rosie.'

'If she was an honest woman she wouldn't be in this position in the first place,' Tom said, his tone one of reason.

'Oh, so your man couldn't have taken precautions?' Anger was making my voice rise. 'He's married with children, I believe – something he failed to tell Rosie – and he didn't even have the sense he was born with to take precautions!' It embarrassed me to be so frank, but I was so angry with Tom's cavalier attitude that I didn't care about the blush that made my cheeks hot.

'I tackled Jenkins about that, and his reply was: "You don't take precautions with a girl you first met in the Red Lion Public House." '

I was taken aback. I imagined Rosie had met Jenkins at the dance in my garden that night. Respectable young girls didn't go into public bars. I got to my feet and picked up my lace gloves and my bag, searching for something to say in mitigation of Rosie. 'Well,' I said hotly, unable to think of a defence, 'this is your problem not mine, sir. Please be sure to do something about it.'

'I'll call and discuss it with you tonight,' Tom said coldly.

I walked out into the sunshine feeling foolish and at a disadvantage and also feeling something else – a sense of having lost something precious to me.

Rosie was waiting for me. 'Did you see my Carl for me?' She was as flushed as any young girl in love, and I tried to make things easier for her.

'I saw Tom. He's going to speak to your Carl Jenkins, see what can be done.'

'Is Carl going to marry me then . . . or what?'

'Leave it all until Tom has had a word. Try not to worry. The men will soon have some answer for us, I'm sure.' I wasn't sure at all.

Rosie looked relieved. She evidently believed in my powers of persuasion more than I did. 'Thank you, Miss Riana. I've got to get out of this mess or my mother will kill me.' It was a phrase I was tired of hearing.

'Well, go and help your mother and act as though nothing's happened. I'll be seeing Tom later, and I'll find out what's going to happen. Try not to worry too much, Rosie, there's a good girl.'

There was no sign of Tom that night, even though I waited for him impatiently. I wanted to get something settled for Rosie's sake. I thought perhaps Jenkins could take Rosie to America, arrange a home for her there. Anything to get her away from the shame of bringing an illegitimate child into the world of a small Welsh village.

In the end, I cleared away the glasses of wine, Mrs Ward's elderberry wine, and switched off the gas light. The mantles popped as they died, and again.

I went to bed disappointed and quivered below the blankets, trying not to cry. I'd wanted to see Tom more than I realized. I wanted to put things right with him to get back on the old warm footing.

I didn't sleep very much. I kept hearing sounds . . . sobs, cries . . . Was it the wind that had whipped up dashing branches and stray bits of wet leaf against the windows, or were there really ghosts in my house, waiting outside my door ready to harm me? I turned my face into the pillow and closed my eyes. This was my house and I shouted, 'Shut up!' into the darkness, and suddenly, all was quiet.

THIRTEEN

The first of September soon arrived, and the art exhibition in the London gallery was a great success. I stood in the bright lights of the elegant room, a glass of champagne in my hand and a smile fixed to my face, and tried to look modest in the warmth of the praise that was heaped on my work. I knew I looked good, different, playing the part of an elegant artist. In one of the old wardrobes in my house I'd found a green silk pants suit, with panels over the trouser legs like an overskirt and a halter top that showed off my pale arms and shoulder length red-blonde hair to perfection.

With it I wore a colourful shawl in peacock greens and purples, so I looked like a picture of a wealthy woman from the nineteen twenties, not a product of the utility age of the war years.

'My dear, you are as ravishing as your paintings.' One of the art critics kissed my hand, and with his head bent he showed his glossy pink bald crown surrounded by grey hair. 'I'm Simon Bleesdale, dear lady.'

He expected me to know of him, and of course I did – he was one of the most influential art critics in London. 'How charming of you to say so.' I tried to sound enthusiastic, but I found his flattery a bit overwhelming.

'Not at all! You are very talented. The ghostliness of the lovely old mansion shines through the paintings. It was almost as if you were possessed when you worked on them.'

I realized, with a flush of pleasure, that he wasn't flattering me at all. His praise was genuine. 'Perhaps you would like to come to one of my ghost weekends?' I suggested. 'Good food, good company and ghosts, if we're lucky. As my guest, of course, Mr Bleesdale,' I added hastily.

'Call me Simon, please, don't stand on formality, and I would be delighted to come to your ghost weekend.

The whole things appeals enormously. Now, dear lady, your public is waiting to meet you! Far be it from me to keep you from your admirers.'

I found myself smiling at, and shaking hands with, people I'd never met before – well-dressed ladies and men with black ties. I received so many compliments I was quite dizzy. And yet my heart was heavy. I wanted Tom to be at my side, Tom to share with me the moment when I stood before my audience with a glass of sparkling champagne in my hand and gave a small speech of thanks to all who'd come to the exhibition.

Mr Readings spoke next, urging customers to buy my work before it became too much in demand and while prices were relatively low. 'Low' was not a word I would have used, each painting was marked at an alarming amount, and yet amazingly they were beginning to sell – and quickly. I saw Mr Readings taking orders and bundles of notes, making records of each sale meticulously in his little notebook.

At last the art lovers departed, and Mr Readings removed his glasses and stared at me as if he'd never seen me before. 'You are the new fashion, my dear, the new Pre-Raphaelite, but with a difference. Your figures are beautiful young things swathed in a deathly haze. Lovely white limbs like those of a ballet dancer, tiny feet not quite touching the ground.' He lifted his glass to me. 'I have found myself a genius. Even Mr Bleesdale bought several canvases, and he has commissioned more. What do you think of that, my dear Miss Evans?'

'I'm delighted and amazed,' I stuttered. And I truly *was* amazed. 'I didn't expect my work to be so popular.'

Of course, Mr Readings would take almost half the money in commission, he'd already made that quite clear, but I accepted that as fair. Mr Readings had launched me into the public, given me a showcase. He had taken a risk on me, and I didn't begrudge him a penny of what he'd truly earned. I'd still receive a princely sum for my work, and I was already planning what I'd do to Aberglasney with it.

'It's very late, dear. You'd better stay in town,' Mr Readings said. His concern, I suspected, was because of the money he could earn from my work, not for my personal safety. 'There is a nice little guest house just along the road, owned by a lady friend of mine. I shall put you up there for the night.'

'Very kind.' I truly was grateful. I didn't fancy the drive home through the dark lonely streets and lanes that led from London to Swansea.

The guest house was warm and comfortable, and Miss Treherne who owned it was obviously besotted by Mr Readings. I really looked at him for the first time. He was tall and quite handsome with grey wings of hair pointing the way to a silver beard. It was clear to me that he would also stay the night at Miss Treherne's little guest house.

I couldn't sleep at first – the house, I realized, was too quiet without the creaks and groans of old Aberglasney – but at last I drifted off: warm and comfortable and filled with cocoa and biscuits, not to mention the champagne.

Miss Treherne herself drove us back to the gallery where I'd left my old van. Her means of transport was an old-fashioned Ford car, but at least it meant I could see something of London itself. Some of the buildings were razed to the ground from the bombing, and yet the early morning cries of the street vendors were cheerful and clear, even in the fog from the smoking chimneys.

I drove back to Swansea at a leisurely pace, eager to get back to my home and yet enjoying the sun as I left the town and encountered the broad countryside. I tested the brakes of the van several times. I'd had enough strange experiences to be wary now, fearing someone was trying to hurt or even kill me. Why? It wasn't for my wealth, that was sure. Before the exhibition I'd had little money, and I was still nowhere near rich.

Was it an effort to stop me finding out the truth about Aberglasney and the deaths of the young maids? That seemed the most likely reason, but then that meant that someone with the guilt of it all, and the knowledge of what really happened, was still in the vicinity of the big old house, the mansion that had become my home . . .

At last, my thoughts turned to Tom, and I felt warm and

comforted. Tom would always protect me; he cared about me, and even though we saw things differently at the moment he was a good friend. More than friends, on my part, which I wouldn't let my mind acknowledge. Our little disagreement would soon be over and done with. We were too close to allow other people's problems to spoil what we had built up.

I remembered how we sat in the shade of the cloisters, the old stone arching above us as solid as the day when the cloisters had been built. What hands had worked on those stones, on the gardens, making a paradise of the private world that surrounded Aberglasney?

And then I thought of Tom's warmth close to mine, his arm touching mine and his occasional kisses . . . they were friendly, but such kisses could quickly turn to passion. Or was I dreaming, wishing, wanting more than Tom had ever thought of offering?

I stopped to drink my bottled water and eat the small sandwiches Miss Treherne had prepared for me. This morning she'd had the glow of a woman who had slept in a lover's arms, and I envied her.

It was peaceful sitting near the grass verge, with the pale sun and the slight chill of the country breeze freshening my skin. I rested a little and then, with a sigh of resignation, I climbed in the van and drove the rest of the way home without stopping.

Tom was standing near the door of the house and my heart lurched as I expected a smile of welcome. Instead, Tom was frowning. 'I was worried about you, Riana. Where have you been all night?' He sounded like an angry father, or at least an older brother.

'I stayed in London, of course.' I was irked. I wasn't a child, I was an artist, the owner of property. What right did he have to question me?

'So you found a man to look after you then?'

'Mr Readings looked after me – the owner of the gallery – so I stayed in London. Have you any objections?' I forced myself to be calmer. 'All my paintings have sold, so at least the trip was worth it.'

'So you celebrated by staying with Mr Readings all night.'

Angry again, I faced him. 'Yes, I stayed all night, but not in the way you are implying.'

'And what do you think I am implying, Miss High-And-Mighty?'

'How dare you lecture me, Tom? You are not my keeper, and you are on my land, so please go back to your billet and stop interfering in my affairs.'

'Affairs being the operative word.'

His sarcasm hurt. 'Oh, just go away! Go on, clear off. You are not welcome at my house!'

I'd said too much. White faced, Tom marched away, his broad shoulders squared, outrage in every line of his tall body. I wanted to call him back, but the words stuck in my throat. How dare he assume that I would stay the night with a man I hardly knew? With any man, for that matter.

I entered the hallway of Aberglasney and was immediately in love with my house again, washed by the tranquillity of the pale thin sunlight falling through the stained tall windows. The house creaked and groaned though there was no one in sight. Even Beatrice seemed to be absent on one of her trips. I wondered where she'd gone, as I often did when she disappeared, but then she was part of the package that came with buying the house. I'd agreed to her staying over sometimes, though she seemed more often here with me than anywhere else, and right now I missed her.

I made some tea and sat in the spotless kitchen drinking it, feeling suddenly alone. Mrs Ward had been here cleaning while I was in London – that was evident in the sparkling cleanliness of the glass in the panelled corner cupboard and the well-swept wooden floor.

I wandered up to my studio taking my cup with me, warming my hands around the china more for comfort than because I was cold. On the landing, I thought I caught a glimpse of white cotton and the drift of floating hair, but when I blinked the corridor was empty. *I'm tired from the long drive*, I thought. *I'd better not begin a new painting today. Perhaps a rest will do me good?*

In my room, I finished the dregs of my tea and then lay

back against the pillows. I must have slept because I thought a lover came to me . . . he was Tom but not Tom. A man a few years older than Tom. A man with laughter lines round his eyes.

When I woke, I wondered what it was all about, and then I stopped worrying about the dream and remembered that Tom and I had quarrelled.

FOURTEEN

I saw Carl Jenkins myself. I didn't want any more quarrels with Tom.

Carl looked shamefaced but mutinous. 'Sorry, Miss Evans, but I took what was freely offered. No man could resist such a lovely young girl. It's just asking too much of humankind.'

'You took precautions to protect her, did you? She was a virgin, wasn't she?' I stumbled over speaking such plain language, but Carl's head bent even lower.

'I didn't know she was a good girl, ma'am. I met her in a public house and –' he shrugged – 'well, I just thought.' He stopped when he saw my expression.

'Was Rosie in the bar?'

'Why, no. She was in a tiny room at the back.'

'The snug?' I didn't wait for a reply. 'It's where the ladies go, officer. It is the custom for respectable women to sit together in a room away from the men and talk and relax. The snug is not a place into which a man usually strays.'

'I didn't know that,' Carl said in a low deep voice.

'So you ruined the girl's reputation, and what are you going to do about it?' He didn't reply. I persisted: 'Can you imagine the shame of bringing an illegitimate child into the village?'

He nodded silently.

'What are you going to do about it?' I demanded.

'What can I do, Miss Evans? I got a wife and children of my own back home. I got enough mouths to feed as it is.'

'Well, isn't that hard luck for you then?'

'What do you mean, ma'am?'

'I mean, this child is going to be your responsibility and so is Rosie. She's talking about having an abortion! It's against the law and dangerous as well. What if she died?'

Carl's head was almost touching his chest now. He was behaving like a chastised child.

'Sort something out.' I almost whispered the words, but they sounded like a clarion call in the pale misty morning air.

'Excuse me, Miss Evans.' Tom loomed out of the mist. 'Where do you think you get off chastising my men?'

'Someone has to if you won't.' I felt myself grow tense. I didn't want to quarrel any more with Tom, but he couldn't speak to me like that and get away with it. 'Jenkins has a responsibility to Rosie, and so have you. I can't let her risk an abortion, and I don't think you can either. Think of the bad publicity the Americans would get if it got into the papers.'

'Are you blackmailing me, Miss Evans?' His voice was icy. I thought of the times Tom and I had sat together close, warm in the summer twilight under the arch of the cloisters, and I felt like crying.

'I suppose I am.' My voice was equally cold. 'Your officer has ruined a girl's reputation. He's insulted her because he didn't know our habits. Here in the village respectable old women and young ladies can sit in what we call the "snug" without being labelled "loose women" . . . but that's what officer Jenkins did, isn't it?'

'That's a matter of opinion.'

'No, it is not!' I would have stamped my foot if I hadn't been standing on grass. 'Rosie was *respectable*,' I said. 'Just ask your officer; he took her innocence.'

Jenkins looked at his feet, and Tom had no choice but to believe what I was saying was true.

There was silence, and then Carl Jenkins spoke in his deep Southern drawl. 'I'll take care of it, sir,' he said, lifting his head. 'I'll take Rosie back home with me, and we'll sort something out for her.'

I sighed in relief. I couldn't wait to see Rosie and tell her it would be all right. Tom, however, turned away and walked off without a word to me. In my mind I made excuses for him: he was embarrassed, upset, feeling guilty at not believing me. And yet, as I turned to go home to

Aberglasney, I felt tears cooling as they ran down my hot face.

Once I was home I managed to tell Rosie the good news, and she closed her eyes in relief. 'I knew he wouldn't let me down,' she breathed. 'He loves me, and I love him. It's going to be all right.'

But the next day Carl Jenkins was killed trying a new modification to one of the plane engines.

FIFTEEN

The next ghost hunt in September was another success. Even more people attended, and though the bedrooms were not quite finished I managed to fit fifty people into Aberglasney House.

Mrs Ward and Rosie did their usual cooking and waiting on tables, and even though Rosie could not hide her devastation at Carl's untimely death she rouged her cheeks and managed to look almost pretty.

One of the ghost hunters, a young man from Yorkshire, took a liking to Rosie's by now rather voluptuous figure and flirted outrageously with her all weekend. Even though Mrs Ward frowned, and tried to freeze young William with a look every time she saw him, he persisted in his attentions until at last, in spite of her mother's displeasure, Rosie agreed to sit with him in the dining room after supper and have a glass of sherry with him.

Later I talked to her. Her blue eyes were shadowed, her face pale beneath her rouge, and in spite of her burgeoning size her mother hadn't yet guessed her condition.

'You have to talk to your mother,' I said. 'Look, I'll help you. I'll have the baby here as much as I can.'

'But –' Rosie was almost in tears – 'there *can't* be a baby. You can imagine how my mum would take it if I brought shame on her!'

'You can't still want to abort it.'

'Why not?' Rosie was uncomprehending.

'It's too late to get rid of it,' I said firmly. 'No doctor will do it now. You are much too far gone. Six or seven months, is it?'

Rosie shrugged helplessly. 'I don't really know.'

Mrs Ward came into the room her dark, bird like eyes bright with suspicion. She put her hand on her daughter's shoulders and shook her. 'You've fallen for a baby, haven't you? Tell me the truth, Rosie, before I smack it out of you.' Rosie started to cry, and her mother shook her roughly once more.

My heart was in my mouth. Mrs Ward was a formidable lady, but I had to speak out. It was clear Rosie couldn't say anything. 'Mrs Ward, please stop manhandling your daughter! You might harm her and the baby.'

Mrs Ward's mouth was a tight line, but she forced herself to speak. 'It would be the best thing. Who's the father, Rosie? Tell me.'

'He's dead, if you must know.' Rosie's voice was a wail of pain. 'I loved him, he was going to take me to America with him, but he's dead! Now are you satisfied?'

Mrs Ward froze. 'An American? Don't tell me your bastard child will be a foreigner!'

'Oh, Mum, can't you care about me for a change? Worry about *my* feelings, not your own?'

I was so sorry for Rosie, and when her mother didn't move I held Rosie in my arms myself.

She appealed to her mother. 'Will you help me, Mum?'

'How *can* I help you?' Mrs Ward was still stiff-backed, but I sensed her attitude had softened.

'I don't know!' Rosie burst into hysterical tears again, and at last Mrs Ward came to her and took her away from me, holding her tightly.

'I'll do my best, we'll go away somewhere, it will be all right,' Mrs Ward said, but her tone was rigidly cool, her brow furrowed with a frown. 'Though how I will be able to support us all without a job, I don't know.'

'You and Rosie can stay here with me,' I said, not being entirely unselfish because I knew I couldn't manage without the two of them to help me with the weekends. 'There are downstairs rooms at the back of the house, unused. We'll do those up between us.'

'But folk will still know. They'll talk about us,' Mrs Ward said quietly.

'Rosie will have to have the baby,' I said firmly. 'She's too far advanced in her pregnancy to abort the child now. I'll talk to Tom. He'll think of something, I'm sure.'

I hadn't spoken to Tom for some days, but I'd wanted an excuse to try to patch things up between us – and this might be it.

However, when I went to see him, Tom was cold and distant. 'If you've come to make a scene, remember I've just lost a good pilot and a good man.'

I wanted to retort that if Carl Jenkins was such a good man, why did he have an affair with a young innocent girl when he had a wife at home? However, I sat down in his office and just took a deep breath instead.

'I've had to write a letter home telling Carl's wife that her husband has been killed.' He spoke defensively, wearily.

'I only wanted to ask your advice,' I said.

His lines of strain softened. 'I'm sorry. I know you're trying to help the girl, and I've been hard on you as well as her. What can I do?'

I shrugged helplessly. 'I don't know.'

He poured us a drink from the bottle in his drawer and sat down again, reaching for my hand as I sat down next to him. It felt comfortable and comforting to have his fingers touching mine, however lightly.

'I wondered if the baby could go to America to be cared for . . . by his own sort,' I finished lamely, knowing I sounded patronizing.

'Black-skinned folk, you mean.' Tom withdrew his hand.

'Yes.' I lifted my chin defensively. 'You can imagine what sort of life the child would have here among a white community, a very insular village community at that.'

Tom sighed. 'I do understand. Perhaps I can arrange something when the child is old enough to travel –' he looked up hopefully – 'unless Rosie wants to go too?'

'I don't think she does. In any case, her mother wouldn't allow it.'

'Her mother can't run her life for ever.'

'I know, but Rosie is young, impressionable . . . Goodness knows what would happen to her if she went away with a baby and tried to manage without her mum.'

'How's the painting going?' He seemed to soften his voice just slightly.

I smiled up at him, longing for him to take me in his arms although he did nothing of the sort. 'Fine. My last exhibition was a great success.'

'I imagine so. After all, you stayed the night in London with your agent . . . or whatever he is.' There was now an edge to Tom's voice that I didn't like very much.

I didn't see why I should explain myself to him but I did anyway. 'That's right. Mr Readings had a lady friend who ran a guest house. I stayed there for the night because it was late and—'

'And your Mr Readings stayed there too, I presume.'

'He did, as a matter of fact.' I tried to gloss over the awkwardness between us. 'He was very pleased at the sales we achieved. Of course, I have to pay him for exhibiting and framing and all that sort of thing, so the profits are virtually halved.'

'Perhaps you have another arrangement – other than money, I mean.'

I took in his meaning, and the hurt made me stand up and step away from him. So that's what he thought of me and my work! That I sold my body in exchange for Mr Readings rustling up a few rich customers, who were then persuaded to buy my paintings. I felt like hitting Tom. He was maligning me and my work as an artist. 'Thanks a million,' I said sarcastically and walked away.

Fuming, I went into the house and walked upstairs to my studio. I heard footsteps running up the stairs behind me, and Rosie came into the room.

'What's happening miss?' She was breathless.

'Air Commander Maybury has agreed to send the baby to America to be brought up by a black family,' I said. 'Now please, Rosie, go away. I have to work if I'm to pay your wages.' I know I sounded sharp, but Tom's harsh and unjustified accusations had wounded me.

I mixed some paints and began to paint: angry colours, bright colours, red and yellow edged with white, the house on fire, flames leaping out of the old roof. And then I painted a faint figure on the roof and covered it with a few layers of a mixture of greyed down and white. She was

almost invisible in a cloud of smoke. I don't know why I
painted it. As far as I knew the house had never been on
fire, but then no one said art should represent real events.
And yet I shivered, hoping I wasn't tempting fate.

It was almost dark by the time I'd stopped work and,
exhausted, I left the studio. When I went downstairs to the
kitchen it was empty. Mrs Ward must have finished for the
night, and she and Rosie had gone home. A tray of cold
meat and pickle was left covered on a tray on the kitchen
table, and an upturned cup was placed in the matching
saucer, ready for me to make myself a cup of tea.

The house was silent, not even the creaking and groaning
of the old boards disturbed the silence. I shivered, feeling
very alone, but a cup of hot tea and some food soon put
me in a better mood.

After, I wandered round the house looking for Beatrice.
There was no sign of her; she was on one of her mysterious 'trips'. I never knew when she would be here or away,
and I felt a momentary irritation. It wouldn't be much
trouble for her to tell me her plans. It was rude to just
vanish!

And then, as if my thoughts had touched her, she was
there outside her door. It hadn't opened or closed, she
was just there. I drew back, startled. Was she a ghost or a
figment of my overworked, overwrought imagination?

'What's wrong, dear? You look as if you've seen a ghost.'
She was so matter-of-fact that I laughed in relief. I was
tired, there were shadows on the landing and I was imagining
things – foolish things like ghosts.

'You startled me, Beatrice,' I said. 'For a moment there,
I thought I was seeing things.'

'Come and sit in my room, dear, you look worried. We
can talk, if you like. I'm a very good listener.'

I thought of my nice cup of tea waiting for me in the
kitchen. I'd made a fresh pot before I'd gone wandering. 'No
thanks, Beatrice,' I said. 'I've got some paperwork to do.'

'Well, I'll say goodbye then, dear.' She spoke softly. 'I'm
going away tonight to visit some of my people, and I'll see
you in a few weeks' time.'

'Beatrice, I've got a ghost-haunting weekend in a few weeks. I want my guests to see you. They are convinced you are not of this world!'

'Are any of us, dear?' Beatrice said and went into her room, closing the door quietly behind her.

I quickly returned to the cheerfulness of the kitchen and sat near the warmth of the open fire. I had a gas stove in there but I loved the coal fire, and now I crouched near it with my cup of tea in my hands.

I must have dozed, because when I opened my eyes my cup was placed neatly on the floor between my feet and from outside I heard the sound of horse's hooves against the drive. I hurried to the front door and looked out in time to see an old-fashioned hansom carriage pulling away. Even as I watched, bewildered, the whole thing slowly vanished, and I was left gaping at the arch that led away from the house.

Was I going mad? Was I working too hard concentrating on ghostly images – imagining the house on fire, haunted? Next I would believe the five young maids were *really* haunting Aberglasney.

I hurried back to the kitchen and poured myself a sherry and sat shivering, afraid even to fetch more coal. I jumped when there was a gentle tapping on the back door. It came again more insistently, and then Tom's voice called out to me.

'Riana, are you in there? Will you let me talk to you? I want to apologize.'

Eagerly, I opened the back door. 'Come in, Tom. Want a cup of tea?' I was so pleased to see a real live human that I couldn't even keep my voice cool.

'You look so pale. What's wrong, Riana?' Tom sat at the table, his big bulk reassuringly solid.

'I'm being silly, Tom, but I thought I saw a hansom cab pulling away from the house.' The words were out before I could prevent them.

Tom smiled. 'I'm afraid that's my fault.'

'How do you mean?' I was unable to keep the tremble out of my voice.

Tom took my hand. 'I'm sorry, Riana. I was silly not to ask old Frank from the village to wait till morning to show it to you. I thought it would help the ghost weekend look more authentic to have an old carriage outside.' He looked rather sheepish. 'It's by way of an apology. I was wrong to accuse you of staying the night and . . . Well, you know. I apologize.'

I smiled forgivingly, although I was still hurt so I chose to ignore his apology. 'Thanks for the carriage – and how silly of me. I actually believed in ghosts for a while.' I spoke lightly. 'Anyway, come and see my latest painting.' I didn't know why I'd said it, I should have sent him packing after his accusations about my morals, but he followed me upstairs and my heart warmed that he was at least friendly to me again.

He stood before the canvas and regarded it, head on one side. I watched him, my heart in my throat. It was strange how much I wanted his approval.

'It's one of your best,' he said at last. 'It's powerful and colourful. The light of the flames is glowing off the canvas, and yet you've managed to put that ghostly image on the roof. It's really wonderful.'

I wanted to hug him. Even now, after my recent successes, I still felt anxious about my work, as if I was a fraud who would one day be caught out.

'Will you have a cup of tea with me, Tom?' I was almost humble, and when Tom put his arm around my shoulders and smiled down at me I wanted to throw myself at him and kiss him and beg him to make love to me. Of course, I did no such thing. I shrugged off his arm and went downstairs, worried that he would think me fast.

We had a cup of tea in companionable silence. I felt better than I'd done for days because Tom was here with me and we weren't quarrelling.

I poured both of us more tea, and Tom spoke at last. 'Tell me about the sale in London,' he said.

'Everything sold,' I said meekly. 'Thanks to Mr Readings.'

'And you stayed in a guest house overnight?'

'That's right. The guest house belongs to Mr Readings' . . . er . . . lady friend,' I added anxiously.

Tom smiled. 'I'm really sorry I implied anything else.'

'So am I.' I spoke a little tartly.

'*Really* sorry. Now, to change the subject, I've made arrangements for Rosie's little child to go to a good family in America.' He didn't look at me. 'It's the best I can do. Airman Jenkins might have been misguided, but he wasn't a bad man. Still, you can be assured the baby will be very well looked after by a good professional childless couple who want a baby very badly.'

'Thank goodness that's settled.' I heaved a sigh of relief. I would be able to tell Rosie in the morning that all was arranged.

'How many months before the child will be born?'

'About two, I think. She doesn't really know herself. She didn't realize there *was* a baby coming until she was well on.' I looked at Tom with half-closed eyes. 'That's how innocent she was.'

'OK, I get the message, Riana. I shouldn't have put the blame on Rosie, I realized that from the start, but I was defending one of my men. You can understand that, surely.'

'Yes, Tom, but you were very hard on Rosie and—' He held up his hand and I stopped speaking.

'Let's just leave it there before we start to argue about it again,' Tom said. 'What about another cup of tea? Or better still a glass of wine or something. You could put on your coat, and we could sit under the cloisters like we did in the summer.'

It was good to sit in the darkness with Tom, huddled against the warmth of his shoulder, knowing we were friends again. I risked a question. 'You didn't really think I'd spent the night with Mr Readings, did you?' My throat was dry, and if I expected Tom to make more and profuse apologies I was mistaken. He made a joke of it.

'Well, I've heard about you artist types! Your flamboyant careless lifestyles and all that.'

I smacked his cheek playfully, and Tom caught my hand and kissed it. It was an erotic gesture, his warm mouth in the palm of my hand, his tongue darting against my skin. I felt myself grow warm and I drew away, startled by my own feelings.

'I think I'm falling in love with you, Miss Evans,' Tom breathed against my cheek.

Enough was enough. I was moved and thrilled, and yet I had the uneasy feeling Tom was still joking with me. I stood up, putting the cold air between us. 'How do I know you haven't got a wife at home like poor Carl Jenkins?'

'How indeed?' Tom touched his forelock. 'But I've told you the truth; there is no wife. Goodnight, Miss Evans, dear Miss Evans, and sweet dreams.' And then he was striding away down my now neat garden towards the barracks.

SIXTEEN

The latest ghost weekend was well under way, and the house was fuller than it had ever been. It was October, and although it was only autumn it felt like deep winter had set in, and fires roared the rooms we used most. As for upstairs, I'd installed electric fires in the bedrooms, not wanting to take the chance of noxious fumes bringing death and destruction to my house. Luckily, the walls were thick stone and the heat seemed contained.

Wine was being drunk, and hearty, cheerful voices could be heard all over the house, but I was lonely. I'd heard that the few remaining Americans were finally packing up to leave Aberglasney, and Tom had not yet spoken to me about it.

As it neared midnight, I extinguished the lights. My guests held torches, as well as candles and box cameras and other equipment designed to detect the presence of spirits, and we all fell silent.

'The blue room is the area of the haunting,' I said in a hushed whisper that carried sibilantly around the silent guests. The colonel as always was at my side, and Mr Bleesdale had finally come along, accompanied by a peroxided young woman with large bosoms who led the crowd towards the stairs.

A serious young man with a notepad and pen had joined the group. His name was Colin Sharp, and he had his college scarf slung in a careless fashion around his neck. He never once smiled, though I suppose he thought his work serious enough. He was working for his doctorate in Pharmacology, which seemed to have nothing at all to do with ghost hunting.

There was a collective gasp as lights could be seen flickering across the landing: five distinct lights shrouded in a haze of mist. Mr Bleesdale faltered and stepped back down into the hall. His lady friend gave a little screech and clung to his arm.

Colin Sharp gave a disgusted mutter. 'Charlatans, frauds, it's a trick to separate you fools from your money. You silly deluded folk don't really believe in ghosts, do you?' He pushed his way up the stairs towards the lights, and when he reached the landing he seemed to be engulfed in the mist, the lights forming a circle around him. The mist grew denser and no one else ventured upstairs.

I was as puzzled as everyone else, and we stood and watched until the mist evaporated and the lights disappeared, and then I heard Mrs Ward shouting for help.

Someone turned the gas lights on, and the one electric light near the front door shed a warm beam into the hallway. The young college student was lying in a heap on the landing, and – with my heart in my mouth – I went up to him. He was pale but breathing, and he seemed to have just fainted, possibly overcome by the beer he'd drunk.

'Did anyone get a picture?' the colonel demanded, but it seemed no one had. With the help of the men I got Colin back into the library, and someone gave him a sip of brandy.

He opened his eyes. 'What happened?' he said dimly. 'Why did I faint away like that? I'm a healthy young man!'

'It was the ghosts,' the young blonde lady chimed in, her face pale under her make-up. 'You should never have challenged them.'

'Don't be silly! What ghosts?' It seemed Colin's memory had been stripped clean of his experiences.

'Help!' Mrs Ward pushed her way towards me. 'It's my Rosie! She's in a bad way. Why are you all still fussing round this obviously drunk young man when my Rosie needs a doctor?'

I knew at once that the baby must be coming. Rosie must be even further along than we'd thought. 'Anyone here a doctor?' I asked, feeling very dramatic. To my surprise, Mr Bravage held up his hand.

'Will I do, dear lady? I'm retired now, but unless there's anyone else I'll offer my services.'

'Thank you so much! Will you follow Mrs Ward? She'll take you to Rosie.' I turned to the other guests. 'Tonight has certainly been very strange, and it's not for me to say what happened here, but I think you all need a drink to settle you down for the night. Please help yourself from the bar.'

The bar was small, newly installed with a few bottles of spirits and a crate of beer under the shelf. I hoped there would be enough to go round. The drink had gone well this evening and would probably be used in a 'medicinal' way after the events of the night.

I went to Rosie's little bedroom, and she was sitting up against the pillows – apparently as well as I was. 'What's all the fuss about?' I asked. 'You seem fine to me.'

'With respects, miss, you haven't had a baby,' Rosie said. 'It comes and goes, like, the pains. One minute everything don't hurt, and then the pitchforks of hell are digging into you.'

I looked at Mr Bravage, who appeared unfamiliar in his shirt sleeves.

He nodded, confirming what Rosie had just told me. 'Perhaps you'll stay and help, Miss Evans?' he said. 'My . . . er . . . niece is not very practical at this sort of thing. The sight of blood makes her faint away.'

'What a surprise!'

My sarcasm was not lost on Mr Bravage. He smiled wryly and said, 'In this life one takes what one can get, dear lady.'

Rosie seemed to crunch up and began to moan, grasping her stomach for dear life.

'Easy, child. Just try to go with the pain.' Mr Bravage gently settled Rosie back against the pillows. 'Conserve your strength, there's a good girl. It may be a few hours yet.'

Rosie looked horrified. 'Hours! But I can't stand all this torture for hours! What can you give me to ease the pain?'

'All I have with me is some indigestion tablets.' Mr Bravage stretched out his hands apologetically. 'I don't carry a bag with me, not any more.'

'I'll see what I can find,' I said, and with a sigh of relief left the room with Rosie's agonized moans following me.

Beatrice was away on one of her trips, but in her room there might be something we could give Rosie. I felt ill at ease as I mounted the stairs and even worse as I went into Beatrice's room. I hated prying, but I had to help Rosie.

There was a little medicine box beside the bed, and hopefully I opened it. Neatly arranged were some bottles all labelled in fine handwriting. I read them one by one, but there seemed nothing that would help Rosie through the pains of childbirth. In the bottom drawer of the little box, however, there was a bottle of laudanum. I put it in my pocket and hurried to the library to talk to my disoriented guest. He was a pharmacist; perhaps he could help.

'Colin, how are you feeling?' I asked.

He looked at me blearily. 'Never better,' he said. He was evidently more than a little drunk.

'Look –' I showed him the small bottle of laudanum – 'is this all right to give to someone in childbirth?'

'Of course, Miss Evans. Laudanum is still being used and will be for some time to come. It is a derivative of opium, you know. Not so potent, but good for toothache or some such thing. Though, I must say, that looks like a very old bottle. Still, it should be all right, I think.'

Reassured, I hurried back to Rosie's room and gave the struggling, red-faced girl a spoonful of laudanum. It seemed to ease the pain, but it made Rosie rather lethargic and sleepy.

'The contractions are not so intense now,' Mr Bravage said. 'What was that medicine you gave her, Miss Evans?'

'Just a painkiller, some laudanum, Colin said it should be all right.'

'That's not good for this sort of situation. It has slowed down the labour, you see. The more severe the contractions, the sooner the baby is delivered safely into this world.'

'I'm so sorry.'

I think we all fell asleep for an hour or two because I heard Rosie groan and I woke up with a suddenness that brought me upright in my chair. Mr Bravage was slumped in his chair snoring, and only Mrs Ward was wide awake – her eyes beady like those of a bird as she stared disapprovingly at me.

'I don't know what you gave my girl, but she's no nearer

to giving birth than she was a few hours ago.' I explained
to her what Colin had told me, and she shook her head and
put the small bottle into her pocket. 'Well, that was no use.'

The house was silent. *Everyone else must be asleep*, I
thought. Not even the 'ghosts' stirred along the landing as
I looked out. The wind had dropped, and a soft rain spat-
tered the windows like gentle tears. I stood at the window
and looked towards the barracks; lights were on, and I realized Tom must still be awake.

I went downstairs into the hall and reached for my coat
and scarf; a walk in the fresh air would do me good. My
head was aching, and I wondered if Rosie would ever
have the baby.

In a way, I would be glad when it was all over and the
child taken to America. But then Tom would be gone too
and with him my hopes and dreams of a future together.
Tom had never made any promises, Tom had said nothing
at all to give me hope, and yet I knew I hadn't imagined
the closeness between us as we'd sat so often under the
cloisters in the gardens of Aberglasney.

Tom was in his room poring over a map as if he couldn't
wait to get away. I felt hurt and betrayed, although I had
no right to feel any of those things.

'Good evening . . . or is it good morning?' I spoke politely
as if to a stranger.

Tom looked at his wrist, at the large watch he wore with
the special dials. 'It's zero four hours,' he said. 'Four o'clock
in the morning.'

'Rosie's still in labour, if you're interested,' I said briskly.
'When you leave, I hope you can take the child with you.'

'Just as well I'm not going just yet then, isn't it?' He
smiled, and I was overwhelmed with a sense of relief – and,
yes, gratitude.

'I suppose so.' I stumbled over the words. 'I suppose
Rosie will have to get the baby used to boiled milk or whatever it is they give babies.'

'What's wrong, Riana? You seemed a little overwrought,'
Tom said.

Suddenly, I was insanely furious. 'Oh, nothing really!' I

said in a loud voice. 'Tonight a man in my party nearly died when we were apparently visited by ghosts, Rosie is about to give birth to a illegitimate baby, and you are sitting calmly down in the barracks not concerning your little self with any part of it!'

'Come on, Riana, let me pour you some coffee. You should have sent for me. I'd have done all I could to help, you know that.'

I wanted to cry, and I wasn't sure why. I watched, stony faced, as he poured me coffee and then gulped the scalding liquid as if it would take the lump away from my throat.

'I'll come up to the house with you and see what's happening.' He took my arm, and I put down my coffee quickly, slopping a little on to the table. We walked up through the gardens in silence.

The lights were still on; my guests were still sitting up drinking with no thoughts of going to bed. I couldn't blame them, for the events of the night had been too exciting for them to give up and go to sleep. My ghost-haunting weekend would be more infamous than ever, I realized. I would have to get more help. Mrs Ward couldn't manage it all alone now that Rosie would be laid up for a while.

As we went into the bedroom, I heard the shrill sound of a baby's cry, and then I gasped in astonishment – the baby lying on the sheets was as white-skinned as I was!

Mr Bravage did some medical things to the baby, and then handed the little being to Rosie.

Tom went up to the bed and took Rosie's hand. 'I think it's time you told us the truth, Rosie.' He spoke firmly, but his voice was kind.

Rosie had tears in her eyes. 'The baby must be following me, sir. Fair, and all that.'

Tom examined the baby's knuckles and elbows and softly touched the fine golden hair. 'Rosie, are you sure the boy is Officer Jenkins' son?'

Rosie's voice was bright. She seemed revived, back to her old flirtatious self. This childbirth was a strange experience all right! 'No, sir, he must be yours.'

I felt the blood drain from my face.

Tom smiled and shook his head. 'Rosie, you and I both know that's not true, honey. Were you having a relationship with anyone else?'

'It's yours, sir. Remember that Army Air Force party in early spring? You were the only other one I danced with beside Carl.' Her laugh tinkled out, and it was as though Rosie had been to a party, not gone through hours of gruelling pain.

'Rosie, stop that at once,' Tom said sternly.

Rosie looked at me. 'Sorry, miss, I know he's your man and all that, but I couldn't help it. I was so flattered when Mr Tom danced with me and held me close an' all.'

'Rosie!' Tom sounded exasperated. 'You can't have a baby just with dancing, you know.'

Blind anger boiled in me. Tom had danced with Rosie, held her close . . . how could he? I didn't wait to hear any more. I ran across the landing and into my bedroom and locked the door behind me. I crept into bed and pulled the blankets up over my face and let the tears flow.

SEVENTEEN

'When are you going to do another exhibition for me, dear Riana?' Mr Readings had become far friendlier since the last exhibition, when all but one of my paintings had sold. Now even that one had gone, and I was so pleased. It had been darker than usual, with blues and greens mixed and lots of velvety leaves with just a few purple irises to give a splash of colour.

Mr Readings seemed to read my mind. 'The last painting of foliage was very good, my dear, but when you put just a touch of ghostliness into the work it sells like hot cakes. Take this one now –' he pointed at my picture of the mansion on fire – 'it could just be a blaze – very nice colour mix, well lit indeed against the dark skies – but that one solitary indistinct figure on the roof makes it so much more than just a house in flames . . . do you see what I mean?'

'I do see what you mean,' I said and meant it. I knew full well that my ghostly pictures had set a new trend of realism with just a touch of the unreal or 'other world' as Mr Readings liked to call it.

'You've hit on something there, Riana. Don't let it go, whatever you do. Somehow the inspiration you show when you paint the "other world" brings life to the work. The painting is so much finer for it. I can't explain it any better than that. It's as if someone else guides your hand.' He shrugged. 'But isn't that the way with most creative people? The spirit moves, and we react to it.'

He laughed at his own joke, but to me it wasn't a joke it was true. Just as Mr Readings said, it was as if someone guided my hand. Suddenly, I was afraid. What if the guiding hand went away? What if I couldn't really paint?

'Well, Riana, when can you have another exhibition ready?'

'I don't know, Mr Readings. When the spirit moves me,

I suppose.' I couldn't help smiling, and he smiled back at me. He really was a very handsome man – humorous, too, now that I knew him better.

While in town I bought a new batch of paints, some canvases and a sketch pad. It all cost money, but these, I reminded myself, were the tools of my trade. I packed them away in my van, and then I went to find a nice cup of tea and somewhere to sit for a few minutes while I tried to make a list of things I wanted for the house.

The November sun, pale and wintry, was nevertheless warm through the bowed glass windows of the tea shop. The cloth on the table was pristine white, and my cup, saucer and teapot were painted with pretty delicate flowers.

I suddenly felt very alone.

Tom. I'd tried to put him out of my mind since the awful night when Rosie had accused him of fathering her baby. He'd protested his innocence, and the baby could just have inherited Rosie's fine white skin and blue eyes, but her words at the baby's birth had made me feel sick and hollow. I knew she was teasing, but a doubt niggled at my mind all the same.

The baby – Rosie had named him John – was still with us. He could hardly go to America to be brought up by a dark-skinned American family, not now. It didn't seem appropriate, in any case. Rosie had bonded with the boy and seemed to love him with such motherliness it would be a shame to part them. Still, Mrs Ward still asserted that John should be adopted.

My stomach seemed to cramp with pain whenever I imagined Tom dancing with Rosie. He hadn't denied that. She had probably been the worse for drink and lapping up the attention.

I finished my tea and asked for the bill, and then I stepped outside into the cold sunshine. My eyes were dazzled by the light, but I was aware of a tall figure blocking my way. 'Tom?'

It was as if he'd been conjured up by my thoughts. My arm was held tightly, and I was led back inside the tea shop. I sank down into the chair I'd just vacated, and Tom sat opposite me.

'Listen to me, Riana. I've never touched Rosie, I don't know why she thinks it a joke to accuse me. Unlike the summer American Army Air Force party, when I spent most of the evening dancing with you, honey, I was only at the spring party for about an hour.'

'You still danced with her,' I said hotly.

'I danced with many of the young ladies present, and then I left. Why should I lie?' Tom challenged.

'I don't know.' I shrugged in bewilderment. 'Just tell me the truth, Tom. What really happened?'

'I was on duty, so I only called in just to show my face. Then I patrolled the grounds until about ten fifteen, as usual.' He shrugged helplessly. 'That's all I can tell you, Riana. It was a long time ago.'

I knew there was no way I could be sure Tom was telling the truth. Carl Jenkins was dead; most of the other men had been sent back to America. 'But the baby is white, no arguing with that,' I said uneasily.

'I think I was the first one to point that out,' Tom said.

'Could the baby be a sort of throwback to another generation?' I think I was being hopeful.

Tom shook his head. 'I don't know. Carl Jenkins's family are all African American, but it's quite possible there was a white connection years ago. Anyway, the child could have Rosie's genes.'

'He could have white blood back along the line,' I said. Carl's name was Jenkins, a British name, after all. But that apart, I didn't like to think of Rosie being in trouble. I bit my lip and looked at Tom. 'What can we do to help her?'

Tom rubbed the gathering lines on his forehead. 'I don't rightly know.'

I rose from my chair. 'Anyway, I have to get back home to Aberglasney. I have a lot to do! There's another haunting party next week.'

Tom's mouth twitched into a familiar smile. 'Why not just ghost *hunting*?' he asked.

'I prefer ghost haunting. It's more descriptive, somehow. Anyway, it brings the guests in, doesn't it?'

'No need to be defensive. I was only asking.'

For a moment we seemed to back on familiar ground, playfully baiting each other, smiling and being happy. I sat down again and asked for another pot of tea. For an hour or two we laughed and joked as we used to, while Tom held my hand and I felt a warm glow of happiness as all our differences seemed swept away. Tom had that magical quality that made me believe everything he said while I was with him. And then, suddenly, he became thoughtful. It was growing dark outside by now, and the magic seemed to vanish. The silence lengthened. and there seemed nothing left to say. 'Well, I'd better get home,' I said eventually.

He made no move to stop me.

'See you, Tom.' I made for the door, and as the bell clanked behind me I half expected Tom to come rushing out after me.

He didn't.

I glanced back and saw that he was walking purposefully towards the centre of town. I wondered, worriedly, where he was going and what he was going to do so far from his barracks. Perhaps he had another lady friend somewhere in the village? Doubt blossomed, and then I told myself I was being silly, paranoid, totally unrealistic. If there had been any talk about Tom and a village girl I would have heard about it. Or would I?

I went to bed miserable and tearful that night and shut my ears to any sounds that the house was making around me.

EIGHTEEN

The colonel, as usual, was the first guest to arrive. And, as usual, he'd brought a huge amount of equipment with him. As he alighted from his taxi he looked up at the windows and waved. I stepped outside to greet him and glanced upwards, but I couldn't see anything. 'Who were you waving at Colonel?' I asked, and he winked at me and tugged his little moustache.

'Never you mind, young Riana, we all see something different in this house. *I* see the ghost of the old lady in Victorian dress.' He rested his cases on the ground, gesturing to the driver to help him inside with them.

'You mean Beatrice?' I said in relief. 'She's no—' I stopped speaking. I didn't have to let him know Beatrice was just a friend and not a ghost at all. She was old and a bit strange, but she was as solid as I was.

At dinner, later, when all my guests had arrived and were seated around the dining tables, Mrs Ward and Rosie served roast lamb and mint sauce. The whole thing seemed to have an air of familiarity about it, and strangely Rosie looked her usual comely self, exactly as she had been before she'd given birth to the baby.

The door blew open, and there was a sound of wailing and crying from upstairs. Everyone left the dinner and rushed out into the hall and up the stairs to see at close quarters the flickering lights. This had happened before; either I was losing my mind, or I was in some terrible nightmare.

Beatrice appeared briefly, but retreated as she saw the people rush towards her, cameras flashing.

The colonel spoke the exact same words he'd spoken before. 'Did you see the Victorian lady? Anyone catch a picture of her? She's called "Beatrice", you know.'

Lights still flickered on the landing, and I found *myself*

repeating exactly the same words I knew I'd used before.
'Here on this landing, the five murdered maids are alleged
to seek release from their chains of death.' My voice was
sepulchral, and everyone fell silent. I *was* going mad.

One lady screamed, the lights vanished, and young
William spoke up bravely. 'Search the rooms, everyone!'

'Mr Bravage, all of you, please do search, and if you
find anything rigged or to be a hoax I will refund your
money.' I felt I was reliving a terrible nightmare, but I had
to speak in my defence. Nothing was rigged, I knew that.

I felt the same sense of fear and unease as I had the first
time all this had happened. Or *was* this the first time it had
happened, and I'd dreamed it before? I didn't know anything
any more.

When we walked back towards the stairs, I hesitated
outside Beatrice's room. I felt the same reluctance to invade
her territory, but Mr Bravage shouted, 'Go on then! Let's
see the lady ghost. Find out if she's alive and kicking!'

I opened Beatrice's door, but she wasn't there. The room
was empty. Relieved, I stepped back and let the other guests
in, led by Mr Bravage. I'd had enough. I clearly remembered
the rest of it: how Mr Bravage had 'sensed a presence' and
then the colonel had smelled decay in the room, a smell I'd
put down to Beatrice's old lavender scent.

Later, as we sat down again to our meal, I still felt the
same dreamlike quality pervading the room. People talked
in loud excited voices. We seemed to move slowly through
the same conversations. I drank a great deal of wine and
went to bed and slept soundly, and in the morning – to my
relief – my guests left, although not before telling me that
Aberglasney was a real find and that I should charge more
for the weekends. It was nothing I hadn't heard before.

Tired beyond belief, I returned to bed and slept like a
baby. When I woke again it was sunrise, and when I eventually left my room everything was back to normal, the
clock was the right time, the date was correct, and I sat
and drank coffee in the silent peace of the dining room and
wondered how I'd dreamed such an odd dream.

But Rosie's baby wasn't a dream; he was stark reality,

and his paternity was still a matter of doubt. I tried to shake off the feeling of despair when I considered that Tom might be the father of Rosie's child.

As it happened, I didn't see anything of Tom for the next few days, and so I concentrated on my painting. I squeezed out the last of my oils, twisting the tubes round a thin stick to force the thickening paint on to my palette. I put a thin wash of ochre on the canvas and then lightly sketched in the stairs and figures of my guests looking upward to where the lights flashed along the landing.

A sense of excitement gripped me. This must have been what my 'dream' or 'vision' or whatever it had been was all about: inspiration for a new painting! Almost without realizing it, I opened my new tubes of paint and worked in the wood of the staircase, adding highlights from the flickering lights above.

The colonel was there, and Mr Bravage, and the new young man who had joined us recently. I painted in the lady who had run screaming back down the stairs and then, with a sigh, put down my brushes. I needed a reviving coffee. I was in the frame of mind where I didn't want to leave my work, but my back ached from standing before the easel and my mouth was too dry.

Mrs Ward was in the kitchen. Her face was long and gloomy. 'I don't know what's going on with Rosie,' she said without stopping her task of drying up dishes. 'She won't talk to me, just hugs that little baby all day and sits and cries over it. I'm at the end of my tether, Miss Riana.' She carefully hung the tea towel over the rail of the cooker and rewrapped her apron with deft, impatient fingers.

'Would it help if Rosie stayed on with me for a while?' The words were out before I'd even considered the implications of what I was offering. A crying baby, a young mother claiming that Tom was the father of her child . . . could I handle the complications of it all?

'That would help, Miss Riana.' The words came out with a rush of relief. 'Perhaps Rosie will talk to you, you being young and all.'

I doubted it. Rosie was claiming that the man I was fond

of had fathered her child. She knew it had hurt me, and I still wasn't sure she was telling the truth, but now I'd made the offer for her to stay I would have to abide by it.

When Rosie came, bag and baggage, to live in the house with me, I stared long and hard at the baby in her arms. He was fair-skinned, but other than that he bore no resemblance to Tom. His hair was turning dark and curly, and his little nose was becoming a proper shape and was a little broad in the nostrils. I suddenly wanted to paint him. Little John with the five maids attending him. I brought my pencils and did some quick sketches while the baby was asleep. He opened his eyes and it was as though he was looking right through me. His eyes were the darkest brown.

I put Rosie to stay in my room because it was the biggest bedroom in the house, and she could put the baby in the cot I'd found in the attic. She would be comfortable there. 'Don't worry if you hear strange noises in the night,' I said, forcing a smile. 'The old house creaks and groans, but it's nothing to worry about.'

'I don't believe in all that ghost nonsense anyway,' Rosie said. 'I've seen the people come and rush around looking for lights and things, and have any of them got any proof of anything? Not one picture, not one sighting, nothing.'

'Oh, that's all right then.' I spoke a little sharply.

Rosie didn't look at me. 'I know it's all put on for the guests, as you call them. All a trick to bring in the money. I don't blame you, mind. I'd probably do the same if I owned this horrible old house.'

'Well, if it's so horrible, why do you want to live here?' I felt my anger rising. Rosie could have plenty of doubts about ghosts, but she shouldn't malign my dear old Aberglasney.

'Anywhere is better than living with my mother, narrow minded prude,' Rosie said.

I left her and went back to the kitchen where Mrs Ward was baking pies for supper. She looked at me with narrowed eyes. 'Complaining already, is she?'

I shrugged. 'She's got the biggest and best bedroom in

the house,' I said tartly. 'There's nothing else I can do to make her welcome.'

'Whatever you do it wouldn't be enough.' She glanced at me. 'I never allowed her to have callers when she lived with me, and if I were you I wouldn't allow any nonsense here.'

I looked at her in surprise. 'But I thought Rosie was in love with Carl Jenkins?'

'Oh, she was, for a time. That's her way, apparently. One today and another one tomorrow.'

'So do you think Tom is the father of her child, Mrs Ward?'

'Not a chance.' She snapped her lips tightly shut, and I knew I'd never get another word out of her on the subject.

That night I heard the usual noises on the landing: doors opening, lights flashing under the crack of the door of my unfamiliar bedroom. But, as usual, I ignored the noises and went to sleep.

The next day I worked on my painting while Rosie took the baby for a walk in the gardens. It was a sunny day in early spring and the light was good through my large studio windows.

I painted baby John and behind him ghostlike spirals of mist, depicting the five maids. There was almost no form to the figures, and yet the painting worked so well that I could see features and shapes in the mist bending over the child.

I sketched a lantern into the painting using my imagination, making a convincing orange-yellow glow shine through the lantern's tiny glass windows. I stood back, wondering how on earth I'd managed to create such a magical painting. I'd gone to art school, worked hard to get my degree, but I'd never been one of the outstanding pupils, the stars-to-be, who the teacher had favoured and respected and pandered to if they were late with their essays. It was Aberglasney that had worked the spell: the atmosphere, the ghostliness, the stone and fabric of the old house. I loved it and felt that it loved me in return.

'Stop being absurd!' I said out loud. And then I heard it:

the giggling, the muffled voices. One was a man's voice, low and somehow coaxing. I froze. Was it true that Beatrice's husband had seduced the young maids and then done away with them?

I realized then that the sounds were coming from the garden. I peered out through my open studio window and below me I could see the baby in the pram, a tiny white-faced creature covered with blankets. And there was Rosie, her pink knees akimbo and the bare backside of an unknown man exposed for all the world to see.

Hastily, I withdrew into my studio and shut the window as if *I* were the guilty one, not Rosie. I held my hand to my mouth, realizing at least that the man wasn't Tom. I knew by the heavy boots Rosie's lover had been wearing and by the rough cap on the mop of unruly hair. And then anger seized me. How dare she do it? Bring a man into my garden and let him . . . do things to her no decent man should be doing, and with the baby at her side! Wasn't she in enough trouble?

I washed my brushes, stood them in an old jam jar to dry and took off my canvas apron. I would have liked an artist's smock, but up until now I hadn't been able to afford one – and anyway, my apron had deep pockets that proved very useful. Restless now, I wanted to run down to Tom and apologize for doubting him. Of course he wasn't the father of Rosie's baby. Perhaps she didn't even know which man was. I stayed in the kitchen, however. I couldn't walk through the gardens in case I embarrassed both Rosie and myself, so I made a cup of tea, thankful that Mrs Ward would have gone home hours ago.

It was a long day, and I was glad to go to bed early and sit up reading *Rebecca* yet again until my eyes grew heavy and I turned off the gas light and went to sleep.

I woke to hear Rosie's baby crying from the next room, so I hastily made myself ready for the day and went to the kitchen to make some breakfast. From downstairs I couldn't hear if Rosie was up and about or not. I didn't know what I'd say to her when I saw her, because I wouldn't have her carrying on, risking yet another unwanted pregnancy, not while she lived under *my* roof.

It was with a feeling of excitement that, some time later, I left the house and walked through the gardens towards the barracks near the boundaries of my land. I had to see Tom and put things right with him, if I could.

He was working at his desk, and the sight of him, his hair fair and silky and his brow creased into furrows as he concentrated, made my heart melt. It hit me then, really hit me: I was in love with Tom, an American pilot who would soon be going home, leaving the country for ever.

'I'm sorry I doubted you,' I said quickly before I could lose my nerve.

He looked up and carefully wiped the ink from the nib of his pen. 'What?'

'I said I'm sorry. I realize I was silly and judgemental accusing you of being the father of Rosie's baby.'

'Well, it showed what you really thought of me. How little faith you have in my character.' His voice held no warmth.

I sat opposite him feeling as if I was applying for a job and feeling more than a little shocked at his coldly spoken words. 'I can't apologize enough,' I said. 'I really shouldn't have listened to her in the first place.'

'You should have had more trust in me.' He didn't give an inch. 'In any case, it hardly matters now. I leave for home at the end of the week. We've finished here, but thank you for your hospitality, Miss Evans.'

I was suddenly ice cold, and yet I felt in a chaos of panic at the same time. He couldn't go and leave me! Not now, when I'd just realized how much he meant to me! But I found myself getting to my feet and holding out my hand. 'Well, thank you for all your help, Tom – clearing the cloisters, the work you and the men did, all that. I'll miss you.' I stumbled over the last few words.

'Riana,' he began, but a loud knocking on the door startled us both.

I withdrew my hand . . . or was Tom the first to move? 'I'd better go and leave you to do your work,' I said.

I left by the back door and returned to the fresh air of the garden. My cheeks felt hot and I knew in my heart that Tom had been about to say something important, but I hurried through the gardens into the house.

Mrs Ward had arrived, with her shopping bag of polish and dusters, and was filling the cupboard under the sink with cleaning materials. 'Morning. You owe me three shillings and sixpence,' she said. 'Where's Rosie and the baby?'

'I don't know,' I said. 'They may not be awake yet. I've been down to see Tom, to say goodbye. The last of the Americans are leaving next week.'

'And good riddance to them,' Mrs Ward said softly. 'Master Tom was all right, kind enough and all that, but he's still a foreigner.' She glanced at me sheepishly. 'Sorry, miss.' Mrs Ward ran the tap and that was the end of the matter.

I didn't feel like working so I went in to the empty sitting room and tried to read the morning paper. There was an article entitled 'The Strange Happenings at Aberglasney', and I read a highly exaggerated account of the drama at the ghost weekend, the 'sighting' of a Victorian lady, and the strange lights on the staircase. Nothing new there, then. It was the same old local gossip, and surely by now some of the villagers must recognize Beatrice – who was eccentric, but certainly very much alive.

The story of the murder was dragged out again at the conclusion of the article and, bored with it all, I threw down the paper. I realized the publicity would do my ghost-haunting weekends a lot of good, but couldn't anyone think of something original to say? I felt a little niggle of resentment: why didn't my paintings get a mention, for instance? They were of the house and its supposed ghosts, and my work had sold well in a London gallery. What's more, the London newspapers had published small pieces about the new artist Mr Readings had discovered, but I supposed that was more to do with the standing of Mr Readings and his gallery than with me.

I closed my eyes and tried to think of other ideas for my weekends. What more could I do but provide good food and accommodation, and the occasional flurry of lights and activity that the guests took to be ghostly visitations?

I think I was drifting into a comfortable haze – half asleep, half awake – when a blood-curdling scream brought me to my feet.

'Help! Get a doctor, an ambulance, Miss Riana. Something dreadful has happened to my Rosie!'

I ran up the stairs, my heart pounding hard in my chest. In my old bedroom, the curtains were still closed and there was a strange smell in the room. I couldn't identify it. Cigarette smoke, perhaps?

Mrs Ward was staring at the empty bed, transfixed with horror. 'She's gone, my Rosie is gone! And the baby too! They've been abducted, or the ghosts have got them, just like those poor maids.' She looked up at me, her face stained with tears. 'They must have meant to take you, Miss Riana. This was *your* room, and my girl was wearing your dressing gown, the one with all the colours and fancy patterns. I saw her wearing it when I brought her a cup of cocoa last night before I went home.'

I suddenly felt cold. Mrs Ward was right. Rosie must have been mistaken for me. 'But the baby, where is he?' The cot was empty.

'My dear, 'elp!' Mrs Ward was incoherent. 'The child has been stolen away! What in the name of heaven and all the angels has happened here in the night?'

I shivered. 'Someone wanted me out of the way.' I mumbled the words through dry lips.

Mrs Ward stared at me with cold accusing eyes. 'My Rosie will be another ghost for you to paint.' Her voice was cold, her hysterics pushed into the recesses of her reserve. 'We'd better get the police and report my daughter and my grandchild missing.' She left the room.

Once the police came, everything degenerated into a scene of noise and chaos. I was ordered out of the room and told not to pollute the crime scene any further.

At the door, a policeman clutched my arm. 'We might need to take your fingerprints, miss.'

'Look on the door handle.' My voice was crisp. 'You'll

find my fingerprints on *everything*, officer. This is my house, and this used to be my room.'

'I see.' He eyed me up and down. 'You are Miss Evans then?'

'That's right.'

'You hold ghost weekends and you sell daubs?' The scornful way he said it implied I would sell my body if I had to.

'If it's any help, Rosie was last seen wearing my dressing gown. She could have been mistaken for me.'

'We'll do the detective work, Miss Evans, and draw our own conclusions. I would advise you to go and make a cup of tea or do something feminine and appropriate.'

'And I would advise *you* not to patronize me, sir.' I straightened, made myself as tall as possible and stared him down. 'Have you brought a senior officer with you?'

'Well, no, Miss Evans. This girl might have left here willingly.' He wasn't quite so sure of himself now.

'Wearing my dressing gown? I doubt that.' I lifted my chin. 'And when a senior officer *does* arrive I will talk to him not to you.'

'Very well, Miss Evans.' He still had an arrogant twist to his lips.

'And my paintings sell for more than you make in a year, so I will not have them called daubs. Aberglasney was on your doorstep, decaying under your stuck-up nose, and yet you didn't have the wit or the drive to restore the old place. Well, I have saved it from ruin, and so long as the way I do it is legal I hope you will respect that.' In that moment I didn't respect myself at all, however. Here I was, bragging about my achievements to a mere constable. What on earth had got into me?

I saw Beatrice on the landing and told her what had happened to Rosie.

She wasn't in the least surprised. 'At least they can't blame her disappearance on poor Eddie. It's this house, you see. It's always been this house.' And with those cryptic words she went into her room and closed her door with a snap of finality.

Mrs Ward was sitting in the kitchen. Her eyes were dry as she pushed a cup of tea towards me. 'Perhaps this is all for the best.' Her voice was low. 'Poor Rosie had no future here, not with the baby and no Americans willing to take the child away. She's run away. That's the answer, it must be! Nothing else makes sense.' Her eyes didn't meet mine. 'And me, well, if I keep my head down and my tongue still, I might survive all the nastiness.'

'Haven't you got a soul, Mrs Ward?' I asked in disbelief at her attitude to losing her daughter and her grandchild.

'Lordy, Miss Riana, I lost that many years ago when I was betrayed by a fine man.' She held her cup in both hands and I saw that she was crying, after all.

'You don't wear a wedding ring, Mrs Ward,' I said suddenly.

'I'm not married.' Her statement was bald, brittle and her eyes filled with tears. 'At least Rosie's been spared the shame, the menial work, the humbleness of being always lowly, a servant, unable even to attend the Lord's house because of the "good people" who don't deign to notice you.'

'You always speak correctly, Mrs Ward. You were well educated, I think.'

'Ah, I was. I was sent to private school by my guilty father. He was married – but not to my mother. History has a strange way of repeating itself, Miss Riana.'

As Mrs Ward put the kettle on again, almost unaware of what she was doing, I saw her in a new light and felt a new closeness to her.

NINETEEN

The police interviewed everyone connected to the ghost weekends and then told me to cancel my booking for the next one, which had been due to take place at the end of November. I wrote letters to my guests and received replies from all of them, rebooking for the Big Christmas weekend. It seemed the disappearance of Rosie and her child had only served to whet the appetite of ghost hunters everywhere. There was even an article in the London papers about the tragedy at the 'house of Riana', now described as a 'famous artist', and one headline reported: 'Another ghost to haunt Aberglasney.'

I was still upset and worried. I missed Rosie, and I found it impossible to hire anyone from the village to come and work for me. Everyone was afraid and suspicious of me and the house, and no one favoured the coming and goings of my guests, even though they brought trade to the village.

Worst of all, Tom had kept out of my way. I knew he was destined to go back to America in a few days, and at the very least I wanted to say goodbye to him. The thought of him leaving filled me with dread; my heart ached at the thought of being without him. I was in love, but an unrequited love that left me hurt and shamed. But, in spite of my pride, I knew I would have to say goodbye to him.

It was a cold, damp day when I made my way down the garden, through the yew-tree tunnel and towards the gates where the barracks stood. To my surprise, some of the buildings had been razed to the ground already. Men were busy laying rolls of grass over the area, almost as though the huts had never been. One of the men looked up and nodded. He was wearing a cherry-red scarf that somehow brightened the day. I wondered who had sent them. Perhaps they were council workers, or maybe Tom had organized the restoring of the ground. Anyway, what did it matter so long as Tom hadn't gone already?

When I saw his familiar figure sitting at the desk, his hair curling into a quiff above his forehead, the strong broad set of his shoulders visible beneath his crisp shirt, I wanted to throw myself into his arms and hug him in relief that he was still there.

He got up when he saw me. 'Riana,' he said and my name fell softly into the cold air of the room. He seemed to straighten his back then, almost as if he was going to salute me. I could see at once he was keeping his distance. Gone was the Tom who had sat with me under the cloisters in the thin balmy air of a summer's night.

'I was very sorry to hear about Rosie,' he said in his best official voice, 'and the child. Does anyone know what's happened to them?'

'The police are investigating,' I replied, and the formality in my own voice placed a huge barrier between us.

There was a long silence, and I searched Tom's face for some sign of softening. I knew I'd been cold to him, stayed away from him without a word, and he was stiff with pride. Even so, if he came and kissed me and told me he loved me, I'd go to the ends of the world with him.

'I just came down to say goodbye,' I found myself saying 'I know you'll be going home soon.'

He looked round distractedly. 'This seems like my home now,' he said, and then he took a deep breath. 'But you are right. I leave tomorrow.'

'And you were going without talking to me?' I was aghast.

'What was there to say?' Tom didn't look at me.

I managed to speak after a while. 'Well, I want to say thanks for everything again. The gardening, the support, your faith in my painting. Everything.'

'My pleasure.' He half bowed.

There seemed nothing left for me to do but go. I went towards the door, just as it was pushed open and two burly policemen came into the office. Before my terrified eyes, they arrested Tom, put him in handcuffs and – without

looking at me – took him outside. I followed, trying to
protest, but the men took no notice of me. They pushed
Tom into a car and slammed the door shut. The car was an
unmarked one, and as it drove away I saw something bright
sticking out of the boot: a red scarf by the look of it.
Suspicions aroused, I memorized the registration number –
or at least some of it – and ran back through the garden to
the house and the phone.

The local police, I learned, had no knowledge of anyone
picking up an American Wing Commander.

I sat abruptly on the chair near the phone table and tried
to sort out my thoughts. Who could have taken Tom . . .
and why?

I went back to Tom's office later that day, thinking perhaps
I would find a clue to what was happening there. The office
was no longer standing, however. It had been taken apart,
prefabricated piece by prefabricated piece, like a jigsaw
puzzle. Someone had been searching the place with complete
thoroughness; not even a pin would have escaped notice.

I looked suspiciously at the workmen, but none of them
was wearing a cherry-red scarf. 'What happened to the Wing
Commander's possessions?' I asked.

The workman shrugged, uncaring. 'Boxed up and sent
on to his home, I suppose,' he said.

I managed a smile. 'Has anyone got a forwarding address?'

'Don't know nothing about that, miss.' He turned away,
finished with the conversation, and in despair I returned to
the house.

What's the police doing here, Miss Riana? Is it about
Rosie?' Mrs Ward was pale with dark shadows under her
eyes. She was evidently more worried about her daughter
than she had let on.

I shook my head. 'We've had four visits from the police
about Rosie and the baby,' I said quietly. 'They'll find her,
don't worry, but this visit by unknown men is something
to do with the Americans.' Though what, I didn't know,
because I would have bet everything I had – even
Aberglasney – that those men had not been real policemen.

'Well, it's those Americans who started the troubles here.' Mrs Ward spoke emphatically. 'We were all right before the war. *Then* the village was quiet and peaceable enough.'

'And what about the five young maids who were murdered?' I asked. 'That wasn't very peaceable, was it?'

'Well, I don't know much about all that.' Mrs Ward turned her face away from me, and I wondered how much she did know. She played her cards very close to her chest, I'd found.

TWENTY

I met Miss Grist again when I went to Swansea the next day. I'd been to the police station to report Tom as missing, and although my comments had been written down by the officer on duty, I felt the sheet of paper would be put in the bin the minute I left. I wandered into the library, and Miss Grist followed me into the reference room. She was wearing a smart white blouse and a dark skirt that appeared almost a uniform. Even her shoes and stockings were black.

She was obviously intrigued by the latest stories about Aberglasney and wanted to know all the details of Rosie's disappearance. She was very friendly, talkative even, and coaxed me to go with her to the staffroom for a cup of coffee during her break and sat uncomfortably close to me.

'How was the room left? Any signs of an intruder?' Her eyes were bright with curiosity. 'Perhaps it was one of those American airmen who abducted her.'

I reined in my sudden burst of irritation. 'We don't know anything more than you do, Miss Grist,' I said. 'One thing I *am* sure about – it wasn't anything to do with the Americans.'

'But this girl had several "assignations" with these men. They say the baby was fathered by one of them.'

'Well, "they" might well be right, but her disappearance was during the night when the house was locked up, and there was no sign of a break-in.' I told myself it was only natural for people to be curious about events at Aberglasney; no doubt Miss Grist was only saying what everyone was thinking.

Her eyes narrowed. 'Are you saying it was the ghosts then, or have you yourself taken the girl somewhere?'

'Why on earth would I? If you have such evidence to back up such suspicions about me you'd better tell it to the police, or else stop being so nosy!' I felt like telling her she was reading too many of the books on the shelves of the library and allowing her imagination to run away with her.

'Did the police suspect you, Miss Evans?'

It was a good question. 'I don't think so. I didn't have a motive, you see. Rosie was my helper. I needed her to work for me.' I spoke wearily now. Miss Grist had the hide of an elephant and wasn't going to give in.

'But she accused the man you loved of being the father of her child. If that wasn't a motive, I don't know what was.'

I put down my cup with a bang against the saucer, and Miss Grist drew back, realizing she'd gone too far. 'Isn't anything private any more? I'll leave you, Miss Grist, and I'll thank you to keep out of my business. I thought it was just idle curiosity on your part, but if even you think I'm capable of abducting a mother and baby, what chance have I with everyone else?'

'I do apologize.' Miss Grist looked distressed. 'I don't believe any of that myself. It's just what people will think and what they will say.'

'Precisely.' I left the library, my cheeks flaming as I walked down the steps and into the chill of the day. It was getting dark already, and there was a hint of snow in the air. I wanted to be home in my house with my dear Tom beside me, Rosie and Mrs Ward working in the kitchen, and guests about to arrive. I wanted everything to be as it was before Rosie had been silly enough to fall for a baby and ruin everything.

I suddenly realized Miss Grist was right. I did have a motive, and one of the strongest types: the vitriol of a woman scorned. How foolish though! Tom wasn't the father. He had always denied it, and I believed him. It was Tom who'd said the baby might not be Carl's son; why would he have pointed that out if he'd had something to hide? All the same, Miss Grist had raised the spectre of jealousy and mistrust in me once again.

I hurried towards the train station at the top of High Street.

A drunken man staggered noisily in the echoing porcelain of the gentleman's toilet, rolling down the steps to disappear beneath road level. The train for Aberglasney was just steaming into the station, and I thanked my lucky stars I didn't have to wait on the bleak cold platform. I sunk into a seat in an empty carriage and thought of the things Miss Grist had said. Was I a suspect? Was I being watched? And what on earth had happened to Tom?

That night I left the light on in my room and took a hot toddy to bed with me. Tonight Aberglasney was quiet: no creaking floorboards, no groaning trees pressing like skeletal fingers against the old windows. And yet I was disturbed and afraid; for the first time I was uneasy in my own house.

The next day I went to the police station again, determined to talk to someone in authority about Tom's disappearance. I sat waiting in the hallway for what seemed hours, but I had decided that I was not going to go away, however long I had to sit there.

At last, a bored detective called me into his room. He switched on a tape recorder, and as I watched the wheels go round I was aware of a policeman standing behind me, guarding the door.

'I'm Inspector Morris. What can we do for you, Miss Evans?'

'I want to report a missing person. Again,' I said, and waited.

The inspector wrote something down, ignoring me completely.

'Do you want any details, or are you going to use mind-reading?'

My sarcasm was lost on him. 'Carry on,' he said.

'Tom Maybury, an American officer, was taken away by men dressed as policemen a few days ago, and there's been no sign of him since.'

There was silence. Morris rifled through some papers. 'There's no record of any such event,' he said.

'So I was told yesterday.' My voice was strong and Morris looked at me sharply.

'I'll write the details down, miss, but this American is nothing to do with us. Perhaps he's gone back to his own country.' His tone indicated that 'his own country' was the best place for him.

I forced a calmness into my voice I didn't feel and wondered how I could get through to this man. 'What if the Americans send someone over here and demand to know what the British police have done to find the officer? They will think we British are very unprofessional.'

The inspector looked a little uneasy. Finally, he wrote something on paper and then looked up at me. 'We'll investigate, of course, but I don't hold out much hope of finding the officer. Our resources here are very limited, you understand.'

'I understand, and thank you so much for your help. I will be sure to tell the American authorities about your understanding and command of the situation.'

This time the sarcasm hit home, and Inspector Morris grew red with embarrassment. 'We've done all we can to help these foreigners,' he snapped, 'and they've repaid us by drinking copious amounts of liquor, being free and easy with our women, and making trouble everywhere they go.'

'Hmm.' I walked to the door and then looked back. 'I think you might have to cut off that piece of tape, don't you?'

Inspector Morris stood up. 'See the lady out, Atkins,' he said abruptly, but he was already fiddling with the tape machine.

I stood outside the tiny police station and breathed in the cold, thin air. It cut like a knife, and I shivered involuntarily. I hurried into the tiny coffee shop and sat down, wrapping my scarf more tightly around my neck.

'Excuse me, may I sit with you? I think I've an apology to make.'

I looked up in surprise. 'Miss Grist! What are you doing down here? Aren't you supposed to be at work today?'

'I realize I spoke out of turn yesterday, and when I saw you at the police station I thought the worst. I thought you were being arrested!'

'Still the soul of tact then?' I said shortly, and Miss Grist pursed her thin lips.

HARRISON COUNTY
PUBLIC LIBRARY
105 North Capitol Ave
Corydon, IN 47112

'I'm *trying* to apologize,' she said. She looked pale and cold, and her eyes were an icy grey as they narrowed against the white of the falling snow. She had made an effort to see me, however, and so I relented.

'Let me buy us a hot pot of coffee,' I suggested.

She smiled at once, and it seemed we were on amicable terms again. I thought it would be helpful if I explained the situation. 'I went to the police to report a missing person,' I said. 'I won't go into it all, but let me assure you I'm not being accused of anything – certainly not Rosie's disappearance or the abduction of her child. She had a key to the house, naturally. I thought it remiss of the police not to ask me that right away.'

'So she might have left of her own accord. Again, I can only apologize.' Miss Grist was frosty again.

'My next ghost weekend will be just before Christmas. Perhaps you'd like to come, Miss Grist? As my guest, of course, though I wonder if you would be kind enough to help me serve the meals. I can't get any village girls up to the house – not since the awful night Rosie disappeared.'

'A superstitious lot, the villagers, and of course I would be delighted to help,' Miss Grist surprised me by saying. She appeared genuinely pleased. She took out a diary and meticulously penned in the date I gave her. 'If there's any secretarial work for me, I'm very good at typing. I could contact your list of guests.' She sounded eager.

'That would be a great help.' And it would; I hated hand-writing all the letters and addressing all the envelopes to my growing list of guests.

'What about the cooking?' she asked. 'That's not one of my great skills, I'm afraid.'

'Mrs Ward does that. Rosie's mother.'

'Oh, is that what Gladys Williams is calling herself now?' There was a spiteful edge to Miss Grist's words. 'No better than she should be, is Gladys. Had an unseemly affair with a foreign gentleman, and poor little Rosie was the result.'

'You know Mrs Ward then, do you?' My tone was severe. I liked Mrs Ward, in spite of her spiky ways, and she was invaluable to me.

'Just gossip, you know,' Miss Grist said. 'Just gossip, that's all. I never met the woman, of course. She and I didn't move in the same circles, you know.'

I realized I didn't like Miss Grist very much. Why on earth had I invited her to my home? I quickly drank the hot, sweet, warming coffee and then picked up my bag and gloves and twisted my scarf around my neck. 'I'd better be getting back.' I tried to smile as Miss Grist rose too.

'I'll come back with you, if I may,' Miss Grist said. 'You can show me around the house, give me your list of guests, and I can get the letters done when I get back to Swansea.'

It made sense, and so Miss Grist walked beside me through the snowy streets and caught the train to Aberglasney. When my house came into view, my heart warmed with pleasure. As we passed the place where the barracks had been, I bit my lip in anxiety; would the police do anything at all to find Tom?

I suspected Inspector Morris would have to go through the motions after what I'd said about the Americans sending someone over to investigate, and I could only hope that Morris would at least do his best to track the men who had taken Tom.

I hesitated among the rubbish left when the workmen removed the huts. Those fake policemen had something to do with Tom's disappearance; who were they, and who had sent them?

A scrap of paper among the rubble caught my eye, and I picked it up. I realized Miss Grist was trying to look over my shoulder at it, and I pushed it quickly into my pocket, not really knowing why I wanted to hide it. All I knew was that I felt lost and empty without Tom and this might be a piece of him.

It was quiet in the house. I hadn't seen any sign of Beatrice for some time. I thought she'd gone away, having taken exception to my guests peering at her, poking into her privacy, but I wished – not for the first time – that she would let me know when she was going away and for how long.

'My, this house is so quiet,' Miss Grist said as she followed me into the hall. I realized we'd been walking through the garden in so great a silence that I'd almost forgotten she was there.

Mrs Ward took one look at Miss Grist and disappeared out of the back door without a word.

'It may be silent now, but it will be full of laughter and noise when my guests come again,' I said, realizing I would be glad when the ghost-haunting weekends began again and filled the house with chatter and warmth and curiosity and all the paraphernalia that went with hunting ghosts.

'I've heard the ghosts are sighted along the upstairs corridor,' Miss Grist said. 'Flickering lights, and all that sort of thing.'

'That's what we've seen sometimes.' I sighed. 'I think the moon makes weird shapes through the trees and that's what causes the flickering lights.'

'Don't you believe in ghosts then, Miss Evans?'

I watched as Miss Grist took off her coat and hung it on the stand in the hall. My heart sank; she obviously intended her stay to be a long one.

She seemed to know the house well – something I hadn't expected – and she made her way to the kitchen and put the kettle on to boil. She gave a deprecating smile. 'I might as well get familiar with things while I'm here.' She almost hugged herself. 'I can hardly wait for the ghost weekend; heaven knows who I'll meet.'

'Mostly elderly colonels and sweet old ladies,' I said dryly. 'They are all intelligent people, mind you, and we do have one young man who might be good company for you.'

Miss Grist brightened up immediately. 'Really? What's his name?'

'I think his name is Colin. And then there's young William, of course. He always comes along to the weekends. He's quite the keen ghost hunter; even keener than the colonel, I sometimes think. Anyway, I'll fetch the list for you.'

She followed me into the study and looked around, as though appraising the house and its contents. I brought the guest list out from its drawer and gave it to her.

Miss Grist put it carefully away in her handbag, and after a moment she spoke again. 'I don't think I'll wait for that cup of tea,' she said. 'I'd better get back to the station, otherwise I'll miss my train.'

I breathed a sigh of relief and quickly opened the door for her, in case she changed her mind.

'See you soon then.' She gave a cheery wave, hurried off along the drive and disappeared through the archway leading to the side gate. She seemed to know her way around my house already. When had she been here, and why pretend she had never visited before? Eventually, I shrugged my questions away. So what if she had been to Aberglasney before? It was *my* house, and all she would be was an occasional guest.

The kettle had boiled so I made some tea and stoked up the fire so I could make some toast. I had some good Welsh salt butter, and my mouth watered at the thought of eating the hot toast with the butter almost liquidizing into it. But then I thought of Tom, and abruptly my appetite faded. Where could he be, and what had happened to him? I almost wished it was the real police who had taken him. At least then I would know he was safe.

I remembered the scrap piece of paper I had picked up from the site of the barracks and took it out of my pocket and tried to read it. The writing was in pencil, the spelling all awry, with letters turned back to front as though written by someone illiterate or foreign.

I took my cup of tea and the note and sat near the fire, but it might as well have been written in Chinese for all the sense I could make of it. I needed a pen and ink and a fresh piece of paper – and perhaps a magnifying glass would help.

At last, seated with all my bits and pieces, I pored over the scrap of paper, slowly writing down what I thought each letter represented. The words made little sense, and at last I realized the note wasn't written in English at all.

I sat up straight as I heard the rattle of the front-door lock, and my heart leaped with a mingling of fear and excitement. Was it Tom returned to me, intruders bent on robbery . . . or worse?

It was Beatrice who stood in the doorway, her white hair covered in misty rain and her funny little bag, wrought with flowers, clutched in her hand. For a moment she did look like the ghost my guests believed she was, and then she spoke. 'Carry my bag to my room for me, dear.' Her voice sounded weak, as if she was very tired.

'Where on earth have you been this time?' I asked irritably. 'Why do you keep coming and going like some sort of ethereal spirit?'

'Just help me to my room, dear, I've only been visiting relatives. Do I have to report to you every time I wish to come and go, then?'

I remembered our bargain, when I'd assured Beatrice she could stay at Aberglasney any time she liked. I decided I was being unfair. 'No, of course not, Beatrice, I'm sorry. I'm a bit touchy today. Such a lot has been happening here. You get changed and rested, and I'll come up with a cup of tea and we'll talk. How's that?'

'Very good, dear. I'm very tired so I might just get into bed, if you don't mind, but we can still talk, if you like.'

'No, the morning will do, Beatrice. I'm being thoughtless.'

I helped her upstairs, and she disappeared into her room, shutting the door pointedly in my face. I shrugged. She was old, and she was entitled to be a bit eccentric.

It was the next day that I saw the advertisement in the *Daily Messenger*. 'Hunt the Ghost,' it read, 'in the beautiful surroundings of Oystermouth Castle in Swansea.' I gasped in disbelief. Someone else was doing a ghost weekend! The headline was followed by a mouth-watering description of the ruined castle near the sea, where the ghost of a minor royal was meant to haunt.

I sighed. I supposed I had to expect competition. My idea had been a good one, but I couldn't keep it to myself for ever. In any case, I had my guest base, my regulars. I would be all right. Still, I hurried to Beatrice's room to show her the newspaper, and she sat up in bed against her pillows, pale and ethereal in her little lace bed cap, and her hand shook as she read the piece.

She threw down the paper at last and shook her head. A stray grey curl drooped over her forehead. I suddenly realized how fond I was of the old lady. 'Makes no difference,' she said. 'Our ghosts are real. Your friends will soon realize and come back to us.'

'But I never expected to lose them in the first place, Beatrice,' I said. 'Do you think they'll desert us then?'

'Something new, my dear, is always an attraction at first, but they'll come back, you'll see.' She stared at me shrewdly. 'Now, what else is there?'

I told her about Rosie, about the terrible night she vanished. 'The police don't seem to be doing very much about it,' I said. 'Nor about the baby. The poor girl and her child seem to have vanished into thin air.'

'I expect the police will carry on the same way they did when Eddie died: show little concern and hope the matter is quickly forgotten.'

There was silence for a moment, and then I dipped into my pocket and brought out the transcription of the note I'd found in the rubble of the barracks. 'Tom's disappeared,' I said. 'I found a note but I can't make sense of it.'

'No wonder you can't read it,' she said. 'It's in very fine, very old Welsh. It's the name of a place in Carmarthen. "Cwm Elwyn." It's an old farmhouse under the mountains, near a winding stream. Of course, you'll go and look there for your Tom.'

'What area, Beatrice? There are many mountains here in Wales and lots of streams too.'

'I don't know!' Beatrice sounded exasperated. 'I'll translate the address for you into English, and then it's up to you.'

'But you think Tom might have been taken there?' I asked hopefully.

'It's a possibility, and only a possibility. This could be the address of someone's mother or grandmother, but I have a feeling Tom is there – somewhere under the shadow of the mountain.'

I was heartened by Beatrice's words. They gave me a sense of hope that I might see Tom again.

'Bring a pen,' Beatrice said, 'and I'll do my best to help.'

She waved me away with a lace-gloved hand, and I
hurried downstairs to find a pen and some notepaper. I felt
excitement flow through me, and I realized again how much
I needed Tom around me, at my side encouraging me. If
only he would say he loved me, I would be the happiest
woman in the world.

I carefully wrote down the address Beatrice gave me,
and when I hastened to the library in town that same day
I found a map and plotted my journey with care. I reckoned it would take half a day to find my way to *Cwm Elwyn*
in *Craig Melyn* and wondered if I would have enough petrol
to take me there. My guest weekend was coming up and I
would need to stock up on supplies, but that wouldn't take
much precious petrol.

The next morning I set off early with my hamper of food
and a Thermos of hot tea on the seat of the van beside me.
I didn't know if Tom would be hungry and thirsty, and I
shuddered at the thought he might not even be alive, but
I began my journey with hope and enthusiasm and headed
in the direction of the mountains of Brecon.

The journey was along country lanes, past endless fields,
but at last the roadway led upward and I felt the air change
from chilly to near freezing. Far below me I saw a long
river snaking through the hills. On one side there was a
castle, and in the middle of the water was a strip of land,
rising like a sleeping animal from the river. A small building
that might have been a church stood on it, and my heart
stopped for a second as I read a crude notice with the
words *Cwm Elwyn* painted on it in large letters that were
blood red.

I stopped my old van on the bank of the river and, to
steady myself, poured a small cup of hot tea. The journey
had taken longer than I'd thought, and soon it would be
dark once more. Nearby, boats were moored – a huddle of
small rowing boats, and some bigger, sturdier boats for
passengers tied to the jetty – but there were no people to
sail them. The place seemed deserted.

I looked desperately at the small island. I had a gut instinct
that Tom was there, and somehow I had to get to him.

I strolled around the boats, and then, quite suddenly, a man appeared at my side.

'Can I help you, miss?' He had a strong accent, definitely Welsh but thick and almost intelligible. In this remote part of the country, Welsh was probably the first language.

'I just wanted to explore the island,' I said. 'Is that a little church out there?'

'It is, miss, but you have to be careful of the tides on this river. They can change with the winds and turn nasty.'

'Could you get me out there?' I searched in my rucksack for my purse.

He waved an extraordinarily large hand in dismissal. 'No need of that. I'll take you out there . . . if you really want to go.'

I smiled in what I thought was a winning way. 'Oh, I do. I love old, haunted places you see.'

He gave me an odd look and gestured me towards one of the boats. It was a small boat with an outboard engine that looked precarious, hanging as it was on the edge of the wooden planking.

At a fairly fast speed, we crossed the river, and I could see the boatman was right: the current swirled the water into circles around us. 'When is the tide due to rise?' I asked, and he looked surprised that I knew anything at all about tidal waters.

'Not for hours yet, miss.' The boat bumped against a mossy bank, and he helped me alight. 'What if I come back for you in –' he looked at his watch – 'say an hour? Will that suit you?'

'Lovely.' I watched as he pulled away from the shore and had the distinct feeling I was being abandoned. I watched until he reached the other side of the shore, and then I turned to explore the island.

The church had steps leading down to a small door. The wooden posts at either side were green, and seaweed grew like strange medieval flowers in the surrounding land. That meant that when the tide came in it covered the church. Everything inside must be soaked and rotten. I realized that if I stayed here too long I would drown.

I pushed hard against the door and almost fell into the smelly, dark, seaweed-slippery porch of the building – if it could be called a building. There were holes in the roof, showing small beams of dull, fading light, and the windows were eroded and cracked by the rush of the water that must continually pound the glass.

'Tom?' My voice was subdued in the sodden surroundings of the church. I walked cautiously along the isle towards the pulpit, feeling the hairs on the back of my neck rising in fear. I don't know what I feared . . . Vampires, perhaps, or at least drowned sailors? But most of all my fear was for Tom. Was he still alive?

'Tom!' I called more loudly, and I heard a small sound above my head.

'Riana, over here.'

I could see Tom at the far end of the church; he was tied to one of the pillars! I hurried along the broken, rotting aisle and saw that he'd got his hands free, but was struggling to untie the rope around his feet.

'Riana, we have to get out of here – and quick. It's going to be high tide tonight, and then the entire island will be under water – at least that's what one of the men who brought me here today said.'

I ran to him and managed, with difficulty, to untie the knots around his feet. He stood up and towered over me, and I resisted the urge to fling myself into his arms. *Tom, please love me*, I thought – and could not tell if I had spoken those thoughts aloud.

TWENTY-ONE

The moon was just a pale shadow in among the misty clouds as I looked up through the holes in the roof of the building at the grey, threatening skies above. I realized I was clinging to Tom, kissing his cheeks, his eyelids, his luscious mouth. At last, he held me away, and I came out of my dream, realizing we were trapped in an old building with the water rising around us.

'We have to get out of here.' Tom's tone was urgent as he held me away from him.

'What's going on, Tom?' I asked. 'Why were you taken here and tied up like a cat about to be drowned?'

'No time for questions. We have to get away before the church is flooded.'

'It's going to be all right.' I smiled at him, which was something of an effort because I was shivering with cold and damp and relief. 'The man with the boat is coming back for me soon.'

'If you believe that, you'll believe anything.'

'You are being melodramatic,' I said. 'Of course he'll come back. Why shouldn't he?'

'They want me dead, that's why, and they don't care if you die too. You are a stranger who has poked her nose into things, and you'd be better out of the way.'

'Who are these people, and why do they want you dead?' I said, almost disbelieving.

'They think I know too much. As I said, there is no time for discussion, Riana. The tide is already creeping under the door. We've got to get away before it's too late.'

I hurried to the door and tried to push it open. It didn't budge. 'It's stuck!'

My words were unnecessary, however, as Tom barged against the slime covered door with all his strength and it failed to open.

'It's been nailed from the outside, probably with a strong beam across it. That must have been after you came in here. As I said, they don't care if you die too.' Tom looked up at the cracked windows. 'That's our best bet. Come on, Riana, we have no time to waste.'

'The river! How are we going to get across if it's in full tide?' I suddenly realized Tom was right; the situation was desperate. Someone wanted us out of the way!

Tom edged off one of his flying boots and began to strike at the glass with the heel. Water was already gushing up to my ankles; it wasn't a very high building, and the tide would soon reach us and be over our heads. The place was now almost pitch black, and it smelled of salt and seaweed and slime. I couldn't stop myself from shivering.

Tom was cursing under his breath in his honeyed American accent, and I resisted the desire to laugh hysterically. He kept hitting the glass, and at last it shattered outwards – like diamonds of light falling into the lapping sea.

Tom began to pull planks of wood from the benches in the gallery. 'Good thing they're rotting. These were once good, strong wooden seats. I'd never have moved them then.' He gasped as he manhandled one of the planks towards the window. 'Use this as a float,' he said, sliding the plank half out of the window.

I looked at the water outside. My feet and legs were already soaked, and the tide was beginning to lap at my waist. Soon it would be too late to get out at all. 'I'll wait for you. Come with me, Tom.'

'Go while you can.' Tom began to prize another plank from the benches, but the water was hampering him now. 'Go!' he said commandingly. He hesitated and then took my face in his hands and kissed me soundly.

'Go. Please, Riana, just go. Save me the pressure of worrying about you as well as myself. I think I must disappear for a while and let my enemies think I'm dead.'

'All right, Tom.' Before I could lose my nerve, I decided he was right I would have to go. I kissed him on his lips; his mouth was cold, but I felt the warmth of his emotions as he hoisted me up and then gently pushed me out through the jagged gap and into the cold sharp air.

I slid the plank into the water and lay on the full length of it. My sweater got stuck on a point of glass and I struggled with it for a moment, and then I gasped as I was in the sea, driven by the rushing tide.

I was lucky. The fierce wind pushed me towards the bank, but as I almost reached safety – after what felt like a lifetime of horror – a wave pushed me off the plank, and I was submerged in the freezing cold muddy water. Fronds of weeds reached curling fingers towards me, but then thankfully another wave drove me towards the bank and I felt the ground under my feet.

Gasping, I hauled myself up out of the freezing water and lay there – panting for breath, soaked and shivering, and almost crying with worry and fear. I scrambled to my knees and looked for Tom on his makeshift raft, but the water had risen even further and was rushing recklessly towards the sea, with no sign of Tom on the boiling surface.

I waited, shivering, for over an hour. Perhaps Tom had come ashore further up the river, I told myself eventually. Perhaps even now he was waiting for me by the car. Hope gave me strength, and with my feet squelching at every step, I made my way back to where I'd left the car. I stopped when I could just see the spiral of the tower of the church, for the rest was under the water.

I began to cry, silent tears that ran unheeded down my freezing cheeks. A piece of seaweed hung from my hair, and I pulled the slimy strand off with a grimace of disgust. I shouted for Tom, but my voice was carried away on the wind.

TWENTY-TWO

My van was where I had left it. Clearly, no one had expected me to survive the floodwater at the church. I climbed inside, wet and shivering and crying with shock. At last, I managed to get home to Aberglasney – but without Tom.

Mrs Ward didn't say a word. She made me some hot sweet tea, and after my bath I changed into a fleecy nightgown and a warm woollen dressing gown and sat in my room, cup in my hand.

Tom had vanished, Rosie and her baby had vanished, and if that wasn't enough to worry about I hadn't sold a painting for some time. I would have to borrow from the bank to finance my next ghost-haunting weekend.

I started to plan the weekend to try to take my mind off Tom. Perhaps he'd been washed downriver? He'd talked about disappearing, and I felt sure in my heart he was still alive. He'd wanted his enemies to think he was dead. I must keep that in my mind, I told myself, and hope and pray that his problems would be resolved soon, and in the meantime I must immerse myself in my plans to make enough money to keep Aberglasney afloat – and that meant working on my ghost weekends.

I stayed in my bed for a few days, getting over a chill and trying to come to terms with my despair about Tom. But at last I knew I had to face life again – alone if necessary. So Mrs Ward and I went shopping together for food in the local market: meat, vegetables, fruit for puddings, cheese and biscuits, and bottles of wine that were cheap but looked good once their contents were poured into my decanters, which appeared like cut crystal in the gaslight. The villagers might scorn Mrs Ward for her past, and me for the present, but they took our money without a flinch.

*   *   *

Mrs Ward was busy setting the long table in the large hall for dinner on the first evening of our renewed ghost-haunting evenings. It was just before Christmas; the air outside was pure – crisp and cold – but inside the downstairs fires roared and flamed with warmth and welcome.

The old colonel was first to arrive, and then Miss Grist turned up, briefly. 'I can't stay,' she said, staring round my empty hall with something like satisfaction. 'Something unexpected has come up.'

The lanterns were lit along the drive and under the archway to the road, and as the car drove Miss Grist away I recognized the driver: it was the young man Colin, who'd come to my last weekend. I felt piqued. Why hadn't he attended my get-together this time? What business could he possibly have with Miss Grist?

The colonel had the answer. 'I don't like to tell you, my dear,' he said and coughed a little, 'but another ghost hunt has been arranged, at a much reduced price to yours, and we were all circulated with letters of invitation. Someone has clearly got hold of your guest list, my dear.'

And I knew full well who that person was. 'Miss Grist,' I said bleakly. 'She's taken my list and used it for her own ends. Where is this ghost hunt taking place, colonel?'

'It's in an old castle. A huge place in a large park. The grounds are extensive, and the guests will not be fed or given any sort of hospitality, but the ghost of a royal duke is reputed to haunt the ruins at this time of year. Apparently, this ghost carries his head underneath his arm. Sounds a bit phoney to me.'

'Thank you for your loyalty, colonel.' I sat at the empty table and thought of all the food we had prepared. In bed that night I cried until I was weary, and I fell asleep knowing I was more in debt, I'd been deserted by people I thought were loyal guests, if not friends, and – worst of all – Tom still hadn't come back and I didn't know if he was alive or drowned beneath the waters of the huge river under the hills.

In the early thin light of the winter's morning, to my surprise cars began to arrive. My guests – full of apologies

– begged to be given shelter and food, and Mr Bravage took me aside and told me what a miserable night they'd had at the castle. 'Frauds!' he said. 'The people were charlatans. They must have thought we were all idiots to believe such an obvious fake.'

'Why, didn't you see the ghost with no head then?' I was trying not to laugh; even saying the words sounded silly.

'Ghost, indeed. You could see at once it was no ghost. The man had his head hidden in a specially adapted coat, and as for the "head" it was that of a plaster mannequin, any fool could see that.' He shook his head. 'A man of my experience, being tricked like that . . . but then I was suspicious when I saw the "ghost". I've been a doctor too long to be fooled by a fake. I ran up the stairs, wrestled with the head, and when it came off I threw it down the stone steps and the wig fell off – and the nose too. Oh, and one ear!'

'A bit like Van Gogh then?'

'Eh?' Mr Bravage looked puzzled for a moment, and then he laughed. 'Oh, I see. The artist chappie who cut off his ear!'

'Did you see Miss Grist from the library there, Mr Bravage?'

'Who? Sorry, I don't know of the lady. Can't help you there, I'm afraid. Oh, she did sign the letter of invitation though. A Miss Grist, you say? Yes, I remember now, that was the lady. She sounded very forbidding too. Not the sort to have a jolly good weekend, with ghosts or no ghosts.'

In the kitchen, Mrs Ward already had the pots steaming on the stove. She looked brighter than she'd done since Rosie disappeared. 'I like it when the house is full,' she said, confirming my hope that she had nothing to do with the list and the other ghost night, and I returned her cheery smile, feeling better myself.

Tom would come back when he was ready, when he'd sorted whatever it was his problem was – I was sure of it. Rosie and the baby would be found safe and well, living with a good-natured man who would take care of her, and I would soon be able to paint again. Already, I had my guests back. Miss Grist's scheme to steal them away from me had failed, and her 'ghost' had been exposed as a fraud.

At least my ghosts were not trickery or deception on my part. Of course, there must be a natural explanation for the lights and the noises from upstairs – the moonlight, and the wind rattling the old house – but nothing *I'd* faked. *Except Beatrice*, a voice whispered in my head. But then I was just withholding the truth about Beatrice. She had once owned the house, and now still felt she had the run of the place. I knew she was tied to it by her dead husband, but it was strange that *he* never seemed to haunt the old house!

We had a jolly – if quiet – weekend, and though my guests drank a lot of mulled wine, and at midnight we ate the delicious mince pies Mrs Ward had made, no ghost or noises or lights bothered us – much to the disappointment of the ghost hunters.

It was almost dawn when the quiet was disturbed by a cry and a series of thumps, and I hurriedly pulled on my warm woollen dressing gown and hurried on to the landing, only to see that the colonel was crumpled at the bottom of the stairs! He was moaning and holding his side, but at least he was alive. I ran to him and knelt down. 'What's happened? Have you had a fall, Colonel Fred?'

'I've had a push, not a fall,' Colonel Fred said indignantly, 'and it was no ghost. It was a human hand I felt in the small of my back. Pushing with some strength, I may tell you!'

I felt along his body for breaks, and though he winced when I touched his side there didn't seem to be anything worse than bruising. 'I'm no nurse,' I said, 'but I did a first-aid course and I think you are going to be all right, but I can ring for an ambulance just in case.'

'No need, my dear Riana. I feel quite all right – just a bit shaken, that's all. I wish I could just find the fool who pushed me.'

Some of the guests helped me to lift Colonel Fred to his feet, and though he was pale and a little trembly he seemed pretty sound on his feet.

'I could do with a large brandy, my dear.' He hobbled

into the sitting room and slumped into an old leather chair.
I brought him a brandy, and he drank it with relish before
holding out his glass for a refill.

'Here, colonel, have the bottle at your side.' I turned to
the others. 'Go back to bed, if you wish. It's only just
dawn.'

There was a chorus of protest, and I looked at Mrs Ward.
'In that case, we'll do breakfast now. Anyone wishing to
stay for lunch, it's on me.'

Mrs Ward stepped forward. 'But if any of you good folk
want to stay an extra night you'll have to pay up, because
I'll need more groceries and such to feed you.'

Mrs Ward had said what I was too embarrassed to say,
and I nodded my agreement.

Everyone wanted to stay, and Mrs Ward put a large bowl
in the centre of the hall table. 'For the takings.'

Her explanation was unnecessary. The guests were already
dipping into wallets and purses with an eagerness that
delighted me.

Later, when my visitors had gone to bathe and dress and
prepare for a good cooked breakfast, I sat with the colonel.
He was still in his striped pyjamas and dressing gown, and
his hand holding the glass to his lips still trembled, but the
colour was coming back into his face.

'I'm going to arrange a bed for you in my back room,'
I said. 'I don't want you climbing stairs today. Mrs Ward
can bring down your things from your room.'

'That might be a good idea, Riana. I'm a bit sore, I must
admit. Who,' he asked, 'would want to harm me?' He was
puzzled, and so was I. 'I'm just an old retired soldier that's
all,' he said, and I looked at him, really looked for the first
time. His moustache and eyebrows were tinged with grey
and so was his hair, but he wasn't really so old – perhaps
sixty or so. If he wasn't so stooped, and if he were to wear
glasses instead of an old-fashioned monocle, he would look
much younger.

'You're not old.' I smiled at him.

He winked at me and then took out his pipe, which added
to his elderly image. 'Compared to you, I'm geriatric, Riana.

You are just a young bud of a girl, so take a tip from me: life isn't all about business and making a "go" of things – important as those things are at your age – it's also about the heart and about love. Which reminds me! Where is that charming American pilot these days? I rather thought he was keen on you.'

'Away on duty, I suppose.' I didn't know why I felt the need to lie to the colonel, but the story of Tom going into the river and wanting to disappear was something I had to respect, even though I didn't understand it.

'He hasn't met with some sort of accident, has he? You look anxious, my dear.'

I hesitated a moment. 'I'd rather not talk about Tom, if you don't mind.' I suppose my tone was cold, discouraging any further questions, because the colonel puffed on his pipe for a moment without answering.

'I wonder if we'll see any ghosts tonight, my dear.' He broke the silence, and I felt relieved. I hoped I hadn't offended him, but being a paying guest didn't allow someone the privilege of enquiring into my private life.

'Perhaps.' I didn't commit myself. Ghosts were touchy beings, if they existed at all.

Breakfast was a noisy, cheerful affair. It seemed that everyone had forgotten Colonel Fred's accident. But I hadn't. I looked around the assorted guests: Mr Bravage, young William, Colin, Mrs Timpson Smith with her neatly-cut hair and rather thin, rouged face. Plump Betty, her cheerful smile making her beautiful, and all the others who as yet were not personalities to me. None of them had any reason to hurt the colonel that I knew of. He must have slipped, missed his step. He liked his drink, and who was to say he hadn't had plenty of that when he went up the stairs?

That evening I had a call from Mr Readings. He wanted to come to Aberglasney to talk to me about another exhibition. I tried to put him off, explaining I had guests, but he was persistent. 'I haven't anything even started yet,' I said at last. 'I've been off my painting for a few weeks.'

'Even more reason for me to talk to you,' he said. 'Oh, and I'll be bringing my lady friend with me, so make it a nice double room, will you?'

I found Mrs Ward reading a postcard in the kitchen. She had a sour look on her face, and when I sat down beside her at the well-scrubbed table, she slid the card over to me. 'From our Rosie,' she said bluntly. 'She's safe and well and so is the baby, and she's living with some man in Ireland.' The anger in her voice was tempered with pain, and I felt like putting my hand over hers to comfort her, but she wasn't the type for sentimental gestures.

'Well, that's a relief,' I said. 'At least she's all right – not murdered, as we all thought.'

'She's without shame, that girl.' Mrs Ward had tears in her voice, though her face was cold and stony. 'I brought her up to be a good girl, but she wouldn't learn from the mistakes I made, would she? She had to go and mess up her life – and the child's too.'

'Don't be too hard on Rosie. She's very young.' I tried to sound soothing.

Mrs Ward replied at once. 'She's no younger than you, Miss Riana, and look at you – making a business for yourself, as well as being a fine painter. I don't see *you* running off to bed any man who comes along and offers.'

I felt the colour bloom in my cheeks. 'No one's offered, Mrs Ward.' I made an effort to smile, but she wasn't amused.

'You are far too respectful of yourself to go to bed with a man without a ring on your finger.'

'Anyway –' I changed the subject – 'we have two more guests coming, so will you make up a double room when you have time, Mrs Ward?'

'Aye, I'll do that after supper. We're having lamb stew and fresh cheese and for the main meal beef and vegetables. I thought we'd finish up with steamed pudding and custard.'

'I don't know how you do it.' I really admired her; no one could coax the local shops into generosity like Mrs Ward.

She lifted her chin in the air and went stiff with pride. 'The villagers know which side their bread is buttered,' she said. 'We are good customers, so it pays to keep the

folks at Aberglasney well supplied.' She allowed herself a
tiny smile. 'And, of course, the Americans created a lot of
trade as well, and it has dawned on the shopkeepers that
now the air force men have all gone back to America they
need our custom.'

'Thank goodness for your contacts.' My words were
heartfelt. In these days of austerity after the war I was lucky
to get ordinary supplies, let alone extras.

Mr Readings and his lady arrived just as Mrs Ward was
serving supper. With the good news about Rosie, I'd finally
managed to hire the services of a village girl to help. She
had the strange name of Treasure, and she really was one
to me. According to Mrs Ward the girl was slow but was
willing – and, as Mrs Ward put it, 'she'll train, given time'.

'My dear Riana.' Mr Readings kissed me on the cheek,
and his lady friend did a little curtsey.

'I hope you'll call me Diane,' she said gently. She had
a Welsh accent, and I was amazed by the coincidence when
she told me she had been brought up close to Aberglasney,
though this was the first time she'd been back in years. She
was a sweet lady and very refined, but I knew she took Mr
Readings to her bed whenever she had the chance.

As usual there was a great deal of chatter at the supper
table, high voices and jolly laughter – that was, until the
wonderful electric lights I'd installed in the ground-floor
rooms went out. I could hear a small scream from plump
Betty.

'Everyone stay calm,' I announced in my best authoritative voice. 'We have oil lamps and candles, so no one
panic.'

Between us, Mrs Ward and I soon had the dining room
lit again. Treasure, meanwhile, stood helpless with fright,
her eyes wide. 'Is it the ghosts of the five maids playing
tricks on us?' She was quaking with fear.

'I do hope so, dear girl,' Colonel Fred said heartily.
'That's what we are all here for, after all.'

'Don't be silly, girl,' Mrs Ward reprimanded. 'Ghosts,
indeed. It's all a load of rubbish.'

'Keep your voice down, Mrs Ward,' I said. 'Don't let my

guests hear you saying such things. We don't want to put them off, do we?'

'But you don't believe in such things, do you?' Mrs Ward eyed me with her usual common-sense expression.

I shrugged. 'Who knows? My guests believe it, and that's why they come to ghost-haunting weekends, so we don't bite the hand that feeds us, do we?'

Mrs Ward nodded sagely. 'Well, I will say I've never been in a house with such strange happenings before.' She spoke loudly so that the guests would hear. 'Shall I serve the pudding now, Miss Riana?'

The sombre mood was dispelled a little as large helpings of steamed syrup pudding were served with rich egg-filled custard. Wine glasses were filled, and soon the business of the failed lights was forgotten and the laughter and sound of voices raised in enjoyment could be heard once more.

Later, as Treasure carried heavy tray-loads of dishes through to the kitchen, the lights came back on and Mr Readings took me to one side.

'Don't worry about paintings until you are ready, my sweet little Riana.' He was a little carried away with the wine. 'Waiting only makes my customers more eager to own one of your precious works.'

Diane came anxiously to Mr Readings' side. 'I don't want to trouble you, dear, but I've a little headache coming on. Do you mind if I go to bed?'

'Of course not, my dear Diane.' Mr Readings turned back to me. 'I would very much like you to think of the next exhibition, however. Perhaps a little more "free" this time, with the ghosts – and the buildings or staircase or whatever – done in an impressionist style.'

Diane was pulling at Mr Readings' sleeve. 'I am a little nervous about going to bed alone. Will you come along with me?'

'Please do go to bed, Mr Readings,' I urged. 'It's been a long drive from London, and I promise to think over what you have said.'

To my relief, he kissed me goodnight on my cheek, and arm in arm the couple went upstairs. I wished all my guests were such early birds, but Colonel Fred was only just setting up his ghost-hunting equipment, while plump Betty was hovering nervously at the foot of the stairs, clinging to the arm of young William.

That night nothing happened, except that I started on a new painting – perhaps inspired by Mr Readings' words or by the need to make some money. The painting was adequate, but had no soul, and I left it half finished and went off to bed. The guests were still making merry downstairs in the sitting room, but I was used to their noise by now and managed to ignore it.

I woke as dawn was creeping into the room and got up quickly and went to the gallery. At once I could see what was wrong with the painting. I squeezed out some fresh oils and – still in my nightgown – began to paint almost in a frenzy of enthusiasm; some might call it inspiration, but paint I did until my eyes began to close again in weariness.

I tiptoed back to my bedroom and fell asleep again, feeling relaxed and content with what I'd achieved.

TWENTY-THREE

I was wakened in the late morning by the appearance of a man at the side of my bed. I opened my mouth to scream and a hand was placed against my lips, a gentle hand. It was Tom.

I held out my arms to him, and he held me close. I could feel the hardness of his body against mine and had the almost uncontrollable desire to pull him under the sheets with me. He released me and sat on the bed, and I felt a sinking feeling of disappointment. I never knew if Tom wanted me in a special way, or just as a friend. 'Thank God you're safe,' I said. 'What's going on?'

'I can't tell you right now, hon. It's a military thing.'

'Rubbish!' There was anger in my voice. 'Why would the military need to try to steal my business from me? To threaten my life and yours? Tell me the truth. I'm not a child.'

'Our lives are linked,' Tom said. 'Whoever is after some information guesses that you know what I know.'

'And what do you know?'

'If I told you, you'd be in as much danger as I am.'

'I *am* in as much danger as you are,' I pointed out. 'From the time I arrived here, someone has tried to harm me. At first I thought the attacks had something to do with Aberglasney, but they have everything to do with you and your military secrets.'

'The two are inextricably linked. Don't you understand?'

'For heaven's sake, Tom, stop talking in riddles. Of course I don't understand.'

'Perhaps that's just as well. You can't tell what you don't know.'

'I wouldn't tell if I did know anything,' I protested.

'Ever had a root canal without anaesthetic?' Tom's voice was wry.

'You mean I could be tortured?' The thought made me wince. 'But the war is over, Tom, and so is all that kind of thing.'

'Maybe.'

I sat up, hugging the sheets and blankets around my shoulders. 'Anyway, why are you here? What's happened? By the way, you smell like you've been sleeping on a rubbish tip!'

'I'm not surprised I smell. I've been hidden on the island, remember?'

'I don't remember much of anything, except that I called and called for you and got no answer. You could have been drowned or captured or anything!'

'I did warn you it was best my enemies thought I was dead, didn't I, honey?'

Suddenly, I was furious with him. Angry that he didn't kiss me, that he didn't tell me he loved me, that he didn't even talk to me as if I was an intelligent adult. 'Stop treating me like a child!' I heard my voice quiver.

Tom took me in his arms, and his kiss was all I could have wished it to be. His mouth parted mine, and I felt my breath become ragged. I wanted him to caress me, make love to me, but he pulled away. 'I need a shower.'

'That's the truth,' I replied.

'You must have an exhibition in London soon,' he said into my ear. 'It's vital you have some work ready within the month. Understood?'

He left me, without another word, and I saw him lower himself from the window and my heart was in my mouth. I didn't know if I should love him or hate him. Did he love me, or was he using me for some scheme of his own? And yet I found myself in my studio, almost as soon as he had left, mixing my paints and obeying his command as if I was a slave girl and he my master.

My other painting was almost dry; soon I would glaze it and it would be finished. This time I did a painting of the stairs – in greys and blues, with just a narrow slant of yellow-orange light, falling from the landing down into the large ornate hall, to give the canvas some colour. A ghostly

shadow sat on the stairs, one arm raised to the balustrade
and a long thin sleeve revealing a slim delicate arm. The
face was hidden by long sweeping hair, which was almost
transparent against the darkness. It was good; even I knew
it was good, perhaps the best thing I'd ever painted. I seemed
to improve with every work I executed. Was I really such
an accomplished artist, I wondered, or was something in
the house urging me on?

My life was full of questions, the main one being did
Tom love me. But I was also worried about my work – was
it natural inspiration or some spiritual intervention? I didn't
know the answers, and yet I finished the painting in two
days: one for the initial composition, and the second day
for making the small changes I thought necessary. There
weren't many: a little flare of light on the sweep of the
hair; the pattern of colour in the carpet briefly revealed in
a narrow patch of light; and one bare long finger highlighted
as it touched the balustrade.

When I had completed the painting, exhausted, I went
to the kitchen, where Mrs Ward had left me a cold pie
and some beef sandwiches. I made a hot cup of tea, realizing I'd eaten nothing all day. I was losing weight, and
I was thin to start with. I could feel the clothes hanging
off me, and so I decided to treat myself to a new frock
when I went into Swansea. I rarely bought clothes so I
had coupons to spare, and suddenly I was filled with the
urge to dress up, have my hair done and put on some
lipstick. What I must have looked like first thing yesterday
morning I dreaded to think. And yet my heart lightened
as I remembered the way Tom's mouth had parted my lips
and how I'd wanted him to love me, to make love to me,
however improper it might be, however wrong and
forward, and me a single girl. Such behaviour could only
have been excused in the war; then death had been an
ever-present threat.

The next morning I was in my studio again when Mrs
Ward came up to me with a tray of Camp coffee that smelled
strong and delicious. 'Have you heard the gossip?' she asked,
her eyes curious as she examined my face.

'No. I've been working hard for my next exhibition.' I made a gesture towards the painting.

She hardly glanced at it. 'More ghosts,' she said with raised eyebrows. 'Anyway, you know Tom, the American air force man?'

'Of course I know Tom.' I was impatient and a little worried. 'What gossip could there possibly be about him?'

'It seems he's run away to London and got involved with an heiress,' she said, watching my face carefully.

I managed to hide my shock. 'Good for him,' I said smoothly. 'I hope he'll be very happy.' I turned away and began to work like a fiend. I was outwardly composed, but inside I felt as if jagged glass was tearing up my heart.

In the next few weeks I found that work was my salvation from the bitterness, anger and jealousy that seemed to eat my soul. My paintings were executed with a frenzy of brush strokes and in strong colours, but always with a shadowy corner and an ethereal being, hardly there, behind a stone arch or similar. Outside the house and in, I painted scenes of the shadowed hallway, the landings, and even the blue room, and wished that Beatrice was there to talk to about my troubles.

Mrs Ward poked and pried, but I remained elusive and avoided her when I could; she seemed to feed off my misery. It seemed to me that she was blooming and I was fading away into nothingness like my ghosts.

The day of the exhibition dawned. In the early morning, a van arrived to take my canvases to London. Gone were the days when I was expected to transport them myself. Now I was treated like royalty, Mr Readings practically putting out the red carpet for me.

Red; that was the colour I would wear, I decided. Once the van had left, I took the train to London and sat in the first-class compartment like a lady born to riches and honours. No one would know I was grieving inside.

I'd heard nothing from Tom – not a word of explanation, not even a plain letter telling me of his whereabouts. I still felt his last kiss on my lips, and I pushed the thought away in case I began to cry.

At Swansea, Miss Grist got into the compartment and gave me a sunny smile as if nothing had ever been wrong between us. 'Lovely crisp day,' she said as she sat down, letting a flurry of cold air in from the corridor before she pushed the door shut and pulled her fur collar around her face. Her hat of soft felt with pretty bird feathers she pulled into place on her brow, and I realized she looked very smart; far from her usual frumpy self. 'I'm actually coming to see your exhibition,' she said, almost preening as she adjusted the hat. 'I thought it was time to see what all the fuss was about.'

'Might you steal my ideas for yourself?' I couldn't help the sarcasm. 'Just as you stole my list of guests. That didn't work, fortunately for me. It seems *your* ghost was a trick.'

'And yours isn't?' She took out a small mirror from her bag and reapplied her lipstick. It was a new lipstick – still very expensive and exclusive after the barrenness of the war years. I couldn't resist staring at it.

'Have you been left an inheritance, Miss Grist?'

'You could say that.' She didn't enlarge. 'Your ghosts?' Her eyebrows were arched. 'Do you really believe the old house is haunted then?'

'I couldn't say.' My tone was cold. 'All I know is there's no trickery involved. Strange things happen of their own accord at Aberglasney.'

'Oh, I know that, dear Miss Evans.' Her tone was almost offensive. 'I also know that your American disappeared and then got engaged to an heiress.' She smiled a thin smile. 'Of course, you didn't know *this*, do you? Tom Maybury is engaged to *me*, Miss Evans. I am the heiress in question.'

'You? Really?' I spoke as calmly as I could, though I was seething inside. I left her as soon as I got off the train, and I waved at Mr Readings as he came to greet me, walking along the platform at a smart pace. I could see his car outside the station; it was old, pre-war, but it gleamed with the loving care he'd lavished upon it.

'Riana, how lovely you look, but you are far too thin! We shall have to feed you up while you are in London.'

Suddenly, Miss Grist was at my side again. 'Well, I must say goodbye, dear Miss Evans,' she said, as though we'd been having an amicable conversation on the train. She smiled at Mr Readings, and from sheer politeness he bowed and took her hand.

'Charmed, dear lady. Charmed, I'm sure.'

As we stood there, a huge Rolls Royce drew up. Miss Grist waved her gloved hand and, with a sweet smile at the chauffeur, stepped inside the magnificent car.

'She must be a lady of good standing and landed gentry to boot. Where did you meet her, Riana?'

'She works part-time at the local library,' I said flatly.

His eyebrows shot up. 'She must be doing that as a hobby or something. By the look of her she's extremely wealthy and has very good taste. You should have invited her to the exhibition.'

'Don't worry, she informs me she's attending,' I said acidly. 'We must make sure she has the best champagne and we must sweet-talk her, though I warn you she's not the sort to buy my work.'

'Humph!' Mr Readings chose to ignore my ire. 'Talking about the exhibition, your work is as colourful and as excellent and individual as always – with just a touch of melancholy, if I might say so.'

'I'm glad you're pleased. I've worked really hard on the exhibition.' I hadn't actually. The work had come easily to me, the brush strokes quick and sure. When I stood at my easel in the studio and painted the house I loved it was as though it was wrapped around me, urging me on, inspiring me in a way I'd never felt before. 'And of course you are entitled to say so! You are exhibiting the paintings for me, after all.'

'And selling them, my dear Riana, and selling them. We shall have a triumphant day tomorrow, you'll see; the opening will be a great event.'

I wondered why I wasn't feeling excited. I used to love the exhibitions; being the centre of attraction still felt like a

new experience for me. Of course, I was still trying to
swallow the shock of being taunted by Miss Grist. Was Tom
really interested in her because she had come into money?
And why had Tom asked me to put on this exhibition in
the first place?

I could feel my hands shaking. My nerves were strung
taut; I felt I would snap into little pieces at any moment.
Tom engaged to be married was pain enough, but Tom
married to a grasping, duplicitous woman like Miss Grist
was impossible to believe!

And then I calmed down. It wasn't true, of course it
wasn't true, none of it was true. Tom was lying low as he'd
planned, so he couldn't be planning to marry anyone. The
way he'd kissed me and held me, the kindness he'd shown
me, the love – yes, *love* . . . He was *my* man. Wasn't he?

I realized then Mr Readings was talking to me.

'You feeling all right, Riana?'

'I'm just tired. That's all, I suppose. Working day and
night on the paintings and then the journey up to London . . .
It's all been a bit wearing, to tell the truth.' My physical
tiredness was nothing compared to my emotional exhaus-
tion, but I had to make some excuse to Mr Readings. 'I'll
be all right after a rest on a cosy bed, so please don't worry.'

'You'll be all right for the exhibition I'm sure, my dear
Riana. Put on your best glad rags and rouge your pretty
cheeks and you'll be just fine.'

That evening at the exhibition I did feel fine. My weariness vanished as I coaxed myself into believing that Miss
Grist was somehow behind the story about Tom and her
sudden wealth. What was she up to now? She'd cheated
me once over my list of guests, so why should she be telling
me the truth now about her engagement? Come to think
about it, I hadn't seen a diamond ring on her finger – just
some huge stones that could have been bought from any
traveller's basket of cheap trinkets.

The exhibition was a great success, and in the end I began
to enjoy myself – although mainly because Miss Grist didn't
show up. I was fawned over and praised and received so

many compliments and smiles that it was a wonder my
head wasn't turned. But I knew something the eager buyers
didn't: it was the influence of Aberglasney that helped me
create such emotive paintings, with the feel of age and
ghostliness and mystery. But still. Seeing the pictures framed
and hanging on the wall of the well-lit opulent gallery I
was impressed myself – and surprised at what I had
achieved.

I sipped at the gin and tonic Mr Readings handed me
and suppressed a grimace at the taste. Alcohol was a luxury
I appreciated, but I would have preferred a nice hot cup of
tea. As it was I slipped my rather utilitarian shoes off when
no one was looking and stood in my stockinged feet, feeling
the softness of the carpet under my toes with a sigh of
pleasure.

'You look very lovely tonight, Riana.' Mr Readings
suddenly stood beside me. 'I didn't realize how tiny you
are, and all that luxuriant red hair! You should have your
portrait painted, young lady. Why not do a self portrait?'

'I couldn't,' I said quickly. 'I can paint other people, but
not myself. I'm afraid I'd find too many faults.' *Or see
through my own image*, I thought, *and see the flawed unsure
being I really was.*

'All right, I'll get young Justin to paint you. A new talent,
Riana. Not as original as you or as talented, but worth
watching all the same. Come, I'll introduce you.'

Still shoeless, I trailed along reluctantly behind Mr
Readings. I didn't want my portrait painted, and I was tired.
All I wanted was to go to the privacy of my room in the
guest house and go to sleep and dream of Tom.

Justin was pleasant and very handsome, in a film star
sort of way. His hair was brilliantined to his head, and his
features were in perfect proportion. He was dressed in a
fine suit and a black bow tie, very proper for the occasion,
but for me Tom's rugged good looks were far more attractive than this picture of male perfection standing before me.
I held out my hand and murmured a greeting.

'Charmed to meet you, Miss Evans.' Justin bent towards
me and kissed both my cheeks in what I thought was a

very French way and somewhat affected for an English man. 'I do love your work,' he enthused, and although I knew as an artist himself he probably meant what he said, I made the appropriate modest replies, and after a few minutes of stilted conversation I tried to move away.

Mr Readings wasn't having it. 'Justin, I would like to make a suggestion. How would you like to paint Riana's portrait?'

Justin stood back a little and regarded me from head to toe in an embarrassingly detached way. 'Yes, I can see a field. Poppies, perhaps, to compliment that lovely red hair.' He rubbed his fingers through my hair until it was wild and curling on my shoulders. 'And a peasant dress,' he said.

'I'll leave the details with you, Justin.' Mr Readings spoke as if I wasn't there.

'Where on earth am I going to get a peasant dress?' I asked, a little piqued.

'Oh, a detail, my dear Riana. Ask that woman, that Mrs Ward, she seems able to pick up just about anything.' Mr Reading smiled. 'I would like to make it a commission. One painting to hang in my gallery permanently.'

'All right,' I said dubiously. 'I'll try, but I'm not promising anything.' Inwardly I groaned. It seemed I would have my portrait painted whether I liked it or not.

The door flew open just then. Some men came into the gallery, and one of them flashed a badge at Mr Readings. 'We have to ask you to come with us, miss,' he said to me. He spoke with such authority that I stepped back, stunned.

'Hang on. I want you to prove you are really policemen before I go anywhere,' I said, remembering the 'policemen' who had taken Tom away.

Mr Readings telephoned the station on my behalf, and then nodded at me. 'They confirmed that these are real policemen.'

'What have I done?' I asked as my arm was caught and I was hustled to the door.

Mr Readings tried to intervene but he was pushed away. 'I shall get you the best lawyer in town, Riana,' Mr Readings said. 'Don't worry! I'll have you free by the morning, and all this nonsense can be explained.'

The pavement was hard and cold beneath my feet; I hadn't had time to find my shoes. I was taken to a big black car and helped – or rather pushed – inside, and five minutes after we'd driven away from the bright lights of the gallery I sat stunned and silent in the back of the car, knowing in my heart that these were not real policemen and wondering if Tom had betrayed me.

TWENTY-FOUR

I was taken to a small house, and although it was dark and I couldn't see much, I could smell the sea, feel the breeze and so I knew I was probably near the coast.

'Just keep quiet.' One of the so-called policemen grinned down at me, and I felt stupid in my evening dress and bare feet, and shivery in the coldness of the bare, utilitarian house.

'What's the charge?' I asked in reply. There was no response, but eventually one of the men asked if I wanted a cup of tea. I nodded helplessly. At least some hot tea would warm me and perhaps comfort me a little.

I was led into a small cell with a single bed and a rickety table as the only furniture. There was a high window – too high to see out of – but at least the sea wasn't coming in, so these men, whoever they were, did not intend to drown me.

The man came back a few minutes later with tea that had been kept in a flask. It tasted metallic, but it was hot and refreshing, and I sat on the bed and drank it gratefully.

He left me then, and I heard the key turning in the lock and guessed there was nothing I could do right now; it was dark and cold and I had no shoes. Better try to sleep and then find a way to escape tomorrow.

I finished my tea and clambered under the bedclothes. They felt a little damp – or maybe it was just the cold – but slowly I began to feel warm and drowsy, and as my eyelids began to droop I realized the lethargy I was feeling was due to some sleeping draught or drug dropped into my tea. I didn't care though. All I wanted to do was let blessed darkness claim me.

I woke to a sharp, chilly but sunny morning, and I had no hangover from the drugged tea. Instead I felt refreshed and calm and ready for some breakfast. Eventually, the policeman who had given me the tea, now in civvies, brought me some: a tray with tea and toast and scrambled eggs that looked as though they were meant to be poached eggs and had gone wrong. All the same, I ate the breakfast with enthusiasm, feeling inexplicably better than I'd done for some time.

It was, I supposed, the sense of having no responsibility for myself or my action, and of having some time to be alone when I could refresh my mind and face my feelings. I had no sense of danger. If the men had meant to hurt me they would have done so by now ... or so I hoped and reasoned. Was it some ransom plan? I decided it must be – otherwise what would anyone want with me?

Later in the morning, however, things took a sinister turn. My hands were tied behind my back and I was blindfolded; that meant I knew the person who wanted to question me. 'Why are you keeping me here?' I was led to a chair and sat down gingerly, afraid of falling. 'If it's money, I haven't got any.'

'It's for your own safety, ma'am, and I'll ask the questions.' The voice was American, deep Southern American with warm, deep overtones. Like Tom's, but not like Tom's. And I wondered again if Tom had set me up.

I waited silently, trying to absorb the sounds and smells around me. I could smell salt and fish and the wash of the waves, and I thought again that we were very near the sea. In the background I could hear feminine tones; obviously, there was a woman in the next room. Her voice was subdued, but again faintly familiar.

'I want information about Tom Maybury. Where is he?'

That surprised me. 'Last I heard he'd got engaged and was being lavished with gifts from his new, rich lady love.' I could hear a touch of bitterness and not a little anger in my voice.

'We all know that's a cover, so what's the truth?'

'I wish I knew,' I said on a sigh. 'How dare you!' My voice was clear and firm. 'I don't know anything about Tom Maybury, and I don't wish to. He was stationed at Aberglasney during the war and we became friends for a while, but then he went away. I have no idea where, and why should I?'

'We don't believe all that rubbish! We know he fell in love with you and the big house you live in.'

'You know more than I do then,' I said doggedly. 'I only wish that was true – the bit about him loving me I mean.' I was babbling now. 'He's engaged to some other woman, remember? Anyway, what's he done?'

I felt the brush of a skirt as someone knelt beside me. So there *was* a woman present!

'We might as well leave you here to die.' The words were whispered more to disguise the voice than anything else, I suspected. The whispering continued eerily in my ear: 'You will be trapped here to starve to death . . .'

After the whispering woman had finished talking, my captors had gagged me – and left me. For a while I made a keening noise, hoping to call Tom to me, until I realized it was impossible to talk coherently, so even if Tom *did* come to save me there was no way I could warn him of the danger. I tried to struggle, but the cords had became twisted and I was only making things worse, so I kept still and rested my head against the thick stone wall. Above me I could hear the beating of rain on the roof, and I had a sense of being here before – and, of course, I had been . . . in a way . . . with Tom. We'd been shut into that derelict church building to drown. But this time I was alone. No one would ever know where I was, and even if by some miracle Tom found out where I'd been taken, he would be caught and captured – perhaps even killed. I struggled again, but it was useless, and so I rested my head once more and tried to think.

I was beginning to despair – for I could hardly breathe with the tightness of the tape over my mouth – when my captors came back for me. I watched in amazement and relief as one of the men silently untied me, and then I was out of the building, gasping in the fresh salty air. I was thrust into a van and lay on the metal floor in the pitch dark, bouncing around for what seemed hours. Anything was better than starving to death alone, I told myself as my elbows hurt more and more and my head felt as if it had been constantly hit with a rock. I must have blacked out, because when I was let out of the van I fell to the ground on my own arched driveway, too numb to stand.

A light fell on me, and Mrs Ward came rushing out of the house. She wrapped a blanket around me and helped me indoors and through to the kitchen, where the welcome sound of the kettle boiling filled my heart with cheer.

'Some men came here, miss,' Mrs Ward said huskily. 'Searched the whole house, they did. Didn't ask permission – just went through, room by room.'

'What were they looking for?' My hands closed around the cup Mrs Ward put in front of me.

'Don't know, Miss Riana, and when I asked they pushed me into the kitchen and shut me in. I kept my mouth shut after that, didn't like the look of those villains at all. Rough men, they were, with glinting evil eyes.'

'Could you give the police a description of them, Mrs Ward?' I asked.

She shook her head, and her mouth twisted in a grimace of regret. 'They had scarves covering their faces, but they had foreign voices and glittering eyes – oh, and dark thick hair, I can tell the police that much.'

'Were they tall men? Fat? Thin? What colour clothes did they wear? What sort of voices did they have . . . were they Americans?'

'American- or Canadian-like, I'd say. Gruff and rough they were. Both big men – broad with big, calloused hands. You know, working men's hands.'

'That's very observant of you, Mrs Ward. Have you called the police?'

'Can't,' she said baldly. 'They cut the wires . . . and,' she added, 'I was too frightened.'

'All right.' I looked round, but everything in the kitchen was as neat and tidy as it had always been.

'They didn't mess things up, I'll say that for them. I did hear a bit of noise from the blue room, mind, as if they were moving furniture, that sort of thing.'

'Good thing Beatrice isn't there, though goodness knows where she is now.'

Mrs Ward shook her head. 'Who can say? Heaven or hell, one of the two.'

'What a funny thing to say, Mrs Ward.'

She frowned back, but before she could make any comment there was the sound of hammering on the front door. 'Oh my Lord, they've come back.' Mrs Ward looked as if she might dive under the table.

I stood up shakily.

'Police!' The voice rang out, and I tensed and put my hand to my lips, beckoning Mrs Ward to be quiet. I wasn't going to be caught like that again.

I crept across the dark hall and peered through the little window. There was a real police car outside and a plain-clothes officer and a uniformed constable standing on the drive.

'I want to see some identification please,' I shouted and obligingly the constable held up a card near the window. I knew anything could be a forgery, but I decided I might as well trust them. Reluctantly, I opened the door, expecting any minute to be thrown back against the wall. But the men walked calmly into the house and stood politely as I examined the card more thoroughly.

'We're from Carmarthen Police Station, miss,' the constable explained. 'We had a call stating there was some sort of disturbance at Aberglasney House.'

'Well –' I was a bit on edge – 'come in, but the "disturbance" is well and truly over. You're too late to apprehend the perpetrators.' I was speaking like a policeman's notebook, but I was still in shock – my clothes still wet from the rain and my skirt sticking to my legs. 'In any case, who reported the matter?'

'Didn't leave a name, miss. They usually don't. But it was a woman; someone with a sore throat, by the sound of it,' he added helpfully.

'We'll search the house, miss.' The detective spoke at last. 'And I suggest you change your clothes before you catch your death.'

I could see he was longing to ask what had happened to me, but didn't quite dare to in case I reported something unpleasant that he didn't wish to deal with right now. He glanced at his watch, confirming my suspicions that he was reluctant to do this job. Had he heard about the ghosts? I wondered.

'Please carry out your search,' I said. 'The criminals have been through the whole house, though they didn't do any damage. Please look carefully for clues. A few more people searching my house won't do any harm.'

'I hear you have parties here, miss?' The constable's face was eager – almost as though he'd heard there were orgies taking place under the elegant roof of my house.

'Not parties,' I said, 'but ghost-haunting evenings, when witches fly and men turn to wolves in the full moon.' I was teasing him, but his eyes widened. 'I have visitors come to see if they can take a picture of the ghosts, the five maids who died here some years ago,' I explained. 'I'm sure you've heard the stories, officer?'

After a swift look at his superior officer, he didn't comment, but his eyes were large.

At last the men began their search of the rooms; of course, they didn't find anything, but in the meantime I was able to change into dry clothing.

We met again, after a remarkably short time, in the hall.

'Nothing out of the ordinary, miss.' The constable was usually the one to speak, as though his superior thought the whole thing beneath him. The constable's next words confirmed the doubts of both men. 'Sure this isn't all a publicity trick, miss, just to get your name in the papers and these parties some free advertising?'

'I'm sure,' I said. 'I was dragged away from a big opening night and I—' I stopped talking, realizing it sounded exactly like a publicity stunt. 'Mr Reading phoned the police station, and someone there confirmed the men who took me away were real police officers.'

'Easy enough to fake,' one of the men said dryly. 'Well, as you don't seem to be in imminent danger, we'll have to leave, but be sure to lock up tonight just in case.'

'Aren't you going to guard the house or anything?'

The well-dressed plain-clothes officer took charge at last. 'This is really not our case, Miss Evans. You were taken from a *London* gallery. We've only come out as a courtesy to our London colleagues, you know.'

'So if I'm murdered in my bed, or abducted again from Aberglasney, it won't be your case then?'

'Goodnight, miss. Call us if you see anything suspicious.' They left abruptly and drove away in a cloud of black smoke.

I closed the door and bolted it and hurried into the kitchen.

'They were about as useful as a cow with a musket!' Mrs Ward said in resignation. 'Sit down, love, and I'll make you a bite to eat.'

'Just some toast and more hot tea, Mrs Ward, please.' I sank down into a chair and put my head in my hands. 'Thank goodness you were here! At least I wasn't alone when those officers came; they thought I made it all up as it was.'

'Aye,' Mrs Ward said dryly.

'What on earth is going on here? What does someone think I know about Tom? I only knew him for a few months. I know we were "fond" of each other . . . Well, I thought he was "fond" of me, anyway, and now he's vanished and it seems he's suspected of all sorts: espionage, perhaps, I just don't know.'

'Forget it now, Riana. Keep all the windows closed and your door locked and I'll double check everything is secured down here.'

I ate the hot buttered toast with relish and then took Mrs Ward's advice and slowly made my way upstairs to my bedroom. I wished Beatrice was here; she and Mrs Ward were the only friends I had now. Could I even trust Mr Readings and his lady friend? I just didn't know any more.

I climbed into my cosy bed, heavy with the blankets, and rubbed my sore head against the softness of the pillows, grateful to be warm and comfortable. My summer days with Tom seemed far away now; the hours we shared in the sun and in the shade of the cloisters when it was too hot seemed a distant dream. And at last I slept.

TWENTY-FIVE

A sort of normality had returned to my life when we had the next ghost-haunting weekend. Beatrice had returned home with her little bag of belongings and, as usual, gave me no inkling of where she had been – but it was clear she loved the house to be full of people, of laughter, and of the cheeriness that came from wine-drinking and the scent of food cooking.

I always took her a small meal on a tray because she refused to join the crowd for dinner. 'Look, dear,' she told me this time, 'the good people who come to these things think I'm a ghost, so don't let's spoil the illusion.' She gave me a sweet smile. 'It's the way I dress. I know I'm eccentric, dear, but that way I'm comfortable.'

I left her then and joined the guests, thinking she had a point. I didn't mind her presence and her constant comings and goings. When she was at Aberglasney, the house, absurd as it might seem, was happy and restful.

My guests were in high spirits, full of the news of my abduction. The actress in me came to the fore, and I told the story of being chained in a strange building, with thugs telling me I would starve and die there, in a dramatic manner that had them all riveted.

Mr Bleesdale was the first to speak. 'Poor Riana, what on earth did those people want from you?'

'They think I know something I shouldn't about the Americans,' I explained. 'Because Tom and I were friends, I was mistaken for some sort of spy. Of course, I don't know much about any of the Americans, except what everyone knows – that they were billeted here during the war.'

'Oh, there was some talk a while back about a new aeroplane engine the Americans were testing. Perhaps it was something to do with the plans,' the colonel said importantly. 'Remember that poor pilot who was killed in a flying accident – Jenkins, was it? Well, he was involved in all this testing business, I heard. That's why his death was kept rather quiet.'

All this was new to me – and a light went off in my head. Tom had never said a word about testing a new type of engine – though why should he have? But perhaps that was why I had been abducted: so my house could be searched for some sort of designs. It didn't explain why Tom had asked me to hold the exhibition in the first place though . . . But I remembered once more that Mrs Ward had told me that the men who'd searched the house had had American accents. Perhaps Tom had learned that the house was to be searched and had wished me out of the way for my own safety. It was just bad luck that I had been targeted by the very men who were after Tom himself!

Another thought struck me, and after dinner was over and the ghost haunting was given up for a good night's sleep I went to see Beatrice. She was sitting on the bed reading, as if she'd been waiting for me. 'You want to know what Edwin did for a living,' she said at once.

'Have you been listening on the stairs?' I asked with wry amusement.

Her smile was sweet. 'No, dear, I'm clairvoyant. Didn't you know?' She nodded. 'He was an engineer and an inventor. He designed a new engine of some sort for an aeroplane, and the Americans – who always had too much money – took it up. The money never came, of course, once my dear husband was accused of murder, though I don't believe he had given the final designs to the Americans before he died.'

I went to sit on the bed, but Beatrice waved me to a chair. 'My old bones are too brittle, dear. Please don't put your weight on the bed.'

'Where are his plans now?'

'If you knew that, dear, you'd be in more trouble than you are now. If you'd known you'd have told those horrible men and they'd have taken the plans from you and Edwin's innocence would never be proven *and* you'd never have got the money from the Americans.'

'But that's your money, Beatrice! If you'd that you wouldn't have needed to sell the house. Anyway, how do you always seem to know everything that goes on?'

'You'll find out all about me, Edwin and the house one day, Riana, I'm counting on it, and then the money will be yours. You own Aberglasney now, and I want you to bring it back to its former glory.'

'I'm doing my best.' I was a little piqued.

'I know that, dear, and I do my best to help by showing myself on the ghost nights, just now and then, to encourage the story that the house is haunted.'

'Don't you think it is then?'

'Of course I do. Don't be silly, dear. Clearly, the house is haunted. It wouldn't be honest to say so otherwise, would it?' Did she wink or was I imagining it?

'Go to bed, Riana,' she said brusquely. 'You seem very tired all of a sudden.'

'I am,' I said. 'It seems to have been a long day.'

If the ghosts came out that night, I never heard them. I slept deeply and dreamlessly and woke in the morning, ready to tackle breakfast with my guests.

'You missed a spectacle, dear Riana.' The colonel greeted me with old-fashioned courtesy, rising from his chair and bowing slightly before tucking into his bacon and eggs once more.

'What do you mean?' I poured some coffee from the pot on the sideboard. Mornings, we'd agreed, were 'help yourself' times, when Mrs Ward brought in platters of food and pots of coffee and left the people who deigned to rise early to fill their own plates. I usually was up from bed in time to help her, but this morning I'd slept late.

'The ladies appeared, dear. The five maids.' The colonel's eyes were quite serious, and I realized he wasn't joking. 'They came along the corridor, drifting like clouds of mist, and then they just disappeared when the young lad William came along to go to his bed.'

'Did he see them too?' I asked innocently, suppressing

an inane desire to laugh. Not surprisingly, Colonel Fred shook his head.

'Unfortunately not. He was too busy trying to load his camera with film. He did see the wreath of mist disappearing into the blue room though.'

'You were very lucky then, colonel. Not many are privileged to see the maids.' I guessed he'd had too many brandies after dinner and the 'mist' had probably been the smoke from his pipe.

'They do say there's going to be a disaster when the maids appear.' Mrs Ward had come into the dining room with fresh coffee and was standing there, her eyes large. *Good old Mrs Ward*, I thought. *Anything to drum up business for the weekends*. I smiled approvingly at her.

'It's true, Riana,' she said in all seriousness. 'They only appear when something bad is going to happen.'

'I've had my guests taken away from me, and I've been kidnapped – I didn't see the maids any time then,' I protested, forgetting the presence of guests. I could have added that my beloved Tom had become engaged to a dreadful, scheming woman too, but that would be giving too much away about my own feelings.

I sat down abruptly and drank my coffee, trying to see beyond Mrs Ward's serious expression.

'You'll see, Riana,' she said soberly.

I ate some toast, nearly choking with every mouthful. Not even the marmalade helped. I drank more coffee, just to keep the guests company

The 'something dreadful' happened very soon; dear Mr Readings was found dead in his gallery.

I travelled up to London for his funeral and stood at the graveside with Diane, who was dry eyed and despairing as she stood and watched his remains being put into the cold earth.

I touched her arm. 'How are you?' A stupid question; I knew it as soon as the words left my mouth.

She stared down at her sensible shoes. 'I'm desolate, dear.' She even used Mr Readings' phrases. 'We were married quietly last week. I've only been his wife for a few days.' Tears blurred her eyes. 'For so long I've wanted him to make an honest woman of me, and now he has died and left me a widow. How can I bear it?'

'I'm sorry, Diane. Are you all right for money? I know Mr Readings will have left you well provided for, but if you need help right now please just tell me.'

'I have my guest house, Riana. It doesn't bring in a fortune, but I'll be far from destitute, and as you say my dear man will have left me well provided for. But what about you? What about your work? Who will market your paintings for you now?'

'I don't know. Don't you worry about that, Diane. I'll manage.'

After the service – during which I shed some tears for the honest, encouraging Mr Readings – we went back to Diane's guest house for a small glass of sherry and some very dry cake her cook had made. The loss of Mr Readings' influence and money was already making a difference. The black market served those who had money to spend very well indeed. Now that Midas touch was lacking, and it showed.

That night I slept at the guest house and drank some more sherry with Diane as she reminisced about the good times she and Mr Readings had shared. It helped her to talk, I could see, and in spite of my tiredness I was happy to listen.

The next morning I travelled home from London, cursing the train that stopped at every small station on the way back to Wales.

As I stepped out of the train, a tall, big shouldered figure came out of the shadows of the station platform. As he came nearer I realized it was Tom. I gasped as he came forward and took my overnight bag and kissed me on the cheek as if I was his maiden aunt.

I pulled away sharply. 'None of that! You are spoken for now, or have you forgotten?'

Tom tapped his nose. 'Don't believe all you hear and only half of what you see,' he said cryptically.

I shook my head and let him lead me to his car, a beaten-up old Ford that I'd never seen before. 'What's happened to all this money you're supposed to have had? Has your new girlfriend spent it? I understood she's some kind of heiress. Or have you come into some sort of plans? Drawings of engines, that sort of thing?'

He just chuckled, but didn't answer.

'What's going on, Tom?' I demanded. 'I think you owe me some sort of explanation.'

He didn't reply, but drove in silence all the way to Aberglasney. I felt a bit intimidated by his closed-in look and didn't ask any more questions.

Once outside my home he stopped the car, took me in his arms and kissed me deeply and thoroughly. I should have slapped his face, but instead I melted into his arms, breathing in the scent of him, the feel of his arms around me, his mouth against mine possessing me. We belonged together. It was unspoken, but known to both of us. What was he doing planning to marry another woman?

'Whatever happens, remember I love you,' he said, and then he opened the door, practically pushed me out of the car, and ground into gears and shot away in a cloud of dust.

Mrs Ward was waiting for me in the doorway. 'Was that Tom?' She was craning her neck to watch the disappearing car.

I didn't answer, wanting to clutch his words and his kiss close to me – something of mine, something precious that I didn't want to share.

'Kettle on, Mrs Ward?' I shrugged off my coat in the hall and let it dangle over the hallstand like a lifeless body. I shivered.

'You're cold, Riana,' Mrs Ward said. 'Come into the kitchen. It's warm there, and I'll make you a nice cup of tea and a sandwich. I have some cold beef and pickle in the larder, will that do?'

I nodded, not wanting to eat anything, but feeling a sandwich might give me some warmth and energy.

'Was the funeral very dreadful?' Mrs Ward asked. 'They usually are.'

'Very dreadful,' I replied. 'In more ways than one. I've lost a dear friend and a patron of the gallery where most of my work was sold.'

'Well, Riana, we'll just have to have more weekends,' Mrs Ward said practically.

'The profit from the weekends will help keep the place going,' I agreed, 'but I needed the money from my work to pay for the improvements to the house.'

'We'll manage.' Mrs Ward looked at me thoughtfully. 'What about taking me in as a lodger?'

'What?' It was something I'd never thought about.

'I only rent Mill Cottage,' she said, 'and you could take rent out of my wages. That would help a bit, wouldn't it?'

'That's very kind of you, Mrs Ward,' I said thoughtfully. Did I really want a live-in lodger? But then my house was open to whoever chose to come to the weekends, and Mrs Ward was with me most of the time anyway – sometimes until late at night.

'I do hate the walk home when it's dark,' she said. It was as if she read my thoughts. 'I wouldn't need much room, mind, just a small place to sleep. After all, I spend most of my time in the kitchen here as it is.'

'Yes, that sounds like a good idea,' I said at last, 'but I don't like the idea of taking money from you for rent.'

'Bless you, I'll be having bed and board, and all I need is a few shilling for a pack of Woodbines every week. In any case,' she said, smiling, 'my lease comes up for renewal soon, and my grumpy old landlord is bound to put the rent up if I sign again.'

'I see. Well, all in all, it sounds as if it will work.' I thought of Mrs Ward being in the house all the time; it would have its detractions, but it would have benefits too – like company when I listened to the radio or had a cup of tea. It wasn't as if I had a husband or a boyfriend or anything close to it; not with Tom playing silly games with me.

I held out my hand and took Mrs Ward's red scrubbed fingers, and yet a strange doubt lingered. Was I doing the right thing?

TWENTY-SIX

Mrs Ward was right about making more money from the house, and fortunately the next ghost-haunting weekend, which would take place in February, was oversubscribed. I had to make a waiting list of people and arrange another weekend quickly.

All the old crowd had priority for this weekend: Colonel Fred, young William, plump Betty, and all the other 'oldies' like Doctor Bravage and Mr Bleesdale. I was able only to allow a few new guests in for the weekend.

Colonel Fred's accident at the Christmas ghost-haunting weekend had hit the newspapers some time ago and caused quite a stir: it seems the public believed he had been attacked by vengeful ghosts; a story he had no doubt fostered. Also, the 'sightings' of the five dead serving maids from the last weekend had made a big story in the newspapers, and now were linked with poor Mr Readings' death. One headline had read: 'CURSED BY THE GHOSTS OF ABERGLASNEY.'

I feared even more for my paintings. No one would want them if they believed the whole enterprise – even buying paintings of mine – was 'cursed'.

The maids, as if on cue, appeared again that night, to the delight and terror of my guests. I even saw shadowy ghostly figures flitting along the landing myself, but I put it down to the flickering lights and the large amounts of sherry I'd consumed. The shadowy figures drifted across the landing wearing sweet cotton nightgowns, but faded to nothing as they reached the stairs. I blinked and put the 'vision' down to imagination. I didn't want to believe that anything bad would happen after seeing the maids, as it had the last time they had been seen.

Young William took photographs on his Brownie camera, clicking away as if he was going to make a fortune for his pictures from the newspapers – and maybe he would.

Beatrice also put in an appearance: peering out of her room with a frown, as if her sleep had been disturbed, and wearing a 'Queen Victoria' kind of sleep bonnet, and then disappearing abruptly with no sound of footsteps, almost as if she was floating on air. I don't know how she managed it, but she was very convincing.

I went into the kitchen and drank some thick coffee, trying to still my reeling brain. Mrs Ward was sitting with her feet up in the rocking chair and didn't sit to attention as she usually did when I came into the room. But now she was a lodger, and lived in, she had every right to make herself comfortable. 'The visitors seeing things again, are they?' she said dryly.

'So am I!' I sank into the old armchair in the corner of the kitchen. 'I don't know what I saw, but it certainly looked like ghosts trailing across the landing and turning into thin air.'

'Trick of the light, I expect.' Mrs Ward took my now empty cup. 'I'll make some more coffee. You've had rather too much alcohol,' she said sagely.

I sighed heavily. 'I expect you're right – or else it was mass hysteria gripping us all.'

'Whatever, it will be good for business.' Mrs Ward was, as ever, practical. She handed me the fresh coffee and sat down again, this time resting her slippers on the thick rug that covered the slate floor. A good fire burned in the grate, and even as I looked at the flames Mrs Ward added more coal. I was only glad she had no more dire warnings about bad things happening when the maids appeared.

The heat made me sleepy, and I let the haziness over-take me. I wanted to paint the maids while they were fresh in my mind or my imagination – whatever it was – but I was far too tired.

Later, I felt arms lift me, and I was being carried upstairs to my bedroom. I could smell Tom. Not the reeking smell of the water and the island, but a fresh-washed tobacco smell, and I put my arms around his neck and clung to him. If it was a dream, I meant to enjoy it.

He kissed me and held me tenderly, and I wanted more from him than kisses and hugs.

'I am not the engaged man everyone thinks I am. You must trust me on that, Riana,' he whispered, his breath sweet against my face.

I felt so young, so in love, and reason flew out through the window. I pressed against him and felt the hardness of his masculine body against my softness. I yielded to him willingly, and that night was the most thrilling, fulfilling night of my life. I felt happy, loved and desirable. That night I had become a woman – and in the morning I was lying in an empty bed.

TWENTY-SEVEN

I painted furiously the next day. A glow of shame was filling me, but my head was clear as an icicle. I knew Tom had made love to me, but did he love me or was he taking advantage of my feelings for him? I was in a pain of rejection, of being a fool . . . and yet there was a certain kind of joy too. I had felt the thrill of possession, of arousing passion, in Tom and in myself. I had wanted him as much as he wanted me, and that night, that experience, would be mine for ever.

Later I had a phone call from the gallery. Diane had taken control of the business! Dear Mr Readings had left it all to her: the gallery, the paintings, the goodwill . . . Everything.

'May I come down to see you, dear Riana?' Diane's voice was still cool with grief, but she told me she wanted to display some of my work at her grand reopening exhibition. 'We'll make it together, Riana,' she said, and I'm sure I heard a catch in her voice. 'My dear man would have wanted us to go on, don't you think?'

'I really do, Diane. Please come and stay as soon as possible. I'll meet you at the station, and Mrs Ward and I will make you very welcome and comfortable, I promise.' I hesitated, running the phone cord through my fingers. 'Just so long as ghosts don't disturb you,' I added, only half joking.

'There's only one ghost that would be important to me, Riana, and that's of my dear Mr Readings himself. If I could see him again just once to tell him how much I care, I could be happy.'

'Come *soon*, Diane.' I didn't know what else to say.

'What about tomorrow?'

'Tomorrow will be wonderful!' I was enthusiastic. I could do with some company, and Diane would be an excellent confidante. I felt I could tell her about Tom and my love for him, and I would see if she could understand the strange way he was behaving. She was an older woman and must be wiser than I was in affairs of the heart.

That night I stayed up late painting, inspired by Diane's news about the gallery. Once again I had a home for my work, a showcase where art lovers could see what I'd done and hopefully appreciate the paintings and buy them.

Diane would explain how long I had to paint the pictures when she arrived; so far I'd only painted the one picture, and even that wasn't finished. At last the lack of light defeated me though, and I cleaned up my pallet and wiped the rims of the tubes of colour and put them aside for the morning.

I stood back and looked at the painting I'd created of the young serving maids, hair flowing over white-gowned slender shoulders, tapering away to a ghostly mist of grey and blue thinned down with white spirit. I sighed; it had worked. The light shone from the candelabra on the landing, the door to the blue room was open, and there was a glimpse of a bed with a distant figure sitting on the quilted cover.

Again I'd painted Beatrice into the picture, all dressed up in her Victorian nightwear – out of time and sequence with the maids, who had died in the nineteen twenties and would have thought themselves modern young women. I'd seen pictures of well-off, elegant women wearing bobbed hair and fox furs, but young women servants wouldn't have been allowed such luxuries, even if they could afford them.

I went to my bedroom and looked at my reflection in the long mirror. My frock had a narrow skirt and a sweetheart neckline. There was nothing elegant about me. My hair was rolled back, and I could have easily passed for a wartime housewife. I untied my hair and it fell wild and loose, hanging down to my waist in vibrant red curls. Now I looked more like an artist. I flung a red scarf around my waist and tied it in a knot, and against the dull grey of my frock it looked good, almost gypsy-like, as if I was going to dance the rest of the night away around a blazing open-air fire with gold earrings sparkling in the dim light.

I sighed and almost hugged myself. What would Tom

think if he could see me now, looking wanton and free, with bare feet and ready to dance? But he had seen me more wanton than this, he had taken me in the very bed I was standing near, and I felt my cheeks grow hot at the memory. I felt thrilled too. He had made me his woman, and whatever happened now he would always be the love of my life, the only love I would ever want.

Diane's visit came and went; we hardly had time to talk about my life. Diane was busy planning the way she would run the gallery, the exhibitions she would hold. 'Of course, Riana, you will be my first and principle artist always,' she promised.

Inspired by her words, for the next few weeks I worked unceasingly on my paintings, barely eating or sleeping, but creating pictures that – in spite of my frenzy – turned out well. They were colourful and atmospheric. It was almost as if I'd entered a new phase in my life . . . and in a way I had.

I saw nothing of Tom in those weeks, but I always felt warm when I thought of him taking me in his arms and making love to me. I was his woman now, whatever he chose to do, and when I saw him again I would tell him so in no uncertain terms.

Love surged through me at the thought of him in his flying jacket and boots. Even soaked and dripping with seaweed, his hair plastered over his face. He was always handsome, and that lovable smile that seemed especially for me was always there, crinkling up his eyes and showing the tantalizing curve of his mouth. How I loved Tom and wanted to make love with him again!

Mrs Ward remonstrated with me one day on a rare visit to the kitchen. 'You should eat more, Riana. I don't know how you keep going. You peck at your food like a bird.'

'Once the exhibition is done I'll relax,' I said. 'I've painted enough pictures now, and I have just one to finish. I'll eat my fill then, don't worry.'

'You have remembered we've got a ghost weekend next week, haven't you?'

I hadn't, but I put on a brave face. 'Don't worry. I'll be ready to ease up by then.'

'What about this exhibition of yours? Won't you be going up to London for the opening about then?'

I made a quick mental calculation. 'No, it's the week after I've got everything organized.' I breathed a sigh of relief; it was pure luck that the two events were a week apart.

The ghost-haunting nights were becoming very well attended now, and a bigger crowd than usual had booked for the next event, giving Mrs Ward and Treasure and me more beds to make up. I had to double up rooms now, as well as the dormitories, with two beds in each. Soon I would be able to furnish other bedrooms – and maybe some more of the unused downstairs rooms – to accommodate more people. Now that I had an outlet for my paintings again, anything was possible. But even with the extra rooms, there still wasn't enough space to fit all the people who wanted to attend the next event – so, thinking of the profit, I decided to arrange an extra ghost-haunting weekend for the week after the exhibition.

I had worked day and night and completed six paintings. The grand reopening exhibition at the gallery would contain a small but select variety of paintings, and if all of mine sold then I'd have some income to spend on the house.

The ghost weekends were bringing in a healthy regular profit, and even though sometimes no supernatural events took place – no sightings, no noises in the night – the reputation Aberglasney had gained for being haunted was well established by now. However, even though no one expected ghosts to appear to order when there were guests staying, so far the 'ghosts' had been extremely cooperative. Even I was beginning to believe there were certain presences in the house that couldn't be explained.

Beatrice believed in the uneasy spirits of the dead serving maids and always did her bit as a 'Victorian ghost' to make some excitement happen on quiet nights. I lived in fear she would be caught – grabbed by the colonel or one of the younger guests, who could move more quickly – but she never was.

Tonight was a cold winter night, with frost designing patterns on the glass in the windows. I knew that next time I painted a picture I would have windows filled with traceries of frost in the background. I did a little pencil sketch that attempted to catch the mood, but frost on glass was going to be difficult to recreate in paint, a challenge. My heart lifted. It was just as Tom was a challenge; all I didn't know about him was a challenge I would love to solve.

This weekend 'young William' had brought a new young lady to hunt ghosts with him, much to the disappointment of some of the other ladies who'd hoped to bag him for themselves – especially 'plump Betty', who fancied herself irresistible to men.

Miss Connie Spears, as we were introduced to young William's girlfriend, was tiny and dark-haired and very slender. She looked as if a puff of wind, let alone a gaggle of ghosts, would blow her over, but she had an incredibly strong voice which she demonstrated after dinner by singing a medley of songs to us.

I wondered how the 'ghosts' were appreciating it and smiled as I thought of Beatrice covering her ears in the bedroom. I'd asked her to join us, but she'd said, 'No –' very firmly – 'I couldn't spoil the image the guests have of me as a ghost,' which made sense, I supposed.

I felt guilty though at leaving her out, and asked Mrs Ward to take some supper on a tray to the blue room.

She shook her head so much that her greying curls came loose from the pins and fell against her face, making her seem much younger. 'You won't catch me going in there,' she announced, folding her arms firmly across her breasts.

'I thought you didn't believe in ghosts!' I was amused, but she obviously wasn't.

'I don't care about ghosts, but have you seen the state of the ceiling in there?'

'What on earth do you mean?'

'Well, you can see the daylight through the hole in the tiles. It must be terrible there when it's cold and raining. You couldn't expect anyone to live there, not even a ghost.'

'But you've seen Beatrice go to and fro on the stair,

surely? She seems to like it in there. She's cosy and warm, and she always has the little electric fire to heat the room. I saw to that myself.'

'More fool you. Of course I've seen *Beatrice*, but she's nutty as a fruit cake, though I'll admit she makes herself useful in those strange clothes of hers, but if you think there are ghosts in the attic then that painting stuff is softening your brain!'

'Don't worry then. I'll take the tray up myself.' I was irritated, but it didn't do to upset such a valuable asset as Mrs Ward.

I caught Beatrice doing some needlework; her fingers were deft, slender and skilled as she stitched away at the embroidery. I glanced up at the ceiling, and I couldn't see any holes there at all. Mrs Ward must have had too many glasses of wine – or else she was making excuses not to climb the stairs. Perhaps she was tired or getting arthritic; it was a good thing I'd brought Treasure in when I did.

'Party going with a swing, if I'm hearing correctly,' Beatrice said dryly. 'Nice enough voice, but we could do with lowering the volume a bit. Who on earth is singing?'

'Young William's new lady friend. You wouldn't think it, but she's tiny and dainty and frail! I don't know where that big voice has room to hide. Anyway, she's adding to the spirit of the weekend. She's at least thirty – much older than William – but he clearly adores her.'

Beatrice raised her eyebrows. 'Likes older women then? Perhaps even I have a chance!' She giggled, and I giggled with her, but I was wise enough not to get too close to her. Beatrice didn't like anyone close to her.

The singing began again, some jazzy tunes from the wartime, and I could hear that Miss Spears was not going to let up.

'Do me a favour, Beatrice,' I suggested. 'Do your bit along the corridor, cause a diversion from Miss Spears' good intentions.'

Beatrice nodded and put down her sewing, waving her hand impatiently at me. 'Depart then, go.'

I thought of kissing her cheek, and then thought better

of it and ran down the stairs. I burst into the dining room, just in time to see Colonel Fred cover his ears. 'Ghosts,' I announced dramatically, 'on the landing. Come quickly, all of you.'

The guests flooded into the hall, and Beatrice was doing her bit – her head raised, her hand pointing at the window. She looked so convincing that I almost believed she *was* a ghost.

Miss Spears, predictably, fainted away, her fall cushioned by the carpet. William knelt at her side to hold a bottle of smelling salts under her nose. Apparently, she was given to fainting spells. Meanwhile the 'ghost' discreetly vanished.

'Look at the window!' the colonel suddenly shouted.

We all stared upward and there, silhouetted in the window, was a face, a ghostly white face. The face of a bearded man! It seemed to hover there for a moment and then disappeared. Even I was shaken, as William's girlfriend fell into a decline again.

'It's the first time we've seen the ghost of a man.' Plump Betty pulled at her corsets, a beam of sheer excitement on her face. 'Ooh, Mr Bravage, might I stand next to you? I am just a little frightened.' She did indeed seem to be trembling.

'Brandies all round,' Colonel Fred declared. 'I've brought a whole casefull with me,' he added as an afterthought.

Rather subdued now, we sat in the large drawing room, quietly discussing the new phenomena. Until now the story of ghosts, of young maids, of the appearances of Beatrice, and of the noises in the night had all seemed a game. I'd been able to explain everything away to myself . . . but not this. The disembodied face of the old man, hovering in an upper window, was really spooky and frightening.

I wandered into the kitchen looking for some aspirin and heard a slight sound behind me. Frightened I'd see a disembodied face staring at me, I was relieved to see a flesh-and-blood man standing there. 'Tom! You're here again.' I hurried towards him. 'What are you doing trying to frighten me like that? What tricks are you playing on us and why? Do you want to ruin my weekends?'

'I don't know what you're talking about, honey.' He sounded genuinely puzzled. 'I've only just driven up in my old army car, so what am I supposed to have done?'

'I don't know what's happening here!' I ran back into the drawing room, where everyone was talking together. Colonel Fred raised his voice as he held forth, and then young William rushed outside to examine the old building for signs of trickery, such as ladders. When he returned to the drawing room, his cheeks red with cold and a sprinkling of snow on his hair, he sank into a chair gasping with fright and lack of breath.

'No sign of intruders. This is no trick, Riana. What we all saw was the ghost of a man, a desperate spirit trying to tell us something!'

'Could it be Edwin Mansel-Atherton, the man accused of the murder of the young maids?' Colonel Fred had, evidently, been reading up on the history of Aberglasney. I shivered, suddenly cold.

I went back to the kitchen where Tom was sitting, leaving my guests to discuss the arrival of a new ghost between themselves.

'What are you doing here?' My tone was sharp. 'The lights of your car must have thrown up images on the window.'

'Don't be silly, Riana. My lights are still hooded. It's an old official car, remember? The lights were kept dim for the blackout, so I don't see how I could have thrown up lights on any window.'

I was embarrassed about accusing him of something he clearly hadn't done . . . and more so about our last meeting when I had fallen into Tom's arms so readily, like a desperate wanton. And yet, even as I tried to be indignant and angry, I wanted to press myself against him and feel his mouth on mine. 'Well, you surprised me, that's all.'

He smiled his crooked charming smile. 'You're getting in the habit of saying that every time we meet,' he commented.

'And we meet so often, don't we, Tom?' I knew I was being sarcastic. 'Not bad for an engaged man with responsibilities, I suppose. Taking your new lady love back to America soon, are you?'

'You are being foolish again,' Tom said. 'Miss Grist is really Mrs Grist. She has a husband who is alive and well and living in the highlands of Scotland. Our "engagement" is a ruse. I can't explain things now.'

'You never can explain! Tom, you say you love me, you *make* love to me, and then you vanish again. Talk to me, please! Just tell me the truth about what's going on.'

He took a deep breath, about to speak, but we were rudely interrupted by a thundering at the door. Tom caught me swiftly in his arms and kissed me. 'Remember, whatever happens, I love you.'

He'd gone then, disappeared like a shadow, leaving me with more questions than answers. All right, he'd gone through a sham engagement with Miss Grist, but why?

When I returned to the drawing room, my guests were standing against the wall, hands in the air, and two men were pointing savage-looking firearms at them!

'What's going on here?' I demanded.

A gun swivelled in my direction and I flinched, taking a step backwards. The men were dressed as soldiers, armed and threatening, but after my previous encounters with bogus police I looked at them doubtfully.

'On the floor!' one of them snapped.

I straightened my back. 'No!' I stated firmly. 'I want to see some identification – if you are genuine soldiers you should have some.'

The man pointing a gun at me appeared agitated and waved his gun about wildly.

I pushed his arm aside and pulled off his mask, and he stared at me in disbelief. 'What are you looking for? Tell me and I might be able to help,' I said calmly.

My guests began to sit down, still wary, their hands clearly visible on the table.

'We have been informed there's an American deserter at large.' One of the soldiers came forward taking charge. 'Has anyone been here in the last half hour?'

'Only the ghost of an old man,' Colonel Fred declared in a roar. 'Proof of identity, if you please, sir.' He bravely approached the man we recognized as leader, and a card was duly produced. The colonel took it, grunting like an old boar. I chuckled, amused by my own unspoken pun, and I was given a frozen look by the man whose mask I'd ripped off.

'Careful, lady,' he said, and then the penny dropped. These men were Americans sure enough, and I could see the flash of dog tags on one soldier's shirt. Tom was an airman . . . though not a soldier, like these men. Something must have shown in my face, because I was pushed into a chair. 'Tell us what you know, ma'am, otherwise things might get a bit nasty here.'

'I don't know anything! I don't even know which man you are talking about, and why should I? I'm getting sick of being attacked in my own house!'

My face was slapped hard, and then all hell broke out as Beatrice came out on to the landing, joined by the misty figures of 'the girls', as I had come to call them.

'The ghosts!' young William shouted, while his girlfriend hid under the table as shots rang out, aimed towards the landing. They made no noticeable difference to the mist, however.

To my relief, now there was no sign of Beatrice. She must have taken cover – as had all the guests, with the exception of William, who was now on the landing trying to grasp hold of the mist with very little success. I saw his hand run clean through one of the shadowy figures, and I saw a glimpse of ghostly hair swinging over a cotton night-gown, and then the images faded and all was silent.

'What the hell was that!' One of the soldiers, white faced and cringing against the wall, was wide-eyed and terrified, his words coming out on a sibilant whisper.

'It's the ghosts of Aberglasney,' I said boldly. 'That's why we're here! This is a ghost-haunting weekend, and you've messed it all up on a wild goose chase. Why would we want spies here? Don't you think we've got enough excitement as it is?'

'I'm out of here!' The soldier without a mask edged towards the door, and I could hear him lighting up a ciga-rette outside, and then he began to run, his feet pounding against the drive.

The leader looked doubtful. 'We should search the place,' he said. 'We need to find out if that cursed airman has been here or not.'

'To hell with all that!' The other soldiers filed out of the house at quick-march.

The leader looked at me apologetically. 'Sorry for the trouble, ma'am.' His gaze was directed at the landing, his eyes wide with disbelief, and he continued talking – almost as if reciting a well-known speech. 'I didn't mean to be so rough, but this man is dangerous. If you see him, keep away from him. He's quite liable to kill you; he's killed before.'

'*Sorry!* What sort of man are you?' The colonel came forward. 'May the ghosts of Aberglasney haunt you for all the days of your life – sir,' he added as an afterthought.

As if on cue, Mrs Ward appeared with a tray of hot drinks, apparently without knowing what had happened. 'Sorry I've been absent for a while, Riana. I fell asleep in my room with the radio on, heard a bit of noise – some banging – and guessed the ghosts had put in an appearance, so I got up.'

'We've been shot at and frightened to death and you didn't know?' I asked in disbelief.

'What! What happened? I'd taken a drink, Riana. It fair knocked me out it did. I'm sorry, but when I woke up I washed my face and came straight down to help.'

'Who gave you a drink?' I asked suspiciously.

The colonel came to rest his hand on Mrs Ward's arm. 'It was my fault,' he said. 'I'm afraid I gave Mrs Ward a cocktail made up of some almost empty bottles – gin, vodka, brandy. I do hope you didn't suffer any ill effects, Mrs Ward.'

She beamed. 'No, I just had a wonderful few hours' rest that's all,' she said happily.

I relaxed. *I must be getting paranoid*, I thought.

The colonel was beaming happily down at Mrs Ward, and my eyes must have opened wide; surely not a romance in the air? Not between pragmatic Mrs Ward and the bluff old colonel?

Mrs Ward's eyes fluttered downward in what looked

suspiciously like a coquettish manner. 'I'd better get these hot drinks served,' she said. Was that a wink?

'Let me help you dear lady.' The colonel and Mrs Ward went around the room handing out tea and coffee, and I sank into a chair, exhausted.

I heard the cars start up outside the door and guessed the soldiers had left. I had no idea what they'd really wanted, but I was angry with them – and with Tom. So far I'd behaved like a weak fool, letting him treat me so casually. He'd only given me the smallest of hints as to his life and his 'activities', and yet my whole life was being disrupted by him. Next time he chose to come calling I'd send him away with a flea in his ear!

Eventually, we all went to our rooms, and from next door I could hear William and his lady friend arguing. I gathered that while William was fascinated by the hall and its unusual residents, Miss Spears was appalled and afraid and wanted to go home to her cottage in the Brecon hills. Frankly, I didn't blame her. It seemed ludicrous to pay to spend a weekend being shot at and frightened half to death!

In the morning, the guests were up bright and early: going on walks in the fresh air, sitting in the library reading, and young William himself was on the landing, looking for bits of string or mirrors or goodness knows what. In spite of being a serious ghost-hunter, he was still trying to discover if there had been some sort of trickery.

I could scarcely believe what had happened myself. It wasn't so much the appearance of ghosts, or the intrusion of the soldiers and the way the men had treated me, that had upset me. It was Tom.

On the other hand, I was tired of being treated roughly, as if I were some sort of traitor. Tonight I would make sure the doors and windows were securely locked. Later, I would get a dog – a big dog that would bark and growl and maybe bite any intruders.

At breakfast the colonel was missing, and worried I went to his room. I knocked and opened the door, and there he was, handling a fierce-looking handgun. He turned and saw me. 'Let anyone insult you again, my dear, and I'll use this on him.' His voice was booming fierce, his handling of the gun was clumsy, and I guessed his title of 'colonel' was 'honorary'.

'I'm going to get a dog,' I said. 'Maybe a *big* dog. At least then we will be warned if anyone tries to break in on us.' *Even Tom*, I thought to myself.

'Very well, Riana, but I think you should report all this to the police.'

'No, no. I don't want to alarm the local people. We might be shut down or something. Our ghost weekends might even be banned!'

The colonel nodded thoughtfully. 'I think you could be right, least said soonest mended, but at least have someone on guard outside. Back and front doors and windows, and someone at the gate perhaps.'

I doubted I could afford all that, but I nodded placatingly. 'We'll have to do something,' I agreed.

I spent the day painting and fuming about Tom and the trouble he'd brought me, while the some of the guests lazed about or read up on the ghosts of Aberglasney and young William took his no-longer lady friend into Swansea to catch a train home. I worked a hasty loose painting of the events of the night before, omitting the shooting incident. That would be hard to explain. Instead, I did the landing scene and below in the hall the mixed reactions of the guests. I spitefully painted in Miss 'Young William' bottom up, crouching under the table, and 'Plump Betty' clutching the arm of Mr Bravage. It worked well, it was good . . . but I didn't like it, so I painted out William's girlfriend and put in a bit of moonlight on the parquet floor instead. It kept the colours muted and blurred and worked much better.

In the afternoon, Diane arrived on a short visit from London and asked to look at my work. She admired my painting, but with a head on one side she regarded it speculatively. 'Not with the "heart" you usually put into your work. Well executed, but something is lacking.' She stood back a bit. 'I know!' She snapped her fingers. 'The face in the window!'

'How do you know about that?'

'I've been talking to some of the others,' she said. 'Betty was full of it. She said it frightened her much more than the ghosts of the young maids. It was an oldish man with a weary face, and "despair was written all over his ghostly features". Her words, not mine.'

Enthused, I quickly painted in the face as I remembered it – pale, hollow-eyed, a grieving expression about the hooded eyes – and I painted in just the hint of tears. I stood back and breathed a sigh of relief; now the painting had meaning, life or death according to how the observer looked at it.

'Good!' Diane said. 'That will sell, as sure as eggs are eggs. I love it.'

'Thanks to your input,' I said, 'it's worked. You have a good eye, Diane, and perhaps even more intuition than dear Mr Readings had.'

'Ah, dear Mr Readings. I miss him like anything, Riana, and I told you, the lovely man left me everything he owned – the house, the business and, most important to me of all, the wedding ring he bought for me.'

I glanced at her hand where the gold band shone in the bright light through my studio windows. Impulsively, I hugged her. 'You were always his wife in every way,' I assured her. 'He loved you very much.'

'I was a mistress for years. I don't suppose I will be accepted in polite society.'

'There's no "polite society" left after the devastation of the war,' I protested.

She looked at me with eyebrows raised. 'You are mistaken, Riana. Snobbery will always exist, whatever the state of the world.'

'Let's go to the kitchen and have Mrs Ward make us a nice mug of hot chocolate, shall we?'

'Hot chocolate! That sounds wonderful. Where do you manage to find such luxuries, Riana?'

'It's Mrs Ward's doing. She conjures up various goodies! I think she's got a list of the local people's misdoings and blackmails them for luxuries.'

We had to make our own hot chocolate, for I saw Mrs Ward out in the vegetable garden, with the colonel helping her to pick spring vegetables for tonight's dinner. I smiled. 'Those two unlikely people are getting on very well, aren't they?' I said.

Diane stood at my side and watched as Mrs Ward's head fell close to the colonel's, clearly examining the produce from the garden. 'They certainly are,' she agreed, somewhat enviously.

It was quiet that night, in stark contrast to the events of the night before. For all that, we sat up in the drawing room, bathed now with firelight, and talked quietly about the ghosts and the strange men who had intruded on us.

'It must be something to do with the American airmen who were stationed here,' William observed, newly knowledgeable after his research trip. 'They intruded into the big houses and took all advantage of all the ladies, offering stockings and food as an inducement to wrongdoing and loose living.'

'That's extremely prudish of you,' Betty said, perhaps feeling she should justify her own kind of approach to men. 'Don't forget that Americans were killed in the war as well as British.'

'I agree,' the colonel said at once. 'There was that young pilot who died when the house was first open to us. Carl Jenkins – was that his name, Riana?'

'That's right.' I thought of Rosie and the furore about her condition and how I'd blamed Tom for it all and felt ashamed. Poor Tom! He did so much for me, and yet I continued to blame him for everything bad that happened. But I couldn't deny, even to myself, that he was tied up in all the mystery. I just hoped it was military secrets and nothing too sinister . . . like arms-smuggling or, even worse, murder and some sort of revenge.

'May I pour some drinks, Riana?' the colonel asked meekly.

'Of course, it's all part of the weekend,' I said quickly. 'Drinks all round, everybody?' That was the latest innovation of mine – to provide a bar and a variety of drinks. I could afford these little additions now.

I helped myself to a small sherry. I felt very tired after my day's painting. It was something I loved doing, but I still wore myself out every time I created a picture. I supposed that I put too much of myself in it. I tensed up at the thought of the haunted face in the window, but when I drank some of the golden sherry it warmed my throat and my stomach and relaxed me a little.

Eventually, the guests departed for bed. It seemed once one made a move, everyone followed, much to my relief.

I visited Beatrice briefly on my own way to bed and asked her, in a whisper, about the events of the night before.

'The man in the window . . . that was my Edwin,' she whispered back. 'He wants you to get on with it and prove he's not a murderer, and then we can all rest in peace.'

I nodded. I had been so bound up in my own problems that I'd forgotten my wish to clear Beatrice's husband.

'Why don't you start by searching the house for suspicious signs,' she said. 'I'm not going to be here tomorrow, so make a start in the blue room. That's where the gals died, you know.'

'All right, Beatrice,' I agreed wearily. 'The guests return home tomorrow so the place will be mine again, and I promise I won't work at all. I'll just make a search of the house and see if I can find anything.' I paused. 'But surely you would have found something by now, Beatrice, if there *was* anything to find?'

'I haven't the ability, dear, nor the strength. You are young and alive, and you can do anything you choose. You'll fight for me. You are the owner of the house now. It's your place to sort everything out, and then we can all rest.'

'Goodnight, Beatrice.' I stumbled out and into my room, and without even undressing I kicked off my shoes, climbed on the bed and immediately fell asleep.

There was the usual bustle of departure in the morning. Even Diane went off home early. Although, of course, William's girlfriend had already left. I felt he would do much better without her presence. As if reading my thoughts, he came up to me. 'A wonderful weekend, Miss Evans. I shall certainly come again, although probably alone. My girlfriend didn't really fit in. She is too sensitive for her own good, you know.'

'I know,' I agreed, finding it difficult to keep my thoughts to myself about his girlfriend's sensitivity. 'Ghosts and armed men aren't everyone's cup of tea,' I said tactfully. 'But I do admire the way you investigated the landing area of the house to find out if there was any trickery involved.'

He blushed.

'It's all right,' I said. 'I doubted the evidence of my own eyes. I don't know, even now, if I was seeing things.'

'If you were, we all were,' William said. 'And we certainly didn't imagine the disembodied face in the window, did we?'

'No.' I made a mental note to start searching the house once the last guest departed.

When it was quiet, I watched Mrs Ward prolonging her farewells to the colonel and smiled to myself as I put the kettle on. The war hadn't managed to kill off all the romance in the world then!

I made a hot pot of coffee, and when Mrs Ward came into the kitchen, her pale cheeks flushed, I poured us a cup. 'You like the colonel, do you?'

The question was superfluous, and Mrs Ward turned away to pour milk in her cup. She shrugged eventually, and I realized it would be wise to drop the subject.

'I'm going to search the house today,' I said firmly. 'I want to look for clues as to what's hidden here.'

'What on earth do you mean?' Mrs Ward gave me her full attention.

'For one thing, why do people keep running in here with guns and things? What are they looking for?'

'It's just because of those Americans, I think,' Mrs Ward said. 'In any case, don't you think we'd have found whatever it is they're looking for, with all the renovation work that's been going on here?'

'You have a point,' I agreed. 'But what on earth do all these armed men think we've got here?'

'Well –' Mrs Ward's voice was dry – 'you've certainly been the target for their violence. If the ghost silliness hadn't happened, they might have begun to torture you for information! I still reckon that Tom bloke has got something to do with it – and him so nice to us, too.'

'I don't think Tom could be involved,' I protested. 'I'm sure he wouldn't want anyone bullied and humiliated, and he was abducted himself at one stage, remember?'

'A cover,' Mrs Ward declared, her lips pursed with disapproval. 'Those Americans caused us enough trouble during the war, and why hasn't that Tom gone back to America with the rest of them, that's what I want to know.'

Again, Mrs Ward had a point. I sighed; there was no use arguing about it. I was too weary and too puzzled and too afraid of what I might find out about Tom to continue with the conversation. Instead, I started a systematic search of the house, starting with the servant's rooms at the top of the house. I found nothing untoward in the recently refurbished and brightly-curtained rooms, however.

I knew Beatrice would be away, so I went to the first floor, entered Beatrice's room, and immediately wondered if there was a window open. Everything felt cold and damp and decayed, and yet when Beatrice chose to be in residence the room felt warm and normal.

I felt dreadful as I searched in drawers and cupboards and even tested the floorboards for anything coming loose – but there was nothing. I left Beatrice's room, having made a thorough search, but feeling uneasy that I'd intruded on her privacy. The blue room, which up until now had been unoccupied, was where the whole thing had begun, the scene of the deaths. The paint was still on the wall, the windows unchanged. So far as I could tell, the room was the same as when the maids had died. Why they hadn't been housed in the servant's quarters at the top of the house, I didn't know. Perhaps the rooms were left to flake away as they weren't needed. But lead from the paint in the blue room had killed the girls, the stories claimed, and indeed it did smell strange in there. I shrugged and went outside and shut the door. There was nothing to find, and I hardly thought it worth searching the other rooms. But I'd promised Beatrice that I would look for evidence of her husband's innocence, and look I would. Perhaps in searching Aberglasney I would find some answers to my own problems.

TWENTY-EIGHT

To my great happiness and relief my paintings continued to sell well, in spite of the gallery having changed hands. The art-loving crowd knew Diane well and trusted her honesty and judgement. One or two of the more senior critics watched on the fringes for a while, expecting – or perhaps hoping – Diane would make mistakes and have to put the valuable gallery up for sale, but that didn't happen.

At the official reopening exhibition, my six new works, including the painting depicting the haunted face in the window, were put on display, with lights fixed above each picture to reflect the colours and the nuances of light, and to highlight the progression of shadow and brightness across the canvas.

There were paintings by some old masters too, including one owned by Diane that I'd seen hanging in her sitting room in the guest house. It must have been a real wrench to part with it, but I knew that Diane needed to make a living as much as I did. Mr Readings would have left her well-provided for, I knew that, but perhaps there was some hold up with releasing all his private fortune to her? Diane had not confided in me, but that she had to sell one of her precious paintings told me enough to know she was short of immediate funds. This thought inspired me to vow to work harder once I returned home.

The exhibition was well attended, both by the curious and by those who genuinely wanted to buy. Silk gowns and fur capes shone under the glittering chandeliers and diamonds sparkled on white fingers: the art-loving crowd from London were out to show how prosperous they were. Nowadays, they arrived in cars, but in the olden days carriages with finely decorated horses would have been waiting outside in the stables, and suddenly I was inspired to paint something from the past.

Diane seemed to dance around the room. There was a smile on her face and a glass of champagne in her hand, though I noticed she didn't drink much of it. And underlying her smile was an air of sadness, because she'd lost the man she loved.

I, on the other hand, was determined to forget Tom. Why should I continue to waste my love and my passion on him when he had disappeared from my life yet again? And yet I ached for him. Not just for his touch, but for the familiarity and friendship we used to share, sitting under the cloisters in the garden Tom and his men had worked to bring into some kind of order.

'Excuse me, Miss Evans. I'm Justin. I'm supposed to paint your portrait, remember?'

I looked up to see a handsome man about my own age staring into my eyes.

'Your work is so atmospheric,' he said. 'Even more so than when I saw it at an earlier exhibition. I have bought one of your new paintings, and may I say that although the face in the picture is ghostly and haunted, the image reminds me of my late father?'

'Your father!' I was fearful and suddenly wary. 'Who was your father?'

'Edwin Mansel-Atherton,' he said. 'Unfortunately, my father is dead, so he's the *late* Edwin Mansel-Atherton. Did Mr Readings mention it when we last met?'

I saw him suddenly as a threat to my future in Aberglasney. After all, might he not be the rightful heir? I liked him very much, but I didn't want him taking my home from me. 'So you've bought my painting?' I said with false brightness.

Just then Diane came and took my arm. 'Some people want to meet the talented lady artist,' she said, hurrying me away. 'You must mingle, dear. You can't stand talking to the most eligible man in London all night, even though he *is* gorgeous!' There was a proprietary air about the way she spoke of Justin, and I imagined she'd met him many times before.

My head was ringing with confusion and questions: most

importantly, was Justin the legal heir to my house? I stopped Diane as she made a beeline for the other art lovers. 'Wait! I'll meet your other clients later. What do you know about Justin Mansel-Atherton?'

Diane appeared puzzled. 'He was a friend of dear Mr Readings. Why? Are you interested in him?'

'In a way,' I said softly, 'but not romantically. I'll tell you all about it after the exhibition.' I'd arranged to stay the night in London with Diane. I could trust Diane and confide in her. She'd find out all she could about Justin – and use her discretion into the bargain. Once I got home I would also question Beatrice about the man, although I would have to be tactful and careful.

Most of the paintings sold that night, leaving only three – one of them mine. I knew I could look forward to some money to spend on the house. Providing, I thought, the house was really mine.

I knew I'd bought it legally, but if Beatrice had no right to sell it then I'd be in trouble. I knew some of these old mansions used to be entailed to the eldest son; I could only hope that wasn't the case with dear old Aberglasney.

Diane was sympathetic and comforting. 'If you've a legal document signed by the owner you must be all right, dear,' she said firmly.

'Yes, but was Beatrice the legal owner? What if Edwin left the house to his eldest son?'

'Don't panic.' Diane poured me a glass of the leftover champagne. 'Justin might be illegitimate. Have you thought of that?'

'I've thought of nothing else.' I sank into a chair with my glass.

Diane sat opposite me. 'I wish dear Mr Readings was here. He'd know who to contact and what the legal position was,' she said. She gave a wan smile. 'And the dear man would have celebrated such a good sale too.'

And *I* wished that Tom was here and was truly mine, instead of blowing hot and cold and vanishing at every turn, and that Justin would disappear from the face of the earth. Unfortunately, wishes didn't always come true.

'Don't worry about it, dear.' Diane's voice intruded on my thoughts. 'At least you've sold your paintings, and you always have that – your talent to paint evocative scenes of Aberglasney.'

'The house is my inspiration,' I said, and I knew I sounded despondent, but I was tired and it was time I went to bed. I kissed Diane's cheek and went to my room, and there I climbed into bed, turned my face into the pillow, and cried bitter, self-pitying tears.

In the morning, everything seemed clearer and much more hopeful. I had a legal document that confirmed I was the owner of Aberglasney. It had been signed and sealed by Beatrice, by me, and by the solicitor. Of course I was the legal owner, and no one could take the house from me.

TWENTY-NINE

S ome days later, when I'd returned home, Justin came to visit. The house seemed to crackle with hostility, and Beatrice, who I'd longed to question about Justin, was away on one of her frequent jaunts. I still couldn't help but wonder where she disappeared to, but whenever I asked her she was vague and unwilling to talk about her life, and I couldn't say I blamed her for that. Still, I dearly wanted to know about Justin and his history.

'Come into the sitting room.' I forced a pleasant smile as Justin handed Mrs Ward his cap. Today he looked like a country squire; I wouldn't have been surprised to see him carrying a gun beneath his arm.

'A tray of coffee, madam?' Mrs Ward was staring suspiciously at Justin, and I wondered if she'd seen him before or if she knew anything about him. I was surprised at her formality; she usually addressed me by my Christian name.

'That would be lovely, Mrs Ward.' I gestured to the sofa. 'Please take a seat Mr . . . er . . . Justin.'

He was staring round at the high ceilings and the beautifully moulded cornice, and I felt an instant antagonism to him. 'You like my house?' I emphasized the 'my', and he smiled as he took a seat.

'I rather think the old place is mine.' His words fell into the room like cold chips of ice. Mrs Ward almost dropped the tray of coffee she was carrying into the room. She frowned, and I shook my head, hoping she wouldn't say anything. She took the hint and retreated, glaring at the visitor.

'I don't understand you,' I said vaguely, unwilling to argue such an important point without professional advice.

'It's quite simple. I am the only son of Edwin Mansel-Atherton, therefore I am his heir.'

'Then why have you taken so long to come to see me or the house – or, for that matter, a solicitor? Is there a will to that effect – that you are heir, I mean?'

'As it happens, I haven't searched for one, and what's more I live in a very fine house in London. What would I do with this place? It takes so much money, and to what effect?' He took a seat as if he owned the place. 'A little bit of tidying and building isn't going to change the bad ambience of the place, is it?' He paused to drink some coffee, and with a grimace of distaste he put down his cup. 'Chicory coffee from a bottle, I take it?'

'The war hasn't long ended, and we are still on rations,' I pointed out, beginning to dislike Justin very much.

'I could let you rent the old place, of course.' He sounded smug.

I stood up, forcing my hands together to stop them shaking. I felt a cold fury turn to a fire in my belly. 'How dare you come here and patronize and whine and then offer me the tenancy of my own house?' My tone was raised.

Justin came towards me and I flinched, expecting a torrent of abuse. I'd got used to being roughly spoken to since I'd bought the house. Instead, Justin took me in his arms and kissed me, deeply and passionately, before I instinctively pushed him away.

'We'll talk again when you are a bit calmer,' he said. He left me, and I heard the door slam after him as I almost fell into a chair.

I painted for the rest of the day, but my heart wasn't in it. I went to bed early, wanting the night to pass.

In the morning, an early sun was shining and I felt refreshed. Feverishly, I searched for the document Beatrice had given me when I'd bought the house, and I sighed with relief when I found it filed away in my desk drawer. I read through it avidly, line by line, trying to learn if there was any loophole in the agreement. After reading and rereading, I could find nothing to disprove the legality of the document. Tomorrow I'd go into Swansea and see the solicitor who had witnessed my signature, I decided, just to be certain.

I was still shaking, however, when I put the agreement away carefully and locked the drawer, hiding the key beneath the clock on the mantelpiece.

A knocking on the door made me freeze. I knew it was Justin before Mrs Ward announced him.

'Do come in.' My tone was frosty as I led the way into the sitting room. 'Please tell me what I can do for you. I'm very busy today.' I sat well away from him, with a low ornate table as a barrier between us. Mrs Ward brought us coffee, and I held my cup like a guard against his undoubted charm and good looks.

'There's no doubt the house is mine,' he said without preamble, 'but I have a solution, seeing as you don't want to rent the old place from me.'

'The house is mine,' I said firmly, 'and I have no intention of arguing about it.'

'What I was thinking,' he said, continuing as if I hadn't spoken, 'is that it would solve everything if we got married. Then there would be no dispute, and the house would belong to both of us.'

I was breathless with the cheek of it. 'What makes you think I would want to marry you?' My tone was angry, and I felt the heat come into my cheeks at his arrogance.

'Well, you would be Mrs Mansel-Atherton for a start. You would have rights to the house, indisputable rights, and no one could take it from you.'

'And you. What would *you* hope to get from such a marriage? My money? A very easy living?' I asked, my voice heavy with sarcasm. 'I've checked, and you have very little money except what you win at cards. You rent a good address in London and put yourself about as a man of means.'

'I have charm and respectability, and *I've* done some checking too. You are – what shall we say? – a fallen woman, aren't you? Rumour has it that you've had at least one man in your bed, not to put too fine a point on it, and some say these weekends you run are an excuse for all sorts of goings on. Didn't one of the girls here have an illegitimate child, for instance?'

I was so angry I could have picked up one of the heavier flower vases and hit him over the head with it. What really upset me was that there was some truth amid all the slander he was spitting out. I put down my cup and got to my feet. 'If you don't leave *my* property at once, I will send Mrs Ward for the police.'

He got up, but laughed irritatingly. 'Poor old Sergeant Price on his bike will take an age to get here, Miss Evans. This is not London, you know, with efficient police cars able to cover the miles quickly – horns blazing out, and blue lights flashing. Face it! You might just lose everything if I take the legal way out of this dilemma.'

I took a deep breath. 'Why don't you come along to the next ghost-haunting weekend and see for yourself what really happens?' I spoke sweetly, and he looked at me suspiciously.

'And be murdered in my bed? I think not.'

'Don't be hysterical and absurd. Alert the police, your friends, the London public to your visit, if you like. Bring cameras, newspaper men, anyone of your dubious circle of acquaintances you like, so that your whereabouts will be well accounted for.' I was issuing a challenge, and he would look weak and silly if he wasn't man enough to take it.

At last, he nodded. 'Very well, I will accept your invitation. And don't worry, I will bring some friends with me.'

'There will be the usual charge, of course.' I wrote the date down for him on a card, and then met his dark eyes. 'Now, if you wouldn't mind leaving, I have a great deal of work to do.'

When he'd gone, I helped myself to some hot coffee and sat thinking about all he'd said. 'How on earth did Justin know about me and Tom? He could easily have learned about Rosie from village gossip, but I had told no one about my one night of passion with Tom except Diane, who I now counted as a close personal friend. Perhaps Mrs Ward knew? But then she was the soul of discretion!

I sat in a chair with my head in my hands and tried to stop the hot tears from brimming in my eyes. If ever I needed Tom's arms around me, his deep reassuring voice, it was now – but as usual he was not with me when I needed him most.

Later I went into town to see Beatrice's solicitor, Mr Jeremy, and to my relief he told me there were no legitimate heirs and that Aberglasney was indisputably and legally mine.

I stared around his dusty office and asked idly if he knew of the murder case where five young serving maids had died.

'Of course I've heard of it, but it's all stuff and nonsense!' he said, waving a pale, effete hand. 'Five young girls don't die of lead poisoning on the same night. Lead poisons the blood slowly, you know.'

'And Mr Mansel-Atherton. Do you think he killed the maids?'

He looked at me over his glasses. 'This is not a legal opinion. I do know old Edwin was a bit of a boy, if you take my meaning, but murder? I think not, Miss Evans.'

'And what about this man who claims he is the heir to Aberglasney?' My mouth was dry as I asked the question.

Mr Jeremy was reluctant to reply. 'I don't wish to defame anyone's character, but the young man could be a by-blow. I mentioned Edwin was a "bit of a lad", didn't I?'

I visited the library next, determined to read through the articles about the murder case again. This time I asked the new young librarian – who had obviously replaced Miss (or was that Mrs?) Grist – for the Bristol and London newspapers, as well as the Cardiff and Swansea editions, to see if there were any other comments about the murder. I took the bundle of newspapers to a table and sat down to read.

In the London issues there was a great deal of coverage of the deaths of the young girls – great columns of print, and a picture of Edwin in his younger days standing outside Aberglasney. The house looked big and grand and as old as the surrounding landscape – almost as though it had grown out of the hills – but the picture of Edwin showed the face of a slim, rather fragile young man wearing spectacles, a beard and a worried frown. There was nothing I didn't already know, however, which was disappointing.

I picked up the *Bristol News* and the same story was repeated – without any pictures of Edwin, but with the gruesome picture of a hangman's noose instead. I was almost ready to hand the newspaper back to the librarian when I noticed Edwin's name in another column: a small piece about some machine he was building. I felt a dart of excitement. The engine, it seemed, was fuelled by something new, something yet untried . . . but no name was given to the fuel. I supposed that was for security reasons. The plans for the engine had been missing since Edwin's death, and it was assumed they were either destroyed or burned.

So the intrusion and searching of my house, my kidnapping, and perhaps, I thought painfully, Tom's interest in me and in Aberglasney, was all because of these missing designs, which could be used to build a new and better aeroplane engine for any future war! The designs must be truly revolutionary, I thought, for the American military to still be so desperate for them, so many years after Edwin's death.

I copied the small column down word for word in careful writing, using the pencil the librarian had pointedly put down before me. I looked up to her when I had finished. 'Miss Grist doesn't work here any more then?' I felt as if I was scratching a sore spot. I would have liked to have known why and how Tom had become mixed up with Miss Grist.

The young woman looked blank. 'We never had a Miss Grist working here, madam.'

'But you did,' I said flatly.

'I'll check, madam, but I'm sure we did not.'

She came back some time later, looking smug. 'The only Miss Grist who came here from time to time was an investigating officer from the police force! She definitely was not a librarian.'

'Thank you.' I tried to digest the information, but nothing fitted. Miss Grist was spiteful, a piece of fluff who had little brain in her head . . . Or had that all been a cover? Was she a very good police investigator indeed?

Eventually I turned my attention back to the papers and

read again about Edwin's engine designs. I felt in my bones I was definitely on to something. If only I could find Tom I could ask him outright, I thought. If only I could find Tom I would be the happiest woman in the whole of the country . . . but I suppressed that lift of my heart.

As I travelled home on the train, I wondered where Justin fitted into all this. Perhaps he, too, was seeking the elusive plans. I supposed they would bring a fortune if sold into the right hands.

To my delight, Beatrice was back. She was stood on the landing as I entered the hallway. She waved to me briefly with her lace-gloved hand and disappeared into her room.

I hurried up the stairs without even taking off my coat and hat, and if Beatrice was surprised to see me so flustered she didn't show it. It was freezing in the room, and I switched on the electric heater I'd installed for her. She raised her eyebrows but said nothing. I crouched in the old basket chair and stared at her. 'I've met Justin,' I said, not willing to be patient. 'Does he have a legal claim to this house?'

'Certainly not!' Beatrice was stiff with hostility. 'He was just a moment of weakness on Edwin's part, the child of a London society lady I believe. Edwin was a very attractive man, you know. The women chased him, even when he was a mature gentleman, and whenever he was on a lecturing tour, I was sitting at home. Alone.'

She twisted her hands together. She still wore her gloves, and I noticed there was a hole in one of the fingers. I would buy her a new pair as soon as I went to Swansea again, I thought absently.

'This Justin might have called himsclf Mansel-Atherton but he's no son of mine. The boy is illegitimate.'

'Did Edwin leave a will?' I was almost afraid to ask. Beatrice was old and rather vague at times, and she might well have a grudge against Edwin's son.

'He didn't have time,' she said. 'He was whisked off to prison so suddenly, you see, but they had to let him out until they did further investigations. But then he forestalled them and took his own life. As I told you.'

'But most people make a will early on in their lives.

I would have thought Mr Mansel-Atherton would be that sort of man.'

'Oh, Edwin was always drawing things,' Beatrice said. 'Always making plans that didn't work. But he lectured well, you know, was invited all over the world, and he was a brilliant engineer.'

I felt my pulse quicken. 'Where did he keep his drawings?'

Beatrice smiled. 'No one knows, dear. He was working on his drawings the night the maids died, and after that everything went crazy here.' She looked at me sadly and then pulled herself upright. 'When he . . . he died, I couldn't afford to employ any more maids – and in any case no one would work here.'

'Where do you go when you leave? Here, I mean.' I was suddenly curious about Beatrice's absences, curious about everything. I had a suspicion that Beatrice was guilty of something, though I didn't know what.

'Why, I go to stay with my friends and family, of course.' She seemed surprised that I'd asked, and suddenly I felt foolish and intrusive.

'I would love to see Edwin's work.' I felt the colour rise to my cheeks, sensing my lie would be obvious, but Beatrice shook her head.

'Yes, have a look around the place any time for his drawings, dear. It's your house, you know! But do search when I'm out visiting. I don't think I could stand the noise and dust if I was here.'

'You could always go to the sitting room or into the garden.' I'd seen her in the garden several times when the weather was good, but she pursed her lips before replying.

'I would prefer you to wait until I was away,' she said firmly. 'I might come across Mrs Ward. I wouldn't like that and neither would she.'

I frowned. I hadn't been aware that Beatrice and Mrs Ward didn't like each other. Mrs Ward hadn't spoken of any falling out. I began to feel uncomfortable sitting in Beatrice's room with my outdoor shoes on, and I got up. 'I'll leave you to get some sleep,' I said. 'I'm sorry to intrude on your privacy, very sorry.'

I hurried downstairs and went into the kitchen. As usual, Mrs Ward was sitting there before the fire, her feet up on a stool.

'Oh, Riana, just come in from Swansea, have you? I'll make you some milky cocoa. It will settle you down for the night.'

I was going to say I'd been talking to Beatrice, but I took the cocoa and came straight to the point. 'Did you know anything about any drawings Edwin Mansel-Atherton made? Plans of engines, that sort of thing?'

Mrs Ward suddenly looked furtive, but then her face cleared. 'Oh, I know what you mean. The drawings that disappeared when he died?'

'That's it.' I looked at her, wondering if I'd imagined the strange look that had come over her face. 'Know anything about them?'

'A lot of rubbish was talked when Mr Edwin died.' She shook her head. 'Who's to say what the truth was? Not me, that's for sure.'

I sighed, suddenly tired and feeling that everyone was an enemy. All the people I thought were friends were keeping the truth from me. I put down my cup. 'It's been a very long day.'

'Oh, I forgot to tell you. Mr Tom called here to see you.' She went to the drawer and took out a note. 'He left this for you.'

I took the note. It was not even in an envelope, and I wondered if Mrs Ward had read it. I went to my room, sat on the bed and devoured the words, feeling a thrill that this was Tom's writing and he'd actually been here in my house.

> Sorry to have missed you. Will call again to explain everything.
>   Love,
>   Tom

It could have been written to anyone; my name was not even on it. I felt like rushing downstairs to ask Mrs Ward:

had Tom delivered it in person? Was it really intended for me? And if so, what did it mean? What was he going to explain – his strange behaviour? And what he was *really* after at Aberglasney?

I kicked off my shoes. I was weary of it all: the mystery of the house and the deaths of the five girls, and of the strangers bursting in any time they chose. I was even tired of my ghost-haunting weekends and the people I'd come to know as friends. Colonel Fred, young William – did all of them spend their time in my house looking for hidden treasure in the form of futuristic designs, rather than looking for ghosts? And the ghosts . . . Were they real, or had it been mass hysteria when we'd all seen the mist and ghostly beings on the landing? I fell back against the pillows and began to cry.

In the morning, I began to paint again – anything to take my mind off the fact that Tom might call. After a restless morning, I had a solitary lunch: some salad and cold potatoes, and a glass of milk. I stood on the doorstep for a while looking along the drive, but there was no sign of anyone arriving. Tom wouldn't come, I knew it in my bones, and at last I went back to the studio and became involved once more in my painting.

I painted the grounds from memory – the cloisters, the now neat gardens, the wooden bench where Tom and I had shared our time and enjoyed each other's company – and the tears welled blurring my eyes. The effect of tears in my eyes altered the painting, and I began to paint in heavy rain sleeting down over the gardens, darkening the stonework on the arches of the cloisters, and making the plants look dark green.

On an impulse, I painted in Beatrice – just a small figure in the distance, bending over the plants, oblivious of the rain. Instinctively, I knew Beatrice didn't worry about the weather. Sometimes she went out in the rain and snow, and very often she would sit in her room, never using the electric fire unless I switched it on for her. I felt a flood of warmth for Beatrice. She was other-worldly in many ways, but so practical, so understanding when occasionally I spoke to her about my fears and about Tom and his strange ways. And the way she put in an appearance when I held my weekends, being a 'ghost' for a few fleeting seconds and then discreetly disappearing! I guessed she must have a hiding place somewhere, because guests often looked into the blue room and she was never there.

I stood back from the painting, and I could see it was all but finished. I would wait for the oils to dry, and then I would put on the finishing touches. As I left, I made sure I locked the studio. I always locked the door now – ever since my paintings had begun to sell well.

Later the sun came out from behind the clouds and the sweet smell of spring flowers filled the garden. The grass needed cutting, the sap was rising in the plants and trees, and after the rain everything looked fresh and green. Suddenly, I ached for Tom – to be in his arms, to feel his body fill mine, to have his mouth claim my lips, and to know that for a short time he was completely mine. *One night of love*. I smiled wryly. Surely that was a cue for a song? I felt wet on my cheeks again, and in a sudden frenzy of anger I wiped them away, unaware I was dabbing ultramarine paint on my cheeks. But then I noticed, in the distance, my guests arriving and I tried to pull myself together. I had completely forgotten that I'd arranged an extra weekend of ghost haunting! Fortunately, Mrs Ward hadn't. As I rushed into the house and into the kitchen, she was busy cooking, I could smell broth made with lamb and saw a fresh piece of cheese cut into chunks in a bowl.

'Oh, thank you for getting on with things, Mrs Ward,' I said. 'What would I do without you? I can see that Treasure is working like a whirlwind too; that girl is invaluable.' I touched Mrs Ward's shoulder. 'What would I do without you?' I said again.

'What indeed? You've been away with the fairies all day, working in your studio. Still, that's how you earn your living – mine too, if the truth be known. We work well as a team, Riana.' She gave me one of her rare smiles, and I knew by the light in her eyes that she was looking forward to seeing Colonel Fred again. 'The *cawl* is ready for the starters, made with lovely fresh veg from the garden and pieces of the lamb to make it tasty,' Mrs Ward said. 'Real Welsh soup is my *cawl*, and fresh cheese cut ready for the dressing. I've got a *joint* of lamb for the main course, and I've picked fresh mint from the garden. As for pudding, I managed to make apple pie and custard, though the custard is a bit on the thin side, mind.'

She looked up at me then and laughed. 'Which tribe have you joined, Riana?'

'What?'

'You're painted up like an Indian brave.'

I hurried to the mirror in the hall and burst out laughing. But then I noticed Mrs Ward's face, reflected behind me, and there was a strange, almost hostile, look in her eyes. 'Do I look that bad?' I asked, and she smiled and the image altered. She was once again the Mrs Ward I knew – never one to give of herself, but loyal and hard working and reliable. 'Anything wrong Mrs Ward?' I turned to her, and she looked down at her shoes. All I could see was the crown of her grey hair, smoothed down tidily as always.

'It's Rosie,' she said. 'She's coming back home.'

'Oh.' I hesitated. 'Aren't you pleased?'

'She says she wants to be free again and young and lovely. She's fed up with being a slave for a man and his impossible family. Her words, not mine.'

I didn't really know what to say. 'She can come here, of course.' I swallowed hard. I could imagine Rosie disrupting the place, flirting and arousing the ire of all the respectable village wives.

'Oh, I don't think that would be wise, Riana,' Mrs Ward surprised me by saying. 'I think she'll stay in London – for a while, anyway.'

'In London? Oh, good.' I felt relieved. I didn't know if I could cope with Rosie's overenthusiastic presence in the house. 'What will she do there?'

'Doubtless she'll meet some gullible man. In the meantime, she'll wait on tables, be a cook, something of that sort.'

I didn't want to enquire further, and fortunately just then there was a knock on the door and the tooting of a horn outside in the yard. 'Looks like more guests are arriving,' I said, sighing heavily. 'We'll talk later if you want, Mrs Ward. And don't worry about Rosie, she'll be all right.'

'I'm not worried about Rosie,' Mrs Ward said bluntly. 'I'm worried about that baby of hers.'

It was good to have the old colonel, Betty, and all my guests arrive and fill the house. Soon the dining room blazed with candles and lamplight and happy diners were drinking wine from sparkling glasses and eating the good food Mrs Ward and Treasure had prepared.

Now the whole house was wired for electricity. It was long overdue, but I knew my guests preferred the old-fashioned lighting that heightened the atmosphere of the old mansion. It was also conducive to ghosts, so it seemed, with the apparent 'happenings' on the landings.

I never saw ghosts when I was alone; I never felt threatened by anything other-worldly in my house. It was the humans I feared and mistrusted.

'How is your romance progressing?' Plump Betty pressed against William with her large bosoms.

'Not very well, as it happens.' William was unusually terse.

Betty wouldn't allow matters to rest there. 'I'm so sorry to hear that, but you are among friends here. You can talk freely to us.'

Colonel Fred leaned forward. 'While that is true, Betty, some things are best left alone, don't you know?' He held the brandy bottle towards William. The colonel had no truck with wine – 'newfangled nonsense' he called it. He loved his brandy and insisted on bringing his own brand, which he always took to his room. He saw me glance at him and the bottle and smiled. 'You see, dear Riana, I have my own spirits to keep me warm of a night. Try some, William. It will help you to relax and sleep.'

William accepted, more for the sake of peace than because he wanted to drink the brandy, but he continued to share the brandy for the rest of the evening. Later, I winked at the colonel, as I could see William was getting merrier and relaxing very well against Betty's plump shoulder. Betty herself was flushed with success. She'd always had a fancy for William.

There were no ghost sightings that night so instead the gathering became a party, with someone putting the gramophone on and playing dance music. I helped the colonel roll back the carpet to reveal the wooden floor, and he took a new guest, a Mrs Lampeter, in his arms and performed a creditable slow foxtrot. Betty inveigled William to dance, and he was propelled round the room with Betty's full bosom projecting into his skinny chest.

I heard the front door open, and my heart beat faster as I hoped Tom had come to see me at last, but it was Justin. He entered the room, immaculately dressed in a dinner suit and a gleaming white shirt with a black bow tie. He held out his hand, and reluctantly I accepted it. 'What brought you here?' I asked none too graciously as we danced.

He smiled down at me and bent to kiss my cheek. 'A very beautiful lady,' he said. I gave him a wry look, and he shook his head, laughing at me. 'No, dear Riana, not you, lovely though you are. Diane wanted me to ask you to give her more paintings. It seems she has a commission for you, so I thought I'd drive down straight away.'

I frowned. Diane knew that Justin wanted my house. Why would she speak to him about coming to see me? 'I think you must be mistaken,' I said icily. 'Diane would contact me herself if she wanted me. I doubt if she'd ask you, of all people, to bring me a message.'

'Ah, but I have won her over.' Justin sounded smug. 'She believes I am the true heir to Aberglasney, and she thinks we should try to get along. It would be in your best interests, seeing as we will be married as soon as you come to your senses.'

'Don't be so silly!' I pushed him away from me. 'I don't even know you why you imagine I should take your word for anything, and why on earth would I want to marry you?'

'Expediency, my dear Riana. We could live here together, and we would be very happy, I'm sure.'

'I take it you have no money and you would let me pay to do up the house and live on my earnings in the meantime. Now, if you are really the legal heir then go fight your case in the courts. Until then, leave me alone.'

I left my guests to party, and on the stairs I encountered Betty leading William to his downfall. She had a wide smile on her face as William fondled her plump rear. There was no sign of ghostly images as I made my way to my bedroom. I lay fully clothed on the quilt and closed my eyes. I could scarcely hear the music from the drawing room, but I wished all my guests a happy night and smiled as I thought of William, who was about to learn what passion was all about. And then I fell asleep.

THIRTY

Once my guests had departed on the Monday morning I dressed and took the train to Swansea and then on to London. I had to see Diane to find out what she was thinking of, encouraging Justin to come to Aberglasney!

Diane was not tucked away in her little sitting room, mourning her dear Mr Readings, but instead she was out visiting his grave, so the maid told me. I thought how fortunate Diane was to still have maids and a cook. I had only Mrs Ward and Treasure, and I was lucky to have them. So I waited, enjoying a cup of real ground coffee instead of the usual Camp coffee I had at home. No doubt Mr Readings had purchased a stock of it before he died, and Diane had found it and was enjoying her usual luxuries.

At last she returned, and in attendance, much to my surprise, was Rosie. Mrs Ward's daughter had changed drastically; she looked neat and respectable. She was struggling with brown paper bags bearing the names of the few good shops that had survived the war.

I put down my cup of very good coffee and hugged Diane. 'Could we have a word in private, please?' I asked meekly. 'Hello, Rosie, how are you?'

'I'm very well, Miss Riana.' This was a Rosie I didn't know: demure, respectful, nicely dressed in a modern full skirt, and with her hair tied up in a ponytail. She looked what she was: a very young girl. Perhaps she'd changed her ways . . . or maybe it was all an act to fool Diane.

'I'll take the bags upstairs.' She edged towards the door. 'I'll be careful to hang everything up for you, don't worry.'

Diane sat down and took off her gloves. 'I think I'll have a cup of coffee with you,' she said. 'I feel a "telling off" might be on the cards.'

'No,' I said. 'Well, not exactly. I just don't want Justin

popping into my house whenever he takes it into his head, that's all. Don't trust him, Diane. Now, tell me, where on earth did you come across Rosie?'

'She just applied for a job, that's all. And as for Justin, he might well have a claim on your house. He is Edwin's son, after all.'

I decided to shelve the matter of Rosie; just now there were more important things to discuss. 'But Justin is not *Beatrice's* son, and she's the one who sold me the house.'

'Just take the document to the solicitor and find out for sure, that's my advice. Justin seems a decent enough young man to me – a little arrogant, maybe, but well intentioned and charming.'

'Did he ever pay you a penny for any of the paintings he's bought?'

'But Riana, he's broke so he never *buys* any paintings. He does some clerical work for me instead. I'm rather sorry for him, really, and if you don't want him I'll have him.' She was smiling, but I could see Justin had charmed her – just as he charmed and fooled everyone except me.

'Well, until everything is sorted I want him to keep out of my way. I don't love him and won't marry him, not even for Aberglasney.'

'Think about it,' Diane said. 'He's handsome and partial to you, and in the old days many women married for expediency.'

'A marriage of convenience, like in books!' I said scathingly. 'Well, I have a career and a house that I've brought to life again. If Justin had a claim, why didn't he come forward when the house was little but a ruin, the gardens overgrown and the Americans stationed at the bottom of the garden?'

Diane lifted her eyebrows. 'At the bottom of the garden? Like *fairies* in books!' She smiled with humour.

'Very funny.' I sighed heavily. 'I know I'm a fool, Diane, but I love Tom. Whatever he's done I can forgive him, if only he loves me as he says he does.'

'Better have one willing suitor who wants to marry you than have a fly-by-night, excuse the pun, like Tom, an

American pilot who might well go home as soon as he finds whatever it is he wants here. At the moment, he's conspicuous by his absence, isn't he?'

There was a gentle knock on the door, and Rosie peeped in. 'Anything you want, Mrs Readings?' she asked.

I looked at Diane in surprise, and when the door closed behind Rosie I had to ask, 'She's very polite to you, isn't she?'

'She's a very good help, and I get on with her well enough.' Diane smiled. 'Mind you, she did quote you as a reference.'

I rather took offence at that. 'The cheeky little madam!'

'I like the way she calls me Mrs Readings. She's about the only one who does.'

'Why did you and he never marry before?' I asked.

'I think dear Mr Readings wanted to keep his options open, dear. He had other "ladies" and I knew it, but I didn't question him on it. He would have been defensive, and I know he didn't want me to be possessive, so I pretended to be as unbothered by our arrangement as he was.' She hung her head. 'But I was never content to remain a mistress – and then, at last, he asked me to marry him, and he died making me a widow almost immediately.' She stopped speaking and looked down at her pale long fingers, with her engagement ring and the band of gold sparkling up at her.

'At least he gave you the ring as a promise,' I said comfortingly as I hugged her. Grief and loss were dreadful emotions. I felt them every time Tom walked in and out of my life.

'We will have a quiet day today.' Diane lifted her head. 'I'll rest if you don't mind and then tomorrow I will come with you to the solicitor in Swansea and we'll sort out the matter of the house.'

'I already saw my solicitor,' I told her. 'He told me that Aberglasney was indisputably mine.'

'Best to be sure,' she insisted. 'You know I'm good at business, Riana, and I'll read the bill of sale properly and ask to see Edwin's will as well.'

'I understand Edwin didn't make a will.' I forced a smile. 'Seems he didn't have time after he was accused of murder.'

We set out early the next day. Diane drove us with skill and speed through the bombed streets of London and out into the country, both of us quiet with our own thoughts until we reached Swansea.

A cart pulled by an old horse drew in beside us as Diane stopped the car alongside the curb outside the solicitor's office, the man shouting out in a raucous voice, 'Rag and bones!' and handing out pennies and farthings for old rags or pots and pans. Anything he could make use of. As I stepped out of the car I could see the poor overladen horse jerk the cart into movement, the creature's head dipping up and down with the effort of moving the weight until the wheels began to roll freely along the street.

To my agitation, the door of the solicitor's office was locked. A policeman stood outside, and I looked up at him questioningly. 'I had an appointment this morning to see Mr—' I got no further as the policeman held up his hand.

'There's been an unfortunate incident in the building, madam. There are fatalities. You must go away. The building inside is unsafe.'

'Fatalities?' I echoed his words and looked at Diane aghast.

'I shall find out what's happened,' she said firmly. 'I have a friend, a top man in the service. I will speak to him.' She took my arm and propelled me to a small, neat tea shop just around the corner from the solicitor's office, and I sat there stunned, meekly drinking tea and waiting for her to come back.

After my third pot of tea, Diane returned. She was pale, and I quickly called for another cup and poured her some hot tea. 'It's bad,' I said, and she nodded.

'There was an explosion. Several people have been killed. The police think it was an unexploded bomb from the war. I'm sorry, Riana. I should have come with you before now.'

'It's not your responsibility,' I said shakily. 'I saw the

lawyer myself and he said everything was legal enough, that Justin was an illegitimate son and had no claim. I wonder how Mr Jeremy is. I do hope he's escaped the explosion.'

'I doubt it,' Diane said. 'It's terrible, they don't know how many people are under the rubble, but as it's a building of offices of legal people, it shouldn't be too hard to make an identification of the deceased.'

'So an unexploded bomb caused all this havoc.' I was quite shaken. 'Poor Mr Jeremy, he was very old. Too old to be working, really.'

Diane gave me a quick look and poured more tea for herself. 'All our young men are still trying to recover from the war. Oh dear, I feel quite shaken. I wish I'd never suggested coming here.'

'Well, you weren't to know there would be an explosion, were you? Look on the bright side, we could have been caught up in it all.'

Diane shivered. 'Don't be so cheerful!' Her tone held a touch of sarcasm, and I smiled to myself. Diane was getting her old spirit back.

Diane became weary of the peace and quiet of Aberglasney after a few days, and on the following Monday we had lunch in Swansea and then I waved her off. I waited until I could no longer see her car in the distance, and then turned to look straight into the dear face of Tom.

'Riana.' There was a world of love and sweetness in his voice, and in spite of myself I wanted to sink into his arms.

We stood looking at each for a long moment, and then we both moved and he was kissing me, holding me as though he would never let me go.

He took me for tea in a simple tea shop, and we sat holding hands over our cooling tea. I knew questions could wait, and I went with him willingly for a walk – along the darkening streets, through Victoria Park, along the sea front – holding hands like lovers. Well, we were lovers, even if we'd made love only once.

He booked us a room in a guest house, and I went with

him willingly. I decided that if I could only have him
sometimes that was better then nothing at all. Did he love
me? I was afraid to ask, but he wanted me, I could see it
in his eyes, and for now that was enough.

He took me gently, slowly, and I revelled in his touch.
Sensations I'd never known before swept my body, tingling
my senses and bringing me to a cascade of desire and a
tumbling of joy as my body and senses were lost and my
mind was bursting with stars. And then, sated, we lay on the
bed alongside each other holding hands, his broad chest rising
and falling with the breathlessness we were both feeling.

In me there was a wonder that any man could rouse such
passion, such burning, melting love. I adored Tom. I loved
every shape of his lean body: his fine buttocks, his strong
legs, his broad chest. I *loved* him.

Later we showered and shared a bottle of precious red
wine in our room. I had no nightclothes with me so I wrapped
myself in one of Tom's shirts and sat cross-legged on the
bed, holding my glass between my fingers. I had never been
so happy in all my life. And then Tom spoke.

'You should marry Justin Mansel-Atherton, you know.'
He said it gravely, with no hint of a smile, and my heart
almost stopped beating.

'What did you say?'

'For your own good, Riana. He's eligible, young, attractive
. . . He might well have a claim to Aberglasney, you know.'

I was tearful and furious all at once. 'You've just made
love to me in the most wonderful way, and now you are
telling me to marry another man! Are you mad?'

He took my hand, and though I tried to pull away he
held on to me. 'Riana, there are people who want me dead,'
he said. 'If I lived with you, even, I'd be putting you at
risk, don't you understand that?'

I dragged my hand free and flopped down on the bed.
'I don't understand anything!' I almost screamed at him. 'I
love you, Tom, don't you know that? You appear and disappear without a thought for my feelings! I don't know
what you are involved with, but I don't care. I just want
to be with you!'

'Sleep on it.' Tom spoke abruptly. He tucked himself inside the bedclothes and turned his back on me. I sat up, staring at his hair, which lay in curls on his neck, for a time. I wanted to touch his hair, kiss his neck, but in the end I closed my eyes, turned away from him and cried myself to sleep.

In the morning Tom had gone, and when, shamed, I went to check out, I found he hadn't even paid the bill properly. He'd left a sheaf of notes as if I was little more than a prostitute.

I hurried to the station. I just wanted to get home, shut myself in my room and try to heal my tattered pride. I didn't want to do anything – no painting, no social weekends with the ghost hunters. Perhaps I would just marry Justin and, as a married woman, get a sensible job and let Justin figure out the best way to keep the house in a good state of repair. If Justin *was* the real heir, I presumed he'd inherit whatever money the Mansel-Athertons had hidden away.

It sounded an easy way out – just hand over responsibility to someone else. I sat listening to the *clackety-clack* of the train, closed my eyes and went over every detail of my night of love with Tom in my head.

THIRTY-ONE

D iane became a frequent visitor to Aberglasney. The trouble was, she always seemed to have Justin in tow – as well as Rosie, who cooed and fussed over Diane as though she were a princess.

Diane enjoyed the ghost weekends and continued to market my paintings, and I thought her respect for Justin and her dreams of him marrying me and making my life easier were sweet but ill placed. The more I saw of Justin, the more I knew I loved Tom, despite everything.

One happy event in my life was that my painting grew in maturity. I put new focus on the house, painted odd corners of the rooms with ghostly images lurking mistily in them. I often painted the old cloisters, which had been built hundreds of years ago, and thought of Tom and me sitting under the arches on a summer's day, when deep shadows and brightly-patterned sunlight had shaped the gardens. I often thought of those days with nostalgia and hurt in my heart.

The grass and flowers had been wild then, and it was because of Tom and his men that the flower beds had begun to have order and shape. Of course, I could afford two gardeners now, who kept the gardens trimmed and neat and weeded, but I knew I would never forget that Tom was the one who had planted my garden and made it beautiful.

I knew I should be pleased with my life. I had good friends – especially Diane, who had my best interests at heart – and I was becoming a 'name' now in the world of art. I was known as the strange young lady who lived with ghosts, but I didn't mind what folk said about me as long as my work was appreciated. I was even commissioned by a minor royal to paint an ancestor sweeping grandly across the lawn at Aberglasney. In spite of myself and my best efforts, the lady ended up bearing a striking resemblance to Beatrice. The painting was returned with a short letter telling me the likeness to the royal lady was not quite right and would I do more work on the face?

I looked at the painted miniature I'd been allowed to borrow and worked with a focused mind, and at last the likeness was almost perfect. This time the painting was accepted and I was paid a handsome sum, which I immediately took to my bank in Swansea, grateful that I was secure for at least another year if I wasn't too enthusiastic with my spending on the house.

Summer came and went, hot and dry and with visitors galore, who were not only coming to see the house but also to visit the beautiful gardens, making use of the newly-restored drive and entrance archway. I saw Tom only twice during the summer, and each time he told me he loved me, took me to bed and made such beautiful love to me that I cried each time.

Now the summer had gone, there was an autumnal touch to the evenings, and the leaves fell like coloured patterns on to the well-manicured grass lawns. I walked the gardens – shuffling through the crisp leaves and kicking them up in heaps like a child.

And then it suddenly became winter once more. The nights drew in and shadows crept across from the cloister into the garden, and I felt that first summer at Aberglasney was long ago and far away.

The house was almost restored to its former glory now; there was electric lighting all over the house, though we still used oil lamps and candelabras for effect on the ghost weekends. My career was blossoming, and all I needed to make my life complete was Tom. But he continued to be evasive.

Justin came often with Diane and stayed at the house, and I had yet to prove by law that Aberglasney was mine. Justin seemed to have given up the idea that he owned the place, but I soon found out that I was completely wrong about that.

I was sitting in the comfort of the drawing room, wondering what to do for a Christmas party this year and enjoying a glass of much needed sherry, when there was a commotion at the door. I stood up abruptly, my senses alert, imagining Tom had arrived to sweep me away.

A flustered Mrs Ward called me into the hallway. 'It's Mr Mansel-Atherton, Riana. He says he's here to stay and that I must take my orders from him.'

Justin stood in the hallway smiling at me, his bags and cases on the floor beside him. 'Sorry, Riana,' he said, grinning. 'I've nowhere else to go, and this house is rightfully mine. So I'm here to stay, whether you like it or not!' He turned to Mrs Ward. 'Make up a room for me, Mrs Ward.'

She hesitated, looking at me uncertainly.

Justin put his hands on his hips in a 'lord of the manor' pose. 'I won't ask again, Mrs Ward.'

She scuttled upstairs, and I could hear her rummaging in the linen cupboard for sheets. I stood there glaring at Justin for a long moment, and then without waiting he strode past me into the sitting room and sat down in the most comfortable armchair! When Mrs Ward returned he ordered a brandy and soda, and she was so frightened by his authoritative manner that she rushed away to do his bidding.

'What do you think you are doing?' I could hardly speak I was so angry. 'How *dare* you come striding in here as if you own the place?'

'Because I *do* own the place! Call the police, if you like. See what *they* say about all this. Just see if they will throw me out!'

'You know they won't be able to do that on the spot. It takes a solicitor and legal papers to determine who really owns Aberglasney,' I stuttered.

'Precisely, and all you own is a pathetic piece of paper signed by a batty old woman. You only got the house because no one contested it. Well, all that is changed now. I'm back, and if I want to live in my house then I have every right to do so. That solicitor chap told me that before he died.'

I shook my head. 'How convenient for you that a bomb killed him before we could sort this out. Well, we'll see about that in the morning! There are other solicitors who deal with wills and that sort of thing.'

'Well, in the meantime, I'll go to my room. And once in, believe me, you won't shift me.'

'We'll see,' I said, overwhelmed by anger. 'I might get someone to throw you out, if I have to.'

'Threats, Miss Evans? Don't overstep the mark or *I* might be the one to do the throwing out.' He bowed to me as though he was a gentleman and left the room.

I could hear him going upstairs, and I stood near the door and shook my fist up the stairs. 'I hope all the ghosts of Aberglasney rise up to haunt you,' I whispered.

Justin must have heard me, because he turned round and smiled spitefully. 'I know the ghosts of Aberglasney much better than you do, Riana darling, and they are not the ones in the spirit world, believe me.'

'What are you talking about, Justin?'

'Past history, Riana. Things you don't understand and don't need to know about.' Justin was as smug as ever. 'Now, I'll say goodnight.'

He disappeared along the corridor, and I went back into the sitting room and refrained from banging the door shut. I sat there and fumed as I heard Justin's footsteps across the landing, wondering if he was attempting to intrude into my studio to look at my unfinished paintings. If he was, he would soon find out that I always kept it locked! It looked as if I was stuck with Justin until I could invoke some legal law that would have him evicted.

In the morning, Justin was seated at the breakfast table with Mrs Ward serving him bacon and eggs and toast as if he was lord of all he surveyed.

'You don't have to wait on Mr Mansel-Atherton,' I said crossly. 'Let him cook his own breakfast, seeing as he's not even paying for board and lodge here.'

'No man pays board and lodge when he owns the house,' Justin said, rebuking me, and Mrs Ward made a hasty retreat to the kitchen.

I followed her. 'When Justin pays your wages you can wait on him as much as you like. Until then, please do what *I* ask.'

'It's difficult for me to take it all in,' she said. 'The Mansel-Atherton family has owned Aberglasney for as long as I can remember.'

'Well, I'm the legal owner now,' I said more gently, 'and I'll prove it. I'll go to a London solicitor if I have to and get Justin thrown out of here.'

'Want breakfast?' Mrs Ward adroitly changed the subject. 'I've just made a fresh pot of tea.'

I sat down. 'I'll have tea and toast,' I said, sulky as a child, 'but I won't eat with that man. I'll stay in here with you.'

'That's all right,' Mrs Ward said, and I felt, churlishly, that she was giving me permission to eat in my own kitchen.

Later, I heard Justin go upstairs, and by the banging and moving of furniture I realized he was searching my house. He wasn't the first one to make a search of Aberglasney; what were they all looking for? Could they *really* all still be looking for Mr Mansel-Atherton's engine designs, after all this time? Of course, I thought, Justin could be looking for proof of his inheritance. My blood ran cold.

I hurried upstairs just as he was going in to the blue room, Beatrice's room. I pushed the door open and there he was on the floor, tapping the boards, a chisel and a hammer lying alongside him.

'What do you think you are doing?' I stared down at him, my hands clenched to my sides, longing to hit him.

'What does it look like?' He sat up and leaned back against the wall. He looked unruffled; Justin always appeared to be in full evening dress, even though he now wore casual trousers and an open-neck shirt. 'I'm searching the old house.'

'But *why*?'

'You must be incredibly stupid, Riana. My father's plans are here somewhere. Designs for a new type of aeroplane engine, so revolutionary and brilliant that I could still make a fortune from them if I discovered them, even now. Everyone wants to get their hands on my father's drawings, from the United States Army Air Forces to the Russians.'

I went cold. Was that why Tom kept returning to me, making love to me, only to learn if I knew about the drawings and where they could be kept? He was in the United States Army Air Forces, after all.

'Sounds as ridiculous as the presence of ghosts to me,' I said 'Now get up from here and get out of my house before I call the police and tell them your intention was to come here and rob me.'

'How would you prove that, Riana my darling? All I would have to do is show the police my birth certificate and they would back off. With my name it would be hard to prove that I am not the rightful owner of the house, wouldn't it?'

'Where's Beatrice when I need her?' I muttered, and Justin turned his back and continued to remove floorboards.

In the kitchen, Mrs Ward was washing the floor, her hair tied up in a scarf and a hint of steel curling pins peeping out over her forehead.

'How can I get rid of that man, Mrs Ward? He's trying to ruin my house! He's busy pulling up floorboards at the moment in the blue room.'

Mrs Ward gave me a quick glance, but remained tight lipped.

I stared at her for a long moment. 'What do you know about these designs that Mr Edwin created? Is it common knowledge that there are lost plans, worth a fortune, hidden in this house?'

She shrugged. 'There was talk when he was taken away by the police, but we villagers didn't know anything about designs and plans and such and no one has ever found anything in the house. If they were to exist though, they'd be worth a mint of money.'

'How do you know that?'

'Just the way that strange men have been here to search. I suspect all this nonsense about lights and ghosts has always been more to do with folks searching the old place than any ghosts.'

I shook my head and tiptoed across the wet floor and went out into the garden to be on my own to think things through.

HARRISON COUNTY
PUBLIC LIBRARY
105 North Capitol Ave
Corydon, IN 47112

I sat under the cloisters. Could it be true that the mysterious noises in the night, the bumps and crashes, had been made by men searching the place all along? And the flickering lights on the landing, so eerie in darkness, were the candles of burglars come to rob Beatrice of what was rightfully hers? I shivered. It seemed as unlikely an explanation as the ghosts.

It was cold in the garden, and a rim of frost edged the stonework. But in a few weeks spring would be coming and the brave yellow of daffodils would make bright splashes across the borders of the gardens. But I was running ahead of myself. I had to plan for my Christmas party for my ghost hunters. My first job was to get rid of Justin. I would ask Diane if she knew of a good lawyer who could look at all the facts – my bill of sale versus Justin's claim to the house because of his name – and learn exactly what the law was about the ownership of Aberglasney.

I would be desolate if Justin proved to be the owner, but I felt my bill of sale was legitimate and legally binding. However, I knew it would take heaven and earth and the might of the law to move Justin out of my home.

THIRTY-TWO

D iane arrived for a visit, but she was in a very funny mood. 'I find Justin very convincing,' she said.

We were sitting on the sofa. It was comfortable and warm in the room, with a glass of good port to keep us company.

'Why on earth are you taking Justin's part?' I was disturbed by Diane's attitude. She seemed to think Justin was the true heir to my house and that I could do worse than to marry him.

'Don't be silly, Riana. I'm thinking of you. He's young, he's ambitious, and as I told you I will be leaving the gallery and all the goodwill of the business to him. He's become very close to me.'

'He's charmed you,' I said bluntly. 'Has he made love to you yet?' As soon as I spoke the words, I regretted them.

'Riana! How could you be so gross? I loved my Mr Readings. You know that the greatest day of my life was when he put a ring on my finger.'

'I'm sorry, that was uncalled for,' I said at once. 'Of course, you wouldn't want a boy like Justin, not after a good man like Mr Readings.' And yet I looked at Diane afresh. She was much younger than Mr Readings, of course. She was a comfortably upholstered but nonetheless attractive widow with lots of money and influence. But then I was being silly. Why would Justin want me and the house if he'd already settled for Diane and her fortune? I hugged Diane and kissed her cheek and told her again how sorry I was . . . and yet and yet, was she really my friend? Was anyone really my friend, including Tom, my dear man? And then there was Mrs Ward . . . She was constantly there at Aberglasney. She had every chance to search the house whenever she cleaned and dusted and changed the linen. Has she discovered any papers? And if so, was she keeping them from me? I was growing paranoid, and I hated it.

Diane persuaded me to go to London, and together we visited her lawyer – who was young and keen and told me my documents regarding Aberglasney were legal and binding. 'Of course, the son has a right to contest the will,' he added, and my spirits sank.

We travelled to the guest house, and once there I sat in a chair my head in my hands. 'You know Justin is forcing himself on me, don't you?' I said miserably.

Diane looked at me sharply. 'You don't mean . . .' Her words trailed away, but she had a glitter in her eyes that I didn't like to see.

'Not physically, of course,' I replied hurriedly. 'I mean that he insists on living in my house, in spite of my protests. Well, today I've got an appointment with another lawyer, Mr Prentice, a fine London lawyer who specializes in houses and wills and such.'

'Why didn't you tell me?' Diane said. 'I've wasted my time advising you and taking you to see my lawyer. What are you thinking of, Riana? Don't you trust me?'

'I trust you, but I don't trust Justin,' I said. 'No doubt he advised you which firm to visit.' She nodded slowly, and I smiled. 'I thought so. You are too trusting, Diane.'

I went to see Mr Prentice on my own because I knew Diane would put Justin's case to him, even if it was only out of a sense of rightness and fairness. The lawyer had modern premises, very unlike Mr Jeremy's dark offices and book-lined study. Mr Prentice sat in a bright light room with two windows and a warm light over a polished, immaculate desk. His ink tray was spotless, no ink blotches stained the burnished wood, and even the nib of his pen was shining as though it had never been used.

Mr Prentice read the bill of sale in silence, absorbing it all quickly and digesting it in silence. At last he spoke. 'Looks legal and binding to me,' he said, and I breathed a sigh of relief. 'So what is the problem, Miss Evans? I assume there is one, or you wouldn't be here.'

I told him about Justin and his claims, and he leaned back in his chair, adjusted his glasses, and listened carefully.

'I visited Aberglasney once,' Mr Prentice remarked, 'on a business matter concerning putting funds into designs for a new type of aeroplane engine. Unfortunately, I couldn't raise the money, but the plans were brilliant, quite brilliant. We haven't seen their like again. But later, if I remember rightly, Mansel-Atherton was accused of murdering five girls.' He paused and lit a cigar. 'All nonsense, of course, not a real shred of evidence against him. I hear the room had been freshly painted. I always thought that if the chimney had been blocked, the lead paint fumes could have killed all the girls in one night, as they lay sleeping in their beds, but not a man like Edwin Mansel-Atherton. He had no motive, for a start. Still, the case ruined him. He killed himself, I believe. Now back to business.'

He paused and picked up a great tome of a book. 'The point is, did Mr Mansel-Atherton ever acknowledge this son in writing? The man had a wonderfully creative brain, so he would know what he was about. Was the father's name on the birth certificate? These questions I must answer before I know for sure what this young man's claims amount to. I will write to you with my findings, Miss Evans, and in the meantime don't worry too much. I think you are pretty safe. Where may I contact this young man?'

'He's in my house, and he won't be moved,' I said, and Mr Prentice frowned.

'He's going to have to be evicted through the law courts then,' he said. 'Or, and officially I didn't tell you this, you could have friends to literally remove him by force.'

That sounded tempting. I could imagine Justin being thrown out on his ear. How indignant he would be that his arrogant pride had been dented! I put my papers away in my bag and got to my feet. 'Well, thank you, Mr Prentice. I will wait to hear from you then. Please be as quick as you can.'

He rose and shook my hand. 'Of course, Miss Evans. I'd be delighted to act for you at once.' His smile was warm, and his hand held mine a little longer than was necessary.

I drew away, blushing. He was a very attractive man, even though he was of mature years. What a pity I was in love with Tom – who didn't appreciate me at all, who came and went at a whim, and who seemed to get me into danger whenever he was around. And yet my heart ached for him.

I left the office walking on air, however. Aberglasney was almost surely mine, and a good-looking man had found me attractive and showed it. I really felt positive for the first time in ages. Also, Mr Prentice had given me an idea to mull over about the death of the maids.

I turned a corner and stopped walking abruptly. Ahead of me was a couple, arm in arm, and I recognized Diane's fashionable hat. I slowed my pace and kept a discreet distance behind them. The man too looked familiar: the hair, the slant of the shoulders, the cut of the clothes . . . it was Justin and Diane! She'd lied about their relationship, making me feel disgusting for even suggesting there was something between them, and there they were together! Thank goodness she hadn't come to see Mr Prentice with me; she would have proved to be a thorn in my side.

I took the underground back to Diane's house and packed my bags as quickly as I could. I didn't even leave her a note; I just wanted to get home as quickly as I could.

It seemed an age before I again stood in the roomy hallway of my house, and I sighed with pleasure. It was all mine, and at last I was beginning to learn the real secrets of Aberglasney.

THIRTY-THREE

There was no sign of Mrs Ward so I made a cup of tea and sat in the kitchen, drinking it thirstily. I'd thought about what Mr Prentice had told me about the death of the young girls, and I realized what he'd said made sense, even it hadn't been the paint itself that had killed them. Hadn't Mr Jeremy told me that lead poisoning took days, not hours? It would be difficult to kill five people at the same time though, that much was true. Wouldn't they scream, run away, or even overpower a man by sheer numbers? In any case, I believed Beatrice. She knew her husband and common sense told me that she spoke the truth. Perhaps Mr Prentice had the truth of it: perhaps the chimney *had* been blocked, and they had suffocated from the fumes of the fire.

I put down my cup and went upstairs with my case, aware for once that the house was deathly quiet. One by one I searched the rooms, poking a brush up chimneys – bringing down lots of dust, and once a very dead bird, but no sign of plans or papers at all.

Lastly I went to Beatrice's room. It was cold and empty, and when I put my hand near the bars of the electric heater there was no warmth in them; Beatrice had not been home.

I sat cross-legged on the floor and poked dispiritedly a little way up the chimney, thinking I was completely on the wrong track. Nothing but soot fell into the hearth, spattering the carpet and my skirt in the process.

The wall was cold behind me as I leaned back against it, exhausted and disappointed. It seemed so logical that if a blocked chimney had been the cause of the deaths of the girls then the papers would be hidden there – preventing the smoke from finding a way out.

I found a newspaper left on the bedside table – proof that neither Mrs Ward nor Treasure dusted in here too often – and spread it over the floor near the fireplace. I decided I would make a determined effort this time! I leaned halfway up the chimney, feeling soot fall in my hair. The brush handle met resistance this time, and – very excited – I pushed harder, feeling like the chimney sweeps of old must have felt.

Suddenly, a huge parcel fell into the grate, covered in a chunk of soot as big as a brick, followed by sheets and sheets of newspaper. A box wrapped in old newspaper lay in the grate, and I stared at it for a moment, not daring to think I'd found the hidden 'treasure'. Was this box really what all the fuss had been about?

I picked up one of the loose newspapers. It was yellow and crumbling, and when I looked at the date I saw it was over twenty years old. As I looked at it, I knew the truth: Edwin had hidden his designs in the chimney, wrapped in old newspaper, all those years ago. But the box, and the papers, had blocked the chimney, causing the deaths of the young maids, who had all slept in the blue room together . . .

I cleaned up the grate as best as I could and took the box to my studio. As I suspected, it contained a sheaf of technical drawings. I meticulously copied the drawings – leaving bits I thought vital out and altering complicated arithmetic that I didn't even understand. A couple of hours passed, but when I had finished I put the original drawings into my art folder, hurried to the blue room and stuffed my 'copies' up the chimney. I was confident no one would make sense out of them, even if they found them.

I heard the front door open, and I knew Justin had come back from London as quickly as he could. He and Diane had realized I must have gone home. I heard voices in the hall and realized Justin had brought company.

I changed and went downstairs to greet my guests. I knew I had to keep a cool head and play Justin's game for now, work out just what he and Diane wanted.

Mrs Ward had returned and she nodded her head to me in apology as she carried a tray of drinks through the hall. 'Sorry I was out when you came home, Riana. I didn't expect you till the morning.' She paused. 'I hope you don't mind, but I've invited the colonel to come over for a drink, ahead of the rest of the ghost people.'

'Of course I don't mind.' I was relieved. Whatever Justin planned, he couldn't do any harm while there were guests in the house. Tomorrow was the Christmas ghost-haunting weekend party, so the house would be overrun.

I noticed my visitors had made themselves at home. Diane had kicked off her shoes and was seated next to Justin. She beamed at me as if nothing was amiss and took a drink with a sigh of satisfaction.

'Why did you run off home so suddenly?' Diane said, looking at me over the rim of her glass.

'A whim?' I said. 'Actually, I saw you and Justin together arm in arm and didn't want to play the gooseberry.'

Diane laughed. 'Well, I suppose I'd better tell you my guilty secret then. Justin is my son.' Diane dropped the bombshell without a blink of her eye, and I stared at her in amazement.

'Your son?' I looked at Justin and saw the same features: the dark hair, the slant of the eyes, the upright carriage.

'You and Edwin Mansel-Atherton then?'

'That's right. We were lovers once, and dear Justin is the result.'

'But Edwin never acknowledged him, did he? And that's why you pressed me to marry him! Diane, I thought you were my friend.'

'Of course I'm your friend, but I'm also a mother. I would love you and Justin to run Aberglasney together. What could be better?'

'But I'm not in love with Justin. I could *never* marry him. Sorry, Justin.'

'Excuse me, Riana.' Mrs Ward came into the room with another tray of drinks. 'Don't forget we've got visitors tomorrow,' she hinted.

I got to my feet. 'Well, if you'll all excuse me, I'd better help Mrs Ward get the bedrooms ready. Help yourselves to drinks.'

'Aye.' Mrs Ward spoke wryly. 'I've been upstairs to put

the linen out, and it looks as if we've had the chimney sweep in some of the bedrooms.'

Justin and Diane gave each other a quick glance. 'We'd better help then.' Diane was the one to speak. 'Come on, Justin. You can help me clean up for dear Riana's sake. We don't want her weekends ruined, do we?'

I knew at once Diane had realized that the chimneys must be where the papers were hidden, so I decided to speak. 'These plans of Mr Mansel-Atherton's. They might be a lever for you to use against me concerning the ownership of Aberglasney, Justin, but I would never marry you. I'm in love with another man.'

'Rubbish!' Diane said softly. 'You haven't started to live yet, Riana.'

'Well, about the designs everyone's making a fuss about. I wondered if they were hidden in the chimneys. I did look, but I found nothing.' I spoke the lie easily, knowing I could be among enemies, not friends.

Diane looked at me for a long time. 'So you've found them then? You're not a very good liar, Riana. Still –' she waved a limp hand at Justin – 'we can talk about this later, but perhaps we should just get out of the way for now. We'll take a drive to the village pub, shall we?'

'Later' I took meant as once I was alone and Diane and Justin could bully me into telling the truth.

'I'm so tired,' I said and declined Diane's invitation, but urged them to go on without me. Once they had left, I rubbed my forehead, and Mrs Ward touched my shoulder. 'Shall I make you a cup of cocoa, Riana? You look so pale.' She made me a drink and then took off her apron. 'I've had enough for today,' she said. 'Kitchen is closed.'

Diane and Justin returned from the pub some time later, having had, I suspected, a good chat about the designs. 'Finished tidying the rooms?' Diane yawned. 'One more drink and then I'll retire for the night,' she said. And, true to her word, once she'd drunk the large gin Mrs Ward had poured her – and Justin had done likewise – she kicked off her shoes and, rather unsteadily, asked Justin to take her arm and lead her up to her room.

'Well, our guests will sleep well tonight.' Mrs Ward kicked off her own shoes and put her feet up on her little stool.

'How can you say that?' I knew I sounded weary. 'They might start searching the place once everything is quiet.'

'I don't think so. I slipped some of that laudanum stuff in their drinks. I could see Mrs Diane's eyes beginning to close when she was going upstairs.' Mrs Ward smiled, and I wondered if she had an ulterior motive in keeping my two guests quiet for the night. What was wrong with me? I was suspecting everyone I came in contact with. Was I in even more danger now I'd found the plans?

I went to bed at last, but I couldn't sleep. I tossed and turned and wanted Tom to come to take me away from everything. But then how was I to know if he cared for me, or if he too only wanted poor Edwin's papers, like all the others? Tom was in the United States Army Air Forces, I reminded myself, and the plans for a new engine would probably help his career along well enough. He could even be a spy! Perhaps that was why he'd been abducted.

I fell asleep at last and dreamed of Mrs Ward, all the ghosts of the dead girls, and poor Edwin, along with a smiling Diane and Justin, holding out a wedding veil towards me as they stood round my bed.

I woke sweating. It was dark and silent and I was alone and very afraid, and it took me a very long time to fall asleep again.

THIRTY-FOUR

There were fewer guests for this year's Christmas ghost-haunting weekend. Colonel Fred, of course, and young William, plump Betty, and most of my 'old faithfuls', as I called them. To my surprise, the handsome lawyer Mr Prentice turned up in a fine shiny car, with a letter and a wink for me. With Diane and Justin, it was a healthy crowd. Almost.

I read the letter quickly and smiled. Mr Prentice had done his research well. Justin had no claim; he was not a Mansel-Atherton at all. The name on the birth certificate read 'Jameson' – Diane's name before she married, I imagined.

I passed the letter to him. He read it and shrugged. 'Ah, well. It was a good try. No hard feelings?' he said airily.

Speechless, I returned to my guests and hid my fears about the designs, about Justin, and about my foolish longing for Tom, and made a show of being happy for my guests. I'd made name cards for everyone, and with good humour everyone pinned them on before we sat down to dinner in the decorated dining room.

The table was graced with a starter of fish and toast. Somehow, with her usual skill, Mrs Ward had managed to acquire some tinned anchovies and a pound of salt butter – the taste was delicious. I knew she'd cooked rabbit and chicken for the main course, with tiny roast potatoes and tinned peas. We'd have tinned fruit and custard for pudding. All in all a good meal, considering the war had not long ended.

After dinner the guests retired to the sitting room where they could relax and smoke and have a drink or two of mulled wine, which I hoped would make them feel more festive, before my little speech and then the ghost hunt would begin. I felt a shiver of apprehension, however. Something was amiss tonight, and though I tried my best to hide it I felt spooked and scared, and I wasn't sure if it was of the living or the dead.

Justin came and sat beside me and put his arm around my shoulders. I looked at him disapprovingly, but it made no difference.

'Where are they?' he said without preamble. 'The drawings, did you find them? I take it from what Mrs Ward said that you've been poking up chimneys here.'

So Justin was my enemy. 'Did you attack me when I first arrived?' I asked, my lips trembling. 'Have you been plotting against me and interfering with my paintings all this time?'

'Hey, hold your horses. I haven't attacked anyone, and no, I haven't done anything to you or your precious paintings. Silly daubs, that's all they are.'

That stung, but I knew he was trying to distract me. 'Go away,' I said. When he did not, I rose and refilled my glass and sat next to the colonel. 'What are you hoping for tonight, Colonel Fred?' I spoke as cheerfully as I could, and he tipped up his glass of brandy and winked at me.

'Who knows, dear lady? I might just make my fortune here tonight.'

'What do you mean?' I asked uneasily.

'Why, I might just capture a ghost on film, Riana. What do you think I mean? Mind you, if anyone gets a good picture it will be young William. He's the clever one here. He's got a very good degree, you know, even though he is a bumbler at times.'

I felt bewildered. I really knew nothing about these people I was accommodating in my house. Who could I trust, and who meant me harm? I wondered if the drawings were safe in my studio, but it wouldn't do to check now; someone would be sure to follow me.

The front doorbell rang out, sounding somehow like the knell of doom. I heard Mrs Ward go to answer it, and then Rosie came into the room, a young child in her arms. His skin had darkened, and his curly hair had also grown darker, and I realized it was her son – hers, and the handsome airman Carl Jenkins.

'I want them, the drawings.' She stood in the middle of
the room, her feet planted firmly on the carpet. 'Carl died
trying out a version this new engine. Not quite correct, the
engine wasn't, because Mr Mansel-Atherton never gave the
Americans all the designs, as he promised. My Carl crashed
his plane because of the mistakes, so by rights my son
should have any money coming from the designs.'

Justin jumped to his feet. 'The drawings might not even
still exist.' He sounded angry. 'My father might have
destroyed them. Have you thought of that?'

'Carl told me about them. They exist all right, and as for
her –' she nodded in my direction – 'doing the place up,
she must have found the drawings by now.'

'Who are you working with Rosie?' Justin demanded.
'Just who is pulling your strings? Is it that other yank, Tom
Maybury?'

I went cold. 'Excuse me,' I interrupted them both. 'Rosie,
there are no drawings, no plans. Not any more. Wise up,
it's all a story. If such plans still existed, the house would
have been saved. It wouldn't have been sold to me in the
first place.'

'Riana's making sense,' the colonel said. 'I don't know
what these drawings are, but they are obviously worth a
considerable amount of money or folk wouldn't be so eager
to find them.'

'What do you know, you silly old man?' Rosie sank into
a chair. She had tears in her eyes – were they genuine?

I looked at her baby's sweet face. His eyes were huge
and dark, and he clung to his mother as if he would never
let her go. Rosie clearly took good care of him, so she
couldn't be all bad. And her man had given his life to trial
Edwin's designs – only without the originals, the Americans
had evidently got the new engine wrong. 'You might as
well stay Rosie,' I said. 'I'll make you up a bed.'

'I can't go anywhere anyway,' Rosie said. 'There's no
inn or hotel that will take me in – not with a black American
child, they won't.'

'You shouldn't have come here,' Mrs Ward interjected.
'Wherever you go there's trouble.'

'Oh, look, little Carl –' Rosie's tone was mocking – 'there's your loving grandmother. Want to hold him, Mother? He's quite civilized. He won't bite or anything.'

'That's enough, Rosie,' I said sharply. 'No one here is prejudiced against you or your son.

'You kidding?' Rosie said. 'I've been shunned by the villagers. No one would put me up, not even for one night.'

'No wonder, calling on good people at this time of night. Where's your sense, girl?' Mrs Ward's tone had softened. 'Come into the kitchen. I'll make you a cup of tea and a bite to eat.'

'I'm so tired, Mum,' Rosie said softly. 'A cup of cocoa in bed would be lovely, thanks.'

'Rosie can have my room, Mrs Ward,' I said. 'The bed is big enough for her and the baby in there.'

'But where will you sleep, Riana?' Mrs Ward asked.

'I'll take the blue room. Beatrice has gone away visiting relatives again.'

'But my dear,' the colonel said, 'that is the room that is most haunted! That's the room we all want to visit!'

'That's fine.' I felt doubtful and superstitiously frightened at the thought of sleeping in what was supposed to be a haunted room, but Beatrice seemed to manage all right when she was here. 'I'll be going to bed later than everyone else, anyway. I always do when I have guests.'

'I'll sleep in the haunted room,' Justin said.

Then young William volunteered. 'Please, Miss Evans, let me sleep in there. I might just get a good picture – a reward for all the weekends I've spent here – and I haven't had a good picture yet.'

There was a clamour of voices, and I held up my hand. 'William wins the prize,' I said. 'He's the youngest and the keenest ghost hunter. He can have the blue room, and I'll take his room.'

William beamed. 'Oh good! I'll stay awake all night with my camera at the ready, just so I don't miss anything.'

'William –' Diane was staring at William suspiciously – 'what is it you actually do for a living? I don't think you've ever mentioned it.'

'It doesn't really matter, Diane,' I interrupted. 'I have a policy of allowing guests to keep their private lives just that.'

'I'm not very good at my job, so I've taken up part-time photography – weddings and such. Perhaps I'll make my mark with that.'

I glared at Diane. 'Happy now? What William does is *his* business.'

It was the early hours of the morning when at last I went to bed. I lay in an uneasy state of mind, wondering who intended to do what harm to me and my house. It was clear Edwin's drawings were at the root of all the mysterious comings and goings, the strange abductions, the threats on my life . . . And what part did Tom have in it all? That was the main reason for my uneasiness.

I went over the facts against him yet again. He was a military man, an airman . . . the drawings would have some significance for him. I turned over on my back and then sat up sharply. I could smell smoke!

I was alert now, and I realized the smoke was curling down the servants' staircase. I ran to the blue room, calling out, 'Fire!'

When I reached the blue room I opened the door gingerly, knowing from the wartime bombing that when air hit flames they could leap and burgeon. To my horror, I could see William kneeling by the blazing fire in the grate, apparently unconscious and overcome with fumes. The fake drawings had fallen from the chimney and begun to burn, setting the room itself alight.

Guilt engulfed me. I'd taken the electric heater out of the room to put in my room, and William must have tried to light the fire. The false drawings were pushed into the chimney, blocking it, and now poor innocent William was suffering the same fate that the five young maids had – suffocated by fumes!

But then William groaned. He was still alive!

Coughing, I dragged William to the door and on to the landing. 'Help, fire!' I shouted loudly. 'Everyone get out of the house!' I managed to pull William's inert body to the stairs and somehow bumped him down them into the hall below. Guests were already coming out of their rooms.

'I'll phone the fire brigade.' The colonel was in his dressing gown, a ruffled Mrs Ward at his side. She too was in her dressing gown, with her hair awry. In other circumstances I would have been amused by her embarrassment – but not now.

'I'll phone,' Mrs Ward said. 'Fred, you help Riana with the young lad.'

Soon we were all on the lawn, shivering against the early morning mist. Rosie cuddled her little boy; his dark eyes were wide with lights glowing in them as he looked up to the house, where the flames were beginning to take hold.

And then the fire brigade arrived, bells clanging, and the police had sent a car which screeched to a halt in the drive. A woman in uniform came towards me. 'I've come because of a suspicious fire, but my intent is also to investigate the death of Mr Mansel-Atherton.'

I knew that voice. I looked up. 'Miss Grist!'

She held a badge towards me. 'I'm Detective Delia Grist as it happens,' she said. 'And we've been observing matters here at Aberglasney for some time. You, with your blundering ways, almost ruined things for us.'

'But why were you posing as a librarian?' I asked.

'It was a cover. I was there merely to observe what you were up to,' Miss Grist said, 'and taking the chance to research the old newspapers. And at the same time, *you* were coming in to do the same research!' She actually smiled. 'To be frank, you were nothing but a pain in the neck. Ah, look, the fire is out. An isolated little fire, I'd say. Now, let's all go into the undamaged part of the house where I can question you all in relative comfort.'

I ushered all my guests into the sitting room and realized the damage had been confined to the top of the floor, where the blue room had been. I realized then that the only guest missing from the room was young William. The ambulance was still outside so he hadn't gone to hospital.

I hurried back to the garden. I could hear coughing from under the yew tree tunnel, and I walked timidly into the darkness, fearing I knew not what. There was a creeping sensation along my scalp, as if all my hairs were standing on end, like those of a frightened cat. I heard soft footfalls behind me, but when I turned no one was there. Gasping with unnamed fear, I stood back against the branches of the yew tree, trying not to breathe too heavily.

I saw a dark shadow then, coming slowly, inexorably towards me. A misshapen figure in the dark. A limping, heavy-breathing figure as if from some nightmare world. And then a glimmer of light illuminated his face. It was twisted and blackened by smoke, and he looked like a monster . . . not the familiar young William I'd always known.

'William, I thought someone had called an ambulance for you.' I spoke nervously as he came to stand inches from my face. He smelt of smoke and dust, and he was like a stranger to me.

'I sent the ambulance away. I didn't want to go to hospital, you interfering witch!'

'But William, I saved your life. I dragged you out of the room and into the fresh air.'

'And you let the designs burn to ashes, you stupid woman. You denied me the chance to make a name for myself. I could kill you!'

He hit me. The blow was so hard that I fell back on to the dew wet grass. I saw William kneeling over me, his strong hands around my throat. My mind refused to accept the sense of it. I couldn't believe it. Young William was the one who had attacked me. He had been my enemy all along.

'You silly bitch.' His tone was venomous. 'Why did you have to buy the house and invite folk in to prance round the place at will? If you hadn't come here, I could have searched in peace.'

He shook me fiercely, his hands tightening around my neck. I was beginning to see sparkles of lights I couldn't draw in any breath

'You've finished me off,' William growled. 'My career is over. I'm an engineer, and I was writing a paper on Edwin

Mansel-Atherton. I could have made my name if it wasn't for your interference! Why didn't you go when I tried to make you? Now I'm going to have to kill you!'

I was beginning to lose consciousness as his fist slammed into my cheek. I was barely able to see, when a dark figure leapt on William dragging him away from me. And then Tom was there, beating the life out of William!

My head started spinning with all the chaos and the smoke and the shocks I suffered and I blacked out . . .

When I came to, the police were taking William away before Tom killed him. Tom knelt beside me and touched my face. 'All right, Riana my darling?'

I thought he was going to propose or at least declare his unending love. Instead he said, 'Where are the designs? Edwin's designs? Tell me, Riana. It's very important.'

My heart sank. 'They are in my studio, in my folder. Does it matter now?'

Tom was running like a deer across the lawn and into the house, and I put my hands over my mouth, unaware that my eye was swelling and turning black. My head was aching with the smoke and fumes, and my throat closing up so much that each breath was an agony. The worst of the whole horrible episode was that I now knew, without doubt, that Tom only wanted me for what he could get out of the designs.

I felt hands lift me to my feet, which helped me to drag more air into my lungs.

Eventually, I was led indoors by the faithful Mrs Ward, who'd come looking for me. 'My poor house,' I croaked.

'Aberglasney isn't badly damaged, Riana, so don't worry about the house. Just worry about your poor little face.'

As we got into the hall, Tom was coming down the staircase, my folder clutched awkwardly to his chest. He flung it open and, discarding my precious sketches, found the papers. 'These are the originals?' He waved them in my face.

'Yes. I did copies and stuffed them back up the chimney in the maids' room,' I said hoarsely. 'Those are the ones that burned.'

'You clever darling!' He kissed me soundly, and I winced

as his fingers touched my bruised cheek. He helped me move, rather shakily, to a chair, and Miss Grist came to my side just as I was about to accuse Tom of being a spy and a traitor. In truth, I didn't care about any of those things though. All that mattered was that he'd played fast and loose with my feelings to get the damned designs for a stupid engine design, which were probably useless now anyway.

'There will be an investigation, of course, but if I'm right then the discovery of these papers up the chimney proves Edwin Mansel-Atherton is an innocent man,' Miss Grist said. 'The maids died because the chimney was blocked. They would have died from carbon-monoxide poisoning,' she explained. But then she added, self-importantly, 'All this should have been reported to the police, of course.'

'The police were here plenty of times – including you, Miss Grist.' I was very aware of Tom standing beside me with the plans in his hands. 'You even tried to ruin my business – so you could search for the plans all the better, I presume?'

'Luckily for you I *was* here,' Miss Grist said, ignoring my accusation, 'or you might not be alive now,' Her tone implied I was stupid and interfering and if I had been strangled then it would have been better for everyone.' She sniffed and added cattily, 'It's well known that carbon-monoxide poisoning causes visions and hallucinations, by the way, Miss Evans. Ghosts indeed!'

At this, everyone – including Justin and Diane, the colonel and Mrs Ward, and all my other guests – gathered around me in support, and I felt ashamed of mistrusting any of them. I looked up at Tom. 'And what is your part in all this?' My tone was hostile. 'Are the designs that important to your precious American air force? More important than I am?'

'I had to get them, honey, don't you see? Even though searching for them myself put me in danger from my own colleagues. The designs make Carl's death the responsibility of the United States Army Air Force, you see. These plans – the originals – prove that the plane Carl was testing wasn't built correctly. The engineers didn't have Mr Mansel-Atherton's complete designs, and so they screwed it up.'

He kissed me, and I stared at him, breathless with love and bewilderment.

'There will be compensation due for his child.' Tom looked at Rosie as she stood, holding the baby close. 'You, Rosie, and your little one, will be cared for always.'

He put both his arms around me and kissed me again. I saw the colonel wink at Mrs Ward, and she had a smile on her thin face.

'More importantly –' Tom drew my attention – 'with the designs out of the way, I knew you would be safe, Riana my love. Not only British and American soldiers, but also an independent searcher wanted the plans badly – someone who wasn't afraid to kill. Until the drawings were found, you stood in the way. You were in danger all the time!'

'That independent someone being William, but why?'

'He'd taken an engineering degree, but he never really made the grade. He'd heard and read a little about the missing designs in an engineering magazine, and he wanted a good look at them. He probably photographed them before he put them in the chimney and lit a fire.'

'But they were the false ones I drew anyway. What good were they?'

'William wouldn't have known that. Not until he'd studied them in detail. He would have plagiarized the bits that he'd thought valuable so he could write a paper on it himself.'

I glanced at stony-faced Miss Grist. 'And this lady?' I asked Tom.

'We worked together on this case, that's all,' he said. 'We did it so we wouldn't blow Detective Grist's cover. Didn't she explain things when she took you to a police safe-house that night of your art exhibition? I knew that some soldiers had plans to search your house, and I wanted you out of the way and safe while they did so, so I asked Detective Grist and her colleagues to take care of you.' He folded me close to him again, and I saw Miss Grist's sneer. I remembered events rather differently. So it had been Miss Grist that night

who had interrogated me about my relationship with Tom
and threatened me with starvation! She had wanted Tom for
herself, but like a man he never saw it. I snuggled into Tom,
but Rosie's voice interrupted my delight and relief.

'Look, there's a ghost! There's really a ghost!' Rosie gasped
with fear.

I turned in Tom's arms, still holding on to him, and
laughed. 'That's only Beatrice,' I said. And then Beatrice
walked towards the big stone wall that surrounded the
garden leading to the graveyard beyond. She waved her
little hand and then walked right through a solid stone wall.

'She's gone home,' I said softly. 'Beatrice has at last been
able to join her dear Edwin.' And I felt a moment's grief
at losing her, but strangely no shock.

Then Tom turned my bruised and battered face gently
towards him and possessed my lips gently but commandingly. And as tears of happiness came to my eyes, my ghost
hunters – my true friends – cheered and clapped, and I
knew there was no need any more for words.

W9-AYG-319

WAYNE STATE UNIV.
Bookstores
8 64
ENGLISH
0205
$ 5.40
NOT RETURNABLE
IF LABEL REMOVED

THE COLLEGE ANTHOLOGY OF

BRITISH AND AMERICAN VERSE

The College Anthology of

BRITISH

and

AMERICAN

VERSE

EDITED BY

A. Kent Hieatt
Columbia University

William Park
Sarah Lawrence College

✦ ✦

Boston, Massachusetts

ALLYN AND BACON, INC.

1964

© COPYRIGHT, 1964, BY ALLYN AND BACON, INC., 150 TREMONT STREET, BOSTON. ALL RIGHTS RESERVED. NO PART OF THIS BOOK MAY BE REPRODUCED IN ANY FORM, BY MIMEOGRAPH OR ANY OTHER MEANS, WITHOUT PERMISSION IN WRITING FROM THE PUBLISHERS.

Library of Congress Catalog Card Number: 64-13963

PRINTED IN THE UNITED STATES OF AMERICA

Acknowledgments

The authors wish to thank the following copyright owners and publishers for permission to reprint certain poems:

MRS. GEORGE BAMBRIDGE—for "Tommy" from *Barrack Room Ballads*, "The King" from *The Seven Seas*, and "Recessional" from *The Five Nations*, by Rudyard Kipling.

CHATTO & WINDUS LTD.—for "The Groundhog" from *Collected Poems* by Richard Eberhart.

THE CUMMINGTON PRESS—for "A Coffee-House Lecture" and "The Lovemaker" by Robert Mezey. Copyright © 1961 by Robert Mezey. Selections reprinted by permission of the Cummington Press, Iowa City, Iowa.

J. M. DENT & SONS LTD.—for "The Force That Through the Green Fuse Drives the Flower," "Especially when the October wind," "A Refusal to Mourn the Death, by Fire, of a Child in London," "Fern Hill," and "Do not go gentle into that good night," by Dylan Thomas.

DOUBLEDAY & COMPANY, INC.—for "Tommy," "The King," and "Recessional" by Rudyard Kipling; for "Dolor," copyright © 1947 by Theodore Roethke, from *The Lost Son and Other Poems* by Theodore Roethke, reprinted by permission of Doubleday & Company, Inc.; for "I Knew a Woman," copyright 1954 by Theodore Roethke, from *Words for the Wind* by Theodore Roethke, reprinted by permission of Doubleday & Company, Inc.

FABER & FABER LTD.—for "The Love Song of J. Alfred Prufrock," "Morning at the Window," "Sweeney Among the Nightingales," "The Waste Land," "Journey of the Magi," and "Gerontion" from *Collected Poems 1909–1962* by T. S. Eliot; for "The Dry Salvages," from *Four Quartets* by T. S. Eliot; for "Musée des Beaux Arts," "Who's Who," "The Cultural Presupposition," "In Memory of W. B. Yeats," "The Unknown Citizen," and "In Praise of Limestone" from *Collected Poems* by W. H. Auden.

FARRAR, STRAUS & COMPANY—for "Words for Hart Crane" from *Life Studies* by Robert Lowell, reprinted by permission of Farrar, Straus & Company, Inc., copyright © 1956, 1959 by Robert Lowell.

[*iv*]

HARCOURT, BRACE & WORLD, INC.—for "The Love Song of J. Alfred Prufrock," "Morning at the Window," "Sweeney Among the Nightingales," "The Waste Land," "Journey of the Magi," and "Gerontion," from *Collected Poems 1909–1962* by T. S. Eliot, copyright, 1936, by Harcourt, Brace & World, Inc., © 1963, 1964, by T. S. Eliot, reprinted by permission of the publishers; for "The Dry Salvages," from *Four Quartets*, copyright, 1943, by T. S. Eliot, reprinted by permission of Harcourt, Brace & World, Inc.; for "Buffalo Bill's," copyright, 1923, 1951, by E. E. Cummings, reprinted from his volume *Poems 1923–1954* by permission of Harcourt, Brace & World, Inc.; for "anyone lived in a pretty how town," copyright, 1940, by E. E. Cummings, reprinted from his volume *Poems 1923–1954* by permission of Harcourt, Brace & World, Inc.; for "next to of course god" and "my sweet old etcetera," copyright, 1926, by Horace Liveright, renewed, 1954, by E. E. Cummings, reprinted from his volume *Poems 1923–1954* by permission of Harcourt, Brace & World, Inc.; for "New Year's Day," "Mr. Edwards and the Spider," "After the Surprising Conversions," and "Salem," from *Lord Weary's Castle*, copyright, 1944, 1946, by Robert Lowell, reprinted by permission of Harcourt, Brace & World, Inc.; for "Bell Speech" from *The Beautiful Changes and Other Poems*, copyright, 1947, by Richard Wilbur, reprinted by permission of Harcourt, Brace & World, Inc.; for "Death of a Toad" from *Ceremony and Other Poems*, copyright, 1948, 1949, 1950, by Richard Wilbur, reprinted by permission of Harcourt, Brace & World, Inc.

HARVARD UNIVERSITY PRESS—for "I like a look of agony," "Success is counted sweetest," "Exultation is the going," "To fight aloud is very brave," "If I shouldn't be alive," "I taste a liquor never brewed," "There's a certain slant of light," "I'm nobody! Who are you?" "The soul selects her own society," "I know that he exists," "After great pain a formal feeling comes," "Departed to judgment," "How many times these low feet staggered," "It was not death," "What soft cherubic creatures," "The first day's night had come," "Twas like a maelstrom with a notch," "I died for beauty," "I heard a fly buzz when I died," "I like to see it lap the miles," "It dropped so low," "Because I could not stop for death," "She rose to his require-ment," "Presentiment is that long shadow on the lawn," "A narrow fellow in the grass," "Crumbling is not an instant's act," "He preached upon 'breadth' till it argued him narrow," "Those dying then," "Apparently with no surprise," "Elysium is as far to," "A clock stopped," "Tell all the truth," "After a hundred years," "I felt a funeral in my brain," "I had not minded walls," "A bird came down the walk," "Finding is the first act," and "They called me to the window," by Emily Dickinson, reprinted by permission of the publishers and the Trustees of Amherst College from *The Poems of Emily Dickinson*, Cambridge, Mass.: The Belknap Press of Harvard University Press, copyright, 1951, 1955, by The President and Fellows of Harvard College.

HOLT, RINEHART AND WINSTON—for "The Wood-Pile," "Stopping by Woods on a Snowy Evening," "Fire and Ice," "Desert Place," "'Out, Out—'," "Neither Far Out Nor In Deep," "Range-Finding," "The Most of It," "Directive," "To Earth-ward," "The Silken Tent," "The Cow in Apple Time," "Provide, Provide," "The Egg and the Machine," "Design," and "All Revelation" from the *Complete Poems of Robert Frost*, copyright 1916, 1921, 1923, 1928, 1930, 1939, 1947, by Holt, Rinehart and Winston, Inc., copyright 1936, 1942 by Robert Frost, copyright renewed 1944, 1951, © 1956 by Robert Frost, reprinted by permission of Holt, Rinehart and Winston, Inc.; for "To an Athlete Dying Young," "'Terence, this is Stupid Stuff,'" "On Wenlock Edge," and "Think no more, lad: be jolly," from *A Shropshire Lad*, authorised edition, from *Complete Poems* by A. E. Housman, copyright © 1959 by Holt, Rinehart and Winston, Inc., reprinted by permission of Holt, Rinehart and Winston, Inc.; for "Eight O'Clock," and "Easter Hymn," from *Complete Poems* by A. E. Housman, copyright 1922 by Holt, Rinehart and Winston,

Inc., copyright 1936 by Barclays Bank Ltd., copyright renewed 1950 by Barclays Bank Ltd., reprinted by permission of Holt, Rinehart and Winston, Inc.

HOUGHTON MIFFLIN COMPANY—for "The Silent Slain" from *Collected Poems of Archibald MacLeish*, reprinted by permission of Houghton Mifflin Company; for "For God While Sleeping" from *All My Pretty Ones* by Anne Sexton, reprinted by permission of Houghton Mifflin Company.

INTERNATIONAL AUTHORS, N.V.—for "Ogres and Pygmies" and "The Portrait" from *Collected Poems* by Robert Graves, © 1955, 1959, International Authors N.V., published by Doubleday & Co. Inc., and Cassell & Co. Ltd.

ALFRED A. KNOPF, INC.—for "Connoisseur of Chaos," "The Glass of Water," and "The Sense of the Sleight-of-Hand Man," reprinted from *The Collected Poems of Wallace Stevens* by permission of Alfred A. Knopf, Inc., copyright 1942, by Wallace Stevens; for "Orpheus," and "April Inventory," reprinted from *Heart's Needle* by W. D. Snodgrass by permission of Alfred A. Knopf, Inc., copyright, 1956, © 1959 by W. D. Snodgrass.

LITTLE, BROWN AND CO.—for "After great pain a formal feeling comes," and "I had not minded walls," by Emily Dickinson, copyright 1929, © 1957 by Mary L. Hampson, from *The Complete Poems of Emily Dickinson*, reprinted by permission of Little, Brown and Co.

LIVERIGHT PUBLISHING CORPORATION—for "To Brooklyn Bridge," "Legend," "Voyages I," and "Voyages VI" from *The Collected Poems of Hart Crane*, by permission of Liveright Publishers, N.Y., copyright © R, 1961, by Liveright Publishing Corp.

THE MACMILLAN COMPANY—for "An Irish Airman Foresees His Death," by William Butler Yeats, reprinted with permission of the publisher from *Collected Poems* by William Butler Yeats, copyright 1919 by The Macmillan Company, renewed 1946 by Bertha Georgie Yeats; for "Easter 1916," "The Second Coming," and "A Prayer for my Daughter," reprinted with permission of the publisher from *Collected Poems* by William Butler Yeats, copyright 1924 by The Macmillan Company, renewed 1952 by Bertha Georgie Yeats; for "Sailing to Byzantium," "Leda and the Swan," "Among School Children," and "Two Songs from a Play," reprinted with permission of the publisher from *Collected Poems* by William Butler Yeats, copyright 1928 by The Macmillan Company, renewed 1956 by Georgie Yeats; for "Dialogue of Self and Soul," "Crazy Jane Talks with the Bishop," "In memory of Eva Gore-Booth and Con Markiewicz," and "Byzantium" reprinted from *Collected Poems* by William Butler Yeats with permission of the publisher, copyright 1933 by The Macmillan Company, renewed 1961 by Bertha Georgie Yeats; for "Neutral Tones," "I Look into My Glass," "Channel Firing," "The Ruined Maid," and "Hap" reprinted with permission of the publisher from *Collected Poems* by Thomas Hardy, copyright 1925 by The Macmillan Company; for "Mr. Flood's Party," reprinted with permission of The Macmillan Company from *Collected Poems* by E. A. Robinson, copyright 1921 by E. A. Robinson, renewed 1949 by Ruth Nivison; for "New England," reprinted with permission of The Macmillan Company from *Collected Poems* by E. A. Robinson, copyright 1925 by E. A. Robinson, renewed 1952 by Ruth Nivison and Barbara R. Holt; for "A Grave," and "Poetry," reprinted with permission of the publisher from *Collected Poems* by Marianne Moore, copyright 1935 by Marianne Moore.

THE MACMILLAN COMPANY OF CANADA LTD.—for "Tommy" from *Barrack Room Ballads*, "The King" from *The Seven Seas*, and "Recessional" from *The Five Nations* by Rudyard Kipling, reprinted by permission of Mrs. George Bambridge, The Macmillan Company of Canada Ltd., and Messrs. Methuen & Co. Ltd.; for

"The Second Coming," "Sailing to Byzantium," "Leda and the Swan," "Crazy Jane Talks with the Bishop," "Among School Children," "Byzantium," "Two Songs from a Play," "In memory of Eva Gore-Booth and Con Markiewicz," "Easter 1916," "A Prayer for my Daughter," "Dialogue of Self and Soul," and "An Irish Airman Foresees His Death," from the *Collected Poems of W. B. Yeats*, reprinted by permission of Mrs. W. B. Yeats, The Macmillan Company of Canada Ltd., and Messrs. Macmillan & Co. Ltd.; for "Neutral Tones," "I Look into My Glass," "Channel Firing," "The Ruined Maid," and "Hap" reprinted from *Collected Poems of Thomas Hardy* by permission of the Trustees of the Hardy Estate, Macmillan & Co. Ltd., London, and The Macmillan Company of Canada Limited.

THE MARVELL PRESS—for "Deceptions" by Philip Larkin, reprinted from *The Less Deceived* by permission of The Marvell Press, Hessle, Yorkshire, England.

NEW DIRECTIONS, PUBLISHERS—for "Spring and All," "The Jungle," "El Hombre," "Poem (As the cat)" and "To Elsie," from *The Collected Earlier Poems of William Carlos Williams*, copyright 1938, 1951, by William Carlos Williams, reprinted by permission of New Directions, Publishers; for "Marriage" from *The Happy Birthday of Death* by Gregory Corso © 1960 by New Directions, reprinted by permission of New Directions, Publishers; for "Hugh Selwyn Mauberley," "In a Station of the Metro," "The Garden," "Portrait d'Une Femme," "The Lake Isle," "The River Merchant's Wife: A Letter" from *Personae: The Collected Poems of Ezra Pound*, copyright 1926, 1954 by Ezra Pound, reprinted by permission of New Directions, Publishers; for "A Refusal to Mourn the Death, by Fire, of a Child in London," "The Force That Through the Green Fuse," "Especially when the October Wind," "Fern Hill," "Do Not Go Gentle" from *The Collected Poems of Dylan Thomas*, copyright © 1957 by New Directions, Publishers, reprinted by permission of New Directions, Publishers.

OXFORD UNIVERSITY PRESS, INC.—for "The Groundhog" from *Collected Poems 1930–1960* by Richard Eberhart, © 1960 by Richard Eberhart, reprinted by permission of Oxford University Press, Inc.; for "God's Grandeur," "Pied Beauty," "The Windhover," "Carrion Comfort," "No Worst, There Is None," "Thou Art Indeed Just, Lord," "That Nature Is a Heraclitean Fire," and "Inversnaid," from *Poems of Gerard Manley Hopkins*, Third Edition, edited by W. H. Gardner, copyright 1948 by Oxford University Press, Inc., reprinted by permission.

RANDOM HOUSE, INC.—for "In Praise of Limestone," copyright 1951 by W. H. Auden, reprinted from *Nones* by W. H. Auden, by permission of Random House, Inc.; for "In Memory of W. B. Yeats," "Musée des Beaux Arts," "The Unknown Citizen," copyright 1960 by W. H. Auden, reprinted from *The Collected Poetry of W. H. Auden*, by permission of Random House, Inc.; for "Who's Who," and "The Cultural Presupposition," copyright 1945 by W. H. Auden, reprinted from *The Collected Poetry of W. H. Auden*, by permission of Random House, Inc.

CHARLES SCRIBNER'S SONS—for "Ode to the Confederate Dead" and "Mr. Pope" reprinted with the permission of Charles Scribner's Sons from *Poems* by Allen Tate, copyright 1932 Charles Scribner's Sons, renewal copyright © 1960, Allen Tate; for "The Clerks" reprinted with the permission of Charles Scribner's Sons from *The Children of the Night* by Edwin Arlington Robinson (Charles Scribner's Sons, 1897).

THE SECOND COMING MAGAZINE—for "A Letter from a Friend" by John N. Morris, which first appeared in *The Second Coming Magazine*, published at 200 West 107th Street, New York City.

THE SEWANEE REVIEW—for "Shh! The Professor is Sleeping" by John N. Morris, which was first printed in *The Sewanee Review*, Summer 1961, copyright © 1961 by The University of the South.

THE SOCIETY OF AUTHORS—for "To an Athlete Dying Young," "On Wenlock Edge," "Think no more, lad," "Terence, this is Stupid Stuff," "Eight O'Clock," and "Easter Hymn" by A. E. Housman, reprinted by permission of The Society of Authors as the literary representative of the estate of the late A. E. Housman and Messrs. Jonathan Cape, Ltd., publishers of A. E. Housman's *Collected Poems.*

WESLEYAN UNIVERSITY PRESS—for "At the Slackening of the Tide," copyright © 1957 by James Wright, reprinted from *Saint Judas* by James Wright, by permission of the Wesleyan University Press.

Preface

This book is a very comprehensive one-volume anthology of poetry which aims at going beyond the usual collection in more than size. Its editors have designed it to meet, within the bounds of economy, as many known needs as could be made consistent with each other, and to meet certain of the most outstanding of these needs better than they have been met before. We consequently believe that *The College Anthology* is effective both at the freshman level and at other undergraduate levels where poetry forms a large part of the subject matter.

Its features are the following: a mainly chronological arrangement; a large and representative selection from two dozen major poets; a supplement, in each period, of poems by various other hands; a very full gathering of modern poetry; a policy of no excerpts (of which one result is that no poem longer than 818 lines is represented); a tendency to sacrifice the representative poem for what we think is the more excellent one when we believe that the two relevant criteria evidently conflict; and an apparatus innocent of critical analysis and restricted to (1) responsible but noninterpretive annotation, (2) a technical appendix, and (3) an index.

The fault usually recognized in older anthologies is that in trying to represent many poets they really represented none: such books gave little space to each poet and excerpted remorselessly from longer poems. Certainly a better method, followed in some recent works, is to concentrate on a small number of major poets so as to give each an ample representation. This kind of inclusiveness has been one of our aims also: on the basis of what is included here, a reader should be able to form a sound idea of the poetic or lyric personality of any of two dozen major poets. He can begin to make those cross references of the imagination and those precise mental comparisons which are so valuable a part of studying one man's work, and he should be able to use the texts here as the basis for a critical essay and as a starting place for the research paper.

But in our experience this kind of selection does not satisfy one of the real needs in many freshman classes, let alone more advanced ones. A teacher often feels the importance of offering one or another kind of poetic experience or excellence which the most usually studied poets do not happen to exemplify. He may not want to consider at length all the varieties of matter which are available in the popular ballads, in Campion, Crashaw, the Cavaliers, Swift, Landor, William Morris, or Kipling, but he is often in the position of wishing to show the one thing which each of them does uniquely, or does better than anyone else. Partly for this reason we have taken some pages from the older type of anthology, and have supplemented the fuller selections in each historical period with isolated poems of particular interest or with larger numbers of poems by poets whom some of us, some of the time, cannot do without. Particularly in modern poetry it has seemed to us that a broad spectrum needs representation in a general anthology. We have ranged widely here, although we are compelled to admit that our choices are sometimes arbitrary because of the length of poems which we wished to include but could not. We have tried to deal reverentially, too, with the already classic modern figures, and not to let our choices be influenced by the economic considerations which come to the fore in printing their poems.

In fine, part of our rationale has been radical inclusiveness on the one side, radical selectivity on the other, because we think that the needs in every classroom are multiple and complex to an extent not usually allowed for, and because anything but a radical option results in just another anthology or in an unmanageably bulky and expensive volume. Admittedly, in trying to satisfy a number of theoretical needs this anthology must be long. But there is an additional pragmatic reason for its being so. The array of perfectly licit aims among teachers who discuss British and American poetry in college classes—even in one course running to a number of sections—is so bewildering that if one is going to lodge them all, one might as well start one's planning with an extensive structure. Although there are excellent works containing a limited selection of great poetry through which one teacher may convey all that a class can usefully absorb in a given time, the selection often does not suit his brother-teacher, or even the same teacher at another time. It is true that nothing provides a broad enough roof to shelter every heart's desire; but, in our teaching and administrative experience, having as much material to work with as is practically obtainable means inestimable dividends in flexibility, aggressive experimentalism, and morale.

One ingredient that we have not included, however, is a critical apparatus. Although there are well-thought-out anthologies which by critical discussion may open an interesting and fairly smooth path towards the central secrets, the present book is for those who wish to choose their own direction, and its organization is humbly chronological.

Much the same may be said of our avoidance of excerpts. Some will say that we have lost more than we have gained by making Chaucer,

Milton, Byron, and Tennyson suffer in consequence, but we have consoled ourselves with the reflection that in all but one of these cases cheap
paperback reprints are presently available.

Our policy on annotations has been to explain scrupulously any
reference within a poem to information which a reader may not possess,
unless we ourselves lack the information and the relevant scholarship
does not provide it. But except in desperate cases we have avoided the
interpretation of meaning, the description of immediate motivating
circumstances in the poet's life or world-view, and the generalization
connecting the poem with its milieu, because we have found these, more
often than not, to be pseudo-explanations and constrictions of the
imagination for the beginner, whose first task and joy should be to come
to grips with a poem's internal logic.

The textual state of any general anthology must always lag behind
the very latest results of specialist scholarship, but we have taken pains to
reproduce or to conflate the best texts available. Generally we have
modified pre-nineteenth-century matter to accord with modern usage,
and have tried to follow the author's detailed intentions for anything
later. For purposes of exemplification we have retained sixteenth-,
seventeenth-, and eighteenth-century pointing and spelling in a few cases
(all noted), and we have followed the manuscript version of Emily
Dickinson's poems, as established by Thomas Johnson.

We thank our wives for their fortitude and help, our friends and
colleagues for their advice, and Miss Deirdre Bodkin and Mrs. Leonard
Nodelman for vigilant typing and clerkship.

Contents

[xiii]

THE RENAISSANCE: SIXTEENTH CENTURY

Contents [*xv*

BEN JONSON

ROBERT HERRICK

THE ROMANTICS

THE MODERNS

THE COLLEGE ANTHOLOGY OF
BRITISH AND AMERICAN VERSE

Medieval Verse;
Popular Ballads

❧ ❧ ❧

Western Wind

Western wind, when wilt thou blow?
The small rain down can rain.
Christ, that my love were in my arms,
And I in my bed again.

Spring Has Come to Town with Love

Lenten ys come with love to toune,
With blosmen and with briddes roune,°   *birdsong*
    That al this blisse bryngeth,
Dayes-yës° in thise dales,   *daisies*
5 Notes sweete of nyghtegales;
    Uch° fowl song singeth.   *each*
The threstelcoc him threteth oo;

Western Wind: The text used is modernized.   1. **Lenten:** Lent falls in the spring.
                                              7. **him . . . oo:** chatters constantly.

[1]

Away is huere° wynter woo,   *their*
When woderove springeth.
10 Thise fowles singeth ferly fele
And wlyteth on huere wynne wele,
That al the wode° ryngeth.   *wood*

The rose rayleth hire rode;
The leves on the lyghte wode
15   Waxen al with wille.
The mone mandeth hire bleo;
The lilie is lossom to seo,
The fenyl° ant the fille.°   *fennel | thyme (?)*
Woweth° thise wilde drakes;   *woo*
20 Miles murgeth huere makes,
On strem that striketh° stille.   *flows*
Mody meneth, so doth mo.
Ichot ycham on of tho
For love that liketh ille.

25 The mone mandeth hire lyght;
So doth the semly sonne bryght,
When briddes singeth breme.°   *loudly*
Dewes donketh the dounes,
Deores with huere derne rounes,
30   Domes forte deme.
Wormes° woweth under cloude;°   *snakes | earth, clod*
Wymmen waxeth wounder proude,
So wel hit wol hem seme.
Yef me shal wonte wille of on,
35 This wunne weole I wole forgon,
Ant wyght in wode be fleme.

9. **woderove:** woodruff, small plant with pleasant odor.
10. **ferly fele:** miraculously many.
11. **wlyteth . . . wele:** warble of their happiness.
13. **rayleth . . . rode:** arrays her coloring, face.
15. **Waxen . . . wille:** grow joyfully.
16. **mandeth . . . bleo:** sends forth her countenance.
17. **lossom to seo:** lovely to see.
20. **Miles . . . makes:** Males (?) gladden their mates.
22. **Mody . . . mo:** The mournful complain; so do others.
23–24. **Ichot . . . ille:** I know that I am one of those who are unhappy on account of love.
28. **donketh . . . dounes:** dampen the hills.
29–30. **Deores . . . deme:** Animals utter soft sounds in secret, to come to settlements together (?).
33. **So . . . seme:** They seem to themselves so well off.
34–36. **Yef . . . fleme:** If I am to lack my will with one of them, I will forgo this joyfulness [around me] and be an exiled man in the wood.

I Sing of a Maiden

I sing of a maiden
    That is makeles,
King of all kings
    To° her sone sche ches.°   *as | chose*

5 He cam also° stille   *as*
    There° his moder was,   *where*
As dew in Aprille
    That falleth on the grass.

He cam also stille
10   To his moderes bour,
As dew in Aprille
    That falleth on the flour.

He cam also stille
    There his moder lay,
15 As dew in Aprille
    That falleth on the spray.°   *branch*

Moder and maiden
    Was never non but sche;
Wel may swich° a lady   *such*
20   Goddes moder be.

Blacksmiths

Swart smeked smithes, smatered° with smoke,   *smeared*
Drive me to deeth with din of here dintes.°   *blows*
Swich noise on nightes ne herde men never,
What knavene° cry and clatering of knockes.   *boys', helpers'*
5 The cammede kongons cryen after "Cole, cole!"
And blowen here bellewes that° al here brain brestes.°   *so that |*
                                             bursts, splits
"Huf, puf," saith that oon, "haf, paf," that other.
They spitten and sprawlen and spellen° many spelles;°   *recite | charms*
They gnawen and gnasshen, they grones togidere,

2. **makeles:** (1) without a husband; (2) without peer; (3) without spot.
10. **bour:** private room, bedchamber.

1. **Swart smeked:** stained black with smoke ("smoked").
5. **cammede kongons:** flat-nosed rascals.

10 And holden hem hote with here hard hamers.
    Of a bole-hide° been here barm-felles,°   *bullhide | aprons*
    Here shankes been shakeled for the fire-flunderes.
    Hevy hamres they han that hard been handled,
    Stark° strokes they striken on a steeled stokke.   *strong*
15 "Lus, bus, las, das," routen by rowe—
    Swich doleful a dreem° the devil it todrive.°   *music | drive off*
    The maister longeth a litel and lassheth a lesse,
    Twineth hem twain and toucheth a treble.
    "Tik, tak, hik, hak, tiket, taket, tik, tak,
20 Lus, bus, lus, das!" Swich lif they leden,
    Alle clothe-meres, Crist hem give sorwe!
    May no man for bren-wateres on night han his rest.

GEOFFREY CHAUCER [1343–1400]

To Rosemond

    Madame, ye been of alle beautee shrine
    As fer as cercled is the mapemounde:
    For as the crystal glorious ye shine,
    And like ruby been youre cheekes rounde.
5   Therwith ye been so merye and so jocounde
    That at a revel whan that I see you daunce
    It is an oinement unto my wounde,
    Though ye to me ne do no daliaunce.

    For though I weepe of teres ful a tine,°   *vat*
10 Yet may that wo myn herte nat confounde;
    Youre semy vois, that ye so smal outtwine,
    Maketh my thought in joye and blis habounde:°   *abound*
    So curteisly I go with love bounde
    That to myself I saye in my penaunce,°   *torment*

10. **holden hem:** keep themselves.
12. **Here ... flunderes:** Their legs are covered against the sparks.
14. **stokke:** stump, block, anvil.
15. **routen by rowe:** sing in turn.
17–18. **The maister ... treble:** The master smith lengthens a half-note and bashes out a quarter-note, repeats both and reaches up to a treble (??).
20–21. **Swich ... sorwe:** They lead such a life, all those mare-clothers (horseshoers), may Christ give them sorrow!
22. **May ... rest:** No one may have his rest at night because of the water-burners (making water seethe and steam as they temper metal in it).

2. **As ... mapemounde:** to the utmost circumference of the round map of the world.
8. **Though ... daliaunce:** though you pay me no attention.
11. **Youre ... outtwine:** your little voice, that you so softly spin out.

15 "Suffiseth me to love you, Rosemounde,
   Though ye to me ne do no daliaunce."

   Was nevere pik walwed in galauntine
   As I in love am walwed and ywounde,°   *entangled*
   For which ful ofte I of myself divine°   *guess*
20 That I am trewe Tristam the secounde;
   My love may not refreide nor affounde;
   I brenne° ay in amorous plesaunce: *burn*
   Do what you list, I wol youre thral° be founde, *slave*
   Though ye to me ne do no daliaunce.

A Ballade Against Woman Inconstant

   Madame, for your newefangelnesse,
   Many a servaunt° have ye put out of grace.   *lover*
   I take my leve of your unstedfastnesse,
   For wel I wot, whyl ye have lyves space,
5 Ye can not love ful half yeer in a place,
   To newe thing your lust is ay so kene;
   In stede of blew, thus may ye were al grene.

   Right as a mirour nothing may enpresse,
   But, lightly as it cometh, so mot it pace,
10 So fareth your love, your werkes bereth witnesse.
   Ther is no feith that may your herte enbrace;
   But, as a wedercok,° that turneth his face   *weathercock*
   With every wind, ye fare, and that is sene;° *seen*
   In stede of blew, thus may ye were al grene.

15 Ye might be shryned, for your brotelnesse,
   Bet than Dalyda, Creseyde or Candace;

17. **Was . . . galauntine:** There was never a pike so submerged in galantine sauce.
20. **trewe Tristam:** faithful Tristram, a knight who was constant in love to Queen Isolt.
21. **refreide . . . affounde:** cool or founder.

Ballade: Despite the Chaucerian character of this poem, it is not completely certain that Chaucer wrote it.
4. **I . . . space:** I know that for as long as you live . . .

5. **in a place:** in one spot.
6. **your . . . kene:** your liking is always so strong.
7. **In . . . grene:** Thus, instead of blue, you may wear nothing but green (blue was the color of constancy, green of new love and fickleness).
8. **Right . . . enpresse:** just as nothing can leave its image on a mirror.
15–16. **Ye . . . Candace:** You might be enshrined as an image of inconstancy more suitably than Delilah, Cressida, or Candace (all signally unfaithful in famous instances).

For ever in chaunging stant your sikernesse;
That tache may no wight fro your herte arace.
If ye lese oon, ye can wel tweyn purchace;
20 Al light for somer (ye woot wel what I mene)
In stede of blew, thus may ye were al grene.

Complaint to His Purse

To you, my purs, and to noon other wight,°   *person*
Complaine I, for ye be my lady dere.
I am so sory, now that ye be light,
For certes, but if ye make me hevy cheere,
5 Me were as lief be laid upon my beere;
For which unto youre mercy thus I crye:
Beeth hevy again, or elles moot° I die.   *must*

Now voucheth sauf this day er it be night
That I of you the blisful soun° may heere,   *sound*
10 Or see youre colour, lik the sonne bright,
That of yelownesse hadde nevere peere.°   *equal*
Ye be my lif, ye be myn hertes steere,°   *guide, rudder*
Queene of confort and of good compaignye:
Beeth hevy again, or elles moot I die.

15 Ye purs, that been to me my lives light
And saviour, as in this world down here,
Out of this tonne helpe me thurgh your might,
Sith that ye wol nat be my tresorere;
For I am shave as neigh° as any frere.   *close*
20 But yet I praye unto youre curteisye:
Beeth hevy again, or elles moot I die.

Lenvoy° de Chaucer   *the envoy*

O conquerour of Brutus Albioun,

17. For . . . sikernesse: What is reliable about you is your changeability.
18. That . . . arace: No one may erase that spot from your heart.
19. If . . . purchace: If you lose one, you can indeed gain two.
20. Al . . . mene: dressed lightly for summer (you well know what I mean) . . .

4. certes . . . cheere: certainly, unless you show me a heavy look . . .

5. Me . . . lief: I would as soon ("beere": bier).
8. voucheth . . . er: Now vouchsafe this day, before . . .
15. lives light: light of my life.
17. tonne: tun, large cask (i.e., predicament).
22. conquerour . . . Albioun: conqueror of England (Henry IV had just seized the throne). Brutus was the legendary founder of Britain.

Which that by line and free eleccioun
Been verray king, this song to you I sende:
25 And ye, that mowen° alle oure harmes amende,   *may*
    Have minde upon my supplicacioun.

J O H N   S K E L T O N [1406?–1529]

Woefully arrayed

    Woefully arrayed,
      My blood, man,
      For thee ran,
    It may not be nay'd:
5   My body blo° and wan,   *ashy*
    Woefully arrayed.

Behold me, I pray thee, with all thy whole reason,
And be not so hard-hearted, and for this encheason,°   *reason*
Sith° I for thy soul sake was slain in good season,   *since*
10 Beguiled and betrayéd by Judas' false treason:
      Unkindly entreated,°   *treated*
      With sharp cord sore freted,
      The Jewes me threted:
    They mowéd,° they grinnéd, they scornéd me,   *grimaced*
15 Condemnéd to death, as thou mayest see,
    Woefully arrayed.

Thus naked am I nailéd, O man, for thy sake!
I love thee, then love me; why sleepest thou? awake!
Remember my tender heart-root for thee brake,
20 With painès my veinès constrainéd to crake:°   *break*
      Thus tuggéd to and fro,
      Thus wrappéd all in woe,
      Whereas never man was so,
    Entreated thus in most cruel wise,
25 Was like a lamb offered in sacrifice,
    Woefully arrayed.

Of sharp thorn I have worn a crown on my head,
So painéd, so strainéd, so rueful, so red,
Thus bobbéd, thus robbéd, thus for thy love dead,

23. **free eleccioun:** uncompelled choice (of   9. **in good season:** promptly.
Parliament).

30　Unfeignéd I deignéd my blood for to shed:
　　　My feet and handès sore
　　　The sturdy nailès bore:
　　　What might I suffer more
　　　Than I have done, O man, for thee?
35　　Come when thou list, welcome to me,
　　　Woefully arrayed.

　　Of recórd thy good Lord I have been and shall be:
　　I am thine, thou art mine, my brother I call thee.
　　Thee love I entirely—see what is befall'n me!
40　Sore beating, sore threating, to make thee, man, all free:
　　　Why art thou unkind?
　　　Why hast not me in mind?
　　　Come yet and thou shalt find
　　　Mine endless mercy and grace—
45　　See how a spear my heart did race,°　　　　　　*destroy*
　　　Woefully arrayed.

　　Dear brother, no other thing I of thee desire
　　But give me thine heart free to reward mine hire:
　　I wrought thee, I bought thee from éternal fire:
50　I pray thee array thee toward my high empíre
　　　Above the orient,°　　　　　　　　　　　　*sun*
　　　Whereof I am regent,
　　　Lord God omnipotent,
　　　With me to reign in endless wealth:
55　　Remember, man, thy soulès health.

　　　Woefully arrayed,
　　　　My blood, man,
　　　　For thee ran,
　　　It may not be nay'd:
60　　　My body blo and wan,
　　　Woefully arrayed.

Lord Randal

"O where hae ye been, Lord Randal, my son?
O where hae ye been, my handsome young man?"
　"I hae been to the wild wood; mother, make my bed soon,
　For I'm weary wi hunting, and fain wald lie down."

4. **fain wald:** gladly would.

5 "Where gat ye your dinner, Lord Randal, my son?
Where gat ye your dinner, my handsome young man?"
  "I dined wi my true love; mother, make my bed soon,
  For I'm weary wi hunting, and fain wald lie down."

  "What gat ye to your dinner, Lord Randal, my son?
10 What gat ye to° your dinner, my handsome young man?"   *for*
  "I gat eels boiled in broo;° mother, make my bed soon,   *broth*
  For I'm weary wi hunting, and fain wald lie down."

  "What became of your bloodhounds, Lord Randal, my son?
What became of your bloodhounds, my handsome young man?"
15   "O they swelld and they died; mother, make my bed soon,
  For I'm weary wi hunting, and fain wald lie down."

  "O I fear ye are poisond, Lord Randal, my son!
O I fear ye are poisond, my handsome young man!"
  "O yes! I am poisond; mother, make my bed soon,
20   For I'm sick at the heart, and I fain wald lie down."

Edward

"Why dois your brand sae drap wi bluid,
    Edward, Edward,
Why dois your brand sae drap wi bluid,
    And why sae sad gang° yee O?"   *go, walk*
5 "O I hae killed my hauke sae guid,
    Mither, mither,
O I hae killed my hauke sae guid,
    And I had nae mair° bot hee O."   *more*

"Your haukis° bluid was nevir sae reid,°   *hawk's / red*
10   Edward, Edward,
Your haukis bluid was never sae reid,
    My deir son I tell thee O."
"O I hae killed my reid-roan steid,
    Mither, mither,
15 O I hae killed my reid-roan steid,
    That erst° was sae fair and frie O."   *before*

"Your steid was auld,° and ye hae gat mair,   *old*
    Edward, Edward,

1. **Why . . . bluid:** Why does your sword
so drip with blood?

Your steid was auld, and ye hae gat mair,
20   Sum other dule ye drie O."
"O I hae killed my fadir deir,
      Mither, mither,
O I hae killed my fadir deir,
   Alas, and wae° is mee O!"   *woe*

25 "And whatten penance wul ye drie for that,
      Edward, Edward,
And whatten penance wul ye drie for that?
   My deir son, now tell me O."
"Ile set my feit° in yonder boat,   *feet*
30   Mither, mither,
Ile set my feit in yonder boat,
   And Ile fare ovir the sea O."

"And what wul ye doe wi your towirs and your ha,°   *hall*
      Edward, Edward,
35 And what wul ye doe wi your towirs and your ha,
   That were sae fair to see O?"
"Ile let thame stand tul they doun fa,°   *fall*
      Mither, mither,
Ile let thame stand tul they doun fa,
40   For here nevir mair maun° I bee O."   *must*

"And what wul ye leive to your bairns° and your wife,   *children*
      Edward, Edward,
And what wul ye leive to your bairns and your wife,
   Whan ye gang ovir the sea O?"
45 "The warldis° room, late them beg thrae life,   *world's*
      Mither, mither,
The warldis room, late them beg thrae life,
   For thame nevir mair wul I see O."

"And what wul ye leive to your ain mither dear,
50   Edward, Edward,
And what wul ye leive to your ain mither dear?
   My deir son, now tell me O."
"The curse of hell frae me sall° ye beir,   *shall*
      Mither, mither,
55 The curse of hell frae me sall ye beir,
   Sic° counseils ye gave to me O."   *such*

20. **dule . . . drie O:** sorrow you suffer.

Barbara Allan

It was in and about the Martinmas time,
  When the green leaves were a falling,
That Sir John Graeme, in the West Country,
  Fell in love with Barbara Allan.

5 He sent his man down through the town,
  To the place where she was dwelling:
"O haste and come to my master dear,
  Gin° ye be Barbara Allan."   *if*

O hooly, hooly rose she up,
10   To the place where he was lying,
And when she drew the curtain by,
  "Young man, I think you're dying."

"O it's I'm sick, and very, very sick,
  And 't is a' for° Barbara Allan:"   *all for*
15 "O the better for me ye's° never be,   *you shall*
  Tho your heart's blood were a spilling.

"O dinna ye mind, young man," said she,
  "When ye was in the tavern a drinking,
That ye made the healths gae° round and round,   *go*
20   And slighted Barbara Allan?"

He turned his face unto the wall,
  And death was with him dealing:
"Adieu, adieu, my dear friends all,
  And be kind to Barbara Allan."

25 And slowly, slowly raise she up,
  And slowly, slowly left him,
And sighing said, she coud not stay,
  Since death of life had reft him.

She had not gane° a mile but twa,°   *gone / two*
30   When she heard the dead-bell ringing,
And every jow° that the dead-bell geid,°   *stroke / gave*
  It cry'd, Woe to Barbara Allan!

"O mother, mother, make my bed!
  O make it saft° and narrow!   *soft*
35 Since my love died for me to-day,
  I'll die for him to-morrow."

1. **Martinmas:** Nov. 11.   16. **spilling:** being destroyed.
9. **hooly:** wholly (*slowly* in another version).

The Three Ravens

There were three ravens sat on a tree,
  Downe a downe, hay downe, hay downe
There were three ravens sat on a tree,
  With a downe.
5 There were three ravens sat on a tree,
They were as blacke as they might be.
  With a downe derrie, derrie, derrie, downe, downe.

The one of them said to his mate,
"Where shall we our breakfast take?"

10 "Down in yonder greene field,
There lies a knight slain under his shield.

"His hounds they lie downe at his feete,
So well they can their master keepe.

"His haukes they flie so eagerly,
15 There's no fowle dare him come nie."°   nigh, near

Downe there comes a fallow doe,
As great with yong as she might goe.

She lift up his bloudy hed,
And kist his wounds that were so red.

20 She got him up upon her backe,
And carried him to earthen lake.

She buried him before the prime,
She was dead herselfe ere even-song time.

Sir Patrick Spens

The king sits in Dumferling toune,
  Drinking the blude-reid wine:
"O whar will I get guid sailor,
  To sail this schip of mine?"

5 Up and spak an eldern° knicht,   old
  Sat at the kings richt kne:
"Sir Patrick Spens is the best sailor,
  That sails upon the se."

2. **Downe . . . downe:** Italicized lines are the refrain. They are read or sung in the same pattern in each following stanza.

21. **earthen lake:** burial place (This may be a corruption of an original place-name).
22. **prime:** first hour of morning.

The king has written a braid° letter,   *broad, stately*
10   And signd it wi his hand,
And sent it to Sir Patrick Spence,
    Was walking on the sand.

The first line that Sir Patrick red,
    A loud lauch lauched he;
15 The next line that Sir Patrick red,
    The teir blinded his ee.°   *eye*

"O wha° is this has don this deid,°   *who | deed*
    This ill deid don to me,
To send me out this time o' the yeir,
20   To sail upon the se!

"Mak hast, mak haste, my mirry men all,
    Our guid schip sails the morne":
"O say na sae,° my master deir,   *so*
    For I feir a deadlie storme.

25 "Late, late yestreen° I saw the new moone,   *yesterday evening*
    Wi the auld moon in hir arme,
And I feir, I feir, my deir master,
    That we will cum to harme."

O our Scots nobles wer richt laith°   *reluctant*
30   To weet° their cork-heild schoone;   *wet*
Bot lang owre a' the play wer playd,
    Thair hats they swam aboone.°   *above*

O lang, lang may their ladies sit,
    Wi thair fans into their hand,
35 Or eir they se Sir Patrick Spence
    Cum sailing to the land.

O lang, lang may the ladies stand,
    Wi thair gold kems° in their hair,   *combs*
Waiting for thair ain deir lords,
40   For they'll se thame na mair.

Haf owre, haf owre to Aberdour,
    It's fiftie fadom deip,
And thair lies guid Sir Patrick Spence,
    Wi the Scots lords at his feit.

---

30. **cork ... schoone:** cork-heeled shoes.   35. **or eir:** before.
31. **lang ... playd:** long before the game   41. **half owre:** halfway over.
was done.

The Demon Lover

"O where have you been, my long, long love,
 This long seven years and mair?"
"O I'm come to seek my former vows
 Ye granted me before."

5 "O hold your tongue of your former vows,
 For they will breed sad strife;
O hold your tongue of your former vows,
 For I am become a wife."

He turned him right and round about,
10   And the tear blinded his ee:°   *eye*
"I wa never hae trodden on Irish ground,
 If it had not been for thee.

"I might hae had a king's daughter,
 Far, far beyond the sea;
15 I might have had a king's daughter,
 Had it not been for love o thee."

"If ye might have had a king's daughter,
 Yersel ye had to blame;
Ye might have taken the king's daughter,
20   For ye kend° that I was nane.   *knew*

"If I was to leave my husband dear,
 And my two babes also,
O what have you to take me to,
 If with you I should go?"

25 "I hae seven ships upon the sea—
 The eighth brought me to land—
With four-and-twenty bold mariners,
 And music on every hand."

She has taken up her two little babes,
30   Kissd them baith° cheek and chin: *both*
"O fair ye weel, my ain two babes,
 For I'll never see you again."

She set her foot upon the ship,
 No mariners could she behold;
35 But the sails were o the taffetie,
 And the masts o the beaten gold.

She had not saild a league, a league,
    A league but barely three,
When dismal grew his countenance,
40   And drumlie° grew his ee.   *threatening*

They had not saild a league, a league,
    A league but barely three,
Until she espied his cloven foot,
    And she wept right bitterlie.

45 "O hold your tongue of your weeping," says he,
    "Of your weeping now let me be;
I will shew you how the lilies grow
    On the banks of Italy."

"O what hills are yon, yon pleasant hills,
50   That the sun shines sweetly on?"
"O yon are the hills of heaven," he said,
    "Where you will never win."

"O whaten a mountain is yon," she said,
    "All so dreary wi frost and snow?"
55 "O yon is the mountain of hell," he cried,
    "Where you and I will go."

He strack the tap-mast wi his hand,
    The fore-mast wi his knee,
And he brake that gallant ship in twain,
60   And sank her in the sea.

The Renaissance:
Sixteenth Century

❧ ❧ ❧

SIR THOMAS WYATT

[1503–1542]

The long love that in my thought doth harbor

The long love that in my thought doth harbor,
And in my heart doth keep his residence,
Into my face presseth with bold pretense
And there encampeth, spreading his banner.
She that me learns to love and suffer,   5
And wills that my trust and lust's negligence
Be reined by reason, shame, and reverence,
With his hardiness takes displeasure.
Wherewithal unto the heart's forest he flieth,
Leaving his enterprise with pain and cry,   10
And there him hideth, and not appeareth.
What may I do, when my master feareth,
But in the field with him to live and die?
For good is the life ending faithfully.

The long . . . harbor: a version of a sonnet
by Petrarch (Sonnetto in vita 91). Compare
Surrey's version, "Love that doth reign
. . ." In both sonnets the lover blushes and
then pales under the influence of the
beloved.

[17]

My galley charged with forgetfulness

My galley, chargèd with forgetfulness,
Thorough sharp seas, in winter nights doth pass,
'Tween rock and rock; and eke mine enemy, alas,
That is my lord, steereth with cruelness;
And every oar, a thought in readiness,   5
As though that death were light in such a case;
An endless wind doth tear the sail apace
Of forcèd sighs and trusty fearfulness;
A rain of tears, a cloud of dark disdain,
Hath done the wearied cords great hinderance,   10
Wreathèd with error and eke with ignorance;
The stars be hid that led me to this pain:
Drowned is Reason, that should me consort;
And I remain, despairing of the port.

Like to these unmeasurable mountains

Like to these unmeasurable mountains,
Is my painful life the burden of ire;
For of great height be they, and high is my desire;
And I of tears, and they be full of fountains;
Under craggy rocks they have full barren plains,   5
Hard thoughts in me my woeful mind doth tire;
Small fruit and many leaves their tops do attire,
Small effect with great trust in me remains.
The boisterous winds oft their high boughs do blast,
Hot sighs from me continually be shed;   10
Cattle in them, and in me love is fed;
Immovable am I, and they are full steadfast;
Of the restless birds they have the tune and note,
And I always plaints that pass thorough my throat.

Who so list to hunt

Who so list to hunt, I know where is an hind;
But as for me, alas, I may no more.

3. **eke ... enemy:** also my enemy (i.e.,
beloved).
13. **consort:** accompany.

by J. Sannazaro (1458–1530): *Rime*, I, iii,
l. 3.
2. **ire:** i.e., the scorn of his beloved.

Like ... mountains: a version of a sonnet   1. **list:** wishes.

The vain travail hath wearied me so sore,
I am of them that farthest come behind.
Yet may I by no means my wearied mind
Draw from the Deer; but as she fleeth afore
Fainting I follow. I leave off, therefore,
Since in a net I seek to hold the wind.
Who list her hunt, I put him out of doubt,
As well as I may spend his time in vain.
And graven with diamonds in letters plain
There is written, her fair neck round about,
Noli me tangere for Caesar's I am
And wild for to hold, though I seem tame.

My lute, awake

My lute, awake, perform the last
Labor that thou and I shall waste,
And end that I have now begun,
For when this song is sung and past,
My lute, be still, for I have done.

As to be heard where ear is none,
As lead to grave in marble stone,
My song may pierce her heart as soon.
Should we then sigh, or sing, or moan?
No, no, my lute, for I have done.

The rocks do not so cruelly
Repulse the waves continually,
As she my suit and affection;
So that I am past remedy,
Whereby my lute and I have done.

Proud of the spoil that thou hast got
Of simple hearts thorough Love's shot,
By whom unkind thou hast them won,
Think not he hath his bow forgot,
Although my lute and I have done.

13. **Noli me tangere:** (Latin) touch me not. The idea of the deer with this inscription around its neck is borrowed from Petrarch, *Rime* 190.
13. **Caesar's:** There is a tradition that Anne Boleyn, later wife of Henry VIII, was Wyatt's mistress for a time.
8. **As . . . stone:** i.e., as easily as soft lead may engrave hard marble.

Vengeance shall fall on thy disdain
That makest but game on earnest pain.
Think not alone under the sun
Unquit to cause thy lovers plain,
Although my lute and I have done.　　　25

Perchance thee lie withered and old
The winter nights that are so cold,
Plaining in vain unto the moon;
Thy wishes then dare not be told,
Care then who list, for I have done.　　　30

And then may chance thee to repent
The time that thou hast lost and spent
To cause thy lovers sigh and swoon;
Then shalt thou know beauty but lent,
And wish and want, as I have done.　　　35

Now cease, my lute, this is the last
Labor that thou and I shall waste,
And ended is that we begun.
Now is the song both sung and past.
My lute, be still, for I have done.　　　40

They flee from me

They flee from me that sometime did me seek,
　　With naked foot stalking in my chamber.
I have seen them gentle, tame, and meek,
　　That now are wild and do not remember
　　That sometime they put themselves in danger　　　5
　　　　To take bread at my hand; and now they range
　　　　Busily seeking with a continual change.

Thankt be fortune, it hath been otherwise
　　Twenty times better; but once, in special,
In thin array, after a pleasant guise,　　　10
　　When her loose gown from her shoulders did fall,

24. **Unquit:** unrevenged.
24. **plain:** lament.

Manuscript Version. The first printed version (1557) was edited so as to give a conventional regularity to the meter: *l.* 2.

in] within. *l.* 3. *I have seen them*] Once I have seen them. *l.* 4. *remember*] once remember. *l.* 5. *they put themselves*] they have put themselves. *l.* 7. *with a*] in. *l.* 11. *from . . . did*] did from. *l.* 13. *therewith . . . did*] And therewithal so sweetly did me kiss. *l.* 15. *I lay*] for I lay broad awaking. *l.* 16. *turned*] turned now.

And she me caught in her arms long and small,
    Therewith all sweetly did me kiss,
    And softly said: "Dear heart, how like you this?"
It was no dream; I lay broad waking: 15
    But all is turned thorough my gentleness
Into a strange fashion of forsaking;
    And I have leave to go of her goodness;
    And she also to use new-fangleness.
        But since that I so kindely am served,   20
        I fain would know what she hath deserved.

Madame, withouten many words

Madame, withouten many words,
Once, I am sure, ye will or no.
And if ye will, then leave your bords,
And use your wit, and show it so;
And with a beck ye shall me call;   5
And if of one that burneth alway
Ye have any pity at all,
Answer him fair with yea or nay.
If it be yea, I shall be fain;
If it be nay, friends as before.   10
Ye shall another man obtain
And I mine own, and yours no more.

EDMUND SPENSER

[*1552?–1599*]

Amoretti

8

More than most fair, full of the living fire
Kindled above unto the Maker near:
No eyes, but joys, in which all powers conspire

---

12. **small:** slim.
20. **kindely:** according to the way of nature; also, ironically, "kindly" in the modern sense.

3. **bords:** tricks.

1. **living fire:** The Neoplatonists pictured the immaterial influence of the Divine as descending beneficially into the universe of time and space as the material light of the sun descends beneficially upon the earth.

That to the world naught else be counted dear.
Through your bright beams doth not the blinded guest　5
Shoot out his darts to base affection's wound;
But angels come, to lead frail minds to rest
In chaste desires on heavenly beauty bound.
You frame my thoughts and fashion me within,
You stop my tongue, and teach my heart to speak,　10
You calm the storm that passion did begin,
Strong through your cause, but by your virtue weak.
Dark is the world where your light shined never;
Well is he born that may behold you ever.

28

The laurel leaf, which you this day do wear,
Gives me great hope of your relenting mind:
For since it is the badge which I do bear,
Ye bearing it do seem to me inclined.
The power thereof, which oft in me I find,　5
Let it likewise your gentle breast inspire
With sweet infusion, and put you in mind
Of that proud maid whom now those leaves attire:
Proud Daphne, scorning Phoebus' lovely fire,
On the Thessalian shore from him did flee,　10
For which the gods in their revengeful ire
Did her transform into a laurel tree.
Then fly no more, fair love, from Phoebus' chase,
But in your breast his leaf and love embrace.

44

When those renoumed noble peers of Greece
Through stubborn pride amongst themselves did jar,
Forgetful of the famous golden fleece,
Then Orpheus with his harp their strife did bar,

5. **blinded guest:** Cupid, representing blind passion.

3. **badge . . . bear:** i.e.., the laurel was associated with poets (hence *laureate*).
9. **fire:** passion; but also heat, as Phoebus was the sun-god.
14. **his . . . love:** both the laurel and poets were sacred to Phoebus.

1. **renoumed:** renowned.
2. **jar:** quarrel.
3. **golden fleece:** the prize which the legendary Argonauts (the peers of Greece) sought.
4. **Orpheus:** mythical Greek musician, whose art had magical power to produce concord.

But this continual cruel civil war,   5
The which my self against myself do make,
Whilst my weak powers of passions warreid are,
No skill can stint, nor reason can aslake.
But when in hand my tuneless harp I take,
Then do I more augment my foes' despite,   10
And grief renew, and passions do awake
To battle, fresh against my self to fight—
'Mongst whom the more I seek to settle peace,
The more I find their malice to increase.

68

Most glorious Lord of life, that on this day
Didst make Thy triumph over death and sin,
And having harrowed hell didst bring away
Captivity thence captive, us to win:
This joyous day, dear Lord, with joy begin,   5
And grant that we for whom thou diddest die
Being with Thy dear blood clean washed from sin,
May live for ever in felicity;
And that, Thy love we weighing worthily,
May likewise love Thee for the same again,   10
And for Thy sake that all like dear didst buy,
With love may one another entertain.
So let us love, dear love, like as we ought;
Love is the lesson which the Lord us taught.

70

Fresh Spring, the herald of love's mighty king,
In whose coat armor richly are displayed
All sorts of flowers the which on earth do spring,
In goodly colors gloriously arrayed:
Go to my love, where she is careless laid,   5
Yet in her winter's bower not well awake;
Tell her the joyous time will not be stayed
Unless she do him by the forelock take.

1. **this day:** Easter.
3. **harrowed:** The harrowing of hell is Christ's releasing of humanity from Satan's prison after the sacrifice of the Cross had made possible a remission of human sin.
11. **like dear:** i.e., with an equal expense of suffering for each one of us.

12. **entertain:** maintain, receive.

2. **coat armor:** tunic worn over armor, showing the device or motto of the wearer: a coat of arms.
5. **careless:** unconcerned.

Bid her therefore herself soon ready make
To wait on Love amongst his lovely crew,   10
Where everyone that misseth then her make
Shall be by him amerced with penance due.
Make haste therefore, sweet love, whilest it is prime,
For none can call again the passed time.

75

One day I wrote her name upon the strand,
But came the waves and washed it away:
Again I wrote it with a second hand,
But came the tide, and made my pains his prey.
Vain man, said she, that doest in vain assay   5
A mortal thing so to immortalize,
For I myself shall like to this decay,
And eek my name be wiped out likewise.
Not so (quoth I), let baser things devise
To die in dust, but you shall live by fame: 10
My verse your virtues rare shall eternize,
And in the heavens write your glorious name.
Where whenas Death shall all the world subdue,
Our love shall live, and later life renew.

Prothalamion

1

Calme was the day, and through the trembling ayre,
Sweete breathing *Zephyrus* did softly play
A gentle spirit, that lightly did delay
Hot *Titans* beames, which then did glyster fayre:
When I whom sullein care,   5
Through discontent of my long fruitlesse stay
In princes court, and expectation vayne
Of idle hopes, which still doe fly away,

11. **make:** mate.
12. **amerced:** punished.
13. **prime:** spring, and also the first hour of morning.

8. **eek:** also.

Prothalamion: (Greek) song of espousal.

Written for the double marriage of the daughters of the Earl of Worcester. The Elizabethan spelling of the original edition is preserved as a specimen to show, roughly, how all the poems of the later 16th and early 17th centuries appeared to their first readers in print.
2. **Zephyrus:** the breeze.
4. **Titans:** the sun's.

Like empty shaddowes, did aflict my brayne,
Walkt forth to ease my payne   10
Along the shoare of silver streaming *Themmes*,
Whose rutty bancke, the which his river hemmes,
Was paynted all with variable flowers,
And all the meades adornd with daintie gemmes,
Fit to decke maydens bowres,   15
And crowne their paramours,
Against the brydale day, which is not long:
    Sweete *Themmes* runne softly, till I end my song.

2

There, in a meadow, by the rivers side,
A flocke of *nymphes* I chaunced to espy,   20
All lovely daughters of the flood thereby,
With goodly greenish locks all loose untyde,
As each had bene a bryde.
And each one had a little wicker basket,
Made of fine twigs entraylèd curiously,   25
In which they gathered flowers to fill their flasket:
And with fine fingers, cropt full feateously
The tender stalkes on hye.
Of every sort, which in that meadow grew,
They gathered some; the violet pallid blew,   30
The little dazie, that at evening closes,
The virgin lillie, and the primrose trew,
With store of vermeil roses,
To decke their bridegroomes posies,
Against the brydale day, which was not long: 35
    Sweete *Themmes* runne softly, till I end my song.

3

With that, I saw two swannes of goodly hewe,
Come softly swimming downe along the Lee;
Two fairer birds I yet did never see:
The snow which doth the top of *Pindus* strew,   40
Did never whiter shew,
Nor *Jove* himselfe when he a swan would be
For love of *Leda*, whiter did appeare:
Yet *Leda* was they say as white as he,
Yet not so white as these, nor nothing neare;   45

12. **rutty**: reedy.

27. **feateously**: dexterously.

38. **Lee**: river flowing into the Thames.
40. **Pindus**: mountains in northern Greece.
43. **Leda**: girl seduced by Zeus in form of a swan.

So purely white they were,
That even the gentle streame, the which them bare,
Seem'd foule to them, and bad his billowes spare
To wet their silken feathers, least they might
Soyle their fayre plumes with water not so fayre,   50
And marre their beauties bright,
That shone as heavens light,
Against their brydale day, which was not long:
    Sweete *Themmes* runne softly, till I end my song.

4

Eftsoones the *nymphes*, which now had flowers their fill,   55
Ran all in haste, to see that silver brood,
As they came floating on the christal flood.
Whom when they sawe, they stood amazèd still,
Their wondring eyes to fill,
Them seem'd they never saw a sight so fayre,   60
Of fowles so lovely, that they sure did deeme
Them heavenly borne, or to be that same payre
Which through the skie draw *Venus* silver teeme,
For sure they did not seeme
To be begot of any earthly seede,   65
But rather angels or of angels breede:
Yet were they bred of *Somers-heat* they say,
In sweetest season, when each flower and weede
The earth did fresh aray,
So fresh they seem'd as day,   70
Even as their brydale day, which was not long:
    Sweete *Themmes* runne softly, till I end my song.

5

Then forth they all out of their baskets drew,
Great store of flowers, the honour of the field,
That to the sense did fragrant odours yeild,   75
All which upon those goodly birds they threw,
And all the waves did strew,
That like old *Peneus* waters they did seeme,
When downe along by pleasant *Tempes* shore
Scattred with flowres, through *Thessaly* they streeme,   80
That they appeare through lillies plenteous store,
Like a brydes chamber flore:

55. **Eftsoones:** at once.
62–63. **payre . . . teeme:** Venus' chariot is usually imagined as being drawn through the air by doves.
67. **Somers-heat:** a pun on "Somerset," the name of the girls' father.

78. **Peneus:** a Greek river, traditionally mentioned in pastoral poetry.

Two of those *nymphes*, meane while, two garlands bound,
Of freshest flowres which in that mead they found,
The which presenting all in trim array,   85
Their snowie foreheads therewithall they crownd,
Whil'st one did sing this lay,
Prepar'd against that day,
Against their brydale day, which was not long:
 Sweete *Themmes* runne softly, till I end my song.   90

6

Ye gentle birdes, the worlds faire ornament,
And heavens glorie, whom this happie hower
Doth leade unto your lovers blisfull bower,
Joy may you have and gentle hearts content
Of your loves couplement: 95
And let faire *Venus*, that is queene of love,
With her heart-quelling sonne upon you smile,
Whose smile they say, hath vertue to remove
All loves dislike, and friendships faultie guile
For ever to assoile.   100
Let endless peace your steadfast hearts accord,
And blessed plentie wait upon your bord,
And let your bed with pleasures chast abound,
That fruitfull issue may to you afford,
Which may your foes confound,   105
And make your joyes redound,
Upon your brydale day, which is not long:
 Sweete *Themmes* run softlie, till I end my song.

7

So ended she; and all the rest around
To her redoubled that her undersong,   110
Which said, their brydale daye should not be long.
And gentle Eccho from the neighbour ground,
Their accents did resound.
So forth those joyous birdes did passe along,
Adowne the Lee, that to them murmurde low,   115
As he would speake, but that he lackt a tong
Yeat did by signes his glad affection show,
Making his streame run slow.
And all the foule which in his flood did dwell
Gan flock about these twaine, that did excell   120
The rest, so far, as *Cynthia* doth shend

97. **sonne**: Cupid. 110. **undersong**: refrain.
121. **Cynthia**: the moon.

The lesser starres. So they enrangèd well,
Did on those two attend,
And their best service lend,
Against their wedding day, which was not long: 125
  Sweete *Themmes* run softly, till I end my song.

8

At length they all to mery *London* came,
To mery London, my most kyndly nurse,
That to me gave this lifes first native sourse:
Though from another place I take my name,   130
An house of auncient fame.
There when they came, whereas those bricky towres,
The which on *Themmes* brode agèd backe doe ryde,
Where now the studious lawyers have their bowers
There whylome wont the Templer Knights to byde,   135
Till they decayd through pride:
Next whereunto there standes a stately place,
Where oft I gaynèd giftes and goodly grace
Of that great lord, which therein wont to dwell,
Whose want too well now feeles my freendles case: 140
But Ah here fits not well
Olde woes but joyes to tell
Against the bridale daye, which is not long:
  Sweete *Themmes* runne softly, till I end my song.

9

Yet therein now doth lodge a noble peer,   145
Great *Englands* glory and the Worlds wide wonder,
Whose dreadful name, late through all *Spaine* did thunder,
And *Hercules* two pillors standing neere,
Did make to quake and feare:
Faire branch of honor, flower of chevalrie,   150
That fillest *England* with thy triumphs fame,
Joy have thou of thy noble victorie,
And endlesse happinesse of thine owne name
That promiseth the same:
That through thy prowesse and victorious armes,   155
Thy country may be freed from forraine harmes:

134–135. **Where . . . Templer Knights:** A site formally occupied by the Knights Templar (suppressed in the 14th century); later used for law students and courts.
139. **great lord:** Earl of Leicester, early patron of Spenser.
140. **case:** subject (not object) of "feeles."

145. **noble peer:** Robert Devereux, Earl of Essex, who had just returned from the capture of Cadiz.
153. **happinesse:** a play on "Devereux" and *heureux* (Fr.: happy).

And great *Elisaes* glorious name may ring
Through al the world, fil'd with thy wide alarmes,
Which some brave muse may sing
To ages following,   160
Upon the brydale day, which is not long:
   Sweete *Themmes* runne softly, till I end my song.

10

From those high towers this noble lord issuing,
Like radiant *Hesper* when his golden hayre
In th'ocean billows he hath bathed fayre,   165
Descended to the rivers open vewing,
With a great traine ensuing.
Above the rest were goodly to bee seene
Two gentle knights of lovely face and feature,
Beseeming well the bower of anie queene,   170
With gifts of wit and ornaments of nature,
Fit for so goodly stature:
That like the twins of *Jove* they seem'd in sight,
Which decke the bauldricke of the heavens bright.
They two, forth pacing to the river side,   175
Received those two faire brides, their loves delight,
Which, at th'appointed tyde,
Each one did make his bryde,
Against their brydale day, which is not long:
   Sweete *Themmes* runne softly, till I end my song.   180

SIR PHILIP SIDNEY

[1554–1586]

Ring out your bells

Ring out your bells, let mourning shows be spread;
   For Love is dead.
     All Love is dead, infected
  With plague of deep disdain;
     Worth, as nought worth, rejected,   5

157. **Elisaes**: Queen Elizabeth I's.
158. **alarmes**: calls to arms.

164. **Hesper**: the morning-star, rising from the ocean which the ancient Greeks thought surrounded all the land in the world.
174. **twins of Jove**: Castor and Pollux, sons of Jove and Leda. They form a constellation in the Zodiac (the "bauldricke" or belt of the heavens).

And Faith fair scorn doth gain.
From so ungrateful fancy,
From such a female franzy,
  From them that use men thus,
  Good Lord, deliver us!   10

Weep, neighbours, weep! do you not hear it said
That Love is dead?
  His death-bed, peacock's folly;
His winding-sheet is shame;
  His will, false-seeming holy;   15
His sole exec'tor, blame.
  From so ungrateful fancy,
  From such a female franzy,
    From them that use men thus,
    Good Lord, deliver us!   20

Let dirge be sung and trentals rightly read,
For Love is dead.
  Sir Wrong his tomb ordaineth
My mistress' marble heart,
  Which epitaph containeth,   25
"Her eyes were once his dart."
  From so ungrateful fancy,
  From such a female franzy,
    From them that use men thus,
    Good Lord, deliver us!   30

Alas! I lie, rage hath this error bred;
Love is not dead.
  Love is not dead, but sleepeth
In her unmatchèd mind,
  Where she his counsel keepeth,   35
Till due desert she find.
  Therefore from so vile fancy,
  To call such wit a franzy,
    Who Love can temper thus,
    Good Lord, deliver us!   40

In wonted walks

In wonted walks, since wonted fancies change,
Some cause there is which of strange cause doth rise;
For in each thing whereto my mind doth range
Part of my pain meseems engraved lies.

13. **peacock:** emblematic of pride and   21. **trentals:** masses for the dead (literally,
show.   thirty masses).

The rocks, which were of constant mind the mark,   5
In climbing steep now hard refusal show;
The shading woods seem now my sun to dark,
And stately hills disdain to look so low.
The restful caves now restless visions give.
In dales I see each way a hard ascent.   10
Like late-mown meads, late cut from joy I live.
Alas, sweet brooks do in my tears augment.
Rocks, woods, hills, caves, dales, meads, brooks answer me:
"Infected minds infect each thing they see."

Astrophel and Stella

1

Loving in truth, and fain in verse my love to show,
That she, dear she, might take some pleasure of my pain,
Pleasure might cause her read, reading might make her know,
Knowledge might pity win, and pity grace obtain,—
I sought fit words to paint the blackest face of woe;   5
Studying inventions fine, her wits to entertain,
Oft turning others' leaves to see if thence would flow
Some fresh and fruitful showers upon my sun-burned brain.
But words came halting forth, wanting invention's stay;
Invention, nature's child, fled step-dame Study's blows,   10
And others' feet still seemed but strangers in my way.
Thus, great with child to speak, and helpless in my throes,
Biting my truant pen, beating myself for spite,
Fool, said my muse to me, look in thy heart and write.

7

When Nature made her chief work, Stella's eyes,
In color black why wrapped she beams so bright?
Would she in beamy black, like painter wise,
Frame daintiest luster mixed of shades and light?
Or did she else that sober hue devise   5
In object best to knit and strength our sight,
Lest, if no veil these brave gleams did disguise,
They, sunlike, should more dazzle than delight?
Or would she her miraculous power show,
That, whereas black seems beauty's contrary,   10

---

1. **fain:** desirous.   9. **stay:** support.

She even in black doth make all beauties flow?
Both so, and thus,—she, minding Love should be
Placed ever there, gave him this mourning weed
To honor all their deaths who for her bleed.

21

Your words, my friend, right healthful caustics, blame
My young mind marred, whom Love doth windlass so;
That mine own writings, like bad servants, show
My wits quick in vain thoughts, in virtue lame;
That Plato I read for naught but if he tame   5
Such coltish years; that to my birth I owe
Nobler desires, lest else that friendly foe,
Great expectation, wear a train of shame;
For since mad March great promise made of me,
If now the May of my years much decline   10
What can be hoped my harvest-time will be?
Sure, you say well, "Your wisdom's golden mine
Dig deep with learning's spade." Now tell me this—
Hath this world aught so fair as Stella is?

35

What may words say, or what may words not say,
Where truth itself must speak like flattery?
Within what bounds can one his liking stay,
Where nature doth with infinite agree?
What Nestor's counsel can my flames allay,   5
Since Reason's self doth blow the coal in me?
And ah, what hope that hope should once see day,
Where Cupid is sworn page to chastity?
Honor is honored, that thou dost possess
Him as thy slave, and now long-needy Fame   10
Doth even grow rich, naming my Stella's name.
Wit learns in thee perfection to express.
Not thou by praise, but praise in thee is raised;
It is a praise to praise, when thou art praised.

13. **weed:** attire.

2. **windlass:** ensnare.
5. **Plato:** particularly his doctrine that love, beginning in the physical, should finally attach itself to the highest spiritual reality.

4. **nature:** world of finite nature; also Stella as a creation of Nature.
5. **Nestor:** an old leader among the Greeks in the *Iliad*, famous for his good counsel.

39

Come sleep! O sleep, the certain knot of peace,
The baiting place of wit, the balm of woe,
The poor man's wealth, the prisoner's release,
Th' indifferent judge between the high and low;
With shield of proof shield me from out the prease   5
Of those fierce darts despair at me doth throw;
O make in me those civil wars to cease;
I will good tribute pay, if thou do so.
Take thou of me smooth pillows, sweetest bed,
A chamber deaf to noise and blind to light,   10
A rosy garland and a weary head;
And if these things, as being thine by right,
Move not thy heavy grace, thou shalt in me,
Livelier than elsewhere, Stella's image see.

71

Who will in fairest book of Nature know
How virtue may best lodged in beauty be,
Let him but learn of love to read in thee,
Stella, those fair lines which true goodness show.
There shall he find all vices' overthrow,   5
Not by rude force, but sweetest sovereignty
Of reason, from whose light those night birds fly,
That inward sun in thine eyes shineth so.
And, not content to be perfection's heir
Thyself, dost strive all minds that way to move,   10
Who mark in thee what is in thee most fair.
So while thy beauty draws the heart to love,
As fast thy virtue bends that love to good.
But, ah, Desire still cries, "Give me some food."

74

I never drank of Aganippe well,
Nor ever did in shade of Tempe sit,
And Muses scorn with vulgar brains to dwell;
Poor layman I, for sacred rites unfit.
Some do I hear of poets' fury tell,   5
But, God wot, wot not what they mean by it;

2. **baiting place:** a stop for food and rest
on a journey.
5. **prease:** press, crowd.

7. **night birds:** "vices" in line 5.

1. **Aganippe:** well at foot of Mount Helicon, sacred to the muses.
2. **Tempe:** a gorge sacred to Apollo, god of poetic inspiration.
6. **God . . . not:** God knows, know not.

And this I swear by blackest brook of hell,
I am no pick-purse of another's wit.
How falls it then that with so smooth an ease
My thoughts I speak; and what I speak doth flow   10
In verse, and that my verse best wits doth please?
Guess we the cause. What, is it thus? Fie, no.
Or so? Much less. How then? Sure thus it is:
My lips are sweet, inspired with Stella's kiss.

76

She comes, and straight therewith her shining orbs do move
Their rays to me, who in her tedious absence lay
Bathed in cold woe; but now appears my shining day,
The only light of joy, the only warmth of love.
She comes with light and warmth, which like Aurora prove—   5
Of gentle face, so that my eyes dare gladly play
With such a rosy morn, whose beams both fresh and gay
Scorch not, but only do dark, chilling spirits remove.
But lo, while I do speak, it groweth noon with me;
Her flamy glittering lights increase with time and place.   10
My heart cries, "Oh, it burns"; mine eyes now dazzled be:
No wind, no shade, no cool—what help then in my case
But with short breath, long looks, stayed feet, and waking head
Pray that my sun go down with meeker beams to bed.

99

When far-spent night persuades each mortal eye,
To whom nor art nor nature granteth light,
To lay his then mark-wanting shafts of sight,
Clos'd with their quivers in sleep's armory;
With windows ope then most my mind doth lie,   5
Viewing the shape of darkness and delight,
Takes in that sad hue, which with th'inward night
Of his 'maz'd powers keeps perfit harmony:
But when birds charm, and that sweet air, which is
Morn's messenger, with rose-enamel'd skies   10
Calls each wight to salute the flow'r of bliss;
In tomb of lids then buried are mine eyes,
Forc'd by their Lord, who is asham'd to find
Such light in sense, with such a darken'd mind.

---

7. **blackest brook:** rivers are a fixed feature   "spheres" suggests the sun.
of the classical Hades.

3. **mark . . . shafts:** arrows lacking a target.
1. **orbs:** eyes; but the general meaning   13. **Lord:** i.e., the lover speaking.

Thou blind man's mark

Thou blind man's mark, thou fool's self-chosen snare,
Fond fancy's scum, and dregs of scattered thought;
Band of all evils, cradle of causeless care;
Thou web of will, whose end is never wrought;
Desire, desire! I have too dearly bought,   5
With price of mangled mind, thy worthless ware;
Too long, too long, asleep thou hast me brought,
Who should my mind to higher things prepare.
But yet in vain thou hast my ruin sought;
In vain thou madest me to vain things aspire;   10
In vain thou kindlest all thy smoky fire;
For virtue hath this better lesson taught,—
Within myself to seek my only hire,
Desiring nought but how to kill desire.

Leave me, O love

Leave me, O love which reachest but to dust;
And thou, my mind, aspire to higher things;
Grow rich in that which never taketh rust,
Whatever fades but fading pleasure brings.
Draw in thy beams, and humble all thy might   5
To that sweet yoke where lasting freedoms be;
Which breaks the clouds and opens forth the light,
That doth both shine and give us sight to see.
O take fast hold; let that light be thy guide
In this small course which birth draws out to death,   10
And think how evil becometh him to slide,
Who seeketh heav'n, and comes of heav'nly breath.
Then farewell, world; thy uttermost I see;
Eternal Love, maintain thy life in me.

1. **mark:** target   12. **heav'nly breath:** the spirit (breath) of the Creator.

CHRISTOPHER MARLOWE
[*1564–1593*]

The Passionate Shepherd to His Love

Come live with me and be my love,
And we will all the pleasures prove
That hills and valleys, dales and fields,
And all the craggy mountains yields.

There will we sit upon the rocks   5
And see the shepherds feed their flocks,
By shallow rivers, to whose falls
Melodious birds sing madrigals.

There will I make thee beds of roses
And a thousand fragrant posies,   10
A cap of flowers, and a kirtle
Embroidered all with leaves of myrtle.

A gown made of the finest wool,
Which from our pretty lambs we pull,
Fair linèd slippers for the cold,   15
With buckles of the purest gold.

A belt of straw and ivy buds
With coral clasps and amber studs:
And if these pleasures may thee move,
Come live with me and be my love.   20

The shepherd swains shall dance and sing
For thy delight each May-morning:
If these delights thy mind may move,
Then live with me and be my love.

Hero and Leander

First Sestiad

On Hellespont, guilty of true love's blood,
In view, and opposite, two cities stood,
Sea-borderers, disjoined by Neptune's might;
The one Abydos, the other Sestos hight.

Hero and Leander: distantly based on the narrative poem of the Alexandrian Greek Musaeus (5th century A.D.). Marlowe calls the divisions of his poems "Sestiads" after Hero's city.
4. **hight:** was called.

At Sestos, Hero dwelt; Hero the fair,   5
Whom young Apollo courted for her hair,
And offered as a dower his burning throne,
Where she should sit for men to gaze upon.
The outside of her garments were of lawn,
The lining purple silk, with gilt stars drawn;   10
Her wide sleeves green, and bordered with a grove
Where Venus in her naked glory strove
To please the careless and disdainful eyes
Of proud Adonis, that before her lies;
Her kirtle blue, whereon was many a stain,   15
Made with the blood of wretched lovers slain.
Upon her head she ware a myrtle wreath,
From whence her veil reached to the ground beneath.
Her veil was artificial flowers and leaves,
Whose workmanship both man and beast deceives;   20
Many would praise the sweet smell as she passed,
When 'twas the odor which her breath forth cast;
And there for honey, bees have sought in vain,
And, beat from thence, have lighted there again.
About her neck hung chains of pebble-stone,   25
Which, lightened by her neck, like diamonds shone.
She ware no gloves, for neither sun nor wind
Would burn or parch her hands, but to her mind,
Or warm or cool them, for they took delight
To play upon those hands, they were so white.   30
Buskins of shells all silvered usèd she,
And branched with blushing coral to the knee,
Where sparrows perched, of hollow pearl and gold,
Such as the world would wonder to behold;
Those with sweet water oft her handmaid fills,   35
Which, as she went, would chirrup through the bills.
Some say, for her the fairest Cupid pined,
And, looking in her face, was strooken blind.
But this is true: so like was one the other,
As he imagined Hero was his mother;   40
And oftentimes into her bosom flew,
About her naked neck his bare arms threw,
And laid his childish head upon her breast,

9. **lawn:** fine, translucent linen.
14. **Adonis:** He scorned Venus' love, and was killed by a boar which he hunted. She mourned him. Both Ovid and Shakespeare tell the story, and Spenser depicts him in his original character as a fertility god, dying and reborn perpetually.
15. **kirtle:** skirt.
19. **artificial:** produced by artifice (with none of the unfavorable modern connotation).
28. **to ... mind:** as she desired.
31. **Buskins:** flexible footwear, reaching almost to the knee.
40. **mother:** Venus.

And with still panting rocked, there took his rest.
So lovely fair was Hero, Venus' nun,   45
As nature wept, thinking she was undone,
Because she took more from her than she left
And of such wondrous beauty her bereft;
Therefore, in sign her treasure suffered wrack,
Since Hero's time hath half the world been black.   50
   Amorous Leander, beautiful and young,
(Whose tragedy divine Musæus sung)
Dwelt at Abydos; since him dwelt there none
For whom succeeding times make greater moan.
His dangling tresses that were never shorn,   55
Had they been cut and unto Colchis borne,
Would have allured the vent'rous youth of Greece
To hazard more than for the Golden Fleece.
Fair Cynthia wished his arms might be her sphere;
Grief makes her pale, because she moves not there. 60
His body was as straight as Circe's wand;
Jove might have sipped out nectar from his hand.
Even as delicious meat is to the taste,
So was his neck in touching, and surpassed
The white of Pelops' shoulder. I could tell ye   65
How smooth his breast was, and how white his belly,
And whose immortal fingers did imprint
That heavenly path, with many a curious dint,
That runs along his back; but my rude pen
Can hardly blazon forth the loves of men,   70
Much less of powerful gods; let it suffice
That my slack muse sings of Leander's eyes,
Those orient cheeks and lips, exceeding his
That leapt into the water for a kiss
Of his own shadow, and despising many,   75
Died ere he could enjoy the love of any.
Had wild Hippolytus Leander seen,
Enamoured of his beauty had he been;
His presence made the rudest peasant melt,

45. **Venus' nun:** Hero, as a devotee of Venus, remains a chaste nun, but Venus is goddess of sexual love.
52. **divine:** The author of the original poem is confused with Musaeus, a mythical offspring of Orpheus, divine prototype of poets.
56. **Colchis:** land of the Golden Fleece, sought by Jason and the other Argonauts.
59. **Cynthia:** goddess of the moon. Her sphere is the enveloping crystalline one that was thought to surround the earth, carrying the moon in orbit.
61. **Circe's wand:** Circe exercised her magic over men with this, transforming them into beasts.
62. **Jove:** He loved his cupbearer, Ganymede.
65. **Pelops:** son of Tantalus. By a plot he was served as a meal to the gods. Reassembled by Hermes, he was given a new shoulder of ivory in place of the eaten one.
73. **orient:** shining.
73. **his:** Narcissus'.
77. **Hippolytus:** He disdained all love.

That in the vast uplandish country dwelt;   80
The barbarous Thracian soldier, moved with nought,
Was moved with him, and for his favor sought.
Some swore he was a maid in man's attire,
For in his looks were all that men desire:
A pleasant smiling cheek, a speaking eye,   85
A brow for love to banquet royally;
And such as knew he was a man, would say,
Leander, thou art made for amorous play;
Why art thou not in love, and loved of all?
Though thou be fair, yet be not thine own thrall.   90
    The men of wealthy Sestos every year,
For his sake whom their goddess held so dear,
Rose-cheeked Adonis, kept a solemn feast.
Thither resorted many a wand'ring guest
To meet their loves; such as had none at all,   95
Came lovers home from this great festival.
For every street, like to a firmament,
Glistered with breathing stars, who, where they went,
Frighted the melancholy earth, which deemed
Eternal heaven to burn, for so it seemed   100
As if another Phaeton had got
The guidance of the sun's rich chariot.
But, far above the loveliest, Hero shined,
And stole away th' enchanted gazer's mind;
For like sea-nymphs' inveigling harmony,   105
So was her beauty to the standers by.
Nor that night-wand'ring pale and wat'ry star
(When yawning dragons draw her thirling car
From Latmos' mount up to the gloomy sky,
Where, crowned with blazing light and majesty,   110
She proudly sits) more over-rules the flood,
Than she the hearts of those that near her stood.
Even as when gaudy nymphs pursue the chase,
Wretched Ixion's shaggy-footed race,
Incensed with savage heat, gallop amain   115
From steep pine-bearing mountains to the plain,
So ran the people forth to gaze upon her,
And all that viewed her were enamoured on her.

81. **Thracian:** These northerners were often early figures of fun for other Greeks.
85. **speaking:** expressive.
101. **Phaeton:** borrowed the horses and chariot of his father the sun god, and, not being able to guide them, nearly destroyed the world.
105. **harmony:** music of the sirens, which drew sailors on the rocks.
107. **star:** moon. She visited her lover on Mount Latmos ("thirling": hurtling).
114. **Ixion:** father of the centaurs, who amorously pursue nymphs. He was chained to a wheel because he pursued Juno.

And as in fury of a dreadful fight,
Their fellows being slain or put to flight,   120
Poor soldiers stand with fear of death dead-strooken,
So at her presence all, surprised and tooken,
Await the sentence of her scornful eyes;
He whom she favors lives, the other dies.
There might you see one sigh, another rage,   125
And some, their violent passions to assuage,
Compile sharp satires; but alas, too late,
For faithful love will never turn to hate.
And many, seeing great princes were denied,
Pined as they went, and thinking on her, died.   130
On this feast day, oh, cursed day and hour!
Went Hero thorough Sestos, from her tower
To Venus' temple, where unhappily,
As after chanced, they did each other spy.
So fair a church as this had Venus none;   135
The walls were of discolored jasper stone,
Wherein was Proteus carvèd, and o'erhead
A lively vine of green sea-agate spread,
Where by one hand light-headed Bacchus hung,
And with the other wine from grapes out-wrung.   140
Of crystal shining fair the pavement was;
The town of Sestos called it Venus' glass;
There might you see the gods in sundry shapes,
Committing heady riots, incest, rapes;
For know that underneath this radiant floor   145
Was Danaë's statue in a brazen tower;
Jove slyly stealing from his sister's bed
To dally with Idalian Ganymed,
And for his love Europa bellowing loud,
And tumbling with the rainbow in a cloud;   150
Blood-quaffing Mars heaving the iron net
Which limping Vulcan and his Cyclops set:
Love kindling fire to burn such towns as Troy;
Silvanus weeping for the lovely boy
That now is turned into a cypress tree,   155
Under whose shade the wood-gods love to be.
And in the midst a silver altar stood;

---

136. **discolored**: variously colored.
138. **lively**: lifelike.
146 ff. **Danaë**: Jove reached her in a shower of gold although she was shut in the top of a tower. Jove's sister was his wife, Juno; for Ganymede, see note to line 62. Jove in the form of a bull pursued Europa. Iris, the rainbow, was his attendant. Mars and Venus were caught together in a net by her husband Vulcan and Vulcan's workers the Cyclopes. Troy was destroyed through the love of Paris and Helen. The wood god Sylvanus loved Cyparissus.

There Hero sacrificing turtles' blood,
Veiled to the ground, veiling her eyelids close,
And modestly they opened as she rose;   160
Thence flew love's arrow with the golden head,
And thus Leander was enamourèd.
Stone still he stood, and evermore he gazed,
Till with the fire that from his count'nance blazed,
Relenting Hero's gentle heart was strook;   165
Such force and virtue hath an amorous look.
    It lies not in our power to love or hate,
For will in us is over-ruled by fate.
When two are stripped, long ere the course begin
We wish that one should lose, the other win;   170
And one especially do we affect
Of two gold ingots, like in each respect.
The reason no man knows, let it suffice,
What we behold is censured by our eyes.
Where both deliberate, the love is slight;   175
Who ever loved, that loved not at first sight?
    He kneeled, but unto her devoutly prayed;
Chaste Hero to herself thus softly said·
Were I the saint he worships, I would hear him;
And as she spake these words, came somewhat near him.   180
He started up; she blushed as one ashamed;
Wherewith Leander much more was inflamed.
He touched her hand; in touching it she trembled;
Love deeply grounded hardly is dissembled.
These lovers parlèd by the touch of hands;   185
True love is mute, and oft amazèd stands.
Thus while dumb signs their yielding hearts entangled,
The air with sparks of living fire was spangled,
And night, deep drenched in misty Acheron,
Heaved up her head, and half the world upon   190
Breathed darkness forth (dark night is Cupid's day).
And now begins Leander to display
Love's holy fire with words, with sighs, and tears,
Which like sweet music entered Hero's ears;
And yet at every word she turned aside,   195
And always cut him off as he replied.
At last, like to a bold sharp sophister,

158. turtles': turtledoves'. They symbolized true love.
161. golden head: Arrows so tipped
inspired true love.
174. censured: judged.
185. parlèd: spoke, deliberated.

186. amazèd: speechless, confused.
189. Acheron: river of the underworld,
from which night ascends to cover the
earth.
197. sophister: practiced arguer, advocate.

With cheerful hope thus he accosted her:
  Fair creature, let me speak without offence;
I would my rude words had the influence   200
To lead thy thoughts as thy fair looks do mine!
Then shouldst thou be his prisoner who is thine.
Be not unkind and fair; misshapen stuff
Are of behavior boisterous and rough.
Oh, shun me not, but hear me ere you go,   205
God knows I cannot force love, as you do.
My words shall be as spotless as my youth,
Full of simplicity and naked truth.
This sacrifice, whose sweet perfume descending
From Venus' altar to your footsteps bending,   210
Doth testify that you exceed her far,
To whom you offer, and whose nun you are.
Why should you worship her? her you surpass
As much as sparkling diamonds flaring glass.
A diamond set in lead his worth retains;   215
A heavenly nymph, beloved of human swains,
Receives no blemish, but ofttimes more grace;
Which makes me hope, although I am but base,
Base in respect of thee, divine and pure,
Dutiful service may thy love procure,   220
And I in duty will excel all other,
As thou in beauty dost exceed Love's mother.
Nor heaven, nor thou, were made to gaze upon;
As heaven preserves all things, so save thou one.
A stately builded ship, well rigged and tall,   225
The ocean maketh more majestical;
Why vowest thou then to live in Sestos here,
Who on love's seas more glorious would appear?
Like untuned golden strings all women are,
Which long time lie untouched, will harshly jar.   230
Vessels of brass, oft handled, brightly shine;
What difference betwixt the richest mine
And basest mold, but use? for both, not used,
Are of like worth. Then treasure is abused,
When misers keep it; being put to loan,   235
In time it will return us two for one.
Rich robes themselves and others do adorn;
Neither themselves nor others, if not worn.
Who builds a palace, and rams up the gate,
Shall see it ruinous and desolate.   240

214. **flaring:** glaring.   233. **mold:** earth, dust.

Ah, simple Hero, learn thyself to cherish!
Lone women, like to empty houses, perish.
Less sins the poor rich man that starves himself
In heaping up a mass of drossy pelf,
Than such as you; his golden earth remains,   245
Which after his decease some other gains;
But this fair gem, sweet in the loss alone,
When you fleet hence, can be bequeathed to none.
Or if it could, down from th' enamelled sky
All heaven would come to claim this legacy,   250
And with intestine broils the world destroy,
And quite confound nature's sweet harmony.
Well therefore by the gods decreed it is
We human creatures should enjoy that bliss.
One is no number; maids are nothing, then,   255
Without the sweet society of men.
Wilt thou live single still? One shalt thou be
Though never-singling Hymen couple thee.
Wild savages, that drink of running springs,
Think water far excels all earthly things,   260
But they that daily taste neat wine, despise it;
Virginity, albeit some highly prize it,
Compared with marriage, had you tried them both,
Differs as much as wine and water doth.
Base bullion for the stamp's sake we allow;   265
Even so for men's impression do we you,
By which alone, our reverend fathers say,
Women receive perfection every way.
This idol which you term virginity
Is neither essence subject to the eye,   270
No, nor to any one exterior sense,
Nor hath it any place of residence,
Nor is 't of earth or mould celestial,
Or capable of any form at all.
Of that which hath no being, do not boast;   275
Things that are not at all, are never lost.
Men foolishly do call it virtuous;
What virtue is it, that is born with us?
Much less can honor be ascribed thereto;
Honor is purchased by the deeds we do.   280
Believe me, Hero, honor is not won
Until some honorable deed be done.

251. **intestine broils:** civil wars.   265. **stamp's sake:** for the sake of the
258. **Hymen:** god of marriage.   image impressed upon it in coinage.
261. **neat:** straight, undiluted.   "Impression" is parallel in the next line.

Seek you, for chastity, immortal fame,
And know that some have wronged Diana's name?
Whose name is it, if she be false or not,   285
So she be fair, but some vile tongues will blot?
But you are fair, ay me, so wondrous fair,
So young, so gentle, and so debonair,
As Greece will think, if thus you live alone,
Some one or other keeps you as his own.   290
Then, Hero, hate me not, nor from me fly
To follow swiftly blasting infamy.
Perhaps thy sacred priesthood makes thee loath;
Tell me, to whom mad'st thou that heedless oath?
To Venus, answered she, and as she spake,   295
Forth from those two tralucent cisterns brake
A stream of liquid pearl, which down her face
Made milk-white paths, whereon the gods might trace
To Jove's high court. He thus replied: The rites
In which love's beauteous empress most delights   300
Are banquets, Doric music, midnight revel,
Plays, masks, and all that stern age counteth evil.
Thee as a holy idiot doth she scorn,
For thou, in vowing chastity, hast sworn
To rob her name and honor, and thereby   305
Commit'st a sin far worse than perjury,
Even sacrilege against her deity,
Through regular and formal purity.
To expiate which sin, kiss and shake hands;
Such sacrifice as this Venus demands.   310
Thereat she smiled, and did deny him so
As, put thereby, yet might he hope for mo.
Which makes him quickly reinforce his speech,
And her in humble manner thus beseech:
Though neither gods nor men may thee deserve,   315
Yet for her sake whom you have vowed to serve,
Abandon fruitless cold virginity,
The gentle queen of love's sole enemy.
Then shall you most resemble Venus' nun,
When Venus' sweet rites are performed and done.   320
Flint-breasted Pallas joys in single life,
But Pallas and your mistress are at strife.

284. **Diana:** goddess of virginity.
293. **loath:** unwilling.
296. **tralucent:** light-transmitting.
298. **might trace:** as on the Milky Way, to heaven.
308. **regular:** according to a rule; like a nun.
312. **put ... mo:** put off his course, yet might hope for more.
321. **Pallas:** Minerva, goddess of reason as opposed to passion.

Love, Hero, then, and be not tyrannous,
But heal the heart that thou hast wounded thus;
Nor stain thy youthful years with avarice;   325
Fair fools delight to be accounted nice.
The richest corn dies if it be not reaped;
Beauty alone is lost, too warily kept.
These arguments he used, and many more,
Wherewith she yielded, that was won before.   330
Hero's looks yielded, but her words made war;
Women are won when they begin to jar.
Thus having swallowed Cupid's golden hook,
The more she strived, the deeper was she strook;
Yet, evilly feigning anger, strove she still,   335
And would be thought to grant against her will.
So having paused a while, at last she said:
Who taught thee rhetoric to deceive a maid?
Ay me! such words as these should I abhor,
And yet I like them for the orator.   340
    With that Leander stooped to have embraced her,
But from his spreading arms away she cast her,
And thus bespake him: Gentle youth, forbear
To touch the sacred garments which I wear.
    Upon a rock, and underneath a hill,   345
Far from the town, where all is whist and still
Save that the sea playing on yellow sand
Sends forth a rattling murmur to the land,
Whose sound allures the golden Morpheus
In silence of the night to visit us,   350
My turret stands; and there, God knows, I play
With Venus' swans and sparrows all the day.
A dwarfish beldame bears me company,
That hops about the chamber where I lie,
And spends the night, that might be better spent,   355
In vain discourse and apish merriment.
Come thither. As she spake this, her tongue tripped,
For unawares, Come thither, from her slipped;
And suddenly her former color changed,
And here and there her eyes through anger ranged.   360
And like a planet moving several ways
At one self instant, she, poor soul, assays,
Loving, not to love at all, and every part
Strove to resist the motions of her heart;

326. **nice:** fastidious, coy.
332. **jar:** argue.
349. **Morpheus:** god of slumber.
361. **several ways:** The apparent movements of the planets are more complicated
than those of stars and had to be explained
in terms of movement "several ways" in
the Ptolemaic system.

And hands so pure, so innocent, nay such   365
As might have made heaven stoop to have a touch,
Did she uphold to Venus, and again
Vowed spotless chastity, but all in vain.
Cupid beats down her prayers with his wings;
Her vows above the empty air he flings;   370
All deep enragèd, his sinewy bow he bent,
And shot a shaft that burning from him went;
Wherewith she, strooken, looked so dolefully,
As made Love sigh to see his tyranny.
And as she wept, her tears to pearl he turned,   375
And wound them on his arm, and for her mourned.
Then towards the palace of the Destinies,
Laden with languishment and grief, he flies,
And to those stern nymphs humbly made request,
Both might enjoy each other, and be blest.   380
But with a ghastly dreadful countenance,
Threat'ning a thousand deaths at every glance,
They answered Love, nor would vouchsafe so much
    As one poor word, their hate to him was such.
Hearken awhile, and I will tell you why: 385
Heaven's wingèd herald, Jove-born Mercury,
The self-same day that he asleep had laid
Enchanted Argus, spied a country maid,
Whose careless hair, instead of pearl t' adorn it,
Glistered with dew, as one that seemed to scorn it; 390
Her breath as fragrant as the morning rose,
Her mind pure, and her tongue untaught to gloze;
Yet proud she was, for lofty pride that dwells
In towered courts is oft in shepherds' cells,
And too too well the fair vermilion knew,   395
And silver tincture of her cheeks, that drew
The love of every swain. On her this god
Enamoured was, and with his snaky rod
Did charm her nimble feet, and made her stay,
The while upon a hillock down he lay,   400
And sweetly on his pipe began to play,
And with smooth speech her fancy to assay;
Till in his twining arms he locked her fast,
And then he wooed with kisses, and at last,
As shepherds do, her on the ground he laid,   405

377. **Destinies:** the three Fates.
388. **Argus:** of the hundred eyes. Mercury made all of them close in sleep and then cut off the head of this guard placed by Juno over another of Jove's loves, Io,
who had been transformed into a cow.
392. **gloze:** deceive.
398. **snaky rod:** caduceus, with serpents intertwined at the top. He had used its magic on Argus.

And tumbling in the grass, he often strayed
Beyond the bounds of shame, in being bold
To eye those parts which no eye should behold.
And like an insolent commanding lover,
Boasting his parentage, would needs discover 410
The way to new Elysium; but she,
Whose only dower was her chastity,
Having striv'n in vain, was now about to cry,
And crave the help of shepherds that were nigh.
Herewith he stayed his fury, and began 415
To give her leave to rise; away she ran;
After went Mercury, who used such cunning,
As she, to hear his tale, left off her running;
Maids are not won by brutish force and might,
But speeches full of pleasure and delight; 420
And knowing Hermes courted her, was glad
That she such loveliness and beauty had
As could provoke his liking, yet was mute,
And neither would deny nor grant his suit.
Still vowed he love, she wanting no excuse 425
To feed him with delays, as women use,
Or thirsting after immortality—
All women are ambitious naturally—
Imposed upon her lover such a task
As he ought not perform, nor yet she ask. 430
A draught of flowing nectar she requested,
Wherewith the king of gods and men is feasted.
He, ready to accomplish what she willed,
Stole some from Hebe (Hebe Jove's cup filled)
And gave it to his simple rustic love; 435
Which being known (as what is hid from Jove?)
He inly stormed, and waxed more furious
Than for the fire filched by Prometheus,
And thrusts him down from heaven; he wand'ring here
In mournful terms, with sad and heavy cheer, 440
Complained to Cupid. Cupid, for his sake,
To be revenged on Jove did undertake;
And those on whom heaven, earth, and hell relies,
I mean the adamantine Destinies,
He wounds with love, and forced them equally 445
To dote upon deceitful Mercury.
They offered him the deadly fatal knife
That shears the slender threads of human life;

411. **Elysium:** paradise.

At his fair-feathered feet the engines laid
Which th' earth from ugly Chaos' den upweighed;   450
These he regarded not, but did entreat
That Jove, usurper of his father's seat,
Might presently be banished into hell,
And aged Saturn in Olympus dwell.
They granted what he craved, and once again   455
Saturn and Ops began their golden reign.
Murder, rape, war, lust, and treachery
Were with Jove closed in Stygian empery.
But long this blessed time continued not;
As soon as he his wishèd purpose got,   460
He, reckless of his promise, did despise
The love of th' everlasting Destinies.
They seeing it, both Love and him abhorred,
And Jupiter unto his place restored.
And but that Learning, in despite of Fate,   465
Will mount aloft, and enter heaven gate,
And to the seat of Jove itself advance,
Hermes had slept in hell with Ignorance;
Yet as a punishment they added this,
That he and Poverty should always kiss.   470
And to this day is every scholar poor;
Gross gold from them runs headlong to the boor.
Likewise, the angry sisters thus deluded,
To avenge themselves on Hermes, have concluded
That Midas' brood shall sit in Honor's chair,   475
To which the Muses' sons are only heir;
And fruitful wits that inaspiring are,
Shall, discontent, run into regions far;
And few great lords in virtuous deeds shall joy,
But be surprised with every garish toy;   480
And still enrich the lofty servile clown,
Who with encroaching guile keeps learning down.
Then muse not Cupid's suit no better sped,
Seeing in their loves the Fates were injurèd.

Second Sestiad

By this, sad Hero, with love unacquainted,
Viewing Leander's face, fell down and fainted.

456. **Saturn:** Before Jove conquered his father Saturn, the latter and his consort Ops ruled over the Golden Age on earth.
458. **Stygian empery:** dark empire of the underworld.
465. **Learning:** of which Mercury is the god.

475. **Midas:** proverbially rich king; everything he touched turned to gold.
476. **Muses' sons:** poets, but also other men of letters and learning.
480. **surprised . . . toy:** captivated by superficial sources of pleasure, not true poetry or learning.

He kissed her and breathed life into her lips,
Wherewith, as one displeased, away she trips.
Yet as she went, full often looked behind, 5
And many poor excuses did she find
To linger by the way, and once she stayed
And would have turned again, but was afraid,
In off'ring parley, to be counted light.
So on she goes, and in her idle flight, 10
Her painted fan of curlèd plumes let fall,
Thinking to train Leander therewithal.
He, being a novice, knew not what she meant,
But stayed, and after her a letter sent,
Which joyful Hero answered in such sort 15
As he had hope to scale the beauteous fort
Wherein the liberal graces locked their wealth,
And therefore to her tower he got by stealth.
Wide open stood the door, he need not climb;
And she herself, before the 'pointed time, 20
Had spread the board, with roses strewed the room,
And oft looked out, and mused he did not come.
At last he came; oh, who can tell the greeting
These greedy lovers had at their first meeting.
He asked, she gave, and nothing was denied; 25
Both to each other quickly were affied.
Look how their hands, so were their hearts united,
And what he did she willingly requited.
Sweet are the kisses, the embracements sweet,
When like desires and affections meet; 30
For from the earth to heaven is Cupid raised,
Where fancy is in equal balance peised.
Yet she this rashness suddenly repented,
And turned aside, and to herself lamented,
As if her name and honor had been wronged 35
By being possessed of him for whom she longed;
Ay, and she wished, albeit not from her heart,
That he would leave her turret and depart.
The mirthful god of amorous pleasure smiled
To see how he this captive nymph beguiled; 40
For hitherto he did but fan the fire,
And kept it down that it might mount the higher.
Now waxed she jealous lest his love abated,
Fearing her own thoughts made her to be hated.
Therefore unto him hastily she goes, 45

12. **train:** draw him after her.   26. **affied:** affianced.
14. **stayed:** stopped.   32. **peised:** weighed.

And like light Salmacis, her body throws
Upon his bosom, where with yielding eyes
She offers up herself, a sacrifice
To slake his anger if he were displeased.
Oh, what god would not therewith be appeased?   50
Like Æsop's cock, this jewel he enjoyed,
And as a brother with his sister toyed,
Supposing nothing else was to be done,
Now he her favor and goodwill had won.
But know you not that creatures wanting sense   55
By nature have a mutual appetence,
And wanting organs to advance a step,
Moved by love's force, unto each other lep?
Much more in subjects having intellect,
Some hidden influence breeds like effect.   60
Albeit Leander, rude in love and raw,
Long dallying with Hero, nothing saw
That might delight him more, yet he suspected
Some amorous rites or other were neglected.
Therefore unto his body hers he clung;   65
She, fearing on the rushes to be flung,
Strived with redoubled strength; the more she strived,
The more a gentle pleasing heat revived,
Which taught him all that elder lovers know;
And now the same gan so to scorch and glow,   70
As in plain terms, yet cunningly, he craved it;
Love always makes those eloquent that have it.
She, with a kind of granting, put him by it,
And ever as he thought himself most nigh it,
Like to the tree of Tantalus she fled,   75
And, seeming lavish, saved her maidenhead.
Ne'er king more sought to keep his diadem,
Than Hero this inestimable gem.
Above our life we love a steadfast friend,
Yet when a token of great worth we send,   80
We often kiss it, often look thereon,
And stay the messenger that would be gone;
No marvel then though Hero would not yield
So soon to part from that she dearly held;
Jewels being lost are found again, this never;   85
'Tis lost but once, and once lost, lost forever.

---

46. Salmacis: embraced her reluctant lover Hermaphroditus closely and was united in one body with him by the gods. **51. Æsop's cock:** found a jewel, but did not know what it was good for.

61. rude: untutored. **75. Tantalus:** In Hades a tree continually withdraws fruit from his hand as he reaches for it.

Now had the morn espied her lover's steeds,
Whereat she starts, puts on her purple weeds,
And, red for anger that he stayed so long,
All headlong throws herself the clouds among.   90
And now Leander, fearing to be missed,
Embraced her suddenly, took leave, and kissed.
Long was he taking leave, and loath to go,
And kissed again, as lovers use to do.
Sad Hero wrung him by the hand and wept,   95
Saying, Let your vows and promises be kept.
Then, standing at the door, she turned about,
As loath to see Leander going out.
And now the sun that through th' horizon peeps,
As pitying these lovers, downward creeps,   100
So that in silence of the cloudy night,
Though it was morning, did he take his flight.
But what the secret trusty night concealed,
Leander's amorous habit soon revealed;
With Cupid's myrtle was his bonnet crowned,   105
About his arms the purple riband wound
Wherewith she wreathed her largely-spreading hair;
Nor could the youth abstain, but he must wear
The sacred ring wherewith she was endowed,
When first religious chastity she vowed;   110
Which made his love through Sestos to be known,
And thence unto Abydos sooner blown
Than he could sail, for incorporeal Fame,
Whose weight consists in nothing but her name,
Is swifter than the wind, whose tardy plumes   115
Are reeking water and dull earthly fumes.
Home, when he came, he seemed not to be there,
But like exilèd air thrust from his sphere,
Set in a foreign place; and straight from thence,
Alcides like, by mighty violence   120
He would have chased away the swelling main
That him from her unjustly did detain.
Like as the sun in a diameter
Fires and inflames objects removèd far,
And heateth kindly, shining lat'rally,   125
So beauty sweetly quickens when 'tis nigh,

104. **habit:** attire.
116. **reeking:** cloudy, smoky. Clouds and rain (?).
118. **air ... sphere:** air removed from its proper place, so as to create a vacuum into which it tries to rush back.
120. **Alcides:** Hercules.

123. **diameter:** burning glass, lens. At the focal point the rays of the sun may start a fire, but between there and the lens, the rays are not so concentrated and only warm in the beneficent and natural ("kindly") fashion.

But being separated and removed,
Burns where it cherished, murders where it loved.
Therefore even as an index to a book,
So to his mind was young Leander's look.   130
Oh, none but gods have power their love to hide;
Affection by the count'nance is descried.
The light of hidden fire itself discovers,
And love that is concealed betrays poor lovers.
His secret flame apparently was seen;   135
Leander's father knew where he had been,
And for the same mildly rebuked his son,
Thinking to quench the sparkles new begun.
But love, resisted once, grows passionate,
And nothing more than counsel lovers hate;   140
For as a hot proud horse highly disdains
To have his head controlled, but breaks the reins,
Spits forth the ringled bit, and with his hooves
Checks the submissive ground, so he that loves,
The more he is restrained, the worse he fares.   145
What is it now but mad Leander dares?
O Hero, Hero! thus he cried full oft,
And then he got him to a rock aloft,
Where having spied her tower, long stared he on 't,
And prayed the narrow toiling Hellespont   150
To part in twain, that he might come and go;
But still the rising billows answered no.
With that he stripped him to the iv'ry skin,
And crying, Love, I come, leaped lively in.
Whereat the sapphire-visaged god grew proud,   155
And made his cap'ring Triton sound aloud,
Imagining that Ganymede, displeased,
Had left the heavens; therefore on him he seized.
Leander strived; the waves about him wound,
And pulled him to the bottom, where the ground   160
Was strewed with pearl, and in low coral groves
Sweet singing mermaids sported with their loves
On heaps of heavy gold, and took great pleasure
To spurn in careless sort the shipwreck treasure.
For here the stately azure palace stood,   165
Where kingly Neptune and his train abode.
The lusty god embraced him, called him love,
And swore he never should return to Jove.
But when he knew it was not Ganymed,

135. apparently: clearly.   Abydos.
150. Hellespont: strait between Sestos and   155. god: Neptune.

For under water he was almost dead,   170
He heaved him up, and looking on his face,
Beat down the bold waves with his triple mace,
Which mounted up, intending to have kissed him,
And fell in drops like tears, because they missed him.
Leander, being up, began to swim,   175
And looking back, saw Neptune follow him;
Whereat aghast, the poor soul gan to cry:
Oh, let me visit Hero ere I die!
The god put Helle's bracelet on his arm,
And swore the sea should never do him harm.   180
He clapped his plump cheeks, with his tresses played,
And smiling wantonly, his love bewrayed.
He watched his arms, and as they opened wide,
At every stroke betwixt them would he slide,
And steal a kiss, and then run out and dance,   185
And as he turned, cast many a lustful glance,
And threw him gaudy toys to please his eye,
And dive into the water, and there pry
Upon his breast, his thighs, and every limb,
And up again, and close beside him swim,   190
And talk of love. Leander made reply:
You are deceived, I am no woman, I.
Thereat smiled Neptune, and then told a tale
How that a shepherd, sitting in a vale,
Played with a boy so fair and kind,   195
As for his love both earth and heaven pined;
That of the cooling river durst not drink
Lest water-nymphs should pull him from the brink;
And when he sported in the fragrant lawns,
Goat-footed satyrs and up-staring fauns   200
Would steal him thence. Ere half this tale was done,
Ay me, Leander cried, th' enamoured sun,
That now should shine on Thetis' glassy bower,
Descends upon my radiant Hero's tower.
Oh, that these tardy arms of mine were wings!   205
And as he spake, upon the waves he springs.
Neptune was angry that he gave no ear,
And in his heart revenging malice bare;
He flung at him his mace, but as it went
He called it in, for love made him repent.   210
The mace returning back, his own hand hit,

179. **Helle:** fell into the Hellespont while
escaping from her stepmother on a winged
ram (producer of the Golden Fleece).

182. **bewrayed:** revealed.
203. **bower:** in the ocean. The sun has
risen high in the sky.

As meaning to be venged for darting it.
When this fresh bleeding wound Leander viewed,
His color went and came, as if he rued
The grief which Neptune felt. In gentle breasts   215
Relenting thoughts, remorse, and pity rests;
And who have hard hearts and obdurate minds
But vicious, hare-brained, and illit'rate hinds?
The god, seeing him with pity to be moved,
Thereon concluded that he was beloved.   220
(Love is too full of faith, too credulous,
With folly and false hope deluding us.)
Wherefore, Leander's fancy to surprise,
To the rich oceän for gifts he flies.
'Tis wisdom to give much; a gift prevails   225
When deep persuading oratory fails.
By this, Leander being near the land,
Cast down his weary feet, and felt the sand.
Breathless albeit he were, he rested not
Till to the solitary tower he got,   230
And knocked and called, at which celestial noise
The longing heart of Hero much more joys
Than nymphs or shepherds when the timbrel rings,
Or crooked dolphin when the sailor sings;
She stayed not for her robes, but straight arose,   235
And drunk with gladness, to the door she goes;
Where seeing a naked man, she screeched for fear,
(Such sights as this to tender maids are rare)
And ran into the dark herself to hide.
Rich jewels in the dark are soonest spied;   240
Unto her was he led, or rather drawn,
By those white limbs which sparkled through the lawn.
The nearer that he came, the more she fled,
And seeking refuge, slipped into her bed.
Whereon Leander sitting, thus began,   245
Through numbing cold all feeble, faint, and wan:
   If not for love, yet, love, for pity sake,
Me in thy bed and maiden bosom take;
At least vouchsafe these arms some little room,
Who, hoping to embrace thee, cheerly swoom;   250
This head was beat with many a churlish billow,
And therefore let it rest upon thy pillow.
Herewith affrighted Hero shrunk away,
And in her lukewarm place Leander lay,

233. **timbrel:** kind of tambourine, for   242. **lawn:** translucent linen.
rural festivities.   250. **swoom:** swam.

Whose lively heat like fire from heaven fet,   255
Would animate gross clay, and higher set
The drooping thoughts of base declining souls,
Than dreary Mars carousing nectar bowls.
His hands he cast upon her like a snare;
She, overcome with shame and sallow fear,   260
Like chaste Diana, when Actæon spied her,
Being suddenly betrayed, dived down to hide her;
And as her silver body downward went,
With both her hands she made the bed a tent,
And in her own mind thought herself secure,   265
O'ercast with dim and darksome coverture.
And now she lets him whisper in her ear,
Flatter, entreat, promise, protest, and swear;
Yet ever as he greedily assayed
To touch those dainties, she the harpy playd,   270
And every limb did, as a soldier stout,
Defend the fort and keep the foeman out;
For though the rising iv'ry mount he scaled,
Which is with azure circling lines empaled,
Much like a globe (a globe may I term this,   275
By which love sails to regions full of bliss)
Yet there with Sisyphus he toiled in vain,
Till gentle parley did the truce obtain.
Wherein Leander on her quivering breast,
Breathless spoke something, and sighed out the rest;   280
Which so prevailed, as he with small ado
Enclosed her in his arms and kissed her too.
And every kiss to her was as a charm,
And to Leander as a fresh alarm,
So that the truce was broke, and she, alas,   285
Poor silly maiden, at his mercy was.
Love is not full of pity, as men say,
But deaf and cruel where he means to prey.
Even as a bird, which in our hands we wring,
Forth plunges and oft flutters with her wing,   290
She trembling strove; this strife of hers, like that
Which made the world, another world begat
Of unknown joy. Treason was in her thought,
And cunningly to yield herself she sought.
Seeming not won, yet won she was at length;   295
In such wars women use but half their strength.

255. **fet:** fetched.
261. **Actæon:** spied on the goddess of virginity while she was bathing.
270. **harpy:** The harpies prevented King Phineus from eating his food.
277. **Sisyphus:** condemned in Hades to roll rocks uphill, which continually rolled down again.

Leander now, like Theban Hercules,
Entered the orchard of th' Hesperides,
Whose fruit none rightly can describe but he
That pulls or shakes it from the golden tree.   300
And now she wished this night were never done,
And sighed to think upon th' approaching sun;
For much it grieved her that the bright daylight
Should know the pleasure of this blessed night,
And them like Mars and Erycine displayed,   305
Both in each other's arms chained as they laid.
Again she knew not how to frame her look,
Or speak to him who in a moment took
That which so long so charily she kept;
And fain by stealth away she would have crept,   310
And to some corner secretly have gone,
Leaving Leander in the bed alone.
But as her naked feet were whipping out,
He on the sudden clinged her so about,
That mermaid-like unto the floor she slid,   315
One half appeared, the other half was hid.
Thus near the bed she blushing stood upright,
And from her countenance behold ye might
A kind of twilight break, which through the hair,
As from an orient cloud, glimpse here and there;   320
And round about the chamber this false morn
Brought forth the day before the day was born.
So Hero's ruddy cheek Hero betrayed,
And her all naked to his sight displayed;
Whence his admiring eyes more pleasure took   325
Than Dis on heaps of gold fixing his look.
By this, Apollo's golden harp began
To sound forth music to the oceän;
Which watchful Hesperus no sooner heard,
But he the day-bright-bearing car prepared,   330
And ran before, as harbinger of light,
And with his flaring beams mocked ugly night
Till she, o'ercome with anguish, shame, and rage,
Danged down to hell her loathsome carriage.
                    Desunt nonnulla.   335

297. **Hercules:** He took from the garden of the gods (Hesperides) the golden apples which were Juno's marriage gift.
305. **Erycine:** Venus. Vulcan caught her and Mars together by the use of a network of chains.
309. **charily:** carefully.
326. **Dis:** god of the underworld, rich with treasures of buried minerals.
329. **Hesperus:** the morning-star.
330. **car:** chariot.
335. **Desunt nonnulla:** (Lat.) Some parts are missing. Marlowe left no more of the poem than this.

WILLIAM SHAKESPEARE

[*1564–1616*]

Sonnets

3

Look in thy glass, and tell the face thou viewest
Now is the time that face should form another,
Whose fresh repair if now thou not renewest,
Thou dost beguile the world, unbless some mother.
For where is she so fair whose uneared womb   5
Disdains the tillage of thy husbandry?
Or who is he so fond will be the tomb
Of his self-love, to stop posterity?
Thou art thy mother's glass, and she in thee
Calls back the lovely April of her prime.   10
So thou through windows of thine age shalt see,
Despite of wrinkles, this thy golden time.
But if thou live rememb'red not to be,
Die single, and thine image dies with thee.

30

When to the sessions of sweet silent thought
I summon up remembrance of things past,
I sigh the lack of many a thing I sought,
And with old woes new wail my dear time's waste.
Then can I drown an eye, unused to flow,   5
For precious friends hid in death's dateless night,
And weep afresh love's long since canceled woe,
And moan the expense of many a vanished sight.
Then can I grieve at grievances foregone,
And heavily from woe to woe tell o'er   10
The sad account of forebemoanèd moan,
Which I new-pay as if not paid before.
But if the while I think on thee, dear friend,
All losses are restored and sorrows end.

5. **uneared**: unplowed.

1. **sessions**: sittings of a court.

6. **dateless**: endless.
8. **expense**: expending, loss; but this word, and *canceled*, *tell* (i.e., "count," as in *teller*), *account*, etc. create a financial metaphor.

35

No more be grieved at that which thou hast done:
Roses have thorns, and silver fountains mud,
Clouds and eclipses stain both moon and sun,
And loathsome canker lives in sweetest bud.
All men make faults, and even I in this,   5
Authorizing thy trespass with compare,
Myself corrupting, salving thy amiss,
Excusing thy sins more than thy sins are.
For to thy sensual fault I bring in sense—
Thy adverse party is thy advocate—   10
And 'gainst myself a lawful plea commence.
Such civil war is in my love and hate,
That I an accessory needs must be
To that sweet thief which sourly robs from me.

55

Not marble, nor the gilded monuments
Of princes, shall outlive this powerful rime;
But you shall shine more bright in these contents
Than unswept stone, besmeared with sluttish time.
When wasteful war shall statues overturn,   5
And broils root out the work of masonry,
Nor Mars his sword nor war's quick fire shall burn
The living record of your memory.
'Gainst death and all-oblivious enmity
Shall you pace forth; your praise shall still find room   10
Even in the eyes of all posterity
That wear this world out to the ending doom.
So, till the judgment that yourself arise,
You live in this, and dwell in lovers' eyes.

64

When I have seen by Time's fell hand defaced
The rich-proud cost of outworn buried age;
When sometime lofty towers I see down-razed,
And brass eternal slave to mortal rage;

6. **Authorizing ... compare:** justifying your sins by comparing them with the faults of other good things.
10. **Thy ... advocate:** i.e., reason, ordinarily the enemy of sensual sin, becomes its lawyer.

4. **unswept stone:** a stone monument, grown dusty with time.
6. **broils:** tumult, civil strife.
12. **ending doom:** the Last Judgment.

When I have seen the hungry ocean gain   5
Advantage on the kingdom of the shore,
And the firm soil win of the watery main,
Increasing store with loss, and loss with store;
When I have seen such interchange of state,
Or state itself confounded to decay;   10
Ruin hath taught me thus to ruminate,
That Time will come and take my love away.
This thought is as a death, which cannot choose
But weep to have that which it fears to lose.

65

Since brass, nor stone, nor earth, nor boundless sea,
But sad mortality o'er-sways their power.
How with this rage shall beauty hold a plea,
Whose action is no stronger than a flower?
O! how shall summer's honey breath hold out   5
Against the wrackful siege of batt'ring days,
When rocks impregnable are not so stout,
Nor gates of steel so strong, but Time decays?
O fearful meditation! where, alack,
Shall Time's best jewel from Time's chest lie hid?   10
Or what strong hand can hold his swift foot back?
Or who his spoil of beauty can forbid?
O, none, unless this miracle have might,
That in black ink my love may still shine bright.

73

That time of year thou mayst in me behold
When yellow leaves, or none, or few, do hang
Upon those boughs which shake against the cold,
Bare ruined choirs where late the sweet birds sang.
In me thou see'st the twilight of such day   5
As after sunset fadeth in the west,
Which by and by black night doth take away,
Death's second self, that seals up all in rest.
In me thou see'st the glowing of such fire,

10. **state:** dignity, high rank.

1–2. **Since brass ... power:** i.e., since

there are none of these things which are not subject to ending and death.
8. **but Time decays:** but that Time shall destroy them.

That on the ashes of his youth doth lie 10
As the deathbed whereon it must expire,
Consumed with that which it was nourished by.
This thou perceivest, which makes thy love more strong,
To love that well which thou must leave ere long.

94

They that have power to hurt and will do none,
That do not do the thing they most do show,
Who, moving others, are themselves as stone,
Unmovèd, cold, and to temptation slow—
They rightly do inherit Heaven's graces 5
And husband nature's riches from expense.
They are the lords and owners of their faces,
Others but stewards of their excellence.
The summer's flower is to the summer sweet,
Though to itself it only live and die, 10
But if that flower with base infection meet,
The basest weed outbraves his dignity.
For sweetest things turn sourest by their deeds;
Lilies that fester smell far worse than weeds.

97

How like a winter hath my absence been
From thee, the pleasure of the fleeting year!
What freezings have I felt, what dark days seen!
What old December's bareness everywhere!
And yet this time removed was summer's time, 5
The teeming autumn, big with rich increase,
Bearing the wanton burthen of the prime,
Like widowed wombs after their lords' decease.
Yet this abundant issue seemed to me
But hope of orphans and unfathered fruit, 10
For summer and his pleasures wait on thee,
And, thou away, the very birds are mute;
Or if they sing, 'tis with so dull a cheer
That leaves look pale, dreading the winter's near.

12. **Consumed ... by:** extinguished by the ashes of the fuel that fed it.

7. **wanton ... prime:** the crops engendered by spring.

8. **stewards:** temporary guardians.

107

Not mine own fears, nor the prophetic soul
Of the wide world dreaming on things to come,
Can yet the lease of my true love control,
Supposed as forfeit to a cónfined doom.
The mortal moon hath her eclipse endured,   5
And the sad augurs mock their own presage.
Incertainties now crown themselves assured,
And peace proclaims olives of endless age.
Now with the drops of this most balmy time
My love looks fresh, and Death to me subscribes,   10
Since, spite of him, I'll live in this poor rhyme
While he insults o'er dull and speechless tribes.
And thou in this shalt find thy monument,
When tyrants' crests and tombs of brass are spent.

116

Let me not to the marriage of true minds
Admit impediments. Love is not love
Which alters when it alteration finds,
Or bends with the remover to remove:
O, no! it is an ever-fixed mark,   5
That looks on tempests and is never shaken;
It is the star to every wandering bark,
Whose worth's unknown, although his height be taken.
Love's not Time's fool, though rosy lips and cheeks
Within his bending sickle's compass come;   10
Love alters not with his brief hours and weeks,
But bears it out even to the edge of doom.
If this be error, and upon me proved,
I never writ, nor no man ever loved.

118

Like as, to make our appetites more keen,
With eager compounds we our palate urge;

5–6. **The mortal . . . presage:** Apparently the meaning is that Queen Elizabeth I (often referred to as Cynthia—the moon) has passed successfully through her astrologically dangerous year, and that the prophets mock their own direful predictions.
10. **subscribes:** yields.

7. **Whose . . . taken:** The value of the star is unknown, although measuring this unknown value's height above the horizon is a guide to the navigator.
10. **compass:** circumference.
12. **doom:** the Last Judgment.

2. **eager:** bitter.

As to prevent our maladies unseen
We sicken to shun sickness when we purge—
Even so, being full of your ne'er-cloying sweetness,   5
To bitter sauces did I frame my feeding,
And sick of welfare found a kind of meetness
To be diseased, ere that there was true needing.
Thus policy in love, to anticipate
The ills that were not, grew to faults assured,   10
And brought to medicine a healthful state,
Which, rank of goodness, would by ill be cured.
But thence I learn, and find the lesson true,
Drugs poison him that so fell sick of you.

129

The expense of spirit in a waste of shame
Is lust in action; and till action, lust
Is perjured, murderous, bloody, full of blame,
Savage, extreme, rude, cruel, not to trust;
Enjoyed no sooner but despisèd straight;   5
Past reason hunted, and no sooner had,
Past reason hated, as a swallowed bait,
On purpose laid to make the taker mad.
Mad in pursuit, and in possession so;
Had, having, and in quest to have, extreme;   10
A bliss in proof; and proved, a very woe;
Before, a joy proposed; behind, a dream.
All this the world well knows, yet none knows well
To shun the Heaven that leads men to this Hell.

130

My Mistress' eyes are nothing like the sun;
Coral is far more red than her lips' red;
If snow be white, why then her breasts are dun;
If hairs be wires, black wires grow on her head.
I have seen roses damasked, red and white,   5
But no such roses see I in her cheeks;

4. purge: take cathartics.
7. welfare: well-being.
12. rank of: grown too large, luxuriant, with.

1. expense: expending.
1. waste: desert; also a using up.

11. in proof: when put to the test; in the act.

1. My Mistress': In this "anti-Petrarchan" sonnet, the usual comparisons of the sonneteers are deflated. Many others, including Petrarch himself, wrote such pieces.
5. damasked: variegated.

And in some perfumes is there more delight
Than in the breath that from my mistress reeks.
I love to hear her speak, yet well I know
That music hath a far more pleasing sound;   10
I grant I never saw a goddess go;
My mistress, when she walks, treads on the ground:
And yet, by heaven, I think my love as rare
As any she belied with false compare.

138

When my love swears that she is made of truth,
I do believe her, though I know she lies,
That she might think me some untutor'd youth,
Unlearned in the world's false subtleties.
Thus vainly thinking that she thinks me young,   5
Although she knows my days are past the best,
Simply I credit her false-speaking tongue:
On both sides thus is simple truth supprest.
But wherefore says she not she is unjust?
And wherefore say not I that I am old?   10
O, love's best habit is in seeming trust,
And age in love loves not to have years told:
Therefore I lie with her, and she with me,
And in our faults by lies we flatter'd be.

144

Two loves I have of comfort and despair,
Which like two spirits do suggest me still:
The better angel is a man right fair,
The worser spirit a woman, colored ill.
To win me soon to hell, my female evil   5
Tempteth my better angel from my side,
And would corrupt my saint to be a devil,
Wooing his purity with her foul pride.
And whether that my angel be turned fiend
Suspect I may, but not directly tell;   10

8. **reeks:** sends out its odor (not necessarily unpleasant).
11. **go:** walk.

11. **habit:** outward appearance, clothing.
13. **lie:** have sexual intercourse.

9. **unjust:** untrue.

2. **suggest me still:** tempt me constantly.
4. **ill:** dark.

But being both from me, both to each friend,   11
I guess one angel in another's hell:
Yet this shall I ne'er know, but live in doubt,
Till my bad angel fire my good one out.

146

Poor soul, the center of my sinful earth,
Rebuke these rebel powers that thee array!
Why dost thou pine within and suffer dearth,
Painting thy outward walls so costly gay?
Why so large cost, having so short a lease,   5
Dost thou upon thy fading mansion spend?
Shall worms, inheritors of this excess,
Eat up thy charge? Is this thy body's end?
Then, soul, live thou upon thy servant's loss,
And let that pine to aggravate thy store;   10
Buy terms divine in selling hours of dross:
Within be fed, without be rich no more.
So shalt thou feed on Death, that feeds on men,
And Death once dead, there's no more dying then.

Fear no more the heat o' the sun

Fear no more the heat o' the sun,
   Nor the furious winter's rages;
Thou thy wordly task hast done,
   Home art gone and ta'en thy wages.
Golden lads and girls all must,   5
As chimney-sweepers, come to dust.

Fear no more the frown o' the great;
   Thou art past the tyrant's stroke;
Care no more to clothe and eat;
   To thee the reed is as the oak.   10
The sceptre, learning, physic, must
All follow this, and come to dust.

---

11. **from me . . . friend:** away from me, and friends to each other.
14. **fire:** drive out by hellish fire.

2. **array:** clothe.

10. **aggravate:** increase.

Fear no more: lament for Imogen, *Cymbeline*, IV, ii, 258 ff.
6. **As:** like.
11. **physic:** science of medicine.

Fear no more the lightning-flash,
   Nor the all-dreaded thunder-stone;
Fear not slander, censure rash;   15
   Thou hast finish'd joy and moan.
All lovers young, all lovers must
Consign to thee, and come to dust.

No exorciser harm thee!
Nor no witchcraft charm thee!   20
Ghost unlaid forbear thee!
Nothing ill come near thee!
Quiet consummation have,
And renownèd be thy grave!

Full fathom five

Full fathom five thy father lies;
   Of his bones are coral made;
Those are pearls that were his eyes:
   Nothing of him that doth fade,
But doth suffer a sea change   5
Into something rich and strange.
Sea nymphs hourly ring his knell:
   Burthen. Ding-dong.
Hark! now I hear them,—Ding-dong, bell.

Where the bee sucks

Where the bee sucks, there suck I:
In a cowslip's bell I lie;
There I couch when owls do cry.
On the bat's back I do fly
After summer merrily.   5
Merrily, merrily shall I live now
Under the blossom that hangs on the bough.

14. thunder-stone: meteorite, which by falling was supposed to make the sound of thunder.
18. Consign: agree.

Full ... five: sung by Ariel to Ferdinand, whose father has apparently drowned, *The Tempest*, I, ii, 396 ff.
8. Burthen: chorus, sung by other voices.

Where ... sucks: sung by Ariel, a spirit, in anticipation of his freedom, *The Tempest*, V, i, 88 ff.

The Phoenix and Turtle

Let the bird of loudest lay,
On the sole Arabian tree,
Herald sad and trumpet be,
To whose sound chaste wings obey.

But thou shriking harbinger,   5
Foul precurrer of the fiend,
Augur of the fever's end,
To this troop come thou not near.

From this session interdict
Every fowl of tyrant wing,   10
Save the Eagle, feath'red king:
Keep the obsequy so strict.

Let the priest in surplice white,
That defunctive music can,
Be the death-divining Swan,   15
Lest the requiem lack his right.

And thou treble-dated Crow,
That thy sable gender mak'st,
With the breath thou giv'st and tak'st,
'Mongst our mourners shalt thou go.   20

Here the anthem doth commence:
Love and Constancy is dead,
Phoenix and the Turtle fled,
In a mutual flame from hence.

So they lov'd as love in twain,   25
Had the essence but in one;
Two distincts, division none:
Number there in love was slain.

Phoenix and Turtle: The fable of the Phoenix is that this wonderful bird, of which there was only one example, went after 1,000 years to a unique ("sole" in line 2) tree and in a spicy nest burned itself, then rose young again from the ashes. It was supposedly virtuous, and was early associated with Christian ideas of rebirth and eternal life. Shakespeare modifies the legend. The virtuous turtledove was regarded as a constant lover.

6. **precurrer:** precursor. The screech owl is meant. It was supposed to foretell death ("fever's end," line 7).
14. **That ... can:** which can sing funeral music. The swan was supposed to sing only once, just before its own death.
16. **right:** rite; also rightful ceremony.
17–19. **treble-dated ... tak'st:** The crow was supposed to live nine times as long as man, and to breed chastely, by interchange of breath.

Hearts remote, yet not asunder;
Distance and no space was seen,   30
'Twixt this Turtle and his Queen;
But in them it were a wonder.

So between them Love did shine,
That the Turtle saw his right
Flaming in the Phoenix sight,   35
Either was the Other's mine.

Property was thus appalled,
That the self was not the same;
Single Nature's double name,
Neither two nor one was called.   40

Reason, in itself confounded,
Saw division grow together,
To themselves yet either neither,
Simple were so well compounded,

That it cried, How true a twain,   45
Seemeth this concordant one!
Love hath Reason, Reason none,
If what parts, can so remain.

Whereupon it made this *threne*,
To the Phoenix and the Dove,   50
Co-Supremes and stars of Love,
A chorus to their tragic scene.

Threnos

Beauty, Truth, and Rarity,
Grace in all simplicity,
Here enclos'd, in cinders lie.   55

Death is now the Phoenix nest,
And the Turtle's loyal breast,
To eternity doth rest,

Leaving no posterity:
'Twas not their infirmity,   60
But was married Chastity.

32. **But:** except.
34. **right:** his rightful property, himself.
37. **Property:** the term in logic for the quality or characteristic of anything.

49. **threne:** threnody, dirge.
52. **scene:** the stage; tragedy in the exalted dramatic sense is one implication.

Truth may seem, but cannot be,
Beauty brag, but 'tis not she:
Truth and Beauty buried be.

To this urn let those repair,   65
That are either true or fair,
For those dead birds, sigh a prayer.

HENRY HOWARD,

EARL OF SURREY [1517–1547]

Complaint of a Lover Rebuked

Love that liveth and reigneth in my thought,
That built his seat within my captive breast,
Clad in the arms wherein with me he fought,
Oft in my face he doth his banner rest.
She that me taught to love and suffer pain,   5
My doubtful hope and eke my hot desire
With shamefast cloak to shadow and refrain,
Her smiling grace converteth straight to ire;
And coward love then to the heart apace
Taketh his flight, whereas he lurks and plains 10
His purpose lost, and dare not show his face.
For my lord's guilt thus faultless bide I pains;
Yet from my lord shall not my foot remove:
Sweet is his death that takes his end by love.

My friend, the things that do attain

My friend, the things that do attain
 The happy life be these, I find;
The riches left, not got with pain;
 The fruitful ground, the quiet mind;

The equal friend; no grudge, no strife;   5
 No charge of rule, nor governance;
Without disease the healthy life;
 The household of continuance;

Complaint: See another version ("The long love that in my thought doth harbor") by Thomas Wyatt of the same Italian sonnet, and the notes to it.

My friend: adaptation of an epigram (X, 47) by the Latin poet Martial.

The mean diet, no dainty fare;
  Wisdom joined with simpleness;   10
The night dischargèd of all care,
  Where wine the wit may not oppress;

The faithful wife, without debate;
  Such sleeps as may beguile the night.
Content thyself with thine estate;   15
  Neither wish death, nor fear his might.

SIR WALTER RALEGH [1552–1618]

The Nymph's Reply to the Shepherd

If all the world and love were young,
And truth in every shepherd's tongue,
These pretty pleasures might me move
To live with thee and be thy love.

Time drives the flocks from field to fold,   5
When rivers rage and rocks grow cold,
And Philomel becometh dumb;
The rest complains of cares to come.

The flowers do fade, and wanton fields
To wayward winter reckoning yields.   10
A honey tongue, a heart of gall,
Is fancy's spring, but sorrow's fall.

Thy gowns, thy shoes, thy beds of roses,
Thy cap, thy kirtle, and thy posies
Soon break, soon wither, soon forgotten: 15
In folly ripe, in reason rotten.

Thy belt of straw and ivy buds,
Thy coral clasps and amber studs,
All these in me no means can move
To come to thee and be thy love.   20

Nymph's . . . Reply: See Christopher Marlowe's (?) "The Passionate Shepherd to His Love," to which this is a reply.
7. **Philomel:** nightingale.

But could youth last and love still breed,
Had joys no date nor age no need,
Then these delights my mind might move
To live with thee and be thy love.

Nature, that washed her hands in milk

Nature, that washed her hands in milk,
And had forgot to dry them,
Instead of earth took snow and silk,
At Love's request to try them,
If she a mistress could compose   5
To please Love's fancy out of those.

Her eyes he would should be of light,
A violet breath, and lips of jelly;
Her hair not black, nor overbright,
And of the softest down her belly;   10
As for her inside he'd have it
Only of wantonness and wit.

At Love's entreaty such a one
Nature made, but with her beauty
She hath framed a heart of stone;   15
So as Love, by ill destiny,
Must die for her whom Nature gave him,
Because her darling would not save him.

But Time (which Nature doth despise,
And rudely gives her Love the lie,   20
Makes Hope a fool, and Sorrow wise)
His hands do neither wash nor dry;
But being made of steel and rust,
Turns snow and silk and milk to dust.

The light, the belly, lips, and breath,   25
He dims, discolors, and destroys;
With those he feeds but fills not death,
Which sometimes were the food of joys.
Yea, Time doth dull each lively wit,
And dries all wantonness with it.   30

22. **date:** end.

Oh, cruel Time! which takes in trust
Our youth, our joys, and all we have,
And pays us but with age and dust;
Who in the dark and silent grave
When we have wandered all our ways   35
Shuts up the story of our days.

The Passionate Man's Pilgrimage

Give me my scallop-shell of quiet,
My staff of faith to walk upon,
My scrip of joy, immortal diet,
My bottle of salvation,
My gown of glory, hope's true gage,   5
And thus I'll take my pilgrimage.

Blood must be my body's balmer,
No other balm will there be given,
Whilst my soul like a white palmer
Travels to the land of heaven,   10
Over the silver mountains,
Where spring the nectar fountains;
And there I'll kiss
The bowl of bliss,
And drink my eternal fill   15
On every milken hill.
My soul will be a-dry before,
But after it will ne'er thirst more;
And by the happy blissful way
More peaceful pilgrims I shall see,   20
That have shook off their gowns of clay
And go appareled fresh like me.
I'll bring them first
To slake their thirst,
And then to taste those nectar suckets,   25
At the clear wells
Where sweetness dwells,
Drawn up by saints in crystal buckets.
And when our bottles and all we
Are filled with immortality,   30
Then the holy paths we'll travel,
Strewed with rubies thick as gravel,

1. **shell:** worn as a badge by pilgrims.   9. **palmer:** pilgrim.
3. **scrip:** bag.   25. **suckets:** sweets.

Ceilings of diamonds, sapphire floors,
High walls of coral, and pearl bowers.

From thence to heaven's bribeless hall   35
Where no corrupted voices brawl,
No conscience molten into gold,
Nor forged accusers bought and sold,
No cause deferred, nor vain-spent journey,
For there Christ is the king's attorney,   40
Who pleads for all without degrees,
And he hath angels, but no fees.
When the grand twelve million jury
Of our sins and sinful fury,
'Gainst our souls black verdicts give,   45
Christ pleads his death, and then we live.
Be thou my speaker, taintless pleader,
Unblotted lawyer, true proceeder,
Thou movest salvation even for alms,
Not with a bribèd lawyer's palms.   50

And this is my eternal plea
To him that made heaven, earth, and sea,
Seeing my flesh must die so soon,
And want a head to dine next noon,
Just at the stroke when my veins start and spread,   55
Set on my soul an everlasting head.
Then am I ready, like a palmer fit,
To tread those blest paths which before I writ.

JOHN LYLY [1553–1606]

Cupid and my Campaspe

Cupid and my Campaspe played
At cards for kisses; Cupid paid:
He stakes his quiver, bow, and arrows,
His mother's doves, and team of sparrows;
Loses them too; then down he throws   5
The coral of his lips, the rose
Growing on 's cheek (but none knows how);

39. **cause:** law-suit.
41. **degrees:** rank.
42. **angels:** pun on name of coin.
54. **want a head:** Ralegh refers to his

imminent execution, ordered by Elizabeth I.

Cupid . . .: song from Lyly's comedy
Alexander and Campaspe.

With these, the crystal of his brow,
And then the dimple on his chin;
All these did my Campaspe win.   10
At last he set her both his eyes:
She won, and Cupid blind did rise.
    O Love, has she done this to thee?
    What shall, alas, become of me?

ROBERT SOUTHWELL [1561–1595]

The Burning Babe

As I in hoary winter's night stood shivering in the snow,
Surpris'd I was with sudden heat which made my heart to glow;
And lifting up a fearful eye to view what fire was near,
A pretty Babe all burning bright did in the air appear;
Who, scorched with excessive heat, such floods of tears did shed,   5
As though his floods should quench his flames which with his tears
        were fed.
"Alas!" quoth he, "but newly born in fiery heats I fry,
Yet none approach to warm their hearts or feel my fire but I.
My faultless breast the furnace is, the fuel wounding thorns;
Love is the fire, and sighs the smoke, the ashes shame and scorns;   10
The fuel Justice layeth on, and Mercy blows the coals;
The metal in this furnace wrought are men's defiled souls;
For which, as now on fire I am to work them to their good,
So will I melt into a bath to wash them in my blood."
With this he vanish'd out of sight and swiftly shrunk away,   15
And straight I called unto mind that it was Christmas Day.

SAMUEL DANIEL [1562–1619]

Ulysses and the Siren

Siren

Come, worthy Greek, Ulysses, come,
    Possess these shores with me;
The winds and seas are troublesome,
    And here we may be free.

7. **fry**: burn.   **Ulysses . . . Siren:** Ulysses successfully re-
                                     sisted the sirens' songs, which drew other
                                     mariners to destruction on the rocks.

Here may we sit and view their toil   5
    That travail on the deep,
And joy the day in mirth the while,
    And spend the night in sleep.

Ulysses

Fair nymph, if fame or honor were
    To be attained with ease,   10
Then would I come and rest with thee,
    And leave such toils as these.
But here it dwells, and here must I
    With danger seek it forth;
To spend the time luxuriously   15
    Becomes not men of worth.

Siren

Ulysses, O be not deceived
    With that unreal name;
This honor is a thing conceived,
    And rests on others' fame;   20
Begotten only to molest
    Our peace, and to beguile
The best thing of our life, our rest,
    And give us up to toil.

Ulysses

Delicious nymph, suppose there were   25
    Nor honor nor report,
Yet manliness would scorn to wear
    The time in idle sport.
For toil doth give a better touch,
    To make us feel our joy;   30
And ease finds tediousness, as much
    As labor, yields annoy.

Siren

Then pleasure likewise seems the shore
    Whereto tends all your toil,
Which you forgo to make it more,   35
    And perish oft the while.

19. **conceived**: only imagined.

Who may disport them diversly,
  Find never tedious day,
And ease may have variety
  As well as action may.   40

Ulysses

But natures of the noblest frame
  These toils and dangers please,
And they take comfort in the same
  As much as you in ease,
And with the thoughts of actions past   45
  Are recreated still;
When pleasure leaves a touch at last
  To show that it was ill.

Siren

That doth opinion only cause
  That's out of custom bred,   50
Which makes us many other laws
  Than ever nature did.
No widows wail for our delights,
  Our sports are without blood;
The world, we see, by warlike wights   55
  Receives more hurt than good.

Ulysses

But yet the state of things require
  These motions of unrest,
And these great spirits of high desire
  Seem born to turn them best,   60
To purge the mischiefs that increase
  And all good order mar;
For oft we see a wicked peace
  To be well changed for war.

Siren

Well, well, Ulysses, then I see   65
  I shall not have thee here,
And therefore I will come to thee,
  And take my fortunes there.
I must be won that cannot win,
  Yet lost were I not won;   70
For beauty hath created been
  T' undo, or be undone.

MICHAEL DRAYTON [1563–1631]

Since there's no help

Since there's no help, come let us kiss and part;
Nay, I have done, you get no more of me,
And I am glad, yea glad with all my heart
That thus so cleanly I myself can free;
Shake hands forever, cancel all our vows,   5
And when we meet at any time again,
Be it not seen in either of our brows
That we one jot of former love retain.
Now at the last gasp of love's latest breath,
When, his pulse failing, passion speechless lies,   10
When faith is kneeling by his bed of death,
And innocence is closing up his eyes,
Now if thou wouldst, when all have given him over,
From death to life thou mightst him yet recover.

THOMAS CAMPION [1567–1620]

My sweetest Lesbia

My sweetest Lesbia, let us live and love;
And though the sager sort our deeds reprove,
Let us not weigh them. Heaven's great lamps do dive
Into their west, and straight again revive;
But, soon as once set is our little light,   5
Then must we sleep one ever-during night.

If all would lead their lives in love like me,
Then bloody swords and armour should not be;
No drum nor trumpet peaceful sleeps should move,
Unless alarm came from the camp of love.   10
But fools do live and waste their little light,
And seek with pain their ever-during night.

Lesbia: the beloved (as named in his
poetry) of the Latin poet Catullus. This
song is based on one of his poems.

When timely death my life and fortune ends,
Let not my hearse be vexed with mourning friends;
But let all lovers, rich in triumph, come   15
And with sweet pastimes grace my happy tomb.
And, Lesbia, close up thou my little light,
And crown with love my ever-during night.

When to her lute Corinna sings

When to her lute Corinna sings,
Her voice revives the leaden strings,
And doth in highest notes appear
As any challenged echo clear;
But when she doth of mourning speak,   5
Even with her sighs the strings do break.

And as her lute doth live or die,
Led by her passion, so must I:
For when of pleasure she doth sing,
My thoughts enjoy a sudden spring,   10
But if she doth of sorrow speak,
Even from my heart the strings do break.

When thou must home to shades of underground

When thou must home to shades of underground,
    And there arrived, a new admirèd guest,
The beauteous spirits do engirt thee round,
    White Iope, blithe Helen, and the rest,
To hear the stories of thy finished love   5
From that smooth tongue, whose music hell can move:

Then wilt thou speak of banqueting delights,
    Of masks and revels which sweet youth did make,
Of tourneys and great challenges of knights,
    And all these triumphs for thy beauty's sake.   10
When thou hast told these honours done to thee,
Then tell, O! tell, how thou didst murder me.

---

13. **timely:** imposed by time.

4. **Iope:** name for a lovely dead woman, chosen in imitation of a similar line of the

Latin poet Propertius (*Elegies*, II, *l.* 28). Also another name for Cassiopeia, daughter of Aeolus.
6. **hell . . . move:** i.e., can move hell.

There is a garden in her face

There is a garden in her face,
Where roses and white lilies grow;
  A heav'nly paradise is that place,
Wherein all pleasant fruits do flow.
    There cherries grow which none may buy   5
    Till "cherry-ripe!" themselves do cry.

Those cherries fairly do enclose
Of orient pearl a double row,
  Where when her lovely laughter shows,
They look like rosebuds filled with snow.   10
    Yet them nor peer nor prince can buy,
    Till "cherry-ripe!" themselves do cry.

Her eyes like angels watch them still;
Her brows like bended bows do stand,
  Threat'ning with piercing frowns to kill   15
All that attempt with eye or hand
    Those sacred cherries to come nigh,
    Till "cherry-ripe!" themselves do cry.

I care not for these ladies

I care not for these ladies
That must be woo'd and pray'd;
Give me kind Amaryllis,
The wanton country maid.   5
Nature art disdaineth;
Her beauty is her own.
  Her when we court and kiss
  She cries, "Forsooth, let go!"
  But when we come where comfort is,
  She never will say, "No!"   10

If I love Amaryllis
She gives me fruit and flowers,
But if we love these ladies
We must give golden showers.
Give them gold that sell love;   15

6. **cherry-ripe:** street-vendors' cry.

Give me the nutbrown lass
  Who, when we court and kiss,
  She cries, "Forsooth, let go!"
  But when we come where comfort is,
  She never will say, "No!"   20

These ladies must have pillows
And beds by strangers wrought;
Give me a bower of willows,
Of moss and leaves unbought,
And fresh Amaryllis   25
With milk and honey fed,
  Who, when we court and kiss,
  She cries "Forsooth, let go!"
  But when we come where comfort is,
  She never will say, "No!"   30

THOMAS NASHE [1567–1601]

A Litany in Time of Plague

Adieu, farewell earth's bliss,
This world uncertain is;
Fond are life's lustful joys,
Death proves them all but toys,
None from his darts can fly.   5
I am sick, I must die.
  Lord, have mercy on us!

Rich men, trust not in wealth,
Gold cannot buy you health;
Physic himself must fade,   10
All things to end are made.
The plague full swift goes by;
I am sick, I must die.
  Lord, have mercy on us!

Beauty is but a flower   15
Which wrinkles will devour:
Brightness falls from the air,

3. **Fond:** foolish.   10. **Physic:** art of medicine.
4. **toys:** trifles.

Queens have died young and fair,
Dust hath closed Helen's eye.
I am sick, I must die.   20
   Lord, have mercy on us!

Strength stoops unto the grave,
Worms feed on Hector brave,
Swords may not fight with fate.
Earth still holds ope her gate;   25
Come! come! the bells do cry.
I am sick, I must die.
   Lord, have mercy on us!

Wit with his wantonness
Tasteth death's bitterness;   30
Hell's executioner
Hath no ears for to hear
What vain art can reply.
I am sick, I must die.
   Lord, have mercy on us!   35

Haste, therefore, each degree,
To welcome destiny.
Heaven is our heritage,
Earth but a player's stage;
Mount we unto the sky.   40
I am sick, I must die.
   Lord, have mercy on us!

36. **degree:** class.

The Renaissance:
Seventeenth Century

JOHN DONNE
[1572–1631]

The Good Morrow

I wonder, by my troth, what thou and I
Did, till we loved? Were we not weaned till then,
But sucked on country pleasures, childishly?
Or snorted we in the seven sleepers' den?
'Twas so; but this, all pleasures fancies be.   5
If ever any beauty I did see,
Which I desired, and got, 'twas but a dream of thee.

And now good morrow to our waking souls,
Which watch not one another out of fear;
For love all love of other sights controls,   10
And makes one little room an everywhere.
Let sea-discoverers to new worlds have gone,
Let maps to other, worlds on worlds have shown,
Let us possess one world; each hath one, and is one.

4. **snorted . . . den:** The Seven Sleepers of Ephesus were said to have slept in a cave for nearly 200 years.
5. **but this:** except for this.

8. **good morrow:** good morning.
13. **Let . . . shown:** Allow that maps have shown worlds on worlds to others.

My face in thine eye, thine in mine appears,   15
And true plain hearts do in the faces rest;
Where can we find two better hemispheres
Without sharp North, without declining West?
Whatever dies was not mixed equally;
If our two loves be one, or thou and I   20
Love so alike that none do slacken, none can die.

Song

Go and catch a falling star,
    Get with child a mandrake root,
Tell me where all past years are,
    Or who cleft the devil's foot,
Teach me to hear mermaids singing,   5
Or to keep off envy's stinging,
      And find
      What wind
Serves to advance an honest mind.

If thou be'st born to strange sights,   10
    Things invisible to see,
Ride ten thousand days and nights,
    Till age snow white hairs on thee.
Thou, when thou return'st, wilt tell me,
All strange wonders that befell thee,   15
      And swear
      No where
Lives a woman true and fair.

If thou find'st one, let me know;
    Such a pilgrimage were sweet.   20
Yet do not; I would not go,
    Though at next door we might meet.
Though she were true when you met her,
And last till you write your letter,
      Yet she   25
      Will be
False, ere I come, to two or three.

19. **Whatever . . . equally:** Absolutely homogeneous matter ("mixed equally") was supposed to be everlasting.

2. **mandrake root:** a root shaped like the lower half of the human body. It was considered an aphrodisiac.

5. **mermaids singing:** To listen to the sirens' song was to be tempted to destruction on the rocks where they lived.

The Sun Rising

Busy old fool, unruly sun,
　　Why dost thou thus
Through windows and through curtains call on us?
Must to thy motions lovers' seasons run?
　　Saucy pedantic wretch, go chide   5
　　Late schoolboys and sour prentices,
　Go tell court-huntsmen that the king will ride,
　Call country ants to harvest offices;
Love, all alike, no season knows, nor clime,
Nor hours, days, months, which are the rags of time.   10

Thy beams, so reverend, and strong
　　Why shouldst thou think?
I could eclipse and cloud them with a wink,
But that I would not lose her sight so long;
　　If her eyes have not blinded thine,   15
　　Look, and tomorrow late tell me
　Whether both the Indias of spice and mine
　Be where thou left'st them, or lie here with me.
Ask for those kings whom thou saw'st yesterday,
And thou shalt hear, all here in one bed lay.   20

She is all states, and all princes I;
　　Nothing else is.
Princes do but play us; compared to this,
All honor's mimic, all wealth alchemy.
　　Thou, sun, art half as happy as we,   25
　　In that the world's contracted thus;
　Thine age asks ease, and since thy duties be
　To warm the world, that's done in warming us.
Shine here to us, and thou art everywhere;
This bed thy center is, these walls thy sphere.   30

The Indifferent

I can love both fair and brown,
Her whom abundance melts, and her whom want betrays,
Her who loves loneness best, and her who masks and plays,

---

6. **prentices:** apprentices.
8. **offices:** duties.
17. **Indias . . . mine:** East Indies of spice, and Western Hemisphere of gold mines.

30. **center . . . sphere:** The earth was supposed to lie at the center, around which the sun was carried in its sphere.

Her whom the country form'd, and whom the town,
   Her who believes, and her who tries,   5
   Her who still weeps with spongy eyes,
   And her who is dry cork and never cries;
I can love her, and her, and you, and you;
I can love any, so she be not true.

   Will no other vice content you?   10
Will it not serve your turn to do as did your mothers?
Or have you all old vices spent, and now would find out others?
   Or doth a fear that men are true torment you?
      O we are not; be not you so.
      Let me, and do you, twenty know.   15
      Rob me, but bind me not, and let me go.
   Must I, who come to travail through you,
   Grow your fix'd subject because you are true?

   Venus heard me sigh this song,
And by love's sweetest part, variety, she swore   20
She heard not this till now, and that it should be so no more.
   She went, examin'd, and return'd ere long,
      And said, "Alas, some two or three
      Poor heretics in love there be,
      Which think to 'stablish dangerous constancy,   25
   But I have told them, 'Since you will be true,
   You shall be true to them who're false to you.'"

The Canonization

For God's sake hold your tongue and let me love,   *ADDRESSED*
   Or chide my palsy or my gout,   *TO* y[ou] *(SING)*
My five gray hairs or ruin'd fortune flout,
   With wealth your state, your mind with arts improve,
      Take you a course, get you a place,   5
      Observe His Honour, or His Grace,
   Or the King's real, or his stamped face
   Contemplate, what you will, approve,
   So you will let me love.

---

5. **tries:** finds out by trial (instead of taking on faith).

5. **Take ... place:** take a definite line; get a position.
7. **Or ... face:** the King's face at court, or money with his face on it.

Alas, alas, who's injur'd by my love?   10
  What merchant's ships have my sighs drown'd?
Who says my tears have overflow'd his ground?   *you (Pl.)*
  When did my colds a forward spring remove?   *society*
    When did the heats which my veins fill
    Add one more to the plaguey Bill?   15
Soldiers find wars, and Lawyers find out still
  Litigious men, which quarrels move,
  Though she and I do love.

Call us what you will, we are made such by love;
  Call her one, me another fly,   20
We are tapers too, and at our own cost die,
  And we in us find th' Eagle and the Dove.
    The Phoenix riddle hath more wit
    By us: we two being one, are it.
So to one neutral thing both sexes fit;   25
  We die and rise the same, and prove
  Mysterious by this love.

We can die by it, if not live by love,
  And if unfit for tombs and hearse
Our legend be, it will be fit for verse;   30
  And if no piece of Chronicle we prove,
    We'll build in sonnets pretty rooms;
    As well a well-wrought urn becomes
The greatest ashes, as half-acre tombs,
  And by these hymns, all shall approve   35
  Us *Canoniz'd* for Love:

And thus invoke us; You whom reverend love
  Made one another's hermitage;
You, to whom love was peace, that now is rage;
  Who did the whole world's soul contract, and drove   40
    Into the glasses of your eyes
    (So made such mirrors and such spies
That they did all to you epitomize,)
  Countries, Towns, Courts: Beg from above
  A pattern of your love!   45

---

15. **plaguey Bill:** list of those dead of the plague.
20. **fly:** proverbially subject to mortality.
24. **Phoenix:** a mythical bird of no sex. It lived a thousand years, then burned itself and was reborn from the ashes.

21. **die:** i.e., in our meaning, to have intercourse.
30. **legend:** most specifically, the story of a saint's life and martyrdom (see "canonized," below).

Break of Day

'Tis true, 'tis day; what though it be?
Oh, wilt thou therefore rise from me?
   Why should we rise because 'tis light?
   Did we lie down because 'twas night?
Love which in spite of darkness brought us hither   5
Should, in despite of light, keep us together.

Light hath no tongue, but is all eye;
If it could speak as well as spy,
   This were the worst that it could say:
   That, being well, I fain would stay,   10
And that I loved my heart and honor so,
That I would not from him that had them go.

Must business thee from hence remove?
Oh, that's the worst disease of love;
   The poor, the foul, the false, love can   15
   Admit, but not the busied man.
He which hath business and makes love, doth do
Such wrong as when a married man doth woo.

A Valediction: Of Weeping

   Let me pour forth
My tears before thy face whilst I stay here,
For thy face coins them, and thy stamp they bear,
And by this mintage they are something worth,
   For thus they be   5
   Pregnant of thee;
Fruits of much grief they are, emblems of more:
When a tear falls, that *thou* falls which it bore;
So thou and I are nothing then, when on a diverse shore.

   On a round ball   10
A workman that hath copies by, can lay
An Europe, Afric, and an Asia,
And quickly make that which was nothing, all;
   So doth each tear
   Which *thee* doth wear,   15
A globe, yea world, by that impression grow,
Till thy tears mix'd with mine do overflow
This world: by waters sent from thee, my heaven dissolvèd so.

O more than moon,
Draw not up seas to drown me in thy sphere,   20
Weep me not dead in thine arms, but forbear
To teach the sea what it may do too soon;
     Let not the wind
     Example find
To do me more harm than it purposeth;   25
Since thou and I sigh one another's breath,
Whoe'er sighs most is cruelest, and hastes the other's death.

Love's Alchemy

Some that have deeper digged love's mine than I,
Say where his centric happiness doth lie;
     I have loved, and got, and told,
But should I love, get, tell, till I were old,
I should not find that hidden mystery.   5
     O, 'tis imposture all:
And as no chemic yet the elixir got,
     But glorifies his pregnant pot,
     If by the way to him befall
Some odoriferous thing, or medicinal;   10
     So lovers dream a rich and long delight,
     But get a winter-seeming summer's night.

Our ease, our thrift, our honor, and our day,
Shall we for this vain bubble's shadow pay?
     Ends love in this, that my man   15
Can be as happy as I can if he can
Endure the short scorn of a bridegroom's play?
     That loving wretch that swears,
'Tis not the bodies marry, but the minds,
     Which he in her angelic finds,   20
     Would swear as justly that he hears,
In that day's rude hoarse minstrelsy, the spheres.
     Hope not for mind in women; at their best
     Sweetness and wit they are but mummy, possessed.

7-8. **And as no chemic ... pot:** As no alchemist yet found the panacea for all ills, but still glorifies his productive pot, shaped like a pregnant woman.
15. **man:** servant.
22. **minstrelsy . . . spheres:** the coarse music and singing of the wedding celebration, against the perfect music said to be made by the concentric crystalline spheres that were supposed to carry the heavenly bodies around the earth.
24. **mummy:** powdered parts of a mummy, used as a medicine (cf. *l.* 10).

The Flea

Mark but this flea, and mark in this
How little that which thou deny'st me is;
   It sucked me first, and now sucks thee,
And in this flea our two bloods mingled be.
   Thou know'st that this cannot be said   5
A sin, nor shame, nor loss of maidenhead;
   Yet this enjoys before it woo,
And pampered, swells with one blood made of two,   *MAGE of PREGNACY*
And this, alas, is more than we would do.

   O stay, three lives in one flea spare,   10
Where we almost, yea more than married are.
   This flea is you and I, and this
Our marriage bed and marriage temple is;
   Though parents grudge, and you, we're met
And cloistered in these living walls of jet.   15
   Though use make you apt to kill me,
Let not to that, self-murder added be,
And sacrilege: three sins in killing three.

   Cruel and sudden, hast thou since
Purpled thy nail in blood of innocence?   20
   Wherein could this flea guilty be,
Except in that drop which it suck'd from thee?
   Yet thou triumph'st, and say'st that thou
Find'st not thyself nor me the weaker now.
   'Tis true. Then learn how false fears be: 25
Just so much honor, when thou yield'st to me,
Will waste, as this flea's death took life from thee.

The Bait

Come live with me and be my love,
And we will some new pleasures prove,
Of golden sands and crystal brooks,
With silken lines and silver hooks.

16. **use:** custom.

The Bait: See "The Passionate Shepherd to His Love," by Marlowe (?), to which this is an answer; also Ralegh's "Nymph's Reply to the Shepherd."

There will the river whispering run,   5
Warmed by thy eyes more than the sun;
And there the enamored fish will stay,
Begging themselves they may betray.

When thou wilt swim in that live bath,
Each fish, which every channel hath,   10
Will amorously to thee swim,
Gladder to catch thee, than thou him.

If thou to be so seen beest loath,
By sun or moon, thou darkenest both;
And if myself have leave to see,   15
I need not their light, having thee.

Let others freeze with angling reeds,
And cut their legs with shells and weeds,
Or treacherously poor fish beset
With strangling snare or windowy net.   20

Let coarse bold hands from slimy nest
The bedded fish in banks out-wrest,
Or curious traitors, sleave-silk flies,
Bewitch poor fishes' wandering eyes.

For thee, thou need'st no such deceit,   25
For thou thyself art thine own bait;
That fish that is not catched thereby,
Alas, is wiser far than I.

The Apparition

When by thy scorn, O murderess, I am dead,
   And that thou thinkst thee free
   From all solicitation from me,
Then shall my ghost come to thy bed,
   And thee, feigned vestal, in worse arms shall see.   5

Then thy sick taper will begin to wink,
   And he whose thou art then, being tired before,
Will, if thou stir or pinch to wake him, think
     Thou call'st for more,
And in false sleep will from thee shrink,   10

5. **vestal:** sacred virgin in ancient Rome.

And then, poor aspen wretch, neglected, thou
  Bathed in a cold, quicksilver sweat wilt lie
    A verier ghost than I.
What I will say, I will not tell thee now,
Lest that preserve thee; and since my love is spent,   15
I'd rather thou shouldst painfully repent
Than by my threatenings rest still innocent.

A Valediction: Forbidding Mourning

As virtuous men pass mildly away,
  And whisper to their souls to go,
Whilst some of their sad friends do say,
  "The breath goes now," and some say, "No,"

So let us melt and make no noise,   5
  No tear-floods nor sigh-tempests move;
'Twas profanation of our joys
  To tell the laity our love.

Moving of th' earth brings harms and fears;
  Men reckon what it did and meant;   10
But trepidation of the spheres,
  Though greater far, is innocent.

Dull sublunary lovers' love,
  Whose soul is sense, cannot admit
Absence, because it doth remove   15
  Those things which elemented it.

But we by a love so much refined
  That ourselves know not what it is,
Interassurèd of the mind,
  Care less eyes, lips, and hands to miss.   20

Our two souls, therefore, which are one,
  Though I must go, endure not yet
A breach, but an expansion,
  Like gold to airy thinness beat.

11. **aspen:** trembling, like aspen leaves.

9–12. **Moving . . . innocent:** Earthquakes have immediate effects; the much wider-ranging apparent irregularities in the movement of heavenly bodies go disregarded.
13. **sublunary:** earthly, not heavenly, because beneath (within) the sphere of the moon, the nearest heavenly body.
16. **elemented:** composed (because material).

If they be two, they are two so   25
  As stiff twin compasses are two;
Thy soul, the fix'd foot, makes no show
  To move, but doth if th' other do.

And though it in the center sit,
  Yet when the other far doth roam,   30
It leans and hearkens after it,
  And grows erect as that comes home.

Such wilt thou be to me, who must,
  Like th' other foot, obliquely run;
Thy firmness makes my circle just,   35
  And makes me end where I begun.

The Ecstasy

Where, like a pillow on a bed,
  A pregnant bank swelled up to rest
The violet's reclining head,
  Sat we two, one another's best.
Our hands were firmly cèmented   5
  With a fast balm, which thence did spring;
Our eye-beams twisted, and did thread
  Our eyes upon one double string;
So to entergraft our hands, as yet
  Was all the means to make us one,   10
And pictures in our eyes to get
  Was all our propagation.
As, 'twixt two equal armies, fate
  Suspends uncertain victory,
Our souls, which to advance their state   15
  Were gone out, hung 'twixt her and me.
And whilst our souls negotiate there,
  We like sepulchral statues lay;
All day, the same our postures were,
  And we said nothing, all the day.   20
If any, so by love refined
  That he soul's language understood,
And by good love were grown all mind,
  Within convenient distance stood,
He, though he knew not which soul spake,   25
  Because both meant, both spake the same,

Might thence a new concoction take
   And part far purer than he came.
This ecstasy doth unperplex,
   We said, and tell us what we love: 30
We see by this it was not sex,
   We see we saw not what did move;
But as all several souls contain
   Mixture of things, they know not what,
Love these mixed souls doth mix again   35
   And makes both one, each this and that.
A single violet transplant,
   The strength, the color, and the size,
All which before was poor and scant,
   Redoubles still, and multiplies.   40
When love with one another so
   Interinanimates two souls,
That abler soul, which thence doth flow,
   Defects of loneliness controls.
We then, who are this new soul, know   45
   Of what we are composed, and made,
For the atomies of which we grow
   Are souls, whom no change can invade.
But O alas! so long, so far,
   Our bodies why do we forbear?   50
They are ours, though they are not we; we are
   The intelligences, they the spheres.
We owe them thanks, because they thus
   Did us, to us, at first convey,
Yielded their forces, sense, to us,   55
   Nor are dross to us, but allay.
On man heaven's influence works not so,
   But that it first imprints the air;
So soul into the soul may flow,
   Though it to body first repair.   60
As our blood labors to beget
   Spirits, as like souls as it can,
Because such fingers need to knit
   That subtle knot, which makes us man,

27. **new concoction:** a purification of the elements constituting him.
32. **move:** move us.
47. **atomies:** atoms.
52. **intelligences . . . spheres:** Each of the concentric spheres supposed to carry the heavenly bodies around the earth was thought to be controlled by an animating soul, or intelligence.
56. **dross . . . allay:** The bodies here are not impurities to the soul, but strengthening qualities (alloy).
61. **blood . . . beget:** Animal spirits from the blood were supposed to link body and soul.

So must pure lovers' souls descend   65
    To affections, and to faculties,
Which sense may reach and apprehend;
    Else a great prince in prison lies.
SOUL   To our bodies turn we then, that so
    Weak men on love revealed may look;   70
Love's mysteries in souls do grow,
    But yet the body is his book.
And if some lover, such as we,
    Have heard this dialogue of one,
Let him still mark us, he shall see   75
    Small change when we're to bodies gone.

The Funeral

Whoever comes to shroud me, do not harm
        Nor question much
That subtle wreath of hair which crowns mine arm;
The mystery, the sign, you must not touch,
        For 'tis my outward soul,   5
Viceroy to that, which then to heaven being gone,
        Will leave this to control
And keep these limbs, her provinces, from dissolution.

For if the sinewy thread my brain lets fall
        Through every part   10
Can tie those parts and make me one of all,
These hairs, which upward grew, and strength and art
        Have, from a better brain,
Can better do't; except she meant that I
        By this should know my pain,   15
As prisoners then are manacled, when they're condemned to die.

Whate'er she meant by't, bury it with me,
        For since I am
Love's martyr, it might breed idolatry
If into others' hands these relics came.   20
        As 'twas humility
T' afford to it all which a soul can do,
        So 'tis some bravery
That since you would save none of me, I bury some of you.

66. **affections; faculties:** emotions; the senses.

19–20. **Love's . . . came:** To what extent the remains and possessions (relics) of saints and martyrs might be venerated without superstitious idolatry has been a vexed question, particularly in Donne's time.

21–24. **As 'twas humility . . . you:** it was humble to claim that the beloved's hair functioned as his soul; it is defiant to bury her hair after she would have none of him.

JOHN DONNE

The Relic

When my grave is broke up again
Some second guest to entertain
(For graves have learned that womanhead
To be to more than one a bed)
    And he that digs it spies   5
A bracelet of bright hair about the bone,
    Will he not let us alone,
And think that there a loving couple lies,
Who thought that this device might be some way
To make their souls at the last busy day   10
Meet at this grave, and make a little stay?

If this fall in a time or land
Where mis-devotion doth command,
Then he that digs us up will bring
Us to the bishop and the king   15
    To make us relics; then
Thou shalt be a Mary Magdalen, and I
    A something else thereby.
All women shall adore us, and some men;
And since at such time miracles are sought,   20
I would have that age by this paper taught
What miracles we harmless lovers wrought.

First, we loved well and faithfully,
Yet knew not what we loved, nor why;
Difference of sex no more we knew   25
    Than our guardian angels do;
    Coming and going, we
Perchance might kiss, but not between those meals;
    Our hands ne'er touched the seals
Which nature, injured by late law, sets free.   30
These miracles we did; but now, alas,
All measure and all language I should pass,
Should I tell what a miracle she was.

---

1. **broke up again:** Graves were sometimes re-used, the original bones being removed. 13–16. **mis-devotion . . . relics:** A Protestant reference to the supposed Catholic veneration of relics: see "The Funeral," *l.* 20, note.
17–18. **Mary Magdalen . . . else:** traditionally, the sinning and then penitent figure of Luke 7: 36–50 and the sister of Martha of Luke 10: 38. The "something else" is an obscure but scandalous reference to Christ. 28. **meals:** i.e., intercourse. 29. **seals:** i.e., of sex. The meaning of the next line is obscure.

A Lecture Upon the Shadow

Stand still, and I will read to thee
A lecture, Love, in love's philosophy.
   These three hours that we have spent
   Walking here, two shadows went
Along with us, which we ourselves produc'd;   5
But, now the sun is just above our head,
   We do those shadows tread,
And to brave clearness all things are reduc'd.
   So whilst our infant loves did grow,
   Disguises did, and shadows, flow   10
From us and our cares; but now 'tis not so.

That love hath not attain'd the high'st degree
Which is still diligent lest others see.

   Except our loves at this noon stay,
We shall new shadows make the other way.   15
   As the first were made to blind
   Others, these which come behind
Will work upon ourselves and blind our eyes.
If our loves faint and westwardly decline,
   To me thou falsely thine,   20
And I to thee mine actions shall disguise.
   The morning shadows wear away,
   But these grow longer all the day,
But O, love's day is short if love decay!

Love is a growing, or full constant light,   25
And his first minute after noon is night.

Satire III, Religion

Kind pity chokes my spleen; brave scorn forbids
Those tears to issue which swell my eyelids;
I must not laugh, nor weep sins and be wise;
Can railing then cure these worn maladies?
Is not our mistress, fair religion,   5
As worthy of all our souls' devotion
As virtue was to the first blinded age?

1. **spleen:** anger.
7. **virtue:** Virtue was the aim of the pagan world ("blind" because not having Christian revelation); religious truth and practice, that of the world after Christ.

Are not heaven's joys as valiant to assuage
Lusts as earth's honor was to them? Alas,
As we do them in means, shall they surpass   10
Us in the end? and shall thy father's spirit
Meet blind philosophers in heaven, whose merit
Of strict life may be imputed faith, and hear
Thee, whom he taught so easy ways and near
To follow, damn'd? O, if thou dar'st, fear this;   15
This fear great courage and high valor is.
Dar'st thou aid mutinous Dutch, and dar'st thou lay
Thee in ships, wooden sepulchers, a prey
To leaders' rage, to storms, to shot, to dearth?
Dar'st thou dive seas and dungeons of the earth?   20
Hast thou courageous fire to thaw the ice
Of frozen North discoveries? and thrice
Colder then salamanders, like divine
Children in th' oven, fires of Spain and the line,
Whose countries limbecks to our bodies be,   25
Canst thou for gain bear? and must every he
Which cries not "Goddess!" to thy mistress draw,
Or eat thy poisonous words? Courage of straw!
O desperate coward, wilt thou seem bold and
To thy foes and His, who made thee to stand   30
Sentinel in his world's garrison, thus yield,
And for forbidden wars leave th' appointed field?
Know thy foes: the foul Devil, whom thou
Strivest to please, for hate, not love, would allow
Thee fain his whole realm to be quit; and as   35
The world's all parts wither away and pass,
So the world's self, thy other lov'd foe, is
In her decrepit wane, and thou, loving this,
Dost love a withered and worn strumpet; last,
Flesh, itself's death, and joys which flesh can taste   40
Thou lovest, and thy fair goodly soul, which doth
Give this flesh power to taste joy, thou dost loathe.
Seek true religion, O, where? Mirreus,
Thinking her unhous'd here and fled from us,

17. **aid . . . Dutch:** against the Spanish.
23–24. **salamanders; Children:** Salamanders were supposed to be unaffected by fire; Shadrach, Meshach, and Abednego were put in a fiery furnace without harm to themselves.
24. **line:** equator, with its heat. The fires of Spain were those of the Inquisition.
25. **limbecks:** retorts, for heating and distilling.
27. **draw:** i.e., draw his sword.

34–35. **would . . . quit:**   would willingly allow his whole realm to be transferred to you.
43. **Mirreus, etc.:** Mirreus is the example of the Roman Catholic for the wrong reasons; Crantz, of the Geneva Presbyterian; Graius, of the adherent of a state religion (the English church, beginning with Henry VIII, in this case); Phrygius, of the skeptic; and Graccus, of the universalist.

Seeks her at Rome; there, because he doth know   45
That she was there a thousand years ago;
He loves her rags so, as we here obey
The statecloth where the prince sat yesterday.
Crantz to such brave loves will not be inthrall'd,
But loves her only who at Geneva is call'd   50
Religion, plain, simple, sullen, young,
Contemptuous, yet unhandsome; as, among
Lecherous humors, there is one that judges
No wenches wholesome but coarse country drudges.
Graius stays still at home here, and because   55
Some preachers, vile ambitious bawds, and laws,
Still new like fashions, bid him think that she
Which dwells with us is only perfect, he
Embraceth her whom his godfathers will
Tender to him, being tender; as wards still   60
Take such wives as their guardians offer, or
Pay values. Careless Phrygius doth abhor
All, because all cannot be good; as one,
Knowing some women whores, dares marry none.
Gracchus loves all as one, and thinks that so   65
As women do in divers countries go
In divers habits, yet are still one kind,
So doth, so is, religion; and this blind-
Ness too much light breeds; but unmoved, thou
Of force must one, and forced but one allow,   70
And the right; ask thy father which is she,
Let him ask his; though truth and falsehood be
Near twins, yet truth a little elder is;
Be busy to seek her; believe me this,
He's not of none, nor worst, that seeks the best.   75
To adore, or scorn an image, or protest,
May all be bad. Doubt wisely; in strange way
To stand inquiring right is not to stray;
To sleep, or run wrong, is. On a huge hill,
Cragged and steep, Truth stands, and he that will   80
Reach her, about must and about must go,
And what the hill's suddenness resists, win so.
Yet strive so that before age, death's twilight,

---

48. **statecloth:** symbol of kingly power.
49. **brave:** full of outward splendor.
53. **Lecherous humors:** those of lecherous
inclinations.
60. **Tender to him:** i.e., at his infant
baptism.
62. **Pay values:** pay part of their estate

held in trust, as a legal penalty for not
accepting a guardian's choice.
70. **Of force:** necessarily.
81. **about must and about:** cannot go
straight up, but must spiral towards the
top, so as not to have an impossibly steep
climb.

Thy soul rest, for none can work in that night.
To will implies delay, therefore now do.   85
Hard deeds, the body's pains; hard knowledge too
The mind's endeavors reach, and mysteries
Are like the sun, dazzling, yet plain to all eyes.
Keep the truth which thou hast found; men do not stand
In so ill case that God hath with his hand   90
Signed kings blank charters to kill whom they hate;
Nor are they vicars, but hangmen, to fate.
Fool and wretch, wilt thou let thy soul be tied
To man's laws, by which she shall not be tried
At the last day? Will it then boot thee   95
To say a Philip or a Gregory,
A Harry or a Martin, taught thee this?
Is not this excuse for mere contraries
Equally strong? Cannot both sides say so?
That thou mayest rightly obey power, her bounds know;   100
Those past, her nature and name is chang'd; to be
Then humble to her is idolatry.
As streams are, power is; those blest flowers that dwell
At the rough stream's calm head, thrive and do well,
But having left their roots, and themselves given   105
To the stream's tyrannous rage, alas, are driven
Through mills and rocks and woods, and at last, almost
Consum'd in going, in the sea are lost.
So perish souls, which more choose men's unjust
Power from God claim'd, than God himself to trust.   110

Holy Sonnets

5

I am a little world made cunningly
Of elements, and an angelic sprite;
But black sin hath betrayed to endless night
My world's both parts, and O, both parts must die.

86–87. **Hard . . . reach:** The body's pains achieve hard deeds; the mind's endeavors achieve hard knowledge.
92. **Nor . . . fate:** Kings and popes who kill where they find opposition to their own religion are not divinely appointed representatives of fate, but only fate's hangmen, at the best.
96–97. **Philip . . . Martin:** respectively, the oppressive Catholic King of Spain, the Pope, Henry VIII, Martin Luther.

You which beyond that heaven which was most high   5
Have found new spheres, and of new lands can write,
Pour new seas in mine eyes, that so I might
Drown my world with my weeping earnestly,
Or wash it if it must be drowned no more.
But O, it must be burnt! Alas, the fire   10
Of lust and envy have burnt it heretofore,
And made it fouler; let their flames retire,
And burn me, O Lord, with a fiery zeal
Of Thee and Thy house, which doth in eating heal.

7

At the round earth's imagin'd corners, blow
Your trumpets, angels, and arise, arise
From death, you numberless infinities
Of souls, and to your scatter'd bodies go,
All whom the flood did, and fire shall o'erthrow,   5
All whom war, dearth, age, agues, tyrannies,
Despair, law, chance hath slain, and you whose eyes
Shall behold God and never taste death's woe.
But let them sleep, Lord, and me mourn a space,
For if above all these my sins abound,   10
'Tis late to ask abundance of thy grace
When we are there. Here on this lowly ground
Teach me how to repent, for that's as good
As if thou'dst seal'd my pardon with thy blood.

9

If poisonous minerals, and if that tree
Whose fruit threw death on else immortal us,
If lecherous goats, if serpents envious
Cannot be damned, Alas? why should I be?
Why should intent or reason, born in me,   5
Make sins, else equal, in me more heinous?
And mercy being easy, and glorious
To God, in his stern wrath why threatens he?
But who am I, that dare dispute with thee,
O God? O! of thine only worthy blood,   10

5–6. **You** ... **write:** the astronomers and explorers.

9. **must** ... **no more:** God promised Noah not to flood the earth again.
10. **burnt:** in hell-fire.

And my tears, make a heavenly Lethean flood,   11
And drown in it my sin's black memory;
That thou remember them, some claim as debt,
I think it mercy, if thou wilt forget.

10

Death, be not proud, though some have callèd thee
Mighty and dreadful, for thou art not so;
For, those whom thou think'st thou dost overthrow,
Die not, poor Death, nor yet canst thou kill me.
From rest and sleep, which but thy pictures be,   5
Much pleasure; then from thee much more must flow;
And soonest our best men with thee do go,
Rest of their bones, and soul's delivery.
Thou art slave to Fate, Chance, kings, and desperate men,
And dost with poison, war, and sickness dwell,   10
And poppy or charms can make us sleep as well
And better than thy stroke. Why swell'st thou then?
One short sleep past, we wake eternally,
And death shall be no more. Death, thou shalt die!

12

Why are we by all creatures waited on?
Why do the prodigal elements supply
Life and food to me, being more pure than I,
Simple, and further from corruption?
Why brook'st thou, ignorant horse, subjection?   5
Why dost thou bull, and boar so seelily
Dissemble weakness, and by one man's stroke die,
Whose whole kind, you might swallow and feed upon?
Weaker I am, woe is me, and worse than you,
You have not sinned, nor need be timorous.   10
But wonder at a greater wonder, for to us
Created nature doth these things subdue,
But their Creator, whom sin, nor nature tied,
For us, his Creatures, and his foes, hath died.

11. **Lethean:** Drinking of the River Lethe
was supposed by the ancients to give forgetfulness to souls entering the Lower
Regions.

12. **poppy:** opium.

6. **seelily:** foolishly, simple-mindedly.

14

Batter my heart, three personed God; for you
As yet but knock, breathe, shine, and seek to mend;
That I may rise and stand, o'erthrow me and bend
Your force to break, blow, burn and make me new.
I, like an usurped town, to another due,   5
Labour to admit you, but Oh, to no end;
Reason, your viceroy in me, me should defend,
But is captived and proves weak or untrue.
Yet dearly I love you and would be loved fain,
But am betrothed unto your enemy: 10
Divorce me, untie or break that knot again,
Take me to you, imprison me, for I
Except you enthrall me, never shall be free,
Nor ever chaste, except you ravish me.

Hymn to God My God, In My Sickness

Since I am coming to that holy room
        Where with thy choir of saints for evermore
I shall be made thy music, as I come
        I tune the instrument here at the door,
        And what I must do then, think here before.   5

Whilst my physicians by their love are grown
        Cosmographers, and I their map, who lie
Flat on this bed, that by them may be shown
        That this is my Southwest discovery
        Per fretum febris, by these straits to die,   10

I joy that in these straits I see my West;
        For though their currents yield return to none,
What shall my West hurt me? As West and East
        In all flat maps (and I am one) are one,
        So death doth touch the resurrection.   15

9. **Southwest discovery:** literally, a strait
by which America might be passed so as
to circumnavigate the world and turn
"West" to "East." Read further.

10. **Per fretum febris:** (Lat.) by the strait
(also violence) of fever.

14. **maps:** i.e., of the world.

Is the Pacific Sea my home? Or are
　　The Eastern riches? Is Jerusalem?
Anian and Magellan and Gibraltar,
　　All straits, and none but straits, are ways to them,
　　Whether where Japhet dwelt, or Cham or Shem.   20

We think that Paradise and Calvary,
　　Christ's Cross and Adam's tree, stood in one place.
Look, Lord, and find both Adams met in me;
　　As the first Adam's sweat surrounds my face,
　　May the last Adam's blood my soul embrace.   25

So, in his purple wrapp'd, receive me, Lord,
　　By these his thorns give me his other crown;
And as to other's souls I preach'd thy word,
　　Be this my text, my sermon to mine own:
　　Therefore that he may raise, the Lord throws down.   30

BEN JONSON

[*1573?–1637*]

To Penshurst

Thou are not, Penshurst, built to envious show
　　Of touch or marble, nor canst boast a row
Of polished pillars, or a roof of gold;
　　Thou hast no lantern whereof tales are told,
Or stairs or courts; but stand'st an ancient pile,   5
　　And, these grudged at, art reverenced the while.
Thou joy'st in better marks, of soil, of air,
　　Of wood, of water; therein thou art fair.
Thou hast thy walks for health as well as sport;
　　Thy mount, to which the Dryads do resort,   10
Where Pan and Bacchus their high feasts have made
　　Beneath the broad beech, and the chestnut shade,
That taller tree, which of a nut was set
　　At his great birth, where all the Muses met.

18. **Anian:** Bering Straits.
20. **Japhet . . . Shem:** The descendants of these sons of Noah were said to have settled, respectively, Europe, Africa, and Asia.
25. **last Adam:** Christ.

Penshurst: country seat of the Sidney family (to which Sir Philip belonged).
2. **touch:** touchstone, a pure, black rock.
4. **lantern:** small tower or cupola in roof, with windows around sides.
14. **his great birth:** Sir Philip Sidney's.

There in the writhèd bark are cut the names   15
    Of many a sylvan, taken with his flames;
And thence the ruddy satyrs oft provoke
    The lighter fauns to reach thy Lady's oak.
Thy copse too, named of Gamage, thou hast there,
    That never fails to serve thee seasoned deer   20
When thou wouldst feast, or exercise thy friends.
    The lower land, that to the river bends,
Thy sheep, thy bullocks, kine, and calves do feed;
    The middle grounds thy mares and horses breed.
Each bank doth yield thee conies; and the tops,   25
    Fertile of wood, Ashore and Sidney's copse,
To crown thy open table, doth provide
    The purpled pheasant with the speckled side;
The painted partridge lies in every field,
    And, for thy mess, is willing to be killed.   30
And if the high-swollen Medway fail thy dish,
    Thou hast thy ponds that pay thee tribute fish,
Fat agèd carps that run into thy net,
    And pikes, now weary their own kind to eat,
As loath the second draught or cast to stay,   35
    Officiously at first themselves betray;
Bright eels that emulate them, and leap on land
    Before the fisher, or into his hand.
Then hath thy orchard fruit, thy garden flowers
    Fresh as the air, and new as are the hours.   40
The early cherry, with the later plum,
    Fig, grape, and quince, each in his time doth come;
The blushing apricot and woolly peach
    Hang on thy walls, that every child may reach.
And though thy walls be of the country stone,   45
    They'are reared with no man's ruin, no man's groan;
There's none that dwell about them wish them down,
    But all come in, the farmer and the clown,
And no one empty handed, to salute
    Thy lord and lady, though they have no suit.   50
Some bring a capon, some a rural cake,
    Some nuts, some apples; some that think they make
The better cheeses bring 'em, or else send
    By their ripe daughters whom they would commend
This way to husbands, and whose baskets bear   55
    An emblem of themselves in plum or pear.

16. **sylvan . . . flames:** rustic in love.   36. **Officiously:** dutiably.
25. **conies:** rabbits.   48. **clown:** yokel.
35. **to stay:** to await (second cast of net).   50. **suit:** request.

But what can this, more than express their love,
    Add to thy free provisions, far above
The need of such, whose liberal board doth flow
    With all that hospitality doth know?   60
Where comes no guest but is allowed to eat
    Without his fear, and of thy lord's own meat;
Where the same beer and bread, and self-same wine
    That is his lordship's shall be also mine.
And I not fain to sit, as some this day   65
    At great men's tables, and yet dine away.
Here no man tells my cups, nor, standing by,
    A waiter doth my gluttony envy,
But gives me what I call and lets me eat;
    He knows below he shall find plenty of meat.   70
Thy tables hoard not up for the next day,
    Nor when I take my lodging need I pray
For fire or lights or livery; all is there
    As if thou then wert mine, or I reigned here;
There's nothing I can wish, for which I stay.   75
    That found King James, when hunting late this way
With his brave son, the prince, they saw thy fires
    Shine bright on every hearth as the desires
Of thy Penates had been set on flame
    To entertain them, or the country came   80
With all their zeal to warm their welcome here.
    What great I will not say, but sudden cheer
Didst thou then make 'em! and what praise was heaped
    On thy good lady then! who therein reaped
The just reward of her high huswifery;   85
    To have her linen, plate, and all things nigh
When she was far, and not a room but dressed
    As if it had expected such a guest!
These, Penshurst, are thy praise, and yet not all.
    Thy lady's noble, fruitful, chaste withal;   90
His children thy great lord may call his own,
    A fortune in this age but rarely known.
They are and have been taught religion; thence
    Their gentler spirits have sucked innocence.
Each morn and even they are taught to pray   95
    With the whole household, and may every day

65–66. **And I . . . away:** I do not like to sit,
as some do, at a great man's table and yet
dine elsewhere (be served a different meal
from those at the head of the table).

67. **tells:** counts.
73. **livery:** provisions.
75. **stay:** wait.
79. **Penates:** Roman household gods.

Read, in their virtuous parents' noble parts,
  The mysteries of manners, arms, and arts.
Now, Penshurst, they that will proportion thee
  With other edifices when they see   100
Those proud, ambitious heaps and nothing else,
  May say their lords have built, but thy lord dwells.

To the Memory of My Beloved
Master William Shakespeare
and What He Hath Left Us

To draw no envy, Shakespeare, on thy name,
  Am I thus ample to thy book and fame,
While I confess thy writings to be such
  As neither man nor Muse can praise too much;
'Tis true, and all men's suffrage. But these ways   5
  Were not the paths I meant unto thy praise,
For seeliest ignorance on these may light,
  Which when it sounds at best but echoes right;
Or blind affection which doth ne'er advance
  The truth, but gropes and urgeth all by chance;   10
Or crafty malice might pretend this praise,
  And think to ruin where it seemed to raise.
These are as some infamous bawd or whore
  Should praise a matron; what could hurt her more?
But thou art proof against them, and indeed   15
  Above th' ill fortune of them, or the need.
I, therefore, will begin. Soul of the age!
  The applause, delight, the wonder of our stage!
My Shakespeare, rise; I will not lodge thee by
  Chaucer, or Spenser, or bid Beaumont lie   20
A little further to make thee a room;
  Thou art a monument, without a tomb,
And art alive still, while thy book doth live
  And we have wits to read and praise to give.
That I not mix thee so, my brain excuses—   25
  I mean with great but disproportioned Muses,—
For if I thought my judgement were of years
  I should commit thee surely with thy peers,

97. **parts:** qualities.
99. **proportion:** compare.

5. **suffrage:** agreement.
7. **seeliest:** most simple-minded.
9. **affection:** passion.
26. **disproportioned:** not comparable.

And tell how far thou didst our Lyly outshine,
   Or sporting Kyd, or Marlowe's mighty line.   30
And though thou hadst small Latin and less Greek,
   From thence to honor thee I would not seek
For names, but call forth thund'ring Æschylus,
   Euripides, and Sophocles to us,
Pacuvius, Accius, him of Cordova dead,   35
   To life again, to hear thy buskin tread
And shake a stage; or, when thy socks were on,
   Leave thee alone for thy comparison
Of all that insolent Greece or haughty Rome
   Sent forth, or since did from their ashes come.   40
Triumph, my Britain, thou hast one to show
   To whom all scenes of Europe homage owe.
He was not of an age, but for all time!
   And all the Muses still were in their prime,
When like Apollo he came forth to warm   45
   Our ears, or like a Mercury to charm!
Nature herself was proud of his designs,
   And joyed to wear the dressing of his lines,
Which were so richly spun, and woven so fit,
   As since, she will vouchsafe no other wit;   50
The merry Greek, tart Aristophanes,
   Neat Terence, witty Plautus, now not please,
But antiquated and deserted lie
   As they were not of nature's family.
Yet must I not give nature all; thy art,   55
   My gentle Shakespeare, must enjoy a part;
For though the poet's matter nature be,
   His art doth give the fashion; and that he
Who casts to write a living line, must sweat
   (Such as thine are) and strike the second heat   60
Upon the Muses' anvil, turn the same,
   And himself with it, that he thinks to frame;
Or for the laurel he may gain a scorn,
   For a good poet's made, as well as born;
And such wert thou. Look how the father's face   65
   Lives in his issue; even so the race

29–30. **Lyly . . . Marlowe:** John Lyly, Thomas Kyd, Christopher Marlowe, Elizabethan dramatists.
35. **Pacuvius . . . Cordova:** The first two were Roman tragedians of the 2nd century B.C.; the third is Seneca the Tragedian (1st century A.D.).
36–37. **buskin, socks:** standing for tragedy and comedy respectively.
42. **scenes:** stages.
44. **Muses . . . prime:** i.e., English poetry was in its first youth.
51–52. **Aristophanes . . . Plautus:** (1) Greek writer of comedy (5th–4th century B.C.), (2,3) Roman writers of comedy (3rd–2nd century B.C.).

Of Shakespeare's mind and manners brightly shines
  In his well-turnèd and true-filèd lines,
In each of which he seems to shake a lance,
  As brandished at the eyes of ignorance.   70
Sweet swan of Avon! what a sight it were
  To see thee in our waters yet appear,
And makes those flights upon the banks of Thames
  That so did take Eliza, and our James!
But stay, I see thee in the hemisphere   75
  Advanced, and made a constellation there!
Shine forth, thou star of poets, and with rage
  Or influence chide or cheer the drooping stage;
Which since thy flight from hence, hath mourned like night,
  And despairs day, but for thy volume's light.   80

On My First Son

Farewell, thou child of my right hand, and joy;
  My sin was too much hope of thee, loved boy.
Seven years thou wert lent to me, and I thee pay,
  Exacted by thy fate, on the just day.
Oh, could I lose all father now! For why   5
  Will man lament the state he should envy?
To have so soon 'scaped world's and flesh's rage,
  And if no other misery, yet age!
Rest in soft peace, and asked, say, Here doth lie
  Ben Jonson his best piece of poetry.   10
For whose sake henceforth all his work be such
  As what he loves may never like too much.

Epitaph on Elizabeth, L. H.

Wouldst thou hear what man can say·
In a little? Reader, stay.
Underneath this stone doth lie
As much beauty as could die;
Which in life did harbor give   5
To more virtue than doth live.

69. **shake a lance:** pun on "Shakespeare."
73. **banks of Thames:** where most of the theaters were.
74. **Eliza . . . James:** Elizabeth I and King James.
76. **constellation:** like the heroes of ancient myth.
78. **influence:** i.e., the astrological kind.

1. **child . . . hand:** This is the literal meaning of Hebrew "Benjamin."
4. **just day:** The son died on his seventh birthday.
5. **father:** feelings of a father.
12. **may never . . . much:** cf. *l.* 2.

If at all she had a fault,
Leave it buried in this vault.
One name was Elizabeth;
Th' other, let it sleep with death: 10
Fitter, where it died, to tell,
Than that it lived at all. Farewell.

An Epitaph on Salomon Pavy, A Child of Queen Elizabeth's Chapel

Weep with me, all you that read
    This little story;
And know, for whom a tear you shed
    Death's self is sorry.
'Twas a child that so did thrive   5
    In grace and feature,
As heaven and nature seemed to strive
    Which owned the creature.
Years he numbered scarce thirteen
    When fates turned cruel,   10
Yet three filled zodiacs had he been
    The stage's jewel:
And did act (what now we moan)
    Old men so duly,
As, sooth, the Parcae thought him one,   15
    He played so truly.
So, by error, to his fate
    They all consented;
But, viewing him since, alas, too late!
    They have repented;   20
And have sought, to give new birth,
    In baths to steep him;
But, being so much too good for earth,
    Heaven vows to keep him.

Elizabeth's Chapel: Children were employed here originally as choristers, but later they were used as a troupe of child-actors, performing parts for every age and sex.
11. three . . . zodiacs: time during which sun made the circle of the zodiac three times; three years.
15. Parcae: the Fates, who determine length of life.
21–22. to give . . . him: by magic, as Medea did for Aeson; she persuaded the daughters of Pelias to try the same process on their father, who died.

Queen and Huntress

Queen and huntress, chaste and fair,
Now the sun is laid to sleep,
Seated in thy silver chair
State in wonted manner keep;
  Hesperus entreats thy light,   5
  Goddess excellently bright.

Earth, let not thy envious shade
Dare itself to interpose;
Cynthia's shining orb was made
Heaven to clear, when day did close;   10
  Bless us then with wishèd sight,
  Goddess excellently bright.

Lay thy bow of pearl apart,
And thy crystal shining quiver;
Give unto the flying hart   15
Space to breathe, how short soever,
  Thou that mak'st a day of night,
  Goddess excellently bright.

Song: To Celia

Drink to me only with thine eyes,
  And I will pledge with mine;
Or leave a kiss but in the cup,
  And I'll not look for wine.
The thirst, that from the soul doth rise,   5
  Doth ask a drink divine.
But might I of Jove's nectar sup,
  I would not change for thine.

I sent thee, late, a rosy wreath,
  Not so much honoring thee,   10
As giving it a hope, that there
  It could not wither'd be.
But thou thereon did'st only breathe,
  And sent'st it back to me.
Since when, it grows, and smells, I swear,   15
  Not of itself, but thee.

Queen and Huntress: In Jonson's masque *Cynthia's Revels*, this is sung by Hesperus, the evening star, to the moon—Cynthia, goddess of chastity and the hunt, identified with Elizabeth I in her time.

7. **shade:** i.e., eclipse.

Song: To Celia: derived from isolated passages in *Epistles* of Philostratus (3rd century A.D.).

Come, My Celia

Come, my Celia, let us prove,
While we can, the sports of love;
Time will not be ours forever:
He at length our good will sever.
Spend not, then, his gifts in vain;   5
Suns that set may rise again,
But if once we lose this light,
'Tis with us perpetual night.
Why should we defer our joys?
Fame and rumor are but toys.   10
Cannot we delude the eyes
Of a few poor household spies?
Or his easier ears beguile,
Thus removèd by our wile?
'Tis no sin love's fruits to steal;   15
But the sweet thefts to reveal,
To be taken, to be seen,
These have crimes accounted been.

Doing a filthy pleasure is

Doing a filthy pleasure is, and short;
And done, we straight repent us of the sport.
Let us not, then, rush blindly on unto it
Like lustful beasts, that only know to do it,
For lust will languish, and that heat decay.   5
But thus, thus, keeping endless holiday,
Let us together closely lie, and kiss;
There is no labor, nor no shame in this.
This hath pleased, doth please, and long will please; never
Can this decay, but is beginning ever.   10

The Triumph of Charis

See the chariot at hand here of love,
    Wherein my lady rideth!   '
Each that draws is a swan or a dove,
    And well the car love guideth.

Come, My Celia: paraphrased from the Roman poet Catullus (1st century B.C.). Song sung by villain (in Jonson's comedy *Volpone*) in seduction scene.

Doing . . . is: after a Latin poem attributed by Jonson to Petronius Arbiter (1st century A.D.) but actually by another.

As she goes, all hearts do duty   5
  Unto her beauty;
And enamored, do wish, so they might
  But enjoy such a sight,
That they still were to run by her side,
Through swords, through seas, whither she would ride.   10

Do but look on her eyes, they do light
  All that love's world compriseth!
Do but look on her hair, it is bright
  As love's star when it riseth!
Do but mark, her forehead's smoother   15
  Than words that soothe her;
And from her arched brows such a grace
  Sheds itself through the face,
As alone there triumphs to the life
All the gain, all the good, of the elements' strife.   20

Have you seen but a bright lily grow,
  Before rude hands have touched it?
Ha' you marked but the fall o' the snow
  Before the soil hath smutched it?
Ha' you felt the wool of beaver?   25
  Or swan's down ever?
Or have smelt o' the bud o' the briar?
  Or the nard i' the fire?
Or have tasted the bag of the bee?
O so white! O so soft! O so sweet is she!   30

Still to be neat

Still to be neat, still to be dressed,
As you were going to a feast;
Still to be powdered, still perfumed;
Lady, it is to be presumed,
Though art's hid causes are not found,   5
All is not sweet, all is not sound.

Give me a look, give me a face
That makes simplicity a grace;
Robes loosely flowing, hair as free;
Such sweet neglect more taketh me   10
Than all th' adulteries of art.
They strike mine eye, but not my heart.

28. **nard**: aromatic preparation.   **Still to be neat**: sung by Clerimont in Jonson's comedy *Epicoene*.
1. **Still**: continually.

It is not growing like a tree

It is not growing like a tree
In bulk, doth make men better be;
Or standing long an oak, three hundred year,
To fall a log at last, dry, bald, and sear:
    A lily of a day   5
    Is fairer far in May;
Although it fall and die that night,
It was the plant and flower of light.
In small proportions we just beauties see,
And in short measures life may perfect be.   10

Ask not to know this man

Ask not to know this man. If fame should speak
His name in any metal, it would break.
Two letters were enough the plague to tear
Out of his grave, and poison every ear.
A parcel of court dirt, a heap and mass   5
Of all vice hurled together, there he was:
Proud, false, and treacherous, vindictive, all
    That thought can add, unthankful, the laystall
Of putrid flesh alive! Of blood, the sink!
And so I leave to stir him, lest he stink.   10

ROBERT HERRICK

[1591–1674]

Delight in Disorder

A sweet disorder in the dress
Kindles in clothes a wantonness.
A lawn about the shoulders thrown
Into a fine distraction;
An erring lace, which here and there   5
Enthralls the crimson stomacher;

Ask . . . man: In Jonson's collection *Under-
Wood*, this is called "A Little Shrub
Growing By."
2. **metal:** plaque on his tomb.
8. **laystall:** dung heap.

3. **lawn:** fine linen (as a scarf).
6. **stomacher:** separate piece for the center
front of a bodice.

A cuff neglectful, and thereby
Ribbons to flow confusedly;
A winning wave, deserving note,
In the tempestuous petticoat;   10
A careless shoestring, in whose tie
I see a wild civility
Do more bewitch me than when art
Is too precise in every part.

Upon Julia's Clothes

Whenas in silks my Julia goes
Then, then (methinks) how sweetly flows
That liquefaction of her clothes.

Next, when I cast mine eyes and see
That brave vibration each way free;   5
O how that glittering taketh me!

Upon Julia's Voice

So smooth, so sweet, so silv'ry is thy voice,
As, could they hear, the damned would make no noise,
But listen to thee, walking in thy chamber,
Melting melodious words to lutes of amber.

To the Virgins, to Make Much of Time

Gather ye rosebuds while ye may,
   Old time is still a-flying,
And this same flower that smiles to-day,
   To-morrow will be dying.

The glorious lamp of heaven, the sun,   5
   The higher he's a-getting,
The sooner will his race be run,
   And nearer he's to setting.

That age is best which is the first,
   When youth and blood are warmer;   10
But being spent, the worse, and worst
   Times still succeed the former.

5. **brave:** making a fine show.   2. **damned:** who roar in the pains of hell.

Then be not coy, but use your time,
    And while ye may, go marry;
For having lost but once your prime,   15
    You may for every tarry.

Corinna's Going A-Maying

Get up, get up for shame, the blooming morn
Upon her wings presents the god unshorn.
    See how Aurora throws her fair
    Fresh-quilted colors through the air:
    Get up, sweet-slug-a-bed, and see   5
    The dew-bespangling herb and tree.
Each flower has wept, and bow'd toward the east,
Above an hour since; yet you not drest,
    Nay! not so much as out of bed?
    When all the birds have matins said,   10
    And sung their thankful hymns: 'tis sin,
    Nay, profanation to keep in,
When as a thousand virgins on this day,
Spring, sooner than the lark, to fetch in May.

Rise; and put on your foliage, and be seen   15
To come forth, like the springtime, fresh and green;
    And sweet as Flora. Take no care
    For jewels for your gown, or hair:
    Fear not; the leaves will strew
    Gems in abundance upon you: 20
Besides, the childhood of the day has kept,
Against you come, some orient pearls unwept:
    Come, and receive them while the light
    Hangs on the dew-locks of the night:
    And Titan on the eastern hill   25
    Retires himself, or else stands still
Till you come forth. Wash, dress, be brief in praying:
Few beads are best, when once we go a-Maying.

A-Maying: May Day observances go back to pagan times, when they related to fertility rites. In Herrick's time they continued to have a religious or ritual overtone, which he exploits here.
2. god unshorn: Apollo's locks were never cut.
3. Aurora: the dawn.

17. **Flora:** goddess of flowers.
22. **Against:** until.
22. **orient pearls:** Eastern ("orient") pearls were the most precious; "orient" refers also to the dawn and sunrise.
25. **Titan:** sun.
28. **beads:** loosely, prayers.

Come, my Corinna, come; and coming, mark
How each field turns a street; each street a park   30
    Made green, and trimm'd with trees: see how
    Devotion gives each house a bough,
    Or branch: each porch, each door, ere this,
    An ark, a tabernacle is
Made up of white-thorn neatly interwove;   35
As if here were those cooler shades of love.
    Can such delights be in the street,
    And open fields, and we not see 't?
    Come, we'll abroad; and let's obey
    The proclamation made for May: 40
And sin no more, as we have done, by staying;
But my Corinna, come, let's go a-Maying.

There's not a budding boy, or girl, this day,
But is got up, and gone to bring in May.
    A deal of youth, ere this, is come   45
    Back, and with white-thorn laden home.
    Some have dispatched their cakes and cream,
    Before that we have left to dream:
And some have wept, and woo'd, and plighted troth,
And chose their priest, ere we can cast off sloth: 50
    Many a green gown has been given;
    Many a kiss, both odd and even:
    Many a glance too has been sent
    From out the eye, Love's firmament:
Many a jest told of the keys betraying   55
This night, and locks picked, yet w' are not a-Maying.

Come, let us go, while we are in our prime;
And take the harmless folly of the time.
    We shall grow old apace, and die
    Before we know our liberty.   60
    Our life is short; and our days run
    As fast away as does the sun:
And as a vapor, or a drop of rain
Once lost, can ne'er be found again:
    So when or you or I are made   65
    A fable, song, or fleeting shade;
    All love, all liking, all delight
    Lies drown'd with us in endless night.
Then while time serves, and we are but decaying;
Come, my Corinna, come, let's go a-Maying.   70

---

34. **ark**: the Hebrew Ark of the Covenant   48. **left to dream**: stopped dreaming.
(see Exodus 25: 10–21).   51. **green**: from lying in the grass.

The Funeral Rites of the Rose

The Rose was sick and, smiling, died;
And, being to be sanctified,
About the bed there sighing stood
The sweet and flowering sisterhood:
Some hung the head, while some did bring,   5
To wash her, water from the spring;
Some laid her forth, while other wept,
But all a solemn fast there kept.
The holy sisters, some among,
The sacred dirge and trental sung.   10
But ah! what sweets smelt everywhere,
As Heaven had spent all perfumes there.
At last, when prayers for the dead
And rites were all accomplishèd,
They, weeping, spread a lawny loom,   15
And closed her up as in a tomb.

Another Grace for a Child

Here a little child I stand,
Heaving up my either hand;
Cold as paddocks though they be,
Here I lift them up to thee,
For a benison to fall   5
On our meat, and on us all. *Amen.*

His Desire

Give me a man that is not dull,
When all the world with rifts is full;
But unamazed dares clearly sing,
Whenas the roof's a-tottering;
And, though it falls, continues still   5
Tickling the cittern with his quill.

4. **sisterhood:** literally, the sisters of a nunnery.
10. **trental:** very loosely, a dirge.
15. **lawny loom:** a piece of fine linen, as a shroud.

3. **paddocks:** frogs.
5. **benison:** blessing.

6. **cittern:** a pear-shaped guitar, plucked with a "quill."

The Bad Season Makes the Poet Sad

Dull to myself, and almost dead to these
My many fresh and fragrant mistresses:
Lost to all music now, since everything
Puts on the semblance here of sorrowing.
Sick is the land to th' heart, and doth endure   5
More dangerous faintings by her desp'rate cure.
But if that golden age would come again,
And Charles here rule, as he before did reign;
If smooth and unperplexed the seasons were,
As when the sweet Maria livèd here;   10
I should delight to have my curls half drowned
In Tyrian dews, and head with roses crowned;
And once more yet, ere I am laid out dead,
Knock at a star with my exalted head.

GEORGE HERBERT

[*1593–1633*]

Easter Wings

Lord, who createdst man in wealth and store,
Though foolishly he lost the same,
Decaying more and more
Till he became
Most poor: 5
With thee
O let me rise,
As larks, harmoniously,
And sing this day thy victories;
Then shall the fall further the flight in me.   10

---

8. **Charles I:** The Stuart king who was deprived of power by the Puritan faction (and beheaded in 1649, after this poem was written). His queen, Henrietta Maria, is mentioned in *l.* 10.

14. **exalted:** lifted up, made joyous.

Easter Wings: one of Herbert's "shaped verses," in which the appearance on the page has to do with the subject.

My tender age in sorrow did begin;
And still with sicknesses and shame
Thou didst so punish sin,
That I became
Most thin.   15
With thee
Let me combine
And feel this day thy victory;
For, if I imp my wing on thine,
Affliction shall advance the flight in me.   20

Prayer (I)

Prayer the Church's banquet, angels' age,
    God's breath in man returning to his birth,
    The soul in paraphrase, heart in pilgrimage,
The Christian plummet sounding heav'n and earth;
Engine against th' Almighty, sinner's tower,   5
    Reversed thunder, Christ-side-piercing spear,
    The six-days-world transposing in an hour,
A kind of tune, which all things hear and fear;
Softness, and peace, and joy, and love, and bliss,
    Exalted manna, gladness of the best,   10
    Heaven in ordinary, man well dressed,
The milky way, the bird of paradise,
    Church-bells beyond the stars heard, the soul's blood,
    The land of spices; something understood.

Jordan (I)

Who says that fictions only and false hair
Become a verse? Is there in truth no beauty?
Is all good structure in a winding stair?
May no lines pass, except they do their duty
    Not to a true, but painted chair?   5

19. **imp:** (falconry) to mount extra pinions on a bird's wing.

11. **Heaven in ordinary:** heaven in daily life.

1. **angels' age:** Because prayer reaches from the finite into the infinite, it suggests this age, which is infinite.
7. **six . . . hour:** Created in six days, the world may be transformed by prayer in an hour.

Jordan: referring to crossing the Jordan, into the Promised Land of simplicity and truth, and out of false and showy complexity.
5. **Not . . . chair:** Bowing down before a real throne is justified; before a throne in a painting it is not.

Is it no verse, except enchanted groves
And sudden arbors shadow coarse-spun lines?
Must purling streams refresh a lover's loves?
Must all be veiled while he that reads, divines,
    Catching the sense at two removes?   10

Shepherds are honest people; let them sing:
Riddle who list, for me, and pull for prime:
I envy no man's nightingale or spring;
Nor let them punish me with loss of rhyme,
    Who plainly say, *My God, My King.*   15

Church Monuments

While that my soul repairs to her devotion,
Here I entomb my flesh, that it betimes
May take acquaintance of this heap of dust;
To which the blast of death's incessant motion,
Fed with the exhalation of our crimes,   5
Drives all at last. Therefore I gladly trust

My body to this school, that it may learn
To spell his elements, and find his birth
Written in dusty heraldry and lines;
Which dissolution sure doth best discern,   10
Comparing dust with dust, and earth with earth.
These laugh at jet and marble, put for signs

To sever the good fellowship of dust,
And spoil the meeting. What shall point out them,
When they shall bow, and kneel, and fall down flat   15
To kiss those heaps, which now they have in trust?
Dear flesh, while I do pray, learn here thy stem
And true descent; that when thou shalt grow fat,

6–7. **except . . . lines?:** unless artificial and showy features (as in landscape-gardening) take attention from the bad structure of the verses?
12. **pull for prime:** make a wild guess, without reasonable justification, as in the card-game primero.

2. **Here:** near a dust-covered, stately tomb-monument in a church.
12–16. **These . . . trust:** The signs of dissolution laugh at the pompous tomb's shining black stone and white marble, which only prevent a meeting of the dust of the corpse below with the other dust of the ages above. Who will notice that pomp when the tomb falls in at, or before, the Last Judgment?
17. **stem:** derivation.

And wanton in thy cravings, thou mayst know,
That flesh is but the glass, which holds the dust   20
That measures all our time; which also shall
Be crumbled into dust. Mark, here below,
How tame those ashes are, how free from lust,
That thou mayst fit thyself against thy fall.

The Windows

Lord, how can man preach thy eternal word?
　　He is a brittle, crazy glass;
Yet in thy temple thou dost him afford
　　This glorious and transcendent place,
　　To be a window through thy grace.   5

But when thou dost anneal in glass thy story,
　　Making thy life to shine within
The holy preacher's, then the light and glory
　　More reverend grows, and more doth win,
　　Which else shows waterish, bleak, and thin.   10

Doctrine and life, colors and light in one,
　　When they combine and mingle, bring
A strong regard and awe; but speech alone
　　Doth vanish like a flaring thing,
　　And in the ear, not conscience, ring.   15

Ana $\left\{ \begin{matrix} Mary \\ Army \end{matrix} \right\}$ gram

How well her name an *Army* doth present,
In whom the Lord of Hosts did pitch his tent!

Virtue

Sweet day, so cool, so calm, so bright,
The bridal of the earth and sky:
The dew shall weep thy fall to-night,
　　For thou must die.

20. **glass:** hourglass.

2. **crazy:** full of cracks.
6–15. **But when . . . ring:** Generally, Herbert is saying that just as stained glass is an improvement on the plain kind, so is the preacher who lives his Christian doctrine (i.e., teaching) better than the one who merely preaches it.

Sweet rose, whose hue angry and brave 5
Bids the rash gazer wipe his eye;
Thy root is ever in its grave,
    And thou must die.

Sweet spring, full of sweet days and roses,
A box where sweets compacted lie; 10
My music shows ye have your closes,
    And all must die.

Only a sweet and virtuous soul,
Like seasoned timber, never gives;
But though the whole world turn to coal, 15
    Then chiefly lives.

Man

My God, I heard this day,
That none doth build a stately habitation,
    But he that means to dwell therein.
    What house more stately hath there been,
Or can be, than is Man? to whose creation 5
    All things are in decay.

    For Man is ev'ry thing,
And more: He is a tree, yet bears more fruit;
    A beast, yet is, or should be more:
    Reason and speech we only bring, 10
Parrots may thank us, if they are not mute;
    They go upon the score.

    Man is all symmetry,
Full of proportions, one limb to another,
    And all to all the world besides:
    Each part may call the furthest, brother: 15
For head with foot hath private amity,
    And both with moons and tides.

5. **brave:** making a fine show.
11. **My . . . closes:** i.e., the music of this poem shows that you, too, have your final cadences.
15. **coal:** burning coals.

7–12. *2nd stanza:* Man is a little image of the universe, but also in one way superior to it: to vegetable creation, and also animal (only we bring reason *and* speech; parrots talk, but only by rote). *3rd stanza:* Both man and the universe are symmetrical, and correspond to each other: as the head relates to the foot, so does the moon to the tides.

Nothing hath got so far,
But Man hath caught and kept it, as his prey.   20
His eyes dismount the highest star:
He is in little all the sphere.
Herbs gladly cure our flesh, because that they
Find their acquaintance there.

For us the winds do blow,   25
The earth doth rest, heav'n move, and fountains flow.
Nothing we see, but means our good,
As our delight, or as our treasure:
The whole is, either our cupboard of food,
Or cabinet of pleasure.   30

The stars have us to bed;
Night draws the curtain, which the sun withdraws;
Music and light attend our head.
All things unto our flesh are kind
In their descent and being; to our mind   35
In their ascent and cause.

Each thing is full of duty:
Waters united are our navigation;
Distinguished, our habitation;
Below, our drink; above, our meat;   40
Both are our cleanliness. Hath one such beauty?
Then how are all things neat?

More servants wait on Man,
Than he'll take notice of: in ev'ry path
He treads down that which doth befriend him,   45
When sickness makes him pale and wan.
Oh mighty love! Man is one world, and hath
Another to attend him.

Since then, my God, thou hast
So brave a palace built; O dwell in it,   50
That it may dwell with thee at last!
Till then, afford us so much wit;
That, as the world serves us, we may serve thee,
And both thy servants be.

24. **acquaintance:** i.e., the correspondence in pattern between man (the microcosm) and universal nature (the macrocosm).
34–36. **unto ... flesh ... cause:** are good, as they exist, for our bodies; are good, in the perception of their relation to their Creator, for our minds.
39. **Distinguished:** i.e., by separating the waters, God created dry land.
40. **above, our meat:** the rain makes the earth productive ("meat": food).
41–42. **Hath ... neat:** If one element is so beautifully adjusted to our needs, how much more beautiful that all elements are so adjusted ("neat").
50. **brave:** splendid.

The Collar

I struck the board, and cried "No more;
    I will abroad.
  What, shall I ever sigh and pine?
My lines and life are free; free as the road,
    Loose as the wind, as large as store.   5
    Shall I be still in suit?
Have I no harvest but a thorn
  To let me blood, and not restore
What I have lost with cordial fruit?
    Sure there was wine   10
Before my sighs did dry it; there was corn
  Before my tears did drown it;
Is the year only lost to me?
  Have I no bays to crown it,
No flowers, no garlands gay? all blasted,   15
    All wasted?
Not so, my heart; but there is fruit,
    And thou hast hands.
  Recover all thy sigh-blown age
On double pleasures; leave thy cold dispute   20
  Of what is fit and not; forsake thy cage,
    Thy rope of sands
Which petty thoughts have made; and made to thee
  Good cable, to enforce and draw,
    And be thy law,   25
While thou didst wink and wouldst not see.
    Away! take heed;
    I will abroad.
  Call in thy death's-head there, tie up thy fears;
    He that forbears   30
  To suit and serve his need
    Deserves his load."
But as I rav'd and grew more fierce and wild
    At every word,
Methought I heard one calling "Child,"   35
    And I replied, "My Lord."

---

1. **board:** table.
6. **still . . . suit:** continually applying for favor.
7. **thorn:** Christ's crown of thorns.
9. **cordial:** warming, heart-supporting.
11. **corn:** grain; i.e., bread, food.
14. **bays:** laurel wreaths.

22–25. **rope . . . law:** a not truly restraining rope (cf. "collar" of the title) which petty thought has imagined to be strong cable to force, pull, and be law to the speaker.
29. **death's-head:** *memento mori:* a skull as a reminder of death.

Love (III)

Love bade me welcome, yet my soul drew back,
     Guilty of dust and sin.
But quick-eyed Love, observing me grow slack
     From my first entrance in,
Drew nearer to me, sweetly questioning   5
     If I lacked anything.

"A guest," I answered, "worthy to be here."
     Love said, "You shall be he."
"I, the unkind, ungrateful? Ah, my dear,
     I cannot look on thee."   10
Love took my hand, and smiling did reply,
     "Who made the eyes but I?"

"Truth, Lord, but I have marred them; let my shame
     Go where it doth deserve."
"And know you not," says Love, "who bore the blame?"
     "My dear, then I will serve."   15
"You must sit down," says Love, "and taste my meat."
     So I did sit and eat.

Redemption

Having been tenant long to a rich Lord,
     Not thriving, I resolved to be bold,
     And make a suit unto him, to afford
A new small-rented lease, and cancel th' old.

In heaven at his manour I him sought: 5
     They told me there, that he was lately gone
     About some land, which he had dearly bought
Long since on earth, to take possession.

I straight returned, and knowing his great birth,
     Sought him accordingly in great resorts;   10
     In cities, theatres, gardens, parks, and courts:
At length I heard a ragged noise and mirth

     Of thieves and murderers: there I him espied,
     Who straight, "Your suit is granted," said, and died.

3. **suit**: request.

Affliction (I)

When first thou didst entice to thee my heart,
　　　　I thought the service brave:
So many joys I writ down for my part,
　　　　Besides what I might have
Out of my stock of natural delights,　　　　　5
Augmented with thy gracious benefits.

I looked on thy furniture so fine,
　　　　And made it fine to me:
Thy glorious household-stuff did me entwine,
　　　　And 'tice me unto thee.　　　　　10
Such stars I counted mine: both heav'n and earth
Paid me my wages in a world of mirth.

What pleasures could I want, whose King I served,
　　　　Where joys my fellows were?
Thus argued into hopes, my thoughts reserved　　15
　　　　No place for grief or fear.
Therefore my sudden soul caught at the place,
And made her youth and fierceness seek thy face.

At first thou gav'st me milk and sweetnesses;
　　　　I had my wish and way:　　　　　20
My days were straw'd with flow'rs and happiness;
　　　　There was no month but May.
But with my years sorrow did twist and grow,
And made a party unawares for woe.

My flesh began unto my soul in pain,　　　　25
　　　　"Sicknesses cleave my bones;
Consuming agues dwell in ev'ry vein,
　　　　And tune my breath to groans."
Sorrow was all my soul; I scarce believed,
Till grief did tell me roundly, that I lived.　　30

When I got health, thou took'st away my life,
　　　　And more; for my friends die:
My mirth and edge was lost; a blunted knife
　　　　Was of more use than I.
Thus thin and lean without a fence or friend,　　35
I was blown through with ev'ry storm and wind.

2. **brave:** splendid.　　　　35. **fence:** protection.

Whereas my birth and spirit rather took
  The way that takes the town;
Thou didst betray me to a ling'ring book,
  And wrap me in a gown.   40
I was entangled in the world of strife,
Before I had the power to change my life.

Yet, for I threat'ned oft the siege to raise,
  Not simp'ring all mine age,
Thou often didst with academic praise   45
  Melt and dissolve my rage.
I took thy sweet'ned pill, till I came where
I could not go away, nor persevere.

Yet lest perchance I should too happy be
  In my unhappiness,   50
Turning my purge to food, thou throwest me
  Into more sicknesses.
Thus doth thy power cross-bias me, not making
Thine own gift good, yet me from my ways taking.

Now I am here, what thou wilt do with me 55
  None of my books will show:
I read, and sigh, and wish I were a tree;
  For sure then I should grow
To fruit or shade: at least some bird would trust
Her household to me, and I should be just. 60

Yet, though thou troublest me, I must be meek;
  In weakness must be stout.
Well, I will change the service, and go seek
  Some other master out.
Ah my dear God! though I am clean forgot, 65
Let me not love thee, if I love thee not.

38–40. **town . . . gown:** traditional contrast between life in the world and life in the university (Cambridge, in this case).
44. **Not simp'ring:** not smiling complaisantly throughout life.
51. **Turning . . . food:** turning cathartics into food.
53. **cross-bias me:** turn me repeatedly from the way I would go.

JOHN MILTON

[*1608–1674*]

Another on the University Carrier

Here lieth one who did most truly prove
That he could never die while he could move,
So hung his destiny never to rot
While he might still jog on and keep his trot,
Made of sphere-metal, never to decay   5
Until his revolution was at stay.
Time numbers motion, yet (without a crime
'Gainst old truth) motion numbered out his time:
And, like an engine moved with wheel and weight,
His principles being ceased, he ended straight;   10
Rest, that gives all men life, gave him his death,
And too much breathing put him out of breath;
Nor were it contradiction to affirm
Too long vacation hastened on his term.
Merely to drive the time away he sickened,   15
Fainted, and died, nor would with ale be quickened.
"Nay," quoth he, on his swooning bed out-stretched,
"If I may not carry, sure I'll ne'er be fetched,
but vow though the cross doctors all stood hearers,
For one Carrier put down, to make six bearers."   20
Ease was his chief disease, and, to judge right,
He died for heaviness that his cart went light.
His leisure told him that his time was come,
And lack of load made his life burdensome,
That even to his last breath (there be that say't)   25
As he were pressed to death, he cried, "More weight!"
But had his doings lasted as they were,
He had been an immortal Carrier.
Obedient to the moon he spent his date
In course reciprocal, and had his fate   30

Carrier: When Milton was a student at Cambridge, a university carrier, charged with carting goods to and from London, was ordered to stop his work because of the plague there. He died during his enforced vacation, and Milton, like other undergraduates, wrote a poem on the subject.
5. sphere-metal: the eternal substance of the concentric spheres which carried the heavenly bodies in their revolution around the earth, according to Ptolemaic astronomy.
12. breathing: pause for rest.
14. term: end, but also school term.
29. Obedient ... Moon: His schedule as a carrier must have corresponded to the fourteen-day period (fortnight) of the moon's cycle.

Linked to the mutual flowing of the seas;
Yet (strange to think) his wain was his increase.   32
His letters are delivered all and gone;
Only remains this superscription.

L'Allegro

Hence, loathèd Melancholy,
  Of Cerberus and blackest Midnight born
In Stygian cave forlorn
  'Mongst horrid shapes, and shrieks, and sights unholy!
Find out some uncouth cell,   5
  Where brooding Darkness spreads his jealous wings.
And the night-raven sings;
  There, under ebon shades and low-browed rocks,
As ragged as thy locks,
  In dark Cimmerian desert ever dwell.   10
But come, thou Goddess fair and free,
In Heaven yclept Euphrosyne,
And by men heart-easing Mirth;
Whom lovely Venus, at a birth,
With two sister Graces more,   15
To ivy-crownèd Bacchus bore:
Or whether (as some sager sing)
The frolic wind that breathes the spring,
Zephyr, with Aurora playing,
As he met her once a-Maying,   20
There, on beds of violets blue,
And fresh-blown roses washed in dew,
Filled her with thee, a daughter fair,
So buxom, blithe, and debonair.
Haste thee, Nymph, and bring with thee   25
Jest, and youthful jollity,
  Quips and cranks and wanton wiles,
Nods and becks and wreathèd smiles,
Such as hang on Hebe's cheek,
  And love to live in dimple sleek;   30

---

32. **wain:** wagon, but also waning, as of the moon.

L'Allegro: roughly, the cheerful or merry man.
2. **Cerberus:** the three-headed dog of hell in ancient mythology.
3. **Stygian:** literally, of the River Styx; black, dark.

10. **Cimmerian:** pertaining to a people living in twilight on the edge of the world (according to ancient myth).
15. **Graces:** the three Graces attend Venus.
19. **Aurora:** the dawn.
24. **buxom; debonair:** gay; gentle, courteous.
29. **Hebe:** youth, cupbearer to gods.

Sport that wrinkled Care derides,
And Laughter holding both his sides.
Come, and trip it as you go,
On the light fantastic toe;
And in thy right hand lead with thee   35
The mountain-nymph, sweet Liberty;
And, if I give thee honour due,
Mirth, admit me of thy crew,
To live with her, and live with thee,
In unreprovèd pleasures free;   40
To hear the lark begin his flight,
And, singing, startle the dull night,
From his watch-tower in the skies,
Till the dappled dawn doth rise;
Then to come, in spite of sorrow,   45
And at my window bid good-morrow,
Through the sweet-briar or the vine,
Or the twisted eglantine;
While the cock, with lively din,
Scatters the rear of darkness thin;   50
And to the stack, or the barn-door,
Stoutly struts his dames before:
Oft listening how the hounds and horn
Cheerly rouse the slumbering morn,
From the side of some hoar hill,   55
Through the high wood echoing shrill:
Sometimes walking, not unseen,
By hedgerow elms, on hillocks green,
Right against the eastern gate
Where the great Sun begins his state,   60
Robed in flames and amber light,
The clouds in thousand liveries dight;
While the plowman, near at hand,
Whistles o'er the furrowed land,
And the milkmaid singeth blithe,   65
And the mower whets his scythe,
And every shepherd tells his tale
Under the hawthorn in the dale.
Straight mine eye hath caught new pleasures,
Whilst the landscape round it measures: 70
Russet lawns, and fallows grey,
Where the nibbling flocks do stray;
Mountains on whose barren breast

36. **Liberty:** free and easy behavior.

The labouring clouds do often rest;
Meadows trim, with daisies pied;   75
Shallow brooks, and rivers wide;
Towers and battlements it sees
Bosomed high in tufted trees,
Where perhaps some beauty lies,
The cynosure of neighbouring eyes.   80
Hard by a cottage chimney smokes
From betwixt two agèd oaks,
Where Corydon and Thyrsis met
Are at their savoury dinner set
Of herbs and other country messes,   85
Which the neat-handed Phyllis dresses;
And then in haste her bower she leaves,
With Thestylis to bind the sheaves;
Or, if the earlier season lead,
To the tanned haycock in the mead.   90
Sometimes, with secure delight,
The upland hamlets will invite,
When the merry bells ring round,
And the jocund rebecks sound
To many a youth and many a maid   95
Dancing in the chequered shade,
And young and old come forth to play
On a sunshine holiday,
Till the livelong daylight fail:
Then to the spicy nut-brown ale: 100
With stories told of many a feat,
How Faery Mab the junkets eat.
She was pinched and pulled, she said;
And by the Friar's lantern led,
Tells how the drudging goblin sweat   105
To earn his cream-bowl duly set,
When in one night, ere glimpse of morn,
His shadowy flail hath threshed the corn
That ten day-labourers could not end;
Then lies him down, the lubber fiend,   110
And, stretched out all the chimney's length,
Basks at the fire his hairy strength,
And crop-full out of doors he flings,

83–88. **Corydon, Thyrsis, Phyllis, Thestylis:** traditional shepherds' names in classical poetry.
94. **rebecks:** fiddles.
102. **Faery Mab . . . junkets:** The queen of fairies eats the junkets left overnight.

103–114. **she, he:** Peasants tell how the fairies pinched, and how, led by the will-o'-the-wisp, the hobgoblin threshes a great quantity of wheat to earn a bowl of cream left for him, then rests beside the fire until dawn (*lubber:* gross, clumsy).

Ere the first cock his matin rings.
Thus done the tales, to bed they creep,   115
By whispering winds soon lulled asleep.
Towered cities please us then,
And the busy hum of men,
Where throngs of knights and barons bold,
In weeds of peace, high triumphs hold,   120
With store of ladies, whose bright eyes
Rain influence, and judge the prize
Of wit or arms, while both contend
To win her grace whom all commend.
There let Hymen oft appear   125
In saffron robe, with taper clear,
And pomp, and feast, and revelry,
With mask and antique pageantry;
Such sights as youthful poets dream
On summer eves by haunted stream.   130
Then to the well-trod stage anon,
If Jonson's learnèd sock be on,
Or sweetest Shakespeare, Fancy's child,
Warble his native wood-notes wild.
And ever, against eating cares,   135
Lap me in soft Lydian airs,
Married to immortal verse,
Such as the meeting soul may pierce,
In notes with many a winding bout
Of linkèd sweetness long drawn out   140
With wanton heed and giddy cunning,
The melting voice through mazes running,
Untwisting all the chains that tie
The hidden soul of harmony;
That Orpheus' self may heave his head   145
From golden slumber on a bed
Of heaped Elysian flowers, and hear
Such strains as would have won the ear
Of Pluto to have quite set free
His half-regained Eurydice.   150
These delights if thou canst give,
Mirth, with thee I mean to live.

120. **weeds:** garments.
122. **Rain influence:** like stars, raining astrological influence.
125. **Hymen:** god of marriage, typically dressed in yellow (here meant to appear in a masque, a stylized, symbolic dramatic entertainment).
132. **sock:** symbolizing comedy.

136. **Lydian:** roughly, the softest, most melting kind of music.
145–150. **Orpheus . . . Eurydice:** Orpheus, the mythical Greek musician, won the promise of his wife from the underworld because of the sweetness of his music, but lost her at the last minute.

JOHN MILTON

Il Penseroso

Hence, vain deluding Joys,
   The brood of Folly without father bred!
How little you bested,
   Or fill the fixèd mind with all your toys!
Dwell in some idle brain,   5
   And fancies fond with gaudy shapes possess,
As thick and numberless
   As the gay motes that people the sun-beams,
Or likest hovering dreams,
   The fickle pensioners of Morpheus' train.   10
But, hail! thou Goddess sage and holy,
Hail, divinest Melancholy!
Whose saintly visage is too bright
To hit the sense of human sight,
And therefore to our weaker view   15
O'erlaid with black, staid Wisdom's hue;
Black, but such as in esteem
Prince Memnon's sister might beseem,
Or that starred Ethiop queen that strove
To set her beauty's praise above   20
The Sea-Nymphs, and their powers offended.
Yet thou art higher far descended:
Thee bright-haired Vesta long of yore
To solitary Saturn bore;
His daughter she; in Saturn's reign   25
Such mixture was not held a stain.
Oft in glimmering bowers and glades
He met her, and in secret shades
Of woody Ida's inmost grove,
Whilst yet there was no fear of Jove.   30
Come, pensive Nun, devout and pure,
Sober, steadfast, and demure,
All in a robe of darkest grain,
Flowing with majestic train,

Il Penseroso: the pensive man, the thinker, who wishes to penetrate beneath the surface of transitory appearances.
3. **bested:** help.
4. **toys:** trifles.
6. **fond:** foolish.
10. **Morpheus:** god of sleep.
12. **Melancholy:** not just sadness, but also the spirit which, with the aid of all learning and knowledge, attempts to know final truth. See Albrecht Dürer's famous print of Melancholy.

18. **Memnon's sister:** Hemera, little-known sister of the Ethiopian prince who fought on the Trojan side in the *Iliad*.
19. **starred . . . queen:** Cassiopeia ("fated," but also put into a constellation).
23–24. **Vesta . . . Saturn:** purity combined with the father of the gods (a *saturnine* complexion signified melancholy). Milton invents the myth.
29. **Ida:** mountain in Crete (where Jove was born, according to one story, and overcame his father Saturn).

And sable stole of cypress lawn   35
Over thy decent shoulders drawn.
Come; but keep thy wonted state,
With even step, and musing gait,
And looks commercing with the skies,
Thy rapt soul sitting in thine eyes: 40
There, held in holy passion still,
Forget thyself to marble, till
With a sad leaden downward cast
Thou fix them on the earth as fast.
And join with thee calm Peace and Quiet,   45
Spare Fast, that oft with gods doth diet,
And hears the Muses in a ring
Aye round about Jove's altar sing;
And add to these retired Leisure,
That in trim gardens takes his pleasure;   50
But first and chiefest, with thee bring
Him that yon soars on golden wing,
Guiding the fiery-wheelèd throne,
The Cherub Contemplation;
And the mute Silence hist along,   55
'Less Philomel will deign a song,
In her sweetest, saddest plight,
Smoothing the rugged brow of Night,
While Cynthia checks her dragon yoke
Gently o'er th' accustomed oak.   60
Sweet bird, that shunn'st the noise of folly,
Most musical, most melancholy!
Thee, chauntress, oft the woods among
I woo, to hear thy even-song;
And, missing thee, I walk unseen   65
On the dry smooth-shaven green
To behold the wandering moon,
Riding near her highest noon,
Like one that had been led astray
Through the heaven's wide pathless way,   70
And oft, as if her head she bowed,
Stooping through a fleecy cloud.
Oft, on a plat of rising ground,

35. **sable . . . lawn:** black stole of dark, fine linen.
36. **decent:** proper.
53–54. **Guiding . . . Contemplation:** From the vision of the wheels a voice speaks to Ezekiel, telling him to eat a scroll, in which melancholy knowledge is written.
It tastes like honey (Ezekiel 1: 9–10; 2: 10).
56. **Philomel:** the nightingale. Philomel, raped by her sister's husband, was kept silent by the removal of her tongue. She and her sister were turned to birds.
59. **Cynthia:** the moon.

I hear the far-off curfew sound,
Over some wide-watered shore,   75
Swinging slow with sullen roar;
Or, if the air will not permit,
Some still removèd place will fit,
Where glowing embers through the room
Teach light to counterfeit a gloom,   80
Far from all resort of mirth,
Save the cricket on the hearth,
Or the bellman's drowsy charm
To bless the doors from nightly harm.
Or let my lamp, at midnight hour,   85
Be seen in some high lonely tower,
Where I may oft outwatch the Bear,
With thrice great Hermes, or unsphere
The spirit of Plato, to unfold
What worlds or what vast regions hold   90
The immortal mind that hath forsook
Her mansion in this fleshly nook;
And of those demons that are found
In fire, air, flood, or underground,
Whose power hath a true consent   95
With planet or with element.
Sometime let gorgeous Tragedy
In sceptered pall come sweeping by,
Presenting Thebes, or Pelops' line,
Or the tale of Troy divine,   100
Or what (though rare) of later age
Ennobled hath the buskined stage.
But, O sad Virgin! that thy power
Might raise Musaeus from his bower;
Or bid the soul of Orpheus sing   105
Such notes as, warbled to the string,
Drew iron tears down Pluto's cheek,
And made Hell grant what love did seek;

83. **bellman:** the night watchman, ringing the hours.
87. **outwatch . . . Bear:** This constellation never sleeps: it is above the horizon all night in our latitudes.
88. **thrice . . . Hermes:** Hermes Trismegistus, the pseudo-author of various books (3rd–4th centuries) of secret lore and magic.
88. **unsphere:** bring hither from whatever sphere he now exists in.
93. **of those demons:** i.e., spirit of those demons (what is meant are beings, familiar in Renaissance magic, who have affinities with each of the four elements, and four planets).
99–100. **Thebes . . . divine:** ancient Greek tragedies, presenting Oedipus, Agamemnon, Orestes, Electra, and their mythical companions.
102. **buskined:** tragic.
103. **Virgin:** melancholy.
104–105. **Musaeus; Orpheus:** On Orpheus, see *L'Allegro, ll.* 145–50, note; the legendary Greek poet Musaeus was supposed to have been his pupil.

Or call up him that left half-told
The story of Cambuscan bold,   110
Of Camball, and of Algarsife,
And who had Canacè to wife,
That owned the virtuous ring and glass,
And of the wondrous horse of brass
On which the Tartar king did ride;   115
And if aught else great bards beside
In sage and solemn tunes have sung,
Of tourneys, and of trophies hung,
Of forests, and enchantments drear,
Where more is meant than meets the ear.   120
Thus, Night, oft see me in thy pale career,
Till civil-suited Morn appear,
Not tricked and frounced, as she was wont
With the Attic boy to hunt,
But kerchiefed in a comely cloud,   125
While rocking winds are piping loud,
Or ushered with a shower still,
When the gust hath blown his fill,
Ending on the rustling leaves,
With minute-drops from off the eaves.   130
And, when the sun begins to fling
His flaring beams, me, Goddess, bring
To archèd walks of twilight groves,
And shadows brown, that Sylvan loves,
Of pine, or monumental oak,   135
Where the rude axe with heavèd stroke
Was never heard the nymphs to daunt,
Or fright them from their hallowed haunt.
There, in close covert, by some brook,
Where no profaner eye may look,   140
Hide me from day's garish eye,
While the bee with honeyed thigh,
That at her flowery work doth sing,
And the waters murmuring,
With such consort as they keep,   145
Entice the dewy-feathered Sleep.
And let some strange mysterious dream
Wave at his wings, in airy stream

109–115. **him . . . half-told:** Geoffrey Chaucer failed to finish *The Squire's Tale*, in which the romantic and magical story of Cambuskan begins.
113. **virtuous:** possessing magical strength.
116–120. **great bards . . . ear:** This sounds like a description of Edmund Spenser's *Faerie Queene*, which impressed Milton strongly.
123–124. **Not tricked . . . hunt:** not adorned and with hair curled, as when she hunted with Cephalus (whom she loved).
134. **Sylvan:** god of forests.
145. **consort:** musical accompaniment.

Of lively portraiture displayed,
Softly on my eyelids laid;   150
And, as I wake, sweet music breathe
Above, about, or underneath,
Sent by some Spirit to mortals good,
Or th' unseen Genius of the wood.
But let my due feet never fail   155
To walk the studious cloister's pale,
And love the high embowèd roof,
With antique pillars massy-proof,
And storied windows richly dight,
Casting a dim religious light.   160
There let the pealing organ blow,
To the full-voiced choir below,
In service high and anthems clear,
As may with sweetness, through mine ear,
Dissolve me into ecstasies,   165
And bring all Heaven before mine eyes.
And may at last my weary age
Find out the peaceful hermitage,
The hairy gown and mossy cell,
Where I may sit and rightly spell   170
Of every star that heaven doth shew,
And every herb that sips the dew,
Till old experience do attain
To something like prophetic strain.
These pleasures, Melancholy, give;   175
And I with thee will choose to live.

Lycidas

*In this monody the author bewails a learned
friend, unfortunately drowned in his passage
from Chester on the Irish Seas, 1637. And by
occasion foretells the ruin of our corrupted
clergy then in their height.*

Yet once more, O ye laurels, and once more
Ye myrtles brown, with ivy nevèr sere,
I come to pluck your berries harsh and crude,
And with forced fingers rude,

154. **Genius:** guardian spirit.
156. **pale:** enclosure.
170. **spell:** study.

Lycidas: This stock pastoral name is

given in this pastoral elegy to Edward
King, the friend referred to in the note
above who attended Cambridge at the
same time as Milton.
1–2. **laurels, myrtles, ivy:** evergreens
associated with poetry.

Shatter your leaves before the mellowing year.   5
Bitter constraint, and sad occasion dear,
Compels me to disturb your season due:
For Lycidas is dead, dead ere his prime,
Young Lycidas, and hath not left his peer.
Who would not sing for Lycidas? He knew   10
Himself to sing, and build the lofty rhyme.
He must not float upon his watery bier
Unwept, and welter to the parching wind,
Without the meed of some melodious tear.
    Begin then, sisters of the sacred well,   15
That from beneath the seat of Jove doth spring,
Begin, and somewhat loudly sweep the string.
Hence with denial vain and coy excuse;
So may some gentle muse
With lucky words favor my destined urn,   20
And as he passes turn,
And bid fair peace be to my sable shroud.
For we were nursed upon the self-same hill,
Fed the same flock, by fountain, shade, and rill.
    Together both, ere the high lawns appeared   25
Under the opening eyelids of the morn,
We drove afield, and both together heard
What time the gray-fly winds her sultry horn,
Battening our flocks with the fresh dews of night,
Oft till the star that rose, at evening, bright,   30
Toward heaven's descent had sloped his westering wheel.
Meanwhile the rural ditties were not mute,
Tempered to the oaten flute;
Rough satyrs danced, and fauns with cloven heel,
From the glad sound would not be absent long,   35
And old Damaetas loved to hear our song.
    But O the heavy change, now thou art gone,
Now thou art gone, and never must return!
Thee, shepherd, thee the woods and desert caves,
With wild thyme and the gadding vine o'ergrown,   40
And all their echoes mourn.
The willows and the hazel copses green
Shall now no more be seen,

6. **dear:** moving; dire.
13. **welter:** toss about.
14. **meed:** reward.
15. **sisters . . . well:** the Muses dwelling at one or another of the springs associated with poetic inspiration.
28. **What time . . . horn:** the heat of the day, when flys buzz most.
29. **Battening:** feeding.
36. **Damaetas:** a stock pastoral name, probably representing someone at Cambridge.
40. **gadding:** straggling.

Fanning their joyous leaves to thy soft lays.
As killing as the canker to the rose,   45
Or taint-worm to the weanling herds that graze,
Or frost to flowers, that their gay wardrobe wear,
When first the white-thorn blows:
Such, Lycidas, thy loss to shepherd's ear.
   Where were ye, nymphs, when the remorseless deep   50
Closed o'er the head of your loved Lycidas?
For neither were ye playing on the steep,
Where your old bards, the famous druids, lie,
Nor on the shaggy top of Mona high,
Nor yet where Deva spreads her wizard stream: 55
Ay me, I fondly dream!
"Had ye been there"—for what could that have done?
What could the Muse herself that Orpheus bore,
The Muse herself for her enchanting son
Whom universal nature did lament,   60
When by the rout that made the hideous roar,
His gory visage down the stream was sent,
Down the swift Hebrus to the Lesbian shore?
   Alas! What boots it with uncessant care
To tend the homely slighted shepherd's trade,   65
And strictly meditate the thankless Muse?
Were it not better done, as other use,
To sport with Amaryllis in the shade,
Or with the tangles of Neaera's hair?
Fame is the spur that the clear spirit doth raise   70
(That last infirmity of noble mind)
To scorn delights, and live laborious days;
But the fair guerdon when we hope to find,
And think to burst out into sudden blaze,
Comes the blind Fury with the abhorrèd shears,   75
And slits the thin-spun life. "But not the praise,"
Phoebus replied, and touched my trembling ears:
"Fame is no plant that grows on mortal soil,
Nor in the glistering foil

53. **druids:** Milton thought of them as ancient priests, prophets, and poets of England, now dead: hence the association with Lycidas, and with Orpheus, below.
54–55. **Mona:** Angelesy, near where King's ship sank; **Deva:** the River Dee, near where it set out.
58–63. **Orpheus . . . shore:** The mythical Greek poet was torn to pieces by a maddened crowd ("rout") of Thracian women; his head floated to Lesbos.
59. **enchanting:** singing, making magic (Orpheus accomplished supernatural feats

with his music).
64. **boots:** profits.
66. **meditate . . . Muse:** write poetry.
68–69. **Amaryllis, Neaera:** stock names for lovely girls.
73. **guerdon:** reward.
75. **Fury . . . shears:** that one (Atropos) of the three Fates who cuts the thread of life.
77. **Phoebus:** god of poetic inspiration. He touches the speaker's ears to make the spoken word memorable.
79. **foil:** trashy glitter.

Set off to the world, nor in broad rumor lies,   80
But lives and spreads aloft by those pure eyes
And perfect witness of all-judging Jove;
As he pronounces lastly on each deed,
Of so much fame in heaven expect thy meed."
    O fountain Arethuse, and thou honored flood,   85
Smooth-sliding Mincius, crowned with vocal reeds,
That strain I heard was of a higher mood.
But now my oat proceeds,
And listens to the herald of the sea,
That came in Neptune's plea.   90
He asked the waves and asked the felon-winds,
What hard mishap hath doomed this gentle swain,
And questioned every gust of rugged wings
That blows from off each beakèd promontory.
They knew not of his story,   95
And sage Hippotades their answer brings:
That not a blast was from his dungeon strayed;
The air was calm, and on the level brine,
Sleek Panopë with all her sisters played.
It was that fatal and perfidious bark   100
Built in the eclipse, and rigged with curses dark,
That sunk so low that sacred head of thine.
    Next Camus, reverend sire, went footing slow,
His mantle hairy, and his bonnet sedge,
Inwrought with figures dim, and on the edge   105
Like to that sanguine flower inscribed with woe.
"Ah, who hath reft," quoth he, "my dearest pledge?"
Last came, and last did go,
The pilot of the Galilean Lake;
Two massy keys he bore of metals twain   110
(The golden opes, the iron shuts amain).
He shook his mitered locks, and stern bespake:

---

82. **witness ... Jove:** One's deeds are rewarded eternally by a just God. The notion of the eternity of poetry, unlike other earthly things, is a favorite one in the Renaissance.
85–88. **O fountain ... proceeds** (paraphrased): Fountain Arethusa (associated with the pastoral poetry of Theocritus) and River Mincius (associated with pastoral poetry of Vergil), what Phoebus told me was a digression, above the lowly reach of pastoral poetry, to which I now return with my humble pipe.
89–90. **herald ... plea:** Triton comes to proclaim Neptune innocent.
92. **swain:** country youth; i.e., King, in pastoral terms.

96. **Hippotades:** god of the winds.
99. **Panopë:** chief of the sea-nymphs.
101. **eclipse:** time of ill omen.
103. **Camus:** river Cam, which flows through Cambridge.
106. **sanguine flower:** The hyacinth was supposed by the Greeks to bear marks meaning "Alas!" because the flower had grown from the blood of a youth unintentionally killed by Phoebus.
109. **pilot:** St. Peter, who had been a fisherman, who had the key of admission to heaven as his symbol, and who is supposed to be the first Bishop of Rome (hence he may discuss the clergy)
112. **mitered:** A bishop wears a miter.

"How well could I have spared for thee, young swain,
Enow of such as for their bellies' sake
Creep, and intrude, and climb into the fold!   115
Of other care they little reckoning make,
Than how to scramble at the shearers' feast,
And shove away the worthy bidden guest.
Blind mouths, that scarce themselves know how to hold
A sheep hook, or have learned aught else the least   120
That to the faithful herdman's art belongs!
What recks it them? What need they? They are sped,
And when they list, their lean and flashy songs
Grate on their scrannel pipes of wretched straw.
The hungry sheep look up and are not fed,   125
But swollen with wind, and the rank mist they draw,
Rot inwardly, and foul contagion spread;
Besides what the grim wolf with privy paw
Daily devours apace, and nothing said;
But that two-handed engine at the door   130
Stands ready to smite once, and smite no more."
    Return, Alpheus, the dread voice is past,
That shrunk thy streams; return, Sicilian Muse,
And call the vales, and bid them higher cast
Their bells and flowerets of a thousand hues.   135
Ye valleys low, where the mild whispers use
Of shades and wanton winds and gushing brooks,
On whose fresh lap the swart star sparely looks,
Throw hither all your quaint enameled eyes,
That on the green turf suck the honeyed showers,   140
And purple all the ground with vernal flowers.
Bring the rathe primrose that forsaken dies,
The tufted crow-toe, and pale jessamine,
The white pink, and the pansy freaked with jet,
The growing violet,   145
The musk-rose, and the well-attired woodbine,
With cowslips wan that hang the pensive head,
And every flower that sad embroidery wears.

114. **Enow:** enough, plenty.
120. **sheep hook:** A bishop's staff is made to look like a sheep hook, since he is the shepherd, or pastor, of those under his care.
122. **What . . . sped:** What difference does it make to them? They have what they want.
123. **list:** wish.
124. **scrannel:** harsh.
128. **wolf:** Milton means the Church of Rome, acting secretly, or (perhaps) Satan.
130. **engine:** meaning not clear.

132–133. **Return . . . Muse:** Milton, after another digression, asks for the return of the definitely pastoral spirit: Alpheus was the river that had been in love with the nymph (then the fountain) Arethusa. The "Sicilian Muse" refers to the pastoral poetry of Theocritus.
138. **swart star:** Sirius, the dog star, is supposed to wither vegetation in late summer.
142. **rathe:** early.
144. **freaked:** speckled.

Bid amaranthus all his beauty shed,
And daffodillies fill their cups with tears,   150
To strew the laureate hearse where Lycid lies.
For so to interpose a little ease,
Let our frail thoughts dally with false surmise.
Ay me! Whilst thee the shores and sounding seas
Wash far away, where'er thy bones are hurled,   155
Whether beyond the stormy Hebrides,
Where thou perhaps under the whelming tide
Visitest the bottom of the monstrous world;
Or whether thou to our moist vows denied,
Sleepest by the fable of Bellerus old,   160
Where the great vision of the guarded mount
Looks toward Namancos and Bayona's hold;
Look homeward, Angel, now, and melt with ruth.
And, O ye dolphins, waft the hapless youth.
    Weep no more, woeful shepherds, weep no more,   165
For Lycidas your sorrow is not dead,
Sunk though he be beneath the watery floor,
So sinks the day-star in the ocean bed,
And yet anon repairs his drooping head,
And tricks his beams, and with new-spangled ore   170
Flames in the forehead of the morning sky:
So Lycidas sunk low, but mounted high,
Through the dear might of him that walked the waves
Where, other groves and other streams along,
With nectar pure his oozy locks he laves,   175
And hears the unexpressive nuptial song,
In the blest kingdoms meek of joy and love.
There entertain him all the saints above
In solemn troops and sweet societies
That sing, and singing in their glory move,   180
And wipe the tears forever from his eyes.
Now, Lycidas, the shepherds weep no more;
Henceforth thou art the genius of the shore,

149. **amaranthus:** a plant that was supposed never to shed.
153. **false surmise:** namely, that the corpse has been recovered from the sea for proper burial.
156. **Hebrides:** islands far to the north of where King died.
158. **monstrous:** filled with sea-monsters.
160. **Bellerus:** a fabulous giant, supposed to be buried in the sea far to the south.
161–162. **Where ... hold:** where, at St. Michael's Mount, this archangel who judges souls justly and is a warrior looks towards the coast of Spain, England's Catholic enemy.
163. **Look ... ruth:** Michael is urged to look back in the opposite direction and to exchange justice for mercy ("ruth") towards the soul of Lycidas.
164. **dolphins:** They were supposed to have carried the singer Arion on their backs.
168. **day-star:** sun.
170. **tricks:** dresses.
176. **unexpressive ... song:** A song which can not be sung by human tongue greets the souls of the blessed at the marriage feast of Christ, the Lamb, in Revelation 19.
183. **genius:** guardian spirit.

In thy large recompense, and shalt be good
To all that wander in that perilous flood.   185
   Thus sang the uncouth swain to the oaks and rills,
While the still morn went out with sandals gray;
He touched the tender stops of various quills,
With eager thought warbling his Doric lay.
And now the sun had stretched out all the hills,   190
And now was dropped into the western bay.
At last he rose, and twitched his mantle blue:
Tomorrow to fresh woods, and pastures new.

How soon hath Time

How soon hath Time, the subtle thief of youth,
Stoln on his wings my three and twentieth year!
My hasting days fly on with full career,
But my late spring no bud or blossom shew'th.
Perhaps my semblance might deceive the truth,   5
That I to manhood am arrived so near,
And inward ripeness doth much less appear,
That some more timely-happy spirits indu'th.
Yet be it less or more, or soon or slow,
It shall be still in strictest measure even,   10
To that same lot, however mean, or high,
Toward which Time leads me, and the will of Heaven;
All is, if I have grace to use it so,
As ever in my great Taskmaster's eye.

On the New Forcers of Conscience Under the Long Parliament

Because you have thrown off your prelate lord,
And with stiff vows renounced his liturgy
To seize the widowed whore Plurality
From them whose sin ye envied, not abhorred,

186. **uncouth:** simple.
188. **quills:** the oaten stalks from which the shepherd singer's pipe is made.
189. **Doric:** the Greek dialect of the earliest pastoral poets.

8. **indu'th:** endows.

On the New . . .: Milton attacks the new Presbyterian faction which has replaced the Episcopalian faction under the Puritan Long Parliament.
1. **lord:** bishops (as under the Episcopalian faction).
3. **Plurality:** the holding of more than one living (i.e., a parish with its revenues) at one time.

Dare ye for this adjure the civil sword   5
To force our consciences that Christ set free,
And ride us with a classic hierarchy
Taught ye by mere A. S. and Rutherford?
Men whose life, learning, faith, and pure intent
Would have been held in high esteem with Paul   10
Must now be named and printed heretics
By shallow Edwards and Scotch what d'ye call:
But we do hope to find out all your tricks,
Your plots and packing worse than those of Trent,
       That so the Parliament   15
May with their wholesome and preventive shears
Clip your phylacteries, though balk your ears,
       And succor our just fears
When they shall read this clearly on your charge:
New presbyter is but *old priest* writ large.   20

Cromwell, our chief of men

Cromwell, our chief of men, who through a cloud
Not of war only, but detractions rude,
Guided by faith and matchless fortitude,
To peace and truth thy glorious way hast ploughed,
And on the neck of crownèd Fortune proud   5
Hast reared God's trophies, and his work pursued,
While Darwen stream, with blood of Scots imbrued,
And Dunbar field, resounds thy praises loud,
And Worcester's laureate wreath: yet much remains
To conquer still; Peace hath her victories   10
No less renowned than War: new foes arise,
Threatening to bind our souls with secular chains.
Help us to save free conscience from the paw
Of hireling wolves, whose Gospel is their maw.

---

7. hierarchy: The Presbyterian synods (governing bodies) had much the same powers as bishops.
8. A. S., Rutherford: Adam Stuart, Samuel Rutherford, Presbyterian writers.
12. Edwards, Scotch what d'ye call: Thomas Edwards and some Scotch writer with a name that a southern Englishman would consider unpronounceable.
14. Trent: the Catholic church council held in response to the Protestant Reformation.
17. phylacteries: meant here as a sign of superstition (They are scrolls, containing texts, worn by Orthodox Jews).

7–9. Darwen, Dunbar, Worcester: victories of Cromwell. A laurel wreath was given to victors in ancient times.

On the Late Massacre in Piedmont

Avenge, O Lord, thy slaughtered saints, whose bones
Lie scattered on the Alpine mountains cold;
Even them who kept thy truth so pure of old,
When all our fathers worshipped stocks and stones,
Forget not: in thy book record their groans   5
Who were thy sheep, and in their ancient fold
Slain by the bloody Piedmontese, that rolled
Mother with infant down the rocks. Their moans
The vales redoubled to the hills, and they
To heaven. Their martyred blood and ashes sow   10
O'er all the Italian fields, where still doth sway
The triple tyrant; that from these may grow
A hundredfold, who, having learnt thy way,
Early may fly the Babylonian woe.

Lawrence, of virtuous father virtuous son

Lawrence, of virtuous father virtuous son,
Now that the fields are dank, and ways are mire,
Where shall we sometimes meet, and by the fire
Help waste a sullen day? What may be won
From the hard season gaining, time will run   5
On smoother, till Favonius re-inspire
The frozen earth, and clothe in fresh attire
The lily and the rose, that neither sowed nor spun.
What neat repast shall feast us, light and choice,
Of Attic taste, with wine, whence we may rise   10
To hear the lute well toucht, or artful voice
Warble immortal notes and Tuscan air?
He who of those delights can judge, and spare
To interpose them oft, is not unwise.

On the Late Massacre . . .: In 1655 an ancient sect, the Waldensians, with beliefs resembling the Protestant ones, were partly massacred by Catholics in northern Italy (Piedmont) and southern France.
12. triple tyrant: The Pope's tiara has three crowns, one above the other.
14. Babylonian: Protestants then referred to the Church of Rome as the "whore of Babylon" (Revelation 17–18).

virtuous father: Henry Lawrence, Puritan statesman.
6. Favonius: the west-wind, associated with spring.
8. lily . . . spun: See Matthew 7: 28.
10. Attic: Athenian; according to the taste of the ancient Greeks.
12. Tuscan air: Italian song.

When I consider how my light is spent

When I consider how my light is spent
Ere half my days, in this dark world and wide,
And that one talent which is death to hide,
Lodged with me useless, though my soul more bent
To serve therewith my Maker, and present   5
My true account, lest he returning chide,
"Doth God exact day-labour, light denied?"
I fondly ask; but Patience, to prevent
That murmur, soon replies, "God doth not need
Either man's work or his own gifts; who best   10
Bear his mild yoke, they serve him best. His state
Is kingly. Thousands at his bidding speed
And post o'er land and ocean without rest:
They also serve who only stand and wait."

Methought I saw my late espoused saint

Methought I saw my late espousèd saint
Brought to me like Alcestis from the grave
Whom Jove's great son to her glad husband gave,
Rescued from Death by force, though pale and faint.
Mine, as whom washed from spot of childbed taint   5
Purification in the old law did save,
And such as yet once more I trust to have
Full sight of her in Heaven without restraint,
Came vested all in white, pure as her mind.
Her face was veiled; yet to my fancied sight   10
Love, sweetness, goodness, in her person shined
So clear as in no face with more delight.
But, oh! as to embrace me she inclined,
I waked, she fled, and day brought back my night.

3. **talent:** The parable of the talents is punningly referred to in *l.* 6 (Matthew 25: 14–30).
8. **fondly:** foolishly.

late espoused: Milton's second wife died two years after their marriage.
2. **Alcestis:** Hercules rescued her from the underworld and restored her to her husband, for whose sake she had died.
6. **old law:** See Leviticus 12.

On Time

Fly, envious Time, till thou run out thy race;
Call on the lazy leaden-stepping hours,
Whose speed is but the heavy plummet's pace;
And glut thy self with what thy womb devours,
Which is no more than what is false and vain,   5
And merely mortal dross;
So little is our loss,
So little is thy gain.
For when as each thing bad thou hast entombed,
And last of all, thy greedy self consumed,   10
Then long Eternity shall greet our bliss
With an individual kiss;
And Joy shall overtake us as a flood,
When every thing that is sincerely good
And perfectly divine,   15
With Truth, and Peace, and Love shall ever shine
About the supreme Throne
Of him, t' whose happy-making sight alone,
When once our heav'nly-guided soul shall climb,
Then all this earthy grossness quit,   20
Attired with stars, we shall for ever sit,
    Triumphing over Death, and Chance, and thee O Time.

WILLIAM BROWNE OF TAVISTOCK [1591–1643]

On the Countess Dowager of Pembroke

Underneath this sable hearse
Lies the subject of all verse:
Sidney's sister, Pembroke's mother;
Death, ere thou hast slain another
Fair and learn'd and good as she,   5
Time shall throw a dart at thee.

Marble piles let no man raise
To her name, for after-days.
Some kind woman, born as she,
Reading this, like Niobe   10
Shall turn marble, and become
Both her mourner and her tomb.

3. **Sidney's ... mother:** sister of Sir Philip Sidney and mother of William Herbert, third Earl of Pembroke.

10. **Niobe:** After Apollo and Diana had killed her twelve children, she turned to stone and continued to weep.

HENRY KING [1592–1669]

The Exequy

Accept, thou shrine of my dead saint,
Instead of dirges, this complaint;
And for sweet flowers to crown thy hearse,
Receive a strew of weeping verse
From thy grieved friend, whom thou might'st see   5
Quite melted into tears for thee.

Dear loss! since thy untimely fate
My task hath been to meditate
On thee, on thee; thou art the book,
The library whereon I look,   10
Though almost blind. For thee, loved clay,
I languish out, not live, the day,
Using no other exercise
But what I practise with mine eyes;
By which wet glasses I find out   15
How lazily time creeps about
To one that mourns; this, only this,
My exercise and business is.
So I compute the weary hours
With sighs dissolvèd into showers.   20

Nor wonder if my time go thus
Backward and most preposterous;
Thou hast benighted me; thy set
This eve of blackness did beget,
Who wast my day, though overcast   25
Before thou hadst thy noon-tide passed;
And I remember must in tears,
Thou scarce hadst seen so many years
As day tells hours. By thy clear sun
My love and fortune first did run;   30
But thou wilt never more appear
Folded within my hemisphere,
Since both thy light and motion
Like a fled star is fall'n and gone;

Exequy: literally, funeral rite.   23. set: as in "sunset."
2. complaint: lament.

And 'twixt me and my soul's dear wish   35
An earth now interposèd is,
Which such a strange eclipse doth make
As ne'er was read in almanac.

I could allow thee for a time
To darken me and my sad clime;   40
Were it a month, a year, or ten,
I would thy exile live till then,
And all that space my mirth adjourn,
So thou wouldst promise to return,
And putting off thy ashy shroud,   45
At length disperse this sorrow's cloud.

But woe is me! the longest date
Too narrow is to calculate
These empty hopes; never shall I
Be so much blest as to descry   50
A glimpse of thee, till that day come
Which shall the earth to cinders doom,
And a fierce fever must calcine
The body of this world like thine,
My little world. That fit of fire   55
Once off, our bodies shall aspire
To our souls' bliss; then we shall rise
And view ourselves with clearer eyes
In that calm region where no night
Can hide us from each other's sight.   60

Meantime, thou hast her, earth; much good
May my harm do thee. Since it stood
With heaven's will I might not call
Her longer mine, I give thee all
My short-lived right and interest   65
In her whom living I loved best;
With a most free and bounteous grief,
I give thee what I could not keep.
Be kind to her, and prithee look
Thou write into thy doomsday book   70
Each parcel of this rarity
Which in thy casket shrined doth lie.

See that thou make thy reck'ning straight,
And yield her back again by weight;
For thou must audit on thy trust   75

Each grain and atom of this dust,
As thou wilt answer Him that lent,
Not gave thee, my dear monument.

So close the ground, and 'bout her shade
Black curtains draw, my bride is laid.   80

Sleep on, my love, in thy cold bed,
Never to be disquieted!
My last good-night! Thou wilt not wake
Till I thy fate shall overtake;
Till age, or grief, or sickness must   85
Marry my body to that dust
It so much loves, and fill the room
My heart keeps empty in thy tomb.
Stay for me there, I will not fail
To meet thee in that hollow vale.   90
And think not much of my delay;
I am already on the way,
And follow thee with all the speed
Desire can make, or sorrows breed.
Each minute is a short degree,   95
And ev'ry hour a step towards thee.
At night when I betake to rest,
Next morn I rise nearer my west
Of life, almost by eight hours' sail,
Than when sleep breathed his drowsy gale.   100

Thus from the sun my bottom steers,
And my day's compass downward bears;
Nor labor I to stem the tide
Through which to thee I swiftly glide.

'Tis true, with shame and grief I yield,   105
Thou like the van first tookst the field,
And gotten hath the victory
In thus adventuring to die
Before me, whose more years might crave
A just precèdence in the grave.   110
But hark! my pulse like a soft drum
Beats my approach, tells thee I come;
And slow howe'er my marches be,
I shall at last sit down by thee.

79. **shade**: spirit, ghost.   106. **van**: vanguard in battle.
101. **bottom**: ship.

The thought of this bids me go on,   115
And wait my dissolution
With hope and comfort. Dear, forgive
The crime, I am content to live
Divided, with but half a heart,
Till we shall meet and never part.   120

THOMAS CAREW [1595?–1639?]

An Elegy upon the Death of
the Dean of St. Paul's, Dr. John Donne

Can we not force from widowed poetry,
Now thou art dead, great Donne, one elegy
To crown thy hearse? Why yet did we not trust,
Though with unkneaded dough-baked prose, thy dust,
Such as th' unscissored lect'rer from the flower   5
Of fading rhet'ric, short-lived as his hour,
Dry as the sand that measures it, might lay
Upon the ashes, on the funeral day?
Have we nor tune nor voice? Didst thou dispense
Through all our language both the words and sense?   10
'Tis a sad truth. The pulpit may her plain
And sober Christian precepts still retain;
Doctrines it may, and wholesome uses, frame,
Grave homilies and lectures, but the flame
Of thy brave soul, that shot such heat and light   15
As burnt our earth and made our darkness bright,
Committed holy rapes upon the will,
Did through the eye the melting heart distil,
And the deep knowledge of dark truths so teach
As sense might judge where fancy could not reach,   20
Must be desired forever. So the fire
That fills with spirit and heat the Delphic choir,
Which, kindled first by the Promethean breath,
Glowed here a while, lies quenched now in thy death.

5. **unscissored lect'rer:** unshorn reader, reciter (preacher). (Unshorn, because grief-stricken (?) or incapable of shearing his rhetoric to proper shape (?).) The "sand" refers to the hourglass used by the preacher to time himself. The construction of the sentence seems unclear.
21. **desired:** missed.
22. **Delphic:** Apollo, inspirer of poets, had a shrine at Delphi.
23. **Promethean:** Prometheus stole fire from heaven for the use of mortals.

The Muses' garden, with pedantic weeds   25
O'erspread, was purged by thee; the lazy seeds
Of servile imitation thrown away,
And fresh invention planted; thou didst pay
The debts of our penurious bankrupt age;
Licentious thefts, that make poetic rage   30
A mimic fury, when our souls must be
Possessed, or with Anacreon's ecstasy,
Or Pindar's, not their own; the subtle cheat
Of sly exchanges, and the juggling feat
Of two-edged words, or whatsoever wrong   35
By ours was done the Greek or Latin tongue,
Thou hast redeemed, and opened us a mine
Of rich and pregnant fancy; drawn a line
Of masculine expression, which had good
Old Orpheus seen, or all the ancient brood   40
Our superstitious fools admire, and hold
Their lead more precious than thy burnished gold,
Thou hadst been their exchequer, and no more
They each in other's dung had searched for ore.
Thou shalt yield no precèdence, but of time   45
And the blind fate of language, whose tuned chime
More charms the outward sense; yet thou mayst claim
From so great disadvantage greater fame,
Since to the awe of thy imperious wit
Our troublesome language bends, made only fit   50
With her tough thick-ribbed hoops to gird about
Thy giant fancy, which had proved too stout
For their soft melting phrases. As in time
They had the start, so did they cull the prime
Buds of invention many a hundred year,   55
And left the rifled fields, besides the fear
To touch their harvest; yet from those bare lands
Of what was only thine, thy only hands,
And that their smallest work, have gleanèd more
Than all those times and tongues could reap before.   60
    But thou art gone, and thy strict laws will be
Too hard for libertines in poetry;
They will recall the goodly exiled train
Of gods and goddesses, which in thy just reign
Was banished nobler poems; now with these,   65

32–33. **Anacreon, Pindar:** ancient Greek   of all poets.
lyric poets.   62. **libertines:** slack non-observers of rules
40. **Orpheus:** ancient mythical prototype

The silenced tales i' th' *Metamorphoses*,
Shall stuff their lines, and swell the windy page,
Till verse, refined by thee in this last age,
Turn ballad-rhyme, or those old idols be
Adored again with new apostasy.   70
   Oh, pardon me, that break with untuned verse
The reverend silence that attends thy hearse,
Whose solemn awful murmurs were to thee,
More than these rude lines, a loud elegy,
That did proclaim in a dumb eloquence   75
The death of all the arts; whose influence,
Grown feeble, in these panting numbers lies,
Gasping short-winded accents, and so dies.
So doth the swiftly turning wheel not stand
In th' instant we withdraw the moving hand,   80
But some short time retain a faint weak course,
By virtue of the first impulsive force;
And so, whilst I cast on thy funeral pile
Thy crown of bays, oh, let it crack awhile,
And spit disdain, till the devouring flashes   85
Suck all the moisture up, then turn to ashes.
   I will not draw the envy to engross
All thy perfections, or weep all the loss;
Those are too numerous for one elegy,
And this too great to be expressed by me.   90
Let others carve the rest; it shall suffice
I on thy grave this epitaph incise:
   Here lies a king that ruled as he thought fit
   The universal monarchy of wit;
   Here lies two flamens, and both those the best,   95
   Apollo's first, at last the true God's priest.

A Song

Ask me no more where Jove bestows,
When June is past, the fading rose:
For in your beauty's orient deep,
These flowers, as in their causes, sleep.

66. **Metamorphoses:** collection of mytho-
logical tales by Latin poet Ovid, much used
by poets before and after Donne.
73. **awful:** awed.
84. **bays:** laurel crown of the poet.
87. **engross:** write down.
95. **flamens:** priests (in Roman religion).

3. **orient:** shining; also precious, such as
the products and the pearls imported from
the East.
4. **in . . . causes:** i.e., in potentiality; in
that which brings them into being, according to Aristotelian philosophy.

Ask me no more whither do stray   5
The golden atoms of the day:
For in pure love heaven did prepare
Those powders to enrich your hair.

Ask me no more whither doth haste
The nightingale, when May is past: 10
For in your sweet dividing throat
She winters, and keeps warm her note.

Ask me no more where those stars light,
That downwards fall in dead of night:
For in your eyes they sit, and there   15
Fixèd become as in their sphere.

Ask me no more if east or west
The phoenix builds her spicy nest:
For unto you at last she flies,
And in your fragrant bosom dies.   20

EDMUND WALLER [1606–1687]

Song

Go, lovely rose!
Tell her that wastes her time and me
That now she knows,
When I resemble her to thee,
How sweet and fair she seems to be.   5

Tell her that's young
And shuns to have her graces spied,
That hadst thou sprung
In deserts where no men abide,
Thou must have uncommended died.   10

Small is the worth
Of beauty from the light retired;
Bid her come forth,
Suffer herself to be desired,
And not blush so to be admired.   15

11. **dividing**: singing: modulating, trilling.
18. **phoenix**: mythical bird which lived 1,000 years, then burned itself in a nest of twigs from spice trees and bushes, and was reborn from the ashes.

Then die, that she
The common fate of all things rare
May read in thee;
How small a part of time they share
That are so wondrous sweet and fair!   20

On a Girdle

That which her slender waist confined
Shall now my joyful temples bind;
No monarch but would give his crown
His arms might do what this has done.

It was my heaven's extremest sphere,   5
The pale which held that lovely deer.
My joy, my grief, my hope, my love,
Did all within this circle move!

A narrow compass, and yet there
Dwelt all that's good and all that's fair;   10
Give me but what this riband bound,
Take all the rest the sun goes round.

SIR JOHN SUCKLING [1609–1642]

Song

Why so pale and wan, fond lover?
    Prithee, why so pale?
Will, when looking well can't move her,
    Looking ill prevail?
    Prithee, why so pale?   5

Why so dull and mute, young sinner?
    Prithee, why so mute?
Will, when speaking well can't win her,
    Saying nothing do 't?
    Prithee, why so mute?   10

5. **extremest sphere:** farthest, all-encom-   6. **pale:** fence of a deer-park.
passing sphere of the concentric ones
surrounding the earth, according to Ptolemaic astronomy.

Quit, quit for shame! This will not move;
　　This cannot take her.
If of herself she will not love,
　　Nothing can make her:
　　The devil take her!　　　　　　　　　15

Out Upon It

Out upon it! I have loved
　　Three whole days together.
And am like to love three more,
　　If it prove fair weather.

Time shall molt away his wings　　　　　5
　　Ere he shall discover
In the whole wide world again
　　Such a constant lover.

But the spite on't is, no praise
　　Is due at all to me:　　　　　　　　10
Love with me had made no stays,
　　Had it any been but she.

Had it any been but she,
　　And that very face,
There had been at least ere this　　　　15
　　A dozen dozen in her place.

Song

No, no, fair heretic, it needs must be
　　But an ill love in me
　　And worse for thee;
For were it in my power
To love thee now this hour　　　　　　5
　　More than I did the last,
I would then so fall
　　I might not love at all.
Love that can flow, and can admit increase,
Admits as well an ebb, and may grow less.　　10

1. **heretic:** i.e., to the true doctrine of love.

True love is still the same. The torrid zones,
   And those more frigid ones,
     It must not know:
For love grown cold or hot
   Is lust, or friendship, not   15
     The thing we have.
For that's a flame would die
Held down, or up too high.
Then think I love more than I can express,
And would love more could I but love thee less.

A Ballad upon a Wedding

I tell thee, Dick, where I have been,
Where I the rarest things have seen,
   Oh, things without compare!
Such sights again cannot be found
In any place on English ground,   5
   Be it at wake or fair.

At Charing Cross, hard by the way
Where we, thou know'st, do sell our hay,
   There is a house with stairs;
And there did I see coming down   10
Such folk as are not in our town,
   Vorty at least, in pairs.

Amongst the rest, one pest'lent fine,
His beard no bigger though than thine,
   Walked on before the rest;   15
Our landlord looks like nothing to him,
The King, God bless him, 'twould undo him
   Should he go still so dressed.

At course-a-park, without all doubt,
He should have first been taken out   20
   By all the maids i' th' town;
Though lusty Roger there had been,
Or little George upon the Green,
   Or Vincent of the Crown.

Ballad: Suckling describes through the mouth of a bumpkin what appears to be an actual marriage of two historical noble persons. The "Dick" to whom it is addressed may refer, under the disguise of another countryman, to the fellow-poet Richard Lovelace.
7. **Charing Cross:** suburban point of London then.
12. **Vorty:** forty (Kentish dialect often used to suggest rusticity).
13. **Pest'lent:** i.e., extremely.
17. **undo:** bankrupt.
18. **still:** continually.
19. **course-a-park:** a country game in which a girl chooses a boy to chase her.

But wot you what? the youth was going   25
To make an end of all his wooing,
  The parson for him stayed;
Yet by his leave, for all his haste,
He did not so much wish all past,
  Perchance, as did the maid.   30

The maid—and thereby hangs a tale:
For such a maid no Whitsun ale
  Could ever yet produce;
No grape that's kindly ripe could be
So round, so plump, so soft as she,   35
  Nor half so full of juice.

Her finger was so small the ring
Would not stay on, which they did bring,
  It was too wide a peck;
And to say truth, for out it must,   40
It looked like the great collar, just,
  About our young colt's neck.

Her feet beneath her petticoat,
Like little mice, stole in and out,
  As if they feared the light;   45
But oh, she dances such a way!
No sun upon an Easter day
  Is half so fine a sight.

He would have kissed her once or twice,
But she would not, she was nice,   50
  She would not do't in sight;
And then she looked as who should say,
I will do what I list to-day,
  And you shall do't at night.

Her cheeks so rare a white was on,   55
No daisy makes comparison,
  Who sees them is undone;
For streaks of red were mingled there,
Such as are on a Katherne pear,
  The side that's next the sun.   60

---

32. Whitsun ale: country feast at Whitsun-
tide.

34. kindly: according to its kind, by course
of nature.
50. nice: particular, proper.

Her lips were red, and one was thin,
Compared to that was next her chin,
   Some bee had stung it newly:
But Dick, her eyes so guard her face
I durst no more upon them gaze   65
   Then on the sun in July.

Her mouth so small, when she does speak
Thou'dst swear her teeth her words did break,
   That they might passage get;
But she so handled still the matter,   70
They came as good as ours, or better,
   And are not spent a whit.

If wishing should be any sin,
The parson himself had guilty been,
   She looked that day so purely;   75
And did the youth so oft the feat
At night, as some did in conceit,
   It would have spoiled him surely.

Passion o' me, how I run on!
There's that that would be thought upon,   80
   I trow, besides the bride.
The business of the kitchen's great,
For it is fit that man should eat,
   Nor was it there denied.

Just in the nick the cook knocked thrice,   85
And all the waiters in a trice
   His summons did obey;
Each serving-man, with dish in hand,
Marched boldly up like our trained band,
   Presented, and away.   90

When all the meat was on the table,
What man of knife or teeth was able
   To stay to be entreated?
And this the very reason was—
Before the parson could say grace,   95
   The company was seated.

89. **trained band:** militia.

Now hats fly off, and youths carouse,
Healths first go round, and then the house,
   The bride's came thick and thick;
And when 'twas named another's health,   100
Perhaps he made it hers by stealth,
   And who could help it, Dick?

O' th' sudden up they rise and dance,
Then sit again and sigh and glance,
   Then dance again, and kiss;   105
Thus several ways the time did pass,
   Whilst ev'ry woman wished her place,
   And ev'ry man wished his.

By this time all were stolen aside
To counsel and undress the bride,   110
   But that he must not know;
But yet 'twas thought he guessed her mind,
And did not mean to stay behind
   Above an hour or so.

When in he came, Dick, there she lay   115
Like new-fallen snow melting away
   ('Twas time, I trow, to part);
Kisses were now the only stay,
Which soon she gave, as who would say,
   God b' w' ye, with all my heart.   120

But just as heavens would have, to cross it,
In came the bridesmaids with the posset;
   The bridegroom eat in spite,
For, had he left the women to 't,
It would have have cost two hours to do 't,   125
   Which were too much that night.

At length the candle's out, and now
All that they had not done they do;
   What that is, who can tell?
But I believe it was no more   130
Than thou and I have done before
   With Bridget and with Nell.

118. **stay**: delay.
120. **God b' w' ye**: God be with you (i.e., "good-bye": she wishes to hurry them).

122. **posset**: milk, liquor, spices compounded: traditional on the wedding night.

WILLIAM CARTWRIGHT [1611–1643]

No Platonic Love

Tell me no more of minds embracing minds,
  And hearts exchanged for hearts;
That spirits spirits meet, as winds do winds,
  And mix their subt'lest parts;
That two unbodied essences may kiss,   5
And then like Angels, twist and feel one Bliss.

I was that silly thing that once was wrought
  To practice this thin love;
I climb'd from sex to soul, from soul to thought;
  But thinking there to move,   10
Headlong I rolled from thought to soul, and then
From soul I lighted at the sex again.

As some strict down-looked men pretend to fast,
  Who yet in closets eat;
So lovers who profess they spirits taste,   15
  Feed yet on grosser meat;
I know they boast they souls to souls convey,
Howe'r they meet, the body is the way.

Come, I will undeceive thee: they that tread
  Those vain aerial ways,   20
Are like young heirs and alchemists misled
  To waste their wealth and days,
For searching thus to be for ever rich,
They only find a med'cine for the itch.

RICHARD CRASHAW [1613?–1649]

In the Holy Nativity of Our Lord God
A Hymn Sung as by the Shepherds

Chorus

  Come, we shepherds, whose blest sight
  Hath met Love's noon in Nature's night;
  Come, lift we up our loftier song
  And wake the sun that lies too long.

Platonic love: Neoplatonists held that love ruled the universe, but was the more excellent the more it ascended from the corporeal to the spiritual and divine. The doctrine is nearly everywhere in earlier poems of the Renaissance.
14. **closets:** small private rooms.

To all our world of well-stolen joy 5
He slept, and dreamt of no such thing,
  While we found out heaven's fairer eye
And kissed the cradle of our King.
  Tell him he rises now too late
To show us aught worth looking at. 10

  Tell him we now can show him more
Than he e'er showed to mortal sight,
  Than he himself e'er saw before,
Which to be seen needs not his light.
  Tell him, Tityrus, where th'hast been 15
Tell him, Thyrsis, what th'hast seen.

Tityrus. Gloomy night embraced the place
Where the noble Infant lay.
  The Babe looked up and showed His face;
In spite of darkness, it was day. 20
  It was Thy day, Sweet! and did rise
Not from the east, but from Thine eyes.

Chorus. It was Thy day, Sweet, etc.

Thyrsis. Winter chid aloud, and sent
The angry North to wage his wars; 25
  The North forgot his fierce intent,
And left perfumes instead of scars.
  By those sweet eyes' persuasive powers
Where he meant frost he scattered flowers.

Cho. By those sweet eyes', etc. 30

Both. We saw Thee in Thy balmy nest,
Young dawn of our eternal day;
  We saw Thine eyes break from their east
And chase the trembling shades away.
  We saw Thee, and we blest the sight, 35
We saw Thee by Thine own sweet light.

Tit. Poor world, said I, what wilt thou do
To entertain this starry Stranger?
  Is this the best thou canst bestow—
A cold, and not too cleanly, manger? 40
  Contend, the powers of heaven and earth,
To fit a bed for this huge birth!

Cho. Contend, the powers, etc.

6. **He:** the sun, often known as the eye of heaven.   15–16. **Tityrus, Thyrsis:** conventional names for shepherds in pastoral poetry.

Thyr. Proud world, said I, cease your contest,
And let the mighty Babe alone;   45
   The phoenix builds the phoenix' nest,
Love's architecture is his own;
   The Babe whose birth embraves this morn,
Made His own bed e'er He was born.

Cho. The Babe whose, etc.   50

Tit. I saw the curled drops, soft and slow,
Come hovering o'er the place's head,
   Offering their whitest sheets of snow
To furnish the fair Infant's bed.
   Forbear, said I; be not too bold;   55
Your fleece is white, but 'tis too cold.

Cho. Forbear, said I, etc.

Thyr. I saw the obsequious seraphim
Their rosy fleece of fire bestow,
   For well they now can spare their wing   60
Since Heaven itself lies here below.
   Well done, said I; but are you sure
Your down, so warm, will pass for pure?

Cho. Well done, said I, etc.

Tit. No, no, your King's not yet to seek   65
Where to repose His royal head;
   See, see how soon His new-bloomed cheek
'Twixt mother's breasts is gone to bed!
   Sweet choice, said we; no way but so
Not to lie cold, yet sleep in snow.   70

Cho. Sweet choice, said we, etc.

Both. We saw Thee in Thy balmy nest,
Bright dawn of our eternal day;
   We saw Thine eyes break from their east
And chase the trembling shades away.   75
   We saw Thee, and we blest the sight,
We saw Thee by Thine own sweet light.

Cho. We saw Thee, etc.

46–47. **phoenix . . . own:** as this mythical bird (often a symbol of Christ) builds the nest in which it dies and is reborn, so Christ chose out this one.

48. **embraves:** makes glorious.
58. **obsequious seraphim:** obedient angels with wings of fire.

Full Chorus

Welcome, all wonders in one sight!
Eternity shut in a span!   80
   Summer in winter! day in night!
Heaven in earth! and God in man!
   Great little one, whose all-embracing birth
Lifts earth to heaven, stoops heaven to earth!

   Welcome, though nor to gold nor silk,   85
To more than Caesar's birthright is;
   Two sister-seas of virgin-milk
With many a rarely-tempered kiss,
   That breathes at once both maid and mother,
Warms in the one, cools in the other.   90

   She sings Thy tears asleep, and dips
Her kisses in Thy weeping eye;
   She spreads the red leaves of Thy lips
That in their buds yet blushing lie;
   She 'gainst those mother-diamonds tries   95
The points of her young eagle's eyes.

   Welcome, though not to those gay flies
Gilded i'th'beams of earthly kings,
   Slippery souls in smiling eyes—
But to poor shepherds, homespun things,   100
   Whose wealth's their flock, whose wit, to be
Well read in their simplicity.

   Yet, when young April's husband showers
Shall bless the fruitful Maia's bed,
   We'll bring the first-born of her flowers   105
To kiss Thy feet and crown Thy head.
   To Thee, dread Lamb! whose love must keep
The shepherds, more than they the sheep.

   To Thee, meek Majesty, soft King
Of simple graces and sweet loves,   110
   Each of us his lamb will bring,
Each his pair of silver doves;
   Till burnt at last in fire of Thy fair eyes,
Ourselves become our own best sacrifice!

97–102. **not ... simplicity:** not to ephemeral courtiers, given a specious importance and splendour ("gilded") by the favoring eyebeams of a king, but to shepherds, who are honest and simple. 104. **Maia:** May, thought of as the wife of April, and fructified by his rains.

On Our Crucified Lord, Naked and Bloody

They've left Thee naked, Lord; O that they had:
This garment too I would they had denied.
Thee with Thyself they have too richly clad,
Opening the purple wardrobe of Thy side.
  O never could be found garments too good   5
  For Thee to wear, but these, of Thine own blood.

Luke 11

Blessed be the paps which thou hast sucked.

Suppose he had been tabled at thy teats,
  Thy hunger feels not what He eats;
He'll have his teat ere long (a bloody one),
  The Mother then must suck the Son.

RICHARD LOVELACE [1618–1657]

To Althea, from Prison

When Love with unconfinèd wings
  Hovers within my gates,
And my divine Althea brings
  To whisper at the grates;
When I lie tangled in her hair   5
  And fetter'd to her eye,
The birds that wanton in the air
  Know no such liberty.

When flowing cups run swiftly round
  With no allaying Thames,   10
Our careless heads with roses crown'd,
  Our hearts with loyal flames;
When thirsty grief in wine we steep,
  When healths and draughts go free,
Fishes that tipple in the deep   15
  Know no such liberty.

9–10. cups ... Thames: wine undiluted 11. careless: without cares.
with water.

When, like committed linnets, I
  With shriller throat shall sing
The sweetness, mercy, majesty
  And glories of my King;   20
When I shall voice aloud how good
  He is, how great should be,
Enlargèd winds, that curl the flood,
  Know no such liberty.

Stone walls do not a prison make,   25
  Nor iron bars a cage;
Minds innocent and quiet take
  That for an hermitage:
If I have freedom in my love
  And in my soul am free,   30
Angels alone, that soar above,
  Enjoy such liberty.

To Lucasta, Going to the Wars

Tell me not, sweet, I am unkind,
  That from the nunnery
Of thy chaste breast and quiet mind,
  To war and arms I fly.

True, a new mistress now I chase,   5
  The first foe in the field;
And with a stronger faith embrace
  A sword, a horse, a shield.

Yet this inconstancy is such
  As you too shall adore;   10
I could not love thee, dear, so much,
  Loved I not honor more.

ABRAHAM COWLEY [1618–1667]

Drinking

The thirsty earth soaks up the rain,
And drinks and gapes for drink again;
The plants suck in the earth, and are
With constant drinking fresh and fair;

---

17. **committed**: imprisoned. Caged finches are supposed to sing more than free ones.
23. **Enlargèd**: freed. There was a classical tradition that the inactive winds were imprisoned in a cave by the wind god.

The sea itself, which one would think   5
Should have but little need of drink,
Drinks ten thousand rivers up,
So filled that they o'erflow the cup.
The busy sun—and one would guess
By's drunken fiery face no less—   10
Drinks up the sea, and when he's done,
The moon and stars drink up the sun:
They drink and dance by their own light,
They drink and revel all the night.
Nothing in nature's sober found,   15
But an eternal health goes round.
Fill up the bowl, then, fill it high!
Fill all the glasses there: for why
Should every creature drink but I?
Why, man of morals, tell me why?   20

ANDREW MARVELL [1621–1678]

The Garden

How vainly men themselves amaze
To win the palm, the oak, or bays,
And their uncessant labors see
Crowned from some single herb or tree,
Whose short and narrow vergèd shade   5
Does prudently their toils upbraid;
While all flowers and all trees do close
To weave the garlands of repose.

Fair quiet, have I found thee here,
And innocence, thy sister dear!   10
Mistaken long, I sought you then
In busy companies of men;
Your sacred plants, if here below,
Only among the plants will grow.
Society is all but rude,   15
To this delicious solitude.

2. **palm, oak, bays:** emblems of achievement ("bays": laurels).

No white nor red was ever seen
So am'rous as this lovely green.
Fond lovers, cruel as their flame,
Cut in these trees their mistress' name;   20
Little, alas, they know or heed
How far these beauties hers exceed!
Fair trees! wheres' e'er your barks I wound,
No name shall but your own be found.

When we have run our passion's heat,   25
Love hither makes his best retreat.
The gods that mortal beauty chase,
Still in a tree did end their race:
Apollo hunted Daphne so,
Only that she might laurel grow;   30
And Pan did after Syrinx speed,
Not as a nymph, but for a reed.

What wondrous life is this I lead!
Ripe apples drop about my head;
The luscious clusters of the vine   35
Upon my mouth do crush their wine;
The nectarine and curious peach
Into my hands themselves do reach;
Stumbling on melons as I pass,
Ensnared with flowers, I fall on grass.   40

Meanwhile the mind from pleasure less
Withdraws into its happiness;
The mind, that ocean where each kind
Does straight its own resemblance find,
Yet it creates, transcending these,   45
Far other worlds and other seas,
Annihilating all that's made
To a green thought in a green shade.

Here at the fountain's sliding foot,
Or at some fruit tree's mossy root,   50
Casting the body's vest aside,
My soul into the boughs does glide;

28. **Still:** continually.
29–32. **Apollo . . . reed:** The nymphs
Daphne and Syrinx were thus transformed
to save them from their pursuers. Laurel is
sacred to Apollo; Pan used reeds to make
his pipes.

43–44. **mind . . . find:** As all terrestrial
creatures were supposed to have their
counterparts in the sea, so everything in
nature finds its counterpart in the mind's
ideas. (This statement is only a preliminary
concession to the one following.)

There like a bird it sits and sings,
Then whets, then combs its silver wings;
And till prepared for longer flight,   55
Waves in its plumes the various light.

Such was that happy garden-state,
While man there walked without a mate;
After a place so pure and sweet,
What other help could yet be meet!   60
But 'twas beyond a mortal's share
To wander solitary there;
Two paradises 'twere, in one,
To live in paradise alone.

How well the skillful gard'ner drew   65
Of flowers and herbs this dial new,
Where, from above, the milder sun
Does through a fragrant zodiac run;
And as it works, th' industrious bee
Computes its time as well as we.   70
How could such sweet and wholesome hours
Be reckoned but with herbs and flowers?

Bermudas

Where the remote Bermudas ride
In th' ocean's bosom unespy'd,
From a small boat that rowed along,
The list'ning winds receiv'd this song:

  "What should we do but sing His praise,   5
That led us through the watery maze,
Unto an isle so long unknown,
And yet far kinder than our own?
Where He the huge sea-monsters wracks,
That lift the deep upon their backs.   10
He lands us on a grassy stage,
Safe from the storms, and prelate's rage.

---

56. **various:** i.e., as contrasted to the single white light of eternity.

66–68. **dial . . . run:** presumably a floral pattern of a clock (or possibly the daily and seasonal change in the flowers), through the patterns of which the sun moves as it does through the constellations of the zodiac.

12. **prelate's:** i.e., bishop's (Marvell, adhering to the Puritan side, opposed episcopal rule).

He gave us this eternal spring,
Which here enamels everything,
And sends the fowls to us in care,   15
On daily visits through the air.
He hangs in shades the orange bright,
Like golden lamps in a green night,
And does in the pomegranates close
Jewels more rich than Ormus shows.   20
He makes the figs our mouths to meet,
And throws the melons at our feet.
But apples plants of such a price,
No tree could ever bear them twice.
With cedars, chosen by His hand,   25
From Lebanon, he stores the land,
And makes the hollow seas, that roar
Proclaim the ambergris on shore.
He cast (of which we rather boast)
The Gospel's pearl upon our coast   30
And in these rocks for us did frame
A temple, where to sound His name.
Oh let our voice His praise exalt,
Till it arrive at Heaven's vault,
Which thence (perhaps) rebounding, may   35
Echo beyond the Mexique Bay."

    Thus sung they, in the English boat,
An holy and a cheerful note;
And all the way, to guide their chime,
With falling oars they kept the time.   40

Mourning

You, that decipher out the fate
    Of human offsprings from the skies,
What mean these infants which, of late,
    Spring from the stars of Chlora's eyes?

Her eyes confused, and doubled o'er   5
    With tears suspended ere they flow,
Seem bending upwards to restore
    To Heaven, whence it came, their woe.

20. **Ormus:** port in Iran where jewels were
traded.
23. **apples:** pineapples.
29. **rather boast:** boast more willingly than
of the other things mentioned.

36. **Mexique Bay:** Bay of Mexico.

1. **You:** astrologers.

When, molding of the watery spheres,
　　Slow drops untie themselves away,   10
As if she with those precious tears
　　Would strew the ground where Strephon lay.

Yet some affirm, pretending art,
　　Her eyes have so her bosom drowned,
Only to soften, near her heart,   15
　　A place to fix another wound.

And while vain pomp does her restrain
　　Within her solitary bower,
She courts herself in amorous rain,
　　Herself both Danaë and the shower.   20

Nay others, bolder, hence esteem
　　Joy now so much her master grown,
That whatsoever does but seem
　　Like grief is from her windows thrown.

Nor that she pays, while she survives,   25
　　To her dead love this tribute due,
But casts abroad these donatives
　　At the installing of a new.

How wide they dream! the Indian slaves,
　　That sink for pearl through seas profound,   30
Would find her tears yet deeper waves
　　And not of one the bottom sound.

I yet my silent judgment keep,
　　Disputing not what they believe;
But sure as oft as women weep   35
　　It is to be supposed they grieve.

To His Coy Mistress

Had we but world enough, and time,
This coyness, lady, were no crime.
We would sit down and think which way
To walk, and pass our long love's day;
Thou by the Indian Ganges' side   5

9. **molding . . . spheres:** copying the shape
of the sphere of water, which, theoretically, surrounds the earth as the spheres of
the planets and stars do at a greater
distance.

20. **Danaë:** Although imprisoned in the
top of a tower, she was approached by
Zeus in a shower of gold.
27. **donatives:** gifts to the crowd, at some
festival.

Shouldst rubies find; I by the tide
Of Humber would complain. I would
Love you ten years before the Flood;
And you should, if you please, refuse
Till the conversion of the Jews.   10
My vegetable love should grow
Vaster than empires, and more slow.
An hundred years should go to praise
Thine eyes, and on thy forehead gaze;
Two hundred to adore each breast,   15
But thirty thousand to the rest;
An age at least to every part,
And the last age should show your heart.
For, lady, you deserve this state,
Nor would I love at lower rate.   20
    But at my back I always hear
Time's wingèd chariot hurrying near;
And yonder all before us lie
Deserts of vast eternity.
Thy beauty shall no more be found,   25
Nor in thy marble vault shall sound
My echoing song; then worms shall try
That long preserved virginity,
And your quaint honor turn to dust,
And into ashes all my lust.   30
The grave's a fine and private place,
But none, I think, do there embrace.
    Now therefore, while the youthful hue
Sits on thy skin like morning dew,
And while thy willing soul transpires   35
At every pore with instant fires,
Now let us sport us while we may;
And now, like am'rous birds of prey,
Rather at once our time devour,
Than languish in his slow-chapped power.   40
Let us roll all our strength, and all
Our sweetness, up into one ball;
And tear our pleasures with rough strife
Thorough the iron gates of life.
Thus, though we cannot make our sun   45
Stand still, yet we will make him run.

7. **Humber:** an humble stream (on which stands Hull, Marvell's home), contrasting with the huge, distant Ganges. **complain:** make my plaint.
10. **conversion:** not supposed to occur until the Last Judgment.
19. **state:** dignity.
35. **transpires:** breathes forth.
40. **slow-chapped:** slow-jawed.

HENRY VAUGHAN [1621–1693]

The Retreat

Happy those early days when I
Shined in my angel-infancy!
Before I understood this place
Appointed for my second race,
Or taught my soul to fancy aught   5
But a white celestial thought;
When yet I had not walked above
A mile or two from my first love,
And looking back at that short space,
Could see a glimpse of his bright face;   10
When on some gilded cloud or flower
My gazing soul would dwell an hour,
And in those weaker glories spy
Some shadows of eternity;
Before I taught my tongue to wound   15
My conscience with a sinful sound,
Or had the black art to dispense
A sev'ral sin to ev'ry sense;
But felt through all this fleshly dress
Bright shoots of everlastingness.   20
    Oh, how I long to travel back
And tread again that ancient track!
That I might once more reach that plain
Where first I left my glorious train,
From whence th' enlightened spirit sees   25
That shady city of palm trees.
But, ah, my soul with too much stay
Is drunk, and staggers in the way.
Some men a forward motion love,
But I by backward steps would move,   30
And when this dust falls to the urn,
In that state I came, return.

4. **second race:** after a prenatal existence
with God.
18. **sev'ral:** separate.
23–26. **plain . . . trees:** Moses saw Jericho,
city of palm trees, in the plain at the border
of the Promised Land, but could not reach
it (Deuteronomy 34: 3).

Regeneration

A ward, and still in bonds, one day
    I stole abroad;
It was high spring, and all the way
    Primrosed and hung with shade;
      Yet was it frost within,   5
        And surly winds
Blasted my infant buds, and sin
    Like clouds eclipsed my mind.

Stormed thus, I straight perceived my spring
    Mere stage, and show,   10
My walk a monstrous, mountained thing,
    Roughcast with rocks and snow;
      And as a pilgrim's eye,
        Far from relief,
Measures the melancholy sky,   15
    Then drops and rains for grief,

So sighed I upwards still; at last
    'Twixt steps and falls
I reached the pinnacle, where placed
    I found a pair of scales;   20
      I took them up and laid
        In th' one, late pains;
The other smoke and pleasures weighed,
    But proved the heavier grains.

With that some cried, "Away!" Straight I   25
    Obeyed, and led
Full cast, a fair, fresh field could spy;
    Some called it Jacob's bed,
      A virgin soil which no
        Rude feet ere trod,   30
Where, since he stepped there, only go
    Prophets and friends of God.

23. **smoke:** insignificant, evanescent things, like pleasure, to be weighed against the speaker's "pains" of repentance.
28. **Jacob's bed:** place which Jacob identified as the gate of heaven, where he saw angels ascending and descending a ladder to heaven and received God's promise (Genesis 28: 11–17).

Here I reposed; but scarce well set,
　　A grove descried
Of stately height, whose branches met   35
　　And mixed on every side;
　　I entered, and once in,
　　　Amazed to see 't,
Found all was changed, and a new spring
　　Did all my senses greet.   40

The unthrift sun shot vital gold,
　　A thousand pieces,
And heaven its azure did unfold,
　　Checkered with snowy fleeces;
　　The air was all in spice,   45
　　　And every bush
A garland wore; thus fed my eyes,
　　But all the ear lay hush.

Only a little fountain lent
　　Some use for ears,   50
And on the dumb shades language spent,
　　The music of her tears;
　　I drew her near, and found
　　　The cistern full
Of divers stones, some bright and round,   55
　　Others ill-shaped and dull.

The first, pray mark, as quick as light
　　Danced through the flood,
But the last, more heavy than the night,
　　Nailed to the center stood;   60
　　I wondered much, but tired
　　　At last with thought,
My restless eye that still desired
　　As strange an object brought.

It was a bank of flowers, where I descried,   65
　　Though 'twas midday,
Some fast asleep, others broad-eyed
　　And taking in the ray;
　　Here, musing long, I heard
　　　A rushing wind   70
Which still increased, but whence it stirred
　　No where I could not find.

I turned me round, and to each shade
    Dispatched an eye
To see if any leaf had made   75
    Least motion or reply,
    But while I listening sought
      My mind to ease
By knowing where 'twas, or where not,
    It whispered, "Where I please."   80

"Lord," then said I, "on me one breath,
And let me die before my death!"

The World

I saw eternity the other night
Like a great ring of pure and endless light,
    All calm as it was bright;
And round beneath it, time in hours, days, years,
    Driv'n by the spheres,   5
Like a vast shadow moved, in which the world
    And all her train were hurled:
The doting lover in his quaintest strain
    Did there complain;
Near him his lute, his fancy, and his flights,   10
    Wit's sour delights,
With gloves and knots, the silly snares of pleasure,
    Yet his dear treasure,
All scattered lay, while he his eyes did pore
    Upon a flower.   15

The darksome statesman, hung with weights and woe,
Like a thick midnight fog moved there so slow
    He did not stay, nor go;
Condemning thoughts, like sad eclipses, scowl
    Upon his soul,   20
And clouds of crying witnesses without
    Pursued him with one shout;

80. **Where I please:** "The wind bloweth where it listeth," etc. (John 3: 8). "Wind": breath, spirit of God.

5. **spheres:** According to pre-Copernican astronomy, all the heavenly bodies were carried around the earth on concentric, crystalline spheres; beyond the outermost was Eternity.

12. **knots:** love knots.

Yet digged the mole, and lest his ways be found
    Worked underground,
Where he did clutch his prey, but One did see   25
    That policy;
Churches and altars fed him; perjuries
    Were gnats and flies;
It rained about him blood and tears, but he
    Drank them as free.   30

The fearful miser on a heap of rust
Sat pining all his life there, did scarce trust
    His own hands with the dust,
Yet would not place one piece above, but lives
    In fear of thieves.   35
Thousands there were as frantic as himself,
    And hugged each one his pelf:
The downright epicure placed heav'n in sense,
    And scorned pretense;
While others, slipped into a wide excess,   40
    Said little less;
The weaker sort slight trivial wares enslave,
    Who think them brave;
And poor despisèd truth sat counting by
    Their victory.   45

Yet some, who all this while did weep and sing,
And sing and weep, soared up into the ring;
    But most would use no wing.
O fools, said I, thus to prefer dark night
    Before true light,   50
To live in grots and caves, and hate the day
    Because it shows the way,
The way which from this dead and dark abode
    Leads up to God,
A way where you might tread the sun, and be   55
    More bright than he.
But as I did their madness so discuss,
    One whispered thus:
This ring the bridegroom did for none provide
    But for his bride.   60

23. **mole:** i.e., the statesman.
26. **policy:** concealed stratagem.
30. **as free:** As freely as they came.
31. **rust:** here, earthly treasures ("where moth and rust doth corrupt").
34. **place:** invest.

43. **brave:** gorgeous.
44. **counting by:** taking account of.
55. **tread:** stand higher than.
59–60. **ring . . . bride:** reference to the marriage of Christ and his church (Revelation 19: 7–9).

The Restoration and Eighteenth Century

JOHN DRYDEN

[1631–1700]

Mac Flecknoe
or, A Satire upon the True-Blue-Protestant
Poet T.S.

All human things are subject to decay,
And, when fate summons, monarchs must obey.
This Flecknoe found, who, like Augustus, young
Was called to empire, and had governed long;
In prose and verse was owned, without dispute, 5
Through all the realms of *Nonsense*, absolute.
This aged prince, now flourishing in peace,
And blest with issue of a large increase,
Worn out with business, did at length debate
To settle the succession of the State; 10
And, pondering which of all his sons was fit
To reign, and wage immortal war with wit,

Mac Flecknoe: the son of Flecknoe, an Irish priest, known as a bad poet, who had died in 1678. T. S. is Thomas Shadwell (1640–1692). It is not known if Dryden attacked these two for personal reasons. In 1682 Shadwell may have written "The Medal of John Bayes," attacking Dryden's "The Medal," but there is reason to believe that "Mac Flecknoe" was written as early as 1678.
3. **Augustus:** the first Roman emperor, only thirty when he began his long and peaceful reign.

Cried: "'Tis resolved; for nature pleads, that he
Should only rule, who most resembles me.
Sh—— alone my perfect image bears,   15
Mature in dulness from his tender years:
Sh—— alone, of all my sons, is he
Who stands confirmed in full stupidity.
The rest to some faint meaning make pretence,
But Sh—— never deviates into sense.   20
Some beams of wit on other souls may fall,
Strike through, and make a lucid interval;
But Sh——'s genuine night admits no ray,
His rising fogs prevail upon the day.
Besides, his goodly fabric fills the eye,   25
And seems designed for thoughtless majesty;
Thoughtless as monarch oaks that shade the plain,
And, spread in solemn state, supinely reign.
Heywood and Shirley were but types of thee,
Thou last great prophet of tautology.   30
Even I, a dunce of more renown than they,
Was sent before but to prepare thy way:
And, coarsely clad in Norwich drugget came
To teach the nations in thy greater name.
My warbling lute, the lute I whilom strung,   35
When to King John of Portugal I sung,
Was but the prelude to that glorious day,
When thou on silver Thames didst cut thy way,
With well-timed oars, before the royal barge,
Swelled with the pride of thy celestial charge;   40
And big with hymn, commander of a host,
The like was ne'er in Epsom blankets tossed.
Methinks I see the new Arion sail,
The lute still trembling underneath thy nail.
At thy well-sharpened thumb, from shore to shore   45
The treble squeaks for fear, the basses roar;
Echoes from Pissing Alley Sh—— call,
And Sh—— they resound from Aston Hall.
About thy boat the little fishes throng,
As at the morning toast that floats along.   50

29. **Heywood and Shirley:** Jacobean dramatists, both of whom were prolific writers. They had probably fallen out of fashion.
33. **Norwich drugget:** a rough cloth.
36. **Portugal:** Flecknoe had visited Portugal.
42. **Epsom Blanket:** Being tossed in a blanket was a comical punishment for pretension. An Epsom blanket refers to Shadwell's play, *Epsom Wells*.
43. **Arion:** a Greek musician of about 700 B.C. Reportedly his song so charmed the dolphins that they once rescued him from drowning.
47. **Pissing Alley:** an alley in London between the Strand and Hollowell Street. Aston Hall has not been identified.

Sometimes, as prince of thy harmonious band,
Thou wield'st thy papers in thy threshing hand.
St. André's feet ne'er kept more equal time,
Not even the feet of thy own *Psyche's* rhyme,
Though they in number as in sense excel;   55
So just, so like tautology, they fell,
That, pale with envy, Singleton forswore ⎫
The lute and sword, which he in triumph bore, ⎬
And vowed he ne'er would act Villerius more." ⎭
Here stopt the good old sire, and wept for joy,   60
In silent raptures of the hopeful boy.
All arguments, but most his plays, persuade,
That for anointed dulness he was made.
    Close to the walls which fair Augusta bind,
(The fair Augusta much to fears inclined,)   65
An ancient fabric, raised to inform the sight,
There stood of yore, and Barbican it hight;
A watch-tower once, but now, so fate ordains,
Of all the pile an empty name remains.
From its old ruins brothel-houses rise,   70
Scenes of lewd loves, and of polluted joys,
Where their vast courts the mother-strumpets keep,
And, undisturbed by watch, in silence sleep.
Near these a Nursery erects its head,
Where queens are formed, and future heroes bred;   75
Where unfledged actors learn to laugh and cry; ⎫
Where infant punks their tender voices try, ⎬
And little Maximins the gods defy. ⎭
Great Fletcher never treads in buskins here,
Nor greater Jonson dares in socks appear;   80
But gentle Simkin just reception finds
Amidst this monument of vanished minds;
Pure clinches the suburban Muse affords,
And Panton waging harmless war with words.
Here Flecknoe, as a place to fame well known,   85
Ambitiously designed his Sh———'s throne;

53. **St. André's:** a well-known dancing master.
54. **Psyche's:** an opera by Shadwell.
57. **Singleton:** a contemporary singer, one of whose roles was Villerius in Davenant's *Siege of Rhodes.*
64. **Augusta:** London, fearful of Popish intrigues and plots.
73. **watch:** the night-watch, similar to the police.
74. **Nursery:** the actual name of the actor's school on this site.
78. **Maximin:** the hero of Dryden's own play *Tyrannic Love.*
79. **Fletcher:** John Fletcher (1579–1625) and Ben Jonson were admired as writers of tragedy and comedy respectively. The buskin and sock were the shoes worn in ancient times by tragic and comic actors.
81. **Simkin:** a clown in a contemporary farce.
83. **clinches:** puns.
84. **Panton:** a celebrated punster.

For ancient Dekker prophesied long since, }
That in this pile should reign a mighty prince, }
Born for a scourge of wit, and flail of sense; }
To whom true dulness should some *Psyches* owe,   90
But worlds of *Misers* from his pen should flow;
Humorists and *Hypocrites*, it should produce,
Whole Raymond families, and tribes of Bruce.
   Now Empress Fame had published the renown
Of Sh————'s coronation through the town.   95
Roused by report of Fame, the nations meet,
From near Bunhill, and distant Watling Street.
No Persian carpets spread the imperial way,
But scattered limbs of mangled poets lay;
From dusty shops neglected authors come,   100
Martyrs of pies, and relics of the bum.
Much Heywood, Shirley, Ogleby, there lay,
But loads of Sh———— almost choked the way,
Bilked stationers for yeomen stood prepared,
And Herringman was captain of the guard.   105
The hoary prince in majesty appeared,
High on a throne of his own labors reared.
At his right hand our young Ascanius sate,
Rome's other hope, and pillar of the State.
His brows thick fogs, instead of glories, grace,   110
And lambent dulness played around his face.
As Hannibal did to the altars come,
Sworn by his sire a mortal foe to Rome;
So Sh———— swore, nor should his vow be vain,
That he till death true dulness would maintain;   115
And, in his father's right, and realm's defence,
Ne'er to have peace with wit, nor truce with sense.
The king himself the sacred unction made,
As king by office, and as priest by trade.
In his sinister hand, instead of ball,   120
He placed a mighty mug of potent ale;
Love's Kingdom to his right he did convey,
At once his scepter, and his rule of sway;
Whose righteous lore the prince had practised young,
And from whose loins recorded *Psyche* sprung.   125

87. **Dekker:** Thomas Dekker (1572?–1632) an Elizabethan dramatist and pamphleteer.
90–92. **Psyches . . . Hypocrites:** *Psyche, The Miser,* and *Humorists* are plays by Shadwell. The reference to *Hypocrites* has not been explained.
93. **Raymond . . . Bruce:** characters in Shadwell's plays.
102. **Ogleby:** a notoriously bad poet.
104. **Bilked:** cheated.
105. **Herringman:** Shadwell's publisher.
108. **Ascanius:** Shadwell, here imagined as the son of Aeneas.
122. **Love's Kingdom:** the only play of Flecknoe's ever acted.

His temples, last, with poppies were o'erspread,
That nodding seemed to consecrate his head.
Just at that point of time, if fame not lie,
On his left hand twelve reverend owls did fly.
So Romulus, 'tis sung, by Tiber's brook,   130
Presage of sway from twice six vultures took.
The admiring throng loud acclamations make,
And omens of his future empire take.
The sire then shook the honors of his head,
And from his brows damps of oblivion shed   135
Full on the filial dulness: long he stood,   ⎫
Repelling from his breast the raging god;   ⎬
At length burst out in this prophetic mood: ⎭
    "Heavens bless my son! from Ireland let him reign
To far Barbadoes on the western main;   140
Of his dominion may no end be known,
And greater than his father's be his throne;
Beyond *Love's Kingdom* let him stretch his pen!"
He paused, and all the people cried, "Amen."
Then thus continued he: "My son, advance   145
Still in new impudence, new ignorance.
Success let others teach, learn thou from me
Pangs without birth, and fruitless industry.
Let *Virtuosos* in five years be writ,
Yet not one thought accuse thy toil of wit.   150
Let gentle George in triumph tread the stage,
Make Dorimant betray, and Loveit rage;
Let Cully, Cockwood, Fopling, charm the pit,
And in their folly show the writer's wit.
Yet still thy fools shall stand in thy defence,   155
And justify their author's want of sense.
Let them be all by thy own model made
Of dulness, and desire no foreign aid;
That they to future ages may be known,
Not copies drawn, but issue of thy own: 160
Nay, let thy men of wit too be the same,
All full of thee, and differing but in name.
But let no alien Sedley interpose,
To lard with wit thy hungry *Epsom* prose.
And when false flowers of rhetoric thou wouldst cull,   165

---

130. **Romulus:** legendary founder of Rome.
149. **Virtuosos:** a play by Shadwell which satirized the Royal Society.
151. **George:** Sir George Etherege (1635?–1691), one of the best writers of comedy.

152–53. **Dorimant . . . Fopling:** characters in Etherege's plays.
163. **Sedley:** Sir Charles Sedley (1639?–1701), the noted wit who was suspected of helping Shadwell compose *Epsom Wells*.

Trust nature, do not labor to be dull,
But write thy best, and top; and, in each line,
Sir Formal's oratory will be thine:
Sir Formal, though unsought, attends thy quill,
And does thy northern dedications fill.   170
Nor let false friends seduce thy mind to fame,
By arrogating Jonson's hostile name.
Let father Flecknoe fire thy mind with praise,
And uncle Ogleby thy envy raise.
Thou art my blood, where Jonson has no part: 175
What share have we in nature, or in art?
Where did his wit on learning fix a brand,
And rail at arts he did not understand?
Where made he love in Prince Nicander's vein,
Or swept the dust in *Psyche's* humble strain?   180
Where sold he bargains, 'whip-stitch, kiss my arse,'
Promised a play and dwindled to a farce?
When did his Muse from Fletcher scenes purloin,
As thou whole Etherege dost transfuse to thine?
But so transfused, as oil on water's flow,   185
His always floats above, thine sinks below.
This is thy province, this thy wondrous way,
New humors to invent for each new play:
This is that boasted bias of thy mind,
By which one way, to dulness, 'tis inclined;   190
Which makes thy writings lean on one side still,
And, in all changes, that way bends thy will.
Nor let thy mountain-belly make pretense
Of likeness; thine's a tympany of sense.
A tun of man in thy large bulk is writ,   195
But sure thou'rt but a kilderkin of wit.
Like mine, thy gentle numbers feebly creep;
Thy tragic Muse gives smiles, thy comic sleep.
With whate'er gall thou sett'st thyself to write,
Thy inoffensive satires never bite,   200
In thy felonious heart though venom lies,
It does but touch thy Irish pen, and dies.
Thy genius calls thee not to purchase fame

---

168. **Sir Formal:** Sir Formal Trifle, a florid orator in Shadwell's *Virtuoso*.
170. **northern dedications:** Shadwell frequently dedicated his works to the Duke of Newcastle and his family.
179. **Prince Nicander:** a character in *Psyche*.
181. **bargains:** Selling bargains consisted of answering innocent questions with coarse phrases. Such phrases are used repeatedly by one of Shadwell's humorous characters in *The Virtuoso*.
189–192. These four lines parody lines in Shadwell's *Humorists*. Dryden has substituted "dulness" for "humor."
194. **tympany:** an inflation or distention, as well as a drum.
196. **kilderkin:** a small measure.

In keen iambics, but mild anagram.
Leave writing plays, and choose for thy command   205
Some peaceful province in acrostic land.
There thou may'st wings display and altars raise,
And torture one poor word ten thousand ways.
Or, if thou wouldst thy different talents suit,
Set thy own songs, and sing them to thy lute."   210
    He said:—but his last words were scarcely heard;⎫
For Bruce and Longvil had a trap prepared,   ⎬
And down they sent the yet declaiming bard.   ⎭
Sinking he left his drugget robe behind,
Borne upwards by a subterranean wind.   215
The mantle fell to the young prophet's part,
With double portion of his father's art.

To the Memory of Mr. Oldham

Farwell, too little and too lately known,
Whom I began to think and call my own:
For sure our souls were near allied, and thine
Cast in the same poetic mold with mine.
One common note on either lyre did strike,   5
And knaves and fools we both abhorred alike.
To the same goal did both our studies drive:
The last set out the soonest did arrive.
Thus Nisus fell upon the slippery place,
Whilst his young friend performed and won the race.   10
O early ripe! to thy abundant store
What could advancing age have added more?
It might (what nature never gives the young)
Have taught the numbers of thy native tongue.
But satire needs not those, and wit will shine   15
Through the harsh cadence of a rugged line.
A noble error, and but seldom made,
When poets are by too much force betray'd.
Thy generous fruits, though gathered ere their prime, ⎫
Still showed a quickness; and maturing time   ⎬ 20
But mellows what we write to the dull sweets of rhyme. ⎭

212. **Bruce and Longvil**: the two characters in *The Virtuoso* who entice Sir Formal Trifle to stand upon a trap door which they release after he delivers a speech.
214. **drugget**: a coarse cloth.

Oldham: John Oldham, one of the most gifted Restoration wits, died in December, 1683, at the age of thirty. The following year his *Remains in Verse and Prose* were published, containing as a preface this tribute by Dryden.
9. **Nisus**: a character in the *Aeneid* who participates in the footraces with his friend Euryalus. Both are later killed.

Once more, hail, and farewell! farewell, thou young,
But ah! too short, Marcellus of our tongue!
Thy brows with ivy and with laurels bound;
But fate and gloomy night encompass thee around.   25

Song for Saint Cecilia's Day

(*November 22, 1687*)

I

From harmony, from heavenly harmony
    This universal frame began:
    When Nature underneath a heap
      Of jarring atoms lay
    And could not heave her head,   5
The tuneful voice was heard from high:
    "Arise, ye more than dead."
Then cold and hot and moist and dry
    In order to their stations leap,
    And Music's power obey.   10
From harmony, from heavenly harmony
    This universal frame began:
    From harmony to harmony
Through all the compass of the notes it ran,
The diapason closing full in man.   15

II

What passion cannot Music raise and quell?
    When Jubal struck the corded shell
    His listening brethren stood around,
    And, wondering, on their faces fell
    To worship that celestial sound.   20
Less than a god they thought there could not dwell
    Within the hollow of that shell,
    That spoke so sweetly, and so well.
What passion cannot Music raise and quell?

23. **Marcellus:** Virgil wrote a tribute to this nephew of Augustus who died in his twentieth year.

Saint Cecilia: the patroness of music, traditionally depicted playing the organ. Dryden's ode was originally set to music by Giovanni Battista Draghi.
17. **Jubal:** Genesis 4: 21, father of all who play harp and organ.

III

The Trumpet's loud clangor   25
    Excites us to arms,
With shrill notes of anger,
    And mortal alarms.
The double double double beat
    Of the thund'ring Drum   30
Cries, "Hark! the foes come;
Charge, charge, 'tis too late to retreat!"

IV

The soft complaining Flute
In dying notes discovers
The woes of hopless lovers;   35
Whose dirge is whisper'd by the warbling Lute.

V

Sharp Violins proclaim
Their jealous pangs and desperation,
Fury, frantic indignation,
Depth of pains, and height of passion,   40
    For the fair, disdainful dame.

VI

But oh! what art can teach,
What human voice can reach
    The sacred Organ's praise?
Notes inspiring holy love,   45
Notes that wing their heavenly ways
    To mend the choirs above.

VII

Orpheus could lead the savage race
And trees uprooted left their place,
    Sequacious of the Lyre.   50
But bright Cecilia raised the wonder higher:
When to her Organ vocal breath was given,
An angel heard, and straight appeared
    Mistaking earth for heaven.

---

48. Orpheus: legendary Greek musician   **50. Sequacious:** inclined to follow a leader.
whose songs could charm all nature.

Grand Chorus

As from the power of sacred lays   55
    The spheres began to move,
And sung the great Creator's praise
    To all the blest above;
So when the last and dreadful hour
This crumbling pageant shall devour,   60
The trumpet shall be heard on high,
The dead shall live, the living die,
And music shall untune the sky.

Song to a Fair, Young Lady, Going Out of the Town in the Spring

I

Ask not the cause, why sullen Spring
    So long delays her flowers to bear;
Why warbling birds forget to sing,
    And winter storms invert the year?
Chloris is gone; and Fate provides   5
To make it Spring, where she resides.

II

Chloris is gone, the Cruel Fair;
    She cast not back a pitying eye:
But left her lover in despair;
    To sigh, to languish, and to die.   10
Ah, how can those fair eyes endure
To give the wounds they will not cure!

III

Great God of Love, why hast thou made
    A face that can all hearts command,
That all religions can invade,   15
    And change the laws of every land?
Where thou hadst placed such power before,
Thou shouldst have made her mercy more.

IV

When Chloris to the Temple comes,
   Adoring crowds before her fall;   20
She can restore the dead from tombs,
   And every life but mine recall.
I only am by Love designed
To be the victim for mankind.

ALEXANDER POPE

[*1688–1744*]

An Essay on Criticism

Part I

'Tis hard to say, if greater want of skill
Appear in writing or in judging ill;
But, of the two, less dang'rous is th' offence
To tire our patience, than mislead our sense.
Some few in that, but numbers err in this,   5
Ten censure wrong for one who writes amiss;
A fool might once himself alone expose,
Now one in verse makes many more in prose.
   'Tis with our judgments as our watches, none
Go just alike, yet each believes his own.   10
In Poets as true genius is but rare,
True Taste as seldom is the Critic's share;
Both must alike from Heaven derive their light,
These born to judge, as well as those to write.
Let such teach others who themselves excel,   15
And censure freely who have written well.
Authors are partial to their wit, 'tis true,
But are not Critics to their judgment too?
   Yet if we look more closely, we shall find
Most have the seeds of judgment in their mind: 20
Nature affords at least a glimm'ring light;
The lines, though touched but faintly, are drawn right.

Pope: The texts of Pope's poems are based
on the 1751 edition of his *Works*.

But as the slightest sketch, if justly traced, ⎫
Is by ill-colouring but the more disgraced, ⎬
So by false learning is good sense defaced: ⎭   25
Some are bewildered in the maze of schools,
And some made coxcombs Nature meant but fools.
In search of wit these lose their common sense,
And then turn Critics in their own defence:
Each burns alike, who can or cannot write,   30
Or with a Rival's, or an Eunuch's spite.
All fools have still an itching to deride,
And fain would be upon the laughing side.
If Mævius scribble in Apollo's spite,
There are who judge still worse than he can write   35
   Some have at first for Wits, then Poets past,
Turned Critics next, and proved plain fools at last.
Some neither can for Wits nor Critics pass,
As heavy mules are neither horse nor ass.
Those half-learned witlings, num'rous in our isle,   40
As half-formed insects on the banks of Nile;
Unfinished things, one knows not what to call,
Their generation's so equivocal:
To tell' em, would a hundred tongues require,
Or one vain wit's, that might a hundred tire.   45
   But you who seek to give and merit fame,
And justly bear a Critic's noble name,
Be sure yourself and your own reach to know,
How far your genius, taste, and learning go;
Launch not beyond your depth, but be discreet,   50
And mark that point where sense and dulness meet.
   Nature to all things fixed the limits fit,
And wisely curbed proud man's pretending wit.
As on the land while here the ocean gains,
In other parts it leaves wide sandy plains;   55
Thus in the soul while memory prevails,
The solid power of understanding fails;
Where beams of warm imagination play,
The memory's soft figures melt away.
One science only will one genius fit;   60
So vast is art, so narrow human wit:
Not only bounded to peculiar arts,

34. **Mævius:** a scribbling contemporary of Virgil and Horace.
41. **Nile:** an allusion to the ancient belief that forms of life generated themselves spontaneously out of the Nile's slime.
44. **Tell:** count.
60. **One science:** one branch of knowledge or learning.

But oft in those confined to single parts.
Like Kings we lose the conquests gained before,
By vain ambition still to make them more;   65
Each might his sev'ral province well command,
Would all but stoop to what they understand.
    First follow Nature, and your judgment frame
By her just standard, which is still the same:
Unerring NATURE, still divinely bright,   70
One clear, unchanged, and universal light,
Life, force, and beauty, must to all impart,
At once the source, and end, and test of Art.
Art from that fund each just supply provides
Works without show, and without pomp presides   75
In some fair body thus th' informing soul
With spirits feeds, with vigour fills the whole,
Each motion guides, and every nerve sustains;
Itself unseen, but in the effects, remains.
Some, to whom Heaven in wit has been profuse,   80
Want as much more, to turn it to its use;
For wit and judgment often are at strife,
Though meant each other's aid, like man and wife.
'Tis more to guide, than spur the Muse's steed;
Restrain his fury, than provoke his speed;   85
The wingèd courser, like a gen'rous horse,
Shows most true mettle when you check his course.
    Those RULES of old discovered, not devised,
Are Nature still, but Nature methodized;
Nature, like Liberty, is but restrained   90
By the same Laws which first herself ordained.
    Hear how learned Greece her useful rules indites,
When to repress, and when indulge our flights:
High on Parnassus' top her sons she showed,
And pointed out those arduous paths they trod;   95
Held from afar, aloft, th' immortal prize,
And urged the rest by equal steps to rise.
Just precepts thus from great examples given,
She drew from them what they derived from Heaven.
The generous Critic fanned the Poet's fire,   100
And taught the world with reason to admire.
Then Criticism the Muses' handmaid proved,
To dress her charms, and make her more beloved:
But following wits from that intention strayed,
Who could not win the mistress, wooed the maid;   105

84. **Muse's steed:** Pegasus, the winged   94. **Parnassus:** hill sacred to Apollo and
horse of poetic inspiration.   the Muses.

Against the Poets their own arms they turned,
Sure to hate most the men from whom they learned.
So modern 'Pothecaries, taught the art
By Doctor's bills to play the Doctor's part,
Bold in the practice of mistaken rules,   110
Prescribe, apply, and call their masters fools.
Some on the leaves of ancient authors prey,
Nor time nor moths e'er spoiled so much as they.
Some drily plain, without invention's aid,
Write dull receipts how poems may be made.   115
These leave the sense, their learning to display,
And those explain the meaning quite away.
    You then whose judgment the right course would steer,
Know well each ANCIENT's proper character;
His Fable, Subject, scope in every page;   120
Religion, Country, genius of his Age:
Without all these at once before your eyes,
Cavil you may, but never criticise.
Be Homer's works your study and delight,
Read them by day, and meditate by night;   125
Thence form your judgment, thence your maxims bring,
And trace the Muses upward to their spring.
Still with itself compared, his text peruse;
And let your comment be the Mantuan Muse.
    When first young Maro in his boundless mind   130
A work t' outlast immortal Rome designed,
Perhaps he seemed above the critic's law,
And but from Nature's fountains scorned to draw:
But when t' examine every part he came,
Nature and Homer were, he found, the same.   135
Convinced, amazed, he checks the bold design;⎫
And rules as strict his laboured work confine, ⎬
As if the Stagirite o'erlooked each line.   ⎭
Learn hence for ancient rules a just esteem;
To copy nature is to copy them.   140
    Some beauties yet no Precepts can declare,
For there's a happiness as well as care.
Music resembles Poetry, in each   ⎫
Are nameless graces which no methods teach,⎬
And which a master-hand alone can reach. ⎭   145

108. **'Pothecaries:** apothecaries or drug-
gists.
109. **bills:** prescriptions.
115. **receipts:** recipes.
120. **Fable:** plot or story.
121. **genius:** spirit.

129. **Mantuan:** Virgil, or young Maro as
he is called in the next line, was born near
Mantua.
138. **Stagirite:** Aristotle, greatest of ancient
critics, was born in Stagira.

If, where the rules not far enough extend,
(Since rules were made but to promote their end)
Some lucky Licence answer to the full
Th' intent proposed, that Licence is a rule.
Thus Pegasus, a nearer way to take,   150
May boldly deviate from the common track;
From vulgar bounds with brave disorder part,
And snatch a grace beyond the reach of art,
Which without passing through the judgment, gains
The heart, and all its end at once attains.   155
In prospects thus, some objects please our eyes,⎫
Which out of nature's common order rise,   ⎬
The shapeless rock, or hanging precipice.   ⎭
Great Wits sometimes may gloriously offend,
And rise to faults true Critics dare not mend.   160
But though the Ancients thus their rules invade,
(As Kings dispense with laws themselves have made)
Moderns, beware! or if you must offend
Against the precept, ne'er transgress its End;
Let it be seldom, and compelled by need;   165
And have, at least, their precedent to plead.
The Critic else proceeds without remorse,
Seizes your fame, and puts his laws in force.
     I know there are, to whose presumptuous thoughts
Those freer beauties, even in them, seem faults.   170
Some figures monstrous and mis-shaped appear,
Considered singly, or beheld too near,
Which, but proportioned to their light, or place,
Due distance reconciles to form and grace.
A prudent chief not always must display   175
His powers in equal ranks, and fair array,
But with th' occasion and the place comply,
Conceal his force, nay seem sometimes to fly.
Those oft are stratagems which error seem,
Nor is it Homer nods, but we that dream.   180
     Still green with bays each ancient Altar stands,
Above the reach of sacrilegious hands;
Secure from Flames, from Envy's fiercer rage,
Destructive War, and all-involving Age.
See, from each clime the learned their incense bring!   185
Hear, in all tongues consenting Pæans ring!
In praise so just let every voice be joined,
And fill the general chorus of mankind.
Hail, Bards triumphant! born in happier days;
Immortal heirs of universal praise!   190

Whose honours with increase of ages grow,
As streams roll down, enlarging as they flow;
Nations unborn your mighty names shall sound,
And worlds applaud that must not yet be found!
Oh may some spark of your celestial fire,   195
The last, the meanest of your sons inspire,
(That on weak wings, from far, pursues your flights;
Glows while he reads, but trembles as he writes)
To teach vain Wits a science little known,
T' admire superior sense, and doubt their own!   200

Part II

Of all the Causes which conspire to blind
Man's erring judgment, and misguide the mind,
What the weak head with strongest bias rules
Is *Pride*, the never-failing vice of fools.
Whatever Nature has in worth denied,   205
She gives in large recruits of needful Pride;
For as in bodies, thus in souls, we find
What wants in blood and spirits, swelled with wind:
Pride, where Wit fails, steps in to our defence,
And fills up all the mighty Void of sense.   210
If once right reason drives that cloud away,
Truth breaks upon us with resistless day.
Trust not yourself; but your defects to know,
Make use of every friend—and every foe.
A *little learning* is a dang'rous thing;   215
Drink deep, or taste not the Pierian spring:
There shallow draughts intoxicate the brain,
And drinking largely sobers us again.
Fired at first sight with what the Muse imparts,
In fearless youth we tempt the heights of Arts,   220
While from the bounded level of our mind
Short views we take, nor see the lengths behind;
But more advanced, behold with strange surprise
New distant scenes of endless science rise!
So pleased at first the tow'ring Alps we try,   225
Mount o'er the vales, and seem to tread the sky,
Th' eternal snows appear already past,
And the first clouds and mountains seem the last:
But, those attained, we tremble to survey
The growing labours of the lengthened way,   230

206. **recruits:** supplies.   Olympus, sacred to the Muses.
216. **Pierian:** the spring in Pieria on Mt.   220. **tempt:** attempt.

Th' increasing prospect tires our wand'ring eyes,
Hills peep o'er hills, and Alps on Alps arise!
   A perfect Judge will read each work of Wit
With the same spirit that its author writ:
Survey the WHOLE, nor seek slight faults to find   235
Where natures moves, and rapture warms the mind:
Nor lose, for that malignant dull delight,
The gen'rous pleasure to be charmed with Wit.
But in such lays as neither ebb, nor flow,
Correctly cold, and regularly low,   240
That shunning faults, one quiet tenour keep;
We cannot blame indeed—but we may sleep.
In Wit, as Nature, what affects our hearts
Is not th' exactness of peculiar parts;
'Tis not a lip, or eye, we beauty call,   245
But the joint force and full result of all.
Thus when we view some well-proportioned dome,
(The world's just wonder, and even thine, O Rome!)
No single parts unequally surprise,
All comes united to th' admiring eyes;   250
No monstrous height, or breadth, or length appear;
The Whole at once is bold, and regular.
   Whoever thinks a faultless piece to see,
Thinks what ne'er was, nor is, nor e'er shall be.
In every work regard the writer's End,   255
Since none can compass more than they intend;
And if the means be just, the conduct true,
Applause, in spight of trivial faults, is due;
As men of breeding, sometimes men of wit,
T' avoid great errors, must the less commit: 260
Neglect the rules each verbal Critic lays,
For not to know some trifles, is a praise.
Most Critics, fond of some subservient art,
Still make the Whole depend upon a Part:
They talk of principles, but notions prize,   265
And all to one loved Folly sacrifice.
   Once on a time, La Mancha's Knight, they say,
A certain bard encount'ring on the way,
Discoursed in terms as just, with looks as sage,
As e'er could Dennis of the Grecian stage;   270
Concluding all were desperate sots and fools,

---

247. dome: Michelangelo's dome of St.
Peter's.
267. La Mancha's: Don Quixote; the
incident referred to is taken from de
Avellaneda's sequel to Part I of Cervantes'
novel.
270. Dennis: John Dennis (1657–1734), a
well-known and outspoken critic of
Pope's time. See *ll.* 585–87.

Who durst depart from Aristotle's rules.
Our Author, happy in a judge so nice,
Produced his Play, and begged the Knight's advice;
Made him observe the subject, and the plot,   275
The manners, passions, unities; what not?
All which, exact to rule, were brought about,
Were but a Combat in the lists left out.
"What! leave the Combat out?" exclaims the Knight;
Yes, or we must renounce the Stagirite.   280
"Not so by Heaven" (he answers in a rage),
"Knights, squires, and steeds, must enter on the stage."
So vast a throng the stage can ne'er contain.
"Then build a new, or act it in a plain."
    Thus Critics, of less judgment than caprice,   285
Curious not knowing, not exact but nice,
Form short Ideas; and offend in arts
(As most in manners) by a love to parts.
    Some to *Conceit* alone their taste confine,
And glitt'ring thoughts struck out at every line;   290
Pleased with a work where nothing's just or fit;
One glaring Chaos and wild heap of wit.
Poets like painters, thus, unskilled to trace
The naked nature and the living grace,
With gold and jewels cover every part,   295
And hide with ornaments their want of art.
True Wit is Nature to advantage dressed,
What oft was thought, but ne'er so well expressed;
Something, whose truth convinced at sight we find,
That gives us back the image of our mind.   300
As shades more sweetly recommend the light,
So modest plainness sets off sprightly wit.
For works may have more wit than does 'em good,
As bodies perish through excess of blood.
    Others for *Language* all their care express,   305
And value books, as women men, for Dress:
Their praise is still,—the Style is excellent:
The Sense, they humbly take upon content.
Words are like leaves; and where they most abound,
Much fruit of sense beneath is rarely found: 310
False Eloquence, like the prismatic glass,
Its gaudy colours spreads on every place;
The face of Nature we no more survey,

---

286. **nice:** overly delicate.   307. **still:** always.
289. **Conceit:** In Pope's time, elaborate,   308. **take ... content:** accept   without
far-fetched similes.   question.

All glares alike, without distinction gay:
But true Expression, like th' unchanging Sun,⎫   315
Clears and improves whate'er it shines upon, ⎬
It gilds all objects, but it alters none.   ⎭
Expression is the dress of thought, and still
Appears more decent, as more suitable;
A vile conceit in pompous words expressed,   320
Is like a clown in regal purple dressed:
For diff'rent styles with diff'rent subjects sort,
As several garbs with country, town, and court.
Some by old words to fame have made pretence,
Ancients in phrase, mere moderns in their sense;   325
Such laboured nothings, in so strange a style,
Amaze th' unlearned, and make the learnèd smile.
Unlucky, as Fungoso in the Play,   ⎫
These sparks with awkward vanity display   ⎬
What the fine gentleman wore yesterday;   ⎭   330
And but so mimic ancient wits at best,
As apes our grandsires, in their doublets drest.
In words, as fashions, the same rule will hold;
Alike fantastic, if too new, or old:
Be not the first by whom the new are tried,   335
Nor yet the last to lay the old aside.
    But most by Numbers judge a Poet's song;
And smooth or rough, with them is right or wrong:
In the bright Muse though thousand charms conspire,
Her Voice is all these tuneful fools admire;   340
Who haunt Parnassus but to please their ear,
Not mend their minds; as some to Church repair,
Not for the doctrine, but the music there.
These equal syllables alone require,
Though oft the ear the open vowels tire;   345
While expletives their feeble aid do join;
And ten low words oft creep in one dull line:
While they ring round the same unvaried chimes,
With sure returns of still expected rhymes;
Where'er you find "the cooling western breeze,"   350
In the next line, it "whispers through the trees:"
If crystal streams "with pleasing murmurs creep,"
The reader's threatened (not in vain) with "sleep:"
Then, at the last and only couplet fraught
With some unmeaning thing they call a thought,   355

328. **Fungoso:** from Ben Jonson's *Every Man in his Humour.*

A needless Alexandrine ends the song
That, like a wounded snake, drags its slow length along.
Leave such to tune their own dull rhymes, and know
What's roundly smooth or languishingly slow;
And praise the easy vigour of a line,   360
Where Denham's strength, and Waller's sweetness join.
True ease in writing comes from art, not chance,
As those move easiest who have learned to dance.
'Tis not enough no harshness gives offence,
The sound must seem an Echo to the sense: 365
Soft is the strain when Zephyr gently blows,
And the smooth stream in smoother numbers flows;
But when loud surges lash the sounding shore,
The hoarse, rough verse should like the torrent roar:
When Ajax strives some rock's vast weight to throw,   370
The line too labours, and the words move slow;
Not so, when swift Camilla scours the plain,
Flies o'er th' unbending corn, and skims along the main.
Hear how Timotheus' varied lays surprise,
And bid alternate passions fall and rise!   375
While, at each change, the son of Libyan Jove
Now burns with glory, and then melts with love,
Now his fierce eyes with sparkling fury glow,
Now sighs steal out, and tears begin to flow:
Persians and Greeks like turns of nature found,   380
And the world's victor stood subdued by Sound!
The power of Music all our hearts allow,
And what Timotheus was, is DRYDEN now.
    Avoid Extremes; and shun the fault of such,
Who still are pleased too little or too much.   385
At every trifle scorn to take offence,
That always shows great pride, or little sense;
Those heads, as stomachs, are not sure the best,
Which nauseate all, and nothing can digest.
Yet let not each gay Turn thy rapture move;   390
For fools admire, but men of sense approve:
As things seem large which we through mists descry,
Dulness is ever apt to magnify.

356. Alexandrine: a line containing six iambic feet.
361. Denham ... Waller: Dryden and Pope both thought Sir John Denham (1615–1669) and Edmund Waller (1606–1687) had contributed to the improvement of English poetry.
370. Ajax: strongest of the Greeks who besieged Troy.
372. Camilla: female warrior in the *Aeneid*.
374. Timotheus: a Theban musician to Alexander the Great, from Dryden's "Alexander's Feast."
376. Libyan Jove: Alexander.
380. like ... nature: similar movements or expressions of feeling.

Some foreign writers, some our own despise;
The Ancients only, or the Moderns prize.   395
Thus Wit, like Faith, by each man is applied
To one small sect, and all are damned beside.
Meanly they seek the blessing to confine,
And force that sun but on a part to shine,
Which not alone the southern wit sublimes,   400
But ripens spirits in cold northern climes;
Which from the first has shone on ages past,
Enlights the present, and shall warm the last;
Though each may feel increases and decays,
And see now clearer and now darker days.   405
Regard not then if Wit be old or new,
But blame the false, and value still the true.
    Some ne'er advance a Judgment of their own,
But catch the spreading notion of the Town;
They reason and conclude by precedent,   410
And own stale nonsense which they ne'er invent.
Some judge of authors' names, not works, and then
Nor praise nor blame the writings, but the men.
Of all this servile herd the worst is he
That in proud dulness joins with Quality.   415
A constant Critic at the great man's board,
To fetch and carry nonsense for my Lord.
What woful stuff this madrigal would be,
In some starved hackney sonneteer, or me?
But let a Lord once own the happy lines,   420
How the wit brightens! how the style refines!
Before his sacred name flies every fault,
And each exalted stanza teems with thought!
    The Vulgar thus through Imitation err;
As oft the Learned by being singular;   425
So much they scorn the crowd, that if the throng
By chance go right, they purposely go wrong;
So Schismatics the plain believers quit,
And are but damned for having too much wit.
Some praise at morning what they blame at night;   430
But always think the last opinion right.
A Muse by these is like a mistress used,
This hour she's idolised, the next abused;
While their weak heads like towns unfortified,
'Twixt sense and nonsense daily change their side.   435

428. **Schismatics:** those who leave the
Established Church or attempt to cause
divisions in it.

Ask them the cause; they're wiser still, they say;
And still to-morrow's wiser than to-day.
We think our fathers fools, so wise we grow;
Our wiser sons, no doubt, will think us so.
Once School-divines this zealous isle o'er-spread;   440
Who knew most Sentences, was deepest read;
Faith, Gospel, all, seemed made to be disputed,
And none had sense enough to be confuted:
Scotists and Thomists, now, in peace remain,
Amidst their kindred cobwebs in Duck-lane.   445
If Faith itself has diff'rent dresses worn,
What wonder modes in Wit should take their turn?
Oft, leaving what is natural and fit,
The current folly proves the ready wit;
And authors think their reputation safe,   450
Which lives as long as fools are pleased to laugh.
    Some valuing those of their own side or mind,
Still make themselves the measure of mankind:
Fondly we think we honour merit then,
When we but praise ourselves in other men.   455
Parties in Wit attend on those of State,
And public faction doubles private hate.
Pride, Malice, Folly, against Dryden rose,
In various shapes of Parsons, Critics, Beaus;
But sense survived, when merry jests were past;   460
For rising merit will buoy up at last.
Might he return, and bless once more our eyes,
New Blackmores and new Milbourns must arise:
Nay should great Homer lift his awful head,
Zoilus again would start up from the dead.   465
Envy will merit, as its shade, pursue;
But like a shadow, proves the substance true;
For envied Wit, like Sol eclipsed, makes known
Th' opposing body's grossness, not its own,
When first that sun too powerful beams displays,   470
It draws up vapours which obscure its rays;
But even those clouds at last adorn its way,
Reflect new glories, and augment the day.

---

440. **School-divines:** Scholastics, medieval theologians.
441. **Sentences:** views of the church fathers, from Peter Lombard's *Book of Sentences.*
444. **Scotists . . . Thomists:** Followers of the medieval theologians Duns Scotus (c. 1265–1308) and St. Thomas Aquinas (c. 1227–1274).
445. **Duck-lane:** a place where old and second-hand books were sold.
463. **Blackmores . . . Milbourns:** Sir Richard Blackmore, a dull epic poet and one of the critics who attacked Dryden (and Pope) for immorality. The Rev. Luke Milbourne attacked Dryden's translation of the *Aeneid.*
465. **Zoilus:** a Greek grammarian of the 3rd or 4th century B.C., notorious for his criticism of Homer.

Be thou the first true merit to befriend;
His praise is lost, who stays, till all commend.   475
Short is the date, alas, of modern rhymes,
And 'tis but just to let them live betimes.
No longer now that golden age appears,
When Patriarch-wits survived a thousand years:
Now length of Fame (our second life) is lost,   480
And bare threescore is all even that can boast;
Our sons their fathers' failing language see,
And such as Chaucer is, shall Dryden be.
So when the faithful pencil has designed
Some bright Idea of the master's mind,   485
Where a new world leaps out at his command,
And ready Nature waits upon his hand;
When the ripe colours soften and unite,
And sweetly melt into just shade and light;
When mellowing years their full perfection give,   490
And each bold figure just begins to live,
The treach'rous colours the fair art betray,
And all the bright creation fades away!
    Unhappy Wit, like most mistaken things,
Atones not for that envy which it brings.   495
In youth alone its empty praise we boast,
But soon the short-lived vanity is lost:
Like some fair flower the early spring supplies,
That gaily blooms, but even in blooming dies.
What is this Wit, which must our cares employ?   500
The owner's wife, that other men enjoy;
Then most our trouble still when most admired,
And still the more we give, the more required;
Whose fame with pains we guard, but lose with ease,
Sure some to vex, but never all to please;   505
'Tis what the vicious fear, the virtuous shun,
By fools 'tis hated, and by knaves undone!
    If Wit so much from Ign'rance undergo,
Ah let not Learning too commence its foe!
Of old, those met rewards who could excel,   510
And such were praised who but endeavoured well:
Though triumphs were to generals only due,
Crowns were reserved to grace the soldiers too.
Now, they who reach Parnassus' lofty crown,
Employ their pains to spurn some others down;   515

483. **Chaucer . . . be:** Because of changes in the English Language, 300 years hence Dryden will be as obscure as Chaucer is now.

And while self-love each jealous writer rules,
Contending wits become the sport of fools:
But still the worst with most regret commend,
For each ill Author is as bad a Friend.
To what base ends, and by what abject ways,   520
Are mortals urged through sacred lust of praise!
Ah ne'er so dire a thirst of glory boast,
Nor in the Critic let the Man be lost.
Good-nature and good-sense must ever join;
To err is human, to forgive, divine.   525
    But if in noble minds some dregs remain
Not yet purged off, of spleen and sour disdain;
Discharge that rage on more provoking crimes,
Nor fear a dearth in these flagitious times.
No pardon vile Obscenity should find.   530
Though wit and art conspire to move your mind;
But Dulness with Obscenity must prove
As shameful sure as Impotence in love.
In the fat age of pleasure, wealth and ease,
Sprung the rank weed, and thrived with large increase: 535
When love was all an easy Monarch's care;
Seldom at council, never in a war:
Jilts ruled the state, and statesmen farces writ;
Nay wits had pensions, and young Lords had wit:
The Fair sate panting at a Courtier's play,   540
And not a Mask went unimproved away:
The modest fan was lifted up no more,
And Virgins smiled at what they blushed before.
The following licence of a Foreign reign
Did all the dregs of bold Socinus drain;   545
Then unbelieving priests reformed the nation,
And taught more pleasant methods of salvation;
Where Heaven's free subjects might their rights dispute,
Lest God himself should seem too absolute:
Pulpits their sacred satire learned to spare,   550

---

521. **sacred ... Praise:** a phrase from *Aeneid*, III ("sacred": accursed).
536. **Monarch:** Charles II; the following lines describe Restoration manners and morals.
538. **Jilts:** mistresses.
540. **Fair:** the fair sex.
541. **Mask:** women wore masks to the theater.
544. **Foreign:** William III was Dutch.
545. **Socinus:** Laelius Socinus (Lelio Sozzini, 1525–1562) and his nephew Fausto Sozzini rejected the doctrine of Christ's divinity and atonement for sin. William III was tolerant towards Dissenters, many of whom held these beliefs. His administration also refused to renew the Licensing Act, which restricted printers and acted as a means of censorship.
550. **sacred satire:** criticism of men from God's point of view.

And Vice admired to find a flatt'rer there!
Encouraged thus, Wit's Titans braved the skies,
And the press groaned with licensed blasphemies.
These monsters, Critics! with your darts engage,
Here point your thunder, and exhaust your rage!　　　　555
Yet shun their fault, who, scandalously nice,
Will needs mistake an author into vice;
All seems infected that th' infected spy,
As all looks yellow to the jaundiced eye.

Part III

Learn then what MORALS Critics ought to show,　　　　560
For 'tis but half a Judge's task, to know.
'Tis not enough, taste, judgment, learning, join;
In all you speak, let truth and candour shine:
That not alone what to your sense is due
All may allow; but seek your friendship too.　　　　565
Be silent always when you doubt your sense;
And speak, though sure, with seeming diffidence:
Some positive, persisting fops we know,
Who, if once wrong, will needs be always so;
But you, with pleasure own your errors past,　　　　570
And make each day a Critic on the last.
'Tis not enough, your counsel still be true;
Blunt truths more mischief than nice falsehoods do;
Men must be taught as if you taught them not,
And things unknown proposed as things forgot.　　　　575
Without Good Breeding, truth is disapproved;
That only makes superior sense beloved.
Be niggards of advice on no pretence;
For the worst avarice is that of sense.
With mean complacence ne'er betray your trust,　　　　580
Nor be so civil as to prove unjust.
Fear not the anger of the wise to raise;
Those best can bear reproof, who merit praise.
'Twere well might critics still this freedom take,
But Appius reddens at each word you speak,　　　　585
And stares, tremendous, with a threat'ning eye,
Like some fierce Tyrant in old tapestry.
Fear most to tax an Honourable fool,
Whose right it is, uncensured, to be dull;

---

552. **Wit's Titans:** Deists and Freethinkers.
553. **licensed:** permitted to be published.
585. **Appius:** John Dennis, author of the
poorly received play, *Appius and Virginia.*
Appius, like Dennis, was sensitive to
criticism.

Such, without wit, are Poets when they please,　　　　590
As without learning they can take Degrees.
Leave dangerous truths to unsuccessful Satires,
And flattery to fulsome Dedicators,
Whom, when they praise, the world believes no more,
Than when they promise to give scribbling o'er.　　　　595
'Tis best sometimes your censure to restrain,
And charitably let the dull be vain:
Your silence there is better than your spite,
For who can rail so long as they can write?
Still humming on, their drowsy course they keep,　　　　600
And lashed so long, like tops, are lashed asleep.
False steps but help them to renew the race,
As, after stumbling, Jades will mend their pace.
What crowds of these, impenitently bold,
In sounds and jingling syllables grown old,　　　　605
Still run on Poets, in a raging vein,
Even to the dregs and squeezings of the brain,
Strain out the last dull droppings of their sense,
And rhyme with all the rage of Impotence.
　　Such shameless Bards we have; and yet 'tis true　　　　610
There are as mad abandoned Critics too.
The bookful blockhead, ignorantly read,
With loads of learnèd lumber in his head,
With his own tongue still edifies his ears,
And always list'ning to himself appears.　　　　615
All books he reads, and all he reads assails,
From Dryden's Fables down to Durfey's Tales.
With him, most authors steal their works, or buy;
Garth did not write his own Dispensary.
Name a new Play, and he's the Poet's friend,　　　　620
Nay showed his faults—but when would Poets mend?
No place so sacred from such fops is barred,
Nor is Paul's church more safe than Paul's churchyard:
Nay, fly to Altars; there they'll talk you dead:
For Fools rush in where Angels fear to tread.　　　　625
Distrustful sense with modest caution speaks,
It still looks home, and short excursions makes;
But rattling nonsense in full volleys breaks,

601. **lashed asleep:** a top sleeps when its motion is imperceptible.
603. **Jades . . . pace:** nags will travel faster.
617. **Durfey:** Thomas Durfey (1653–1723) published his own adaptations of Continental novels.

619. **Garth:** Samuel Garth (1661–1719), doctor and author of the mock-heroic *Dispensary*, which satirized the medical profession. Blackmore and others claimed he was a copier.

And never shocked, and never turned aside,
Bursts out, resistless, with a thund'ring tide. 630
    But where's the man, who counsel can bestow,
Still pleased to teach, and yet not proud to know?
Unbiased, or by favour, or by spite;
Not dully prepossessed, nor blindly right;
Though learned, well-bred; and though well-bred, sincere, 635
Modestly bold, and humanly severe:
Who to a friend his faults can freely show,
And gladly praise the merit of a foe?
Blest with a taste exact, yet unconfined;
A knowledge both of books and human kind: 640
Gen'rous converse; a soul exempt from pride;
And love to praise, with reason on his side?
    Such once were Critics; such the happy few,
Athens and Rome in better ages knew.
The mighty Stagirite first left the shore, 645
Spread all his sails, and durst the deeps explore:
He steered securely, and discovered far,
Led by the light of the Mæonian Star.
Poets, a race long unconfined, and free,
Still fond and proud of savage liberty, 650
Received his laws; and stood convinced 'twas fit,
Who conquered Nature, should preside o'er Wit.
    Horace still charms with graceful negligence,
And without method talks us into sense,
Will, like a friend, familiarly convey 655
The truest notions in the easiest way.
He, who supreme in judgment, as in wit,
Might boldly censure, as he boldly writ,
Yet judged with coolness, though he sung with fire;
His Precepts teach but what his works inspire. 660
Our Critics take a contrary extreme,
They judge with fury, but they write with fle'me:
Nor suffers Horace more in wrong Translations
By Wits, than Critics in as wrong Quotations.
    See Dionysius Homer's thoughts refine, 665
And call new beauties forth from every line!
    Fancy and art in gay Petronius please,

---

648. **Mæonian Star:** Homer, supposedly born in Maeonia in Lydia.
662. **fle'me:** phlegm, the cold and moist humour, causing sluggishness.

665. **Dionysius:** Dionysius of Halicarnassus, 1st century B.C. rhetorician and historian who lived and wrote in Rome.
667. **Petronius:** Roman satirist, 1st century A.D.

The scholar's learning, with the courtier's ease.
   In grave Quintilian's copious work, we find
The justest rules, and clearest method joined: 670
Thus useful arms in magazines we place,
All ranged in order, and disposed with grace,
But less to please the eye, than arm the hand,
Still fit for use, and ready at command.
   Thee, bold Longinus! all the Nine inspire,   675
And bless their Critic with a Poet's fire.
An ardent Judge, who zealous in his trust,
With warmth gives sentence, yet is always just;
Whose own example strengthens all his laws;
And is himself that great Sublime he draws.   680
   Thus long succeeding Critics justly reigned,
Licence repressed, and useful laws ordained.
Learning and Rome alike in empire grew;
And Arts still followed where her Eagles flew;
From the same foes, at last, both felt their doom,   685
And the same age saw Learning fall, and Rome.
With Tyranny, then Superstition joined,
As that the body, this enslaved the mind;
Much was believed, but little understood,
And to be dull was construed to be good;   690
A second deluge Learning thus o'er-run,
And the Monks finished what the Goths begun.
   At length Erasmus, that great injured name,
(The glory of the Priesthood, and the shame!)
Stemmed the wild torrent of a barb'rous age,   695
And drove those holy Vandals off the stage.
   But see! each Muse, in Leo's golden days,
Starts from her trance, and trims her withered bays,
Rome's ancient Genius, o'er its ruins spread,
Shakes off the dust, and rears his rev'rend head.   700
Then Sculpture and her sister-arts revive;
Stones leaped to form, and rocks began to live;
With sweeter notes each rising Temple rung;
A Raphael painted, and a Vida sung.
Immortal Vida: on whose honoured brow   705
The Poet's bays and Critic's ivy grow:

669. Quintilian: Roman grammarian and rhetorician, 1st century A.D.
675. Longinus: Greek philosopher of the 3rd century A.D., long thought to be author of a treatise on the sublime.
693. Erasmus: Though Erasmus (1466–1536) remained loyal to the Roman Catholic Church, he attacked the clergy and encouraged free enquiry.
697. Leo: Leo X, Pope from 1513 to 1521, was a great patron of artists and writers.
704. Vida: M. Hieronymus Vida of Cremona (1490?–1566) a Latin poet, wrote didactic poems and an art of poetry in verse.

Cremona now shall ever boast thy name,
As next in place to Mantua, next in fame!
   But soon by impious arms from Latium chased,
Their ancient bounds the banished Muses passed;   710
Thence Arts o'er all the northern world advance,
But Critic-learning flourished most in France:
The rules a nation, born to serve, obeys;
And Boileau still in right of Horace sways.
But we, brave Britons, foreign laws despised,   715
And kept unconquered, and uncivilised;
Fierce for the liberties of wit, and bold,
We still defied the Romans, as of old.
Yet some there were, among the sounder few
Of those who less presumed, and better knew,   720
Who durst assert the juster ancient cause,
And here restored Wit's fundamental laws.
Such was the Muse, whose rules and practice tell,
"Nature's chief Master-piece is writing well."
Such was Roscommon, not more learned than good,   725
With manners gen'rous as his noble blood;
To him the wit of Greece and Rome was known,
And every author's merit, but his own.
Such late was Walsh—the Muse's judge and friend,
Who justly knew to blame or to commend;   730
To failings mild, but zealous for desert;
The clearest head, and the sincerest heart.
This humble praise, lamented shade! receive,
This praise at least a grateful Muse may give:
The Muse, whose early voice you taught to sing,   735
Prescribed her heights, and pruned her tender wing,
(Her guide now lost) no more attempts to rise,
But in low numbers short excursions tries:
Content, if hence th' unlearned their wants may view,
The learned reflect on what before they knew: 740
Careless of censure, nor too fond of fame;
Still pleased to praise, yet not afraid to blame,
Averse alike to flatter, or offend;
Not free from faults, nor yet too vain to mend.

---

714. **Boileau:** Nicolas Boileau-Depreaux (1636–1711), a French critic and poet, who like Horace and Vida wrote an art of poetry in verse.
724. **Nature's . . . well:** from the "Essay on Poetry" by John Sheffield, Duke of Buckingham, one of Pope's friends.

725. **Roscommon:** Wentworth Dillon, 4th Earl of Roscommon (1633?–1685) translated Horace's "Art of Poetry."
729. **Walsh:** William Walsh (1663–1708), poet and critic who befriended and advised the young Pope.

The Rape of the Lock

An Heroic-Comical Poem

Nolueram, Belinda, tuos violare capillos;
Sed juvat, hoc precibus me tribuisse tuis.
[Martial, *Epigrams* XII, 84]

Canto I

What dire offense from am'rous causes springs,
What mighty contests rise from trivial things,
I sing—This verse to Caryll, Muse! is due;
This ev'n Belinda may vouchsafe to view:
Slight is the subject, but not so the praise,   5
If She inspire, and He approve my lays.
  Say what strange motive, Goddess! could compel
A well-bred Lord t' assault a gentle Belle?
Oh say what stranger cause, yet unexplored,
Could make a gentle Belle reject a Lord?   10
In tasks so bold, can little men engage,
And in soft bosoms dwells such mighty Rage?
  Sol through white curtains shot a tim'rous ray,
And op'd those eyes that must eclipse the day;
Now lap-dogs give themselves the rousing shake,   15
And sleepless lovers, just at twelve, awake:
Thrice rung the bell, the slipper knocked the ground,
And the pressed watch returned a silver sound.
Belinda still her downy pillow pressed,
Her guardian SYLPH prolonged the balmy rest.   20
'Twas He had summoned to her silent bed
The morning-dream that hovered o'er her head.
A youth more glitt'ring than a Birth-night Beau
(That even in slumber caused her cheek glow),
Seemed to her ear his winning lips to to lay,   25

Rape . . . Lock: The poem is based on an actual incident. Because Lord Petre (the Baron) cut off a lock of Miss Arabella Fermor's (Belinda's) hair, a quarrel resulted between the families of the two. Pope's friend, John Caryll, urged Pope to write something which might allay the passions on both sides. The first version of the poem, only two cantos long, appeared in 1712. By 1717 Pope had expanded it to its present length.
Nolerum . . . tuis: "I was loth, Belinda, to violate your locks, but I am pleased to have granted that much to your prayers." Trans. Tillotson. Pope substituted Belinda for Martial's Polytimus.
17. slipper . . . ground: to summon the inattentive servants.
20. Sylph: Pope fashioned Rosicrucian lore about the spirits—Sylphs, Gnomes, Nymphs, and Salamanders—into the "machinery" expected in an epic poem.
23. Birth-night Beau: At royal birthday parties, everyone wore his most splendid clothes.

And thus in whispers said, or seemed to say.
　Fairest of mortals, thou distinguished care
Of thousand bright Inhabitants of Air!
If e'er one Vision touched thy infant thought,
Of all the Nurse and all the Priest have taught,   30
Of airy Elves by moonlight shadows seen,
The silver token, and the circled green,
Or virgins visited by Angel-powers,
With golden crowns and wreaths of heavenly flowers,
Hear and believe! thy own importance know,   35
Nor bound thy narrow views to things below.
Some secret truths, from learned pride concealed,
To Maids alone and Children are reveal'd:
What though no credit doubting Wits may give?
The Fair and Innocent shall still believe.   40
Know, then, unnumbered Spirits round thee fly,
The light Militia of the lower sky;
These, though unseen, are ever on the wing,
Hang o'er the Box, and hover round the Ring.
Think what an equipage thou hast in Air,   45
And view with scorn two Pages and a Chair.
As now your own, our beings were of old,
And once inclosed in Woman's beauteous mold;
Thence, by a soft transition, we repair
From earthly Vehicles to these of air.   50
Think not, when Woman's transient breath is fled,
That all her vanities at once are dead;
Succeeding vanities she still regards,
And though she plays no more, o'erlooks the cards.
Her joy in gilded Chariots, when alive,   55
And love of Ombre, after death survive.
For when the Fair in all their pride expire,
To their first Elements their Souls retire:
The Sprites of fiery Termagants in flame
Mount up, and take a Salamander's name.   60
Soft yielding Minds to water glide away,
And sip, with Nymphs, their elemental tea.
The graver Prude sinks downward to a Gnome,
In search of mischief still on Earth to roam.

---

32. **silver . . . green:** the silver coin left by
fairies in payment for skimming the cream
off jugs of milk. Bright rings of grass were
thought to be caused by elves dancing.
44. **Box . . . Ring:** theater box and riding
ring.

46. **Chair:** sedan chair.
56. **Ombre:** from the Spanish "hombre"
(man), a popular three-handed card game.
In Canto III Pope accurately describes a
hand being played.

The light Coquettes in Sylphs aloft repair,   65
And sport and flutter in the fields of Air.
   Know farther yet; whoever fair and chaste
Rejects mankind, is by some Sylph embraced.
For Spirits, freed from mortal law, with ease
Assume what sexes and what shapes they please.   70
What guards the purity of melting Maids,
In courtly balls, and midnight masquerades,
Safe from the treacherous friend, the daring spark,
The glance by day, the whisper in the dark,
When kind occasion prompts their warm desires,   75
When music softens, and when dancing fires?
'Tis but their Sylph, the wise Celestials know,
Though Honour is the word with Men below.
   Some Nymphs there are, too conscious of their face,
For life predestined to the Gnomes' embrace.   80
These swell their prospects and exalt their pride,
When offers are disdained, and love denied.
Then gay Ideas crowd the vacant brain;
While Peers and Dukes, and all their sweeping train,
And Garters, Stars, and Coronets appear,   85
And in soft sounds, Your Grace salutes their ear.
'Tis these that early taint the female soul,
Instruct the eyes of young Coquettes to roll,
Teach Infant-Cheeks a bidden blush to know,
And little Hearts to flutter at a Beau.   90
   Oft, when the world imagine women stray,
The Sylphs through mystic mazes guide their way,
Through all the giddy circle they pursue,
And old impertinence expel by new.
What tender maid but must a victim fall   95
To one man's treat, but for another's ball?
When Florio speaks, what virgin could withstand,
If gentle Damon did not squeeze her hand?
With varying vanities, from every part,
They shift the moving Toyshop of their heart;   100
Where wigs with wigs, with sword-knots sword-knots strive,
Beaux banish beaux, and coaches coaches drive.
This erring mortals Levity may call,
Oh blind to truth! the Sylphs contrive it all.
   Of these am I, who thy protection claim,   105
A watchful sprite, and Ariel is my name.

101. **sword-knots:** ribbons tied to the hilts
of swords.

Late, as I ranged the crystal wilds of air,
In the clear Mirror of thy ruling Star
I saw, alas! some dread event impend,
Ere to the main this morning sun descend,   110
But heaven reveals not what, or how, or where:
Warned by the Sylph, oh pious maid, beware!
This to disclose is all thy guardian can.
Beware of all, but most beware of Man!
   He said; when Shock, who thought she slept too long,   115
Leapt up, and waked his mistress with his tongue.
'Twas then, Belinda! if Report say true,
Thy eyes first opened on a Billet-doux;
Wounds, Charms, and Ardors were no sooner read,
But all the vision vanished from thy head.   120
   And now, unveil'd, the Toilet stands displayed,
Each silver vase in mystic order laid.
First, robed in white, the Nymph intent adores
With head uncovered, the Cosmetic Powers.
A heavenly image in the glass appears,   125
To that she bends, to that her eyes she rears;
Th' inferior Priestess, at her altar's side,
Trembling begins the sacred Rites of Pride.
Unnumbered treasures ope at once, and here
The various offerings of the world appear;   130
From each she nicely culls with curious toil,
And decks the Goddess with the glitt'ring spoil.
This casket India's glowing gems unlocks,
And all Arabia breathes from yonder box.
The tortoise here and elephant unite,   135
Transformed to combs, the speckled, and the white.
Here Files of Pins extend their shining rows,
Puffs, Powders, Patches, Bibles, Billet-doux.
Now awful Beauty put on all its arms;
The fair each moment rises in her charms,   140
Repairs her smiles, awakens every grace,
And calls forth all the wonders of her face;
Sees by degrees a purer blush arise,
And keener lightnings quicken in her eyes.
The busy Sylphs surround their darling Care,   145
These set the head, and those divide the hair,
Some fold the sleeve, while others plait the gown;
And Betty's praised for labors not her own.

---

118. Billet-doux: love letter.

Canto II

Not with more glories, in th' ethereal plain,
The Sun first rises o'er the purpled main,
Than issuing forth, the rival of his beams
Launched on the bosom of the silver Thames.
Fair Nymphs, and well-dressed Youths around her shone,   5
But every eye was fixed on her alone.
On her white breast a sparkling cross she wore,
Which Jews might kiss, and Infidels adore.
Her lively looks a sprightly mind disclose,
Quick as her eyes, and as unfixed as those: 10
Favors to none, to all she smiles extends;
Oft she rejects, but never once offends.
Bright as the sun, her eyes the gazers strike,
And, like the sun, they shine on all alike.
Yet graceful ease, and sweetness void of pride,   15
Might hide her faults, if Belles had faults to hide:
If to her share some female errors fall,
Look on her face, and you'll forget 'em all.
     This Nymph, to the destruction of Mankind,
Nourished two Locks which graceful hung behind   20
In equal curls, and well conspired to deck
With shining ringlets the smooth ivory neck.
Love in these labyrinths his slaves detains,
And mighty hearts are held in slender chains.
With hairy springes we the birds betray,   25
Slight lines of hair surprise the finny prey,
Fair tresses man's imperial race insnare,
And Beauty draws us with a single hair.
     Th' adventurous Baron the bright locks admired;
He saw, he wished, and to the prize aspired.   30
Resolved to win, he meditates the way,
By force to ravish, or by fraud betray;
For when success a Lover's toil attends,
Few ask, if fraud or force attained his ends.
     For this, ere Phoebus rose, he had implored   35
Propitious Heaven, and every power adored,
But chiefly Love—to Love an altar built,
Of twelve vast French Romances, neatly gilt.
There lay three garters, half a pair of gloves;
And all the trophies of his former loves;   40
With tender Billet-doux he lights the pyre,

(*Canto II*) 4. **Thames:** Belinda will travel   25. **springes:** snares.
to Hampton Court, the royal palace about   35. **Phoebus:** the sun.
fourteen miles upstream from London.

And breathes three am'rous sighs to raise the fire.
Then prostrate falls, and begs with ardent eyes
Soon to obtain, and long possess the prize:
The Powers gave ear, and granted half his prayer,   45
The rest, the winds dispersed in empty air.
  But now secure the painted vessel glides,
The sunbeams trembling on the floating tides,
While melting music steals upon the sky,
And softened sounds along the waters die.   50
Smooth flow the waves, the Zephyrs gently play,
Belinda smiled, and all the world was gay.
All but the Sylph—with careful thoughts oppressed,
Th' impending woe sat heavy on his breast.
He summons straight his Denizens of air;   55
The lucid squadrons round the sails repair:
Soft o'er the shrouds aerial whispers breathe,
That seem'd but Zephyrs to the train beneath.
Some to the sun their insect wings unfold,
Waft on the breeze, or sink in clouds of gold.   60
Transparent forms, too fine for mortal sight,
Their fluid bodies half dissolved in light,
Loose to the wind their airy garments flew,
Thin glitt'ring textures of the filmy dew,
Dipped in the richest tincture of the skies,   65
Where light disports in ever-mingling dyes,
While ev'ry beam new transient colours flings,
Colours that change whene'er they wave their wings.
Amid the circle, on the gilded mast,
Superior by the head, was Ariel placed;   70
His purple pinions op'ning to the sun,
He raised his azure wand, and thus begun.
  Ye Sylphs and Sylphids, to your chief give ear,
Fays, Fairies, Genii, Elves, and Demons hear!
Ye know the spheres and various tasks assigned   75
By laws eternal to th' aerial kind.
Some in the fields of purest Æther play,
And bask and whiten in the blaze of day.
Some guide the course of wand'ring orbs on high,
Or roll the planets through the boundless sky.   80
Some less refined, beneath the moon's pale light
Pursue the stars that shoot athwart the night,
Or suck the mists in grosser air below,
Or dip their pinions in the painted bow,

56. **repair:** gather.

Or brew fierce tempests on the wintry main,   85
Or o'er the glebe distil the kindly rain.
Others on earth o'er human race preside,
Watch all their ways, and all their actions guide:
Of these the chief the care of Nations own,
And guard with arms divine the British Throne.   90
   Our humbler province is to tend the Fair,
Not a less pleasing, though less glorious care.
To save the powder from too rude a gale,
Nor let th' imprisoned essences exhale;
To draw fresh colors from the vernal flowers;   95
To steal from rainbows e'er they drop in showers
A brighter wash; to curl their waving hairs,
Assist their blushes, and inspire their airs;
Nay oft, in dreams, invention we bestow,
To change a Flounce, or add a Furbelow.   100
   This day, black omens threat the brightest Fair,
That e'er deserved a watchful Spirit's care;
Some dire disaster, or by force, or slight;
But what, or where, the fates have wrapped in night.
Whether the Nymph shall break Diana's law,   105
Or some frail China jar receive a flaw;
Or stain her honour, or her new brocade;
Forget her prayers, or miss a masquerade;
Or lose her heart, or necklace, at a ball;
Or whether Heaven has doomed that Shock must fall.   110
Haste, then, ye spirits! to your charge repair:
The flutt'ring fan be Zephyretta's care;
The drops to thee, Brillante, we consign;
And, Momentilla, let the watch be thine;
Do thou, Crispissa, tend her favourite Lock;   115
Ariel himself shall be the guard of Shock.
   To fifty chosen Sylphs, of special note,
We trust th' important charge, the Petticoat:
Oft have we known that seven-fold fence to fail,
Though stiff with hoops, and armed with ribs of whale;   120
Form a strong line about the silver bound,
And guard the wide circumference around.
   Whatever spirit, careless of his charge,
His post neglects, or leaves the Fair at large,
Shall feel sharp vengeance soon o'ertake his sins,   125

86. **glebe:** field.
91. **Fair:** fair sex.
97. **wash:** face lotion.
100. **Flounce; Furbelow:** ornamental material sewn on a gown.
105. **Diana's law:** chastity.
115. **Crispissa:** to crisp meant to curl.

Be stopped in vials, or transfixed with pins;
Or plunged in lakes of bitter washes lie,
Or wedged whole ages in a bodkin's eye:
Gums and Pomatums shall his flight restrain,
While clogged he beats his silken wings in vain;   130
Or alum styptics with contracting power
Shrink his thin essence like a rivel'd flower:
Or as Ixion fixed, the wretch shall feel
The giddy motion of the whirling mill,
In fumes of burning Chocolate shall glow,   135
And tremble at the sea that froths below!
   He spoke; the Spirits from the sails descend;
Some, orb in orb, around the Nymph extend,
Some thrid the mazy ringlets of her hair,
Some hang upon the pendants of her ear;   140
With beating hearts the dire event they wait,
Anxious, and trembling for the birth of Fate.

Canto III

Close by those meads, for ever crowned with flowers,
Where Thames with pride surveys his rising towers,
There stands a structure of majestic frame,
Which from the neighb'ring Hampton takes its name.
Here Britain's statesmen oft the fall foredoom   5
Of foreign tyrants, and of Nymphs at home;
Here Thou, Great Anna! whom three realms obey,
Dost sometimes counsel take—and sometimes Tea.
   Hither the heroes and the nymphs resort,
To taste awhile the pleasures of a Court;   10
In various talk th' instructive hours they passed,
Who gave the ball, or paid the visit last:
One speaks the glory of the British Queen,
And one describes a charming Indian screen;
A third interprets motions, looks, and eyes;   15
At every word a reputation dies.
Snuff, or the fan, supply each pause of chat,
With singing, laughing, ogling, and all that.
   Meanwhile declining from the noon of day,
The sun obliquely shoots his burning ray;   20
The hungry Judges soon the sentence sign,
And wretches hang that jurymen may dine;

128. **bodkin's:** a bodkin is a blunt needle with a large eye.
132. **rivel'd:** shriveled.
133. **Ixion:** He was bound to an ever-turning wheel for insulting Juno.

139. **thrid:** thread.

(*Canto III*) 7. **Anna:** Queen Anne (1702–1714). The Union of Scotland with England and Wales took place in 1707.

The merchant from th' Exchange returns in peace,
And the long labors of the toilet cease.
Belinda now, whom thirst of fame invites,   25
Burns to encounter two advent'rous Knights,
At Ombre singly to decide their doom;
And swells her breast with conquests yet to come.
Straight the three bands prepare in arms to join,
Each band the number of the Sacred Nine.   30
Soon as she spreads her hand, th' aerial guard
Descend, and sit on each important card:
First Ariel perched upon a Matadore,
Then each, according to the rank they bore;
For Sylphs, yet mindful of their ancient race,   35
Are, as when women, wond'rous fond of place.
    Behold, four Kings in majesty revered,
With hoary whiskers and a forky beard;
And four fair Queens whose hands sustain a flower,
Th' expressive emblem of their softer power,   40
Four Knaves in garbs succinct, a trusty band,
Caps on their heads, and halberds in their hand;
And particolored troops, a shining train,
Draw forth to combat on the velvet plain.
    The skilful Nymph reviews her force with care;   45
Let Spades be trumps! she said, and trumps they were.
    Now move to war her sable Matadores,
In show like leaders of the swarthy Moors.
Spadillio first, unconquerable Lord!
Led off two captive trumps, and swept the board.   50
As many more Manillio forced to yield,
And marched a victor from the verdant field.
Him Basto followed, but his fate more hard
Gained but one trump and one Plebeian card.
With his broad saber next, a chief in years,   55
The hoary Majesty of Spades appears;
Puts forth one manly leg, to sight revealed;
The rest, his many-colored robe concealed.
The rebel Knave, who dares his prince engage,
Proves the just victim of his royal rage.   60

---

27. **Ombre:** The ombre was the challenger (here Belinda), who claimed he could take more tricks than the other two. The game is fully described in Geoffrey Tillotson's edition of the poem.
29. **three ... join:** The three dealt hands prepare to join in combat.
30. **Sacred Nine:** the nine Muses.
33. **Matadore:** The three highest cards were called matadores; the ace of spades, the ace of clubs, and one other decided by whether trumps were red or black. In this game the two of spades is the third matador.
49. **Spadillio:** actually spadille, literally little sword, the ace of spades.
51. **Manillio:** the two of spades.
53. **Basto:** the ace of clubs.

E'en mighty Pam, that Kings and Queens o'erthrew,
And mow'd down armies in the fights of Lu,
Sad chance of war! now, destitute of aid,
Falls undistinguished by the victor Spade!
    Thus far both armies to Belinda yield;   65
Now to the Baron fate inclines the field.
His warlike Amazon her host invades,
Th' imperial consort of the crown of Spades.
The Club's black Tyrant first her victim died,
Spite of his haughty mien, and barb'rous pride: 70
What boots the regal circle on his head,
His giant limbs, in state unwieldy spread?
That long behind he trails his pompous robe,
And, of all monarchs, only grasps the globe?
    The Baron now his Diamonds pours apace;   75
Th' embroidered King who shows but half his face,
And his refulgent Queen, with pow'rs combined
Of broken troops an easy conquest find.
Clubs, Diamonds, Hearts, in wild disorder seen,
With throngs promiscuous strow the level green.   80
Thus when dispersed a routed army runs,
Of Asia's troops, and Afric's sable sons,
With like confusion different nations fly,
Of various habit, and of various dye,
The pierced battalions dis-united fall,   85
In heaps on heaps; one fate o'erwhelms them all.
    The Knave of Diamonds tries his wily arts,
And wins (oh shameful chance!) the Queen of Hearts.
At this, the blood the Virgin's cheek forsook,
A livid paleness spreads o'er all her look;   90
She sees, and trembles at th' approaching ill,
Just in the jaws of ruin, and Codille.
And now (as oft in some distempered State)
On one nice Trick depends the gen'ral fate.
An Ace of Hearts steps forth: The King unseen   95
Lurked in her hand, and mourn'd his captive Queen:
He springs to vengeance with an eager pace,
And falls like thunder on the prostrate Ace.
The Nymph exulting fills with shouts the sky;
The walls, the woods, and long canals reply.   100
    Oh thoughtless mortals! ever blind to fate,
Too soon dejected, and too soon elate!

61. **Pam:** the jack of clubs, high card in
Lu.
80. **strow:** strew.

92. **Codille:** defeat, the elbow or knee
given to the challenger who fails.
95. **Ace:** when black suits were trump,
red aces were lower than red face cards.

Sudden, these honours shall be snatched away,
And cursed for ever this victorious day.
　For lo! the board with cups and spoons is crowned,　　　105
The berries crackle, and the mill turns round;
On shining Altars of Japan they raise
The silver lamp; the fiery spirits blaze.
From silver spouts the grateful liquors glide,
While China's earth receives the smoking tide.　　　　　110
At once they gratify their scent and taste,
And frequent cups prolong the rich repast.
Straight hover round the Fair her Airy Band;
Some, as she sipped, the fuming liquor fanned,
Some o'er her lap their careful plumes displayed,　　　　115
Trembling, and conscious of the rich brocade.
Coffee (which makes the politician wise,
And see through all things with his half-shut eyes),
Sent up in vapors to the Baron's brain
New stratagems, the radiant Lock to gain.　　　　　　120
Ah cease, rash youth! desist ere 'tis too late,
Fear the just Gods, and think of Scylla's fate!
Changed to a bird, and sent to flit in air,
She dearly pays for Nisus' injured hair!
　But when to mischief mortals bend their will,　　　　125
How soon they find fit instruments of ill!
Just then, Clarissa drew with tempting grace
A two-edged weapon from her shining case;
So Ladies in Romance assist their Knight,
Present the spear, and arm him for the fight.　　　　　130
He takes the gift with rev'rence, and extends
The little engine on his fingers' ends;
This just behind Belinda's neck he spread,
As o'er the fragrant steams she bends her head.
Swift to the Lock a thousand Sprites repair,　　　　　135
A thousand wings, by turns, blow back the hair;
And thrice they twitched the diamond in her ear;
Thrice she looked back, and thrice the foe drew near.
Just in that instant, anxious Ariel sought
The close recesses of the Virgin's thought;　　　　　　140
As on the nosegay in her breast reclined,
He watched th' Ideas rising in her mind,
Sudden he viewed, in spite of all her art,

---

106. **berries . . . mill:** coffee beans and grinder.
107. **Altars of Japan:** lacquered tables in the Japanese style.

122–24. **Scylla's . . . hair:** She was transformed into a bird because she plucked a lock of her father's hair and gave it to his enemy, Minos, whom she loved.

An earthly lover lurking at her heart.
Amazed, confused, he found his power expired,   145
Resigned to fate, and with a sigh retired.
   The Peer now spreads the glitt'ring Forfex wide,
T' enclose the Lock; now joins it, to divide.
E'en then, before the fatal engine closed,
A wretched Sylph too fondly interposed,   150
Fate urged the shears, and cut the Sylph in twain
(But airy substance soon unites again),
The meeting points the sacred hair dissever
From the fair head, for ever, and for ever!
   Then flashed the living lightning from her eyes,   155
And screams of horror rend th' affrighted skies.
Not louder shrieks to pitying Heav'n are cast,
When husbands, or when lap-dogs breathe their last;
Or when rich China vessels fall'n from high,
In glitt'ring dust and painted fragments lie!   160
   Let wreaths of triumph now my temples twine
(The victor cried) the glorious Prize is mine!
While fish in streams, or birds delight in air,
Or in a coach and six the British Fair,
As long as Atalantis shall be read,   165
Or the small pillow grace a Lady's bed,
While visits shall be paid on solemn days,
When num'rous wax-lights in bright order blaze,
While nymphs take treats, or assignations give,
So long my honor, name, and praise shall live!   170
What Time would spare, from Steel receives its date,
And monuments, like men, submit to Fate!
Steel could the labor of the Gods destroy,
And strike to dust th' imperial tow'rs of Troy;
Steel could the works of mortal Pride confound,   175
And hew triumphal arches to the ground.
What wonder then, fair Nymph! thy hairs should feel,
The conquering force of unresisted Steel?

Canto IV

But anxious cares the pensive Nymph oppressed,
And secret passions labor'd in her breast.
Not youthful kings in battle seized alive,
Not scornful virgins who their charms survive,
Not ardent lovers robbed of all their bliss,   5

147. **Forfex:** scissors.
165. **Atalantis:** *The New Atalantis* (1709) by Mary Manley was a thinly disguised allegory about contemporary court and political scandal.

Not ancient ladies when refused a kiss,
Not tyrants fierce that unrepenting die,
Not Cynthia when her manteau's pinned awry,
E'er felt such rage, resentment, and despair,
As Thou, sad Virgin! for thy ravished Hair.   10
   For, that sad moment, when the Sylphs withdrew
And Ariel weeping from Belinda flew,
Umbriel, a dusky, melancholy sprite,
As ever sullied the fair face of light,
Down to the central earth, his proper scene,   15
Repaired to search the gloomy Cave of Spleen.
   Swift on his sooty pinions flits the Gnome,
And in a vapour reached the dismal dome.
No cheerful breeze this sullen region knows,
The dreaded East is all the wind that blows.   20
Here, in a grotto, sheltered close from air,
And screened in shades from day's detested glare,
She sighs for ever on her pensive bed,
Pain at her side, and Megrim at her head.
   Two handmaids wait the throne: alike in place,   25
But differing far in figure and in face.
Here stood Ill-nature like an ancient maid,
Her wrinkled form in black and white arrayed;
With store of prayers, for mornings, nights, and noons,
Her hand is filled; her bosom with lampoons.   30
   There Affectation, with a sickly mien,
Shows in her cheek the roses of eighteen,
Practiced to lisp, and hang the head aside,
Faints into airs, and languishes with pride;
On the rich quilt sinks with becoming woe,   35
Wrapped in a gown, for sickness, and for show.
The Fair-ones feel such maladies as these,
When each new night-dress gives a new disease.
   A constant Vapour o'er the palace flies;
Strange Phantoms rising as the mists arise;   40
Dreadful, as hermit's dreams in haunted shades,
Or bright, as visions of expiring maids.
Now glaring fiends, and snakes on rolling spires,
Pale specters, gaping tombs, and purple fires:
Now lakes of liquid gold, Elysian scenes,   45
And crystal domes, and angels in machines.

(*Canto IV*) 8. **manteau:** negligee or loose garment.
16. **Spleen:** ill humor, low spirits, also called vapors.

24. **Megrim:** migraine, also melancholy.
43–46. **Now ... machines:** The vision of spleen corresponds to contemporary operatic and stage effects.

Unnumbered throngs on every side are seen,
Of bodies changed to various forms by Spleen.
Here living Tea-pots stand, one arm held out,
One bent; the handle this, and that the spout:
A Pipkin there, like Homer's Tripod walks;
Here sighs a Jar, and there a Goose-pie talks;
Men prove with child, as powerful Fancy works,
And Maids turned Bottles, call aloud for corks.

    Safe passed the Gnome through this fantastic band,
A branch of healing spleenwort in his hand.
Then thus addressed the Power: "Hail, wayward Queen!
Who rule the sex to fifty from fifteen,
Parent of vapours and of female wit,
Who give th' hysteric, or poetic fit,
On various tempers act by various ways,
Make some take physic, others scribble plays;
Who cause the proud their visits to delay,
And send the godly in a pet, to pray.
A Nymph there is, that all thy power disdains,
And thousands more in equal mirth maintains.
But oh! if e'er thy Gnome could spoil a grace,
Or raise a pimple on a beauteous face,
Like Citron-waters matrons' cheeks inflame,
Or change complexions at a losing game;
If e'er with airy horns I planted heads,
Or rumpled petticoats, or tumbled beds,
Or caused suspicion when no soul was rude,
Or discomposed the head-dress of a Prude,
Or e'er to costive lap-dog gave disease,
Which not the tears of brightest eyes could ease:
Hear me, and touch Belinda with chagrin;
That single act gives half the world the spleen."

    The Goddess with a discontented air
Seems to reject him, though she grants his prayer.
A wondrous Bag with both her hands she binds,
Like that where once Ulysses held the winds;
There she collects the force of female lungs,
Sighs, sobs, and passions, and the war of tongues.
A Vial next she fills with fainting fears,
Soft sorrows, melting griefs, and flowing tears.

50

55

60

65

70

75

80

85

---

51. **Pipkin . . . walks:** In the *Iliad*, XVIII,
Vulcan furnishes the gods with walking
tripods. A pipkin is an earthen pot.
56. **spleenwort:** a fern, thought to ward off
spleen.
69. **Citron-waters:** brandy flavored with
orange or lemon.

75. **costive:** constipated.
82. **Ulysses . . . winds:** In the *Odyssey*, X,
Aeolus gives Ulysses a bag containing all
the winds adverse to his voyage home.
When in sight of Ithaca, Ulysses' companions open the bag, releasing the winds
which drive the ship far into the west.

The Gnome rejoicing bears her gifts away,
Spreads his black wings, and slowly mounts to day.
   Sunk in Thalestris' arms the Nymph he found,
Her eyes dejected and her hair unbound. 90
Full o'er their heads the swelling Bag he rent,
And all the Furies issued at the vent.
Belinda burns with more than mortal ire,
And fierce Thalestris fans the rising fire.
"O wretched maid!" she spread her hands, and cried 95
(While Hampton's echoes, "Wretched maid!" replied),
"Was it for this you took such constant care
The bodkin, comb, and essence to prepare?
For this your locks in paper durance bound,
For this with torturing irons wreathed around? 100
For this with fillets strained your tender head,
And bravely bore the double loads of lead?
Gods! shall the ravisher display your hair,
While the Fops envy, and the Ladies stare!
Honour forbid! at whose unrivaled shrine 105
Ease, pleasure, virtue, all, our sex resign.
Methinks already I your tears survey,
Already hear the horrid things they say,
Already see you a degraded toast,
And all your honour in a whisper lost! 110
How shall I, then, your helpless fame defend?
'Twill then be infamy to seem your friend!
And shall this prize, th' inestimable prize,
Exposed through crystal to the gazing eyes,
And heightened by the diamond's circling rays, 115
On that rapacious hand for ever blaze?
Sooner shall grass in Hyde-Park Circus grow,
And Wits take lodgings in the sound of Bow;
Sooner let earth, air, sea, to Chaos fall,
Men, monkeys, lap-dogs, parrots, perish all!" 120
   She said; then raging to Sir Plume repairs,
And bids her Beau demand the precious hairs:
(Sir Plume of amber snuff-box justly vain,
And the nice conduct of a clouded cane)
With earnest eyes, and round unthinking face, 125
He first the snuff-box open'd, then the case,
And thus broke out—"My Lord, why, what the devil?

---

94. **Thalestris:** a friend named for the Queen of the Amazons.
117. **Hyde . . . Circus:** fashionable riding ring in Hyde Park, London.

118. **Wits . . . Bow:** St. Mary-le-Bow Church is not in an elegant neighborhood. Supposedly all born within hearing of its bells are cockneys.

Z—ds! damn the lock! 'fore Gad, you must be civil!
Plague on 't! 'tis past a jest—nay prithee, Pox!
Give her the hair"—he spoke, and rapped his box.   130
   "It grieves me much" (replied the Peer again)
"Who speaks so well should ever speak in vain.
But by this Lock, this sacred Lock I swear
(Which never more shall join its parted hair;
Which never more its honours shall renew,   135
Clipped from the lovely head where late it grew),
That while my nostrils draw the vital air,
This hand, which won it, shall for ever wear."
He spoke, and speaking, in proud triumph spread
The long-contended honours of her head.   140
   But Umbriel, hateful Gnome! forbears not so;
He breaks the vial whence the sorrows flow.
Then see! the Nymph in beauteous grief appears,
Her eyes half-languishing, half-drowned in tears;
On her heaved bosom hung her drooping head,   145
Which, with a sigh, she raised; and thus she said:
"Forever cursed be this detested day,
Which snatched my best, my favourite curl away!
Happy! ah ten times happy, had I been,
If Hampton Court these eyes had never seen!   150
Yet am not I the first mistaken maid,
By love of Courts to num'rous ills betrayed.
Oh had I rather unadmired remained
In some lone isle, or distant Northern land;
Where the gilt Chariot never marks the way,   155
Where none learn Ombre, none e'er taste Bohea!
There kept my charms concealed from mortal eye,
Like roses that in deserts bloom and die.
What moved my mind with youthful Lords to roam?
O had I stayed, and said my prayers at home!   160
'Twas this, the morning Omens seemed to tell,
Thrice from my trembling hand the patch-box fell;
The tott'ring China shook without a wind,
Nay, Poll sat mute, and Shock was most unkind!
A Sylph too warned me of the threats of Fate,   165
In mystic visions, now believed too late!
See the poor remnants of these slighted hairs!
My hands shall rend what ev'n thy rapine spares:
These, in two sable ringlets taught to break,
Once gave new beauties to the snowy neck;   170

---

156. **Bohea:** an expensive black tea.

The sister lock now sits uncouth, alone,
And in its fellow's fate foresees its own;
Uncurled it hangs, the fatal shears demands,
And tempts once more thy sacrilegious hands.
O hadst thou, Cruel! been content to seize   175
Hairs less in sight, or any hairs but these!"

Canto V

She said: the pitying audience melt in tears.
But Fate and Jove had stopped the Baron's ears.
In vain Thalestris with reproach assails,
For who can move when fair Belinda fails?
Not half so fixed the Trojan could remain,   5
While Anna begged and Dido raged in vain.
Then grave Clarissa graceful waved her fan;
Silence ensued, and thus the Nymph began.
"Say, why are Beauties prais'd and honour'd most,
The wise man's passion, and the vain man's toast?   10
Why deck'd with all that land and sea afford,
Why Angels called, and Angel-like adored?
Why round our coaches crowd the white-gloved Beaus,
Why bows the side-box from its inmost rows?
How vain are all these glories, all our pains,   15
Unless good Sense preserve what Beauty gains;
That men may say, when we the front-box grace,
'Behold the first in virtue, as in face!'
Oh! if to dance all night, and dress all day,
Charmed the small-pox, or chased old age away;   20
Who would not scorn what housewife's cares produce,
Or who would learn one earthly thing of use?
To patch, nay ogle, might become a Saint,
Nor could it sure be such a sin to paint.
But since, alas! frail Beauty must decay,   25
Curled or uncurled, since locks will turn to gray,
Since painted, or not painted, all shall fade,
And she who scorns a man, must die a maid;
What then remains but well our power to use,
And keep good-humour still whate'er we lose?   30
And trust me, Dear! good-humour can prevail,
When airs, and flights, and screams, and scolding fail.
Beauties in vain their pretty eyes may roll;
Charms strike the sight, but merit wins the soul."

(Canto V) 6. **Anna . . . vain:** In the *Aeneid*,
IV, Aeneas abandoned Dido despite the
pleas of her sister Anna.

So spoke the Dame, but no applause ensu'd;   35
Belinda frowned, Thalestris called her Prude.
"To arms, to arms!" the fierce Virago cries,
And swift as lightning to the combat flies.
All side in parties, and begin th' attack;
Fans clap, silks rustle, and tough whalebones crack;   40
Heroes' and Heroines' shouts confus'dly rise,
And bass, and treble voices strike the skies.
No common weapons in their hands are found,
Like Gods they fight, nor dread a mortal wound.
So when bold Homer makes the Gods engage,   45
And heav'nly breasts with human passions rage;
'Gainst Pallas, Mars; Latona, Hermes arms;
And all Olympus rings with loud alarms:
Jove's thunder roars, Heaven trembles all around,
Blue Neptune storms, the bellowing Deeps resound;   50
Earth shakes her nodding towers, the ground gives way,
And the pale ghosts start at the flash of day!
Triumphant Umbriel on a sconce's height
Clapped his glad wings, and sat to view the fight:
Propped on the bodkin spears, the Sprites survey   55
The growing combat, or assist the fray.
While through the press enraged Thalestris flies,
And scatters deaths around from both her eyes,
A Beau and Witling perished in the throng,
One died in metaphor, and one in song.   60
"O cruel Nymph! a living death I bear,"
Cried Dapperwit, and sunk beside his chair.
A mournful glance Sir Fopling upwards cast,
"Those eyes are made so killing"—was his last.
Thus on Mæander's flow'ry margin lies   65
Th' expiring swan, and as he sings he dies.
When bold Sir Plume had drawn Clarissa down,
Chloe stepped in, and killed him with a frown;
She smiled to see the doughty hero slain,
But at her smile, the Beau revived again.   70
Now Jove suspends his golden scales in air,
Weighs the Men's wits against the Lady's hair;
The doubtful beam long nods from side to side;

45–52. **Homer ... day:** the battle of the gods, *Iliad*, XX.
53. **sconce's:** a bracket candlestick secured to the wall.
64. **Those ... killing:** an air from the popular opera *Camilla* by M. A. Buonocini.

65–66. **Mæander ... dies:** In Ovid's *Epistle VII*, the swan dies singing the lament of "Dido to Aeneas."
71. **Jove ... air:** In both the *Iliad* and the *Aeneid* Zeus (Jove) determines the outcome of battle by means of a scale.

At length the Wits mount up, the Hairs subside.
   See fierce Belinda on the Baron flies,   75
With more than usual lightning in her eyes;
Nor fear'd the Chief th' unequal fight to try,
Who sought no more than on his foe to die.
But this bold Lord with manly strength indued,
She with one finger and a thumb subdued: 80
Just where the breath of life his nostrils drew,
A charge of snuff the wily virgin threw;
The Gnomes direct, to every atom just,
The pungent grains of titillating dust.
Sudden, with starting tears each eye o'erflows,   85
And the high dome re-echoes to his nose.
   Now meet thy fate, incensed Belinda cried,
And drew a deadly bodkin from her side.
(The same, his ancient personage to deck,
Her great great grandsire wore about his neck   90
In three seal-rings; which after, melted down,
Formed a vast buckle for his widow's gown:
Her infant grandame's whistle next it grew,
The bells she jingled, and the whistle blew;
Then in a bodkin graced her mother's hairs,   95
Which long she wore, and now Belinda wears).
   "Boast not my fall" (he cried) "insulting foe!
Thou by some other shalt be laid as low.
Nor think, to die dejects my lofty mind;
All that I dread is leaving you behind!   100
Rather than so, ah let me still survive,
And burn in Cupid's flames—but burn alive."
   "Restore the Lock!" she cries; and all around
"Restore the Lock!" the vaulted roofs rebound.
Not fierce Othello in so loud a strain   105
Roared for the handkerchief that caus'd his pain.
But see how oft ambitious aims are crossed,
And chiefs contend 'till all the prize is lost!
The Lock, obtained with guilt, and kept with pain,
In every place is sought, but sought in vain: 110
With such a prize no mortal must be blessed,
So Heaven decrees! with Heaven who can contest?
   Some thought it mounted to the lunar sphere,
Since all things lost on earth are treasur'd there.
There Heroes' wits are kept in pond'rous vases,   115
And beaus' in snuff-boxes and tweezer-cases.
There broken vows, and death-bed alms are found,
And lovers' hearts with ends of riband bound,

The courtier's promises, and sick man's prayers,
The smiles of harlots, and the tears of heirs,   120
Cages for gnats, and chains to yoke a flea,
Dried butterflies, and tomes of casuistry.
    But trust the Muse—she saw it upward rise,
Though marked by none but quick, poetic eyes:
(So Rome's great founder to the Heavens withdrew,   125
To Proculus alone confessed in view).
A sudden star, it shot through liquid air,
And drew behind a radiant trail of hair.
Not Berenice's Locks first rose so bright,
The Heavens bespangling with disheveled light.   130
The Sylphs behold it kindling as it flies,
The pleased pursue its progress through the skies.
    This the beau-monde shall from the Mall survey,
And hail with music its propitious ray.
This the blest Lover shall for Venus take,   135
And send up vows from Rosamonda's Lake.
This Partridge soon shall view in cloudless skies,
When next he looks through Galileo's eyes;
And hence th' egregious wizard shall foredoom
The fate of Louis, and the fall of Rome.   140
    Then cease, bright Nymph! to mourn thy ravish'd hair,
Which add new glory to the shining sphere!
Not all the tresses that fair head can boast,
Shall draw such envy as the Lock you lost.
For, after all the murders of your eye,   145
When, after millions slain, yourself shall die;
When those fair suns shall set, as set they must,
And all those tresses shall be laid in dust;
This Lock, the Muse shall consecrate to Fame,
And 'midst the stars inscribe Belinda's name.   150

125–26. **Rome's . . . view:** According to Livy, I, xvi, after Romulus ascended directly to heaven, Proculus, to keep order and restore hope, told the citizens he had received a message from Romulus saying that Rome would be the capital of the world.
129. **Berenice's Locks:** According to legend, Berenice, a 3rd-century B.C. Egyptian sorceress, sacrificed a lock of her hair to the gods so that her husband might return safely from war. The lock was transformed into a constellation.
133. **Mall:** a walk in St. James's Park, London.
136. **Rosamonda's Lake:** a lake in St. James's Park.
137. **Partridge:** an almanac maker, a butt for the jokes of Swift and Pope.

Epistle to Dr. Arbuthnot

P.   Shut, shut the door, good John! fatigued, I said,
Tie up the knocker, say I'm sick, I'm dead.
The Dog-star rages! nay 'tis past a doubt,
All Bedlam, or Parnassus, is let out:
Fire in each eye, and papers in each hand,   5
They rave, recite, and madden round the land.
       What walls can guard me, or what shades can hide?
They pierce my thickets, through my Grot they glide;
By land, by water, they renew the charge;
They stop the chariot, and they board the barge.   10
No place is sacred, not the Church is free;
Even Sunday shines no Sabbath-day to me;
Then from the Mint walks forth the Man of rhyme,
Happy to catch me just at Dinner-time.
       Is there a Parson, much bemused in beer,   15
A maudlin Poetess, a rhyming Peer,
A Clerk, foredoomed his father's soul to cross,
Who pens a Stanza, when he should *engross*?
Is there, who, locked from ink and paper, scrawls
With desp'rate charcoal round his darkened walls?   20
All fly to Twit'nam, and in humble strain
Apply to me, to keep them mad or vain.
Arthur, whose giddy son neglects the Laws,
Imputes to me and my damned works the cause:
Poor Cornus sees his frantic wife elope,   25
And curses Wit, and Poetry, and Pope.
       Friend to my Life! (which did not you prolong,
The world had wanted many an idle song)
What *Drop* or *Nostrum* can this plague remove?
Or which must end me, a Fool's wrath or love?   30
A dire dilemma! either way I'm sped,
If foes, they write, if friends, they read me dead.

Dr. Arbuthnot: Dr. John Arbuthnot (1667–1735) physician to Queen Anne and to Pope, was a wit in his own right and an original member, along with Pope and Swift, of the satiric Scriblerus Club.
1. **John:** John Serle, Pope's gardener.
3. **Dog-star:** Sirius, which appears in August, is associated with heat and madness.
4. **Bedlam; Parnassus:** Bethlehem Hospital for the insane; the mountain sacred to the Muses.
8. **Grot:** Near his small villa in Twickenham Pope had built an elaborate grotto where he often went to meditate or compose his poems.
13. **Mint:** a place in Southwark where debtors could not be arrested during the week; they could not be arrested anywhere on Sunday.
21. **Twit'nam:** Twickenham.
23. **Arthur:** Arthur Moore, a politician whose son James Moore Smyth had without permission used some of Pope's verses in a play.
25. **Cornus:** Latin for horn, the emblem of the cuckold.
29. **Nostrum:** medicine.

Seized and tied down to judge, how wretched I!
Who can't be silent, and who will not lie.
To laugh, were want of goodness and of grace,   35
And to be grave, exceeds all Power of face.
I sit with sad civility, I read
With honest anguish, and an aching head;
And drop at last, but in unwilling ears,
This saving counsel, "Keep your piece nine years."   40
  "Nine years!" cries he, who high in Drury-lane,
Lulled by soft Zephyrs through the broken pane,
Rhymes ere he wakes, and prints before *Term* ends,
Obliged by hunger, and request of friends:
"The piece, you think, is incorrect? why, take it,   45
I'm all submission, what you'd have it, make it."
  Three things another's modest wishes bound,
My Friendship, and a Prologue, and ten pound.
  Pitholeon sends to me: "You know his Grace,
I want a Patron; ask him for a Place."   50
  —Pitholeon libeled me—"but here's a letter
Informs you, Sir, 'twas when he knew no better.
Dare you refuse him? Curll invites to dine,
He'll write a *Journal*, or he'll turn Divine."
  Bless me! a packet.—"'Tis a stranger sues,   55
A Virgin Tragedy, an Orphan Muse."
If I dislike it, "Furies, death and rage!"
If I approve, "Commend it to the Stage."
There (thank my stars) my whole Commission ends,
The Players and I are, luckily, no friends.   60
Fired that the house reject him, "'Sdeath I'll print it,
And shame the fools—Your Int'rest, Sir, with Lintot!"
"Lintot, dull rogue! will think your price too much:"
"Not, Sir, if you revise it, and retouch."
All my demurs but double his Attacks;   65
At last he whispers, 'Do; and we go snacks.'
Glad of a quarrel, straight I clap the door,
"Sir, let me see your works and you no more."
'Tis sung, when Midas' Ears began to spring,

41. **Drury-lane:** in the vicinity of Drury Lane Theatre; high because he lives in a garret.
43. **Term:** a session of the law courts. The publishing season coincided with these sessions.
49. **Pitholeon:** a foolish poet of ancient Rhodes who prided himself on his knowledge of Greek. Pope probably means Leonard Welsted, who translated Longinus and also slandered Pope.
53. **Curll:** Edmund Curll, a disreputable bookseller, solicited abusive and scandalous biographies.
54. **Journal . . . divine:** He will attack Pope in the *London Journal* or write a theological treatise.
62. **Lintot:** Bernard Lintot, one of Pope's publishers.
66. **snacks:** shares.

(Midas, a sacred person and a king)   70
His very Minister who spied them first,
(Some say his Queen) was forced to speak, or burst.
And is not mine, my friend, a sorer case,
When every coxcomb perks them in my face?
A. Good friend, forbear! you deal in dang'rous things.   75
I'd never name Queens, Ministers, or Kings;
Keep close to Ears, and those let asses prick;
'Tis nothing—P. Nothing? if they bite and kick?
Out with it, DUNCIAD! let the secret pass,
That secret to each fool, that he's an Ass: 80
The truth once told (and wherefore should we lie?)
The Queen of Midas slept, and so may I.
    You think this cruel? take it for a rule,
No creature smarts so little as a fool.
Let peals of laughter, Codrus! round thee break,   85
Thou unconcerned canst hear the mighty crack:
Pit, Box, and gall'ry in convulsions hurled,
Thou stand'st unshook amidst a bursting world.
Who shames a Scribbler? break one cobweb through,
He spins the slight, self-pleasing thread anew: 90
Destroy his fib or sophistry, in vain,
The creature's at his dirty work again,
Throned in the centre of his thin designs,
Proud of a vast extent of flimsy lines!
Whom have I hurt? has Poet yet, or Peer,   95
Lost the arched eye-brow, or Parnassian sneer?
And has not Colley still his Lord, and whore?
His Butchers Henley, his free-masons Moore?
Does not one table Bavius still admit?
Still to one Bishop Philips seem a wit?   100
Still Sappho—A. Hold! for God's sake—you'll offend,
No Names!—be calm!—learn prudence of a friend!

---

70. **Midas:** Apollo gave Midas, King of Lydia, the ears of an ass for preferring Pan's music to his. When Midas's barber discovered the transformation, he almost burst until he whispered the news into a hole in the ground. By changing the legend Pope seems to be implicating King George II, Queen Caroline, and the King's Minister, Sir Robert Walpole.
79. **Dunciad:** Pope's mock-epic, satirizing his enemies and the literary fools of the day.
85. **Codrus:** a poet ridiculed by Virgil and Juvenal.
97. **Colley:** Colley Cibber, the poet laureate.
98. **Butchers ... Moore:** John Henley,
known as "Orator" Henley, an independent preacher, who on Easter Sunday 1729 gave a sermon to the butchers of Newport Market. James Moore Smyth often headed the processions of the Freemasons.
99. **Bavius:** enemy of Horace and Virgil.
100. **Philips:** The poet Ambrose Philips, known as "Namby Pamby," had been employed by Hugh Boulton, Bishop of Armagh.
101. **Sappho:** Lady Mary Wortley Montagu. In his "Essay on Women," Pope had attacked her under this character. She replied in a satiric poem of her own, attacking Pope's physical defects.

I too could write, and I am twice as tall;
But foes like these—P.   One Flatt'rer's worse than all.
Of all mad creatures, if the learned are right,   105
It is the slaver kills, and not the bite.
A fool quite angry is quite innocent:
Alas! 'tis ten times worse when they *repent*.
    One dedicates in high heroic prose,
And ridicules beyond a hundred foes: 110
One from all Grubstreet will my fame defend,
And, more abusive, calls himself my friend.
This prints my *Letters*, that expects a bribe,
And others roar aloud, "Subscribe, subscribe."
    There are, who to my person pay their court: 115
I cough like *Horace*, and, though lean, am short,
Ammon's great son one shoulder had too high,
Such *Ovid's* nose, and 'Sir! you have an Eye'—
Go on, obliging creatures, make me see
All that disgraced my Betters, met in me.   120
Say for my comfort, languishing in bed,
"Just so immortal *Maro* held his head:"
And when I die, be sure you let me know
Great *Homer* died three thousand years ago.
    Why did I write? what sin to me unknown   125
Dipt me in ink, my parents', or my own?
As yet a child, nor yet a fool to fame,
I lisped in numbers, for the numbers came.
I left no calling for this idle trade,
No duty broke, no father disobeyed.   130
The Muse but served to ease some friend, not Wife,
To help me through this long disease, my Life,
To second, ARBUTHNOT! thy Art and Care,
And teach the Being you preserved, to bear.
    But why then publish? *Granville* the polite,   135
And knowing *Walsh*, would tell me I could write;
Well-natured *Garth* inflamed with early praise;
And *Congreve* loved, and *Swift* endured my lays;

111. **Grubstreet:** Street inhabited by hack writers; a term denoting such authors.
113. **Letters:** Some of Pope's letters had been surreptitiously printed by Curll.
114. **Subscribe:** The quantity of prior subscriptions often determined how many copies of a new book would be printed.
115. **person:** Pope was an asthmatic hunchbacked dwarf.
117. **Ammon's great son:** Alexander the Great.
118. **Ovid's nose:** a pun; family name was Naso.
122. **Maro:** Virgil.

128. **numbers:** poetic meter.
135-141. **Granville . . . St.   John:** Pope lists the distinguished wits and patrons of poetry friendly to Dryden and the youthful Pope: Charles Granville, Lord Lansdowne; William Walsh, poet and critic; Sir Samuel Garth, like Arbuthnot a physician and writer; William Congreve, the playwright; Charles Talbot, Duke of Shrewsbury; Lord Sommers; John Sheffield, Duke of Buckingham; Francis Atterbury, the Tory Bishop of Rochester; Henry St. John, Viscount Bolingbroke.

The courtly *Talbot, Somers, Sheffield* read;
Even mitred *Rochester* would nod the head,   140
And *St. John's* self (great *Dryden's* friends before)
With open arms received one Poet more.
Happy my studies, when by these approved!
Happier their author, when by these beloved!
From these the world will judge of men and books,   145
Not from the *Burnets, Oldmixons,* and *Cookes.*
    Soft were my numbers; who could take offense,
While pure Description held the place of Sense?
Like gentle *Fanny's* was my flowery theme,
A painted mistress, or a purling stream.   150
Yet then did *Gildon* draw his venal quill;—
I wished the man a dinner, and sat still.
Yet then did *Dennis* rave in furious fret;
I never answered,—I was not in debt.
If want provoked, or madness made them print,   155
I waged no war with *Bedlam* or the *Mint.*
    Did some more sober Critic come abroad;
If wrong, I smiled; if right, I kissed the rod.
Pains, reading, study, are their just pretense,
And all they want is spirit, taste, and sense.   160
Commas and points they set exactly right,
And 'twere a sin to rob them of their mite.
Yet ne'er one sprig of laurel graced these ribalds,
From slashing *Bentley* down to pidling *Tibalds:*
Each wight, who reads not, and but scans and spells,   165
Each Word-catcher, that lives on syllables,
Even such small Critics some regard may claim,
Preserved in *Milton's* or in *Shakespeare's* name.
Pretty! in amber to observe the forms
Of hairs, or straws, or dirt, or grubs, or worms!   170
The things, we know, are neither rich nor rare,
But wonder how the devil they got there.
    Were others angry: I excused them too;
Well might they rage, I gave them but their due.

146. **Burnets . . . Cookes:** Thomas Burnet, John Oldmixon, and Thomas Cooke, according to Pope: "Authors of secret and scandalous History."
149. **Fanny's:** Lord Hervey, who like Pope wrote epistles from forsaken mistresses in the manner of "Eloisa to Abelard."
151. **Gildon:** Charles Gildon, a critic who Pope believed had attacked him at the instigation of Addison.
153. **Dennis:** The outspoken critic John Dennis had often attacked Pope.

164. **Bentley . . . Tibalds:** In his edition of *Paradise Lost,* Richard Bentley (1662–1742), a classical scholar, had bracketed all the passages he believed had been falsely inserted in the poem. The Scriblerus Club thought him the perfect pedant. Lewis Theobald (pronounced "Tibald") (1688–1744), a better scholar than Pope, had exposed the errors in Pope's edition of Shakespeare. Pope retaliated by making him the first hero of *The Dunciad;* in later editions he was replaced by Colley Cibber.

A man's true merit 'tis not hard to find;   175
But each man's secret standard in his mind,
That Casting-weight pride adds to emptiness,
This, who can gratify? for who can *guess*?
The Bard whom pilfered Pastorals renown,
Who turns a Persian tale for half a Crown,   180
Just writes to make his barrenness appear,
And strains, from hard-bound brains, eight lines a year;
He, who still wanting, though he lives on theft,
Steals much, spends little, yet has nothing left:
And He, who now to sense, now nonsense leaning,   185
Means not, but blunders round about a meaning:
And He, whose fustian's so sublimely bad,
It is not Poetry, but prose run mad:
All these, my modest Satire bade *translate*,
And owned that nine such Poets made a *Tate*.   190
How did they fume, and stamp, and roar, and chafe!
And swear, not ADDISON himself was safe.
     Peace to all such! but were there One whose fires
True Genius kindles, and fair Fame inspires;
Blest with each talent and each art to please,   195
And born to write, converse, and live with ease:
Should such a man, too fond to rule alone,
Bear, like the Turk, no brother near the throne.
View him with scornful, yet with jealous eyes,
And hate for arts that caused himself to rise;   200
Damn with faint praise, assent with civil leer,
And without sneering, teach the rest to sneer;
Willing to wound, and yet afraid to strike,
Just hint a fault, and hesitate dislike;
Alike reserved to blame, or to commend,   205
A tim'rous foe, and a suspicious friend;
Dreading even fools, by Flatt'rers besieged,
And so obliging, that he ne'er obliged;
Like *Cato*, give his little Senate laws,
And sit attentive to his own applause;   210
While Wits and Templars every sentence raise,
And wonder with a foolish face of praise:—

177. **Casting-weight:** the weight that tips the scales.
179–180. **Bard . . . Crown:** Ambrose Philips, whose pastorals appeared at the same time as Pope's.
190. **nine . . . Tate:** from the saying "it takes nine tailors to make a man." Nahum Tate (1652–1715) was poet laureate from 1692 until his death. He gave *King Lear* a happy ending.

192. **Addison:** Joseph Addison (1672–1719), co-author of the *Tatler* and the *Spectator*, was perhaps the most influential writer of his day. In the lines which follow Pope describes him as Atticus.
209. **Cato:** the name of Addison's classical tragedy, much admired in 1713. This line is similar to one Pope himself wrote for the Prologue of the play.
211. **Templars:** law students.

Who but must laugh, if such a man there be?
Who would not weep, if ATTICUS were he?
   What though my Name stood rubric on the walls,   215
Or plaistered posts, with claps, in capitals?
Or smoking forth, a hundred hawker's load,
On wings of winds came flying all abroad?
I sought no homage from the Race that write;
I kept, like *Asian* Monarchs, from their sight: 220
Poems I heeded (now be-rhymed so long)
No more than thou, great GEORGE! a birth-day song.
I ne'er with wits or witlings passed my days,
To spread about the itch of verse and praise;
Nor like a puppy, daggled through the town,   225
To fetch and carry sing-song up and down;
Nor at Rehearsals sweat, and mouthed, and cried,
With handkerchief and orange at my side.
But sick of fops, and poetry, and prate,
To *Bufo* left the whole *Castalian* state.   230
   Proud as *Apollo* on his forkèd hill,
Sat full-blown *Bufo*, puffed by every quill;
Fed with soft Dedication all day long,
Horace and he went hand in hand in song.
His Library (where busts of Poets dead   235
And a true *Pindar* stood without a head,)
Received of wits an undistinguished race,
Who first his judgment asked, and then a place:
Much they extolled his pictures, much his seat,
And flattered every day, and some days eat: 240
Till grown more frugal in his riper days,
He paid some bards with port, and some with praise;
To some a dry rehearsal was assigned,
And others (harder still) he paid in kind.
Dryden alone (what wonder?) came not nigh,   245
Dryden alone escaped this judging eye:
But still the *Great* kindness in reserve,
He helped to bury whom he helped to starve.
   May some choice patron bless each grey goose quill!
May every *Bavius* have his *Bufo* still!   250
So, when a Statesman wants a day's defense,
Or Envy holds a whole week's war with Sense,

---

214. **Atticus:** Addison. Atticus was a
wealthy man of letters and a friend of
Cicero.
215. **rubric:** in red letters.
216. **claps:** posters.
222. **George:** King George II.
230. **Bufo . . . state:** Bufo, signifying a
buffoon. Castalia was a spring on Parnassus.
231. **forkèd hill:** Parnassus had two peaks,
one sacred to Apollo, the other to Bacchus.
236. **Pindar:** Greek lyric poet of the early
5th century B.C.

Or simple pride for flatt'ry makes demands,
May dunce by dunce be whistled off my hands!
Blest be the *Great*! for those they take away,   255
And those they left me; for they left me GAY;
Left me to see neglected Genius bloom,
Neglected die, and tell it on his tomb:
Of all thy blameless life the sole return
My Verse, and QUEENSB'RY weeping o'er thy urn!   260
     Oh let me live my own, and die so too!
(To live and die is all I have to do:)
Maintain a Poet's dignity and ease,
And see what friends, and read what books I please;
Above a Patron, though I condescend   265
Sometimes to call a minister my friend.
I was not born for Courts or great affairs;
I pay my debts, believe, and say my prayers;
Can sleep without a Poem in my head;
Nor know, if *Dennis* be alive or dead.   270
     Why am I asked what next shall see the light?
Heavens! was I born for nothing but to write?
Has Life no joys for me? or, (to be grave)
Have I no friend to serve, no soul to save?
"I found him close with *Swift*"—'Indeed? no doubt,'   275
(Cries prating *Balbus*) 'something will come out.'
'Tis all in vain, deny it as I will.
"No, such a Genius never can lie still;"
And then for mine obligingly mistakes
The first Lampoon Sir *Will.* or *Bubo* makes.   280
Poor guiltless I! and can I choose but smile,
When every Coxcomb knows me by my *Style*?
     Curst be the verse, how well soe'er it flow,
That tends to make one worthy man my foe,
Give Virtue scandal, Innocence a fear,   285
Or from the soft-eyed Virgin steal a tear!
But he who hurts a harmless neighbor's peace,
Insults fallen worth, or Beauty in distress,
Who loves a Lie, lame slander helps about,
Who writes a Libel, or who copies out: 290
That Fop, whose pride affects a patron's name,
Yet absent, wounds an author's honest fame:
Who can *your* merit *selfishly* approve,
And show the *sense* of it without the *love*;

256. **Gay**: John Gay (1685–1732), author
of the *Beggar's Opera*, spent his last year's
under the patronage of the Duchess of
Queensberry.

280. **Sir ... Bubo**: Sir William Yonge, a
Whig politician and poet; George Bubb
(Bubo) Doddington, a Whig patron of
letters.

Who has the vanity to call you friend,   295
Yet wants the honor, injured, to defend;
Who tells whate'er you think, whate'er you say,
And, if he lie not, must at least betray:
Who to the *Dean*, and *silver bell* can swear,
And sees at *Canons* what was never there;   300
Who reads, but with a lust to misapply,
Make Satire a Lampoon, and Fiction, Lie.
A lash like mine no honest man shall dread,
But all such babbling blockheads in his stead.
    Let *Sporus* tremble—A.   What? that thing of silk,   305
Sporus, that mere white curd of Ass's milk?
Satire or sense, alas! can *Sporus* feel?
Who breaks a butterfly upon a wheel?
P.   Yet let me flap this bug with gilded wings,
This painted child of dirt, that stinks and stings;   310
Whose buzz the witty and the fair annoys,
Yet wit ne'er tastes, and beauty ne'er enjoys:
So well-bred spaniels civilly delight
In mumbling of the game they dare not bite.
Eternal smiles his emptiness betray,   315
As shallow streams run dimpling all the way.
Whether in florid impotence he speaks,
And, as the prompter breathes, the puppet squeaks;
Or at the ear of *Eve*, familiar Toad,
Half froth, half venom, spits himself abroad,   320
In puns, or politics, or tales, or lies,
Or spite, or smut, or rhymes, or blasphemies.
His wit all see-saw, between *that* and *this*,
Now high, now low, now master up, now miss,
And he himself one vile Antithesis.   325
Amphibious thing! that acting either part,
The trifling head or the corrupted heart,
Fop at the toilet, flatt'rer at the board,
Now trips a Lady, and now struts a Lord.
Eve's tempter thus the Rabbins have exprest,   330
A Cherub's face, a reptile all the rest;
Beauty that shocks you, parts that none will trust;
Wit that can creep, and pride that licks the dust.

299–300. **Dean...Canons:** Pope was falsely accused of having Cannons, the Duke of Chandos's estate, in mind when he satirized Timon's villa in his "Moral Essay IV." There Pope says that Timon's chapel has a silver bell and a dean who never offends his polite audience.

305. **Sporus:** a boy whom Nero publicly married; in this poem Lord Hervey, the effeminate Whig nobleman and friend of Queen Caroline.
330. **Rabbins:** rabbis; Jewish authorities on doctrine.

Not Fortune's worshipper, nor fashion's fool,
Not Lucre's madman, nor Ambition's tool,   335
Not proud, nor servile;—be one Poet's praise,
That, if he pleased, he pleased by manly ways:
That Flatt'ry, even to Kings, he held a shame,
And thought a Lie in verse or prose the same.
That not in Fancy's maze he wandered long,   340
But stooped to Truth, and moralized his song:
That not for Fame, but Virtue's better end,
He stood the furious foe, the timid friend,
The damning critic, half approving wit,
The coxcomb hit, or fearing to be hit;   345
Laughed at the loss of friends he never had,
The dull, the proud, the wicked, and the mad;
The distant threats of vengeance on his head
The blow unfelt, the tear he never shed;
The tale revived, the lie so oft o'erthrown,   350
Th' imputed trash, and dulness not his own;
The morals blackened when the writings scape,
The libeled person, and the pictured shape;
Abuse, on all he loved, or loved him, spread,
A friend in exile, or a father, dead;   355
The whisper, that to greatness still too near,
Perhaps, yet vibrates on his Sov'reign's ear:—
Welcome for thee, fair *Virtue!* all the past;
For thee, fair *Virtue!* welcome even the *last!*
  A.   But why insult the poor, affront the great?   360
P.   A knave's a knave, to me, in every state:
Alike my scorn, if he succeed or fail,
Sporus at court, or *Japhet* in a jail,
A hireling scribbler, or a hireling peer,
Knight of the post corrupt, or of the shire;   365
If on a Pillory, or near a Throne,
He gain his Prince's ear, or lose his own.
  Yet soft by nature, more a dupe than wit,
Sappho can tell you how this man was bit;
This dreaded Sat'rist *Dennis* will confess   370
Foe to his pride, but friend to his distress:
So humble, he has knocked at *Tibbald's* door,
Has drunk with *Cibber*, nay, has rhymed for *Moore.*
Full ten years slandered, did he once reply?

---

363. **Japhet:** Japhet Crook, a forger.
365. **Knight ... post:** one who got his
living by selling false evidence.
369. **bit:** fooled.

371. **friend ... distress:** Pope wrote a
prologue for Dennis's play *The Provoked
Husband*, performed in 1733 for Dennis's
benefit.

Three thousand suns went down on *Welsted's* lie.   375
To please a Mistress one aspersed his life;
He lashed him not, but let her be his wife.
Let *Budgel* charge low *Grubstreet* on his quill,
And write whate'er he pleased, except his Will;
Let the two *Curlls* of Town and Court, abuse   380
His father, mother, body, soul, and muse.
Yet why? that Father held it for a rule,
It was a sin to call our neighbor fool:
That harmless Mother thought no wife a whore:
Hear this, and spare has family, *James Moore*!   385
Unspotted names, and memorable long!
If there be force in Virtue, or in Song.
    Of gentle blood (part shed in Honour's cause,
While yet in *Britain* Honour had applause)
Each parent sprung—A.   What fortune, pray?—P.
    Their own,   390
And better got, than *Bestia's* from the throne.
Born to no Pride, inheriting no Strife,
Nor marrying Discord in a noble wife,
Stranger to civil and religious rage,
The good man walked innoxious through his age.   395
Nor Courts he saw, no suits would ever try,
Nor dared an Oath, nor hazarded a Lie.
Un-learned, he knew no schoolman's subtle art,
No language, but the language of the heart.
By Nature honest, by Experience wise,   400
Healthy by temp'rance, and by exercise;
His life, though long, to sickness past unknown,
His death was instant, and without a groan.
O grant me, thus to live, and thus to die!
Who sprung from Kings shall know less joy than I.   405
    O Friend! may each domestic bliss be thine!
Be no unpleasing Melancholy mine:
Me, let the tender office long engage,
To rock the cradle of reposing Age,
With lenient arts extend a Mother's breath,   410

375. **Three ... lie:** Pope's own note says that Welsted falsely accused him of causing a lady's death and of libelling the Duke of Chandos after receiving £500 from that nobleman.
376. **one:** not known.
378–79. **Budgel ... Will:** Eustace Budgel thought that Pope had attacked him in the *Grub Street Journal* for forging Dr. Matthew Tindal's will and taking that man's estate away from his heirs.
380. **two Curlls:** the publisher and Lord Hervey.
391. **Bestia:** L. Calpurnius Bestia, a Roman consul bribed by Jurgurtha into a dishonorable peace. Here the Duke of Marlborough.
397. **Oath:** As a Catholic, Pope's father would neither swear an oath against the Pope nor one to the Anglican Church.
410. **Mother's breath:** At the time he wrote these lines, Pope was nursing his dying mother.

Make Langour smile, and smooth the bed of Death,
Explore the thought, explain the asking eye,
And keep a while one parent from the sky!
On cares like these if length of days attend,
May Heaven, to bless those days, preserve my friend,   415
Preserve him social, cheerful, and serene,
And just as rich as when he served a Queen.
A. Whether that blessing be denied or given,
Thus far was right, the rest belongs to Heaven.

Engraved on the Collar of a Dog, Which I Gave to His Royal Highness

I am his Highness' dog at Kew;   1
Pray tell me, sir, whose dog are you?

JOHN WILMOT, EARL OF ROCHESTER
[1647–1680]

The Maimed Debauchee

1

As some brave *Admiral*, in former war
  Deprived of force, but prest with courage still,
Two rival fleets appearing from afar,
  Crawls to the top of an adjacent hill;

2

From whence (with thoughts full of concern) he views   5
  The wise, and daring, conduct of the fight:
And each bold action to his mind renews,
  His present glory, and his past delight.

3

From his fierce eyes flashes of rage he throws,
  As from black clouds when lightning breaks away,   10
Transported thinks himself amidst his foes,
  And absent yet enjoys the bloody day.

Royal Highness: Prince Frederick, son of George II.

1. **Kew:** a royal palace and garden about nine miles up the Thames from London.

4

So when my days of impotence approach,
  And I'm by love and wine's unlucky chance,
Driven from the pleasing billows of debauch,   15
  On the dull shore of lazy temperance

5

My pains at last some respite shall afford,
  While I behold the battles you maintain:
When fleets of glasses sail around the board,
  From whose broad-sides volleys of wit shall rain.   20

6

Nor shall the sight of honourable scars,
  Which my too forward valour did procure,
Frighten new-listed soldiers from the wars,
  Past joys have more than paid what I endure.

7

Should some brave youth (worth being drunk) prove nice,   25
  And from his fair inviter meanly shrink,
'Twould please the ghost of my departed vice,
  If, at my counsel, he repent and drink.

8

Or should some cold-complexioned sot forbid,
  With his dull morals, our night's brisk alarms;   30
I'll fire his blood by telling what I did,
  When I was strong, and able to bear arms.

9

I'll tell of whores attack'd their lords at home,
  Bawds' quarters beaten up, and fortress won;
Windows demolished, watches overcome,   35
  And handsome ills by my contrivance done.

10

With tales like these I will such heat inspire,
  As to important mischief shall incline;
I'll make him long some ancient church to fire,
  And fear no lewdness they're called to by wine.   40

11

Thus statesman-like I'll saucily impose,
  And, safe from danger, valiantly advise;
Sheltered in impotence urge you to blows,
  And, being good for nothing else, be wise.

MATTHEW PRIOR [1664–1721]

An Ode

The merchant, to secure his treasure,
  Conveys it in a borrowed name:
Euphelia serves to grace my measure;
  But Cloe is my real flame.

My softest verse, my darling lyre,   5
  Upon Euphelia's toilet lay;
When Cloe noted her desire,
  That I should sing, that I should play.

My lyre I tune, my voice I raise;
  But with my numbers mix my sighs: 10
And whilst I sing Euphelia's praise,
  I fixed my soul on Cloe's eyes.

Fair Cloe blushed: Euphelia frowned:
  I sung and gazed: I played and trembled:
And Venus to the loves around   15
  Remarked, how ill we all dissembled.

JONATHAN SWIFT [1667–1745]

A Description of the Morning

Now hardly here and there an hackney-coach
Appearing, showed the ruddy morn's approach.
Now Betty from her master's bed had flown,
And softly stole to discompose her own.

---

3. **measure:** song.   10. **numbers:** meter, or the song itself.

The slipshod prentice from his master's door,   5
Had pared the dirt, and sprinkled round the floor.
Now Moll had whirled her mop with dext'rous airs,
Prepared to scrub the entry and the stairs.
The youth with broomy stumps began to trace
The kennel-edge, where wheels had worn the place.   10
The smallcoal-man was heard with cadence deep,
'Till drowned in shriller notes of chimney-sweep,
Duns at his lordship's gate began to meet,
And brickdust Moll had screamed through half the street.
The turnkey now his flock returning sees,   15
Duly let out a'nights to steal for fees.
The watchful bailiffs take their silent stands,
And school-boys lag with satchels in their hands.

The Progress of Beauty

When first Diana leaves her bed
Vapors and steams her looks disgrace,
A frowzy dirty coloured red
Sits on her cloudy wrinkled face.

But by degrees when mounted high   5
Her artificial face appears
Down from her window in the sky
Her spots are gone, her visage clears.

'Twixt earthly females and the moon
All parallels exactly run;   10
If Celia should appear too soon
Alas, the nymph would be undone.

To see her from her pillow rise
All reeking in a cloudy steam,
Cracked lips, foul teeth, and gummy eyes,   15
Poor Strephon, how would he blaspheme!

The soot or powder which was wont
To make her hair look black as jet,
Falls from her tresses on her front
A mingled mass of dirt and sweat.   20

10. **kennel-edge:** gutter.
13. **Duns:** creditors seeking payment.

chastity.
11. **Celia:** in Latin, heaven.
16. **Strephon:** conventional name for an amorous shepherd.

1. **Diana:** the moon and the goddess of

Three colours, black, and red, and white,
So graceful in their proper place,
Remove them to a different light
They form a frightful hideous face,

For instance; when the lily slips   25
Into the precincts of the rose,
And takes possession of the lips,
Leaving the purple to the nose.

So Celia went entire to bed,
All her complexions safe and sound,   30
But when she rose, the black and red
Though still in sight, had changed their ground.

The black, which would not be confined
A more inferior station seeks
Leaving the fiery red behind,   35
And mingles in her muddy cheeks.

The paint by perspiration cracks,
And falls in rivulets of sweat,
On either side you see the tracks,
While at her chin the confluents met.   40

A skillful housewife thus her thumb
With spittle while she spins, anoints,
And thus the brown Meanders come
In trickling streams betwixt her joints.

But Celia can with ease reduce   45
By help of pencil, paint and brush
Each colour to its place and use,
And teach her cheeks again to blush.

She knows her early self no more
But filled with admiration, stands,   50
As other painters oft adore
The workmanship of their own hands.

Thus after four important hours
Celia's the wonder of her sex;
Say, which among the heavenly powers   55
Could cause such wonderful effects.

---

40. **confluents:** tributaries, also pimples or pustules run together.

43. **Meander:** river near Troy, synonymous with winding stream.

Venus, indulgent to her kind
Gave women all their hearts could wish
When first she taught them where to find
White lead, and Lusitanian dish.   60

Love with white lead cements his wings,
White lead was sent us to repair
Two brightest, brittlest earthly things
A lady's face, and China ware.

She ventures now to lift the sash,   65
The window is her proper sphere;
Ah lovely nymph be not too rash,
Nor let the beaux approach too near.

Take pattern by your sister star,
Delude at once and bless our sight,   70
When you are seen, be seen from far,
And chiefly choose to shine by night.

In the Pell-mell when passing by,
Keep up the glasses of your chair,
Then each transported fop will cry,   75
G-d d-m me Jack, she's wondrous fair.

But, art no longer can prevail
When the materials all are gone,
The best mechanic hand must fail
Where nothing's left to work upon.   80

Matter, as wise logicians say,
Cannot without a form subsist,
And form, say I, as well as they,
Must fail if matter brings no grist.

And this is fair Diana's case   85
For, all astrologers maintain
Each night a bit drops off her face
When mortals say she's in her wane.

While Partridge wisely shows the cause
Efficient of the moon's decay,   90
That Cancer with his pois'nous claws
Attacks her in the Milky Way:

60. **White lead: Lusitanian:** cosmetic; Portuguese.
73. **Pell-mell:** Pall Mall, in St. James's Park.
74. **chair:** sedan chair.

89. **Partridge:** John Partridge, astrologer and almanac writer, satirized by Swift in the *Bickerstaff Papers*.
91. **Cancer:** the crab, one of the signs of the Zodiac.

But Gadbury in art profound
From her pale cheeks pretends to show
That swain Endymion is not sound,   95
Or else that Mercury's her foe.

But, let the cause be what it will,
In half a month she looks so thin
That Flamstead can with all his skill
See but her forehead and her chin   100

Yet as she wastes, she grows discreet,
Till midnight never shows her head;
So rotting Celia strolls the street
When sober folks are all a-bed.

For sure if this be Luna's fate,   105
Poor Celia, but of mortal race
In vain expects a longer date
To the materials of her face.

When mercury her tresses mows
To think of oil and soot, is vain,   110
No painting can restore a nose,
Nor will her teeth return again.

Two balls of glass may serve for eyes,
White lead can plaster up a cleft,
But these alas, are poor supplies   115
If neither cheeks, nor lips be left.

Ye powers who over love preside,
Since mortal beauties drop so soon,
If you would have us well supplied,
Send us new nymphs with each new moon.   120

The Progress of Poetry

The farmer's goose, who in the stubble,
Has fed without restraint or trouble,
Grown fat with corn and sitting still,
Can scarce get o'er the barn door sill;

93. **Gadbury:** John Gadbury, another astrologer.
95. **Endymion . . . sound:** a youthful shepherd beloved by the moon. He is suspected of having a venereal disease.
96. **Mercury's:** a pun; mercury was used, sometimes with ill effects, as a cure for syphilis.
99. **Flamstead:** John Flamstead, first astronomer royal.
111. **nose:** In its later stages syphilis can attack the cartilage of the nose.

And hardly waddles forth to cool   5
Her belly in the neighboring pool;
Nor loudly cackles at the door,
For cackling shows the goose is poor.
   But when she must be turned to graze,
And round the barren common strays,   10
Hard exercise and harder fare
Soon make my dame grow lank and spare:
Her body light, she tries her wings,
And scorns the ground, and upward springs,
While all the parish, as she flies,   15
Hear sounds harmonious from the skies.
   Such is the poet, fresh in pay
(The third night's profits of his play),
His morning draughts till noon can swill,
Among his brethren of the quill: 20
With good roast beef his belly full,
Grown lazy, foggy, fat, and dull:
Deep sunk in plenty and delight,
What poet e'er could take his flight?
Or stuffed with phlegm up to the throat,   25
What poet e'er could sing a note?
Nor Pegasus could bear the load
Along the high celestial road;
The steed, oppressed, would break his girth,
To raise the lumber from the earth.   30
   But view him in another scene,
When all his drink is Hippocrene,
His money spent, his patrons fail,
His credit out for cheese and ale;
His two-years' coat so smooth and bare,   35
Through every thread it lets in air;
With hungry meals his body pined,
His guts and belly full of wind;
And, like a jockey for a race,
His flesh brought down to flying case: 40
Now his exalted spirit loathes
Encumbrances of food and clothes;
And up he rises like a vapor,
Supported high on wings of paper;
He singing flies, and flying sings,   45
While from below all Grub Street rings.

18. **third . . . play:** the profits from the
third performance went to the author.
27. **Pegasus:** winged horse of poetic
inspiration.

32. **Hippocrene:** a spring at Mt. Helicon,
sacred to the Muses.
40. **case:** trim.
46. **Grub Street:** home of hack writers.

A Satirical Elegy on the
Death of a Late Famous General

His Grace! impossible! what dead!
Of old age too, and in his bed!

And could that Mighty Warrior fall?
And so inglorious, after all!
Well, since he's gone, no matter how,   5
The last loud trump must wake him now:
And, trust me, as the noise grows stronger,
He'd wish to sleep a little longer.
And could he be indeed so old
As by the newspapers we're told?   10
Threescore, I think, is pretty high;
'Twas time in conscience he should die.
This world he cumbered long enough;
He burnt his candle to the snuff;
And that's the reason, some folks think,   15
He left behind so great a stink.

Behold his funeral appears,
Nor widow's sighs, nor orphan's tears,
Wont at such times each heart to pierce,
Attend the progress of his hearse.   20
But what of that, his friends may say,
He had those honors in his day.
True to his profit and his pride,
He made them weep before he died.

Come hither, all ye empty things,   25
Ye bubbles raised by breath of Kings;
Who float upon the tide of state,
Come hither, and behold your fate.
Let pride be taught by this rebuke,
How very mean a thing's a Duke;   30
From all his ill-got honors flung,
Turned to that dirt from whence he sprung.

General: The Duke of Marlborough,
generally despised by the Tory satirists.

SAMUEL JOHNSON [1709–1784]

The Vanity of Human Wishes
The Tenth Satire of Juvenal, Imitated

Let observation with extensive view,
Survey mankind, from China to Peru;
Remark each anxious toil, each eager strife,
And watch the busy scenes of crouded life;
Then say how hope and fear, desire and hate,   5
O'erspread with snares the clouded maze of fate,
Where wav'ring man, betray'd by vent'rous pride,
To tread the dreary paths without a guide;
As treach'rous phantoms in the mist delude,
Shuns fancied ills, or chases airy good.   10
How rarely reason guides the stubborn choice,
Rules the bold hand, or promps the suppliant voice,
How nations sink, by daring schemes oppress'd,
When vengeance listens to the fool's request.
Fate wings with ev'ry wish th' afflictive dart,   15
Each gift of nature, and each grace of art,
With fatal heat impetuous courage glows,
With fatal sweetness elocution flows,
Impeachment stops the speaker's pow'rful breath,
And restless fire precipitates on death.   20
    But scarce observ'd the knowing and the bold,
Fall in the gen'ral massacre of gold;
Wide-wasting pest! that rages unconfin'd,
And crouds with crimes the records of mankind,
For gold his sword the hireling ruffian draws,   25
For gold the hireling judge distorts the laws;
Wealth heap'd on wealth, nor truth nor safety buys,
The dangers gather as the treasures rise.
    Let hist'ry tell where rival kings command,
And dubious title shakes the madded land,   30
When statutes glean the refuse of the sword,
How much more safe the vassal than the lord,
Low skulks the hind beneath the rage of pow'r,
And leaves the wealthy traytor in the Tow'r,

Juvenal: Roman satirist (60?–140). This
text follows eighteenth-century spelling and
capitalization.

Untouch'd his cottage, and his slumbers sound,   35
Tho' confiscation's vulturs hover round.
   The needy traveller, serene and gay,
Walks the wild heath, and sings his toil away.
Does envy seize thee? crush th' upbraiding joy,
Increase his riches and his peace destroy,   40
New fears in dire vicissitude invade,
The rustling brake alarms, and quiv'ring shade,
Nor light nor darkness bring his pain relief,
One shews the plunder, and one hides the thief.
   Yet still one gen'ral cry the skies assails,   45
And gain and grandeur load the tainted gales;
Few know the toiling statesman's fear or care,
Th' insidious rival and the gaping heir.
   Once more, Democritus, arise on earth,
With chearful wisdom and instructive mirth,   50
See motly life in modern trappings dress'd,
And feed with varied fools th' eternal jest:
Thou who couldst laugh where want enchain'd caprice,
Toil crush'd conceit, and man was of a piece;
Where wealth unlov'd without a mourner dy'd;   55
And scarce a sycophant was fed by pride;
Where ne'er was known the form of mock debate,
Or seen a new-made mayor's unwieldy state;
Where change of fav'rites made no change of laws,
And senates heard before they judg'd a cause;   60
How wouldst thou shake at Britain's modish tribe,
Dart the quick taunt, and edge the piercing gibe?
Attentive truth and nature to decry,
And pierce each scene with philosophic eye.
To thee were solemn toys or empty shew,   65
The robes of pleasure and the veils of woe:
All aid the farce, and all thy mirth maintain,
Whose joys are causeless, or whose griefs are vain.
   Such was the scorn that fill'd the sage's mind,
Renew'd at ev'ry glance on humankind;   70
How just that scorn ere yet thy voice declare,
Search every state, and canvass ev'ry pray'r.
   Unnumber'd suppliants croud Preferment's gate,
Athirst for wealth, and burning to be great;
Delusive Fortune hears th' incessant call,   75
They mount, they shine, evaporate, and fall.
On ev'ry stage the foes of peace attend,

42. **brake**: thicket.
49. **Democritus**: Greek philosopher of the late 5th century B.C., known as the laughing philosopher.

Hate dogs their flight, and insult mocks their end.
Love ends with hope, the sinking statesman's door
Pours in the morning worshiper no more;   80
For growing names the weekly scribbler lies,
To growing wealth the dedicator flies,
From every room descends the painted face,
That hung the bright Palladium of the place,
And smoak'd in kitchens, or in auctions sold,   85
To better features yields the frame of gold;
For now no more we trace in ev'ry line
Heroic worth, benevolence divine:
The form distorted justifies the fall,
And detestation rids th' indignant wall.   90
   But will not Britain hear the last appeal,
Sign her foes doom, or guard her fav'rites zeal;
Through Freedom's sons no more remonstrance rings,
Degrading nobles and controuling kings;
Our supple tribes repress their patriot throats,   95
And ask no questions but the price of votes;
With weekly libels and septennial ale,
Their wish is full to riot and to rail.
   In full-blown dignity, see Wolsey stand,
Law in his voice, and fortune in his hand: 100
To him the church, the realm, their pow'rs consign,
Thro' him the rays of regal bounty shine,
Turn'd by his nod the stream of honour flows,
His smile alone security bestows:
Still to new heights his restless wishes tow'r,   105
Claim leads to claim, and pow'r advances pow'r;
Till conquest unresisted ceas'd to please,
And rights submitted, left him none to seize.
At length his sov'reign frowns—the train of state
Mark the keen glance, and watch the sign to hate.   110
Where-e'er he turns he meets a stranger's eye,
His suppliants scorn him, and his followers fly;
At once is lost the pride of aweful state,
The golden canopy, the glitt'ring plate,
The regal palace, the luxurious board,   115
The liv'ried army, and the menial lord.
   With age, with cares, with maladies oppress'd,

84. Palladium: an icon which protects, named after the statue of Pallas Athene which after falling from heaven preserved the Trojans until Diomedes stole it.
97. septennial ale: ale given out during elections, which occur at least once every seven years.

99. Wolsey: Thomas Cardinal Wolsey (1475?–1530), for a while Lord Chancellor under Henry VIII. He built Hampton Court as his own palace.

He seeks the refuge of monastic rest.
Grief aids disease, remember'd folly stings,
And his last sighs reproach the faith of kings.   120
    Speak thou, whose thoughts at humble peace repine,
Shall Wolsey's wealth, with Wolsey's end be thine?
Or liv'st thou now, with safer pride content,
The wisest justice on the banks of Trent?
For why did Wolsey near the steeps of fate,   125
On weak foundations raise th' enormous weight?
Why but to sink beneath misfortune's blow,
With louder ruin to the gulphs below?
    What gave great Villiers to th' assassin's knife,
And fix'd disease on Harley's closing life?   130
What murder'd Wentworth, and what exil'd Hyde,
By kings protected, and to kings ally'd?
What but their wish indulg'd in courts to shine,
And pow'r too great to keep, or to resign?
    When first the college rolls receive his name,   135
The young enthusiast quits his ease for fame;
Through all his veins the fever of renown
Spreads from the strong contagion of the gown;
O'er Bodley's dome his future labours spread,
And Bacon's mansion trembles o'er his head.   140
Are these thy views? proceed, illustrious youth,
And virtue guard thee to the throne of Truth!
Yet should thy soul indulge the gen'rous heat,
Till captive Science yields her last retreat;
Should Reason guide thee with her brightest ray,   145
And pour on misty Doubt resistless day;
Should no false Kindness lure to loose delight,
Nor Praise relax, nor Difficulty fright;
Should tempting Novelty thy cell refrain,
And Sloth effuse her opiate fumes in vain;   150
Should Beauty blunt on fops her fatal dart,
Nor claim the triumph of a letter'd heart;
Should no Disease thy torpid veins invade,
Nor Melancholy's phantoms haunt thy shade;
Yet hope not life from grief or danger free,   155

129. **Villiers:** George Villiers, 1st Duke of Buckingham, a favorite of Charles I, was assassinated in 1628.
130. **Harley:** Robert Harley, Earl of Oxford and leader of the Tories, was imprisoned by the Whigs in 1715.
131. **Wentworth:** Thomas Wentworth, Earl of Strafford, an adviser to Charles I, was impeached and executed in 1641.
131–32. **Hyde . . . Ally'd:** Edward Hyde, Earl of Clarendon, the famous historian and statesman, was impeached in 1667. His daughter married James II.
139. **Bodley's dome:** the Bodleian Library, Oxford.
140. **Bacon's mansion:** according to legend, the study of Roger Bacon (1214–1294) would collapse when a greater man came to Oxford.

Nor think the doom of man revers'd for thee:
Deign on the passing world to turn thine eyes,
And pause awhile from letters, to be wise;
There mark what ills the scholar's life assail,
Toil, envy, want, the patron, and the jail.   160
See nations slowly wise, and meanly just,
To buried merit raise the tardy bust.
If dreams yet flatter, once again attend,
Hear Lydiat's life, and Galileo's end.
    Nor deem, when learning her last prize bestows   165
The glitt'ring eminence exempt from foes;
See when the vulgar 'scape, despis'd or aw'd,
Rebellion's vengeful talons seize on Laud.
From meaner minds, tho' smaller fines content
The plunder'd palace or sequester'd rent;   170
Mark'd out by dangerous parts he meets the shock,
And fatal Learning leads him to the block:
Around his tomb let Art and Genius weep,
But hear his death, ye blockheads, hear and sleep.
    The festal blazes, the triumphal show,   175
The ravish'd standard, and the captive foe,
The senate's thanks, the gazette's pompous tale,
With force resistless o'er the brave prevail.
Such bribes the rapid Greek o'er Asia whirl'd,
For such the steady Romans shook the world;   180
For such in distant lands the Britons shine,
And stain with blood the Danube or the Rhine;
This pow'r has praise, that virtue scarce can warm,
Till fame supplies the universal charm.
Yet Reason frowns on War's unequal game,   185
Where wasted nations raise a single name,
And mortgag'd states their grandsires wreaths regret,
From age to age in everlasting debt;
Wreaths which at last the dear-bought right convey
To rust on medals, or on stones decay.   190
    On what foundation stands the warrior's pride,
How just his hopes let Swedish Charles decide;
A frame of adamant, a soul of fire,
No dangers fright him, and no labours tire;
O'er love, o'er fear extends his wide domain,   195
Unconquer'd lord of pleasure and of pain;

---

164. **Lydiat's . . . end:** Thomas Lydiat (1572–1646), an Oxford scholar and a royalist, who died in poverty. Galileo was imprisoned as a heretic and died blind.
168. **Laud:** Archbishop of Canterbury, executed by the Puritans in 1645.
170. **sequester'd:** confiscated.
179. **Greek:** Alexander the Great.
192. **Charles:** Charles XII of Sweden (1682–1718).

No joys to him pacific scepters yield,
War sounds the trump, he rushes to the field;
Behold surrounding kings their pow'r combine,
And one capitulate, and one resign;   200
Peace courts his hand, but spreads her charms in vain;
"Think nothing gain'd, he cries, till nought remain,
"On Moscow's walls till Gothic standards fly,
"And all be mine beneath the polar sky."
The march begins in military state,   205
And nations on his eye suspended wait;
Stern Famine guards the solitary coast,
And Winter barricades the realms of Frost;
He comes, not want and cold his course delay;—
Hide, blushing Glory, hide Pultowa's day: 210
The vanquish'd hero leaves his broken bands,
And shews his miseries in distant lands;
Condemn'd a needy supplicant to wait,
While ladies interpose, and slaves debate.
But did not Chance at length her error mend?   215
Did no subverted empire mark his end?
Did rival monarchs give the fatal wound?
Or hostile millions press him to the ground?
His fall was destin'd to a barren strand,
A petty fortress, and a dubious hand;   220
He left the name, at which the world grew pale,
To point a moral, or adorn a tale.
    All times their scenes of pompous woes afford,
From Persia's tyrant to Bavaria's lord.
In gay hostility, and barb'rous pride,   225
With half mankind embattled at his side,
Great Xerxes comes to seize the certain prey,
And starves exhausted regions in his way;
Attendant Flatt'ry counts his myriads o'er,
Till counted myriads sooth his pride no more;   230
Fresh praise is try'd till madness fires his mind,
The waves he lashes, and enchains the wind;
New pow'rs are claim'd, new pow'rs are still bestow'd,
Till rude resistance lops the spreading god;

200. **one . . . resign:** Frederick IV of Denmark was defeated in 1700; Augustus I of Poland, deposed in 1704, was succeeded by Stanislaus I, Charles's choice.
203. **Gothic:** Teutonic or northern.
210. **Pultowa:** where the Russians defeated Charles. Afterwards he fled to Turkey in hopes of forming an alliance against Russia.

219. **barren strand:** He died attacking Fredericksheld in Norway.
220. **dubious hand:** He was rumored to have been killed by an aide-de-camp.
224. **Persia's . . . lord:** Xerxes, who invaded Greece in the 5th century B.C.; Elector Charles Albert of Bavaria contested the crown of Maria Theresa, thus causing the War of the Austrian Succession.

The daring Greeks deride the martial show,   235
And heap their vallies with the gaudy foe;
Th' insulted sea with humbler thoughts he gains,
A single skiff to speed his flight remains;
Th' incumber'd oar scarce leaves the dreaded coast
Through purple billows and a floating host.   240
   The bold Bavarian, in a luckless hour,
Tries the dread summits of Cesarean pow'r,
With unexpected legions bursts away,
And sees defenceless realms receive his sway;
Short sway! fair Austria spreads her mournful charms,   245
The queen, the beauty, sets the world in arms;
From hill to hill the beacons rousing blaze
Spreads wide the hope of plunder and of praise;
The fierce Croatian, and the wild Hussar,
And all the sons of ravage croud the war;   250
The baffled prince in honour's flatt'ring bloom
Of hasty greatness finds the fatal doom,
His foes derision, and his subjects blame,
And steals to death from anguish and from shame.
   Enlarge my life with multitude of days,   255
In health, in sickness, thus the suppliant prays;
Hides from himself his state, and shuns to know,
That life protracted is protracted woe.
Time hovers o'er, impatient to destroy,
And shuts up all the passages of joy: 260
In vain their gifts the bounteous seasons pour,
The fruit autumnal, and the vernal flow'r,
With listless eyes the dotard views the store,
He views, and wonders that they please no more;
Now pall the tastless meats, and joyless wines,   265
And Luxury with sighs her slave resigns.
Approach, ye minstrels, try the soothing strain,
And yield the tuneful lenitives of pain:
No sounds alas would touch th' impervious ear,
Though dancing mountains witness'd Orpheus near;   270
Nor lute nor lyre his feeble pow'rs attend,
Nor sweeter musick of a virtuous friend,
But everlasting dictates croud his tongue,
Perversely grave, or positively wrong.
The still returning tale, and ling'ring jest,   275
Perplex the fawning niece and pamper'd guest,

---

268. **lenitives:** soothing medicines.   270. **Orpheus:** the legendary Greek musician whose song could restore life.

While growing hopes scarce awe the gath'ring sneer,
And scarce a legacy can bribe to hear;
The watchful guests still hint the last offence,
The daughter's petulance, the son's expence,   280
Improve his heady rage with treach'rous skill,
And mould his passions till they make his will.
    Unnumber'd maladies his joints invade,
Lay siege to life and press the dire blockade;
But unextinguish'd Avarice still remains,   285
And dreaded losses aggravate his pains;
He turns, with anxious heart and cripled hands,
His bonds of debt, and mortgages of lands;
Or views his coffers with suspicious eyes,
Unlocks his gold, and counts it till he dies.   290
    But grant, the virtues of a temp'rate prime
Bless with an age exempt from scorn or crime;
An age that melts in unperceiv'd decay,
And glides in modest Innocence away;
Whose peaceful day Benevolence endears,   295
Whose night congratulating Conscience cheers;
The gen'ral fav'rite as the gen'ral friend:
Such age there is, and who could wish its end?
    Yet ev'n on this her load Misfortune flings,
To press the weary minutes flagging wings: 300
New sorrow rises as the day returns,
A sister sickens, or a daughter mourns.
Now kindred Merit fills the sable bier,
Now lacerated Friendship claims a tear.
Year chases year, decay persues decay,   305
Still drops some joy from with'ring life away;
New forms arise, and diff'rent views engage,
Superfluous lags the vet'ran on the stage,
Till pitying Nature signs the last release,
And bids afflicted worth retire to peace.   310
    But few there are whom hours like these await,
Who set unclouded in the gulphs of fate.
From Lydia's monarch should the search descend,
By Solon caution'd to regard his end,
In life's last scene what prodigies surprise,   315
Fears of the brave, and follies of the wise?
From Marlb'rough's eyes the streams of dotage flow,

313–14. **Lydia's . . . end:** Solon, the Athenian lawgiver, told Croesus, King of Lydia, not to consider himself happy until he knew how his life would end. Croesus was overthrown by the Persians. 317. **Marlb'rough:** John Churchill, Duke of Marlborough, whose brilliant generalship defeated the armies of Louis XIV.

And Swift expires a driv'ler and a show.
   The teeming mother, anxious for her race,
Begs for each birth the fortune of a face: 320
Yet Vane could tell what ills from beauty spring;
And Sedley curs'd the form that pleas'd a king.
Ye nymphs of rosy lips and radiant eyes,
Whom Pleasure keeps too busy to be wise,
Whom Joys with soft varieties invite,   325
By day the frolick, and the dance by night,
Who frown with vanity, who smile with art,
And ask the latest fashion of the heart,
What care, what rules your heedless charms shall save,
Each nymph your rival, and each youth your slave?   330
Against your fame with fondness hate combines,
The rival batters, and the lover mines.
With distant voice neglected Virtue calls,
Less heard and less, the faint remonstrance falls;
Tir'd with contempt, she quits the slipp'ry reign,   335
And Pride and Prudence take her seat in vain.
In croud at once, where none the pass defend,
The harmless Freedom, and the private Friend.
The guardians yield, by force superior ply'd;
By Int'rest, Prudence; and by Flatt'ry, Pride.   340
Now Beauty falls betray'd, despis'd, distress'd,
And hissing Infamy proclaims the rest.
   Where then shall Hope and Fear their objects find?
Must dull Suspence corrupt the stagnant mind?
Must helpless man, in ignorance sedate,   345
Roll darkling down the torrent of his fate?
Must no dislike alarm, no wishes rise,
No cries attempt the mercies of the skies?
Enquirer, cease, petitions yet remain,
Which heav'n may hear, nor deem religion vain.   350
Still raise for good the supplicating voice,
But leave to heav'n the measure and the choice.
Safe in his pow'r, whose eyes discern afar
The secret ambush of a specious pray'r.
Implore his aid, in his decisions rest,   355
Secure whate'er he gives, he gives the best.
Yet when the sense of sacred presence fires,
And strong devotion to the skies aspires,
Pour forth thy fervours for a healthful mind,

---

318. **Swift:** he spent the last years of his life in total senility.
321. **Vane:** Anne Vane (1705–1736), mistress of Frederick, Prince of Wales.
322. **Sedley:** Catherine Sedley, mistress of James II.

Obedient passions, and a will resign'd;   360
For love, which scarce collective man can fill;
For patience sov'reign o'er transmuted ill;
For faith, that panting for a happier seat,
Counts death kind Nature's signal of retreat:
These goods for man the laws of heav'n ordain,   365
These goods he grants, who grants the pow'r to gain;
With these celestial wisdom calms the mind,
And makes the happiness she does not find.

To Miss ———

On Her Playing upon the Harpsichord
in a Room Hung with Some Flower-
pieces of Her Own Painting

When Stella strikes the tuneful string
In scenes of imitated spring,
Where Beauty lavishes her powers
On beds of never-fading flowers,
And pleasure propagates around   5
Each charm of modulated sound.
Ah! think not, in the dangerous hour,
The nymph fictitious, as the flower;
But shun, rash youth, the gay alcove,
Nor tempt the snares of wily love.   10
When charms thus press on every sense,
What thought of flight, or of defense?
Deceitful Hope, and vain Desire,
Forever flutter o'er her lyre,
Delighting, as the youth draws nigh,   15
To point the glances of her eye,
And forming, with unerring art,
New chains to hold the captive heart.
But on these regions of delight,
Might Truth intrude with daring flight,   20
Could Stella, sprightly, fair and young,
One moment hear the moral song,
Instruction with her flowers might spring,
And Wisdom warble from her string.
Mark, when from thousand mingled dyes   25
Thou see'st one pleasing form arise,
How active light, and thoughtful shade,

Miss: presumably Miss Alicia Marie   his friend Henry Harvey to send as his
Carpenter. Johnson wrote the poem for   own to the lady.

In greater scenes each other aid;
Mark, when the different notes agree
In friendly contrariety,   30
How passion's well-accorded strife
Gives all the harmony of life;
Thy pictures shall thy conduct frame,
Consistent still, though not the same,
Thy music teach the nobler art   35
To tune the regulated heart.

Translation of Lines by Benserade

In bed we laugh, in bed we cry,
And born in bed, in bed we die;
The near approach a bed may show
Of human bliss to human woe.

A Short Song of Congratulation

Long-expected one and twenty
Lingering year at last is flown,
Pomp and pleasure, pride and plenty,
Great Sir John, are all your own.

Loosened from the minor's tether;   5
Free to mortgage or to sell,
Wild as wind, and light as feather
Bid the slaves of thrift farewell.

Call the Bettys, Kates, and Jennys
Every name that laughs at care,   10
Lavish of your grandsire's guineas,
Show the spirit of an heir.

All that prey on vice and folly
Joy to see their quarry fly,
Here the gamester light and jolly   15
There the lender grave and sly.

Benserade: Isaac de Benserade (1613–1691), poet of the court of Louis XIV. His lines read: Théatre des Ris et des Pleurs, / Lit ou je nais et ou je meurs; / Tu nous fais voir comment Voisins / Sont nos Plaisirs et nos Chagrins. Johnson reportedly translated these lines impromptu. It may prove instructive to compare Johnson's version to one by his friend Mrs. Thrale: Bed where first I drew my Breath, / Bed of Love, Bed of Death; / Thine's the Theatre to show / How near allied are Bliss and Woe.

4. Sir John: Sir John Lade, a nephew of the Thrales, who lived as Johnson predicted.

Wealth, Sir John, was made to wander,
   Let it wander as it will;
See the jockey, see the pander,
   Bid them come, and take their fill.   20

When the bonny blade carouses,
   Pockets full, and spirits high,
What are acres? What are houses?
   Only dirt, or wet or dry.

If the guardian or the mother   25
   Tell the woes of willful waste,
Scorn their counsel and their pother,
   You can hang or drown at last.

THOMAS GRAY [1716–1771]

Ode on a Distant Prospect of Eton College

[*I am a man: sufficient reason for
being miserable.*]
Meander

Ye distant spires, ye antique towers,
   That crown the watry glade,
Where grateful Science still adores
   Her Henry's holy Shade;
And ye, that from the stately brow   5
Of Windsor's heights the expanse below
   Of grove, of lawn, of mead survey,
Whose turf, whose shade, whose flowers among
Wanders the hoary Thames along
   His silver-winding way: 10

Ah, happy hills, ah, pleasing shade,
   Ah, fields beloved in vain,
Where once my careless childhood strayed,
   A stranger yet to pain!
I feel the gales, that from ye blow,   15
A momentary bliss bestow,
   As waving fresh their gladsome wing,
My weary soul they seem to sooth,
And, redolent of joy and youth,
   To breathe a second spring.   20

3. **Science:** knowledge.   4. **Henry's:** Henry VI founded Eton in 1440.

Say, Father Thames, for thou hast seen
    Full many a sprightly race
Disporting on thy margent green
    The paths of pleasure trace,
Who foremost now delight to cleave   25
With pliant arm thy glassy wave?
    The captive linnet which enthrall?
What idle progeny succeed
To chase the rolling circle's speed,
    Or urge the flying ball?   30

While some on earnest business bent
    Their murm'ring labors ply
'Gainst graver hours, that bring constraint
    To sweeten liberty;
Some bold adventurers disdain   35
The limits of their little reign,
    And unknown regions dare descry:
Still as they run they look behind,
They hear a voice in every wind,
    And snatch a fearful joy.   40

Gay hope is theirs by fancy fed,
    Less pleasing when possessed;
The tear forgot as soon as shed,
    The sunshine of the breast:
Theirs buxom health of rosy hue,   45
Wild wit, invention ever-new,
    And lively cheer of vigor born;
The thoughtless day, the easy night,
The spirits pure, the slumbers light,
    That fly the approach of morn.   50

Alas, regardless of their doom,
    The little victims play!
No sense have they of ills to come,
    Nor care beyond to-day:
Yet see how all around 'em wait   55
The Ministers of human fate,
    And black Misfortune's baleful train!
Ah, show them where in ambush stand
To seize their prey the murderous band!
    Ah, tell them, they are men!   60

---

27. **enthrall:** imprison.   29. **rolling circle:** hoop.

These shall the fury Passions tear,
  The vultures of the mind,
Disdainful Anger, pallid Fear,
  And Shame that skulks behind;
Or pining Love shall waste their youth,   65
Or Jealousy with rankling tooth,
  That inly gnaws the secret heart,
And Envy wan, and faded Care,
Grim-visaged, comfortless Despair,
  And Sorrow's piercing dart.   70

Ambition this shall tempt to rise,
  Then whirl the wretch from high,
To bitter Scorn a sacrifice,
  And grinning Infamy.
The stings of Falsehood those shall try,   75
And hard Unkindness' altered eye,
  That mocks the tear it forced to flow;
And keen Remorse with blood defiled,
And moody Madness laughing wild
  Amid severest woe.   80

Lo, in the vale of years beneath
  A grisly troop are seen,
The painful family of Death,
  More hideous than their Queen:
This racks the joints, this fires the veins,   85
That every laboring sinew strains,
  Those in the deeper vitals rage;

Lo, Poverty, to fill the band,
That numbs the soul with icy hand,
  And slow-consuming Age.   90

To each his sufferings: all are men,
  Condemned alike to groan,
The tender for another's pain,
  The unfeeling for his own.
Yet ah! why should they know their fate?   95
Since sorrow never comes too late,
  And happiness too swiftly flies.
Thought would destroy their paradise.
No more; where ignorance is bliss,
  'Tis folly to be wise.   100

On Lord Holland's Seat Near M———e, Kent

Old, and abandoned by each venal friend,
  Here Holland took the pious resolution
To smuggle some few years, and strive to mend
  A broken character and constitution.

On this congenial spot he fixed his choice,   5
  Earl Goodwin trembled for his neighboring sand,
Here seagulls scream and cormorants rejoice,
  And mariners, though shipwrecked, dread to land.

Here reign the blustering North and blighting East,
  No tree is heard to whisper, bird to sing,   10
Yet Nature cannot furnish out the feast,
  Art he invokes new horrors still to bring.

Now moldering fanes and battlements arise,
  Arches and turrets nodding to their fall,
Unpeopled places delude his eyes,   15
  And mimic desolation covers all.

"Ah!" said the sighing peer, "had Bute been true,
  Nor Shelburne's Rigby's, Calcraft's friendship vain,
Far other scenes than these had blessed our view,
  And realized the ruins that we feign.   20

"Purged by the sword and beautified by fire,
  Then had we seen proud London's hated walls;
Owls might have hooted in St. Peter's choir,
  And foxes stunk and littered in St. Paul's."

Elegy Written in a Country Churchyard

The curfew tolls the knell of parting day,
  The lowing herd winds slowly o'er the lea,
The ploughman homeward plods his weary way,
  And leaves the world to darkness and to me.

Holland's . . . Kent: Henry Fox, 1st Baron Holland (1705–1774), was an unscrupulous politician who as Paymaster-General during the Seven Years War amassed a huge private fortune. On his estate near Margate in Kent, Holland built both a villa and gothic ruins: **6. Goodwin . . . sand:** Goodwin Sands, a dangerous shoal nearby, was said to have been at one time fertile land owned by Earl Goodwin. **17–18. Bute . . . vain:** Politicians who had deserted Holland. **23. St. Peter's:** Westminster Abbey, dedicated to St. Peter. **24. St. Paul's:** the cathedral of London.

Now fades the glimmering landscape on the sight,   5
    And all the air a solemn stillness holds,
Save where the beetle wheels his droning flight,
    And drowsy tinklings lull the distant folds:

Save that from yonder ivy-mantled tower
    The moping owl does to the moon complain   10
Of such as, wandering near her secret bower,
    Molest her ancient solitary reign.

Beneath those rugged elms, that yew-tree's shade
    Where heaves the turf in many a mouldering heap,
Each in his narrow cell for ever laid,   15
    The rude forefathers of the hamlet sleep.

The breezy call of incense-breathing morn,
    The swallow twittering from the straw-built shed,
The cock's shrill clarion, or the echoing horn,
    No more shall rouse them from their lowly bed.   20

For them no more the blazing hearth shall burn,
    Or busy housewife ply her evening care:
No children run to lisp their sire's return,
    Or climb his knees the envied kiss to share.

Oft did the harvest to their sickle yield,   25
    Their furrow oft the stubborn glebe has broke:
How jocund did they drive their team afield!
    How bowed the woods beneath their sturdy stroke!

Let not Ambition mock their useful toil,
    Their homely joys, and destiny obscure;   30
Nor Grandeur hear with a disdainful smile
    The short and simple annals of the poor.

The boast of heraldry, the pomp of power,
    And all that beauty, all that wealth e'er gave,
Awaits alike th' inevitable hour:—   35
    The paths of glory lead but to the grave.

Nor you, ye Proud, impute to these the fault
    If Memory o'er their tomb no trophies raise,
Where through the long-drawn aisle and fretted vault
    The pealing anthem swells the note of praise.   40

16. **rude:** uneducated.
26. **glebe:** turf.
38. **trophies:** memorial sculptures, traditionally in the form of captured arms and armor.
39. **fretted:** adorned with ornamental designs.

Can storied urn or animated bust
    Back to its mansion call the fleeting breath?
Can Honour's voice provoke the silent dust,
    Or Flattery soothe the dull cold ear of Death?

Perhaps in this neglected spot is laid   45
    Some heart once pregnant with celestial fire;
Hands, that the rod of empire might have swayed,
    Or waked to ecstasy the living lyre:

But Knowledge to their eyes her ample page
    Rich with the spoils of time, did ne'er unroll;   50
Chill Penury repressed their noble rage,
    And froze the genial current of the soul.

Full many a gem of purest ray serene
    The dark unfathomed caves of ocean bear:
Full many a flower is born to blush unseen,   55
    And waste its sweetness on the desert air.

Some village Hampden, that with dauntless breast
    The little tyrant of his fields withstood,
Some mute inglorious Milton here may rest,
    Some Cromwell, guiltless of his country's blood.   60

Th' applause of list'ning senates to command,
    The threats of pain and ruin to despise,
To scatter plenty o'er a smiling land,
    And read their history in a nation's eyes,

Their lot forbade: nor circumscribed alone   65
    Their growing virtues, but their crimes confined;
Forbade to wade through slaughter to a throne,
    And shut the gates of mercy on mankind;

The struggling pangs of conscious truth to hide,
    To quench the blushes of ingenuous shame,   70
Or heap the shrine of Luxury and Pride
    With incense kindled at the Muse's flame.

Far from the madding crowd's ignoble strife,
    Their sober wishes never learn'd to stray;
Along the cool sequestered vale of life   75
    They kept the noiseless tenor of their way.

57. **Hampden:** John Hampden (1594–
1643), leader of Parliament and opponent
of Charles I.

Yet e'en these bones from insult to protect
    Some frail memorial still erected nigh,
With uncouth rhymes and shapeless sculpture decked,
    Implores the passing tribute of a sigh.   80

Their name, their years, spelt by th' unlettered Muse,
    The place of fame and elegy supply:
And many a holy text around she strews,
    That teach the rustic moralist to die.

For who, to dumb forgetfulness a prey,   85
    This pleasing anxious being e'er resigned,
Left the warm precincts of the cheerful day,
    Nor cast one longing lingering look behind?

On some fond breast the parting soul relies,
    Some pious drops the closing eye requires;   90
E'en from the tomb the voice of Nature cries,
    E'en in our ashes live their wonted fires.

For thee, who, mindful of th' unhonoured dead,
    Dost in these lines their artless tale relate;
If chance, by lonely Contemplation led,   95
    Some kindred spirit shall inquire thy fate,

Haply some hoary-headed swain may say,
    "Oft have we seen him at the peep of dawn
Brushing with hasty steps the dews away,
    To meet the sun upon the upland lawn;   100

"There at the foot of yonder nodding beech
    That wreathes its old fantastic roots so high,
His listless length at noon-tide would he stretch,
    And pore upon the brook that babbles by.

"Hard by yon wood, now smiling as in scorn,   105
    Muttering his wayward fancies he would rove,
Now drooping, woeful-wan, like one forlorn,
    Or crazed with care, or crossed in hopeless love.

"One morn I miss'd him on the custom'd hill,
    Along the heath, and near his favourite tree;   110
Another came; nor yet beside the rill,
    Nor up the lawn, nor at the wood was he;

"The next with dirges due in sad array
    Slow through the church-way path we saw him borne,
Approach and read (for thou canst read) the lay   115
    Graved on the stone beneath yon aged thorn."

The Epitaph

Here rests his head upon the lap of Earth
    A Youth, to Fortune and to Fame unknown;
Fair Science frowned not on his humble birth,
    And Melancholy marked him for her own.   120

Large was his bounty, and his soul sincere;
    Heaven did a recompense as largely send:
He gave to Misery all he had, a tear,
    He gained from Heaven, 'twas all he wished, a friend.

No farther seek his merits to disclose,   125
    Or draw his frailties from their dread abode,
(There they alike in trembling hope repose),
    The bosom of his Father and his God.

WILLIAM COLLINS [1721–1759]

Ode to Evening

If aught of oaten stop, or pastoral song,
May hope, chaste Eve, to soothe thy modest ear,
    Like thy own solemn springs,
    Thy springs and dying gales,

O nymph reserved, while now the bright-haired sun   5
Sits in yon western tent, whose cloudy skirts,
    With brede ethereal wove,
    O'erhang his wavy bed:

Now air is hushed, save where the weak-eyed bat,
With short shrill shriek, flits by on leathern wing,   10
    Or where the beetle winds
    His small but sullen horn,

As oft he rises 'midst the twilight path,
Against the pilgrim borne in heedless hum:
    Now teach me, maid composed,   15
    To breathe some softened strain,

119. **Science:** knowledge.   7. **brede:** embroidery.

Whose numbers, stealing through thy darkening vale,
May not unseemly with its stillness suit,
   As, musing slow, I hail
   Thy genial loved return!   20

For when thy folding-star arising shows
His paly circlet, at his warning lamp
   The fragrant Hours, and elves
   Who slept in flowers the day,

And many a nymph who wreaths her brows with sedge,   25
And sheds the fresh'ning dew, and, lovelier still,
   The pensive Pleasures sweet,
   Prepare thy shadowy car.

Then lead, calm vot'ress, where some sheety lake
Cheers the lone heath, or some time-hallowed pile   30
   Or upland fallows gray
   Reflect its last cool gleam.

But when chill blust'ring winds, or driving rain,
Forbid my willing feet, be mine the hut
   That from the mountain's side   35
   Views wilds, and swelling floods,

And hamlets brown, and dim-discovered spires,
And hears their simple bell, and marks o'er all
   Thy dewy fingers draw
   The gradual dusky veil.   40

While Spring shall pour his show'rs, as oft he wont,
And bathe thy breathing tresses, meekest Eve;
   While Summer loves to sport
   Beneath thy ling'ring light;

While sallow Autumn fills thy lap with leaves;   45
Or Winter, yelling through the troublous air,
   Affrights thy shrinking train,
   And rudely rends thy robes;

So long, sure-found beneath the sylvan shed,
Shall Fancy, Friendship, Science, rose-lipped Health,   50
   Thy gentlest influence own,
   And hymn thy fav'rite name!

21. folding-star: The evening star's appear-   **50. Science:** knowledge.
ance marks the time to herd the sheep into
their fold.

WILLIAM COWPER [1731–1800]

The Castaway

Obscurest night involved the sky,
    The Atlantic billows roared,
When such a destined wretch as I,
    Washed headlong from on board,
Of friends, of hope, of all bereft,   5
His floating home forever left.

No braver chief could Albion boast
    Than he with whom he went,
Nor ever ship left Albion's coast
    With warmer wishes sent.   10
He loved them both, but both in vain,
Nor him beheld, nor her again.

Not long beneath the whelming brine,
    Expert to swim, he lay;
Nor soon he felt his strength decline,   15
    Or courage die away;
But waged with death a lasting strife,
Supported by despair of life.

He shouted: nor his friends had failed
    To check the vessel's course,   20
But so the furious blast prevailed,
    That, pitiless perforce,
They left their outcast mate behind,
And scudded still before the wind.

Some succor yet they could afford;   25
    And such as storms allow,
The cask, the coop, the floated cord,
    Delayed not to bestow.
But he (they knew) nor ship nor shore,
Whate'er they gave, should visit more.   30

---

7. **chief . . . Albion:** George Lord Anson
(1697–1762) who circumnavigated the
world. Years before writing this poem
Cowper read in Anson's *Voyage* (1748) of
a man washed overboard. Albion is
England.

Nor, cruel as it seemed, could he
    Their haste himself condemn,
Aware that flight, in such a sea,
    Alone could rescue them;
Yet bitter felt it still to die   35
Deserted and his friends so nigh.

He long survives, who lives an hour
    In ocean, self-upheld;
And so long he, with unspent power,
    His destiny repelled;   40
And ever, as the minutes flew,
Entreated help, or cried "Adieu!"

At length, his transient respite past,
    His comrades, who before
Had heard his voice in every blast,   45
    Could catch the sound no more:
For then, by toil subdued, he drank
The stifling wave, and then he sank.

No poet wept him; but the page
    Of narrative sincere,   50
That tells his name, his worth, his age,
    Is wet with Anson's tear:
And tears by bards or heroes shed
Alike immortalize the dead.

I therefore purpose not, or dream,   55
    Descanting on his fate,
To give the melancholy theme
    A more enduring date:
But misery still delights to trace
Its semblance in another's case.   60

No voice divine the storm allayed,
    No light propitious shone,
When, snatched from all effectual aid,
    We perished, each alone:
But I beneath a rougher sea,   65
And whelmed in deeper gulfs than he.

ROBERT BURNS [1759–1796]

Green grow the rashes

Chorus

Green grow the rashes, O;
Green grow the rashes, O;
　The sweetest hours that e'er I spend
Are spent amang the lasses, O.

There's nought but care on ev'ry han',　　　　　　5
　In every hour that passes, O:
What signifies the life o' man,
　And 'twere na for the lasses, O?

The war'ly race may riches chase,
　An' riches still may fly them, O;　　　　　　　10
An' tho' at last they catch them fast,
　Their hearts can ne'er enjoy them, O.

But gie me a cannie hour at e'en,
　My arms about my dearie, O;
An' war'ly cares, an' war'ly men,　　　　　　　15
　May a' gae tapsalteerie, O.

For you sae douce, ye sneer at this:
　Ye're nought but senseless asses, O:
The wisest man the warl' e'er saw,
　He dearly loved the lasses, O.　　　　　　　20

Auld Nature swears, the lovely dears
　Her noblest work she classes, O:
Her prentice han' she tried on man,
　An' then she made the lasses, O.

John Anderson, my jo

John Anderson, my jo, John,
　When we were first acquent;
Your locks were like the raven,
　Your bonie brow was brent;

rashes: rushes.
9. **war'ly:** worldly.
13. **cannie:** quiet.
16. **tapsalteerie:** topsy-turvy.

17. **douce:** sober.

jo: sweetheart, dear.
4. **brent:** smooth.

But now your brow is beld, John,   5
  Your locks are like the snow;
But blessings on your frosty pow,
  John Anderson, my jo.

John Anderson, my jo, John,
  We clamb the hill thegither;   10
And mony a cantie day, John,
  We've had wi' ane anither:
Now we maun totter down, John,
  And hand in hand we'll go,
And sleep thegither at the foot,   15
  John Anderson, my jo.

Ae fond kiss

Ae fond kiss, and then we sever;
Ae farewell, and then forever!
Deep in heart-wrung tears I'll pledge thee,
Warring sighs and groans I'll wage thee.
Who shall say that Fortune grieves him,   5
While the star of hope she leaves him?
Me, nae cheerfu' twinkle lights me;
Dark despair around benights me.

I'll ne'er blame my partial fancy,
Naething could resist my Nancy;   10
But to see her was to love her;
Love but her, and love forever.
Had we never loved sae kindly,
Had we never loved sae blindly,
Never met—or never parted—   15
We had ne'er been broken-hearted.

Fare thee weel, thou first and fairest!
Fare thee weel, thou best and dearest!
Thine be ilka joy and treasure,
Peace, enjoyment, love, and pleasure!   20
Ae fond kiss, and then we sever;
Ae farewell, alas, forever!
Deep in heart-wrung tears I'll pledge thee,
Warring sighs and groans I'll wage thee!

5. **beld**: bald.
7. **pow**: head.
11. **cantie**: cheerful.

ae: one.
19. **ilka**: every.

A Red, Red Rose

O my luve is like a red, red rose,
    That's newly sprung in June;
O my luve is like the melodie
    That's sweetly played in tune.

As fair thou art, my bonie lass,   5
    So deep in luve am I;
And I will luve thee still, my dear,
    Till a' the seas gang dry.

Till a' the seas gang dry, my dear,
    And the rocks melt wi' the sun;   10
And I will luve thee still, my dear,
    While the sands o' life shall run.

And fare thee weel, my only luve,
    And fare thee weel a while;
And I will come again, my luve,   15
    Tho' it were ten thousand mile!

Scots wha hae

Scots, wha hae wi' Wallace bled,
Scots, wham Bruce has aften led;
Welcome to your gory bed,
    Or to victorie!
Now's the day, and now's the hour;   5
See the front o' battle lour;
See approach proud Edward's power—
    Chains and slaverie!

Wha will be a traitor knave?
Wha can fill a coward's grave?   10
Wha sae base as be a slave?
    Let him turn and flee!
Wha for Scotland's king and law
Freedom's sword will strongly draw,
Freeman stand or freeman fa',   15
    Let him follow me!

8. **gang:** go.

Scots wha hae: Scots who have. The song purports to be Bruce's address to his army before the battle of Bannockburn, 1314.

By oppression's woes and pains!
By your sons in servile chains!
We will drain our dearest veins,
   But they shall be free!   20
Lay the proud usurpers low!
Tyrants fall in every foe!
Liberty's in every blow!—
   Let us do or die!

For a' That and a' That

Is there, for honest poverty,
   That hings his head, and a' that?
The coward-slave, we pass him by,
   We dare be poor for a' that!
     For a' that, and a' that,   5
       Our toils obscure, and a' that,
     The tank is but the guinea's stamp;
       The man's the gowd for a' that.

What though on hamely fare we dine,
   Wear hodden-gray, and a' that;   10
Gie fools their silks, and knaves their wine,
   A man's a man for a' that.
     For a' that, and a' that,
       Their tinsel show, and a' that,
     The honest man, though e'er sae poor,   15
       Is King o' men for a' that.

Ye see yon birkie, ca'd a lord,
   Wha struts, and stares, and a' that;
Though hundreds worship at his word,
   He's but a coof for a' that: 20
     For a' that, and a' that,
       His riband, star, and a' that.
     The man of independent mind,
       He looks and laughs at a' that.

a': all.
8. gowd: gold.
10. hodden-gray: coarse grey woolen.
17. birkie: fellow.
20. coof: fool.

A prince can mak a belted knight,   25
   A marquis, duke, and a' that;
But an honest man's aboon his might,
   Guid faith, he mauna fa' that!
     For a' that, and a' that,
       Their dignities, and a' that,   30
     The pith o' sense, and pride o' worth,
      Are higher rank than a' that.

Then let us pray that come it may,
   As come it will, for a' that,
That sense and worth o'er a' the earth   35
   Shall bear the gree, and a' that!
     For a' that and a' that,
       It's comin yet, for a' that,
     That man to man the warld o'er,
      Shall brothers be for a' that.   40

Sweet Afton

Flow gently, sweet Afton! among thy green braes,
Flow gently, I'll sing thee a song in thy praise;
My Mary's asleep by thy murmuring stream,
Flow gently, sweet Afton, disturb not her dream.

Thou stock-dove whose echo resounds thro' the glen,   5
Ye wild whistling blackbirds in yon thorny den,
Thou green crested lapwing, thy screaming forbear,
I charge you, disturb not my slumbering Fair.

How lofty, sweet Afton, thy neighbouring hills,
Far mark'd with the courses of clear, winding rills;   10
There daily I wander as noon rises high,
My flocks and my Mary's sweet cot in my eye.

How pleasant thy banks and green valleys below,
Where, wild in the woodlands, the primroses blow;
There oft, as mild ev'ning weeps over the lea,   15
The sweet-scented birk shades my Mary and me.

27. **aboon:** above.
28. **mauna fa':** must not try for.
36. **bear . . . gree:** have the first place.

1. **braes:** banks, hillsides.
16. **birk:** birch.

Thy crystal stream, Afton, how lovely it glides,
And winds by the cot where my Mary resides;
How wanton thy waters her snowy feet lave,
As, gathering sweet flowerets, she stems thy clear wave. 20

Flow gently, sweet Afton, among thy green braes,
Flow gently, sweet river, the theme of my lays;
My Mary's asleep by thy murmuring stream,
Flow gently, sweet Afton, disturb not her dream.

Ye flowery banks

Ye flowery banks o' bonie Doon,
 How can ye blume sae fair?
How can ye chant, ye little birds,
 And I sae fu' o' care?

Thou'll break my heart, thou bonie bird, 5
 That sings upon the bough;
Thou minds me o' the happy days
 When my fause luve was true.

Thou'll break my heart, thou bonie bird,
 That sings beside thy mate; 10
For sae I sat, and sae I sang,
 And wist na o' my fate.

Aft hae I rov'd by bonie Doon,
 To see the woodbine twine,
And ilka bird sang o' its luve, 15
 And sae did I o' mine.

Wi' lightsome heart I pu'd a rose,
 Frae aff its thorny tree;
And my fause luver staw my rose,
 But left the thorn wi' me. 20

7. **minds:** reminds.   18. **Frae aff:** from off.
12. **wist:** knew.   19. **staw:** stole.
15. **ilka:** every

The Romantics

❧ ❧ ❧

WILLIAM BLAKE

[*1757–1827*]

Song

How sweet I roamed from field to field
And tasted all the summer's pride,
'Til I the prince of love beheld
Who in the sunny beams did glide!

He shew'd me lilies for my hair,   5
And blushing roses for my brow;
He led me through his gardens fair,
Where all his golden pleasures grow.

With sweet May dews my wings were wet,
And Phœbus fired my vocal rage;   10
He caught me in his silken net,
And shut me in his golden cage.

He loves to sit and hear me sing,
Then, laughing, sports and plays with me;
Then stretches out my golden wing,   15
And mocks my loss of liberty.

10. **Phœbus:** the sun god, or the sun
personified. Also, the god of poetry.

The Lamb

Little Lamb, who made thee?
　Dost thou know who made thee?
Gave thee life, and bid thee feed,
By the stream and o'er the mead;
Gave thee clothing of delight,　　　　5
Softest clothing, wooly, bright;
Gave thee such a tender voice,
Making all the vales rejoice?
　Little Lamb, who made thee?
　Dost thou know who made thee?　　10

　Little Lamb, I'll tell thee,
　Little Lamb, I'll tell thee:
He is called by thy name,
For He calls Himself a Lamb.
He is meek, and He is mild;　　　　15
He became a little child.
I a child, and thou a lamb,
We are called by His name.
　Little Lamb, God bless thee!
　Little Lamb, God bless thee!　　20

The Little Black Boy

My mother bore me in the southern wild,
And I am black, but O my soul is white;
White as an angel is the English child,
But I am black, as if bereav'd of light.

My mother taught me underneath a tree,　　5
And sitting down before the heat of day,
She took me on her lap and kissed me,
And, pointing to the east, began to say:

"Look on the rising sun—there God does live,
And gives his light, and gives his heat away;　　10
And flowers and trees and beasts and men receive
Comfort in morning, joy in the noon day.

"And we are put on earth a little space,
That we may learn to bear the beams of love;
And these black bodies and this sun-burnt face　　15
Is but a cloud, and like a shady grove.

"For when our souls have learn'd the heat to bear,
The cloud will vanish; we shall hear his voice,
Saying: 'come out from the grove, my love and care,
And round my golden tent like lambs rejoice.'"   20

Thus did my mother say, and kissed me;
And thus I say to little English boy:
When I from black, and he from white cloud free,
And round the tent of God like lambs we joy,

I'll shade him from the heat, till he can bear   25
To lean in joy upon our father's knee;
And then I'll stand and stroke his silver hair,
And be like him, and he will then love me.

The Clod and the Pebble

"Love seeketh not itself to please,
Nor for itself hath any care,
But for another gives its ease,
And builds a heaven in hell's despair."

So sung a little clod of clay,   5
Trodden with the cattle's feet,
But a pebble of the brook
Warbled out these metres meet:

"Love seeketh only self to please,
To bind another to its delight,   10
Joys in another's loss of ease,
And builds a hell in heaven's despite."

The Chimney-Sweeper

A little black thing among the snow,
Crying "weep, weep" in notes of woe!
"Where are thy father and mother, say?"—
"They are both gone up to church to pray.

"Because I was happy upon the heath,   5
And smiled among the winter's snow,
They clothed me in the clothes of death,
And taught me to sing the notes of woe.

"And because I am happy, and dance and sing,
They think they have done me no injury,   10
And are gone to praise God and his Priest and King,
Who make up a heaven of our misery."

The Sick Rose

O Rose, thou art sick:
The invisible worm,
That flies in the night,
In the howling storm,

Has found out thy bed   5
Of crimson joy;
And his dark secret love
Does thy life destroy.

The Tyger

Tyger! Tyger! burning bright
In the forests of the night,
What immortal hand or eye
Could frame thy fearful symmetry?

In what distant deeps or skies   5
Burnt the fire of thine eyes?
On what wings dare he aspire?
What the hand dare seize the fire?

And what shoulder, and what art,
Could twist the sinews of thy heart?   10
And when thy heart began to beat,
What dread hand? and what dread feet?

What the hammer? what the chain?
In what furnace was thy brain?
What the anvil? what dread grasp   15
Dare its deadly terrors clasp?

When the stars threw down their spears,
And water'd heaven with their tears,
Did he smile his work to see?
Did he who made the Lamb make thee?   20

Tyger! Tyger! burning bright
In the forests of the night,
What immortal hand or eye,
Dare frame thy fearful symmetry?

Ah! Sun-Flower

Ah, Sun-flower! weary of time,
Who countest the steps of the Sun;
Seeking after that sweet golden clime
Where the traveller's journey is done;

Where the Youth pined away with desire,   5
And the pale Virgin shrouded in snow,
Arise from their graves, and aspire
Where my Sun-flower wishes to go.

The Garden of Love

I went to the Garden of Love,
And saw what I never had seen:
A chapel was built in the midst,
Where I used to play on the green.

And the gates of this chapel were shut,   5
And "Thou shalt not" writ over the door;
So I turned to the Garden of Love,
That so many sweet flowers bore;

And I saw it was filled with graves,
And tombstones where flowers should be;   10
And priests in black gowns were walking their rounds,
And binding with briars my joys and desires.

London

I wander through each chartered street,
Near where the chartered Thames does flow,
And mark in every face I meet
Marks of weakness, marks of woe.

1. **chartered**: pre-empted or rented.

In every cry of every man,   5
In every infant's cry of fear,
In every voice in every ban,
The mind-forged manacles I hear.

How the chimney-sweeper's cry
Every blackening church appalls;   10
And the hapless soldier's sigh
Runs in blood down palace walls.

But most through midnight streets I hear
How the youthful harlot's curse
Blasts the new born infant's tear,   15
And blights with plagues the marriage hearse.

A Poison Tree

I was angry with my friend:
I told my wrath, my wrath did end.
I was angry with my foe:
I told it not, my wrath did grow.

And I watered it in fears,   5
Night and morning with my tears;
And I sunned it with smiles,
And with soft deceitful wiles.

And it grew both day and night;
Till it bore an apple bright;   10
And my foe beheld it shine,
And he knew that it was mine,

And into my garden stole
When the night had veiled the pole:
In the morning glad I see   15
My foe outstretched beneath the tree.

I saw a chapel all of gold

I saw a chapel all of gold
That none did dare to enter in,
And many weeping stood without,
Weeping, mourning, worshipping.

I saw a serpent rise between   5
The white pillars of the door,
And he forced and forced and forced—
Down the golden hinges tore,

And along the pavement sweet,
Set with pearls and rubies bright,   10
All his slimy length he drew,
Till upon the altar white

Vomiting his poison out
On the bread and on the wine.
So I turned into a sty   15
And laid me down among the swine.

I asked a thief to steal me a peach

I asked a thief to steal me a peach:
He turned up his eyes.
I asked a lithe lady to lie her down:
Holy and meek she cries.

As soon as I went an angel came: 5
He winked at the thief
And smiled at the dame,
And without one word spoke
Had a peach from the tree,
And 'twixt earnest and joke   10
Enjoyed the Lady.

Auguries of Innocence

To see a world in a grain of sand
And a heaven in a wild flower,
Hold infinity in the palm of your hand,
And eternity in an hour.

A robin redbreast in a cage   5
Puts all heaven in a rage.
A dove-house filled with doves and pigeons
Shudders hell through all its regions.
A dog starved at his master's gate
Predicts the ruin of the state.   10
A horse misused upon the road
Calls to heaven for human blood.
Each outcry of the hunted hare

A fibre from the brain does tear.
A skylark wounded in the wing,   15
A cherubim does cease to sing;
The game cock clipped and armed for fight
Does the rising sun affright.
Every wolf's and lion's howl
Raises from hell a human soul.   20
The wild deer wandering here and there,
Keeps the human soul from care.
The lamb misused breeds public strife
And yet forgives the butcher's knife.
The bat that flits at close of eve   25
Has left the brain that won't believe.
The owl that calls upon the night
Speaks the unbeliever's fright.
He who shall hurt the little wren
Shall never be beloved by men.   30
He who the ox to wrath has moved
Shall never be by woman loved.
The wanton boy that kills the fly
Shall feel the spider's enmity.
He who torments the chafer's sprite   35
Weaves a bower in endless night.
The caterpillar on the leaf
Repeats to thee thy mother's grief.
Kill not the moth nor butterfly,
For the last judgment draweth nigh.   40
He who shall train the horse to war
Shall never pass the polar bar.
The beggar's dog and widow's cat,
Feed them and thou wilt grow fat.
The gnat that sings his summer's song   45
Poison gets from slander's tongue.
The poison of the snake and newt
Is the sweat of envy's foot.
The poison of the honey bee
Is the artist's jealousy.   50
The prince's robes and beggar's rags
Are toadstools on the miser's bags.
A truth that's told with bad intent
Beats all the lies you can invent.
It is right it should be so;   55
Man was made for joy and woe;
And when this we rightly know,
Through the world we safely go.

Joy and woe are woven fine,
A clothing for the soul divine;   60
Under every grief and pine
Runs a joy with silken twine.
The babe is more than swadling bands,
Throughout all these human lands;
Tools were made, and born were hands,   65
Every farmer understands.
Every tear from every eye
Becomes a babe in eternity;
This is caught by females bright,
And returned to its own delight.   70
The bleat, the bark, bellow, and roar
Are waves that beat on heaven's shore.
The babe that weeps the rod beneath
Writes revenge in realms of death.
The beggar's rags, fluttering in air,   75
Does to rags the heavens tear.
The soldier, armed with sword and gun,
Palsied strikes the summer's sun.
The poor man's farthing is worth more
Than all the gold on Afric's shore.   80
One mite wrung from the lab'rer's hands
Shall buy and sell the miser's lands;
Or, if protected from on high,
Does that whole nation sell and buy.
He who mocks the infant's faith   85
Shall be mocked in age and death.
He who shall teach the child to doubt
The rotting grave shall never get out.
He who respects the infant's faith
Triumphs over hell and death.   90
The child's toys and the old man's reasons
Are the fruits of the two seasons.
The questioner, who sits so sly
Shall never know how to reply.
He who replies to words of doubt   95
Doth put the light of knowledge out.
The strongest poison ever known
Came from Caesar's laurel crown.
Naught can deform the human race
Like to the armour's iron brace.   100
When gold and gems adorn the plow
To peaceful arts shall envy bow.
A riddle, or the cricket's cry,

Is to doubt a fit reply.
The emmet's inch and eagle's mile   105
Make lame philosophy to smile.
He who doubts from what he sees
Will ne'er believe, do what you please.
If the sun and moon should doubt,
They'd immediately go out.   110
To be in a passion you good may do,
But no good if a passion is in you.
The whore and gambler, by the state
Licensed, build that nation's fate.
The harlot's cry from street to street   115
Shall weave Old England's winding sheet.
The winner's shout, the loser's curse,
Dance before dead England's hearse.
Every night and every morn
Some to misery are born.   120
Every morn and every night
Some are born to sweet delight.
Some are born to sweet delight,
Some are born to endless night.
We are led to believe a lie   125
When we see not through the eye,
Which was born in a night to perish in a night,
When the soul slept in beams of light.
God appears, and God is light,
To those poor souls who dwell in night,   130
But does a human form display
To those who dwell in realms of day.

Mock on, Mock on Voltaire, Rousseau

Mock on, Mock on Voltaire, Rousseau:
Mock on, Mock on; 'tis all in vain!
You throw the sand against the wind,
And the wind blows it back again.

And every sand becomes a Gem   5
Reflected in the beams divine;
Blown back they blind the mocking eye,
But still in Israel's paths they shine.

Voltaire, Rousseau: Voltaire (1694–1778)   two 18th-century writers who attacked
and Jean Jacques Rousseau (1712–1778),   established ideas about religion and society.

The atoms of Democritus
And Newton's particles of light   10
Are sands upon the Red sea shore,
Where Israel's tents do shine so bright.

And did those feet in ancient time

And did those feet in ancient time
Walk upon England's mountains green?
And was the holy lamb of God
On England's pleasant pastures seen?

And did the countenance divine   5
Shine forth upon our clouded hills?
And was Jerusalem builded here
Among these dark satanic mills?

Bring me my bow of burning gold!
Bring me my arrows of desire!   10
Bring me my spear: O clouds, unfold!
Bring me my chariot of fire!

I will not cease from mental fight,
Nor shall my sword sleep in my hand,
Till we have built Jerusalem   15
In England's green and pleasant land.

Epilogue to the Gates of Paradise

(*To the Accuser who is the God of this World*)

Truly, my Satan, thou art but a dunce,
And dost not know the garment from the man;
Every harlot was a virgin once,
Nor can'st thou ever change Kate into Nan.

Tho' thou art worshipped by the names divine   5
Of Jesus and Jehovah, thou art still
The son of morn in weary night's decline,
The lost traveller's dream under the hill.

---

9. **Democritus:** 5th-century B.C. philosopher who believed in the atomic structure of the world.
10. **Newton's ... light:** Newton believed light to be a material substance.

And ... Time: from the Preface to *Milton.*

WILLIAM WORDSWORTH

[*1770–1850*]

Lines Composed a Few Miles Above Tintern Abbey
On Revisiting the Banks of the Wye
During a Tour. July 13, 1798

Five years have past; five summers, with the length
Of five long winters! and again I hear
These waters, rolling from their mountain-springs
With a soft inland murmur.—Once again
Do I behold these steep and lofty cliffs,   5
That on a wild secluded scene impress
Thoughts of more deep seclusion; and connect
The landscape with the quiet of the sky.
The day is come when I again repose
Here, under this dark sycamore, and view   10
These plots of cottage-ground, these orchard-tufts,
Which at this season, with their unripe fruits,
Are clad in one green hue, and lose themselves
'Mid groves and copses. Once again I see
These hedge-rows, hardly hedge-rows, little lines   15
Of sportive wood run wild: these pastoral farms,
Green to the very door; and wreaths of smoke
Sent up, in silence from among the trees!
With some uncertain notice, as might seem
Of vagrant dwellers in the houseless woods,   20
Or of some Hermit's cave, where by his fire
The Hermit sits alone.
                    These beauteous forms
Through a long absence, have not been to me
As is a landscape to a blind man's eye:
But oft, in lonely rooms, and 'mid the din   25
Of towns and cities, I have owed to them
In hours of weariness, sensations sweet,
Felt in the blood, and felt along the heart;
And passing even into my purer mind,
With tranquil restoration:—feelings too   30
Of unremembered pleasure: such, perhaps,

Banks of the Wye: in Monmouthshire, near
the Welsh border. Wordsworth had been
twenty-three on his previous visit.

As have no slight or trivial influence
On that best portion of a good man's life,
His little, nameless, unremembered acts
Of kindness and of love. Nor less, I trust,   35
To them I may have owed another gift,
Of aspect more sublime; that blessed mood,
In which the burthen of the mystery,
In which the heavy and the weary weight
Of all this unintelligible world,   40
Is lightened:—that serene and blessed mood,
In which the affections gently lead us on,—
Until, the breath of this corporeal frame
And even the motion of our human blood
Almost suspended, we are laid asleep   45
In body, and become a living soul:
While with an eye made quiet by the power
Of harmony, and the deep power of joy,
We see into the life of things.
                    If this
Be but a vain belief, yet, oh! how oft   50
In darkness and amid the many shapes
Of joyless daylight; when the fretful stir
Unprofitable, and the fever of the world,
Have hung upon the beatings of my heart—
How oft, in spirit, have I turned to thee,   55
O sylvan Wye! thou wanderer thro' the woods,
How often has my spirit turned to thee!

   And now, with gleams of half-extinguished thought,
With many recognitions dim and faint,
And somewhat of a sad perplexity,   60
The picture of the mind revives again:
While here I stand, not only with the sense
Of present pleasure, but with pleasing thoughts
That in this moment there is life and food
For future years. And so I dare to hope,   65
Though changed, no doubt, from what I was when first
I came among these hills; when like a roe
I bounded o'er the mountains, by the sides
Of the deep rivers, and the lonely streams,
Wherever nature led: more like a man   70
Flying from something that he dreads, than one
Who sought the thing he loved. For nature then
(The coarser pleasures of my boyish days,
And their glad animal movements all gone by)

To me was all in all.—I cannot paint   75
What then I was. The sounding cataract
Haunted me like a passion: the tall rock,
The mountain, and the deep and gloomy wood,
Their colours and their forms, were then to me
An appetite; a feeling and a love,   80
That had no need of a remoter charm,
By thought supplied, nor any interest
Unborrowed from the eye.—That time is past,
And all its aching joys are now no more,
And all its dizzy raptures. Not for this   85
Faint I, nor mourn nor murmur; other gifts
Have followed; for such loss, I would believe,
Abundant recompense. For I have learned
To look on nature, not as in the hour
Of thoughtless youth; but hearing oftentimes   90
The still, sad music of humanity,
Nor harsh nor grating, though of ample power
To chasten and subdue. And I have felt
A presence that disturbs me with the joy
Of elevated thoughts; a sense sublime   95
Of something far more deeply interfused,
Whose dwelling is the light of setting suns,
And the round ocean and the living air,
And the blue sky, and in the mind of man;
A motion and a spirit, that impels   100
All thinking things, all objects of all thought,
And rolls through all things. Therefore am I still
A lover of the meadows and the woods,
And mountains; and of all that we behold
From this green earth; of all the mighty world   105
Of eye, and ear,—both what they half create,
And what perceive; well pleased to recognise
In nature and the language of the sense,
The anchor of my purest thoughts, the nurse,
The guide, the guardian of my heart, and soul   110
Of all my moral being.
                          Nor perchance,
If I were not thus taught, should I the more
Suffer my genial spirits to decay:
For thou art with me here upon the banks
Of this fair river; thou my dearest Friend,   115
My dear, dear Friend; and in thy voice I catch

115. **Friend:** Wordsworth's sister Dorothy.

The language of my former heart, and read
My former pleasures in the shooting lights
Of thy wild eyes. Oh! yet a little while
May I behold in thee what I was once,   120
My dear, dear Sister! and this prayer I make,
Knowing that Nature never did betray
The heart that loved her; 'tis her privilege,
Through all the years of this our life, to lead
From joy to joy: for she can so inform   125
The mind that is within us, so impress
With quietness and beauty, and so feed
With lofty thoughts, that neither evil tongues,
Rash judgments, nor the sneers of selfish men,
Nor greetings where no kindness is, nor all   130
The dreary intercourse of daily life,
Shall e'er prevail against us, or disturb
Our cheerful faith, that all which we behold
Is full of blessings. Therefore let the moon
Shine on thee in thy solitary walk;   135
And let the misty mountain-winds be free
To blow against thee: and, in after years,
When these wild ecstasies shall be matured
Into a sober pleasure; when thy mind
Shall be a mansion for all lovely forms,   140
Thy memory be as a dwelling-place
For all sweet sounds and harmonies; oh! then,
If solitude, or fear, or pain, or grief,
Should be thy portion, with what healing thoughts
Of tender joy wilt thou remember me,   145
And these my exhortations! Nor, perchance—
If I should be where I no more can hear
Thy voice, nor catch from thy wild eyes these gleams
Of past existence—wilt thou then forget
That on the banks of this delightful stream   150
We stood together, and that I, so long
A worshipper of Nature, hither came
Unwearied in that service: rather say
With warmer love—oh! with far deeper zeal
Of holier love. Nor wilt thou then forget,   155
That after many wanderings, many years
Of absence, these steep woods and lofty cliffs,
And this green pastoral landscape, were to me
More dear, both for themselves and for thy sake!

149. past existence: Wordsworth's earlier
condition at the time of his first visit.

She dwelt among the untrodden ways

She dwelt among the untrodden ways
    Beside the springs of Dove,
A maid whom there were none to praise
    And very few to love:

A violet by a mossy stone   5
    Half hidden from the eye!
—Fair as a star, when only one
    Is shining in the sky.

She lived unknown, and few could know
    When Lucy ceased to be;   10
But she is in her grave, and, oh,
    The difference to me!

A slumber did my spirit seal

A slumber did my spirit seal;
    I had no human fears:
She seemed a thing that could not feel
    The touch of earthly years.

No motion has she now, no force;   5
    She neither hears nor sees;
Rolled round in earth's diurnal course,
    With rocks, and stones, and trees.

My heart leaps up

My heart leaps up when I behold
    A rainbow in the sky:
So was it when my life began;
So is it now, I am a man;
So be it when I shall grow old,   5
    Or let me die!
The Child is father of the Man;
And I could wish my days to be
Bound each to each by natural piety.

2. **Dove:** There is a river of this name in Wordsworth's beloved Lake Country.

2. **human:** mortal.
7. **diurnal:** daily.

Resolution and Independence

There was a roaring in the wind all night;
The rain came heavily and fell in floods;
But now the sun is rising calm and bright;
The birds are singing in the distant woods:
Over his own sweet voice the stock-dove broods;   5
The jay makes answer as the magpie chatters;
And all the air is filled with pleasant noise of waters.

All things that love the sun are out of doors;
The sky rejoices in the morning's birth;
The grass is bright with rain-drops;—on the moors   10
The hare is running races in her mirth;
And with her feet she from the plashy earth
Raises a mist, that, glittering in the sun,
Runs with her all the way wherever she doth run.

I was a traveller then upon the moor;   15
I saw the hare that raced about with joy;
I heard the woods and distant waters roar,
Or heard them not, as happy as a boy:
The pleasant season did my heart employ:
My old remembrances went from me wholly;   20
And all the ways of men so vain and melancholy.

But, as it sometimes chanceth, from the might
Of joy in minds that can no further go,
As high as we have mounted in delight
In our dejection do we sink as low,   25
To me that morning did it happen so;
And fears, and fancies, thick upon me came;
Dim sadness—and blind thoughts, I knew not, nor could name.

I heard the sky-lark warbling in the sky;
And I bethought me of the playful hare: 30
Even such a happy child of earth am I;
Even as these blissful creatures do I fare;
Far from the world I walk, and from all care;
But there may come another day to me—
Solitude, pain of heart, distress, and poverty.   35

My whole life I have lived in pleasant thought,
As if life's business were a summer mood;
As if all needful things would come unsought
To genial faith, still rich in genial good;
But how can he expect that others should   40
Build for him, sow for him, and at his call
Love him, who for himself will take no heed at all?

I thought of Chatterton, the marvelous boy,
The sleepless soul that perished in his pride;
Of him, who walked in glory and in joy   45
Following his plough, along the mountainside:
By our own spirits are we deified:
We poets in our youth begin in gladness;
But thereof come in the end despondency and madness.

Now, whether it were by peculiar grace,   50
A leading from above, a something given,
Yet it befell, that, in this lonely place,
When I with these untoward thoughts had striven,
Beside a pool bare to the eye of heaven
I saw a man before me unawares: 55
The oldest man he seemed that ever wore gray hairs.

As a huge stone is sometimes seen to lie
Couched on the bald top of an eminence;
Wonder to all who do the same espy,
By what means it could thither come, and whence;   60
So that it seems a thing endued with sense:
Like a sea-beast crawled forth, that on a shelf
Of rock or sand reposeth, there to sun itself;

Such seemed this man, not all alive nor dead,
Nor all asleep—in his extreme old age: 65
His body was bent double, feet and head
Coming together in life's pilgrimage;
As if some dire constraint of pain, or rage
Of sickness felt by him in times long past,
A more than human weight upon his frame had cast.   70

---

39. **genial:** characterized by genius.
43. **Chatterton:** Thomas Chatterton (1752–
1770), at seventeen, supposedly committed
suicide because of his lack of success as a
poet; actually he may have died from an
overdose of mercury attempting to cure
himself of syphilis.
45. **him:** Robert Burns.

Himself he propped, limbs, body and pale face,
Upon a long gray staff of shaven wood:
And, still as I drew near with gentle pace,
Upon the margin of that moorish flood
Motionless as a cloud the old man stood;   75
That heareth not the loud winds when they call,
And moveth altogether, if it move at all.

At length, himself unsettling, he the pond
Stirred with his staff and fixedly did look
Upon the muddy water, which he conned,   80
As if he had been reading in a book:
And now a stranger's privilege I took;
And, drawing to his side, to him did say
"This morning gives us promise of a glorious day."

A gentle answer did the old man make,   85
In courteous speech which forth he slowly drew:
And him with further words I thus bespake,
"What occupation do you there pursue?
This is a lonesome place for one like you."
Ere he replied, a flash of mild surprise   90
Broke from the sable orbs of his yet vivid eyes.

His words came feebly, from a feeble chest,
But each in solemn order followed each,
With something of a lofty utterance dressed;
Choice word, and measured phrase, above the reach   95
Of ordinary men; a stately speech;
Such as grave Livers do in Scotland use,
Religious men, who give to God and man their dues.

He told, that to these waters he had come
To gather leeches, being old and poor: 100
Employment hazardous and wearisome!
And he had many hardships to endure:
From pond to pond he roamed, from moor to moor;
Housing, with God's good help, by choice or chance;
And in this way he gained an honest maintenance.   105

The old man still stood talking by my side;
But now his voice to me was like a stream
Scarce heard; nor word from word could I divide;

100. **leeches:** then used for bloodletting,
a popular treatment.

And the whole body of the man did seem
Like one whom I had met with in a dream; 110
Or like a man from some far region sent,
To give me human strength, by apt admonishment.

My former thoughts returned: the fear that kills;
And hope that is unwilling to be fed;
Cold, pain and labor, and all fleshly ills; 115
And mighty poets in their misery dead.
Perplexed, and longing to be comforted,
My question eagerly did I renew,
"How is it that you live, and what is it you do?"

He with a smile did then his words repeat; 120
And said, that, gathering leeches, far and wide
He travelled; stirring thus about his feet
The waters of the pools where they abide.
"Once I could meet with them on every side;
But they have dwindled long by slow decay; 125
Yet still I persevere, and find them where I may."

While he was talking thus, the lonely place,
The old man's shape, and speech, all troubled me:
In my mind's eye I seemed to see him pace
About the weary moors continually, 130
Wandering about alone and silently.
While I these thoughts within myself pursued,
He, having made a pause, the same discourse renewed.

And soon with this he other matter blended,
Cheerfully uttered, with demeanor kind, 135
But stately in the main; and when he ended,
I could have laughed myself to scorn to find
In that decrepit man so firm a mind.
"God," said I, "be my help and stay secure;
I'll think of the leech-gatherer on the lonely moor!" 140

Yew Trees

There is a Yew Tree, pride of Lorton Vale,
Which to this day stands single, in the midst
Of its own darkness, as it stood of yore:
Not loath to furnish weapons for the bands

Yew: used for bows, with which the English
won many early victories.
1. **Lorton Vale:** in the Lake Country.

Of Umfraville or Percy ere they marched   5
To Scotland's heaths; or those that crossed the sea
And drew their sounding bows at Azincour,
Perhaps at earlier Crecy, or Poictiers.
Of vast circumference and gloom profound
This solitary Tree! a living thing   10
Produced too slowly ever to decay;
Of form and aspect too magnificent
To be destroyed. But worthier still of note
Are those fraternal Four of Borrowdale,
Joined in one solemn and capacious grove;   15
Huge trunks! and each particular trunk a growth
Of intertwisted fibers serpentine
Up-coiling, and inveterately convolved;
Nor uninformed with Phantasy, and looks
That threaten the profane—a pillared shade,   20
Upon whose grassless floor of red-brown hue,
By sheddings from the pining umbrage tinged
Perennially—beneath whose sable roof
Of boughs, as if for festal purpose decked
With unrejoicing berries—ghostly Shapes   25
May meet at noontide; Fear and trembling Hope,
Silence and Foresight; Death the Skeleton
And Time the Shadow—there to celebrate,
As in a natural temple scattered o'er
With altars undisturbed of mossy stone,   30
United worship; or in mute repose
To lie, and listen to the mountain flood
Murmuring from Glaramara's inmost caves.

I wandered lonely as a cloud

I wandered lonely as a cloud
That floats on high o'er vales and hills,
When all at once I saw a crowd,
A host, of golden daffodils,
Beside the lake, beneath the trees,   5
Fluttering and dancing in the breeze.

Continuous as the stars that shine
And twinkle on the milky way,
They stretch'd in never-ending line
Along the margin of a bay: 10
Ten thousand saw I at a glance
Tossing their heads in sprightly dance.

The waves beside them danced, but they
Out-did the sparkling waves in glee:—
A Poet could not but be gay   15
In such a jocund company!
I gazed—and gazed—but little thought
What wealth the show to me had brought:

For oft, when on my couch I lie
In vacant or in pensive mood,   20
They flash upon that inward eye
Which is the bliss of solitude;
And then my heart with pleasure fills
And dances with the daffodils.

Ode

Intimations of Immortality from Recollections of Early Childhood

*The Child is father of the Man;
And I could wish my days to be
Bound each to each by natural piety.*

I

There was a time when meadow, grove, and stream,
The earth, and every common sight,
        To me did seem
        Apparelled in celestial light,
The glory and the freshness of a dream.   5
It is not now as it hath been of yore;—
        Turn whereso'er I may,
        By night or day,
The things which I have seen I now can see no more.

II

        The Rainbow comes and goes,   10
        And lovely is the Rose,
        The Moon doth with delight
Look round her when the heavens are bare;
        Waters on a starry night
        Are beautiful and fair;   15
        The sunshine is a glorious birth;
        But yet I know, where'er I go,
That there hath past away a glory from the earth.

III

Now, while the birds thus sing a joyous song,
   And while the young lambs bound   20
      As to the tabor's sound,
To me alone there came a thought of grief:
A timely utterance gave that thought relief,
     And I again am strong:
The cataracts blow their trumpets from the steep;   25
No more shall grief of mine the season wrong;
I hear the Echoes through the mountains throng,
The Winds come to me from the fields of sleep,
     And all the earth is gay;
       Land and sea   30
    Give themselves up to jollity,
     And with the heart of May
   Doth every Beast keep holiday;—
      Thou Child of Joy,
Shout round me, let me hear thy shouts, thou happy
      Shepherd-boy!   35

IV

Ye blessed Creatures, I have heard the call
   Ye to each other make; I see
The heavens laugh with you in your jubilee;
   My heart is at your festival,
    My head hath its coronal,   40
The fulness of your bliss, I feel—I feel it all.
     Oh evil day! if I were sullen
     While Earth herself is adorning,
      This sweet May-morning,
     And the Children are culling   45
      On every side,
   In a thousand valleys far and wide,
   Fresh flowers; while the sun shines warm,
And the Babe leaps up on his Mother's arm:—
    I hear, I hear, with joy I hear!   50
    —But there's a Tree, of many, one,
A single Field which I have looked upon,
Both of them speak of something that is gone:
     The Pansy at my feet
     Doth the same tale repeat: 55
Whither is fled the visionary gleam?
Where is it now, the glory and the dream?

---

21. **tabor:** something like a tambourine.   40. **coronal:** garland of wild flowers.

V

Our birth is but a sleep and a forgetting:
The Soul that rises with us, our life's Star,
        Hath had elsewhere its setting,   60
            And cometh from afar:
        Not in entire forgetfulness,
        And not in utter nakedness,
But trailing clouds of glory do we come
            From God, who is our home: 65
Heaven lies about us in our infancy!
Shades of the prison-house begin to close
            Upon the growing Boy,
But He beholds the light, and whence it flows,
            He sees it in his joy;   70
The Youth, who daily farther from the east
        Must travel, still is Nature's Priest,
        And by the vision splendid
        Is on his way attended;
At length the Man perceives it die away,   75
And fade into the light of common day.

VI

Earth fills her lap with pleasures of her own;
Yearnings she hath in her own natural kind,
And, even with something of a Mother's mind,
            And no unworthy aim,   80
        The homely Nurse doth all she can
To make her Foster-child, her Inmate Man,
        Forget the glories he hath known,
And that imperial palace whence he came.

VII

Behold the Child among his new-born blisses,   85
A six years' Darling of a pigmy size!
See, where 'mid work of his own hand he lies,
Fretted by sallies of his mother's kisses,
With light upon him from his father's eyes!
See, at his feet, some little plan or chart,   90
Some fragment from his dream of human life,
Shaped by himself with newly-learned art;
        A wedding or a festival,
        A mourning or a funeral;

81. **homely:** simple, friendly.   88. **Fretted:** teased.

And this hath now his heart,   95
And unto this he frames his song:
Then will he fit his tongue
To dialogues of business, love, or strife;
But it will not be long
Ere this be thrown aside,   100
And with new joy and pride
The little Actor cons another part;
Filling from time to time his "humorous stage"
With all the Persons, down to palsied Age,
That Life brings with her in her equipage;   105
As if his whole vocation
Were endless imitation.

VIII

Thou, whose exterior semblance doth belie
Thy Soul's immensity;
Thou best Philosopher, who yet dost keep   110
Thy heritage, thou Eye among the blind,
That, deaf and silent, read'st the eternal deep,
Haunted forever by the eternal mind,—
Mighty Prophet! Seer blest!
On whom those truths do rest,   115
Which we are toiling all our lives to find,
In darkness lost, the darkness of the grave;
Thou, over whom thy Immortality
Broods like the Day, a Master o'er a Slave,
A Presence which is not to be put by;   120
Thou little Child, yet glorious in the might
Of heaven-born freedom on thy being's height,
Why with such earnest pains dost thou provoke
The years to bring the inevitable yoke,
Thus blindly with thy blessedness at strife?   125
Full soon thy Soul shall have her earthly freight,
And custom lie upon thee with a weight,
Heavy as frost, and deep almost as life!

IX

O joy! that in our embers
Is something that doth live,   130
That Nature yet remembers
What was so fugitive!

103. **humorous**: displaying all the humors,
or different kinds of character. Quoted
from the Elizabethan Samuel Daniel.

The thought of our past years in me doth breed
Perpetual benediction: not indeed
For that which is most worthy to be blest;   135
Delight and liberty, the simple creed
Of Childhood, whether busy or at rest,
With new-fledged hope still fluttering in his breast:—
    Not for these I raise
      The song of thanks and praise;   140
   But for those obstinate questionings
   Of sense and outward things,
   Fallings from us, vanishings;
   Blank misgivings of a Creature
Moving about in worlds not realized,   145
High instincts before which our mortal Nature
Did tremble like a guilty Thing surprised:
    But for those first affections,
    Those shadowy recollections,
     Which, be they what they may,   150
Are yet the fountain light of all our day,
Are yet a master light of all our seeing;
    Uphold us, cherish, and have power to make
Our noisy years seem moments in the being
Of the eternal Silence: truths that wake,   155
     To perish never;
Which neither listlessness, nor mad endeavor,
    Nor Man nor Boy,
Nor all that is at enmity with joy,
Can utterly abolish or destroy!   160
    Hence in a season of calm weather
    Though inland far we be,
Our Souls have sight of that immortal sea
    Which brought us hither,
    Can in a moment travel thither,   165
And see the Children sport upon the shore,
And hear the mighty waters rolling evermore.

          X

Then sing, ye Birds, sing, sing a joyous song!
    And let the young Lambs bound
    As to the tabor's sound!   170
We in thought will join your throng,
    Ye that pipe and ye that play,
    Ye that through your hearts to-day
    Feel the gladness of the May!

What though the radiance which was once so bright   175
Be now for ever taken from my sight,
   Though nothing can bring back the hour
Of splendor in the grass, of glory in the flower;
     We will grieve not, rather find
     Strength in what remains behind;   180
     In the primal sympathy
     Which having been must ever be;
     In the soothing thoughts that spring
     Out of human suffering;
     In the faith that looks through death,   185
In years that bring the philosophic mind.

XI

And O, ye Fountains, Meadows, Hills, and Groves,
Forbode not any severing of our loves!
Yet in my heart of hearts I feel your might;
I only have relinquished one delight   190
To live beneath your more habitual sway.
I love the Brooks which down their channels fret,
Even more than when I tripped lightly as they;
The innocent brightness of a new-born Day
     Is lovely yet;   195
The Clouds that gather round the setting sun
Do take a sober coloring from an eye
That hath kept watch o'er man's mortality;
Another race hath been, and other palms are won.
Thanks to the human heart by which we live,   200
Thanks to its tenderness, its joys, and fears,
To me the meanest flower that blows can give
Thoughts that do often lie too deep for tears.

The Solitary Reaper

    Behold her, single in the field,
    Yon solitary Highland Lass!
    Reaping and singing by herself;
    Stop here, or gently pass!
    Alone she cuts and binds the grain   5
    And sings a melancholy strain;
    Oh listen! for the vale profound
    Is overflowing with the sound.

199. **palms:** prizes for achievement.

No nightingale did ever chaunt
More welcome notes to weary bands　　　　10
Of travellers in some shady haunt,
Among Arabian sands:
A voice so thrilling ne'er was heard
In spring-time from the cuckoo-bird
Breaking the silence of the seas　　　　15
Among the farthest Hebrides.

Will no one tell me what she sings?—
Perhaps the plaintive numbers flow
For old, unhappy, far-off things,
And battles long ago:　　　　20
Or is it some more humble lay,
Familiar matter of to-day?
Some natural sorrow, loss, or pain,
That has been, and may be again?

Whate'er the theme, the maiden sang　　　　25
As if her song could have no ending;
I saw her singing at her work,
And o'er the sickle bending;—
I listened, motionless and still;
And, as I mounted up the hill,　　　　30
The music in my heart I bore,
Long after it was heard no more.

Personal Talk

I

I am not One who much or oft delight
To season my fireside with personal talk,—
Of friends, who live within an easy walk,
Or neighbors, daily, weekly, in my sight:
And, for my chance-acquaintance, ladies bright,　　　　5
Sons, mothers, maidens withering on the stalk,
These all wear out of me, like Forms, with chalk
Painted on rich men's floors, for one feastnight.
Better than such discourse doth silence long,
Long, barren silence, square with my desire;　　　　10

17. **what . . . sings:** According to Dorothy
Wordsworth's description of the reading
which inspired this poem, the girl was
singing in Gaelic.

Personal Talk: roughly, gossip.

To sit without emotion, hope, or aim,
In the loved presence of my cottage-fire,
And listen to the flapping of the flame,
Or kettle whispering its faint undersong.

II

"Yet life," you say, "is life; we have seen and see,   15
And with a living pleasure we describe;
And fits of sprightly malice do but bribe
The languid mind into activity.
Sound sense, and love itself, and mirth and glee
Are fostered by the comment and the gibe."   20
Even be it so; yet still among your tribe,
Our daily world's true Worldlings, rank not me!
Children are blest, and powerful; their world lies
More justly balanced; partly at their feet,
And part far from them: sweetest melodies   25
Are those that are by distance made more sweet;
Whose mind is but the mind of his own eyes,
He is a Slave; the meanest we can meet!

III

Wings have we,—and as far as we can go
We may find pleasure: wilderness and wood,   30
Blank ocean and mere sky, support that mood
Which with the lofty sanctifies the low.
Dreams, books, are each a world; and books, we know,
Are a substantial world, both pure and good:
Round these, with tendrils strong as flesh and blood,   35
Our pastime and our happiness will grow.
There find I personal themes, a plenteous store,
Matter wherein right voluble I am,
To which I listen with a ready ear;
Two shall be named, pre-eminently dear,—   40
The gentle Lady married to the Moor;
And heavenly Una with her milk-white Lamb.

IV

Nor can I not believe but that hereby
Great gains are mine; for thus I live remote
From evil-speaking; rancor, never sought,   45
Comes to me not; malignant truth, or lie.

41. **Lady:** Desdemona, married to Othello, in Shakespeare's *Othello*.
42. **Una:** After many adventures, she is espoused to the Redcross Knight in Edmund Spenser's *Faerie Queene*, I. She signifies variously truth and the true church.

Hence have I genial seasons, hence have I
Smooth passions, smooth discourse, and joyous thought:
And thus from day to day my little boat
Rocks in its harbor, lodging peaceably.   50
Blessing be with them—and eternal praise,
Who gave us nobler loves, and nobler cares—
The Poets, who on earth have made us heirs
Of truth and pure delight by heavenly lays!
Oh! might my name be numbered among theirs,   55
Then gladly would I end my mortal days.

Composed Upon Westminster Bridge

September 3, 1802

Earth has not anything to show more fair:
Dull would he be of soul who could pass by
A sight so touching in its majesty:
This City now doth, like a garment, wear
The beauty of the morning; silent, bare,   5
Ships, towers, domes, theatres, and temples lie
Open unto the fields, and to the sky;
All bright and glittering in the smokeless air.
Never did sun more beautifully steep
In his first splendour, valley, rock, or hill;   10
Ne'er saw I, never felt, a calm so deep!
The river glideth at his own sweet will:
Dear God! the very houses seem asleep;
And all that mighty heart is lying still!

It is a beauteous evening

It is a beauteous evening, calm and free;
The holy time is quiet as a nun
Breathless with adoration; the broad sun
Is sinking down in its tranquility;
The gentleness of heaven broods o'er the sea: 5
Listen! the mighty Being is awake,
And doth with his eternal motion make
A sound like thunder—everlastingly.
Dear child! dear girl! that walkest with me here,

Westminster Bridge: crossing the Thames near Westminster Abbey and the Houses of Parliament.

9. child: Wordsworth's companion on the beach at Calais in the autumn of 1802 was his natural daughter by Annette Vallon.

If thou appear untouched by solemn thought,   10
Thy nature is not therefore less divine:
Thou liest in Abraham's bosom all the year,
And worship'st at the Temple's inner shrine,
God being with thee when we know it not.

London, 1802

Milton! thou shouldst be living at this hour;
England hath need of thee; she is a fen
Of stagnant waters: altar, sword, and pen,
Fireside, the heroic wealth of hall and bower,
Have forfeited their ancient English dower   5
Of inward happiness. We are selfish men;
Oh! raise us up, return to us again;
And give us manners, virtue, freedom, power.
Thy soul was like a Star, and dwelt apart:
Thou hadst a voice whose sound was like the sea: 10
Pure as the naked heavens, majestic, free,
So didst thou travel on life's common way,
In cheerful godliness; and yet thy heart
The lowliest duties on herself did lay.

Nuns fret not

Nuns fret not at their convent's narrow room;
And hermits are contented with their cells;
And students with their pensive citadels;
Maids at the wheel, the weaver at his loom,
Sit blithe and happy; bees that soar for bloom,   5
High as the highest Peak of Furness-fells,
Will murmur by the hour in foxglove bells:
In truth, the prison, unto which we doom
Ourselves, no prison is: and hence for me,
In sundry moods, 'twas pastime to be bound   10
Within the Sonnet's scanty plot of ground;
Pleased if some Souls (for such there needs must be)
Who have felt the weight of too much liberty,
Should find brief solace there, as I have found.

12. **Abraham's bosom**: where souls were   6. **Furness**: south of the Lake Country, in
to rest after death (Luke 16: 22).   northern Lancashire.

The world is too much with us

The world is too much with us; late and soon,
Getting and spending, we lay waste our powers:
Little we see in Nature that is ours;
We have given our hearts away, a sordid boon!
The Sea that bares her bosom to the moon;   5
The winds that will be howling at all hours,
And are up-gathered now like sleeping flowers;
For this, for everything, we are out of tune;
It moves us not.—Great God! I'd rather be
A Pagan, suckled in a creed outworn,   10
So might I, standing on this pleasant lea,
Have glimpses that would make me less forlorn;
Have sight of Proteus rising from the sea;
Or hear old Triton blow his wreathèd horn.

Mutability

From low to high doth dissolution climb,
And sink from high to low, along a scale
Of awful notes, whose concord shall not fail;
A musical but melancholy chime,
Which they can hear who meddle not with crime,   5
Nor avarice, nor over-anxious care.
Truth fails not; but her outward forms that bear
The longest date do melt like frosty rime
That in the morning whiten'd hill and plain
And is no more; drop like the tower sublime   10
Of yesterday, which royally did wear
His crown of weeds, but could not even sustain
Some casual shout that broke the silent air,
Or the unimaginable touch of Time.

---

4. **sordid boon:** i.e., the giving is sordid, not the gift.

13–14. **Proteus, Triton:** sea-creatures of classical narrative and myth.

SAMUEL TAYLOR COLERIDGE

[*1772–1834*]

The Rime of the Ancient Mariner

Part I

An ancient Mariner meeteth three Gallants bidden to a wedding-feast, and detaineth one.

It is an ancient Mariner,
And he stoppeth one of three.
"By thy long grey beard and glittering eye,
Now wherefore stopp'st thou me?

The Bridegroom's doors are opened wide, 5
And I am next of kin;
The guests are met, the feast is set:
May'st hear the merry din."

He holds him with his skinny hand,
"There was a ship," quoth he. 10
"Hold off! unhand me, greybeard loon!"
Eftsoons his hand drop he.

The Wedding-Guest is spellbound by the eye of the old seafaring man, and constrained to hear his tale.

He holds him with his glittering eye—
The Wedding-Guest stood still,
And listens like a three year's child: 15
The Mariner hath his will.

The Wedding-Guest sat on a stone:
He cannot choose but hear;
And thus spake on that ancient man,
The bright-eyed Mariner. 20

"The ship was cheered, the harbour cleared,
Merrily did we drop
Below the kirk, below the hill,
Below the lighthouse top.

The Mariner tells how the ship sailed southward with a good wind and fair weather, till it reached the line.

The Sun came up upon the left, 25
Out of the sea came he!
And he shone bright, and on the right
Went down into the sea.

Higher and higher every day,
Till over the mast at noon—"
The Wedding-Guest here beat his breast,   30
For he heard the loud bassoon.

The Wedding-
Guest heareth
the bridal
music; but the
Mariner contin-
ueth his tale.

The Bride hath paced into the hall,
Red as a rose is she;
Nodding their heads before her goes   35
The merry minstrelsy.

The Wedding-Guest he beat his breast,
Yet he cannot choose but hear;
And thus spake on that ancient man,
The bright-eyed Mariner.   40

The ship driven
by a storm
toward the
South Pole.

"And now the STORM-BLAST came, and he
Was tyrannous and strong:
He struck with his o'ertaking wings,
And chased us south along.

With sloping masts and dipping prow,   45
As who pursued with yell and blow
Still treads the shadow of his foe
And forward bends his head,
The ship drove fast, loud roared the blast,
And southward aye we fled.   50

And now there came both mist and snow
And it grew wondrous cold:
And ice, mast-high, came floating by,
As green as emerald.

The land of ice,
and of fearful
sounds, where
no living thing
was to be seen.

And through the drifts the snowy clifts   55
Did send a dismal sheen:
Nor shapes of men nor beasts we ken—
The ice was all between.

The ice was here, the ice was there,
The ice was all around: 60
It cracked and growled, and roared and howled,
Like noises in a swound!

Till a great sea-
bird, called the
Albatross, came
through the
snow-fog, and
was received
with great joy
and hospitality.

At length did cross an Albatross:
Thorough the fog it came;
As if it had been a Christian soul,   65
We hailed it in God's name.

It ate the food it ne'er had eat,
And round and round it flew.
The ice did split with a thunder-fit;
The helmsman steered us through! 70

And lo! the Albatross proveth a bird of good omen, and followeth the ship as it returned northward through fog and floating ice.

And a good south wind sprung up behind;
The Albatross did follow,
And every day, for food or play,
Came to the mariners' hollo!

In mist or cloud, on mast or shroud,
It perched for vespers nine; 75
Whiles all the night, through fog-smoke white,
Glimmered the white Moon-shine."

The ancient Mariner inhospitably killeth the pious bird of good omen.

"God save thee, ancient Mariner!
From the fiends that plague thee thus!— 80
Why look'st thou so?"—"With my crossbow
I shot the Albatross.

Part II

The Sun now rose upon the right:
Out of the sea came he,
Still hid in mist, and on the left 85
Went down into the sea.

And the good south wind still blew behind,
But no sweet bird did follow,
Nor any day for food or play
Came to the mariners' hollo! 90

His shipmates cry out against the ancient Mariner for killing the bird of good luck.

And I had done a hellish thing,
And it would work 'em woe:
For all averred, I had killed the bird
That made the breeze to blow.
Ah wretch! said they, the bird to slay, 95
That made the breeze to blow!

But when the fog cleared off, they justify the same, and thus make themselves accomplices in the crime.

Nor dim nor red, like God's own head,
The glorious Sun uprist:
Then all averred, I had killed the bird
That brought the fog and mist. 100
'Twas right, said they, such birds to slay,
That bring the fog and mist.

*The fair breeze
continues; the
ship enters the
Pacific Ocean
and sails north-
ward, even till
it reaches the
Line.*

The fair breeze blew, the white foam flew,
The furrow followed free;
We were the first that ever burst   105
Into that silent sea.

*The ship hath
been suddenly
becalmed.*

Down dropt the breeze, the sails dropt down,
'Twas sad as sad could be;
And we did speak only to break
The silence of the sea!   110

All in a hot and copper sky,
The bloody Sun, at noon,
Right up above the mast did stand,
No bigger than the Moon.

Day after day, day after day,   115
We stuck, nor breath nor motion;
As idle as a painted ship
Upon a painted ocean.

*And the Alba-
tross begins to
be avenged.*

Water, water, everywhere,
And all the boards did shrink;   120
Water, water, everywhere,
Nor any drop to drink.

The very deep did rot: O Christ!
That ever this should be!
Yea, slimy things did crawl with legs   125
Upon the slimy sea.

About, about, in reel and rout
The death-fires danced at night;
The water, like a witch's oils,
Burnt green, and blue, and white.   130

And some in dreams assurèd were

*A Spirit had
followed them;
one of the in-
visible inhabi-
tants of this
planet, neither*

Of the Spirit that plagued us so;
Nine fathom deep he had followed us
From the land of mist and snow.

*departed souls nor angels; concerning whom the learned Jew, Josephus, and the Platonic Constantino-
politan, Michael Psellus, may be consulted. They are very numerous, and there is no climate or element
without one or more.*

And every tongue, through utter drought,   135
Was withered at the root;
We could not speak, no more than if
We had been choked with soot.

The shipmates, in their sore distress, would fain throw the whole guilt on the ancient Mariner; in sign whereof they hang the dead sea-bird round his neck.

Ah! well-a-day! what evil looks
Had I from old and young!   140
Instead of the cross, the Albatross
About my neck was hung.

Part III

There passed a weary time. Each throat
Was parched, and glazed each eye.
A weary time! a weary time!   145

The ancient Mariner beholdeth a sign in the element afar off.

How glazed each weary eye!
When looking westward, I beheld
A something in the sky.

At first it seemed a little speck,
And then it seemed a mist;   150
It moved and moved, and took at last
A certain shape, I wist.

A speck, a mist, a shape, I wist!
And still it neared and neared:
As if it dodged a water-sprite,   155
It plunged and tacked and veered.

As its nearer approach it seemeth him to be a ship; and at a dear ransom he freeth his speech from the bonds of thirst.

With throats unslaked, with black lips baked,
We could not laugh nor wail;
Through utter drought all dumb we stood!
I bit my arm, I sucked the blood,   160
And cried, A sail! a sail!

With throats unslaked, with black lips baked,
Agape they heard me call:

A flash of joy;

Gramercy! they for joy did grin,
And all at once their breath drew in,   165
As they were drinking all.

And horror follows. For can it be a ship that comes onward without wind or tide?

See! See! (I cried) she tacks no more!
Hither to work us weal;
Without a breeze, without a tide,
She steadies with upright keel!   170

The western wave was all a-flame.
The day was well nigh done!
Almost upon the western wave
Rested the broad bright Sun;
When that strange shape drove suddenly   175
Betwixt us and the Sun.

*It seemeth him
but the skeleton
of a ship.*

And straight the Sun was flecked with bars,
(Heaven's Mother send us grace!)
As if through a dungeon-grate he peered
With broad and burning face.   180

Alas! (thought I, and my heart beat loud)
How fast she nears and nears!
*And its ribs are
seen as bars on
the face of the
setting Sun.*
Are those her sails that glance in the Sun,
Like restless gossameres!

*The Spectre-
Woman and her
Death-mate,
and no other on
board the
skeleton ship.*
Are those her ribs through which the Sun   185
Did peer, as through a grate?
And is that Woman all her crew?
Is that a DEATH? and are there two?
Is DEATH that woman's mate?

*Like vessel, like
crew!*

*Death and Life-
in-Death have
diced for the
ship's crew, and
she (the latter)
winneth the an-
cient Mariner.*
Her lips were red, her looks were free,   190
Her locks were yellow as gold:
Her skin was as white as leprosy,
The Nightmare LIFE-IN-DEATH was she,
Who thicks man's blood with cold.

The naked hulk alongside came   195
And the twain were casting dice;
'—The game is done! I've won, I've won!—'
Quoth she, and whistles thrice.

*No twilight
within the
courts of the
Sun.*
The Sun's rim dips; the stars rush out:
At one stride comes the dark;   200
With far-heard whisper, o'er the sea,
Off shot the spectre-bark.

We listened and looked sideways up!
Fear at my heart, as at a cup,
My life-blood seemed to sip!   205
The stars were dim, and thick the night,
The steersman's face by his lamp gleamed white;
From the sails the dew did drip—
*At the rising of
the Moon.*
Till clomb above the eastern bar
The hornèd Moon, with one bright star   210
Within the nether tip.

*One after
another,*
One after one, by the star-dogged Moon,
Too quick for groan or sigh,
Each turned his face with a ghastly pang,
And cursed me with his eye.   215

His shipmates drop down dead;

Four times fifty living men,
(And I heard nor sigh nor groan)
With heavy thump, a lifeless lump,
They dropped down one by one.

But Life-in-Death begins her work on the ancient Mariner.

The souls did from their bodies fly,—   220
They fled to bliss or woe!
And every soul, it passed me by,
Like the whizz of my crossbow!"

Part IV

The Wedding-Guest feareth that a spirit is talking to him;

"I fear thee, ancient Mariner!
I fear thy skinny hand!   225
And thou art long, and lank, and brown,
As is the ribbed sea-sand.

I fear thee and thy glittering eye,
And thy skinny hand, so brown."—

But the ancient Mariner assureth him of his bodily life, and proceedeth to relate his horrible penance.

"Fear not, fear not, thou Wedding-Guest!   230
This body dropt not down.

Alone, alone, all, all alone,
Alone on a wide wide sea!
And never a saint took pity on
My soul in agony.   235

He despiseth the creatures of the calm,

The many men, so beautiful!
And they all dead did lie:
And a thousand thousand slimy things
Lived on; and so did I.

And envieth that they should live, and so many lie dead.

I looked upon the rotting sea,   240
And drew my eyes away;
I looked upon the rotting deck,
And there the dead men lay.

I looked to Heaven, and tried to pray;
But or ever a prayer had gusht,   245
A wicked whisper came, and made
My heart as dry as dust.

I closed my lids, and kept them close,
And the balls like pulses beat;
For the sky and the sea, and the sea and the sky,   250
Lay like a load on my weary eye,
And the dead were at my feet.

*But the curse
liveth for him
in the eye of
the dead men.*
The cold sweat melted from their limbs,
Nor rot nor reek did they;
The look with which they looked on me   255
Had never passed away.

An orphan's curse would drag to hell
A spirit from on high;
But oh! more horrible than that
Is a curse in a dead man's eye!   260
Seven days, seven nights, I saw that curse,
And yet I could not die.

*In his loneliness
and fixedness he
yearneth to-
wards the jour-
neying Moon,
and the Stars
that still sojourn,
yet still move on-
ward; and every-
where the blue
sky belongs to
them, and is
their appointed
rest, and their
native country
and their own
natural homes,
which they enter
unannounced, as
lords that are certainly expected and yet there is a silent joy at their arrival.*
The moving Moon went up the sky,
And nowhere did abide:
Softly she was going up,   265
And a star or two beside—

Her beams bemocked the sultry main,
Like April hoar-frost spread;
But where the ship's huge shadow lay,
The charmèd water burnt alway   270
A still and awful red.

*By the light of
the Moon he
beholdeth God's
creatures of the
great calm.*
Beyond the shadow of the ship,
I watched the water-snakes:
They moved in tracks of shining white,
And when they reared, the elfish light   275
Fell off in hoary flakes.

Within the shadow of the ship
I watched their rich attire:
Blue, glossy green, and velvet black,
They coiled and swam; and every track   280
Was a flash of golden fire.

*Their beauty
and their happi-
ness.*
O happy living things! no tongue
Their beauty might declare:
A spring of love gushed from my heart,
*He blesseth
them in his
heart.*
And I blessed them unaware: 285
Sure my kind saint took pity on me,
And I blessed them unaware.

*The spell begins
to break.*
The selfsame moment I could pray;
And from my neck so free
The Albatross fell off, and sank   290
Like lead into the sea.

Part V

Oh sleep! it is a gentle thing,
Beloved from pole to pole!
To Mary Queen the praise be given!
She sent the gentle sleep from Heaven,   295
That slid into my soul.

By grace of the holy Mother, the ancient Mariner is refreshed with rain.

The silly buckets on the deck,
That had so long remained,
I dreamt that they were filled with dew;
And when I awoke, it rained.   300

My lips were wet, my throat was cold,
My garments all were dank;
Sure I had drunken in my dreams,
And still my body drank.

I moved, and could not feel my limbs: 305
I was so light—almost
I thought that I had died in sleep,
And was a blessèd ghost.

He heareth sounds and seeth strange sights and commotions in the sky and the element.

And soon I saw a roaring wind:
It did not come anear;   310
But with its sound it shook the sails,
That were so thin and sere.

The upper air burst into life!
And a hundred fire-flags sheen,
To and fro they were hurried about!   315
And to and fro, and in and out,
The wan stars danced between.

And the coming wind did roar more loud,
And the sails did sigh like sedge;
And the rain poured down from one black cloud;   320
The Moon was at its edge.

The thick black cloud was cleft, and still
The Moon was at its side:
Like waters shot from some high crag,
The lightning fell with never a jag,   325
A river steep and wide.

The bodies of the ship's crew are inspired, and the ship moves on;

The loud wind never reached the ship,
Yet now the ship moved on!
Beneath the lightning and the Moon
The dead men gave a groan.   330

They groaned, they stirred, they all uprose,
Nor spake, nor moved their eyes;
It had been strange, even in a dream,
To have seen those dead men rise.

The helmsman steered, the ship moved on;   335
Yet never a breeze up-blew;
The mariners all 'gan work the ropes,
Where they were wont to do;
They raised their limbs like lifeless tools—
We were a ghastly crew.   340

The body of my brother's son
Stood by me, knee to knee:
The body and I pulled at one rope,
But he said nought to me."

"I fear thee, ancient Mariner!"   345
"Be calm, thou Wedding-Guest!

But not by the souls of the men, nor by daemons of earth or middle air, but by a blessed troop of angelic spirits, sent down by the invocation of the guardian saint.

'Twas not those souls that fled in pain,
Which to their corses came again,
But a troop of spirits blest:

For when it dawned—they dropt their arms,   350
And clustered round the mast;
Sweet sounds rose slowly through their mouths,
And from their bodies passed.

Around, around, flew each sweet sound,
Then darted to the Sun;   355
Slowly the sounds came back again,
Now mixed, now one by one.

Sometimes a-dropping from the sky
I heard the sky-lark sing;
Sometimes all little birds that are,   360
How they seemed to fill the sea and air
With their sweet jargoning!

And now 'twas like all instruments,
Now like a lonely flute;
And now it is an angel's song,   365
That makes the heavens be mute.

348. corses: corpses.

It ceased; yet still the sails made on
A pleasant noise till noon,
A noise like of a hidden brook
In the leafy month of June,   370
That to the sleeping woods all night
Singeth a quiet tune.

Till noon we quietly sailed on,
Yet never a breeze did breathe:
Slowly and smoothly went the ship,   375
Moved onward from beneath.

*The lonesome
Spirit from the
South-pole car-
ries on the ship
as far as the
Line, in obedi-
ence to the an-
gelic troop, but
still requireth
vengeance.*

Under the keel nine fathom deep,
From the land of mist and snow,
The Spirit slid: and it was he
That made the ship to go.   380
The sails at noon left off their tune,
And the ship stood still also.

The Sun, right up above the mast,
Had fixed her to the ocean:
But in a minute she 'gan stir,   385
With a short uneasy motion—
Backwards and forwards half her length
With a short uneasy motion.

Then, like a pawing horse let go,
She made a sudden bound: 390
It flung the blood into my head,
And I fell down in a swound.

*The Polar
Spirit's fellow
daemons, the
invisible inhabi-
tants of the ele-
ment, take part
in his wrong;
and two of them
relate, one to
the other, that
penance long
and heavy for
the ancient
Mariner hath
been accorded
to the Polar
Spirit, who re-
turneth south-
ward.*

How long in that same fit I lay,
I have not to declare;
But ere my living life returned,   395
I heard and in my soul discerned
Two voices in the air.

'Is it he?' quoth one, 'Is this the man?
By him who died on cross,
With his cruel bow he laid full low   400
The harmless Albatross.

The spirit who bideth by himself
In the land of mist and snow,
He loved the bird that loved the man
Who shot him with his bow.'   405

The other was a softer voice,
As soft as honey-dew:
Quoth he, 'The man hath penance done,
And penance more will do.'

Part VI

FIRST VOICE

'But tell me, tell me! speak again,   410
Thy soft response renewing—
What makes that ship drive on so fast?
What is the ocean doing?'

SECOND VOICE

'Still as a slave before his lord,
The ocean hath no blast;   415
His great bright eye most silently
Up to the Moon is cast—

If he may know which way to go;
For she guides him smooth or grim.
See, brother, see! how graciously   420
She looketh down on him.'

FIRST VOICE

The Mariner hath been cast into a trance; for the angelic power causeth the vessel to drive northward faster than human life could endure.

'But why drives on that ship so fast,
Without or wave or wind?'

SECOND VOICE

'The air is cut away before,
And closes from behind.

Fly, brother, fly! more high, more high!
Or we shall be belated:
For slow and slow that ship will go,
When the Mariner's trance is abated.'   425

The supernatural motion is retarded; the Mariner awakes, and his penance begins anew.

I woke, and we were sailing on   430
As in a gentle weather:
'Twas night, calm night, the Moon was high;
The dead men stood together.

All stood together on the deck,
For a charnel-dungeon fitter: 435
All fixed on me their stony eyes,
That in the Moon did glitter.

The pang, the curse, with which they died,
Had never passed away:
I could not draw my eyes from theirs,
Nor turn them up to pray.   440

The curse is finally expiated.

And now this spell was snapt: once more
I viewed the ocean green,
And looked far forth, yet little saw
Of what had else been seen—   445

Like one that on a lonesome road
Doth walk in fear and dread,
And having once turned round walks on,
And turns no more his head;
Because he knows a frightful fiend   450
Doth close behind him tread.

But soon there breathed a wind on me,
Nor sound nor motion made:
Its path was not upon the sea,
In ripple or in shade.   455

It raised my hair, it fanned my cheek
Like a meadow-gale of spring—
It mingled strangely with my fears,
Yet it felt like a welcoming.

Swiftly, swiftly flew the ship,   460
Yet she sailed softly too:
Sweetly, sweetly blew the breeze—
On me alone it blew.

And the ancient Mariner beholdeth his native country.

Oh! dream of joy! is this indeed
The lighthouse top I see?   465
Is this the hill? is this the kirk?
Is this mine own countree?

We drifted o'er the harbour-bar,
And I with sobs did pray—
O let me be awake, my God!   470
Or let me sleep alway.

The harbour-bay was clear as glass,
So smoothly was it strewn!
And on the bay the moonlight lay,
And the shadow of the Moon.   475

The rock shone bright, the kirk no less,
That stands above the rock:
The moonlight steeped in silentness
The steady weathercock.

And the bay was white with silent light,   480
Till rising from the same,
Full many shapes, that shadows were,
In crimson colours came.

*The angelic
spirits leave the
dead bodies, and
appear in their
own forms of
light.*

A little distance from the prow
Those crimson shadows were: 485
I turned my eyes upon the deck—
O, Christ! what saw I there!

Each corse lay flat, lifeless and flat,
And, by the holy rood!
A man all light, a seraph-man,   490
On every corse there stood.

This seraph-band, each waved his hand:
It was a heavenly sight!
They stood as signals to the land,
Each one a lovely light;   495

This seraph-band, each waved his hand,
No voice did they impart—
No voice; but oh! the silence sank
Like music on my heart.

But soon I heard the dash of oars,   500
I heard the Pilot's cheer;
My head was turned perforce away,
And I saw a boat appear.

The Pilot and the Pilot's boy,
I heard them coming fast: 505
Dear Lord in Heaven! it was a joy
That dead men could not blast.

I saw a third—I heard his voice:
It is the Hermit good!
He singeth loud his godly hymns   510
That he makes in the wood.
He'll shrieve my soul, he'll wash away
The Albatross's blood.

Part VII

The Hermit of the Wood

This Hermit good lives in that wood
Which slopes down to the sea.   515
How loudly his sweet voice he rears!
He loves to talk with the marineres
That come from a far countree.

He kneels at morn, and noon, and eve—
He hath a cushion plump: 520
It is the moss that wholly hides
The rotted old oak-stump.

The skiff-boat neared: I heard them talk,
'Why this is strange, I trow!
Where are those lights so many and fair,   525
That signal made but now?'

Approacheth the ship with wonder.

'Strange, by faith!' the Hermit said—
'And they answered not our cheer!
The planks look warped! and see those sails,
How thin they are and sere!   530
I never saw aught like to them,
Unless perchance it were

Brown skeletons of leaves that lag
My forest-brook along;
When the ivy-tod is heavy with snow,   535
And the owlet whoops to the wolf below,
That eats the she-wolf's young.'

'Dear Lord! it hath a fiendish look—'
(The Pilot made reply)
'I am a-feared'—'Push on, push on!'   540
Said the Hermit cheerily.

The boat came closer to the ship,
But I nor spake nor stirred;
The boat came close beneath the ship,
And straight a sound was heard.   545

The ship suddenly sinketh.

Under the water it rumbled on,
Still louder and more dread:
It reached the ship, it split the bay;
The ship went down like lead.

*The ancient
Mariner is saved
in the Pilot's
boat.*

Stunned by that loud and deadful sound,   550
Which sky and ocean smote,
Like one that hath been seven days drowned
My body lay afloat;
But swift as dreams, myself I found
Within the Pilot's boat.   555

Upon the whirl, where sank the ship,
The boat spun round and round;
And all was still, save that the hill
Was telling of the sound.

I moved my lips—the Pilot shrieked   560
And fell down in a fit;
The holy Hermit raised his eyes,
And prayed where he did sit.

I took the oars: the Pilot's boy,
Who now doth crazy go,   565
Laughed loud and long, and all the while
His eyes went to and fro.
'Ha! ha!' quoth he, 'full plain I see,
The Devil knows how to row.'

And now, all in my own countree,   570
I stood on the firm land!
The Hermit stepped forth from the boat,
And scarcely he could stand.

*The ancient
Mariner earn-
estly entreateth
the Hermit to
shrieve him; and
the penance of
life falls on
him.*

'O shrieve me, shrieve me, holy man!'
The Hermit crossed his brow.   575
'Say quick,' quoth he, 'I bid thee say—
What manner of man are thou?'

Forthwith this frame of mine was wrenched
With a woeful agony,
Which forced me to begin my tale;   580
And then it left me free.

*And ever and
anon through-
out his future
life an agony
constraineth
him to travel
from land to
land.*

Since then, at an uncertain hour,
That agony returns:
And still my ghastly tale is told,
This heart within me burns.   585

574. **shrieve:** to free from guilt.

I pass, like night, from land to land;
I have strange power of speech;
That moment that his face I see,
I know the man that must hear me:
To him my tale I teach.   590

What loud uproar bursts from that door!
The wedding-guests are there:
But in the garden-bower the bride
And bride-maids singing are:
And hark the little vesper bell,   595
Which biddeth me to prayer!

O Wedding-Guest! this soul hath been
Alone on a wide wide sea:
So lonely 'twas, that God himself
Scarce seemèd there to be.   600

O sweeter than the marriage-feast,
'Tis sweeter far to me,
To walk together to the kirk
With a goodly company!—

To walk together to the kirk,   605
And all together pray,
While each to his great Father bends,
Old men, and babes, and loving friends,
And youths and maidens gay!

And to teach, by his own example, love and reverence to all things that God made and loveth.

Farewell, farewell! but this I tell   610
To thee, thou Wedding Guest!
He prayeth well, who loveth well
Both man and bird and beast.

He prayeth best, who loveth best
All things both great and small;   615
For the dear God who loveth us,
He made and loveth all."

The Mariner, whose eye is bright,
Whose beard with age is hoar,
Is gone: and now the Wedding-Guest   620
Turned from the bridegroom's door.

He went like one that hath been stunned,
And is of sense forlorn:
A sadder and a wiser man,
He rose the morrow morn.   625

Frost at Midnight

The Frost performs its secret ministry,
Unhelped by any wind. The owlet's cry
Came loud—and hark, again! loud as before.
The inmates of my cottage, all at rest,
Have left me to that solitude, which suits   5
Abstruser musings: save that at my side
My cradled infant slumbers peacefully.
'Tis calm indeed; so calm, that it disturbs
And vexes meditation with its strange
And extreme silentness. Sea, hill, and wood,   10
This populous village! Sea, and hill, and wood,
With all the numberless goings-on of life,
Inaudible as dreams! the thin blue flame
Lies on my low-burnt fire, and quivers not;
Only that film, which fluttered on the grate,   15
Still flutters there, the sole unquiet thing.
Methinks, its motion in this hush of nature
Gives it dim sympathies with me who live,
Making it a companionable form,
Whose puny flaps and freaks the idling Spirit   20
By its own moods interprets, everywhere
Echo or mirror seeking of itself,
And makes a toy of Thought.
                                    But O! how oft,
How oft, at school, with most believing mind,
Presageful, have I gazed upon the bars,   25
To watch that fluttering stranger! and as oft
With unclosed lids, already had I dreamt
Of my sweet birth-place, and the old church-tower,
Whose bells, the poor man's only music, rang
From morn to evening, all the hot Fair-day,   30
So sweetly, that they stirred and haunted me
With a wild pleasure, falling on mine ear
Most like articulate sounds of things to come!
So gazed I, till the soothing things, I dreamt,
Lulled me to sleep, and sleep prolonged my dreams!   35
And so I brooded all the following morn,
Awed by the stern preceptor's face, mine eye
Fixed with mock study on my swimming book:
Save if the door half opened, and I snatched

A hasty glance, and still my heart leaped up,   40
For still I hoped to see the *stranger's* face,
Townsman, or aunt, or sister more beloved,
My playmate when we both were clothed alike!

    Dear Babe, that sleepest cradled by my side,
Whose gentle breathings, heard in this deep calm,   45
Fill up the interspersèd vacancies
And momentary pauses of the thought!
My babe so beautiful! it thrills my heart
With tender gladness, thus to look at thee,
And think that thou shalt learn far other lore,   50
And in far other scenes! For I was reared
In the great city, pent 'mid cloisters dim,
And saw nought lovely but the sky and stars.
But *thou*, my babe! shalt wander like a breeze
By lakes and sandy shores, beneath the crags   55
Of ancient mountain, and beneath the clouds,
Which image in their bulk both lakes and shores
And mountain crags: so shalt thou see and hear
The lovely shapes and sounds intelligible
Of that eternal language, which thy God   60
Utters, who from eternity doth teach
Himself in all, and all things in himself.
Great universal Teacher! he shall mold
Thy spirit, and by giving make it ask.

    Therefore all seasons shall be sweet to thee,   65
Whether the summer clothe the general earth
With greenness, or the redbreast sit and sing
Betwixt the tufts of snow on the bare branch
Of mossy apple-tree, while the nigh thatch
Smokes in the sun-thaw; whether the eave-drops fall   70
Heard only in the trances of the blast,
Or if the secret ministry of frost
Shall hang them up in silent icicles,
Quietly shining to the quiet Moon.

Kubla Khan

    In Xanadu did Kubla Khan
A stately pleasure-dome decree:
Where Alph, the sacred river, ran
Through caverns measureless to man
    Down to a sunless sea.   5

So twice five miles of fertile ground
With walls and towers were girdled round:
And there were gardens bright with sinuous rills,
Where blossomed many an incense-bearing tree;
And here were forests ancient as the hills,   10
Enfolding sunny spots of greenery.

But oh! that deep romantic chasm which slanted
Down the green hill athwart a cedarn cover!
A savage place! as holy and enchanted
As e'er beneath a waning moon was haunted   15
By woman wailing for her demon-lover!
And from this chasm, with ceaseless turmoil seething,
As if this earth in fast thick pants were breathing,
A mighty fountain momently was forced:
Amid whose swift half-intermitted burst   20
Huge fragments vaulted like rebounding hail,
Or chaffy grain beneath the thresher's flail:
And 'mid these dancing rocks at once and ever
It flung up momently the sacred river.
Five miles meandering with a mazy motion   25
Through wood and dale the sacred river ran,
Then reached the caverns measureless to man,
And sank in tumult to a lifeless ocean:
And 'mid this tumult Kubla heard from far
Ancestral voices prophesying war!   30
　　The shadow of the dome of pleasure
　　Floated midway on the waves;
　　Where was heard the mingled measure
　　From the fountain and the caves.
It was a miracle of rare device,   35
A sunny pleasure-dome with caves of ice!

　　A damsel with a dulcimer
　　In a vision once I saw:
　　It was an Abyssinian maid,
　　And on her dulcimer she played,   40
　　Singing of Mount Abora.
　　Could I revive within me
　　Her symphony and song,
　　To such a deep delight 'twould win me,
That with music loud and long,   45
I would build that dome in air,

37. **dulcimer:** a musical instrument made of
wires stretched over a sounding board and
played with two light hammers.

That sunny dome! those caves of ice!
And all who heard should see them there,
And all should cry, Beware! Beware!
His flashing eyes, his floating hair!   *50*
Weave a circle round him thrice,
And close your eyes with holy dread,
For he on honey-dew hath fed,
And drunk the milk of Paradise.

Dejection: An Ode

[*Written April 4, 1802*]

> Late, late yestreen I saw the new Moon,
> With the old Moon in her arms;
> And I fear, I fear, my Master dear!
> We shall have a deadly storm.
>   *Ballad of Sir Patrick Spence.*

I

Well! If the Bard was weather-wise, who made
    The grand old ballad of Sir Patrick Spence,
    This night, so tranquil now, will not go hence
Unroused by winds, that ply a busier trade
Than those which mould yon cloud in lazy flakes,   5
Or the dull sobbing draft, that moans and rakes
Upon the strings of this Æolian lute,
    Which better far were mute.
    For lo! the New-moon winter-bright!
    And overspread with phantom light,   10
    (With swimming phantom light o'erspread
    But rimmed and circled by a silver thread)
I see the old Moon in her lap, foretelling
    The coming-on of rain and squally blast.
And oh! that even now the gust were swelling,   15
    And the slant night-shower driving loud and fast!
Those sounds which oft have raised me, whilst they awed,
    And sent my soul abroad,
Might now perhaps their wonted impulse give,
Might startle this dull pain, and make it move and live!   20

7. **Æolian lute:** a box containing tuned
strings on which the wind produces tones.

II

A grief without a pang, void, dark, and drear,
  A stifled, drowsy, unimpassioned grief,
  Which finds no natural outlet, no relief,
    In word, or sigh, or tear—
O Lady! in this wan and heartless mood,   25
To other thoughts by yonder throstle woo'd,
  All this long eve, so balmy and serene,
Have I been gazing on the western sky,
  And its peculiar tint of yellow green:
And still I gaze—and with how blank an eye!   30
And those thin clouds above, in flakes and bars,
That give away their motion to the stars;
Those stars, that glide behind them or between,
Now sparkling, now bedimmed, but always seen:
Yon crescent Moon, as fixed as if it grew   35
In its own cloudless, starless lake of blue;
I see them all so excellently fair,
I see, not feel, how beautiful they are!

III

  My genial spirits fail;
    And what can these avail   40
To lift the smothering weight from off my breast?
    It were a vain endeavour,
    Though I should gaze for ever
On that green light that lingers in the west:
I may not hope from outward forms to win   45
The passion and the life, whose fountains are within.

IV

O Lady! we receive but what we give,
And in our life alone does Nature live:
Ours is her wedding garment, ours her shroud!
  And would we aught behold, of higher worth,   50
Than that inanimate cold world allowed
To the poor loveless ever-anxious crowd,
  Ah! from the soul itself must issue forth
A light, a glory, a fair luminous cloud
    Enveloping the Earth—   55
And from the soul itself must there be sent
  A sweet and potent voice, of its own birth,
Of all sweet sounds the life and element!

26. **throstle**: European song thrush.

V

O pure of heart! thou need'st not ask of me
What this strong music in the soul may be!   60
What, and wherein it doth exist,
This light, this glory, this fair luminous mist,
This beautiful and beauty-making power.
    Joy, virtuous Lady! Joy that ne'er was given,
Save to the pure, and in their purest hour,   65
Life, and Life's effluence, cloud at once and shower,
Joy, Lady! is the spirit and the power,
Which wedding Nature to us gives in dower
    A new Earth and new Heaven,
Undreamt of by the sensual and the proud—   70
Joy is the sweet voice, Joy the luminous cloud—
        We in ourselves rejoice!
And thence flows all that charms or ear or sight,
    All melodies the echoes of that voice,
All colours a suffusion from that light.   75

VI

There was a time when, though my path was rough,
    This joy within me dallied with distress,
And all misfortunes were but as the stuff
    Whence Fancy made me dreams of happiness:
For hope grew round me, like the twining vine,   80
And fruits, and foliage, not my own, seemed mine.
But now afflictions bow me down to earth:
Nor care I that they rob me of my mirth;
        But oh! each visitation
Suspends what nature gave me at my birth,   85
    My shaping spirit of Imagination.
For not to think of what I needs must feel,
    But to be still and patient, all I can;
And haply by abstruse research to steal
    From my own nature all the natural man—   90
    This was my sole resource, my only plan:
Till that which suits a part infects the whole,
And now is almost grown the habit of my soul.

VII

Hence, viper thoughts, that coil around my mind,
        Reality's dark dream!   95
I turn from you, and listen to the wind,
    Which long has raved unnoticed. What a scream
Of agony by torture lengthened out

That lute sent forth! Thou Wind, that rav'st without
 Bare crag, or mountain-tairn, or blasted tree,   100
Or pine-grove whither woodman never clomb,
Or lonely house, long held the witches' home,
 Methinks were fitter instruments for thee,
Mad Lutanist! who in this month of showers,
Of dark-brown gardens, and of peeping flowers,   105
Mak'st Devils' yule, with worse than wintry song,
The blossoms, buds, and timorous leaves among.
 Thou Actor, perfect in all tragic sounds!
Thou mighty Poet, e'en to frenzy bold!
  What tell'st thou now about?   110
  'Tis of the rushing of an host in rout,
 With groans, of trampled men, with smarting wounds—
At once they groan with pain, and shudder with the cold!
But hush! there is a pause of deepest silence!
 And all that noise, as of a rushing crowd,   115
With groans, and tremulous shudderings—all is over—
 It tells another tale, with sounds less deep and loud!
  A tale of less affright,
  And tempered with delight,
As Otway's self had framed the tender lay,—   120
  'Tis of a little child
  Upon a lonesome wild,
Not far from home, but she hath lost her way:
And now moans low in bitter grief and fear,
And now screams loud, and hopes to make her mother hear. 125

VIII

'Tis midnight, but small thoughts have I of sleep:
Full seldom may my friend such vigils keep!
Visit her, gentle Sleep! with wings of healing,
 And may this storm be but a mountain-birth,
May all the stars hang bright above her dwelling,   130
 Silent as though they watched the sleeping Earth!
  With light heart may she rise,
  Gay fancy, cheerful eyes,
 Joy lift her spirit, joy attune her voice;
To her may all things live, from pole to pole,   135
Their life the eddying of her living soul!
 O simple spirit, guided from above,
Dear Lady! friend devoutest of my choice,
Thus mayest thou ever, evermore rejoice.

---

100. **tairn**: lake.   120. **Otway**: Thomas Otway (1652–1685)
                 dramatist famous for tragedies of pathos.

On Donne's Poetry

With Donne, whose muse on dromedary trots,
Wreathe iron pokers into true-love knots;
Rhyme's sturdy cripple, fancy's maze and clue,
Wit's forge and fire-blast, meaning's press and screw.

Work Without Hope

Lines Composed 21st February 1825

All Nature seems at work. Slugs leave their lair—
The bees are stirring—birds are on the wing—
And Winter slumbering in the open air,
Wears on his smiling face a dream of Spring!
And I the while, the sole unbusy thing,   5
Nor honey make, nor pair, nor build, nor sing.

Yet well I ken the banks where amaranths blow,
Have traced the fount whence streams of nectar flow.
Bloom, O ye amaranths! bloom for whom ye may,
For me ye bloom not! Glide, rich streams, away!   10
With lips unbrightened, wreathless brow, I stroll:
And would you learn the spells that drowse my soul?
Work without Hope draws nectar in a sieve,
And Hope without an object cannot live.

PERCY BYSSHE SHELLEY

[1792–1822]

Ozymandias

I met a traveller from an antique land
Who said: Two vast and trunkless legs of stone
Stand in the desert. Near them, on the sand,
Half sunk, a shattered visage lies, whose frown,
And wrinkled lip, and sneer of cold command,   5

Ozymandias: Ramses II, the Pharaoh of Egypt who opposed the Israelites. His statue, reported to be the largest in the ancient world, bore this inscription: "I am Ozymandias, king of kings; if anyone wishes to know what I am and where I lie, let him surpass me in some of my exploits."

Tell that its sculptor well those passions read
Which yet survive, stamped on these lifeless things,
The hand that mocked them and the heart that fed:
And on the pedestal these words appear:
"My name is Ozymandias, king of kings: 10
Look on my works, ye Mighty, and despair!"
Nothing beside remains. Round the decay
Of that colossal wreck, boundless and bare
The lone and level sands stretch far away.

Stanzas Written in Dejection, Near Naples

I

The sun is warm, the sky is clear,
    The waves are dancing fast and bright,
Blue isles and snowy mountains wear
    The purple noon's transparent might,
    The breath of the moist earth is light,   5
Around its unexpanded buds;
    Like many a voice of one delight,
The winds, the birds, the ocean floods,
The City's voice itself is soft like Solitude's.

2

I see the Deep's untrampled floor   10
    With green and purple seaweeds strown;
I see the waves upon the shore,
    Like light dissolved in star-showers, thrown:
    I sit upon the sands alone—
The lightning of the noontide ocean   15
    Is flashing round me, and a tone
Arises from its measured motion,
How sweet! did any heart now share in my emotion.

3

Alas! I have nor hope nor health,
    Nor peace within nor calm around,   20
Nor that content surpassing wealth
    The sage in meditation found,
    And walked with inward glory crowned—
Nor fame, nor power, nor love, nor leisure.
    Others I see whom these surround—   25
Smiling they live, and call life pleasure;—
To me that cup has been dealt in another measure.

4

Yet now despair itself is mild,
　Even as the winds and waters are;
I could lie down like a tired child,　　　　　　　　　30
　　And weep away the life of care
　　Which I have borne and yet must bear,
Till death like sleep might steal on me,
　And I might feel in the warm air
My cheek grow cold, and hear the sea　　　　　　　35
Breathe o'er my dying brain its last monotony.

5

Some might lament that I were cold,
　As I, when this sweet day is gone,
Which my lost heart, too soon grown old,
　　Insults with this untimely moan;　　　　　　　40
　　They might lament—for I am one
Whom men love not,—and yet regret,
　Unlike this day, which, when the sun
Shall on its stainless glory set,
Will linger, though enjoyed, like joy in memory yet.　　45

England in 1819

An old, mad, blind, despised, and dying king—
Princes, the dregs of their dull race, who flow
Through public scorn—mud from a muddy spring;
Rulers who neither see, nor feel, nor know,
But leechlike to their fainting country cling,　　　　　5
Till they drop, blind in blood, without a blow;
A people starved and stabbed in the untilled field—
An army, which liberticide and prey
Makes as a two-edged sword to all who wield;
Golden and sanguine laws which tempt and slay;　　10
Religion Christless, Godless—a book sealed;
A Senate—Time's worst statute unrepealed—
Are graves, from which a glorious Phantom may
Burst, to illumine our tempestuous day.

1. **king:** George III, d. 1820.
7. **people . . . field:** a reference to the "Peterloo Massacre." In 1819 government cavalry attacked an orderly workers' meeting held in St. Peter's field, Manchester, killing nine, injuring several hundred.
12. **statute:** a discriminatory law against Roman Catholics.
13. **Phantom:** revolution.

Ode to the West Wind

1

O wild West Wind, thou breath of Autumn's being,
Thou, from whose unseen presence the leaves dead
Are driven, like ghosts from an enchanter fleeing.

Yellow, and black, and pale, and hectic red,
Pestilence-stricken multitudes: O thou,   5
Who chariotest to their dark wintry bed

The wingèd seeds, where they lie cold and low,
Each like a corpse within its grave, until
Thine azure sister of the Spring shall blow.

Her clarion o'er the dreaming earth, and fill   10
(Driving sweet buds like flocks to feed in air)
With living hues and odours plain and hill:

Wild Spirit, which art moving everywhere;
Destroyer and preserver; hear, oh hear!

2

Thou on whose stream, mid the steep sky's commotion,   15
Loose clouds like earth's decaying leaves are shed,
Shook from the tangled boughs of Heaven and Ocean,

Angels of rain and lightning: there are spread
On the blue surface of thine aëry surge,
Like the bright hair uplifted from the head   20

Of some fierce Maenad, even from the dim verge
Of the horizon to the zenith's height,
The locks of the approaching storm. Thou dirge

Of the dying year, to which this closing night
Will be the dome of a vast sepulchre,   25
Vaulted with all thy congregated might

Of vapours, from whose solid atmosphere
Black rain, and fire, and hail will burst: oh, hear!

21. **Maenad:** a frenzied female votary of
Dionysus, god of wine and vegetation.

3

Thou who didst waken from his summer dreams
The blue Mediterranean, where he lay,   30
Lulled by the coil of his crystalline streams,

Beside a pumice isle in Baiae's bay,
And saw in sleep old palaces and towers
Quivering within the wave's intenser day,

All overgrown with azure moss and flowers   35
So sweet, the sense faints picturing them! Thou
For whose path the Atlantic's level powers

Cleave themselves into chasms, while far below
The sea-blooms and the oozy woods which wear
The sapless foliage of the ocean, know   40

Thy voice, and suddenly grow gray with fear,
And tremble and despoil themselves: oh, hear!

4

If I were a dead leaf thou mightest bear;
If I were a swift cloud to fly with thee;
A wave to pant beneath thy power, and share   45

The impulse of thy strength, only less free
Than thou, O uncontrollable! If even
I were as in my boyhood, and could be

The comrade of thy wanderings over Heaven,
As then, when to outstrip thy skiey speed   50
Scarce seemed a vision; I would ne'er have striven

As thus with thee in prayer in my sore need.
Oh, lift me as a wave, a leaf, a cloud!
I fall upon the thorns of life! I bleed!

A heavy weight of hours has chained and bowed   55
One too like thee; tameless, and swift, and proud.

5

Make me thy lyre, even as the forest is:
What if my leaves are falling like its own!
The tumult of thy mighty harmonies

32. **Baiae:** a bay near Naples.   57. **lyre:** a wind harp.

Will take from both a deep, autumnal tone,   60
Sweet though in sadness. Be thou, Spirit fierce,
My spirit! Be thou me, impetuous one!

Drive my dead thoughts over the universe
Like withered leaves to quicken a new birth!
And, by the incantation of this verse,   65

Scatter, as from an unextinguished hearth
Ashes and sparks, my words among mankind!
Be through my lips to unawakened earth

The trumpet of a prophecy! O, Wind,
If Winter comes, can Spring be far behind?   70

Adonais

An Elegy On The Death of John Keats,
Author Of Endymion, Hyperion, Etc.

[Thou wert the morning star among the living,
    Ere thy fair light had fled—
Now, having died, thou art as Hesperus, giving
    New splendor to the dead.]

I

I weep for Adonais—he is dead!
O, weep for Adonais! though our tears
Thaw not the frost which binds so dear a head!
And thou, sad Hour, selected from all years
To mourn our loss, rouse thy obscure compeers,   5
And teach them thine own sorrow! Say: "With me
Died Adonais; till the Future dares
Forget the Past, his fate and fame shall be
An echo and a light unto eternity!"

Adonais: derived from Adonis, the lover of Venus slain by a wild boar, and possibly from Adonai, an Old Testament name for God. Adonis himself has been worshipped as a vegetable deity. In this poem Adonais is John Keats, who Shelley thought had been mortally wounded by the unfavorable reception given *Endymion* in *The Quarterly Review.*

Thou . . . dead: Shelley's translation of a Greek epigram he had placed at the head of the poem. He refers to the planet Venus, which has a dual identity, the morning star Lucifer and the evening star Hesperus or Vesper.

2

Where wert thou, mighty Mother, when he lay,   10
When thy Son lay, pierced by the shaft which flies
In darkness? where was lorn Urania
When Adonais died? With veilèd eyes,
'Mid listening Echoes, in her Paradise
She sate, while one, with soft enamoured breath,   15
Rekindled all the fading melodies,
With which, like flowers that mock the corse beneath,
He had adorned and hid the coming bulk of death.

3

O, weep for Adonais—he is dead!
Wake, melancholy Mother, wake and weep!   20
Yet wherefore? Quench within their burning bed
Thy fiery tears, and let thy loud heart keep
Like his, a mute and uncomplaining sleep;
For he is gone, where all things wise and fair
Descend;—oh, dream not that the amorous Deep   25
Will yet restore him to the vital air;
Death feeds on his mute voice, and laughs at our despair.

4

Most musical of mourners, weep again!
Lament anew, Urania!—He died,
Who was the Sire of an immortal strain,   30
Blind, old, and lonely, when his country's pride,
The priest, the slave, and the liberticide,
Trampled and mocked with many a loathèd rite
Of lust and blood; he went, unterrified,
Into the gulf of death; but his clear Sprite   35
Yet reigns o'er earth: the third among the sons of light.

5

Most musical of mourners, weep anew!
Not all to that bright station dared to climb;
And happier they their happiness who knew,
Whose tapers yet burn through that night of time   40
In which suns perished; others more sublime,
Struck by the envious wrath of man or God,
Have sunk, extinct in their refulgent prime;
And some yet live, treading the thorny road,
Which leads, through toil and hate, to Fame's serene abode.   45

10. **Mother:** Urania, muse of astronomy, whom Shelley merges with Uranian Aphrodite or Heavenly Venus.
17. **corse:** corpse.

29. **He:** Milton.
36. **third:** Milton is the third of the "sons of light," the successor of Homer and Dante.

6

But now, thy youngest, dearest one has perished,
The nursling of thy widowhood, who grew,
Like a pale flower by some sad maiden cherished,
And fed with true-love tears, instead of dew;
Most musical of mourners, weep anew!   50
Thy extreme hope, the loveliest and the last,
The bloom, whose petals, nipped before they blew,
Died on the promise of the fruit, is waste;
The broken lily lies—the storm is overpast.

7

To that high Capital, where kingly Death   55
Keeps his pale court in beauty and decay,
He came; and bought, with price of purest breath,
A grave among the eternal.—Come away!
Haste, while the vault of blue Italian day
Is yet his fitting charnel-roof! while still   60
He lies, as if in dewy sleep he lay;
Awake him not! surely he takes his fill
Of deep and liquid rest, forgetful of all ill.

8

He will awake no more, oh, never more!—
Within the twilight chamber spreads apace   65
The shadow of white Death, and at the door
Invisible Corruption waits to trace
His extreme way to her dim dwelling-place;
The eternal Hunger sits, but pity and awe
Soothe her pale rage, nor dares she to deface   70
So fair a prey, till darkness, and the law
Of change, shall o'er his sleep the mortal curtain draw.

9

O, weep for Adonais!—The quick Dreams,
The passion-wingèd Ministers of thought,
Who were his flocks, whom near the living streams   75
Of his young spirit he fed, and whom he taught
The love which was its music, wander not,—
Wander no more, from kindling brain to brain,
But droop there, whence they sprung; and mourn their lot
Round the cold heart, where, after their sweet pain   80
They ne'er will gather strength, or find a home again.

49. **dew:** an allusion to Keats's *Isabella*.   55. **Capital:** Rome.

10

And one with trembling hands clasps his cold head,
And fans him with her moonlight wings, and cries:
"Our love, our hope, our sorrow, is not dead;
See, on the silken fringe of his faint eyes,   85
Like dew upon a sleeping flower, there lies
A tear some Dream has loosened from his brain.
Lost Angel of a ruined Paradise!
She knew not 'twas her own; as with no stain
She faded, like a cloud which had outwept its rain.   90

11

One from a lucid urn of starry dew
Washed his light limbs as if embalming them;
Another clipped her profuse locks, and threw
The wreath upon him, like an anadem,
Which frozen tears instead of pearls begem;   95
Another in her wilful grief would break
Her bow and wingèd reeds, as if to stem
A greater loss with one which was more weak;
And dull the barbèd fire against his frozen cheek.

12

Another Splendour on his mouth alit,   100
That mouth, whence it was wont to draw the breath
Which gave it strength to pierce the guarded wit,
And pass into the panting heart beneath
With lightning and with music: the damp death
Quenched its caress upon his icy lips;   105
And, as a dying meteor stains a wreath
Of moonlight vapour, which the cold night clips,
It flushed through his pale limbs, and passed to its eclipse.

13

And others came . . . Desires and Adorations,
Wingèd Persuasions and veiled Destinies,   110
Splendours, and Glooms, and glimmering Incarnations
Of hopes and fears, and twilight Phantasies;
And Sorrow, with her family of Sighs,
And Pleasure, blind with tears, led by the gleam
Of her own dying smile instead of eyes,   115
Came in slow pomp;—the moving pomp might seem
Like pageantry of mist on an autumnal stream.

94. **anadem**: garland.   107. **clips**: embraces.

14

All he had loved, and moulded into thought,
From shape, and hue, and odour, and sweet sound,
Lamented Adonais. Morning sought   120
Her eastern watch-tower, and her hair unbound,
Wet with the tears which should adorn the ground,
Dimmed the aërial eyes that kindle day;
Afar the melancholy thunder moaned,
Pale Ocean in unquiet slumber lay,   125
And the wild winds flew round, sobbing in their dismay.

15

Lost Echo sits amid the voiceless mountains,
And feeds her grief with his remembered lay,
And will no more reply to winds or fountains,
Or amorous birds perched on the young green spray,   130
Or herdsman's horn, or bell at closing day;
Since she can mimic not his lips, more dear
Than those for whose disdain she pined away
Into a shadow of all sounds;—a drear
Murmur, between their songs, is all the woodmen hear.   135

16

Grief made the young Spring wild, and she threw down
Her kindling buds, as if she Autumn were,
Or they dead leaves; since her delight is flown,
For whom should she have waked the sullen year?
To Phoebus was not Hyacinth so dear   140
Nor to himself Narcissus, as to both
Thou, Adonais: wan they stand and sere
Amid the faint companions of their youth,
With dew all turned to tears; odour, to sighing ruth.

17

Thy spirit's sister, the lorn nightingale,   145
Mourns not her mate with such melodious pain;
Not so the eagle, who like thee could scale
Heaven, and could nourish in the sun's domain
Her mighty youth with morning, doth complain,
Soaring and screaming round her empty nest,   150
As Albion wails for thee: the curse of Cain
Light on his head who pierced thy innocent breast,
And scared the angel soul that was its earthly guest!

133. **those:** Narcissus, for whom Echo pined away into a mere voice.
140. **Phoebus . . . Hyacinth:** Phoebus Apollo, to commemorate his grief for Hyacinth's death, signed the flower which grew where Hyacinth died with the letters AI, signifying woe.
144. **ruth:** pity.
147–49. **eagle . . . morning:** According to legend, if the eagle flew near the sun his old age would be burnt away.
151. **Albion:** England.

18

Ah, woe is me! Winter is come and gone,
But grief returns with the revolving year;   155
The airs and streams renew their joyous tone;
The ants, the bees, the swallows, reappear;
Fresh leaves and flowers deck the dead Seasons' bier;
The amorous birds now pair in every brake,
And build their mossy homes in field and brere;   160
And the green lizard, and the golden snake,
Like unimprisoned flames, out of their trance awake.

19

Through wood and stream and field and hill and Ocean
A quickening life from the Earth's heart has burst,
As it has ever done, with change and motion   165
From the great morning of the world when first
God dawned on Chaos; in its stream immersed
The lamps of Heaven flash with a softer light;
All baser things pant with life's sacred thirst;
Diffuse themselves; and spend in love's delight   170
The beauty and the joy of their renewèd might.

20

The leprous corpse, touched by this spirit tender,
Exhales itself in flowers of gentle breath;
Like incarnations of the stars, when splendour
Is changed to fragrance, they illumine death   175
And mock the merry worm that wakes beneath;
Naught we know, dies. Shall that alone which knows
Be as a sword consumed before the sheath
By sightless lightning?—the intense atom glows
A moment, then is quenched in a most cold repose.   180

21

Alas! that all we loved of him should be,
But for our grief, as if it had not been,
And grief itself be mortal! Woe is me!
Whence are we, and why are we? of what scene
The actors or spectators? Great and mean   185
Meet massed in death, who lends what life must sorrow.
As long as skies are blue, and fields are green,
Evening must usher night, night urge the morrow,
Month follow month with woe, and year wake year to sorrow.

159. **brake:** thicket.   160. **brere:** briar.

22

He will awake no more, oh, never more!   190
"Wake thou," cried Misery, "childless Mother, rise
Out of thy sleep, and slake, in thy heart's core,
A wound more fierce than his with tears and sighs."
And all the Dreams that watched Urania's eyes,
And all the Echoes whom their sister's song   195
Had held in holy silence, cried: "Arise!"
Swift as a Thought by the snake Memory stung,
From her ambrosial rest the fading Splendour sprung.

23

She rose like an autumnal Night, that springs
Out of the East, and follows wild and drear   200
The golden Day, which, on eternal wings,
Even as a ghost abandoning a bier,
Had left the Earth a corpse. Sorrow and fear
So struck, so roused, so rapt Urania;
So saddened round her like an atmosphere   205
Of stormy mist; so swept her on her way
Even to the mournful place where Adonais lay.

24

Out of her secret Paradise she sped,
Through camps and cities rough with stone and steel,
And human hearts, which to her aëry tread   210
Yielding not, wounded the invisible
Palms of her tender feet where'er they fell:
And barbèd tongues, and thoughts more sharp than they,
Rent the soft Form they never could repel,
Whose sacred blood, like the young tears of May,   215
Paved with eternal flowers that undeserving way.

25

In the death-chamber for a moment Death,
Shamed by the presence of that living Might,
Blushed to annihilation, and the breath
Revisited those lips, and life's pale light   220
Flashed through those limbs, so late her dear delight.
"Leave me not wild and drear and comfortless,
As silent lightning leaves the starless night!
Leave me not!" cried Urania: her distress
Roused Death: Death rose and smiled, and met her vain caress.   225

192. **slake**: to reduce, to lessen the tension.   204. **rapt**: lifted or transported.

26

"Stay yet awhile! speak to me once again;
Kiss me, so long but as a kiss may live;
And in my heartless breast and burning brain
That word, that kiss, shall all thoughts else survive,
With food of saddest memory kept alive,   230
Now thou art dead, as if it were a part
Of thee, my Adonais! I would give
All that I am to be as thou now art!
But I am chained to Time, and cannot thence depart!

27

"Oh gentle child, beautiful as thou wert,   235
Why didst thou leave the trodden paths of men
Too soon, and with weak hands though mighty heart
Dare the unpastured dragon in his den?
Defenceless as thou wert, oh, where was then
Wisdom the mirrored shield, or scorn the spear?   240
Or hadst thou waited the full cycle, when
Thy spirit should have filled its crescent sphere,
The monsters of life's waste had fled from thee like deer.

28

"The herded wolves, bold only to pursue;
The obscene ravens, clamorous o'er the dead;   245
The vultures to the conqueror's banner true,
Who feed where Desolation first has fed,
And whose wings rain contagion;—how they fled,
When like Apollo, from his golden bow,
The Pythian of the age one arrow sped   250
And smiled!—The spoilers tempt no second blow;
They fawn on the proud feet that spurn them lying low.

29

"The sun comes forth, and many reptiles spawn;
He sets, and each ephemeral insect then
Is gathered into death without a dawn,   255
And the immortal stars awake again;
So is it in the world of living men:
A godlike mind soars forth, in its delight
Making earth bare and veiling heaven, and when
It sinks, the swarms that dimmed or shared its light   260
Leave to its kindred lamps the spirit's awful night."

228. **heartless:** She has given her heart to Adonais.
250. **Pythian:** Apollo earned this name when he slew the dragon Python. Byron is the modern Pythian because in his satiric poems he slaughters the modern dragons, the critics.

30

Thus ceased she: and the mountain shepherds came,
Their garlands sere, their magic mantles rent;
The Pilgrim of Eternity, whose fame
Over his living head like Heaven is bent,   265
An early but enduring monument,
Came, veiling all the lightnings of his song
In sorrow: from her wilds Ierne sent
The sweetest lyrist of her saddest wrong,
And love taught grief to fall like music from his tongue.   270

31

Midst others of less note, came one frail Form,
A phantom among men, companionless
As the last cloud of an expiring storm
Whose thunder is its knell; he, as I guess,
Had gazed on Nature's naked loveliness,   275
Actaeon-like, and now he fled astray
With feeble steps o'er the world's wilderness,
And his own thoughts, along that rugged way,
Pursued, like raging hounds, their father and their prey.

32

A pardlike Spirit beautiful and swift—   280
A Love in desolation masked;—a Power
Girt round with weakness;—it can scarce uplift
The weight of the superincumbent hour;
It is a dying lamp, a falling shower,
A breaking billow;—even whilst we speak   285
Is it not broken? On the withering flower
The killing sun smiles brightly; on a cheek
The life can burn in blood, even while the heart may break.

33

His head was bound with pansies overblown,
And faded violets, white, and pied, and blue;   290
And a light spear topped with a cypress cone,
Round whose rude shaft dark ivy tresses grew
Yet dripping with the forest's noonday dew,
Vibrated, as the ever-beating heart
Shook the weak hand that grasped it; of that crew   295
He came the last, neglected and apart;
A herd-abandoned deer, struck by the hunter's dart.

264. Pilgrim: Byron, so called because of his pilgrim, Childe Harold.
268. Ierne: Ireland, who sends the poet Thomas Moore.
271. Form: Shelley.
276. Actaeon: For seeing Diana naked, the hunter Actaeon was turned into a stag, then torn to pieces by his own hounds.
280. pardlike: leopard-like.
291. light spear: the thyrsus, the leaf-entwined staff of Dionysus.

34

All stood aloof, and at his partial moan
Smiled through their tears; well knew that gentle band
Who in another's fate now wept his own,   300
As, in the accents of an unknown land,
He sung new sorrow; sad Urania scanned
The Stranger's mien, and murmured: "Who art thou?"
He answered not, but with a sudden hand
Made bare his branded and ensanguined brow,   305
Which was like Cain's or Christ's—Oh! that it should be so!

35

What softer voice is hushed over the dead?
Athwart what brow is that dark mantle thrown?
What form leans sadly o'er the white death-bed,
In mockery of monumental stone,   310
The heavy heart heaving without a moan?
If it be He, who, gentlest of the wise,
Taught, soothed, loved, honoured the departed one,
Let me not vex with inharmonious sighs
The silence of that heart's accepted sacrifice.   315

36

Our Adonais has drunk poison—oh!
What deaf and viperous murderer could crown
Life's early cup with such a draught of woe?
The nameless worm would now itself disown:
It felt, yet could escape, the magic tone   320
Whose prelude held all envy, hate, and wrong,
But what was howling in one breast alone,
Silent with expectation of the song,
Whose master's hand is cold, whose silver lyre unstrung.

37

Live thou, whose infamy is not thy fame!   325
Live! fear no heavier chastisement from me,
Thou noteless blot on a remembered name!
But be thyself, and know thyself to be:
And ever at thy season be thou free
To spill the venom when thy fangs o'erflow: 330
Remorse and Self-contempt shall cling to thee;
Hot Shame shall burn upon thy secret brow,
And like a beaten hound tremble thou shalt—as now.

312. **He:** Leigh Hunt, poet, editor, and
friend of both Keats and Shelley.

319. **worm:** Keats's reviewer, as was
customary, remained nameless.
321. **held:** held back.

38

Nor let us weep that our delight is fled
Far from these carrion kites that scream below;   335
He wakes or sleeps with the enduring dead;
Thou canst not soar where he is sitting now.—
Dust to the dust! but the pure spirit shall flow
Back to the burning fountain whence it came,
A portion of the Eternal, which must glow   340
Through time and change, unquenchably the same,
Whilst thy cold embers choke the sordid hearth of shame.

39

Peace, peace! he is not dead, he doth not sleep—
He hath awakened from the dream of life—
'Tis we who, lost in stormy visions, keep   345
With phantoms an unprofitable strife,
And in mad trance strike with our spirit's knife
Invulnerable nothings.—*We* decay
Like corpses in a charnel; fear and grief
Convulse us and consume us day by day,   350
And cold hopes swarm like worms within our living clay.

40

He has outsoared the shadow of our night:
Envy and calumny and hate and pain,
And that unrest which men miscall delight,
Can touch him not and torture not again;   355
From the contagion of the world's slow stain
He is secure, and now can never mourn
A heart grown cold, a head grown grey in vain;
Nor, when the spirit's self has ceased to burn,
With sparkless ashes load an unlamented urn.   360

41

He lives, he wakes—'t is Death is dead, not he;
Mourn not for Adonais.—Thou young Dawn,
Turn all thy dew to splendour, for from thee
The spirit thou lamentest is not gone;
Ye caverns and ye forests, cease to moan!   365
Cease, ye faint flowers and fountains, and thou Air,
Which like a mourning veil thy scarf hadst thrown
O'er the abandoned Earth, now leave it bare
Even to the joyous stars which smile on its despair!

42

He is made one with Nature: there is heard 370
His voice in all her music, from the moan
Of thunder, to the song of night's sweet bird;
He is a presence to be felt and known
In darkness and in light, from herb and stone,
Spreading itself where'er that Power may move 375
Which has withdrawn his being to its own;
Which wields the world with never-wearied love,
Sustains it from beneath, and kindles it above.

43

He is a portion of the loveliness
Which once he made more lovely: he doth bear 380
His part, while the one Spirit's plastic stress
Sweeps through the dull dense world, compelling there
All new successions to the forms they wear;
Torturing the unwilling dross that checks its flight
To its own likeness, as each mass may bear; 385
And bursting in its beauty and its might
From trees and beasts and men into the Heaven's light.

44

The splendours of the firmament of time
May be eclipsed, but are extinguished not;
Like stars to their appointed height they climb, 390
And death is a low mist which cannot blot
The brightness it may veil. When lofty thought
Lifts a young heart above its mortal lair,
And love and life contend in it, for what
Shall be its earthly doom, the dead live there 395
And move like winds of light on dark and stormy air.

45

The inheritors of unfulfilled renown
Rose from their thrones, built beyond mortal thought,
Far in the Unapparent. Chatterton
Rose pale; his solemn agony had not 400

381. **plastic:** forming, developing, and growing.
385. **as ... bear:** as much as each substance is capable of.
399. **Chatterton:** Thomas Chatterton (1752–1770) supposedly committed suicide because of his lack of success as a poet. Actually he may have died from an overdose of mercury attempting to cure himself of syphilis.

Yet faded from him: Sidney, as he fought
And as he fell, and as he lived and loved,
Sublimely mild, a Spirit without spot,
Arose; and Lucan, by his death approved:
Oblivion, as they rose, shrank like a thing reproved.   405

46

And many more, whose names on Earth are dark
But whose transmitted effluence cannot die
So long as fire outlives the parent spark,
Rose, robed in dazzling immortality.
"Thou art become as one of us," they cry,   410
"It was for thee yon kingless sphere has long
Swung blind in unascended majesty,
Silent alone amid an Heaven of Song.
Assume thy wingèd throne, thou Vesper of our throng!"

47

Who mourns for Adonais? oh, come forth,   415
Fond wretch! and know thyself and him aright.
Clasp with thy panting soul the pendulous Earth;
As from a centre, dart thy spirit's light
Beyond all worlds, until its spacious might
Satiate the void circumference; then shrink   420
Even to a point within our day and night;
And keep thy heart light, lest it make thee sink,
When hope has kindled hope, and lured thee to the brink.

48

Or go to Rome, which is the sepulchre,
Oh, not of him, but of our joy; 't is nought   425
That ages, empires, and religions there
Lie buried in the ravage they have wrought;
For such as he can lend,—they borrow not
Glory from those who made the world their prey;
And he is gathered to the kings of thought   430
Who waged contention with their time's decay,
And of the past are all that cannot pass away.

---

401. **Sidney:** Sir Philip Sidney (1554–1586), another young poet, died of a battle-wound.

404. **Lucan:** Marcus Annaeus Lucan (39–65) killed himself when his plot against Nero failed.

49

Go thou to Rome,—at once the Paradise,
The grave, the city, and the wilderness;
And where its wrecks like shattered mountains rise   435
And flowering weeds and fragrant copses dress
The bones of Desolation's nakedness
Pass, till the Spirit of the spot shall lead
Thy footsteps to a slope of green access
Where, like an infant's smile, over the dead,   440
A light of laughing flowers along the grass is spread.

50

And grey walls moulder round, on which dull Time
Feeds, like slow fire upon a hoary brand,
And one keen pyramid with wedge sublime,
Pavilioning the dust of him who planned   445
This refuge for his memory, doth stand
Like flame transformed to marble; and beneath,
A field is spread, on which a newer band
Have pitched in Heaven's smile their camp of death,
Welcoming him we lose with scarce extinguished breath.   450

51

Here pause: these graves are all too young as yet
To have outgrown the sorrow which consigned
Its charge to each; and if the seal is set,
Here, on one fountain of a mourning mind,
Break it not thou! too surely shalt thou find   455
Thine own well full, if thou returnest home,
Of tears and gall. From the world's bitter wind
Seek shelter in the shadow of the tomb.
What Adonais is, why fear we to become?

52

The One remains, the many change and pass;   460
Heaven's light forever shines, Earth's shadows fly;
Life, like a dome of many-coloured glass,
Stains the white radiance of Eternity,
Until Death tramples it to fragments.—Die,
If thou wouldst be with that which thou dost seek!   465
Follow where all is fled!—Rome's azure sky,
Flowers, ruins, statues, music, words, are weak
The glory they transfuse with fitting truth to speak.

439. **slope:** the Protestant cemetery.
444. **pyramid:** the tomb of Gaius Cestus, a tribune of the people.

453–54. **seal ... mind:** Not only Keats but also Shelley's three-year-old son William was buried there.

53

Why linger? why turn back, why shrink, my Heart?
Thy hopes are gone before: from all things here   470
They have departed; thou shouldst now depart!
A light is past from the revolving year,
And man, and woman; and what still is dear
Attracts to crush, repels to make thee wither.
The soft sky smiles,—the low wind whispers near;   475
'T is Adonais calls! oh, hasten thither,
No more let Life divide what Death can join together.

54

That Light whose smile kindles the Universe,
That Beauty in which all things work and move,
That Benediction which the eclipsing Curse   480
Of birth can quench not, that sustaining Love
Which, through the web of being blindly wove
By man and beast and earth and air and sea,
Burns bright or dim, as each are mirrors of
The fire for which all thirst, now beams on me,   485
Consuming the last clouds of cold mortality.

55

The breath whose might I have invoked in song
Descends on me; my spirit's bark is driven,
Far from the shore, far from the trembling throng
Whose sails were never to the tempest given;   490
The massy earth and spherèd skies are riven!
I am borne darkly, fearfully, afar:
Whilst burning through the inmost veil of Heaven,
The soul of Adonais, like a star,
Beacons from the abode where the Eternal are.   495

A Dirge

Rough wind, that moanest loud
    Grief too sad for song;
Wild wind, when sullen cloud
    Knells all the night long;
Sad storm, whose tears are vain,   5
Bare woods, whose branches strain,
Deep caves and dreary main,
    Wail, for the world's wrong!

JOHN KEATS

[*1795–1821*]

On First Looking into Chapman's Homer

Much have I travelled in the realms of gold
  And many goodly states and kingdoms seen;
  Round many western islands have I been
Which bards in fealty to Apollo hold.
Oft of one wide expanse had I been told   5
  That deep-browed Homer ruled as his demesne;
  Yet did I never breathe its pure serene
Till I heard Chapman speak out loud and bold:
Then felt I like some watcher of the skies
  When a new planet swims into his ken;   10
Or like stout Cortez when with eagle eyes
  He stared at the Pacific—and all his men
Looked at each other with a wild surmise—
  Silent, upon a peak in Darien.

Keen, fitful gusts are whispering here and there

Keen, fitful gusts are whispering here and there
  Among the bushes half leafless, and dry;
  The stars look very cold about the sky,
And I have many miles on foot to fare,
Yet feel I little of the cool bleak air,   5
  Or of the dead leaves rustling drearily,
  Or of these silver lamps that burn on high,
Or of the distance from home's pleasant lair:
For I am brimful of the friendliness
  That in a little cottage I have found;   10
Of fair-haired Milton's eloquent distress,
  And all his love for gentle Lycid drowned;
Of lovely Laura in her light green dress,
  And faithful Petrarch gloriously crowned.

Chapman's: George Chapman, Elizabethan translator of the *Iliad*.
6. **demesne:** domain.
7. **serene:** clear air.
11. **Cortez:** actually, Balboa.
14. **Darien:** Panama.

13. **Laura:** the lady of Petrarch's sonnets.
14. **Petrarch:** Italian poet (1304–1374), crowned laureate in Rome, 1340.

JOHN KEATS

On Seeing the Elgin Marbles
for the First Time

My spirit is too weak—mortality
   Weighs heavily on me like unwilling sleep,
   And each imagined pinnacle and steep
Of godlike hardship, tells me I must die
Like a sick eagle looking at the sky.   5
   Yet 'tis a gentle luxury to weep
   That I have not the cloudy winds to keep,
Fresh for the opening of the morning's eye.
Such dim-conceivèd glories of the brain
   Bring round the heart an indescribable feud;   10
So do these wonders a most dizzy pain,
   That mingles Grecian grandeur with the rude
Wasting of old Time—with a billowy main—
   A sun—a shadow of a magnitude.

On the Sea

It keeps eternal whisperings around
   Desolate shores, and with its mighty swell
   Gluts twice ten thousand Caverns, till the spell
Of Hecate leaves them their old shadowy sound.
Often 'tis in such gentle temper found,   5
   That scarcely will the very smallest shell
   Be moved for days from where it sometime fell,
When last the winds of Heaven were unbound.
Oh ye! who have your eye-balls vexed and tired,
   Feast them upon the wideness of the Sea;   10
      Oh ye! whose ears are dinned with uproar rude,
   Or fed too much with cloying melody—
      Sit ye near some old Cavern's Mouth, and brood
Until ye start, as if the sea-nymphs quired!

Elgin: In 1806 Lord Elgin had brought to England many of the remaining statues and friezes of the Parthenon. In 1816 the government purchased them for the British Museum.

4. **Hecate:** goddess of magic and the underworld.

When I have fears that I may cease to be

When I have fears that I may cease to be
  Before my pen has gleaned my teeming brain,
Before high pilèd books, in charact'ry,
  Hold like rich garners the full-ripened grain;
When I behold, upon the night's starred face,   5
  Huge cloudy symbols of a high romance,
And think that I may never live to trace
  Their shadows, with the magic hand of chance;
And when I feel, fair creature of an hour!
  That I shall never look upon thee more,   10
Never have relish in the faery power
  Of unreflecting love!—then on the shore
Of the wide world I stand alone, and think
Till love and fame to nothingness do sink.

To Homer

Standing aloof in giant ignorance,
  Of thee I hear and of the Cyclades,
As one who sits ashore and longs perchance
  To visit dolphin-coral in deep seas.
So thou wast blind!—but then the veil was rent;   5
  For Jove uncurtained Heaven to let thee live,
And Neptune made for thee a spumy tent,
  And Pan made sing for thee his forest-hive;
Aye, on the shores of darkness there is light,
  And precipices show untrodden green;   10
There is a budding morrow in midnight,
  There is a triple sight in blindness keen;
Such seeing hadst thou, as it once befell
To Dian, Queen of Earth, and Heaven, and Hell.

3. **charact'ry**: words or symbols used to express thought.

2. **Cyclades**: a group of Grecian isles.
14. **Dian**: Diana, sometimes worshipped as the goddess of nature, Hell, and the moon.

JOHN KEATS

The Eve of St. Agnes

1

St. Agnes' Eve—Ah, bitter chill it was!
The owl, for all his feathers, was a-cold;
The hare limped trembling through the frozen grass,
And silent was the flock in woolly fold:
Numb were the Beadsman's fingers, while he told   5
His rosary, and while his frosted breath,
Like pious incense from a censer old,
Seemed taking flight for heaven, without a death,
Past the sweet Virgin's picture, while his prayer he saith.

2

His prayer he saith, this patient, holy man;   10
Then takes his lamp, and riseth from his knees,
And back returneth, meagre, barefoot, wan,
Along the chapel aisle by slow degrees:
The sculptured dead, on each side, seem to freeze,
Emprisoned in black, purgatorial rails: 15
Knights, ladies, praying in dumb orat'ries,
He passeth by; and his weak spirit fails
To think how they may ache in icy hoods and mails.

3

Northward he turneth through a little door,
And scarce three steps, ere Music's golden tongue   20
Flattered to tears this agèd man and poor;
But no—already had his deathbell rung;
The joys of all his life were said and sung:
His was harsh penance on St. Agnes' Eve:
Another way he went, and soon among   25
Rough ashes sat he for his soul's reprieve,
And all night kept awake, for sinners' sake to grieve.

St. Agnes: St. Agnes, martyred in the early 4th century, is the patron saint of virgins. On the eve of January 21st, her day, virtuous young girls who perform the proper rites are said to be able to dream of their future husbands.
5. Beadsman: a man employed to pray for his patron.

4

That ancient Beadsman heard the prelude soft;
And so it chanced, for many a door was wide,
From hurry to and fro. Soon, up aloft,   30
The silver, snarling trumpets 'gan to chide:
The level chambers, ready with their pride,
Were glowing to receive a thousand guests:
The carvèd angels, ever eager-eyed,
Stared, where upon their heads the cornice rests,   35
With hair blown back, and wings put cross-wise on their breasts.

5

At length burst in the argent revelry,
With plume, tiara, and all rich array,
Numerous as shadows, haunting faerily
The brain, new stuffed, in youth, with triumphs gay   40
Of old romance. These let us wish away,
And turn, sole-thoughted, to one Lady there,
Whose heart had brooded, all that wintry day,
On love, and winged St. Agnes' saintly care,
As she had heard old dames full many times declare.   45

6

They told her how, upon St. Agnes' Eve,
Young virgins might have visions of delight,
And soft adorings from their loves receive
Upon the honeyed middle of the night,
If ceremonies due they did aright;   50
As, supperless to bed they must retire,
And couch supine their beauties, lily white;
Nor look behind, nor sideways, but require
Of Heaven with upward eyes for all that they desire.

7

Full of this whim was thoughtful Madeline: 55
The music, yearning like a God in pain,
She scarcely heard: her maiden eyes divine,
Fixed on the floor, saw many a sweeping train
Pass by—she heeded not at all: in vain
Came many a tiptoe, amorous cavalier,   60
And back retired; not cooled by high disdain,
But she saw not: her heart was otherwhere:
She sighed for Agnes' dreams, the sweetest of the year.

37. **argent revelry**: silver-clad revelers.

8

She danced along with vague, regardless eyes,
Anxious her lips, her breathing quick and short: 65
The hallowed hour was near at hand: she sighs
Amid the timbrels, and the thronged resort
Of whisperers in anger, or in sport;
'Mid looks of love, defiance, hate, and scorn,
Hoodwinked with faery fancy; all amort,   70
Save to St. Agnes and her lambs unshorn,
And all the bliss to be before tomorrow morn.

9

So, purposing each moment to retire,
She lingered still. Meantime, across the moors,
Had come young Porphyro, with heart on fire   75
For Madeline. Beside the portal doors,
Buttressed from moonlight, stands he, and implores
All saints to give him sight of Madeline,
But for one moment in the tedious hours,
That he might gaze and worship all unseen;   80
Perchance speak, kneel, touch, kiss—in sooth such things have been.

10

He ventures in: let no buzzed whisper tell:
All eyes be muffled, or a hundred swords
Will storm his heart, Love's fev'rous citadel:
For him, those chambers held barbarian hordes,   85
Hyena foemen, and hot-blooded lords,
Whose very dogs would execrations howl
Against his lineage: not one breast affords
Him any mercy in that mansion foul,
Save one old beldame, weak in body and in soul.   90

11

Ah, happy chance! the agèd creature came,
Shuffling along with ivory-headed wand,
To where he stood, hid from the torch's flame,
Behind a broad hall-pillar, far beyond
The sound of merriment and chorus bland: 95
He startled her; but soon she knew his face,
And grasped his fingers in her palsied hand,
Saying, "Mercy, Porphyro! hie thee from this place;
"They are all here to-night the whole blood-thirsty race!

67. **timbrels:** small drums.
70. **all amort:** as though dead.
71. **unshorn:** lambs to be shorn the next
day, in honor of St. Agnes.

90. **beldame:** old, and usually ugly,
woman.
92. **wand:** staff.

12

"Get hence! get hence! there's dwarfish Hildebrand;   100
"He had a fever late, and in the fit
"He cursèd thee and thine, both house and land:
"Then there's that old Lord Maurice, not a whit
"More tame for his grey hairs—Alas me! flit!
"Flit like a ghost away."—"Ah, Gossip dear,   105
"We're safe enough; here in this arm-chair sit,
"And tell me how"—"Good Saints! not here, not here;
"Follow me, child, or else these stones will be thy bier."

13

He followed through a lowly archèd way,
Brushing the cobwebs with his lofty plume,   110
And as she muttered "Well-a—well-a day!"
He found him in a little moonlight room,
Pale, latticed, chill, and silent as a tomb.
"Now tell me where is Madeline," said he,
"O tell me, Angela, by the holy loom   115
"Which none but secret sisterhood may see,
"When they St. Agnes' wool are weaving piously."

14

"St. Agnes! Ah! it is St. Agnes' Eve—
"Yet men will murder upon holy days:
"Thou must hold water in a witch's sieve,   120
"And be liege lord of all the Elves and Fays,
"To venture so: it fills me with amaze
"To see thee, Porphyro!—St. Agnes' Eve!
"God's help! my lady fair the conjuror plays
"This very night: good angels her deceive!   125
"But let me laugh awhile, I've mickle time to grieve."

15

Feebly she laugheth in the languid moon,
While Porphyro upon her face doth look,
Like puzzled urchin on an agèd crone
Who keepeth closed a wondrous riddle-book,   130
As spectacled she sits in chimney nook.
But soon his eyes grew brilliant, when she told
His lady's purpose; and he scarce could brook
Tears, at the thought of those enchantments cold,
And Madeline asleep in lap of legends old.   135

105. **Gossip:** godparent or crony.   133. **brook:** here, restrain.
126. **mickle:** much.

16

Sudden a thought came like a full-blown rose,
Flushing his brow, and in his painèd heart
Made purple riot: then doth he propose
A stratagem, that makes the beldame start:
"A cruel man and impious thou art: 140
"Sweet lady, let her pray, and sleep, and dream
"Alone with her good angels, far apart
"From wicked men like thee. Go, go!—I deem
"Thou canst not surely be the same that thou didst seem."

17

"I will not harm her, by all saints I swear,"   145
Quoth Porphyro: "O may I ne'er find grace
"When my weak voice shall whisper its last prayer,
"If one of her soft ringlets I displace,
"Or look with ruffian passion in her face:
"Good Angela, believe me by these tears;   150
"Or I will, even in a moment's space,
"Awake, with horrid shout, my foemen's ears,
"And beard them, though they be more fanged than wolves and bears."

18

"Ah! why wilt thou affright a feeble soul?
"A poor, weak, palsy-stricken, churchyard thing,   155
"Whose passing-bell may ere the midnight toll;
"Whose prayers for thee, each morn and evening,
"Were never missed."—Thus plaining, doth she bring
A gentler speech from burning Porphyro;
So woeful, and of such deep sorrowing,   160
That Angela gives promise she will do
Whatever he shall wish, betide her weal or woe.

19

Which was, to lead him, in close secrecy,
Even to Madeline's chamber, and there hide
Him in a closet, of such privacy   165
That he might see her beauty unespied,
And win perhaps that night a peerless bride,
While legioned faeries paced the coverlet,
And pale enchantment held her sleepy-eyed.
Never on such a night have lovers met,   170
Since Merlin paid his Demon all the monstrous debt.

158. **plaining:** complaining.

171. **Merlin . . . debt:** probably refers to
Merlin's paying for his magic with his life.

20

"It shall be as thou wishest," said the Dame:
"All cates and dainties shall be storèd there
"Quickly on this feast night: by the tambour frame
"Her own lute thou wilt see: no time to spare,   175
"For I am slow and feeble, and scarce dare
"On such a catering trust my dizzy head.
"Wait here, my child, with patience; kneel in prayer
"The while: Ah! thou must needs the lady wed,
"Or may I never leave my grave among the dead."   180

21

So saying, she hobbled off with busy fear.
The lover's endless minutes slowly passed;
The Dame returned, and whispered in his ear
To follow her; with agèd eyes aghast
From fright of dim espial. Safe at last,   185
Through many a dusky gallery, they gain
The maiden's chamber, silken, hushed, and chaste;
Where Porphyro took covert, pleased amain.
His poor guide hurried back with agues in her brain.

22

Her falt'ring hand upon the balustrade,   190
Old Angela was feeling for the stair,
When Madeline, St. Agnes' charmèd maid,
Rose, like a missioned spirit, unaware:
With silver taper's light, and pious care,
She turned, and down the agèd gossip led   195
To a safe level matting. Now prepare,
Young Porphyro, for gazing on that bed;
She comes, she comes again, like ring-dove frayed and fled.

23

Out went the taper as she hurried in;
Its little smoke, in pallid moonshine, died: 200
She closed the door, she panted, all akin
To spirits of the air, and visions wide:
No uttered syllable, or, woe betide!
But to her heart, her heart was voluble,
Paining with eloquence her balmy side;   205
As though a tongueless nightingale should swell
Her throat in vain, and die, heart-stifled, in her dell.

---

173. **cates:** delicacies.   188. **amain:** mightily.
174. **frame:** a frame for embroidery.   198. **frayed:** frightened.

24

A casement high and triple-arched there was,
All garlanded with carven imag'ries
Of fruits, and flowers, and bunches of knot-grass,   210
And diamonded with panes of quaint device,
Innumerable of stains and splendid dyes,
As are the tiger-moth's deep-damasked wings;
And in the midst, 'mong thousand heraldries,
And twilight saints, and dim emblazonings,   215
A shielded scutcheon blushed with blood of queens and kings.

25

Full on this casement shone the wintry moon,
And threw warm gules on Madeline's fair breast,
As down she knelt for heaven's grace and boon;
Rose-bloom fell on her hands, together pressed,   220
And on her silver cross soft amethyst,
And on her hair a glory, like a saint:
She seemed a splendid angel, newly dressed,
Save wings, for heaven:—Porphyro grew faint:
She knelt, so pure a thing, so free from mortal taint.   225

26

Anon his heart revives: her vespers done,
Of all its wreathèd pearls her hair she frees;
Unclasps her warmèd jewels one by one;
Loosens her fragrant bodice; by degrees
Her rich attire creeps rustling to her knees: 230
Half-hidden, like a mermaid in seaweed,
Pensive awhile she dreams awake, and sees,
In fancy, fair St. Agnes in her bed,
But dares not look behind, or all the charm is fled.

27

Soon, trembling in her soft and chilly nest,   235
In sort of wakeful swoon, perplexed she lay,
Until the poppied warmth of sleep oppressed
Her soothèd limbs, and soul fatigued away;
Flown, like a thought, until the morrow-day;
Blissfully havened both from joy and pain;   240
Clasped like a missal where swart Paynims pray;
Blinded alike from sunshine and from rain,
As though a rose should shut, and be a bud again.

218. **gules:** red vertical stripes.   241. **Paynims:** pagans, especially Moslems.

28

Stolen to this paradise, and so entranced,
Porphyro gazed upon her empty dress,   245
And listened to her breathing, if it chanced
To wake into a slumberous tenderness:
Which when he heard, that minute did he bless,
And breathed himself: then from the closet crept,
Noiseless as fear in a wide wilderness,   250
And over the hushed carpet, silent, stepped,
And 'tween the curtains peeped, where, lo!—how fast she slept.

29

Then by the bedside, where the faded moon
Made a dim, silver twilight, soft he set
A table and, half anguished, threw thereon   255
A cloth of woven crimson, gold, and jet:—
O for some drowsy Morphean amulet!
The boisterous midnight, festive clarion,
The kettledrum, and far-heard clarinet,
Affray his ears, though but in dying tone:—   260
The hall door shuts again, and all the noise is gone.

30

And still she slept an azure-lidded sleep,
In blanchèd linen, smooth, and lavendered,
While he from forth the closet brought a heap
Of candied apple, quince, and plum, and gourd;   265
With jellies soother than the creamy curd,
And lucent syrops, tinct with cinnamon;
Manna and dates, in argosy transferred
From Fez; and spicèd dainties, every one,
From silken Samarcand to cedared Lebanon.   270

31

These delicates he heaped with glowing hand
On golden dishes and in baskets bright
Of wreathèd silver: sumptuous they stand
   In the retirèd quiet of the night,
Filling the chilly room with perfume light.—   275
"And now, my love, my seraph fair, awake!
"Thou art my heaven, and I thine eremite:
"Open thine eyes, for meek St. Agnes' sake,
"Or I shall drowse beside thee, so my soul doth ache."

277. eremite: religious hermit.

32

Thus whispering, his warm unnervèd arm   280
Sank in her pillow. Shaded was her dream
By the dusk curtains:—'twas a midnight charm
Impossible to melt as icèd stream:
The lustrous salvers in the moonlight gleam;
Broad golden fringe upon the carpet lies: 285
It seemed he never, never could redeem
From such a steadfast spell his lady's eyes;
So mused awhile, entoiled in woofèd fantasies.

33

Awakening up, he took her hollow lute,—
Tumultuous,—and, in chords that tenderest be,   290
He played an ancient ditty, long since mute,
In Provence called, "La belle dame sans merci:"
Close to her ear touching the melody;—
Wherewith disturbed, she uttered a soft moan:
He ceased—she panted quick—and suddenly   295
Her blue affrayèd eyes wide open shone:
Upon his knees he sank, pale as smooth-sculptured stone.

34

Her eyes were open, but she still beheld,
Now wide awake, the vision of her sleep:
There was a painful change, that nigh expelled   300
The blisses of her dream so pure and deep,
At which fair Madeline began to weep,
And moan forth witless words with many a sigh;
While still her gaze on Porphyro would keep;
Who knelt, with joinèd hands and piteous eye,   305
Fearing to move or speak, she looked so dreamingly.

35

"Ah, Porphyro!" said she, "but even now
"Thy voice was at sweet tremble in mine ear,
"Made tuneable with every sweetest vow;
"And those sad eyes were spiritual and clear: 310
"How changed thou art! how pallid, chill, and drear!
"Give me that voice again, my Porphyro,
"Those looks immortal, those complainings dear!
"Oh, leave me not in this eternal woe,
"For if thou diest, my Love, I know not where to go."   315

288. **woofèd:** woven.   292. **La ... merci:** the beautiful lady
                                           without pity.

36

Beyond a mortal man impassioned far
At these voluptuous accents, he arose,
Ethereal, flushed, and like a throbbing star
Seen mid the sapphire heaven's deep repose;
Into her dream he melted, as the rose   320
Blendeth its odor with the violet,—
Solution sweet: meantime the frost-wind blows
Like Love's alarum pattering the sharp sleet
Against the windowpanes; St. Agnes' moon hath set.

37

'Tis dark: quick pattereth the flaw-blown sleet.   325
"This is no dream, my bride, my Madeline!"
'Tis dark: the icèd gusts still rave and beat:
"No dream, alas! alas! and woe is mine!
"Porphyro will leave me here to fade and pine.—
"Cruel! what traitor could thee hither bring?   330
"I curse not, for my heart is lost in thine,
"Though thou forsakest a deceivèd thing;—
"A dove forlorn and lost with sick unprunèd wing."

38

"My Madeline! sweet dreamer! lovely bride!
"Say, may I be for aye thy vassal blest?   335
"Thy beauty's shield, heart-shaped and vermeil dyed?
"Ah, silver shrine, here will I take my rest
"After so many hours of toil and quest,
"A famished pilgrim,—saved by miracle.
"Though I have found, I will not rob thy nest   340
"Saving of thy sweet self; if thou think'st well
"To trust, fair Madeline, to no rude infidel.

39

"Hark! 'tis an elfin-storm from faery land,
"Of haggard seeming, but a boon indeed:
"Arise—arise! the morning is at hand;—   345
"The bloated wassailers will never heed:—
"Let us away, my love, with happy speed;
"There are no ears to hear, or eyes to see,—
"Drowned all in Rhenish and the sleepy mead:
"Awake! arise! my love, and fearless be,   350
"For o'er the southern moors I have a home for thee."

---

325. **flaw-blown:** gust-blown.   344. **haggard:** wild, untamed.
336. **vermeil:** vermillion.

40

She hurried at his words, beset with fears,
For there were sleeping dragons all around,
At glaring watch, perhaps, with ready spears—
Down the wide stairs a darkling way they found.—   355
In all the house was heard no human sound.
A chain-drooped lamp was flickering by each door;
The arras, rich with horseman, hawk, and hound,
Fluttered in the besieging wind's uproar;
And the long carpets rose along the gusty floor.   360

41

They glide, like phantoms, into the wide hall;
Like phantoms, to the iron porch, they glide;
Where lay the Porter, in uneasy sprawl,
With a huge empty flagon by his side:
The wakeful bloodhound rose, and shook his hide,   365
But his sagacious eye an inmate owns:
By one, and one, the bolts full easy slide:—
The chains lie silent on the footworn stones;—
The key turns, and the door upon its hinges groans.

42

And they are gone: aye, ages long ago   370
These lovers fled away into the storm.
That night the Baron dreamt of many a woe,
And all his warrior-guests, with shade and form
Of witch, and demon, and large coffin-worm,
Were long be-nightmared. Angela the old   375
Died palsy-twitched, with meagre face deform;
The Beadsman, after thousand aves told,
For aye unsought-for slept among his ashes cold.

Bright star! would I were
steadfast as thou art

Bright star! would I were steadfast as thou art—
    Not in lone splendor hung aloft the night,
And watching, with eternal lids apart,
    Like Nature's patient sleepless Eremite,
The moving waters at their priestlike task   5
    Of pure ablution round earth's human shores,
Or gazing on the new soft fallen mask

4. **Eremite:** religious hermit.

Of snow upon the mountains and the moors—
No—yet still steadfast, still unchangeable,
   Pillowed upon my fair love's ripening breast,   10
To feel forever its soft fall and swell,
   Awake forever in a sweet unrest,
Still, still to hear her tender-taken breath,
And so live ever—or else swoon to death.

On Fame

"You cannot eat your cake and have it too."—Proverb.

I

Fame, like a wayward girl, will still be coy
   To those who woo her with too slavish knees,
But makes surrender to some thoughtless boy,
   And dotes the more upon a heart at ease:
She is a Gipsy, will not speak to those   5
   Who have not learnt to be content without her;
A Jilt, whose ear was never whispered close,
   Who thinks they scandal her who talk about her;
A very Gipsy is she, Nilus-born,
   Sister-in-law to jealous Potiphar;   10
Ye love-sick Bards, repay her scorn for scorn,
   Ye Artists lovelorn, madmen that ye are!
Make your best bow to her and bid adieu,
Then, if she likes it, she will follow you.

II

How fevered is the man, who cannot look
   Upon his mortal days with temperate blood,
Who vexes all the leaves of his life's book,
   And robs his fair name of its maidenhood;
It is as if the rose should pluck herself,   5
   Or the ripe plum finger its misty bloom,
As if a Naiad, like a meddling elf,
   Should darken her pure grot with muddy gloom,
But the rose leaves herself upon the briar,
   For winds to kiss and grateful bees to feed,   10
And the ripe plum still wears its dim attire,
   The undisturbèd lake has crystal space.
   Why then should man, teazing the world for grace,
Spoil his salvation for a fierce miscreed?

I. 9. **Nilus-born:** born out of the Nile's slime.
I. 10. **Potiphar:** In Genesis 39, Potiphar is the Pharaoh's captain of the guard. His wife, unable to seduce Joseph, falsely accuses him of assault. The sister-in-law is Keats's invention, perhaps signifying someone once removed from human turmoil and frustration.
II. 7. **Naiad:** water nymph.

La Belle Dame sans Merci

(*First Version*)

"Ah, what can ail thee, knight-at-arms,
   Alone and palely loitering?
The sedge is withered from the lake,
   And no birds sing.

"Ah, what can ail thee, knight-at-arms!   5
   So haggard and so woe-begone?
The squirrel's granary is full,
   And the harvest's done.

"I see a lily on thy brow,
   With anguish moist and fever dew;   10
And on thy cheek a fading rose
   Fast withereth too."

"I met a lady in the meads
   Full beautiful, a faery's child;
Her hair was long, her foot was light,   15
   And her eyes were wild.

"I made a garland for her head,
   And bracelets too, and fragrant zone;
She looked at me as she did love,
   And made sweet moan.   20

"I set her on my pacing steed,
   And nothing else saw all day long;
For sideways would she lean, and sing
   A faery's song.

"She found me roots of relish sweet,   25
   And honey wild, and manna dew;
And sure in language strange she said,
   I love thee true.

La . . . Merci: "The beautiful lady without
mercy," so named for an actual medieval
song.

"She took me to her elfin grot,
   And there she wept and sighed full sore,   30
And there I shut her wild, wild eyes—
   With kisses four.

"And there she lullèd me asleep,
   And there I dreamed, ah woe betide,
The latest dream I ever dreamed   35
   On the cold hill's side.

"I saw pale kings, and princes too,
   Pale warriors, death-pale were they all;
Who cried—'La belle dame sans merci
   Hath thee in thrall!'   40

"I saw their starved lips in the gloom
   With horrid warning gapèd wide,
And I awoke, and found me here
   On the cold hill's side.

"And this is why I sojourn here   45
   Alone and palely loitering,
Though the sedge is withered from the lake,
   And no birds sing."

On the Sonnet

If by dull rhymes our English must be chained,
   And, like Andromeda, the Sonnet sweet
Fettered, in spite of painèd loveliness;
Let us find out, if we must be constrained,
   Sandals more interwoven and complete   5
To fit the naked foot of poesy;
Let us inspect the lyre, and weigh the stress
Of every chord, and see what may be gained
   By ear industrious, and attention meet;
Misers of sound and syllable, no less   10
Than Midas of his coinage, let us be
   Jealous of dead leaves in the bay-wreath crown;
So, if we may not let the Muse be free,
   She will be bound with garlands of her own.

2. **Andromeda:** an Ethiopian princess
chained as prey for a monster and rescued
by Perseus, who then married her.

JOHN KEATS

Ode to Psyche

O Goddess! hear these tuneless numbers, wrung
  By sweet enforcement and remembrance dear,
And pardon that thy secrets should be sung
  Even into thine own soft-conchèd ear:
Surely I dreamt to-day, or did I see   5
  The wingèd Psyche with awaken'd eyes?
I wander'd in a forest thoughtlessly,
  And, on the sudden, fainting with surprise,
Saw two fair creatures, couchèd side by side
    In deepest grass, beneath the whisp'ring roof   10
    Of leaves and trembled blossoms, where there ran
      A brooklet, scarce espied:

'Mid hush'd, cool-rooted flowers, fragrant-eyed,
  Blue, silver-white, and budded Tyrian,
They lay calm-breathing, on the bedded grass;   15
    Their arms embracèd, and their pinions too;
    Their lips touch'd not, but had not bade adieu,
As if disjoinèd by soft-handed slumber,
And ready still past kisses to outnumber
    At tender eye-dawn of aurorean love: 20
      The wingèd boy I knew;
    But who wast thou, O happy, happy dove?
    His Psyche true!

O latest born and loveliest vision far
  Of all Olympus' faded hierarchy!   25
Fairer than Phoebe's sapphire-region'd star,
  Or Vesper, amorous glow-worm of the sky;
Fairer than these, though temple thou hast none,
    Nor altar heap'd with flowers;
Nor virgin-choir to make delicious moan   30
    Upon the midnight hours;
No voice, no lute, no pipe, no incense sweet
  From chain-swung censer teeming;
No shrine, no grove, no oracle, no heat
  Of pale-mouth'd prophet dreaming.   35

Psyche: a maiden beloved by Cupid. Overcoming Venus's jealousy the two were married, and Psyche became an immortal. She is also a personification of the soul.
4. conchèd: like a sea-shell.
14. Tyrian: purple, because of the purple dye which came from Tyre.
20. aurorean: dawning, from Aurora, goddess of the dawn.
26. Phoebe: Diana, goddess of the moon.
27. Vesper: Venus, the evening star.

O brightest! though too late for antique vows,
   Too, too late for the fond believing lyre,
When holy were the haunted forest boughs,
   Holy the air, the water, and the fire;
Yet even in these days so far retir'd   40
   From happy pieties, thy lucent fans,
   Fluttering among the faint Olympians,
I see, and sing, by my own eyes inspired.
So let me be thy choir, and make a moan
      Upon the midnight hours;   45
Thy voice, thy lute, thy pipe, thy incense sweet
   From swingèd censer teeming;
Thy shrine, thy grove, thy oracle, thy heat
   Of pale-mouth'd prophet dreaming.

Yes, I will be thy priest, and build a fane   50
   In some untrodden region of my mind,
Where branchèd thoughts, new grown with pleasant pain,
   Instead of pines shall murmur in the wind:
Far, far around shall those dark-cluster'd trees
   Fledge the wild-ridged mountains steep by steep;   55
And there by zephyrs, streams, and birds, and bees,
   The moss-lain Dryads shall be lull'd to sleep;
And in the midst of this wide quietness
A rosy sanctuary will I dress
With the wreath'd trellis of a working brain,   60
   With buds, and bells, and stars without a name,
With all the gardener Fancy e'er could feign,
   Who breeding flowers, will never breed the same.
And there shall be for thee all soft delight
   That shadowy thought can win,   65
A bright torch, and a casement ope at night,
   To let the warm Love in!

Ode to a Nightingale

I

My heart aches, and a drowsy numbness pains
   My sense, as though of hemlock I had drunk,
Or emptied some dull opiate to the drains
   One minute past, and Lethe-wards had sunk:

---

50. **fane:** temple.   4. **Lethe-wards:** towards Lethe, the river
                                 of Hades whose waters cause forgetfulness.

'Tis not through envy of thy happy lot,   5
   But being too happy in thine happiness,—
     That thou, light-wingèd Dryad of the trees,
      In some melodious plot
   Of beechen green, and shadows numberless,
     Singest of summer in full-throated ease.   10

2

O, for a draught of vintage! that hath been
   Cool'd a long age in the deep-delved earth,
Tasting of Flora and the country green,
   Dance, and Provençal song, and sunburnt mirth!
O for a beaker full of the warm South,   15
   Full of the true, the blushful Hippocrene,
     With beaded bubbles winking at the brim,
      And purple-stained mouth;
     That I might drink, and leave the world unseen,
     And with thee fade away into the forest dim: 20

3

Fade far away, dissolve, and quite forget
   What thou among the leaves hast never known,
The weariness, the fever, and the fret
   Here, where men sit and hear each other groan;
Where palsy shakes a few, sad, last gray hairs,   25
   Where youth grows pale, and spectre-thin, and dies;
     Where but to think is to be full of sorrow
      And leaden-eyed despairs,
     Where Beauty cannot keep her lustrous eyes,
     Or new Love pine at them beyond tomorrow.   30

4

Away! away! for I will fly to thee,
   Not charioted by Bacchus and his pards,
But on the viewless wings of Poesy,
   Though the dull brain perplexes and retards:
Already with thee! tender is the night,   35
   And haply the Queen-Moon is on her throne,
     Cluster'd around by all her starry fays;
      But here there is no light,
   Save what from heaven is with the breezes blown
     Through verdurous glooms and winding mossy ways.   40

---

7. **Dryad:** wood nymph.
13. **Flora:** goddess of flowers; personification for flowers.

16. **Hippocrene:** the fountain of the Muses on Mt. Helicon.
32. **Bacchus ... pards:** the god of wine, whose chariot is drawn by leopards.

5

I cannot see what flowers are at my feet,
  Nor what soft incense hangs upon the boughs,
But, in embalmèd darkness, guess each sweet
  Wherewith the seasonable month endows
The grass, the thicket, and the fruit-tree wild;   45
  White hawthorn, and the pastoral eglantine;
    Fast fading violets cover'd up in leaves;
      And mid-May's eldest child,
  The coming musk-rose, full of dewy wine,
    The murmurous haunt of flies on summer eves.   50

6

Darkling I listen; and, for many a time
  I have been half in love with easeful Death,
Call'd him soft names in many a musèd rhyme,
  To take into the air my quiet breath;
Now more than ever seems it rich to die,   55
  To cease upon the midnight with no pain,
    While thou art pouring forth thy soul abroad
      In such an ecstasy!
  Still wouldst thou sing, and I have ears in vain—
    To thy high requiem become a sod.   60

7

Thou wast not born for death, immortal Bird!
  No hungry generations tread thee down;
The voice I hear this passing night was heard
  In ancient days by emperor and clown:
Perhaps the self-same song that found a path   65
  Through the sad heart of Ruth, when, sick for home,
    She stood in tears amid the alien corn;
      The same that oft-times hath
  Charm'd magic casements, opening on the foam
    Of perilous seas, in faery lands forlorn.   70

8

Forlorn! the very word is like a bell
  To toll me back from thee to my sole self!
Adieu! the fancy cannot cheat so well
  As she is fam'd to do, deceiving elf.
Adieu! adieu! thy plaintive anthem fades   75

43. embalmèd: perfumed.   66. **Ruth:** in the Bible she forsook her
                                               native land to live in Israel with Naomi,
                                               her mother-in-law.

Past the near meadows, over the still stream,
    Up the hill-side; and now 'tis buried deep
        In the next valley-glades:
Was it a vision, or a waking dream?
Fled is that music:—Do I wake or sleep?   80

Ode on a Grecian Urn

1

Thou still unravish'd bride of quietness,
    Thou foster-child of silence and slow time,
Sylvan historian, who canst thus express
    A flowery tale more sweetly than our rhyme:
What leaf-fring'd legend haunts about thy shape   5
    Of deities or mortals, or of both,
        In Tempe or the dales of Arcady?
What men or gods are these? What maidens loth?
    What mad pursuit? What struggle to escape?
        What pipes and timbrels? What wild ecstasy?   10

2

Heard melodies are sweet, but those unheard
    Are sweeter; therefore, ye soft pipes, play on;
Not to the sensual ear, but, more endear'd,
    Pipe to the spirit ditties of no tone;
Fair youth, beneath the trees, thou canst not leave   15
    Thy song, nor ever can those trees be bare;
        Bold Lover, never, never canst thou kiss,
Though winning near the goal—yet, do not grieve;
    She cannot fade, though thou hast not thy bliss,
        For ever wilt thou love, and she be fair!   20

3

Ah, happy, happy boughs! that cannot shed
    Your leaves, nor ever bid the Spring adieu;
And, happy melodist, unwearièd,
    For ever piping songs for ever new;
More happy love! more happy, happy love!   25
    For ever warm and still to be enjoy'd,
        For every panting, and for ever young;
All breathing human passion far above,
    That leaves a heart high-sorrowful and cloyed,
        A burning forehead, and a parching tongue.   30

7. **Tempe ... Arcady:** In Greek poetry,   10. **timbrels:** small drums or tambourines.
symbols of pastoral beauty.

4

Who are these coming to the sacrifice?
  To what green altar, O mysterious priest,
Lead'st thou that heifer lowing at the skies,
  And all her silken flanks with garlands drest?
What little town by river or sea shore,   35
  Or mountain-built with peaceful citadel,
    Is emptied of this folk, this pious morn?
And, little town, thy streets for evermore
  Will silent be; and not a soul to tell
    Why thou art desolate, can e'er return.   40

5

O Attic shape! Fair attitude! with brede
  Of marble men and maidens overwrought,
With forest branches and the trodden weed;
  Thou, silent form, dost tease us out of thought
As doth eternity: Cold Pastoral!   45
  When old age shall this generation waste,
    Thou shalt remain, in midst of other woe
Than ours, a friend to man, to whom thou say'st,
  "Beauty is truth, truth beauty,"—that is all
    Ye know on earth, and all ye need to know.   50

Ode on Melancholy

1

No, no, go not to Lethe, neither twist
  Wolfs-bane, tight-rooted, for its poisonous wine;
Nor suffer thy pale forehead to be kiss'd
  By nightshade, ruby grape of Proserpine;
Make not your rosary of yew-berries,   5
  Nor let the beetle, nor the death-moth be
    Your mournful Psyche, nor the downy owl
A partner in your sorrow's mysteries;
  For shade to shade will come too drowsily,
    And drown the wakeful anguish of the soul.   10

49. **"Beauty . . . beauty"**: Two versions of this poem appeared in 1820; the second one omits the quotation marks around this phrase.

1. **Lethe**: the river in Hades whose waters cause forgetfulness.
4. **Proserpine**: goddess of the underworld.
7. **Psyche**: the soul, sometimes depicted as a butterfly or moth departing from the mouth of the dead.

2

But when the melancholy fit shall fall
    Sudden from heaven like a weeping cloud,
That fosters the droop-headed flowers all,
    And hides the green hill in an April shroud;
Then glut thy sorrow on a morning rose,   15
    Or on the rainbow of the salt sand-wave,
        Or on the wealth of globèd peonies;
Or if thy mistress some rich anger shows,
    Emprison her soft hand, and let her rave,
        And feed deep, deep upon her peerless eyes.   20

3

She dwells with Beauty—Beauty that must die;
    And Joy, whose hand is ever at his lips
Bidding adieu; and aching Pleasure nigh,
    Turning to poison while the bee-mouth sips:
Ay, in the very temple of Delight   25
    Veil'd Melancholy has her sovran shrine,
        Though seen of none save him whose strenuous tongue
Can burst Joy's grape against his palate fine;
    His soul shall taste the sadness of her might,
        And be amoung her cloudy trophies hung.   30

Ode to Autumn

1

Season of mists and mellow fruitfulness!
    Close bosom-friend of the maturing sun;
Conspiring with him how to load and bless
    With fruit the vines that round the thatch-eaves run;
To bend with apples the moss'd cottage-trees,   5
    And fill all fruit with ripeness to the core;
        To swell the gourd, and plump the hazel shells
    With a sweet kernel; to set budding more
And still more, later flowers for the bees,
Until they think warm days will never cease;   10
    For summer has o'er-brimm'd their clammy cells.

2

Who hath not seen thee oft amid thy store?
  Sometimes whoever seeks abroad may find
Thee sitting careless on a granary floor,
  Thy hair soft-lifted by the winnowing wind;   15
Or on a half-reap'd furrow sound asleep,
  Drowsed with the fume of poppies, while thy hook
    Spares the next swath and all its twinèd flowers;
And sometimes like a gleaner thou dost keep
Steady thy laden head across a brook;   20
Or by a cider-press, with patient look,
  Thou watchest the last oozings, hours by hours.

3

Where are the songs of Spring? Aye, where are they?
  Think not of them,—thou hast thy music too,
While barred clouds bloom the soft-dying day   25
  And touch the stubble-plains with rosy hue;
Then in a wailful choir the small gnats mourn
  Among the river-sallows, borne aloft
    Or sinking as the light wind lives or dies;
And full-grown lambs loud bleat from hilly bourn;   30
Hedge-crickets sing, and now with treble soft
The redbreast whistles from a garden-croft;
  And gathering swallows twitter in the skies.

This living hand

This living hand, now warm and capable
Of earnest grasping, would, if it were cold
And in the icy silence of the tomb,
So haunt thy days and chill thy dreaming nights
That thou wouldst wish thine own heart dry of blood   5
So in my veins red life might stream again,
And thou be conscience-calmed—see here it is—
I hold it towards you.

28. **sallows:** willows.
30. **bourn:** realm.
32. **croft:** an enclosed plot of ground.

This . . . Hand: found written in the margin of the unfinished *Cap and Bells*.

WALTER SAVAGE LANDOR [1775–1864]

Mother, I cannot mind my wheel

Mother, I cannot mind my wheel;
    My fingers ache, my lips are dry:
O, if you felt the pain I feel!
    But O, who ever felt as I?

No longer could I doubt him true—   5
    All other men may use deceit;
He always said my eyes were blue,
    And often swore my lips were sweet.

Rose Aylmer

Ah what avails the sceptred race,
    Ah what the form divine!
What every virtue, every grace!
    Rose Aylmer, all were thine.
Rose Aylmer, whom these wakeful eyes   5
    May weep, but never see,
A night of memories and of sighs
    I consecrate to thee.

On Seeing a Hair of Lucretia Borgia

Borgia, thou once were almost too august
And high for adoration;—now thou'rt dust;
All that remains of thee these plaits infold,
Calm hair, meandering with pellucid gold!

Rose Aylmer: the daughter of Baron Aylmer; she met Landor when she was seventeen. Four years later she died suddenly in India.

Lucretia Borgia: Duchess of Ferrara (1480–1519).
4. **pellucid:** transparent.

Lately our poets

Lately our poets loitered in green lanes,
Content to catch the ballads of the plains;
I fancied I had strength enough to climb
A loftier station at no distant time,
And might securely from intrusion doze   5
Upon the flowers through which Ilissus flows.
In those pale olive grounds all voices cease,
And from afar dust fills the paths of Greece.
My slumber broken and my doublet torn,
I find the laurel also bears a thorn.   10

THOMAS LOVE PEACOCK [1785–1866]

The War-Song of Dinas Vawr

The mountain sheep are sweeter,
But the valley sheep are fatter;
We therefore deemed it meeter
To carry off the latter.
We made an expedition;   5
We met an host, and quelled it;
We forced a strong position,
And killed the men who held it.

On Dyfed's richest valley,
Where herds of kine were brousing,   10
We made a mighty sally,
To furnish our carousing.
Fierce warriors rushed to meet us;
We met them, and o'erthrew them:
They struggled hard to beat us;   15
But we conquered them, and slew them.

As we drove our prize at leisure,
The king marched forth to catch us:
His rage surpassed all measure,
But his people could not match us.   20
He fled to his hall-pillars;
And, ere our force we led off,
Some sacked his house and cellars,
While others cut his head off.

6. **Ilissus:** the river of Athens which waters the olives groves of Attica.

War-Song . . . Vawr: from Peacock's novel *The Misfortunes of Elphin* (1829), laid in medieval Wales (hence the names).

We there, in strife bewild'ring,   25
Spilt blood enough to swim in:
We orphaned many children,
And widowed many women.
The eagles and the ravens
We glutted with our foemen;   30
The heroes and the cravens,
The spearmen and the bowmen.

We brought away from battle,
And much their land bemoaned them,
Two thousand head of cattle,   35
And the head of him that owned them:
Ednyfed, King of Dyfed,
His head was borne before us;
His wine and beasts supplied our feasts,
And his overthrow, our chorus.   40

GEORGE GORDON, LORD BYRON [1788–1824]

She walks in beauty

She walks in beauty, like the night
   Of cloudless climes and starry skies;
And all that's best of dark and bright
   Meet in her aspect and her eyes:
Thus mellowed to that tender light   5
   Which heaven to gaudy day denies.

One shade the more, one ray the less,
   Had half impaired the nameless grace
Which waves in every raven tress
   Or softly lightens o'er her face;   10
Where thoughts serenely sweet express
   How pure, how dear their dwelling-place.

And on that cheek, and o'er that brow
   So soft, so calm, yet eloquent,
The smiles that win, the tints that glow,   15
   But tell of days in goodness spent,
A mind at peace with all below,
   A heart whose love is innocent!

On This Day I Complete My Thirty-Sixth Year

1

'T is time this heart should be unmoved,
  Since others it hath ceased to move:
Yet, though I cannot be beloved,
  Still let me love!

2

My days are in the yellow leaf;   5
  The flowers and fruits of Love are gone;
The worm, the canker, and the grief
  Are mine alone!

3

The fire that on my bosom preys
  Is lone as some Volcanic isle;   10
No torch is kindled at its blaze—
  A funeral pile.

4

The hope, the fear, the zealous care,
  The exalted portion of the pain
And power of love, I cannot share,   15
  But wear the chain.

5

But 't is not *thus*—and 't is not *here*—
  Such thoughts should shake my soul, nor *now*
Where Glory decks the hero's bier,
  Or binds his brow.   20

6

The Sword, the Banner, and the Field,
  Glory and Greece, around me see!
The Spartan, borne upon his shield,
  Was not more free.

7

Awake! (not Greece—she *is* awake!)   25
  Awake, my spirit! Think through *whom*
Thy life-blood tracks its parent lake,
  And then strike home!

On ... Year: written shortly before Byron's
death, when he was taking part in the
Greek war of independence.

20. binds his brow: with the laurel crown,
for valor.

8

Tread those reviving passions down,
   Unworthy manhood!—unto thee   30
Indifferent should the smile or frown
   Of Beauty be.

9

If thou regret'st thy youth, *why live?*
   The land of honourable death
Is here:—up to the Field, and give   35
   Away thy breath!

10

Seek out—less often sought than found—
   A soldier's grave, for thee the best;
Then look around, and choose thy ground,
   And take thy Rest.   40
      Missolonghi, Jan. 22, 1824.

EDGAR ALLAN POE [1809–1849]

To Helen

Helen, thy beauty is to me
   Like those Nicèan barks of yore,
That gently, o'er a perfumed sea,
   The weary, way-worn wanderer bore
To his own native shore.   5

On desperate seas long wont to roam,
   Thy hyacinth hair, thy classic face,
Thy Naiad airs have brought me home
   To the glory that was Greece,
And the grandeur that was Rome.   10

Lo! in yon brilliant window-niche
   How statue-like I see thee stand,
The agate lamp within thy hand!
   Ah! Psyche, from the regions which
Are Holy-Land!   15

2. **Nicèan:** not identified. Poe seems to be choosing the word for its classical and Mediterranean connotations.

7. **hyacinth:** in other works, Poe associates "hyacinth" with black curling tresses.
8. **Naiad:** water nymph.
14. **Psyche:** bride of Cupid; the soul.

The Later Nineteenth Century

❧ ❧ ❧

ALFRED, LORD TENNYSON

[*1809–1892*]

The Kraken

Below the thunders of the upper deep,
Far, far beneath in the abysmal sea,
His ancient, dreamless, uninvaded sleep
The Kraken sleepeth: faintest sunlights flee
About his shadowy sides; above him swell   5
Huge sponges of millennial growth and height;
And far away into the sickly light,
From many a wondrous grot and secret cell
Unnumber'd and enormous polypi
Winnow with giant arms the slumbering green.   10
There hath he lain for ages, and will lie
Battening upon huge sea-worms in his sleep,
Until the latter fire shall heat the deep;
Then once by man and angels to be seen,
In roaring he shall rise and on the surface die.   15

Mariana

"Mariana in the moated grange"—*Measure for Measure*

With blackest moss the flower-plots
    Were thickly crusted, one and all:
The rusted nails fell from the knots
    That held the pear to the gable-wall.
The broken sheds looked sad and strange;   5
    Unlifted was the clinking latch;
    Weeded and worn the ancient thatch
Upon the lonely moated grange.
    She only said, "*My life is dreary,*
      He cometh not," she said;   10
    She said, "*I am aweary, aweary,*
      I would that I were dead!"

Her tears fell with the dews at even;
    Her tears fell ere the dews were dried;
She could not look on the sweet heaven,   15
    Either at morn or eventide.
After the flitting of the bats,
    When thickest dark did trance the sky,
    She drew her casement-curtain by,
And glanced athwart the glooming flats.   20
    She only said, "*The night is dreary,*
      He cometh not," she said;
    She said, "*I am aweary, aweary,*
      I would that I were dead!"

Upon the middle of the night,   25
    Waking she heard the night-fowl crow:
The cock sung out an hour ere light;
    From the dark fen the oxen's low
Came to her: without hope of change,
    In sleep she seemed to walk forlorn,   30
    Till cold wings woke the grey-eyed morn
About the lonely moated grange.
    She only said, "*The day is dreary,*
      He cometh not," she said;
    She said, "*I am aweary, aweary,*   35
      I would that I were dead!"

Mariana . . . grange: from Shakespeare's *Measure for Measure*, III, i, *l.* 277. Mariana waits in a farmhouse for the lover who had betrayed her.

About a stone-cast from the wall
   A sluice with blackened water slept
And o'er it many, round and small,
   The clustered marish-mosses crept.   40
Hard by a poplar shook alway,
   All silver-green with gnarlèd bark:
   For leagues no other tree did mark
The level waste, the rounding grey.
      She only said, "*My life is dreary,*   45
        He cometh not," she said;
      She said, "*I am aweary, aweary,*
        I would that I were dead!"

And ever when the moon was low,
   And the shrill winds were up and away,   50
In the white curtain, to and fro,
   She saw the gusty shadow sway.
But when the moon was very low,
   And wild winds bound within their cell,
   The shadow of the poplar fell   55
Upon her bed, across her brow.
      She only said, "*The night is dreary,*
        He cometh not," she said;
      She said, "*I am aweary, aweary,*
        I would that I were dead!"   60

All day within the dreamy house,
   The doors upon their hinges creaked;
The blue fly sung in the pane; the mouse
   Behind the mouldering wainscot shrieked,
Or from the crevice peered about,   65
   Old faces glimmered through the doors,
   Old footsteps trod the upper floors,
Old voices called her from without.
      She only said, "*My life is dreary,*
        He cometh not," she said;   70
      She said, "*I am aweary, aweary,*
        I would that I were dead!"

The sparrow's chirrup on the roof,
   The slow clock ticking, and the sound
Which to the wooing wind aloof   75
   The poplar made, did all confound

40. **marish:** marsh.

Her sense; but most she loathed the hour
  When the thick-moated sunbeam lay
  Athwart the chambers, and the day
Was sloping toward his western bower.   80
    Then, said she, "*I am very dreary,*
      He will not come," she said;
    She wept, "*I am aweary, aweary,*
      O God, that I were dead!"

Sonnet

She took the dappled partridge flecked with blood,
  And in her hand the drooping pheasant bare.
  And by his feet she held the woolly hare,
And like a master painting where she stood,
Looked some new goddess of an English wood.   5
  Nor could I find an imperfection there,
  Nor blame the wanton act that showed so fair—
To me whatever freak she plays is good.
Hers is the fairest Life that breathes with breath.
  And *their* still plumes and azure eyelids closed   10
    Made quiet Death so beautiful to see
That Death lent grace to Life and Life to Death
  And in one image Life and Death reposed,
    To make my love an Immortality.

You ask me, why, though ill at ease

You ask me, why, though ill at ease,
  Within this region I subsist,
  Whose spirits falter in the mist,
And languish for the purple seas.

It is the land that freemen till,   5
  That sober-suited Freedom chose,
  The land, where girt with friends or foes
A man may speak the thing he will;

A land of settled government,
  A land of just and old renown,   10
  Where Freedom slowly broadens down
From precedent to precedent;

Where faction seldom gathers head,
   But, by degrees to fullness wrought,
   The strength of some diffusive thought   15
Hath time and space to work and spread.

Should banded unions persecute
   Opinion, and induce a time
   When single thought is civil crime,
And individual freedom mute,   20

Though power should make from land to land
   The name of Britain trebly great—
   Though every channel of the State
Should fill and choke with golden sand—

Yet waft me from the harbor-mouth,   25
   Wild wind! I seek a warmer sky,
   And I will see before I die
The palms and temples of the South.

Ulysses

It little profits that an idle king,
By this still hearth, among these barren crags,
Matched with an agèd wife, I mete and dole
Unequal laws unto a savage race,
That hoard, and sleep, and feed, and know not me.   5
I cannot rest from travel; I will drink
Life to the lees. All times I have enjoyed
Greatly, have suffered greatly, both with those
That loved me, and alone; on shore, and when
Through scudding drifts the rainy Hyades   10
Vext the dim sea. I am become a name
For always roaming with a hungry heart;
Much have I seen and known,—cities of men
And manners, climates, councils, governments,
Myself not least, but honoured of them all;   15
And drunk delight of battle with my peers,
Far on the ringing plains of windy Troy.
I am a part of all that I have met;
Yet all experience is an arch wherethrough

Ulysses : He retired to his island of Ithaca after the Trojan War and long wanderings; was said by Dante (*Inferno*, 26) to have gone on a new voyage to the other side of the earth, where his ship foundered. **10. Hyades:** a group of stars said to bring rain when they rose.

Gleams that untravelled world whose margin fades   20
For ever and for ever when I move.
How dull it is to pause, to make an end,
To rust unburnished, not to shine in use!
As though to breathe were life! Life piled on life
Were all too little, and of one to me   25
Little remains; but every hour is saved
From that eternal silence, something more,
A bringer of new things; and vile it were
For some three suns to store and hoard myself,
And this grey spirit yearning in desire   30
To follow knowledge like a sinking star,
Beyond the utmost bound of human thought.
    This is my son, mine own Telemachus,
To whom I leave the sceptre and the isle—
Well-loved of me, discerning to fulfil   35
This labour, by slow prudence to make mild
A rugged people, and through soft degrees
Subdue them to the useful and the good.
Most blameless is he, centred in the sphere
Of common duties, decent not to fail   40
In offices of tenderness, and pay
Meet adoration to my household gods,
When I am gone. He works his work, I mine.
    There lies the port; the vessel puffs her sail:
There gloom the dark, broad seas. My mariners,   45
Souls that have toiled, and wrought, and thought with me—
That ever with a frolic welcome took
The thunder and the sunshine, and opposed
Free hearts, free foreheads—you and I are old;
Old age hath yet his honour and his toil.   50
Death closes all; but something ere the end,
Some work of noble note, may yet be done,
Not unbecoming men that strove with Gods.
The lights begin to twinkle from the rocks:
The long day wanes; the slow moon climbs; the deep   55
Moans round with many voices. Come, my friends,
'T is not too late to seek a newer world.
Push off, and sitting well in order smite
The sounding furrows; for my purpose holds
To sail beyond the sunset, and the baths   60
Of all the western stars, until I die.

60–61. **baths ... stars:** The stars were
said to go down in the great ocean which
was supposed to circle the world.

It may be that the gulfs will wash us down;
It may be we shall touch the Happy Isles,
And see the great Achilles, whom we knew.
Though much is taken, much abides; and though   65
We are not now that strength which in old days
Moved earth and heaven; that which we are, we are;
One equal temper of heroic hearts,
Made weak by time and fate, but strong in will
To strive, to seek, to find, and not to yield.   70

Tithonus

The woods decay, the woods decay and fall,
The vapours weep their burthen to the ground,
Man comes and tills the field and lies beneath,
And after many a summer dies the swan.
Me only cruel immortality   5
Consumes: I wither slowly in thine arms,
Here at the quiet limit of the world,
A white-hair'd shadow roaming like a dream
The ever-silent spaces of the East,
Far-folded mists, and gleaming halls of morn.   10
    Alas! for this grey shadow, once a man—
So glorious in his beauty and thy choice,
Who madest him thy chosen, that he seem'd
To his great heart none other than a God!
I ask'd thee, "Give me immortality."   15
Then didst thou grant mine asking with a smile,
Like wealthy men who care not how they give.
But thy strong Hours indignant work'd their wills,
And beat me down and marr'd and wasted me,
And tho' they could not end me, left me maim'd   20
To dwell in presence of immortal youth,
Immortal age beside immortal youth,
And all I was, in ashes. Can thy love,
Thy beauty, make amends, tho' even now,
Close over us, the silver star, thy guide,   25
Shines in those tremulous eyes that fill with tears
To hear me? Let me go: take back thy gift:

69–70. **strong . . . yield:** Dante puts much the same sentiment in Ulysses' mouth.

Tithonus: Beloved of Aurora, goddess of the dawn, who gained eternal life for him, but not eternal youth. Grown aged, he addresses her here.
4. **swan:** a very long-lived bird.
25. **silver star:** the planet Venus (associated with love) often appears in the east just before sunrise.

Why should a man desire in any way
To vary from the kindly race of men,
Or pass beyond the goal of ordinance   30
Where all should pause, as is most meet for all?
    A soft air fans the cloud apart; there comes
A glimpse of that dark world where I was born.
Once more the old mysterious glimmer steals
From thy pure brows, and from thy shoulders pure,   35
And bosom beating with a heart renew'd.
Thy cheek begins to redden thro' the gloom,
Thy sweet eyes brighten slowly close to mine,
Ere yet they blind the stars, and the wild team
Which love thee, yearning for thy yoke, arise,   40
And shake the darkness from their loosen'd manes,
And beat the twilight into flakes of fire.
    Lo! ever thus thou growest beautiful
In silence, then before thine answer given
Departest, and thy tears are on my cheek.   45
    Why wilt thou ever scare me with thy tears,
And make me tremble lest a saying learnt,
In days far-off, on that dark earth, be true?
"The Gods themselves cannot recall their gifts."
    Ay me! ay me! with what another heart   50
In days far-off, and with what other eyes
I used to watch—if I be he that watch'd—
The lucid outline forming round thee; saw
The dim curls kindle into sunny rings;
Changed with thy mystic change, and felt my blood   55
Glow with the glow that slowly crimson'd all
Thy presence and thy portals, while I lay,
Mouth, forehead, eyelids, growing dewy-warm
With kisses balmier than half-opening buds
Of April, and could hear the lips that kiss'd   60
Whispering I knew not what of wild and sweet,
Like that strange song I heard Apollo sing,
While Ilion like a mist rose into towers.
    Yet hold me not for ever in thine East:
How can my nature longer mix with thine?   65
Coldly thy rosy shadows bathe me, cold
Are all thy lights, and cold my wrinkled feet
Upon thy glimmering thresholds, when the steam
Floats up from those dim fields about the homes

---

29. **kindly:** natural, pertaining to their kind (archaic usage).
39. **team:** the horses that draw Aurora's chariot into the sky at dawn.

62–63. **Apollo . . . towers:** The walls of Troy (Ilion) rose to the music of Apollo.

Of happy men that have the power to die,   70
And grassy burrows of the happier dead.
Release me, and restore me to the ground;
Thou seest all things, thou wilt see my grave:
Thou wilt renew thy beauty morn by morn;
I earth in earth forget these empty courts,   75
And thee returning on thy silver wheels.

Break, Break, Break

Break, break, break,
  On thy cold gray stones, O Sea!
And I would that my tongue could utter
  The thoughts that arise in me.

O well for the fisherman's boy,   5
  That he shouts with his sister at play!
O well for the sailor lad,
  That he sings in his boat on the bay!

And the stately ships go on
  To their haven under the hill;   10
But O for the touch of a vanished hand,
  And the sound of a voice that is still!

Break, break, break
  At the foot of thy crags, O Sea!
But the tender grace of a day that is dead   15
  Will never come back to me.

Locksley Hall

Comrades, leave me here a little, while as yet 'tis early morn:
Leave me here, and when you want me, sound upon the bugle-horn.

'Tis the place, and all around it, as of old, the curlews call,
Dreary gleams about the moorland flying over Locksley Hall;

Locksley Hall, that in the distance overlooks the sandy tracts,   5
And the hollow ocean-ridges roaring into cataracts.

Many a night from yonder ivied casement, ere I went to rest,
Did I look on great Orion sloping slowly to the West.

Many a night I saw the Pleiads, rising through the mellow shade,
Glitter like a swarm of fire-flies tangled in a silver braid.   10

Here about the beach I wandered, nourishing a youth sublime.
With the fairy tales of science, and the long result of time;

When the centuries behind me like a fruitful land reposed;
When I clung to all the present for the promise that it closed;

When I dipped into the future far as human eye could see;   15
Saw the vision of the world, and all the wonder that would be.—

In the spring a fuller crimson comes upon the robin's breast;
In the spring the wanton lapwing gets himself another crest;

In the spring a livelier iris changes on the burnished dove;
In the spring a young man's fancy lightly turns to thoughts of love.   20

Then her cheek was pale and thinner than should be for one so young,
And her eyes on all my motions with a mute observance hung.

And I said, "My cousin Amy, speak, and speak the truth to me,
Trust me, cousin, all the current of my being sets to thee."

On her pallid cheek and forehead came a color and a light,   25
As I have seen the rosy red flushing in the northern night.

And she turned—her bosom shaken with a sudden storm of sighs—
All the spirit deeply dawning in the dark of hazel eyes—

Saying, "I have hid my feelings, fearing they should do me wrong;"
Saying, "Dost thou love me, cousin?" weeping, "I have loved thee
        long."   30

Love took up the glass of Time, and turned it in his glowing hands;
Every moment, lightly shaken, ran itself in golden sands.

Love took up the harp of Life, and smote on all the chords with might;
Smote the chord of Self, that, trembling, passed in music out of sight.

Many a morning on the moorland did we hear the copses ring,   35
And her whisper thronged my pulses with the fulness of the spring.

Many an evening by the waters did we watch the stately ships,
And our spirits rushed together at the touching of the lips.

14. **closed:** enclosed.

O my cousin, shallow-hearted! O my Amy, mine no more!
O the dreary, dreary moorland! O the barren, barren shore!   40

Falser than all fancy fathoms, falser than all songs have sung,
Puppet to a father's threat, and servile to a shrewish tongue!

Is it well to wish thee happy? having known me—to decline
On a range of lower feelings and a narrower heart than mine!

Yet it shall be; thou shalt lower to his level day by day,   45
What is fine within thee growing coarse to sympathize with clay.

As the husband is, the wife is; thou art mated with a clown,
And the grossness of his nature will have weight to drag thee down.

He will hold thee, when his passion shall have spent its novel force,
Something better than his dog, a little dearer than his horse.   50

What is this? his eyes are heavy; think not they are glazed with wine.
Go to him, it is thy duty; kiss him, take his hand in thine.

It may be my lord is weary, that his brain is overwrought;
Soothe him with thy finer fancies, touch him with thy lighter thought.

He will answer to the purpose, easy things to understand—   55
Better thou wert dead before me, though I slew thee with my hand!

Better thou and I were lying, hidden from the heart's disgrace,
Rolled in one another's arms, and silent in a last embrace.

Cursèd be the social wants that sin against the strength of youth!
Cursèd be the social lies that warp us from the living truth!   60

Cursèd be the sickly forms that err from honest Nature's rule!
Cursèd be the gold that gilds the straitened forehead of the fool!

Well—'tis well that I should bluster!—hadst thou less unworthy
        proved—
Would to God—for I had loved thee more than ever wife was loved.

Am I mad, that I should cherish that which bears but bitter fruit?   65
I will pluck it from my bosom, though my heart be at the root.

Never, though my mortal summers to such length of years should come
As the many-wintered crow that leads the changing rookery home.

47. **clown**: boor.

Where is comfort? in division of the records of the mind?
Can I part her from herself, and love her, as I knew her, kind?   70

I remember one that perished; sweetly did she speak and move;
Such a one do I remember, whom to look at was to love.

Can I think of her as dead, and love her for the love she bore?
No—she never loved me truly; love is love for evermore.

Comfort? comfort scorned of devils! this is truth the poet sings,   75
That a sorrow's crown of sorrow is remembering happier things.

Drug thy memories, lest thou learn it, lest thy heart be put to proof,
In the dead unhappy night, and when the rain is on the roof.

Like a dog, he hunts in dreams, and thou art staring at the wall,
Where the dying night-lamp flickers, and the shadows rise and fall.   80

Then a hand shall pass before thee, pointing to his drunken sleep,
To thy widowed marriage-pillows, to the tears that thou wilt weep.

Thou shalt hear the "Never, never," whispered by the phantom years,
And a song from out the distance in the ringing of thine ears;

And an eye shall vex thee, looking ancient kindness on thy pain.   85
Turn thee, turn thee on thy pillow; get thee to thy rest again.

Nay, but Nature brings thee solace; for a tender voice will cry.
'Tis a purer life than thine, a lip to drain thy trouble dry.

Baby lips will laugh me down; my latest rival brings thee rest.
Baby fingers, waxen touches, press me from the mother's breast.   90

Oh, the child too clothes the father with a dearness not his due.
Half is thine and half is his; it will be worthy of the two.

Oh, I see thee old and formal, fitted to thy petty part,
With a little hoard of maxims preaching down a daughter's heart.

"They were dangerous guides, the feelings—she herself was not
          exempt—   95
Truly, she herself had suffered"—Perish in thy self-contempt!

Overlive it—lower yet—be happy! wherefore should I care?
I myself must mix with action, lest I wither by despair.

75. **poet:** Dante, *Inferno*, V, *ll.* 121–23.

What is that which I should turn to, lighting upon days like these?
Every door is barred with gold, and opens but to golden keys.   100

Every gate is thronged with suitors, all the markets overflow.
I have but an angry fancy; what is that which I should do?

I had been content to perish, falling on the foeman's ground.
When the ranks are rolled in vapor, and the winds are laid with sound.

But the jingling of the guinea helps the hurt that Honor feels,   105
And the nations do but murmur, snarling at each other's heels.

Can I but relive in sadness? I will turn that earlier page.
Hide me from my deep emotion, O thou wondrous Mother-Age!

Make me feel the wild pulsation that I felt before the strife,
When I heard my days before me and the tumult of my life;   110

Yearning for the large excitement that the coming years would yield,
Eager-hearted as a boy when first he leaves his father's field,

And at night along the dusky highway near and nearer drawn,
Sees in heaven the light of London flaring like a dreary dawn;

And his spirit leaps within him to be gone before him then,   115
Underneath the light he looks at, in among the throngs of men;

Men, my brothers, men the workers, ever reaping something new;
That which they have done but earnest of the things that they shall do.

For I dipped into the future, far as human eye could see,
Saw the Vision of the world, and all the wonder that would be;   120

Saw the heavens fill with commerce, argosies of magic sails,
Pilots of the purple twilight, dropping down with costly bales;

Heard the heavens fill with shouting, and there rained a ghastly dew
From the nation's airy navies grappling in the central blue;

Far along the world-wide whisper of the southwind rushing warm,   125
With the standards of the peoples plunging through the thunder-
          storm;

Till the war-drum throbbed no longer, and the battle-flags were furled
In the Parliament of man, the Federation of the world.

There the common sense of most shall hold a fretful realm in awe,
And the kindly earth shall slumber, lapped in universal law.   130

So I triumphed ere my passion sweeping through me left me dry,
Left me with the palsied heart, and left me with the jaundiced eye;

Eye, to which all order festers, all things here are out of joint.
Science moves, but slowly, slowly, creeping on from point to point;

Slowly comes a hungry people, as a lion, creeping nigher,   135
Glares at one that nods and winks behind a slowly-dying fire.

Yet I doubt not through the ages one increasing purpose runs,
And the thoughts of men are widened with the process of the suns.

What is that to him that reaps not harvest of his youthful joys,
Though the deep heart of existence beat for ever like a boy's?   140

Knowledge comes, but wisdom lingers, and I linger on the shore,
And the individual withers, and the world is more and more.

Knowledge comes, but wisdom lingers, and he bears a laden breast,
Full of sad experience, moving toward the stillness of his rest.

Hark, my merry comrades call me, sounding on the bugle-horn,   145
They to whom my foolish passion were a target for their scorn.

Shall it not be scorn to me to harp on such a mouldered string?
I am shamed through all my nature to have loved so slight a thing.

Weakness to be wroth with weakness! woman's pleasure, woman's
       pain—
Nature made them blinder motions bounded in a shallower brain: 150

Woman is the lesser man, and all thy passions, matched with mine,
Are as moonlight unto sunlight and as water unto wine—

Here, at least, where nature sickens, nothing. Ah, for some retreat
Deep in yonder shining Orient, where my life began to beat,

Where in wild Mahratta-battle fell my father evil-starred;—   155
I was left a trampled orphan, and a selfish uncle's ward.

Or to burst all links of habit—there to wander far away,
On from island unto island at the gateways of the day.

Larger constellations burning, mellow moons and happy skies,
Breadths of tropic shade and palms in cluster, knots of Paradise. 160

Never comes the trader, never floats an European flag,
Slides the bird o'er lustrous woodland, swings the trailer from the crag;

155. **Mahratta-battle:** The (later) Duke of   162. **trailer:** vine.
Wellington defeated the Mahrattas (Indians
of Bombay region) at the Battle of Assaye
(1803).

Droops the heavy-blossomed bower, hangs the heavy-fruited tree—
Summer isles of Eden lying in dark purple spheres of sea.

There methinks would be enjoyment more than in this march of
    mind, 165
In the steamship, in the railway, in the thoughts that shake mankind.

There the passions cramped no longer shall have scope and breathing
    space;
I will take some savage woman, she shall rear my dusky race.

Iron-jointed, supple-sinewed, they shall dive, and they shall run,
Catch the wild goat by the hair, and hurl their lances in the sun; 170

Whistle back the parrot's call, and leap the rainbows of the brooks,
Not with blinded eyesight poring over miserable books—

Fool, again the dream, the fancy! but I *know* my words are wild,
But I count the gray barbarian lower than the Christian child.

I, to herd with narrow foreheads, vacant of our glorious gains, 175
Like a beast with lower pleasures, like a beast with lower pains!

Mated with a squalid savage—what to me were sun or clime!
I the heir of all the ages, in the foremost files of time—

I that rather held it better men should perish one by one,
Than that earth should stand at gaze like Joshua's moon in Ajalon! 180

Not in vain the distance beacons. Forward, forward let us range,
Let the great world spin for ever down the ringing grooves of change.

Through the shadow of the globe we sweep into the younger day;
Better fifty years of Europe than a cycle of Cathay.

Mother-Age,—for mine I knew not,— help me as when life begun; 185
Rift the hills, and roll the waters, flash the lightnings, weigh the sun.

Oh, I see the crescent promise of my spirit hath not set.
Ancient founts of inspiration well through all my fancy yet.

Howsoever these things be, a long farewell to Locksley Hall!
Now for me the woods may wither, now for me the roof-tree fall. 190

Comes a vapor from the margin, blackening over heath and holt,
Cramming all the blast before it, in its breast a thunderbolt.

Let it fall on Locksley Hall, with rain or hail, or fire or snow;
For the mighty wind arises, roaring sea-ward, and I go.

180. **Joshua:** He commanded the sun and   Ajalon (Joshua 10: 12–13).
moon to stand still while the Israelites   182. **grooves:** railroad tracks.
slaughtered their enemies in the valley of

Lines

Here often, when a child I lay reclined,
　　I took delight in this locality.
Here stood the infant Ilion of the mind,
　　And here the Grecian ships did seem to be.
And here again I come, and only find   5
　　The drain-cut levels of the marshy lea—
Gray sea banks and pale sunsets—dreary wind,
　　Dim shores, dense rains, and heavy-clouded sea!

Tears, idle tears

Tears, idle tears, I know not what they mean,
Tears from the depth of some divine despair
Rise in the heart, and gather to the eyes,
In looking on the happy autumn-fields,
And thinking of the days that are no more.   5

Fresh as the first beam glittering on a sail,
That brings our friends up from the underworld,
Sad as the last which reddens over one
That sinks with all we love below the verge;
So sad, so fresh, the days that are no more.   10

Ah, sad and strange as in dark summer dawns
The earliest pipe of half-awakened birds
To dying ears, when unto dying eyes
The casement slowly grows a glimmering square;
So sad, so strange, the days that are no more.   15

Dear as remembered kisses after death,
And sweet as those by hopeless fancy feigned
On lips that are for others; deep as love,
Deep as first love, and wild with all regret;
O Death in Life, the days that are no more!   20

---

3. **Ilion:** Troy, i.e., a distant, thrilling goal.　　**Tears . . . tears:** a song from the long narrative poem *The Princess* (1847, 1850).

Now sleeps the crimson petal

Now sleeps the crimson petal, now the white;
Nor waves the cypress in the palace walk;
Nor winks the gold fin in the porphry font:
The fire-fly wakens: waken thou with me.

Now droops the milkwhite peacock like a ghost,   5
And like a ghost she glimmers on to me.

Now lies the Earth all Danaë to the stars,
And all thy heart lies open unto me.

Now slides the silent meteor on, and leaves
A shining furrow, as thy thoughts in me.   10

Now folds the lily all her sweetness up,
And slips into the bosom of the lake:
So fold thyself, my dearest, thou, and slip
Into my bosom and be lost in me.

Come down, O maid

Come down, O maid, from yonder mountain height:
What pleasure lives in height (the shepherd sang)
In height and cold, the splendour of the hills?
But cease to move so near the heavens, and cease
To glide a sunbeam by the blasted Pine,   5
To sit a star upon the sparkling spire;
And come, for Love is of the valley, come,
For Love is of the valley, come thou down
And find him; by the happy threshold, he,
Or hand in hand with Plenty in the maize,   10
Or red with spirted purple of the vats,
Or foxlike in the vine; nor cares to walk
With Death and Morning on the Silver Horns,
Nor wilt thou snare him in the white ravine,

Now . . . petal: another song from *The Princess.*
7. Danaë: Although the mortal princess Danaë was imprisoned in the upper room of a tower, Zeus succeeded in consorting with her by descending in a shower of gold.

Come . . . maid: another lyrical interlude from *The Princess.*
10. maize: corn.
12. foxlike . . . vine: reference from the passionate praise of the beloved in Song of Solomon 2: 15.
13. Silver Horns: mountain peaks.

Nor find him dropt upon the firths of ice   15
That huddling slant in furrow-cloven falls
To roll the torrent out of dusky doors:
But follow; let the torrent dance thee down
To find him in the valley; let the wild
Lean-headed Eagles yelp alone, and leave   20
The monstrous ledges there to slope, and spill
Their thousand wreaths of dangling water-smoke
That like a broken purpose waste in air:
So waste not thou; but come; for all the vales
Await thee; azure pillars of the hearth   25
Arise to thee; the children call, and I
Thy shepherd pipe, and sweet is every sound,
Sweeter thy voice, but every sound is sweet;
Myriads of rivulets hurrying thro' the lawn,
The moan of doves in immemorial elms,   30
And murmuring of innumerable bees.

Dedication of Idylls of the King

These to His Memory—since he held them dear,
Perchance as finding there unconsciously
Some image of himself—I dedicate,
I dedicate, I consecrate with tears—
These Idylls.

        And indeed he seems to me   5
Scarce other than my king's ideal knight,
"Who reverenced his conscience as his king;
Whose glory was, redressing human wrong;
Who spake no slander, no, nor listened to it;
Who loved one only and who clave to her—"   10
Her—over all whose realms to their last isle,
Commingled with the gloom of imminent war,
The shadow of his loss drew like eclipse,
Darkening the world. We have lost him; he is gone.

15–17. **firths . . . doors:** apparently an obscure reference to glaciers and the streams that emerge at the bottom of their advancing face.

Dedication: to Prince Albert, consort of Queen Victoria. Written in the year following that of Albert's death (1861). 7–10. "**Who . . . her**": King Arthur's description of the ideals of the knights of the Round Table (*Idylls of the King*, XI, *l.* 472).

We knew him now; all narrow jealousies   15
Are silent, and we see him as he moved,
How modest, kindly, all-accomplished, wise,
With what sublime repression of himself,
And in what limits, and how tenderly;
Not swaying to this faction or to that;   20
Not making his high place the lawless perch
Of winged ambitions, nor a vantage-ground
For pleasure; but through all this tract of years
Wearing the white flower of a blameless life,
Before a thousand peering littlenesses,   25
In that fierce light which beats upon a throne,
And blackens every blot: for where is he,
Who dares foreshadow for an only son
A lovelier life, a more unstained, than his?
Or how should England dreaming of *his* sons   30
Hope more for these than some inheritance
Of such a life, a heart, a mind as thine,
Thou noble Father of her Kings to be,
Laborious for her people and her poor—
Voice in the rich dawn of an ampler day—   35
Far-sighted summoner of War and Waste
To fruitful strifes and rivalries of peace—
Sweet nature gilded by the gracious gleam
Of letters, dear to Science, dear to Art,
Dear to thy land and ours, a Prince indeed,   40
Beyond all titles, and a household name,
Hereafter, through all times, Albert the Good.

    Break not, O woman's-heart, but still endure;
Break not, for thou art Royal, but endure,
Remembering all the beauty of that star   45
Which shone so close beside Thee that ye made
One light together, but has passed and leaves
The Crown a lonely splendor.

                        May all love,
His love, unseen but felt, o'ershadow thee,
The love of all thy sons encompass thee,   50
The love of all thy daughters cherish thee,
The love of all thy people comfort thee,
Till God's love set thee at his side again!

40. **thy land:** originally Saxe-Coburg in
Germany.

In love, if love be Love

In love, if love be Love, if love be ours,
Faith and unfaith can ne'er be equal powers:
Unfaith in aught is want of faith in all.

It is the little rift within the lute,
That by and by will make the music mute,   5
And ever widening slowly silence all.

The little rift within the lover's lute
Or little pitted speck in garnered fruit,
That rotting inward slowly molders all.

It is not worth the keeping: let it go: 10
But shall it? answer, darling, answer, no.
And trust me not at all or all in all.

Crossing the Bar

Sunset and evening star,
   And one clear call for me!
And may there be no moaning of the bar,
   When I put out to sea,

But such a tide as moving seems asleep,   5
   Too full for sound and foam,
When that which drew from out the boundless deep
   Turns again home.

Twilight and evening bell,
   And after that the dark!   10
And may there be no sadness of farewell,
   When I embark;

For tho' from out our bourne of Time and Place
   The flood may bear me far,
I hope to see my Pilot face to face   15
   When I have crossed the bar.

In love . . . Love: Vivien's song to Merlin the Magician, *Idylls of the King*, VI, *ll.* 385–97. It is for selfish purposes that she gains his love and uses his magic to imprison him perpetually.
4. **rift:** crack.

3. **moaning . . . bar:** sound of waves on a sand bar off the coast.
13. **bourne:** boundary, shore.

ROBERT BROWNING

[*1812–1899*]

Porphyria's Lover

The rain set early in to-night,
   The sullen wind was soon awake,
It tore the elm-tops down for spite,
   And did its worst to vex the lake:
   I listened with heart fit to break.   5
When glided in Porphyria; straight
   She shut the cold out and the storm,
And kneeled and made the cheerless grate
   Blaze up, and all the cottage warm;
   Which done, she rose, and from her form   10
Withdrew the dripping cloak and shawl,
   And laid her soiled gloves by, untied
Her hat and let the damp hair fall,
   And, last, she sate down by my side
   And called me. When no voice replied,   15
She put my arm about her waist,
   And made her smooth white shoulder bare,
And all her yellow hair displaced,
   And, stooping, made my cheek lie there,
   And spread, o'er all, her yellow hair,   20
Murmuring how she loved me—she
   Too weak, for all her heart's endeavour,
To set its struggling passion free
   From pride, and vainer ties dissever,
   And give herself to me for ever.   25
But passion sometimes would prevail,
   Nor could to-night's gay feast restrain
A sudden thought of one so pale
   For love of her, and all in vain;
   So, she was come through wind and rain.   30
Be sure I looked up at her eyes
   Happy and proud; at last I knew
Porphyria worshipped me; surprise
   Made my heart swell, and still it grew
   While I debated what to do.   35
That moment she was mine, mine, fair,
   Perfectly pure and good: I found

A thing to do, and all her hair
  In one long yellow string I wound
  Three times her little throat around,   40
And strangled her. No pain felt she;
  I am quite sure she felt no pain
As a shut bud that holds a bee,
  I warily oped her lids: again
  Laughed the blue eyes without a strain.   45
And I untightened next the tress
  About her neck; her cheek once more
Blushed bright beneath my burning kiss:
  I propped her head up as before,
  Only, this time my shoulder bore   50
Her head, which droops upon it still:
  The smiling rosy little head,
So glad it has its utmost will,
  That all it scorned at once is fled,
  And I, its love, am gained instead!   55
Porphyria's love: she guessed not how
  Her darling one wish would be heard.
And thus we sit together now,
  And all night long we have not stirred,
  And yet God has not said a word!   60

Soliloquy of the Spanish Cloister

I

Gr-r-r—there go, my heart's abhorrence!
  Water your damned flower-pots, do!
If hate killed men, Brother Lawrence,
  God's blood, would not mine kill you!
What? your myrtle-bush wants trimming?   5
  Oh, that rose has prior claims—
Needs its leaden vase filled brimming?
  Hell dry you up with its flames!

2

At the meal we sit together:
  Salve tibi! I must hear   10
Wise talk of the kind of weather,
  Sort of season, time of year:

10. **Salve tibi:** "Good day to thee."

Not a plenteous cork-crop: scarcely
  Dare we hope oak-galls, I doubt:
What's the Latin name for "parsley"?   15
  What's the Greek name for Swine's Snout?

3

Whew! We'll have our platter burnished,
  Laid with care on our own shelf!
With a fire-new spoon we're furnished,
  And a goblet for ourself,   20
Rinsed like something sacrificial
  Ere 'tis fit to touch our chaps—
Marked with L. for our initial!
  (He–he! There his lily snaps!)

4

Saint, forsooth! While brown Dolores   25
  Squats outside the Convent bank,
With Sanchicha, telling stories,
  Steeping tresses in the tank,
Blue-black, lustrous, thick like horsehairs,
  —Can't I see his dead eye glow,   30
Bright as 'twere a Barbary corsair's?
  (That is, if he'd let it show!)

5

When he finishes refection,
  Knife and fork he never lays
Cross-wise, to my recollection,   35
  As do I, in Jesu's praise.
I, the Trinity illustrate,
  Drinking watered orange-pulp—
In three sips the Arian frustrate;
  While he drains his at one gulp.   40

6

Oh, those melons? If he's able
  We're to have a feast! so nice!
One goes to the Abbot's table,
  All of us get each a slice.

---

14. **oak-galls:** abnormal growths on oak trees; used for tanning.

39. **Arian:** Arius (256–336) denied the doctrine of the Trinity.

How go on your flowers? None double?   45
   Not one fruit-sort can you spy?
Strange!—And I, too, at such trouble,
   Keep them close-nipped on the sly!

7

There's a great text in Galatians,
   Once you trip on it, entails   50
Twenty-nine distinct damnations,
   One sure, if another fails.
If I trip him just a-dying,
   Sure of heaven as sure can be,
Spin him round and send him flying   55
   Off to hell, a Manichee?

8

Or, my scrofulous French novel,
   On grey paper with blunt type!
Simply glance at it, you grovel
   Hand and foot in Belial's gripe: 60
If I double down its pages
   At the woeful sixteenth print,
When he gathers his greengages,
   Ope a sieve and slip it in't?

9

Or, there's Satan!—one might venture   65
   Pledge one's soul to him, yet leave
Such a flaw in the indenture
   As he'd miss till, past retrieve,
Blasted lay that rose-acacia
   We're so proud of! *Hy, Zy, Hine* . . .   70
'St, there's Vespers! *Plena gratiâ*
   Ave, Virgo! Gr-r-r—you swine!

---

49. Galatians: Possibly Galatians 2 and 3. In Galatians 5: 15–16, St. Paul warns against biting and devouring one another, then lists seventeen lusts of the flesh.
56. Manichee: a follower of the 3rd century Persian, Mani, who believed God and Satan each governed half the universe.
60. Belial: either Satan or one of his henchmen.
71–72. Plena . . . Virgo: "Hail, Virgin, full of grace."

My Last Duchess

Ferrara

That's my last Duchess painted on the wall,
Looking as if she were alive. I call
That piece a wonder, now: Frà Pandolf's hands
Worked busily a day, and there she stands.
Will't please you sit and look at her? I said   5
"Frà Pandolf" by design, for never read
Strangers like you that pictured countenance,
The depth and passion of its earnest glance,
But to myself they turned (since none puts by
The curtain I have drawn for you, but I)   10
And seemed as they would ask me, if they durst,
How such a glance came there; so, not the first
Are you to turn and ask thus. Sir, 'twas not
Her husband's presence only, called that spot
Of joy into the Duchess' cheek: perhaps   15
Frà Pandolf chanced to say "Her mantle laps
Over my Lady's wrist too much," or "Paint
Must never hope to reproduce the faint
Half-flush that dies along her throat": such stuff
Was courtesy, she thought, and cause enough   20
For calling up that spot of joy. She had
A heart—how shall I say?—too soon made glad,
Too easily impressed; she liked whate'er
She looked on, and her looks went everywhere.
Sir, 'twas all one! My favour at her breast,   25
The dropping of the daylight in the West,
The bough of cherries some officious fool
Broke in the orchard for her, the white mule
She rode with round the terrace—all and each
Would draw from her alike the approving speech,   30
Or blush, at least. She thanked men,—good! but thanked
Somehow—I know not how—as if she ranked
My gift of a nine-hundred-years-old name
With anybody's gift. Who'd stoop to blame
This sort of trifling? Even had you skill   35
In speech—(which I have not)—to make your will
Quite clear to such an one, and say "Just this
Or that in you disgusts me; here you miss,

Duchess: Lucrezia, young wife of Alfonso II, Duke of Ferrara, died in 1561 after only three years of marriage. Soon afterwards, the Duke negotiated to marry the niece of the Count of Tyrol.
3. **Frà Pandolf:** an imaginary artist.

Or there exceed the mark"—and if she let
Herself be lessoned so, nor plainly set   40
Her wits to yours, forsooth, and made excuse,
—E'en then would be some stooping, and I choose
Never to stoop. Oh, Sir, she smiled, no doubt
Whene'er I passed her; but who passed without
Much the same smile? This grew; I gave commands;   45
Then all smiles stopped together. There she stands
As if alive. Will't please you rise? We'll meet
The company below, then. I repeat,
The Count your master's known munificence
Is ample warrant that no just pretence   50
Of mine for dowry will be disallowed;
Though his fair daughter's self, as I avowed
At starting, is my object. Nay, we'll go
Together down, Sir! Notice Neptune, tho',
Taming a sea-horse, thought a rarity,   55
Which Claus of Innsbruck cast in bronze for me!

The Bishop Orders His Tomb at Saint Praxed's Church

Rome, 15—

Vanity, saith the preacher, vanity!
Draw round my bed: is Anselm keeping back?
Nephews—sons mine . . . ah God, I know not! Well—
She, men would have to be your mother once,
Old Gandolf envied me, so fair she was!   5
What's done is done, and she is dead beside,
Dead long ago, and I am Bishop since,
And as she died so must we die ourselves,
And thence ye may perceive the world's a dream.
Life, how and what is it? As here I lie   10
In this state-chamber, dying by degrees,
Hours and long hours in the dead night, I ask
"Do I live, am I dead?" Peace, peace seems all.
Saint Praxed's ever was the church for peace;
And so, about this tomb of mine. I fought   15
With tooth and nail to save my niche, ye know:
—Old Gandolf cozened me, despite my care;

56. **Claus . . . Innsbruck:** an unidentified sculptor; Innsbruck was the capital of the Tyrol.

Saint Praxed: named for St. Praxedes, a Roman virgin of the 2nd century who gave her wealth to poor Christians.
1. **Vanity . . . preacher:** Ecclesiastes 1: 2.

Shrewd was that snatch from out the corner South
He graced his carrion with, God curse the same!
Yet still my niche is not so cramped but thence   20
One sees the pulpit o' the epistle-side
And somewhat of the choir, those silent seats,
And up into the aery dome where live
The angels, and a sunbeam's sure to lurk:
And I shall fill my slab of basalt there,   25
And 'neath my tabernacle take my rest,
With those nine columns round me, two and two,
The odd one at my feet where Anselm stands:
Peach-blossom marble all, the rare, the ripe
As fresh-poured red wine of a mighty pulse.   30
—Old Gandolf with his paltry onion-stone,
Put me where I may look at him! True peach,
Rosy and flawless: how I earned the prize!
Draw close: that conflagration of my church
—What then? So much was saved if aught were missed!   35
My sons, ye would not be my death? Go dig
The white-grape vineyard where the oil-press stood,
Drop water gently till the surface sink,
And if ye find . . . Ah God, I know not, I! . . .
Bedded in store or rotten fig-leaves soft,   40
And corded up in a tight olive-frail,
Some lump, ah God, of *lapis lazuli,*
Big as a Jew's head cut off at the nape,
Blue as a vein o'er the Madonna's breast . . .
Sons, all have I bequeathed you, villas, all,   45
That brave Frascati villa with its bath,
So, let the blue lump poise between my knees,
Like God the Father's globe on both his hands
Ye worship in the Jesu Church so gay,
For Gandolf shall not choose but see and burst!   50
Swift as a weaver's shuttle fleet our years:
Man goeth to the grave, and where is he?
Did I say basalt for my slab, sons? Black—
'T was ever antique-black I meant! How else
Shall ye contrast my frieze to come beneath?   55
The bas-relief in bronze ye promised me,
Those Pans and Nymphs ye wot of, and perchance

---

21. **epistle-side:** epistles of the New Testament are read on the right side of the altar as one faces it.
26. **tabernacle:** stone canopy.
31. **onion-stone:** inferior marble.
41. **olive-frail:** woven basket.

42. **lapis lazuli:** light blue stone.
46. **Frascati:** wealthy resort town near Rome.
49. **Jesu:** Jesuit.
51. **Swift . . . years:** Job 7: 6.
53. **Black:** black marble.

Some tripod, thyrsus, with a vase or so,
The Saviour at his sermon on the mount,
Saint Praxed in a glory, and one Pan   60
Ready to twitch the Nymph's last garment off,
And Moses with the tables . . . but I know
Ye mark me not! What do they whisper thee,
Child of my bowels, Anselm? Ah, ye hope
To revel down my villas while I gasp   65
Bricked o'er with beggar's mouldy travertine
Which Gandolf from his tomb-top chuckles at!
Nay, boys, ye love me—all of jasper, then!
'T is jasper ye stand pledged to, lest I grieve
My bath must needs be left behind, alas!   70
One block, pure green as a pistachio-nut,
There's plenty jasper somewhere in the world—
And have I not Saint Praxed's ear to pray
Horses for ye, and brown Greek manuscripts,
And mistresses with great smooth marbly limbs?   75
—That's if ye carve my epitaph aright,
Choice Latin, picked phrase, Tully's every word,
No gaudy ware like Gandolf's second line—
Tully, my masters? Ulpian serves his need!
And then how I shall lie through centuries,   80
And hear the blessed mutter of the mass,
And see God made and eaten all day long,
And feel the steady candle-flame, and taste
Good strong thick stupefying incense-smoke!
For as I lie here, hours of the dead night,   85
Dying in state and by such slow degrees,
I fold my arms as if they clasped a crook,
And stretch my feet forth straight as stone can point,
And let the bedclothes, for a mortcloth, drop
Into great laps and folds of sculptor's-work: 90
And as yon tapers dwindle, and strange thoughts
Grow, with a certain humming in my ears,
About the life before I lived this life,
And this life too, popes, cardinals and priests,
Saint Praxed at his sermon on the mount,   95
Your tall pale mother with her talking eyes,
And new-found agate urns as fresh as day,

---

58. **thyrsus:** staff of Bacchus, god of wine.
60. **glory:** halo.
62. **tables:** tablets of the law.
66. **travertine:** limestone.
77. **Tully:** Marcus Tullius Cicero, whose prose was a model of style.

79. **Ulpian:** Domituus Ulpianus, a jurist of the 3rd century whose Latin style is inferior to Cicero's.
89. **mortcloth:** cloth covering a coffin.

And marble's language, Latin pure, discreet,
—Aha, ELUCESCEBAT quoth our friend?
No Tully, said I, Ulpian at the best!   100
Evil and brief hath been my pilgrimage.
All *lapis*, all, sons! Else I give the Pope
My villas! Will ye ever eat my heart?
Ever your eyes were as a lizard's quick,
They glitter like your mother's for my soul,   105
Or ye would heighten my impoverished frieze,
Piece out its starved design, and fill my vase
With grapes, and add a visor and a Term,
And to the tripod ye would tie a lynx
That in his struggle throws the thyrsus down,   110
To comfort me on my entablature
Whereon I am to lie till I must ask
"Do I live, am I dead?" There, leave me, there!
For ye have stabbed me with ingratitude
To death—ye wish it—God, ye wish it! Stone—   115
Gritstone, a-crumble! Clammy squares which sweat
As if the corpse they keep were oozing through—
And no more *lapis* to delight the world!
Well, go! I bless ye. Fewer tapers there,
But in a row: and, going, turn your backs   120
—Ay, like departing altar-ministrants,
And leave me in my church, the church for peace,
That I may watch at leisure if he leers—
Old Gandolf, at me, from his onion-stone,
As still he envied me, so fair she was!   125

Memorabilia

Ah, did you once see Shelley plain,
    And did he stop and speak to you,
And did you speak to him again?
    How strange it seems and new!

But you were living before that,   5
    And also you are living after;
And the memory I started at—
    My starting moves your laughter!

99. **Elucescebat . . . friend:** "He shone forth," carved on Gandolf's tomb; Cicero would have written "elucebat."
108. **Term:** a pillar adorned with a bust.
116. **Gritstone:** sandstone.

Memorabilia: In a bookstore Browning once met a stranger who mentioned having spoken with Shelley. Browning was so affected by this information that he blanched and stared at the man, who burst into laughter.

I crossed a moor, with a name of its own
    And a certain use in the world no doubt,   10
Yet a hand's-breadth of it shines alone
    'Mid the blank miles round about:

For there I picked up on the heather
    And there I put inside my breast
A moulted feather, an eagle-feather!   15
    Well, I forget the rest.

Andrea del Sarto

(Called "*the Faultless Painter*")

But do not let us quarrel any more,
No, my Lucrezia; bear with me for once:
Sit down and all shall happen as you wish.
You turn your face, but does it bring your heart?
I'll work then for your friend's friend, never fear,   5
Treat his own subject after his own way,
Fix his own time, accept too his own price,
And shut the money into his small hand
When next it takes mine. Will it? tenderly?
Oh, I'll content him,—but to-morrow, love!   10
I often am much wearier than you think,
This evening more than usual, and it seems
As if—forgive now—should you let me sit
Here by the window with your hand in mine
And look a half hour forth on Fiesole,   15
Both of one mind, as married people use,
Quietly, quietly the evening through,
I might get up to-morrow to my work
Cheerful and fresh as ever. Let us try.
To-morrow, how you shall be glad for this!   20
Your soft hand is a woman of itself,
And mine the man's bared breast she curls inside.
Don't count the time lost, neither; you must serve
For each of the five pictures we require:
It saves a model. So! keep looking so—   25
My serpentining beauty, rounds on rounds!
—How could you ever prick those perfect ears,

Andrea del Sarto: a Florentine painter (1486–1531). Browning based his poem on the biography of del Sarto in Giorgio Vasari's *Lives of the Painters.* Vasari had been a student of del Sarto's.
15. **Fiesole:** suburb of Florence.

Even to put the pearl there! oh, so sweet—
My face, my moon, my everybody's moon,
Which everybody looks on and calls his,   30
And, I suppose, is looked on by in turn,
While she looks—no one's: very dear, no less.
You smile? why, there's my picture ready made,
There's what we painters call our harmony!
A common greyness silvers everything,—   35
All in a twilight, you and I alike
—You, at the point of your first pride in me
(That's gone you know),—but I, at every point;
My youth, my hope, my art, being all toned down
To yonder sober pleasant Fiesole.   40
There's the bell clinking from the chapel-top;
That length of convent-wall across the way
Holds the trees safer, huddled more inside;
The last monk leaves the garden; days decrease,
And autumn grows, autumn in everything.   45
Eh? the whole seems to fall into a shape
As if I saw alike my works and self
And all that I was born to be and do,
A twilight piece. Love, we are in God's hand.
How strange now, looks the life he makes us lead;   50
So free we seem, so fettered fast we are!
I feel he laid the fetter: let it lie!
This chamber for example—turn your head—
All that's behind us! You don't understand
Nor care to understand about my art,   55
But you can hear at least when people speak:
And that cartoon, the second from the door
—It is the thing, love! so such things should be—
Behold Madonna!—I am bold to say.
I can do with my pencil what I know,   60
What I see, what at bottom of my heart
I wish for, if I ever wish so deep—
Do easily, too—when I say, perfectly,
I do not boast, perhaps: yourself are judge
Who listened to the Legate's talk last week,   65
And just as much as they used to say in France.
At any rate 'tis easy, all of it;
No sketches first, no studies, that's long past:
I do what many dream of all their lives
—Dream? strive to do, and agonize to do,   70

57. **cartoon:** a large drawing, a study for a
tapestry or fresco.

And fail in doing. I could count twenty such
On twice your fingers, and not leave this town,
Who strive—you don't know how the others strive
To paint a little thing like that you smeared
Carelessly passing with your robes afloat,— 75
Yet do much less, so much less, Someone says,
(I know his name, no matter)—so much less!
Well, less is more, Lucrezia: I am judged.
There burns a truer light of God in them,
In their vexed beating stuffed and stopped-up brain, 80
Heart, or whate'er else, than goes on to prompt
This low-pulsed forthright craftsman's hand of mine.
Their works drop groundward, but themselves, I know,
Reach many a time a heaven that's shut to me,
Enter and take their place there sure enough, 85
Though they come back and cannot tell the world.
My works are nearer heaven, but I sit here.
The sudden blood of these men! at a word—
Praise them, it boils, or blame them, it boils too.
I, painting from myself and to myself, 90
Know what I do, am unmoved by men's blame
Or their praise either. Somebody remarks
Morello's outline there is wrongly traced,
His hue mistaken, what of that? or else,
Rightly traced and well ordered, what of that? 95
Speak as they please, what does the mountain care?
Ah, but a man's reach should exceed his grasp,
Or what's a heaven for? all is silver-grey
Placid and perfect with my art: the worse!
I know both what I want and what might gain, 100
And yet how profitless to know, to sigh
"Had I been two, another and myself,
"Our head would have o'erlooked the world!" No doubt.
Yonder's a work, now, of that famous youth,
The Urbinate who died five years ago. 105
('Tis copied, George Vasari sent it me.)
Well, I can fancy how he did it all,
Pouring his soul, with kings and popes to see,
Reaching, that Heaven might so replenish him,
Above and through his art—for it gives way; 110
That arm is wrongly put—and there again—
A fault to pardon in the drawing's lines,
Its body, so to speak: its soul is right,

---

93. **Morello:** a mountain near Florence.   105. **Urbinate:** Raphael (1483–1520), born in Urbino, painted in Rome.

He means right—that, a child may understand.
Still, what an arm! and I could alter it;   115
But all the play, the insight and the stretch
Out of me, out of me! And wherefore out?
Had you enjoined them on me, given me soul,
We might have risen to Rafael, I and you!
Nay, Love, you did give all I asked, I think—   120
More than I merit, yes, by many times.
But had you—oh, with the same perfect brow,
And perfect eyes, and more than perfect mouth,
And the low voice my soul hears, as a bird
The fowler's pipe, and follows to the snare—   125
Had you, with these the same, but brought a mind!
Some women do so. Had the mouth there urged
"God and the glory! never care for gain.
The present by the future, what is that?
Live for fame, side by side with Agnolo—   130
Rafael is waiting: up to God all three!"
I might have done it for you. So it seems:
Perhaps not. All is as God overrules.
Beside, incentives come from the soul's self;
The rest avail not. Why do I need you?   135
What wife had Rafael, or has Agnolo?
In this world, who can do a thing, will not;
And who would do it, cannot, I perceive:
Yet the will's somewhat—somewhat, too, the power—
And thus we half-men struggle. At the end,   140
God, I conclude, compensates, punishes.
'Tis safer for me, if the award be strict,
That I am something underrated here,
Poor this long while, despised, to speak the truth.
I dared not, do you know, leave home all day,   145
For fear of chancing on the Paris lords.
The best is when they pass and look aside;
But they speak sometimes; I must bear it all.
Well may they speak! That Francis, that first time,
And that long festal year at Fontainebleau!   150
I surely then could sometimes leave the ground,
Put on the glory, Rafael's daily wear,
In that humane great monarch's golden look,—
One finger in his beard or twisted curl

130. **Agnolo:** Michelangelo.
146. **Paris lords:** French nobles who insulted del Sarto. In 1518 Francis I of France invited del Sarto to paint at Fontainebleau, where del Sarto stayed one year. Pressed by Lucrezia to return home, he left France entrusted with funds to buy art for Francis I. Supposedly he spent the money instead on his wife and their little home.

Over his mouth's good mark that made the smile,   155
One arm about my shoulder, round my neck,
The jingle of his gold chain in my ear,
I painting proudly with his breath on me,
All his court round him, seeing with his eyes,
Such frank French eyes, and such a fire of souls   160
Profuse, my hand kept plying by those hearts,—
And, best of all, this, this, this face beyond,
This is the background, waiting on my work,
To crown the issue with a last reward!
A good time, was it not, my kingly days?   165
And had you not grown restless . . . but I know—
'Tis done and past; 'twas right, my instinct said;
Too live the life grew, golden and not grey,
And I'm the weak-eyed bat no sun should tempt
Out of the grange whose four walls make his world.   170
How could it end in any other way?
You called me, and I came home to your heart.
The triumph was, reach and stay there; since if
I reached it ere the triumph, what is lost?
Let my hands frame your face in your hair's gold,   175
You beautiful Lucrezia that are mine!
"Rafael did this, Andrea painted that—
The Roman's is the better when you pray,
But still the other's Virgin was his wife—"
Men will excuse me. I am glad to judge   180
Both pictures in your presence; clearer grows
My better fortune, I resolve to think.
For, do you know, Lucrezia, as God lives,
Said one day Agnolo, his very self,
To Rafael . . . I have known it all these years . . .   185
(When the young man was flaming out his thoughts
Upon a palace-wall for Rome to see,
Too lifted up in heart because of it)
"Friend, there's a certain sorry little scrub
Goes up and down our Florence, none cares how,   190
Who, were he set to plan and execute
As you are, pricked on by your popes and kings,
Would bring the sweat into that brow of yours!"
To Rafael's!—And indeed the arm is wrong.
I hardly dare . . . yet, only you to see,   195
Give the chalk here—quick, thus the line should go!
Ay, but the soul! he's Rafael! rub it out!
Still, all I care for, if he spoke the truth,
(What he? why, who but Michel Agnolo?

Do you forget already words like those?) 200
If really there was such a chance, so lost,—
Is, whether you're—not graceful—but more pleased.
Well, let me think so. And you smile indeed!
This hour has been an hour! Another smile?
If you would sit thus by me every night 205
I should work better, do you comprehend?
I mean that I should earn more, give you more.
See, it is settled dusk now; there's a star;
Morello's gone, the watch-lights show the wall,
The cue-owls speak the name we call them by. 210
Come from the window, love,—come in, at last,
Inside the melancholy little house
We built to be so gay with. God is just.
King Francis may forgive me; oft at nights
When I look up from painting, eyes tired out, 215
The walls become illumined, brick from brick
Distinct, instead of mortar, fierce bright gold,
That gold of his I did cement them with!
Let us but love each other. Must you go?
That Cousin here again? he waits outside 220
Must see you—you, and not with me? Those loans?
More gaming debts to pay? you smiled for that?
Well, let smiles buy me! have you more to spend?
While hand and eye and something of a heart
Are left me, work's my ware, and what's it worth? 225
I'll pay my fancy. Only let me sit
The grey remainder of the evening out,
Idle, you call it, and muse perfectly
How I could paint, were I but back in France,
One picture, just one more—the Virgin's face, 230
Not yours this time! I want you at my side
To hear them—that is, Michel Agnolo—
Judge all I do and tell you of its worth.
Will you? To-morrow, satisfy your friend.
I take the subjects for his corridor, 235
Finish the portrait out of hand—there, there,
And throw him in another thing or two
If he demurs; the whole should prove enough
To pay for this same Cousin's freak. Beside,
What's better and what's all I care about, 240
Get you the thirteen scudi for the ruff.

---

210. **cue-owls**: horned owls, whose cry   241. **scudi**: a scudo is an Italian coin.
sounds like the Italian word liù.

Love, does that please you? Ah, but what does he,
The Cousin! what does he to please you more?
  I am grown peaceful as old age to-night.
I regret little, I would change still less.   245
Since there my past life lies, why alter it?
The very wrong to Francis!—it is true
I took his coin, was tempted and complied,
And built this house and sinned, and all is said.
My father and my mother died of want.   250
Well, had I riches of my own? you see
How one gets rich! Let each one bear his lot.
They were born poor, lived poor, and poor they died:
And I have laboured somewhat in my time
And not been paid profusely. Some good son   255
Paint my two hundred pictures—let him try!
No doubt, there's something strikes a balance. Yes,
You loved me quite enough, it seems tonight.
This must suffice me here. What would one have?
In heaven, perhaps, new chances, one more chance—   260
Four great walls in the New Jerusalem
Meted on each side by the angel's reed,
For Leonard, Rafael, Agnolo and me
To cover—the three first without a wife,
While I have mine! So—still they overcome   265
Because there's still Lucrezia,—as I choose.
Again the Cousin's whistle! Go, my Love.

WALT WHITMAN

[*1819–1892*]

From pent-up aching rivers

From pent-up, aching rivers,
From that of myself, without which I were nothing,
From what I am determin'd to make illustrious, even if I stand sole
    among men,
From my own voice resonant, singing the phallus,
Singing the song of procreation,   5
Singing the need of superb children, and therein superb grown people,
Singing the muscular urge and the blending,

262. **Meted . . . reed:** In Revelation 21:   263. **Leonard:** Leonardo da Vinci.
15, an angel measures the walls of the holy
city with a golden reed.

Singing the bedfellow's song, (O resistless yearning!
O for any and each, the body correlative attracting!
O for you, whoever you are, your correlative body! O it, more than
    all else, you delighting!) 10
From the hungry gnaw that eats me night and day,
From native moments, from bashful pains, singing them,
Singing something yet unfound, though I have diligently sought it,
    many a long year,
Singing the true song of the Soul, fitful, at random,
Renascent with grossest Nature, or among animals, 15
Of that, of them, and what goes with them, my poems informing,
Of the smell of apples and lemons, of the pairing of birds,
Of the wet of woods, of the lapping of waves,
Of the mad pushes of waves upon the land, I them chanting,
The overture lightly sounding, the strain anticipating, 20
The welcome nearness, the sight of the perfect body,
The swimmer swimming naked in the bath, or motionless on his back
    lying and floating,
The female form approaching—I, pensive, love-flesh tremulous, aching,
The divine list, for myself or you, or for any one, making,
The face, the limbs, the index from head to foot, and what it
    arouses, 25
The mystic deliria, the madness amorous, the utter abandonment,
(Hark close, and still, what I now whisper to you,
I love you, O you entirely possess me,
O I wish that you and I escape from the rest, and go utterly off,
    O free and lawless,
Two hawks in the air, two fishes swimming in the sea not more
    lawless than we;) 30
The furious storm through me careering, I passionately trembling,
The oath of the inseparableness of two together, of the woman that
    loves me, and whom I love more than my life, that oath
    swearing,
(O I willingly stake all, for you!
O let me be lost, if it must be so!
O you and I, what is it to us what the rest do or think? 35
What is all else to us? only that we enjoy each other, and exhaust
    each other, if it must be so;)
From the master, the pilot I yield the vessel to,
The general commanding me, commanding all, from him
    permission taking;
From time the programme hastening, (I have loiter'd too long,
    as it is,
From sex, from the warp and from the woof, 40
From privacy, from frequent repinings alone,

From plenty of persons near, and yet the right person not near,
From the soft sliding of hands over me, and thrusting of fingers
      through my hair and beard,
From the long sustain'd kiss upon the mouth or bosom,
From the close pressure that makes me or any man drunk, fainting
      with excess,   45
From what the divine husband knows, from the work of fatherhood;
From exultation, victory, and relief, from the bedfellow's embrace
      in the night,
From the act-poems of eyes, hands, hips, and bosoms,
From the cling of the trembling arm,
From the bending curve and the clinch,   50
From side by side, the pliant coverlid off-throwing,
From the one so unwilling to have me leave, and me just as unwilling
      to leave,
(Yet a moment, O tender waiter, and I return,)
From the hour of shining stars and dropping dews,
From the night, a moment, I, emerging, flitting out,   55
Celebrate you, act divine, and you, children prepared for,
And you, stalwart loins.

Crossing Brooklyn Ferry

1

Flood-tide below me! I see you face to face!
Clouds of the west—sun there half an hour high—I see you also
      face to face.

Crowds of men and women attired in the usual costumes, how curious
      you are to me!
On the ferry-boats the hundreds and hundreds that cross, returning
      home, are more curious to me than you suppose,
And you that shall cross from shore to shore years hence are more to
      me, and more in my meditations, than you might suppose.   5

2

The impalpable sustenance of me from all things at all hours of the day,
The simple, compact, well-join'd scheme, myself disintegrated, every
      one disintegrated yet part of the scheme,
The similitudes of the past and those of the future,
The glories strung like beads on my smallest sights and hearings, on
      the walk in the street and the passage over the river,
The current rushing so swiftly and swimming with me far away,   10
The others that are to follow me, the ties between me and them,
The certainty of others, the life, love, sight, hearing of others.

Others will enter the gates of the ferry and cross from shore to shore,
Others will watch the run of the flood-tide,
Others will see the shipping of Manhattan north and west, and the
      heights of Brooklyn on the south and east,   15
Others will see the islands large and small;
Fifty years hence, others will see them as they cross, the sun half an
      hour high,
A hundred years hence, or ever so many hundred years hence, others
      will see them,
Will enjoy the sunset, the pouring-in of the flood-tide, the falling-back
      to the sea of the ebb-tide.

3

It avails not, time nor place—distance avails not,   20
I am with you, you men and women of a generation, or ever so many
      generations hence,
Just as you feel when you look on the river and sky, so I felt,
Just as any of you is one of a living crowd, I was one of a crowd,
Just as you are refresh'd by the gladness of the river and the bright
      flow, I was refresh'd,
Just as you stand and lean on the rail, yet hurry with the swift current,
      I stood yet was hurried,   25
Just as you look on the numberless masts of ships and the thick-
      stemm'd pipes of steamboats, I look'd.

I too many and many a time cross'd the river of old,
Watched the Twelfth-month sea-gulls, saw them high in the air floating
      with motionless wings, oscillating their bodies,
Saw how the glistening yellow lit up parts of their bodies and left
      the rest in strong shadow,
Saw the slow-wheeling circles and the gradual edging toward the
      south,   30
Saw the reflection of the summer sky in the water,
Had my eyes dazzled by the shimmering track of beams,
Look'd at the fine centrifugal spokes of light round the shape of my
      head in the sunlit water,
Look'd on the haze on the hills southward and south-westward,
Look'd on the vapor as it flew in fleeces tinged with violet,   35
Look'd toward the lower bay to notice the vessels arriving,
Saw their approach, saw aboard those that were near me,
Saw the white sails of schooners and sloops, saw the ships at anchor,
The sailors at work in the rigging or out astride the spars,
The round masts, the swinging motion of the hulls, the slender
      serpentine pennants,   40

The large and small steamers in motion, the pilots in their pilot-houses,
The white wake left by the passage, the quick tremulous whirl of the
    wheels,
The flags of all nations, the falling of them at sunset,
The scallop-edged waves in the twilight, the ladled cups, the
    frolicsome crests and glistening,
The stretch afar growing dimmer and dimmer, the gray walls of the
    granite storehouses by the docks,   45
On the river the shadowy group, the big steam-tug closely flank'd
    on each side by the barges, the hay-boat, the belated lighter,
On the neighboring shore the fires from the foundry chimneys
    burning high and glaringly into the night,
Casting their flicker of black contrasted with wild red and yellow light
    over the tops of houses, and down into the clefts of streets.

4

These and all else were to me the same as they are to you,
I loved well those cities, loved well the stately and rapid river,   50
The men and women I saw were all near to me,
Others the same—others who look back on me because I look'd
    forward to them,
(The time will come, though I stop here to-day and to-night.)

5

What is it then between us?
What is the count of the scores or hundreds of years between us?   55

Whatever it is, it avails not—distance avails not, and place avails not,
I too lived, Brooklyn of ample hills was mine,
I too walk'd the streets of Manhattan island, and bathed in the water
    around it,
I too felt curious abrupt questionings stir within me.
In the day among crowds of people sometimes they came upon me,   60
In my walks home late at night or as I lay in my bed they came upon
    me,
I too had been struck from the float forever held in solution,
I too had receiv'd identity by my body,
That I was I knew was of my body, and what I should be I knew I
    should be of my body.

6

It is not upon you alone the dark patches fall,   65
The dark threw its patches down upon me also,
The best I had done seem'd to me blank and suspicious,
My great thoughts as I supposed them, were they not in reality
    meagre?

Nor is it you alone who knows what it is to be evil,
I am he who knew what it was to be evil,   70
I too knitted the old knot of contrariety,
Blabb'd, blush'd, resented, lied, stole, grudg'd,
Had guile, anger, lust, hot wishes I dared not speak,
Was wayward, vain, greedy, shallow, sly, cowardly, malignant,
The wolf, the snake, the hog, not wanting in me,   75
The cheating look, the frivolous word, the adulterous wish, not
    wanting,
Refusals, hates, postponements, meanness, laziness, none of these wanting,
Was one with the rest, the days and haps of the rest,
Was called by my nighest name by clear loud voices of young men as
    they saw me approaching or passing,
Felt their arms on my neck as I stood, or the negligent leaning of their
    flesh against me as I sat,   80
Saw many I loved in the street or ferry-boat or public assembly, yet
    never told them a word,
Lived the same life with the rest, the same old laughing, gnawing,
    sleeping,
Play'd the part that still looks back on the actor or actress,
The same old role, the role is what we make it, as great as we like,
Or as small as we like, or both great and small.   85

7

Closer yet I approach you,
What thought you have of me now, I had as much of you—I laid in my
    stores in advance,
I consider'd long and seriously of you before you were born.

Who was to know what should come home to me?
Who knows but I am enjoying this?   90
Who knows, for all the distance, but I am as good as looking at you
    now, for all you cannot see me?

8

Ah, what can ever be more stately and admirable to me than mast-
    hemm'd Manhattan?
River and sunset and scallop-edg'd waves of flood-tide?
The sea-gulls oscillating their bodies, the hay-boat in the twilight, and
    the belated lighter?
What gods can exceed these that clasp me by the hand, and with
    voices I love call me promptly and loudly by my nighest
    name as I approach?   95

What is more subtle than this which ties me to the woman or man
    that looks in my face?
Which fuses me into you now, and pours my meaning into you?

We understand then do we not?
What I promis'd without mentioning it, have you not accepted?
What the study could not teach—what the preaching could not
    accomplish is accomplish'd, is it not? 100

9

Flow on, river! flow with the flood-tide, and ebb with the ebb-tide!
Frolic on, crested and scallop-edg'd waves!
Gorgeous clouds of the sunset! drench with your splendor me, or the
    men and women generations after me!
Cross from shore to shore, countless crowds of passengers!
Stand up, tall masts of Mannahatta! stand up, beautiful hills of
    Brooklyn! 105
Throb, baffled and curious brain! throw out questions and answers!
Suspend here and everywhere, eternal float of solution!
Gaze, loving and thirsting eyes, in the house or street or public
    assembly!
Sound out, voices of young men! loudly and musically call me by my
    nighest name!
Live, old life! play the part that looks back on the actor or actress! 110
Play the old role, the role that is great or small according as one
    makes it!
Consider, you who peruse me, whether I may not in unknown ways
    be looking upon you;
Be firm, rail over the river, to support those who lean idly, yet haste
    with the hasting current;
Fly on, sea-birds! fly sideways, or wheel in large circles high in the air;
Receive the summer sky, you water, and faithfully hold it till all
    downcast eyes have time to take it from you! 115
Diverge, fine spokes of light, from the shape of my head, or any one's
    head, in the sunlit water!
Come on, ships from the lower bay! pass up or down, white-sail'd
    schooners, sloops, lighters!
Flaunt away, flags of all nations! be duly lower'd at sunset!
Burn high your fires, foundry chimneys! cast black shadows at night-
    fall! cast red and yellow light over the tops of the houses!
Appearances, now or henceforth, indicate what you are, 120
You necessary film, continue to envelop the soul,
About my body for me, and your body for you, be hung our divinest
    aromas,

Thrive, cities—bring your freight, bring your shows, ample and
    sufficient rivers,
Expand, being than which none else is perhaps more spiritual,
Keep your places, objects that which none else is more lasting.   125

You have waited, you always wait, you dumb, beautiful ministers,
We receive you with free sense at last, and are insatiate henceforward,
Not you any more shall be able to foil us, or withhold yourselves
    from us,
We use you, and do not cast you aside—we plant you permanently
    within us,
We fathom you not—we love you—there is perfection in you also,   130
You furnish your parts toward eternity,
Great or small, you furnish your parts toward the soul.

Out of the cradle endlessly rocking

Out of the cradle endlessly rocking,
Out of the mocking-bird's throat, the musical shuttle,
Out of the Ninth month midnight,
Over the sterile sands and the fields beyond, where the child leaving
    his bed wander'd alone, bareheaded, barefoot,
Down from the shower'd halo,   5
Up from the mystic play of shadows twining and twisting as if they
    were alive,
Out from the patches of briers and blackberries,
From the memories of the bird that chanted to me,
From your memories sad brother, from the fitful risings and fallings
    I heard,
From under that yellow half-moon late-risen and swollen as if with
    tears,   10
From those beginning notes of yearning and love there in the mist,
From the thousand responses of my heart never to cease,
From the myriad thence-arous'd words,
From the word stronger and more delicious than any,
From such as now they start the scene revisiting,   15
As a flock, twittering, rising, or overhead passing,
Borne hither, ere all eludes me, hurriedly,
A man, yet by these tears a little boy again,
Throwing myself on the sand, confronting the waves,
I, chanter of pains and joys, uniter of here and hereafter,   20
Taking all hints to use them, but swiftly leaping beyond them,
A reminiscence sing.

Once Paumanok,
When the lilac-scent was in the air and Fifth-month grass was growing,
Up this seashore in some briers,   25
Two feather'd guests from Alabama, two together,
And their nest, and four light-green eggs spotted with brown,
And every day the he-bird to and fro near at hand,
And every day the she-bird crouch'd on her nest, silent, with bright
        eyes,
And every day I, a curious boy, never too close, never disturbing
        them,   30
Cautiously peering, absorbing, translating.

Shine! shine! shine!
Pour down your warmth, great sun!
While we bask, we two together.
Two together!   35
Winds blow south, or winds blow north,
Day come white, or night come black,
Home, or rivers and mountains from home,
Singing all time, minding no time,
While we two keep together.   40

Till of a sudden,
May-be kill'd, unknown to her mate,
One forenoon that she-bird crouch'd not on the nest,
Nor return'd that afternoon, nor the next,
Nor ever appear'd again.   45

And thenceforward all summer in the sound of the sea,
And at night under the full of the moon in calmer weather,
Over the hoarse surging of the sea,
Or flitting from brier to brier by day,
I saw, I heard at intervals the remaining one, the he-bird,   50
The solitary guest from Alabama.

Blow! blow! blow!
Blow up sea-winds along Paumanok's shore;
I wait and I wait till you blow my mate to me.

Yes, when the stars glisten'd,   55
All night long on the prong of a moss-scallop'd stake,
Down almost amid the slapping waves,
Sat the lone singer wonderful causing tears.

He call'd on his mate,
He pour'd forth the meanings which I of all men know.   60

23. **Paumanok:** Indian name for Long
Island.

Yes my brother I know,
The rest might not, but I have treasur'd every note,
For more than once dimly down to the beach gliding,
Silent, avoiding the moonbeams, blending myself with the shadows,
Recalling now the obscure shapes, the echoes, the sounds and sights
   after their sorts,   65
The white arms out in the breakers tirelessly tossing,
I, with bare feet, a child, the wind wafting my hair,
Listen'd long and long.

Listen'd to keep, to sing, now translating the notes,
Following you my brother.   70

Soothe! soothe! soothe!
Close on its wave soothes the wave behind,
And again another behind embracing and lapping, every one close,
But my love soothes not me, not me.
Low hangs the moon, it rose late,   75
It is lagging—O I think it is heavy with love, with love.

O madly the sea pushes upon the land,
With love, with love.

O night! do I not see my love fluttering out among the breakers?
What is that little black thing I see there in the white? 80

Loud! loud! loud!
Loud I call to you, my love!
High and clear, I shoot my voice over the waves,
Surely you must know who is here, is here,
You must know who I am, my love.   85

Low-hanging moon!
What is that dusky spot in your brown yellow?
O it is the shape, the shape of my mate!
O moon do not keep her from me any longer.

Land! land! O land!   90
Whichever way I turn, O I think you could give me my mate back again
   if you only would,
For I am almost sure I see her dimly whichever way I look.

O rising stars!
Perhaps the one I want so much will rise, will rise with one of you.

O throat! O trembling throat!   95
Sound clearer through the atmosphere!
Pierce the woods, the earth,
Somewhere listening to catch you must be the one I want.

Shake out carols!
Solitary here, the night's carols!   100
Carols of lonesome love! death's carols!
Carols under that lagging, yellow, waning moon!
O under that moon where she droops almost down into the sea!
O reckless despairing carols.

But soft, sink low!   105
Soft! let me just murmur,
And do you wait a moment you husky-nois'd sea,
For somewhere I believe I heard my mate responding to me,
So faint, I must be still, be still to listen,
But not altogether still, for then she might not come immediately to me.   110

Hither my love!
Here I am! here!
With this just-sustain'd note I announce myself to you,
This gentle call is for you my love, for you.

Do not be decoy'd elsewhere,   115
That is the whistle of the wind, it is not my voice,
That is the fluttering, the fluttering of the spray,
Those are the shadows of leaves.

O darkness! O in vain!
O I am very sick and sorrowful.   120

O brown halo in the sky near the moon, drooping upon the sea!
O troubled reflection in the sea!
O throat! O throbbing heart!
And I singing uselessly, uselessly all the night.

O past! O happy life! O songs of joy!   125
In the air, in the woods, over fields,
Loved! loved! loved! loved! loved!
But my mate no more, no more with me!
We two together no more.

The aria sinking,   130
All else continuing, the stars shining,
The winds blowing, the notes of the bird continuous echoing,
With angry moans the fierce old mother incessantly moaning,

On the sands of Paumanok's shore gray and rustling,
The yellow half-moon enlarged, sagging down, drooping, the face
     of the sea almost touching,   135
The boy ecstatic, with his bare feet the waves, with his hair the
     atmosphere dallying,
The love in the heart long pent, now loose, now at last tumultuously
     bursting,
The aria's meaning, the ears, the soul, swiftly depositing,
The strange tears down the cheeks coursing,
The colloquy there, the trio, each uttering,   140
The undertone, the savage old mother incessantly crying,
To the boy's soul's questions sullenly timing, some drown'd secret
     hissing,
To the outsetting bard.

Demon or bird (said the boy's soul,)
Is it indeed toward your mate you sing? or is it really to me?   145
For I, that was a child, my tongue's use sleeping, now I have heard
     you,
Now in a moment I know what I am for, I awake,
And already a thousand singers, a thousand songs, clearer, louder and
     more sorrowful than yours,
A thousand warbling echoes have started to life within me, never to die.

O you singer solitary, singing by yourself, projecting me,   150
O solitary me listening, never more shall I cease perpetuating you,
Never more shall I escape, never more the reverberations,
Never more the cries of unsatisfied love be absent from me,
Never again leave me to be the peaceful child I was before what
     there in the night,
By the sea under the yellow and sagging moon,   155
The messenger there arous'd, the fire, the sweet hell within,
The unknown want, the destiny of me.

O give me the clew! (it lurks in the night here somewhere,)
O if I am to have so much, let me have more!

A word then, (for I will conquer it,)   160
The word final, superior to all,
Subtle, sent up—what is it?—I listen;
Are you whispering it, and have been all the time, you seawaves?
Is that it from your liquid rims and wet sands?

Whereto answering, the sea,   165
Delaying not, hurrying not,
Whisper'd me through the night, and very plainly before daybreak,

Lisp'd to me the low and delicious word death,
And again death, death, death, death,
Hissing melodious, neither like the bird nor like my arous'd child's
    heart,   170
But edging near as privately for me rustling at my feet,
Creeping thence steadily up to my ears and laving me softly all over,
Death, death, death, death, death.

Which I do not forget,
But fuse the song of my dusky demon and brother,   175
That he sang to me in the moonlight on Paumanok's gray beach,
With the thousand responsive songs at random,
My own songs awaked from that hour,
And with them the key, the word up from the waves,
The word of the sweetest song and all songs,   180
That strong and delicious word which, creeping to my feet,
(Or like some old crone rocking the cradle, swathed in sweet garments,
    bending aside,)
The sea whisper'd me.

When I heard the learn'd astronomer

When I heard the learn'd astronomer,
When the proofs, the figures, were ranged in columns before me,
When I was shown the charts and diagrams, to add, divide, and
    measure them,
When I sitting heard the astronomer where he lectured with much
    applause in the lecture-room,
How soon unaccountable I became tired and sick,   5
Till rising and gliding out I wander'd off by myself,
In the mystical moist night-air, and from time to time,
Look'd up in perfect silence at the stars.

I sit and look out

I sit and look out upon all the sorrows of the world, and upon all
    oppression and shame,
I hear secret convulsive sobs from young men at anguish with
    themselves, remorseful after deeds done,
I see in low life the mother misused by her children, dying, neglected,
    gaunt, desperate,
I see the wife misused by her husband, I see the treacherous seducer
    of young women,

I mark the ranklings of jealousy and unrequited love attempted to be
    hid, I see these sights on the earth,   5
I see the workings of battle, pestilence, tyranny, I see martyrs and
    prisoners,
I observe a famine at sea, I observe the sailors casting lots who shall
    be kill'd to preserve the lives of the rest,
I observe the slights and degradations cast by arrogant persons upon
    laborers, the poor, and upon negroes, and the like;
All these—all the meanness and agony without end I sitting look out
    upon,
See, hear, and am silent.   10

The Dalliance of the Eagles

Skirting the river road, (my forenoon walk, my rest,)
Skyward in air a sudden muffled sound, the dalliance of the eagles,
The rushing amorous contact high in space together,
The clinching interlocking claws, a living, fierce, gyrating wheel,
Four beating wings, two beaks, a swirling mass tight grappling,   5
In tumbling turning clustering loops, straight downward falling,
Till o'er the river pois'd, the twain yet one, a moment's lull,
A motionless still balance in the air, then parting, talons loosing,
Upward again on slow-firm pinions slanting, their separate diverse
    flight,
She hers, he his, pursuing.   10

Cavalry Crossing a Ford

A line in long array where they wind betwixt green islands,
They take a serpentine course, their arms flash in the sun—hark
    to the musical clank,
Behold the silvery river, in it the splashing horses loitering stop to
    drink,
Behold the brown-faced men, each group, each person a picture, the
    negligent rest on the saddles,
Some emerge on the opposite bank, others are just entering the
    ford—while,   5
Scarlet and blue and snowy white,
The guidon flags flutter gayly in the wind.

Dalliance: amorous play.   **7. guidon:** a small flag used in the U.S.
                                            Army to distinguish a company.

WALT WHITMAN

When lilacs last in the dooryard bloomed

I

When lilacs last in the dooryard bloomed,
And the great star early droop'd in the western sky in the night,
I mourn'd, and yet shall mourn with ever-returning spring.

Ever-returning spring, trinity sure to me you bring,
Lilac blooming perennial and drooping star in the west,   5
And thought of him I love.

2

O powerful western fallen star!
O shades of night—O moody, tearful night!
O great star disappear'd—O the black murk that hides the star!
O cruel hands that hold me powerless—O helpless soul of me!   10
O harsh surrounding cloud that will not free my soul.

3

In the dooryard fronting an old farm-house near the white-wash'd
    palings,
Stands the lilac-bush tall-growing with heart-shaped leaves of rich
    green,
With many a pointed blossom rising delicate, with the perfume strong
    I love,
With every leaf a miracle—and from this bush in the dooryard,   15
With delicate-color'd blossoms and heart-shaped leaves of rich green,
A sprig with its flower I break.

4

In the swamp in secluded recesses,
A shy and hidden bird is warbling a song.
Solitary the thrush,   20
The hermit withdrawn to himself, avoiding the settlements,
Sings by himself a song.

Song of the bleeding throat,
Death's outlet song of life, (for well dear brother I know,
If thou wast not granted to sing thou would'st surely die.)   25

When ... bloomed: This poem is one of
four elegies entitled "Memories of President Lincoln," written in 1865.

5

Over the breast of the spring, the land, amid cities,
Amid lanes and through old woods, where lately the violets peep'd
      from the ground, spotting the gray debris,
Amid the grass in the fields each side of the lanes, passing the endless
      grass,
Passing the yellow-spear'd wheat, every grain from its shroud in the
      dark-brown fields uprisen,
Passing the apple-tree blows of white and pink in the orchards,   30
Carrying a corpse to where it shall rest in the grave,
Night and day journeys a coffin.

6

Coffin that passes through lanes and streets,
Through day and night with the great cloud darkening the land,
With the pomp of the inloop'd flags with the cities draped in black,   35
With the show of the States themselves as of crape-veil'd women
      standing,
With processions long and winding and the flambeaus of the night,
With the countless torches lit, with the silent sea of faces and the
      unbared heads,
With the waiting depot, the arriving coffin, and the sombre faces,
With dirges through the night, with the thousand voices rising strong
      and solemn,   40
With all the mournful voices of the dirges pour'd around the coffin,
The dim-lit churches and the shuddering organs—where amid these
      you journey,
With the tolling tolling bells' perpetual clang,
Here, coffin that slowly passes,
I give you my sprig of lilac.   45

7

(Nor for you, for one alone,
Blossoms and branches green to coffins all I bring,
For fresh as the morning, thus would I chant a song for you O sane
      and sacred death.

All over bouquets of roses,
O death, I cover you over with roses and early lilies,   50
But mostly and now the lilac that blooms the first,
Copious I break, I break the sprigs from the bushes,
With loaded arms I come, pouring for you,
For you and the coffins all of you O death.)

---

30. **blows:** blossoms.
32. **coffin:** Lincoln's funeral train journeyed across a mourning nation from Washington, D.C. to Springfield, Illinois.

8

O western orb sailing the heaven,　　　　　　　　　　　　　　　55
Now I know what you must have meant as a month since I walk'd,
As I walk'd in silence the transparent shadowy night,
As I saw you had something to tell as you bent to me night after
　　　night,
As you droop'd from the sky low down as if to my side, (while the
　　　other stars all look'd on,)
As we wander'd together the solemn night, (for something I know not
　　　what kept me from sleep,)　　　　　　　　　　　　　　60
As the night advanced, and I saw on the rim of the west how full
　　　you were of woe,
As I stood on the rising ground in the breeze in the cool transparent
　　　night,
As I watch'd where you pass'd and was lost in the netherward black
　　　of the night,
As my soul in its trouble dissatisfied sank, as where you sad orb,
Concluded, dropt in the night, and was gone.　　　　　　　　65

9

Sing on there in the swamp,
O singer bashful and tender, I hear your notes, I hear your call,
I hear, I come presently, I understand you,
But a moment I linger, for the lustrous star has detain'd me,
The star my departing comrade holds and detains me.　　　　70

10

O how shall I warble myself for the dead one there I loved?
And how shall I deck my song for the large sweet soul that has gone?
And what shall my perfume be for the grave of him I love?

Sea-winds blown from east and west,
Blown from the Eastern sea and blown from the Western sea, till
　　　there on the praries meeting,　　　　　　　　　　　　75
These and with these and the breath of my chant,
I'll perfume the grave of him I love.

11

O what shall I hang on the chamber walls?
And what shall the pictures be that I hang on the walls,
To adorn the burial-house of him I love?　　　　　　　　　80

---

56. **Now ... walk'd:** One evening in Washington before Lincoln's assassination, Whitman seeing the evening star low in the sky, felt a premonition of woe.

Pictures of growing spring and farms and homes,
With the Fourth-month eve at sundown, and the gray smoke lucid
    and bright,
With floods of the yellow gold of the gorgeous, indolent, sinking sun,
    burning, expanding the air,
With the fresh sweet herbage under foot, and the pale green leaves
    of the trees prolific,
In the distance the flowing glaze, the breast of the river, with a wind-
    dapple here and there,   85
With ranging hills on the banks, with many a line against the sky, and
    shadows,
And the city at hand with dwellings so dense, and stacks of chimneys,
And all the scenes of life and the workshops, and the workmen
    homeward returning.

12

Lo, body and soul—this land,
My own Manhattan with spires, and the sparkling and hurrying tides,
    and the ships,   90
The varied and ample land, the South and the North in the light,
    Ohio's shores and flashing Missouri,
And ever the far-spreading praries cover'd with grass and corn.

Lo, the most excellent sun so calm and haughty,
The violet and purple morn with just-felt breezes,
The gentle soft-born measureless light,   95
The miracle spreading bathing all, the fulfill'd noon,
The coming eve delicious, the welcome night and the stars,
Over my cities shining all, enveloping man and land.

13

Sing on, sing on you gray-brown bird,
Sing from the swamps, the recesses, pour your chant from the bushes,   100
Limitless out of the dusk, out of the cedars and pines.

Sing on dearest brother, warble your reedy song,
Loud human song, with voice of uttermost woe.

O liquid and free and tender!
O wild and loose to my soul—O wondrous singer!   105
You only I hear—yet the star holds me, (but will soon depart,)
Yet the lilac with mastering odor holds me.

14

Now while I sat in the day and look'd forth,
In the close of the day with its light and the fields of spring, and the
    farmers preparing their crops,
In the large unconscious scenery of my land with its lakes and
    forests, 110
In the heavenly aerial beauty, (after the perturb'd winds and the
    storms,)
Under the arching heavens of the afternoon swift passing, and the
    voices of children and women,
The many-moving sea-tides, and I saw the ships how they sail'd,
And the summer approaching with richness, and the fields all busy
    with labor,
And the infinite separate houses, how they all went on, each with its
    meals and minutia of daily usages, 115
And the streets how their throbbings throbb'd, and the cities pent—
    lo, then and there,
Falling upon them all and among them all, enveloping me with the
    rest,
Appear'd the cloud, appear'd the long black trail,
And I knew death, its thought, and the sacred knowledge of death.

Then with the knowledge of death as walking one side of me, 120
And the thought of death close-walking the other side of me,
And I in the middle as with companions, and as holding the hands of
    companions,
I fled forth to the hiding receiving night that talks not,
Down to the shores of the water, the path by the swamp in the dimness,
To the solemn shadowy cedars and ghostly pines so still. 125

And the singer so shy to the rest receiv'd me.
The gray-brown bird I know receiv'd us comrades three
And he sang the carol of death, and a verse for him I love.

From deep secluded recesses,
From the fragrant cedars and the ghostly pines so still, 130
Came the carol of the bird.
And the charm of the carol rapt me,
As I held as if by their hands my comrades in the night,
And the voice of my spirit tallied the song of the bird,

Come lovely and soothing death, 135
Undulate round the world, serenely arriving, arriving,
In the day, in the night, to all, to each,
Sooner or later delicate death.

Prais'd be the fathomless universe,
For life and joy, and for objects and knowledge curious,   140
And for love, sweet love—but praise! praise! praise!
For the sure-enwinding arms of cool-enfolding death.

Dark mother always gliding near with soft feet,
Have none chanted for thee a chant of fullest welcome?
Then I chant it for thee, I glorify thee above all,   145
I bring thee a song that when thou must indeed come, come unfalteringly.

Approach strong deliveress,
When it is so, when thou hast taken them I joyously sing the dead,
Lost in the loving floating ocean of thee,
Laved in the flood of thy bliss O death.   150

From me to thee glad serenades,
Dances for thee I propose saluting thee, adornments and feastings for thee,
And the sights of the open landscape and the high-spread sky are fitting,
And life and the fields, and the huge and thoughtful night.

The night in silence under many a star,   155
The ocean shore and the husky whispering wave whose voice I know,
And the soul turning to thee O vast and well-veil'd death,
And the body gratefully nestling close to thee.

Over the tree-tops I float thee a song,
Over the rising and sinking waves, over the myriad fields and the
      prairies wide,   160
Over the dense-pack'd cities all and the teeming wharves and ways,
I float this carol with joy, with joy to thee O death.

15

To the tally of my soul,
Loud and strong kept up the gray-brown bird,
With pure deliberate notes spreading filling the night.   165

Loud in the pines and cedars dim,
Clear in the freshness moist and the swamp-perfume,
And I with my comrades there in the night.

While my sight that was bound in my eyes unclosed,
As to long panoramas of visions.   170

And I saw askant the armies,
I saw as in noiseless dreams hundreds of battle-flags,
Borne through the smoke of the battles and pierc'd with missiles I
      saw them,

And carried hither and yon through the smoke, and torn and bloody,
And at last but a few shreds left on the staffs, (and all in silence,)   175
And the staffs all splinter'd and broken.

I saw battle-corpses, myriads of them,
And the white skeletons of young men, I saw them,
I saw the debris and debris of all the slain soldiers of the war,
But I saw they were not as was thought,   180
They themselves were fully at rest, they suffer'd not,
The living remain'd and suffer'd, the mother suffer'd,
And the wife and the child and the musing comrade suffer'd,
And the armies that remain'd suffer'd.

16

Passing the visions, passing the night,   185
Passing, unloosing the hold of my comrades' hands,
Passing the song of the hermit bird and the tallying song of my soul,
Victorious song, death's outlet song, yet varying ever-altering song,
As low and wailing, yet clear the notes, rising and falling, flooding the
        night,
Sadly sinking and fainting, as warning and warning, and yet again
        bursting with joy,   190
Covering the earth and filling the spread of the heaven,
As that powerful psalm in the night I heard from recesses,
Passing, I leave thee lilac with heart-shaped leaves,
I leave thee there in the door-yard, blooming, returning with spring.

I cease from my song for thee,   195
From my gaze on thee in the west, fronting the west, communing
        with thee,
O comrade lustrous with silver face in the night.

Yet each to keep and all, retrievements out of the night,
The song, the wondrous chant of the gray-brown bird,
And the tallying chant, the echo arous'd in my soul,   200
With the lustrous and drooping star with the countenance full of woe,
With the holders holding my hand nearing the call of the bird,
Comrades mine and I in the midst, and their memory
        ever to keep, for the dead I loved so well,
For the sweetest, wisest soul of all my days and lands—and this for
        his dear sake,
Lilac and star and bird twined with the chant of my soul,   205
There in the fragrant pines and the cedars dusk and dim.

This Compost

1

Something startles me where I thought I was safest,
I withdraw from the still woods I loved,
I will not go now on the pastures to walk,
I will not strip the clothes from my body to meet my lover the sea,
I will not touch my flesh to the earth as to other flesh to renew me.   5

O how can it be that the ground itself does not sicken?
How can you be alive you growths of spring?
How can you furnish health you blood of herbs, roots, orchards, grain?
Are they not continually putting distemper'd corpses within you?
Is not every continent work'd over and over with sour dead?   10

Where have you disposed of their carcasses?
Those drunkards and gluttons of so many generations?
Where have you drawn off all the foul liquid and meat?
I do not see any of it upon you to-day, or perhaps I am deceiv'd,
I will run a furrow with my plough, I will press my spade through
    the sod and turn it up underneath,   15
I am sure I shall expose some of the foul meat.

2

Behold this compost! behold it well!
Perhaps every mite has once form'd part of a sick person—yet behold!
The grass of spring covers the prairies,
The bean bursts noiselessly through the mould in the garden,   20
The delicate spear of the onion pierces upward,
The apple-buds cluster together on the apple-branches,
The resurrection of the wheat appears with pale visage out of its graves,
The tinge awakes over the willow-tree and the mulberry-tree,
The he-birds carol mornings and evenings while the she-birds sit on
    their nests,   25
The young of poultry break through the hatch'd eggs,
The new-born of animals appear, the calf is dropt from the cow,
    the colt from the mare,
Out of its little hill faithfully rise the potato's dark green leaves,
Out of its hill rises the yellow maize-stalk, the lilacs bloom in the
    dooryards,
The summer growth is innocent and disdainful above all those strata
    of sour dead.   30

What chemistry!
That the winds are really not infectious,
That this is no cheat, this transparent green-wash of the sea which is
    so amorous after me,
That it is safe to allow it to lick my naked body all over with its
    tongues,
That it will not endanger me with the fevers that have deposited
    themselves in it,   35
That all is clean forever and forever,
That the cool drink from the well tastes so good,
That blackberries are so flavorous and juicy,
That the fruits of the apple-orchard and the orange-orchard, that
    melons, grapes, peaches, plums, will none of them poison me,
That when I recline on the grass I do not catch any disease,   40
Though probably every spear of grass rises out of what was once a
    catching disease.
Now I am terrified at the Earth, it is that calm and patient,
It grows such sweet things out of such corruptions,
It turns harmless and stainless on its axis, with such endless successions
    of diseas'd corpses,
It distills such exquisite winds out of such infused fetor,   45
It renews with such unwitting looks its prodigal, annual, sumptuous
    crops,
It gives such divine materials to men, and accepts such leavings from
    them at last.

A noiseless patient spider

A noiseless patient spider,
I mark'd where on a little promontory it stood isolated,
Mark'd how to explore the vacant vast surrounding,
It launch'd forth filament, filament, filament, out of itself,
Ever unreeling them, ever tirelessly speeding them.   5

And you O my soul where you stand,
Surrounded, detached, in measureless oceans of space,
Ceaselessly musing, venturing, throwing, seeking the spheres to connect
    them,
Till the bridge you will need be form'd, till the ductile anchor hold,
Till the gossamer thread you fling catch somewhere, O my soul.   10

The Dismantled Ship

In some unused lagoon, some nameless bay,
On sluggish, lonesome waters, anchor'd near the shore,
An old, dismasted, gray and batter'd ship, disabled, done,
After free voyages to all the seas of earth, haul'd up at last and
    hawser'd tight,
Lies rusting, mouldering.   5

ARTHUR HUGH CLOUGH [1819–1861]

The Latest Decalogue

Thou shalt have one God only; who
Would be at the expense of two?
No graven images may be
Worshipped, except the currency;
Swear not at all; for, for thy curse   5
Thine enemy is none the worse:
At church on Sunday to attend
Will serve to keep the world thy friend:
Honour thy parents; that is, all
From whom advancement may befall: 10
Thou shalt not kill; but need'st not strive
Officiously to keep alive:
Do not adultery commit;
Advantage rarely comes of it:
Thou shalt not steal; an empty feat,   15
When it's so lucrative to cheat:
Bear not false witness; let the lie
Have time on its own wings to fly:
Thou shalt not covet, but tradition
Approves all forms of competition.   20

Say not, the struggle nought availeth

Say not, the struggle nought availeth,
    The labour and the wounds are vain,
The enemy faints not, nor faileth,
    And as things have been they remain.

Decalogue: the Ten Commandments. In one of Clough's manuscripts these following additional lines conclude the poem: "The sum of all is, thou shalt love, / If anybody, God above: / At any rate shall never labor / *More* than thyself to love thy neighbor."

If hopes were dupes, fears may be liars;   5
  It may be, in yon smoke concealed,
Your comrades chase e'en now the fliers,
  And, but for you, possess the field.

For while the tired waves, vainly breaking,
  Seem here no painful inch to gain,   10
Far back, through creeks and inlets making,
  Comes silent, flooding in, the main,

And not by eastern windows only,
  When daylight comes, comes in the light,
In front, the sun climbs slow, how slowly,   15
  But westward, look, the land is bright.

MATTHEW ARNOLD [1822–1888]

Shakespeare

Others abide our question. Thou art free.
We ask and ask—Thou smilest and art still,
Out-topping knowledge. For the loftiest hill,
Who to the stars uncrowns his majesty,
Planting his stedfast footsteps in the sea,   5
Making the heaven of heavens his dwelling-place,
Spares but the cloudy border of his base
To the foil'd searching of mortality;
And thou, who didst the stars and sunbeams know,
Self-school'd, selfscann'd, self-honour'd, self-secure,   10
Didst walk on earth unguess'd at.—Better so!
All pains the immortal spirit must endure,
All weakness which impairs, all griefs which bow,
Find their sole voice in that victorious brow.

Memorial Verses

April, 1850

Goethe in Weimar sleeps, and Greece,
Long since, saw Byron's struggle cease.
But one such death remain'd to come.
The last poetic verse is dumb—
We stand to-day by Wordsworth's tomb.   5

12. **main:** sea.

1. **Weimar:** in central Germany. Goethe died in 1832, Byron in 1824, Wordsworth in the month and year above.

When Byron's eyes were shut in death,
We bowed our head and held our breath.
He taught us little; but our soul
Had *felt* him like the thunder's roll.
With shivering heart the strife we saw   10
Of passion with eternal law;
And yet with reverential awe
We watch'd the fount of fiery life
Which serv'd for that Titanic strife.

When Goethe's death was told, we said: 15
Sunk, then, is Europe's sagest head.
Physician of the iron age
Goethe has done his pilgrimage.
He took the suffering human race,
He read each wound, each weakness clear;   20
And struck his finger on the place,
And said—*Thou ailest here, and here!*
He look'd on Europe's dying hour
Of fitful dream and feverish power;
His eye plunged down the weltering strife,   25
The turmoil of expiring life—
He said: *The end is everywhere,*
Art still has truth, take refuge there!
And he was happy, if to know
Causes of things, and far below   30
His feet to see the lurid flow
Of terror, and insane distress,
And headlong fate, be happiness.

And Wordsworth!—Ah, pale ghosts, rejoice!
For never has such soothing voice   35
Been to your shadowy world convey'd,
Since erst, at morn, some wandering shade
Heard the clear song of Orpheus come
Through Hades, and the mournful gloom.
Wordsworth is gone from us—and ye,   40
Ah, may ye feel his voice as we!
He too upon a wintry clime
Had fallen—on this iron time
Of doubts, disputes, distractions, fears.
He found us when the age had bound   45
Our souls in its benumbing round;

38. **Orpheus:** mythical singer, the type of all poets. With his music he charmed even Hades, to which he descended to recover Eurydice.

He spoke, and loosed our hearts in tears.
He laid us as we lay at birth
On the cool flowery lap of earth,
Smiles broke from us and we had ease;   50
The hills were round us, and the breeze
Went o'er the sun-lit fields again;
Our foreheads felt the wind and rain.
Our youth return'd; for there was shed
On spirits that had long been dead,   55
Spirits dried up and closely furl'd,
The freshness of the early world.

Ah! since dark days still bring to light
Man's prudence and man's fiery might,
Time may restore us in his course   60
Goethe's sage mind and Byron's force;
But where will Europe's latter hour
Again find Wordsworth's healing power?
Others will teach us how to dare,
And against fear our breast to steel;   65
Others will strengthen us to bear—
But who, ah! who, will make us feel?
The cloud of mortal destiny,
Others will front it fearlessly—
But who, like him, will put it by?   70

Keep fresh the grass upon his grave,
O Rotha, with thy living wave!
Sing him thy best! for few or none
Hears thy voice right, now he is gone.

To Marguerite—Continued

Yes: in the sea of life enisl'd,
With echoing straits between us thrown,
Dotting the shoreless watery wild,
We mortal millions live *alone*.
    The islands feel the enclasping flow,   5
    And then their endless bounds they know.

72. **Rotha**: river near Wordsworth's grave.

To Marguerite: companion poem to
"Isolation. To Marguerite," in which

Arnold records losing the love of a girl
and reflects that he must go back to his
isolation—the common lot, he says,
although others do not realize it so
clearly.

But when the moon their hollows lights,
And they are swept by balms of spring,
And in their glens, on starry nights,
The nightingales divinely sing;   10
And lovely notes, from shore to shore,
Across the sounds and channels pour;

Oh, then a longing like despair
Is to their farthest caverns sent;
For surely once, they feel, we were   15
Parts of a single continent.
Now round us spreads the watery plain
Oh might our marges meet again!

Who order'd, that their longing's fire
Should be, as soon as kindled, cool'd?   20
Who renders vain their deep desire?—
   A God, a God their severance ruled;
And bade betwixt their shores to be
The unplumb'd, salt, estranging sea.

The Scholar Gipsy

"There was very lately a lad in the University of Oxford, who was by his poverty
forced to leave his studies there; and at last to join himself to a company of vaga-
bond gipsies. Among these extravagant people, by the insinuating subtility of his
carriage, he quickly got so much of their love and esteem as that they discovered to
him their mystery. After he had been a pretty while well exercised in the trade,
there chanced to ride by a couple of scholars, who had formerly been of his acquaintance. They quickly spied out their old friend among the gipsies; and he gave them
an account of the necessity which drove him to that kind of life, and told them that
the people he went with were not such impostors as they were taken for, but that
they had a traditional kind of learning among them, and could do wonders by the
power of imagination, their fancy binding that of others: that himself had learned
much of their art, and when he had compassed the whole secret, he intended, he
said, to leave their company, and give the world an account of what he had learned."
—GLANVIL'S *Vanity of Dogmatizing*, 1661.

Go, for they call you, Shepherd, from the hill;
   Go, Shepherd, and untie the wattled cotes:
      No longer leave thy wistful flock unfed,
   Nor let thy bawling fellows rack their throats,
      Nor the cropp'd grasses shoot another head.   5

2. **wattled cotes**: sheep-enclosures of inter-
laced sticks.

But when the fields are still,
And the tired men and dogs all gone to rest,
  And only the white sheep are sometimes seen
  Cross and recross the strips of moon-blanch'd green;
Come, Shepherd, and again renew the quest.   10

Here, where the reaper was at work of late,
  In this high field's dark corner, where he leaves
    His coat, his basket, and his earthen cruse,
  And in the sun all morning binds the sheaves,
    Then here, at noon, comes back his stores to use;   15
    Here will I sit and wait,
While to my ear from uplands far away
  The bleating of the folded flocks is borne,
  With distant cries of reapers in the corn—
All the live murmur of a summer's day.   20

Screen'd in this nook o'er the high, half-reaped field,
  And here till sun-down, Shepherd, will I be.
    Through the thick corn the scarlet poppies peep
  And round green roots and yellowing stalks I see
    Pale blue convolvulus in tendrils creep: 25
    And air-swept lindens yield
Their scent, and rustle down their perfum'd showers
  Of bloom on the bent grass where I am laid,
  And bower me from the August sun with shade;
And the eye travels down to Oxford's towers: 30

And near me on the grass lies Glanvil's book—
  Come, let me read the oft-read tale again,
    The story of that Oxford scholar poor,
  Of pregnant parts and quick inventive brain,
    Who, tired of knocking at preferment's door,   35
    One summer morn forsook
His friends, and went to learn the gipsy-lore,
  And roam'd the world with that wild brotherhood,
  And came, as most men deem'd, to little good,
But came to Oxford and his friends no more.   40

---

10. **Come . . . quest:** See *ll.* 57–63.
13. **cruse:** container for drink.
18. **folded:** in their folds.
28. **bent:** a kind of reedy grass.

34. **Of . . . parts:** of well-filled intellect.
35. **preferment:** being preferred to a church living.

But once, years after, in the country lanes,
  Two scholars whom at college erst he knew
    Met him, and of his way of life enquired.
  Whereat he answer'd, that the gipsy-crew,
    His mates, had arts to rule as they desired   45
      The working of men's brains,
  And they can bind them to what thoughts they will.
  "And I," he said, "the secret of their art,
    When fully learn'd, will to the world impart;
  But it needs heaven-sent moments for this skill."   50

This said, he left them, and return'd no more.—
  But rumours hung about the country-side
    That the lost Scholar long was seen to stray,
  Seen by rare glimpses, pensive and tongue-tied,
    In hat of antique shape, and cloak of grey,   55
      The same the Gipsies wore.
  Shepherds had met him on the Hurst in spring;
    At some lone alehouse in the Berkshire moors,
    On the warm ingle-bench, the smock-frock'd boors
  Had found him seated at their entering.   60

But, 'mid their drink and clatter, he would fly.
  And I myself seem half to know thy looks,
    And put the shepherds, wanderer, on thy trace;
  And boys who in lone wheatfields scare the rooks
    I ask if thou hast pass'd their quiet place;   65
      Or in my boat I lie
  Moor'd to the cool bank in the summer-heats,
    Mid wide grass meadows which the sunshine fills,
    And watch the warm green-muffled Cumner hills,
  And wonder if thou haunt'st their shy retreats.   70

For most, I know, thou lov'st retired ground!
  Thee, at the ferry, Oxford riders blithe,
    Returning home on summer nights, have met
  Crossing the stripling Thames at Bab-lock-hithe,
    Trailing in the cool stream thy fingers wet,   75
      As the punt's rope chops round;
  And leaning backwards in a pensive dream,
    And fostering in thy lap a heap of flowers
    Pluck'd in shy fields and distant Wychwood bowers,
  And thine eyes resting on the moonlit stream: 80

57. **Hurst:** hill near Oxford.   74. **Stripling:** i.e., narrow upper part.
59. **boors:** country people, farmhands.

And then they land, and thou art seen no more!—
  Maidens who from the distant hamlets come
    To dance around the Fyfield elm in May,
  Oft through the darkening fields have seen thee roam,
    Or cross a stile into the public way.   85
      Oft thou hast given them store
  Of flowers—the frail-leaf'd, white anemony,
    Dark bluebells drench'd with dews of summer eves,
    And purple orchises with spotted leaves—
  But none hath words she can report of thee.   90

And, above Godstow Bridge, when hay-time's here
  In June, and many a scythe in sunshine flames,
    Men who through those wide fields of breezy grass
  Where black-wing'd swallows haunt the glittering Thames,
    To bathe in the abandon'd lasher pass,   95
      Have often pass'd thee near
  Sitting upon the river bank o'ergrown;
    Mark'd thine outlandish garb, thy figure spare,
    Thy dark vague eyes, and soft abstracted air—
  But, when they came from bathing, thou wast gone!   100

At some lone homestead in the Cumner hills,
  Where at her open door the housewife darns,
    Thou hast been seen, or hanging on a gate
  To watch the threshers in the mossy barns.
    Children, who early range these slopes and late   105
      For cresses from the rills,
  Have known thee eyeing, all an April day,
    The springing pastures and the feeding kine;
    And mark'd thee, when the stars come out and shine,
  Through the long dewy grass move slow away.   110

In Autumn, on the skirts of Bagley Wood—
  Where most the Gipsies by the turf-edged way
    Pitch their smoked tents, and every bush you see
  With scarlet patches tagg'd and shreds of grey,
    Above the forest ground call'd Thessaly—   115
      The blackbird, picking food,
  Sees thee, nor stops his meal, nor fears at all;
    So often has he known thee past him stray,
    Rapt, twirling in thy hand a wither'd spray,
  And waiting for the spark from heaven to fall.   120

---

95. **lasher pass:** pool formed by water   106. **cresses:** watercress.
spilling over a small dam.

And once, in winter, on the causeway chill
    Where home through flooded fields foot-travellers go,
      Have I not pass'd thee on the wooden bridge,
    Wrapt in thy cloak and battling with the snow,
        Thy face tow'rd Hinksey and its wintry ridge?   125
          And thou hast climb'd the hill
    And gain'd the white brow of the Cumner range;
      Turn'd once to watch, while thick the snowflakes fall,
      The line of festal light in Christ-Church hall—
    Then sought thy straw in some sequester'd grange.   130

But what—I dream! Two hundred years are flown
    Since first thy story ran through Oxford halls,
      And the grave Glanvil did the tale inscribe
    That thou wert wander'd from the studious walls
        To learn strange arts, and join a gipsy-tribe: 135
          And thou from earth art gone
    Long since, and in some quiet churchyard laid—
      Some country nook, where o'er thy unknown grave
      Tall grasses and white flowering nettles wave,
    Under a dark, red-fruited yew-tree's shade.   140

—No, no, thou hast not felt the lapse of hours!
    For what wears out the life of mortal men?
      'Tis that from change to change their being rolls;
    'Tis that repeated shocks, again, again,
        Exhaust the energy of strongest souls,   145
          And numb the elastic powers.
    Till having used our nerves with bliss and teen,
      And tired upon a thousand schemes our wit,
      To the just-pausing Genius we remit
    Our worn-out life, and are—what we have been.   150

Thou hast not lived, why should'st thou perish, so?
    Thou hadst *one* aim, *one* business, *one* desire;
      Else wert thou long since number'd with the dead!
    Else hadst thou spent, like other men, thy fire!
        The generations of thy peers are fled,   155
          And we ourselves shall go;
    But thou possessest an immortal lot,
      And we imagine thee exempt from age
      And living as thou liv'st on Glanvil's page,
    Because thou hadst—what we, alas! have not.   160

129. **Christ . . . hall:** the dining hall of Christ Church College.
147. **teen:** sorrow.

149. **Genius:** a being who receives life back at death and sends it forth in other forms. Spenser, *Faerie Queene*, III, vi, Stanzas 31-32.

For early didst thou leave the world with powers
  Fresh, undiverted to the world without,
    Firm to their mark, not spent on other things;
  Free from the sick fatigue, the languid doubt,
    Which much to have tried, in much been baffled, brings.   165
      O life unlike to ours!
  Who fluctuate idly without term or scope,
    Of whom each strives, nor knows for what he strives,
    And each half lives a hundred different lives;
  Who wait like thee, but not, like thee, in hope.   170

Thou waitest for the spark from heaven! and we,
  Light half-believers of our casual creeds,
    Who never deeply felt, nor clearly will'd,
  Whose insight never has borne fruit in deeds,
    Whose vague resolves never have been fulfill'd;   175
      For whom each year we see
  Breeds new beginnings, disappointments new;
    Who hesitate and falter life away,
    And lose to-morrow the ground won to-day—
  Ah! do not we, wanderer! await it too?   180

Yes, we await it!—but it still delays,
  And then we suffer; and amongst us one,
    Who most has suffer'd, takes dejectedly
  His seat upon the intellectual throne;
    And all his store of sad experience he   185
      Lays bare of wretched days;
  Tells us his misery's birth and growth and signs,
    And how the dying spark of hope was fed,
    And how the breast was soothed, and how the head,
  And all his hourly varied anodynes.   190

This for our wisest! and we others pine,
  And wish the long unhappy dream would end,
    And waive all claim to bliss, and try to bear;
  With close-lipp'd patience for our only friend,
    Sad patience, too near neighbour to despair—   195
      But none has hope like thine!
  Thou through the fields and through the woods dost stray,
    Roaming the country side, a truant boy,
    Nursing thy project in unclouded joy,
  And every doubt long blown by time away.   200

O born in days when wits were fresh and clear,
  And life ran gaily as the sparkling Thames;
    Before this strange disease of modern life,
  With its sick hurry, its divided aims,
    Its heads o'ertax'd, its palsied hearts, was rife—   205
      Fly hence, our contact fear!
Still fly, plunge deeper in the bowering wood!
  Averse, as Dido did with gesture stern
  From her false friend's approach in Hades turn,
Wave us away, and keep thy solitude.   210

Still nursing the unconquerable hope,
  Still clutching the inviolable shade,
    With a free, onward impulse brushing through,
  By night, the silver'd branches of the glade—
    Far on the forest skirts, where none pursue,   215
      On some mild pastoral slope
Emerge, and resting on the moonlit pales,
  Freshen thy flowers, as in former years
  With dew, or listen with enchanted ears,
From the dark dingles, to the nightingales.   220

But fly our paths, our feverish contact fly!
  For strong the infection of our mental strife,
    Which, though it gives no bliss, yet spoils for rest;
  And we should win thee from thy own fair life,
    Like us distracted, and like us unblest.   225
      Soon, soon thy cheer would die,
Thy hopes grow timorous, and unfix'd thy powers,
  And thy clear aims be cross and shifting made:
  And then thy glad perennial youth would fade,
Fade, and grow old at last, and die like ours.   230

Then fly our greetings, fly our speech and smiles!
  —As some grave Tyrian trader, from the sea,
    Described at sunrise an emerging prow
  Lifting the cool-hair'd creepers stealthily,
    The fringes of a southward-facing brow   235
      Among the Ægean isles;
And saw the merry Grecian coaster come,
  Freighted with amber grapes, and Chian wine,
  Green bursting figs, and tunnies steep'd in brine—
And knew the intruders on his ancient home,   240

208. Dido: When Aeneas visits Hades, this queen of Carthage thus turns away from him, the lover who had rejected her. Virgil, *Aeneid*, vi, *ll*. 450–76.

220. dingles: small deep valleys.

The young light-hearted masters of the waves—
   And snatch'd his rudder, and shook out more sail,
   And day and night held on indignantly
O'er the blue Midland water with the gale,
   Betwixt the Syrtes and soft Sicily,   245
      To where the Atlantic raves
Outside the western straits; and unbent sails
   There, where down cloudy cliffs, through sheets of foam,
   Shy traffickers, the dark Iberians come;
And on the beach undid his corded bales.   250

Dover Beach

The sea is calm to-night.
The tide is full, the moon lies fair
Upon the straits;—on the French coast, the light
Gleams and is gone; the cliffs of England stand,
Glimmering and vast, out in the tranquil bay.   5
Come to the window, sweet is the night air!

Only, from the lone line of spray
Where the sea meets the moon-blanch'd land,
Listen, you hear the grating roar
Of pebbles which the waves draw back, and fling,   10
At their return, up the high strand,
Begin, and cease, and then again begin,
With tremulous cadence slow, and bring
The eternal note of sadness in.

Sophocles long ago   15
Heard it on the Ægæan, and it brought
Into his mind the turbid ebb and flow
Of human misery; we
Find also in the sound a thought,
Hearing it by this distant northern sea.   20

242. **snatch'd:** the subject is the Tyrian trader of *l*. 232.
249. **Iberians:** ancient inhabitants of Spain and Portugal, with some resemblance to gypsies.

15. **Sophocles:** The tragedian makes this comparison in his *Antigone*, *ll*. 583 ff.

The Sea of Faith
Was once, too, at the full, and round earth's shore
Lay like the fold of a bright girdle furl'd
But now I only hear
Its melancholy, long, withdrawing roar,   25
Retreating, to the breath
Of the night-wind down the vast edges drear
And naked shingles of the world.

Ah, love, let us be true
To one another! for the world, which seems   30
To lie before us like a land of dreams,
So various, so beautiful, so new,
Hath really neither joy, nor love, nor light,
Nor certitude, nor peace, nor help from pain;
And we are here as on a darkling plain   35
Swept with confused alarms of struggle and flight,
Where ignorant armies clash by night.

The Last Word

Creep into thy narrow bed,
Creep, and let no more be said!
Vain thy onset! all stands fast;
Thou thyself must break at last.

Let the long contention cease!   5
Geese are swans and swans are geese.
Let them have it how they will!
Thou art tired; best be still!

They out-talked thee, hissed thee, tore thee.
Better men fared thus before thee;   10
Fired their ringing shot and passed,
Hotly charged—and broke at last.

Charge once more, then, and be dumb!
Let the victors, when they come,
When the forts of folly fall,   15
Find thy body by the wall.

GEORGE MEREDITH [1828–1909]

Am I failing?

Am I failing? For no longer can I cast
A glory round about this head of gold.
Glory she wears, but springing from the mould;
Not like the consecration of the Past!
Is my soul beggared? Something more than earth   5
I cry for still: I cannot be at peace
In having Love upon a mortal lease.
I cannot take the woman at her worth!
Where is the ancient wealth wherewith I clothed
Our human nakedness, and could endow   10
With spiritual splendour a white brow
That else had grinned at me the fact I loathed?
A kiss is but a kiss now! and no wave
Of a great flood that whirls me to the sea.
But, as you will! we'll sit contentedly,   15
And eat our pot of honey on the grave.

Lucifer in Starlight

On a starred night Prince Lucifer uprose.
Tired of his dark dominion, swung the fiend
Above the rolling ball in cloud part screened,
Where sinners hugged their spectre of repose.
Poor prey to his hot fit of pride were those.   5
And now upon his western wing he leaned,
Now his huge bulk o'er Afric's sands careened,
Now the black planet shadowed Arctic snows.
Soaring through wider zones that pricked his scars
With memory of the old revolt from Awe,   10
He reached a middle height, and at the stars,
Which are the brain of heaven, he looked, and sank.
Around the ancient track marched, rank on rank,
The army of unalterable law.

Am . . . failing?: No. 29 in the sonnet-
sequence *Modern Love*.
3. mould: earth.

5. hot . . . pride: This is said to have
caused his initial revolt against God (see
l. 10).

Winter Heavens

Sharp is the night, but stars with frost alive
Leap off the rim of earth across the dome.
It is a night to make the heavens our home
More than the nest whereto apace we strive.
Lengths down our road each fir-tree seems a hive,   5
In swarms outrushing from the golden comb.
They waken waves of thoughts that burst to foam:
The living throb in me, the dead revive.
Yon mantle clothes us: there, past mortal breath,
Life glistens on the river of the death.   10
It folds us, flesh and dust; and have we knelt,
Or never knelt, or eyed as kine the springs
Of radiance, the radiance enrings:
And this is the soul's haven to have felt.

LEWIS CARROLL [1832–1898]

Jabberwocky

from *Through the Looking Glass*, Chapter 1.

'Twas brillig, and the slithy toves
    Did gyre and gimble in the wabe;
All mimsy were the borogoves,
    And the mome raths outgrabe.

"Beware the Jabberwock, my son!   5
    The jaws that bite, the claws that catch!
Beware the Jubjub bird, and shun
    The frumious Bandersnatch!"

He took his vorpal sword in hand;
    Long time the manxome foe he sought—   10
So rested he by the Tumtum tree,
    And stood awhile in thought.

And, as in uffish thought he stood,
    The Jabberwock, with eyes of flame,
Came whiffling through the tulgey wood,   15
    And burbled as it came!

2. **Leap . . . rim:** rise above the horizon   12. **kine:** cattle (looking desirously at a
as the earth turns.   spring of water).
6. **comb:** honeycomb.

One, two! One, two! And through and through
  The vorpal blade went snicker-snack!
He left it dead, and with its head
  He went galumphing back.   20

"And hast thou slain the Jabberwock?
  Come to my arms, my beamish boy!
O frabjous day! Callooh! Callay!"
  He chortled in his joy.

'Twas brillig, and the slithy toves   25
  Did gyre and gimble in the wabe;
All mimsy were the borogroves,
  And the mome raths outgrabe.

WILLIAM MORRIS [1834–1896]

The Haystack in the Floods

Had she come all the way for this,
To part at last without a kiss?
Yea, had she borne the dirt and rain
That her own eyes might see him slain
Beside the haystack in the floods?   5

Along the dripping leafless woods,
The stirrup touching either shoe,
She rode astride as troopers do;
With kirtle kilted to her knee,
To which the mud splash'd wretchedly;   10
And the wet dripp'd from every tree
Upon her head and heavy hair,
And on her eyelids broad and fair;
The tears and rain ran down her face.

By fits and starts they rode apace,   15
And very often was his place
Far off from her; he had to ride
Ahead, to see what might betide
When the roads cross'd; and sometimes, when
There rose a murmuring from his men,   20
Had to turn back with promises;
Ah me! she had but little ease;

And often for pure doubt and dread
She sobb'd, made giddy in the head
By the swift riding; while, for cold,   25
Her slender fingers scarce could hold
The wet reins: yea, and scarcely, too,
She felt the foot within her shoe
Against the stirrup: all for this,
To part at last without a kiss   30
Beside the haystack in the floods.

For when they near'd that old soak'd hay,
They saw across the only way
That Judas, Godmar, and the three
Red running lions dismally   35
Grinn'd from his pennon, under which,
In one straight line along the ditch,
They counted thirty heads.

                                        So then,
While Robert turn'd round to his men,
She saw at once the wretched end,   40
And, stooping down, tried hard to rend
Her coif the wrong way from her head,
And hid her eyes; while Robert said:
"Nay, love, 'tis scarcely two to one,
At Poictiers where we made them run   45
So fast—why, sweet my love, good cheer,
The Gascon frontier is so near,
Nought after this."

                                        But, "O," she said,
"My God! my God! I have to tread
The long way back without you; then   50
The court at Paris; those six men;
The gratings of the Chatelet;
The swift Seine on some rainy day
Like this, and people standing by,
And laughing, while my weak hands try   55
To recollect how strong men swim.
All this, or else a life with him,
For which I should be damned at last,
Would God that this next hour were past!"

---

42. **coif:** close-fitting cap.
45. **Poictiers:** great battle at which the English defeated the French in 1356.
47. **Gascon frontier:** Gascony was held by England.

52. **Chatelet:** prison in Paris.
53. **Seine:** Women were thrown in to determine whether they were witches. If they drowned, they were innocent.

He answer'd not, but cried his cry,   60
"St. George for Marny!" cheerily;
And laid his hand upon her rein.
Alas! no man of all his train
Gave back that cheery cry again;
And, while for rage his thumb beat fast   65
Upon his sword-hilt, some one cast
About his neck a kerchief long,
And bound him.

               Then they went along
To Godmar; who said: "Now, Jehane,
Your lover's life is on the wane   70
So fast, that, if this very hour
You yield not as my paramour,
He will not see the rain leave off—
Nay, keep your tongue from gibe and scoff,
Sir Robert, or I slay you now."   75

She laid her hand upon her brow,
Then gazed upon the palm, as though
She thought her forehead bled, and—"No."
She said, and turn'd her head away,
As there were nothing else to say,   80
And everything were settled: red
Grew Godmar's face from chin to head:
"Jehane, on yonder hill there stands
My castle, guarding well my lands:
What hinders me from taking you,   85
And doing that I list to do
To your fair wilful body, while
Your knight lies dead?"

              A wicked smile
Wrinkled her face, her lips grew thin,
A long way out she thrust her chin: 90
"You know that I should strangle you
While you were sleeping; or bite through
Your throat, by God's help—ah!" she said,
"Lord Jesus, pity your poor maid!
For in such wise they hem me in,   95
I cannot choose but sin and sin,
Whatever happens: yet I think
They could not make me eat or drink,
And so should I just reach my rest,"
"Nay, if you do not my behest,   100

O Jehane! though I love you well,"
Said Godmar, "would I fail to tell
All that I know?" "Foul lies," she said.
"Eh? lies my Jehane? by God's head,
At Paris folks would deem them true!   105
Do you know, Jehane, they cry for you,
'Jehane the brown! Jehane the brown!
Give us Jehane to burn or drown!'—
Eh—gag me Robert!—sweet my friend,
This were indeed a piteous end   110
For those long fingers, and long feet,
And long neck, and smooth shoulders sweet:
An end that few men would forget
That saw it—So, an hour yet:
Consider, Jehane, which to take   115
Of life or death!"

                     So, scarce awake,
Dismounting, did she leave that place,
And totter some yards: with her face
Turn'd upward to the sky she lay,
Her head on a wet heap of hay,   120
And fell asleep: and while she slept
And did not dream, the minutes crept
Round to the twelve again; but she,
Being waked at last, sigh'd quietly,
And strangely childlike came, and said: 125
"I will not." Straightway Godmar's head,
As though it hung on strong wires, turn'd
Most sharply round, and his face burn'd.

For Robert—both his eyes were dry,
He could not weep, but gloomily   130
He seem'd to watch the rain; yea, too,
His lips were firm; he tried once more
To touch her lips; she reach'd out, sore
And vain desire so tortured them,
The poor grey lips, and now the hem   135
Of his sleeve brush'd them.

                     With a start
Up Godmar rose, thrust them apart;
From Robert's throat he loosed the bands
Of silk and mail; with empty hands
Held out, she stood and gazed, and saw,   140

The long bright blade without a flaw
Glide out from Godmar's sheath, his hand
In Robert's hair; she saw him bend
Back Robert's head; she saw him send
The thin steel down; the blow told well,   145
Right backward the knight Robert fell,
And moan'd as dogs do, being half dead,
Unwitting, as I deem: so then
Godmar turn'd grinning to his men,
Who ran, some five or six, and beat   150
His head to pieces at their feet.
Then Godmar turn'd again and said:
"So, Jehane, the first fitte is read!
Take note, my lady, that your way
Lies backward to the Chatelet!"   155
She shook her head and gazed awhile
At her cold hands with a rueful smile,
As though this thing had made her mad.

This was the parting that they had
Beside the haystack in the floods.   160

BRET HARTE [1836–1902]

Mrs. Judge Jenkins

(Being the Only Genuine Sequel to "Maud Muller")

Maud Muller all that summer day
Raked the meadow sweet with hay;

Yet, looking down the distant lane,
She hoped the Judge would come again.

But when he came, with smile and bow,   5
Maud only blushed, and stammered, "Ha-ow?"

And spoke of her "pa," and wondered whether
He'd give consent they should wed together.

153. **fitte:** division of a narrative poem.

Maud Muller: In Whittier's poem "Maud Muller" Judge Jenkins and Maud, the country maid, spend their lives lamenting because their chance meeting did not result in marriage.

Old Muller burst in tears, and then
Begged that the Judge would lend him "ten";   10

For trade was dull, and wages low,
And the "craps," this year, were somewhat slow.

And ere the languid summer died,
Sweet Maud became the Judge's bride.

But on the day that they were mated,   15
Maud's brother Bob was intoxicated;

And Maud's relations, twelve in all,
Were very drunk at the Judge's hall;

And when the summer came again,
The young bride bore him babies twain;   20

And the Judge was blest, but thought it strange
That bearing children made such a change;

For Maud grew broad and red and stout,
And the waist that his arm once clasped about

Was more than he now could span; and he   25
Sighed as he pondered, ruefully,

How that which in Maud was native grace
In Mrs. Jenkins was out of place;

And thought of the twins, and wished that they
Looked less like the men who raked the hay   30

On Muller's farm, and dreamed with pain,
Of the day he wandered down the lane.

And looking down that dreary track,
He half regretted that he came back;

For, had he waited, he might have wed   35
Some maiden fair and thoroughbred;

For there be women fair as she,
Whose verbs and nouns do more agree.

Alas for maiden! alas for judge!
And the sentimental,—that's one-half "fudge"; 40

For Maud soon thought the Judge a bore,
With all his learning and all his lore;

And the Judge would have bartered Maud's fair face
For more refinement and social grace.

If, of all the words of tongue and pen, 45
The saddest are, "It might have been,"

More sad are these we daily see:
"It is, but hadn't ought to be."

WILLIAM ERNEST HENLEY [1849–1903]

Madam Life's a piece in bloom

Madam Life's a piece in bloom
   Death goes dogging everywhere:
She's the tenant of the room,
   He's the ruffian on the stair.

You shall see her as a friend, 5
   You shall bilk him once or twice;
But he'll trap you in the end,
   And he'll stick you for her price.

With his kneebones at your chest,
   And his knuckles in your throat, 10
You would reason—plead—protest!
   Clutching at her petticoat;

But she's heard it all before,
   Well she knows you've had your fun,
Gingerly she gains the door, 15
   And your little job is done.

46. It . . . been: Whittier wrote "For of
all sad words of tongue and pen / The
saddest are these; 'It might have been.'"

RUDYARD KIPLING [1865–1936]

Tommy

I went into a public-'ouse to get a pint o' beer,
The publican 'e up an' sez, "We serve no redcoats here."
The girls be'ind the bar they laughed an' giggled fit to die,
I outs into the street again an' to myself sez I:

    O it's Tommy this, an' Tommy that, an' "Tommy, go away";   5
    But it's "Thank you, Mister Atkins," when the band begins to play,
    The band begins to play, my boys, the band begins to play,
    O it's "Thank you, Mister Atkins," when the band begins to play.

I went into a theatre as sober as could be,
They gave a drunk civilian room, but 'adn't none for me;   10
They sent me to the gallery or round the music-'alls,
But when it comes to fightin', Lord! they'll shove me in the stalls!

    For it's Tommy this, an' Tommy that, an' "Tommy, wait outside";
    But it's "Special train for Atkins" when the trooper's on the tide,
    The troopship's on the tide, my boys, the troopship's on the tide,   15
    O it's "Special train for Atkins" when the trooper's on the tide.

Yes, makin' mock o' uniforms that guard you while you sleep
Is cheaper than them uniforms, an' they're starvation cheap;
An' hustlin' drunken soldiers when they're goin' large a bit
Is five times better business than paradin' in full kit.   20

    Then it's Tommy this, an' Tommy that, an' "Tommy, 'ow's yer
        soul?"
    But it's "Thin red line of 'eroes" when the drums begin to roll,
    The drums begin to roll, my boys, the drums begin to roll,
    O it's "Thin red line of 'eroes" when the drums begin to roll.

We aren't no thin red 'eroes, nor we aren't no blackguards too,   25
But single men in barricks, most remarkable like you;
An' if sometimes our conduck isn't all your fancy paints,
Why, single men in barricks don't grow into plaster saints;

    While it's Tommy this, an' Tommy that, an' "Tommy, fall be'ind,"
    But it's "Please to walk in front, sir," when there's trouble in the
        wind,   30
    There's trouble in the wind, my boys, there's trouble in the wind,
    O it's "Please to walk in front, sir," when there's trouble in the
        wind.

You talk o' better food for us, an' schools, an' fires, an' all:
We'll wait for extry rations if you treat us rational.
Don't mess about the cook-room slops, but prove it to our face   35
The Widow's Uniform is not the soldier-man's disgrace.

> For it's Tommy this, an' Tommy that, an' "Chuck him out,
>   the brute!"
> But it's "Savior of 'is country" when the guns begin to shoot;
> An' it's Tommy this, an' Tommy that, an' anything you please;
> An' Tommy ain't a bloomin' fool—you bet that Tommy sees!   40

The King

"Farewell, Romance!" the Cave-men said;
    "With bone well carved he went away,
"Flint arms the ignoble arrowhead,
    "And jasper tips the spear today.
"Changed are the Gods of Hunt and Dance,   5
"And He with these. Farewell, Romance!"

"Farewell, Romance!" the Lake-folk sighed;
    "We lift the weight of flatling years;
"The caverns of the mountain-side
    "Hold Him who scorns our hutted piers.   10
"Lost hills whereby we dare not dwell,
"Guard ye His rest. Romance, farewell!"

"Farewell, Romance!" the Soldier spoke;
    "By sleight of sword we may not win,
"But scuffle 'mid uncleanly smoke   15
    "Of arquebus and culverin.
"Honor is lost, and none may tell
"Who paid good blows. Romance, farewell!"

"Farewell, Romance!" the Traders cried;
    "Our keels have lain with every sea;   20
"The dull-returning wind and tide
    "Heave up the wharf where we would be;
"The known and noted breezes swell
"Our trudging sails. Romance, farewell!"

16. **arquebus, culverin:** early firearm and
cannon.

"Good-by, Romance!" the Skipper said;   25
  "He vanished with the coal we burn;
"Our dial marks full-steam ahead,
  "Our speed is timed to half a turn.
"Sure as the ferried barge we ply
"'Twixt port and port. Romance, good-by!"   30

"Romance!" the season-tickets mourn,
  "*He* never ran to catch his train,
"But passed with coach and guard and horn—
  "And left the local—late again!"
Confound Romance! . . . And all unseen   35
Romance brought up the nine-fifteen.

His hand was on the lever laid,
  His oil-can soothed the worrying cranks,
His whistle waked the snowbound grade,
  His fog-horn cut the reeking Banks;   40
By dock and deep and mine and mill
The Boy-god reckless labored still!

Robed, crowned and throned, He wove his spell,
  Where heart-blood beat or hearth-smoke curled,
With unconsidered miracle,   45
  Hedged in a backward-gazing world;
Then taught his chosen bard to say:
"Our King was with us—yesterday!"

Recessional

God of our fathers, known of old,
  Lord of our far-flung battle-line—
Beneath whose awful hand we hold
  Dominion over palm and pine—
Lord God of Hosts, be with us yet,   5
Lest we forget—lest we forget!

The tumult and the shouting dies—
  The captains and the kings depart—
Still stands Thine ancient sacrifice,
  An humble and a contrite heart.   10
Lord God of Hosts, be with us yet,
Lest we forget—lest we forget!

Recessional: term for hymn sung as clergy and choir proceed out at end of service. This poem was published at the end of Queen Victoria's Diamond Jubilee celebration (1897).

Far-called our navies melt away—
  On dune and headland sinks the fire—
Lo, all our pomp of yesterday   15
  Is one with Nineveh and Tyre!
Judge of the Nations, spare us yet,
Lest we forget—lest we forget!

If, drunk with sight of power, we loose
  Wild tongues that have not Thee in awe—   20
Such boasting as the Gentiles use,
  Or lesser breeds without the Law—
Lord God of Hosts, be with us yet,
Lest we forget—lest we forget!

For heathen heart that puts her trust   25
  In reeking tube and iron shard,
All valiant dust that builds on dust,
  And, guarding, calls not thee to guard,
For frantic boast and foolish word—
Thy mercy on Thy People, Lord!   30

ERNEST DOWSON [1867–1900]

Non Sum Qualis Eram Bonae sub Regno Cynarae

Last night, ah, yesternight, betwixt her lips and mine
There fell thy shadow, Cynara! thy breath was shed
Upon my soul between the kisses and the wine;
And I was desolate and sick of an old passion,
  Yea, I was desolate and bowed by head: 5
I have been faithful to thee, Cynara! in my fashion.

All night upon mine heart I felt her warm heart beat,
Night-long within mine arms in love and sleep she lay;
Surely the kisses of her bought red mouth were sweet;
But I was desolate and sick of an old passion,   10
  When I awoke and found the dawn was gray:
I have been faithful to thee, Cynara! in my fashion.

21. **Gentiles:** heathen.

Non . . . Cynarae: "I am not what I was under the rule of good Cynara." A quotation from Horace (*Odes*, IV, i, *ll.* 3–4). He asks Venus no longer to trouble him; he is older, and not what he was when the girl Cynara ruled him.

I have forgot much, Cynara! gone with the wind,
Flung roses, roses riotously with the throng,
Dancing, to put thy pale, lost lilies out of mind;   15
But I was desolate and sick of an old passion,
     Yea, all the time, because the dance was long:
I have been faithful to thee, Cynara! in my fashion.

I cried for madder music and for stronger wine,
But when the feast is finished and the lamps expire,   20
Then falls thy shadow, Cynara! the night is thine;
And I am desolate and sick of an old passion,
     Yea, hungry for the lips of my desire:
I have been faithful to thee, Cynara! in my fashion.

The Moderns

EMILY DICKINSON

[*1830–1886*]

Success is counted sweetest

Success is counted sweetest
By those who ne'er succeed.
To comprehend a nectar
Requires sorest need.

Not one of all the purple Host 5
Who took the Flag today
Can tell the definition
So clear of Victory

As he defeated—dying—
On whose forbidden ear 10
The distant strains of triumph
Burst agonized and clear!

Exultation is the going

Exultation is the going
On an island soul to sea,
Past the houses—past the headlands—
Into deep Eternity—

Bred as we, among the mountains, 5
Can the sailor understand
The divine intoxication
Of the first league out from land?

How many times these low feet staggered

How many times these low feet staggered—
Only the soldered mouth can tell—
Try—can you stir the awful rivet—
Try—can you lift the hasps of steel!

Stroke the cool forehead—hot so often—   5
Lift—if you care—the listless hair—
Handle the adamantine fingers
Never a thimble—more—shall wear—

Buzz the dull flies—on the chamber window—
Brave—shines the sun through the freckled pane—   10
Fearless—the cobweb swings from the ceiling—
Indolent Housewife—in Daisies—lain!

I taste a liquor never brewed

I taste a liquor never brewed—
From Tankards scooped in Pearl—
Not all the Frankfort Berries
Yield such an Alcohol!

Inebriate of Air—am I—   5
And Debauchee of Dew—
Reeling—thro endless summer days—
From inns of Molten Blue—

When "Landlords" turn the drunken Bee
Out of the Foxglove's door—   10
When Butterflies—renounce their "drams"—
I shall but drink the more!

Till Seraphs swing their snowy Hats—
And Saints—to windows run—
To see the little Tippler   15
From Manzanilla come!

7. **adamantine:** immovable, unyielding.   16. **Manzanilla:** a flower of the camomile
                                               family; also a sherry.

There's a certain Slant of light

There's a certain Slant of light,
Winter Afternoons—
That oppresses, like the Heft
Of Cathedral Tunes—

Heavenly Hurt, it gives us— 5
We can find no scar,
But internal difference,
Where the Meanings, are—

None may teach it—Any—
'Tis the Seal Despair— 10
An imperial affliction
Sent us of the Air—

When it comes, the Landscape listens—
Shadows—hold their breath—
When it goes, 'tis like the Distance 15
On the look of Death—

I felt a Funeral, in my Brain

I felt a Funeral, in my Brain,
And Mourners to and fro
Kept treading—treading—till it seemed
That Sense was breaking through—

And when they all were seated, 5
A Service, like a Drum—
Kept beating—beating—till I thought
My Mind was going numb—

And then I heard them lift a Box
And creak across my Soul 10
With those same Boots of Lead, again,
Then Space—began to toll,

As all the Heavens were a Bell,
And Being, but an Ear,
And I, and Silence, some strange Race 15
Wrecked, solitary, here—

3. **Heft:** weight.

And then a Plank in Reason, broke,
And I dropped down, and down—
And hit a World, at every plunge,
And Finished knowing—then—   20

A Clock stopped

A Clock stopped—
Not the Mantel's—
Geneva's farthest skill
Cant put the puppet bowing—
That just now dangled still—   5

An awe came on the Trinket!
The Figures hunched, with pain—
Then quivered out of Decimals—
Into Degreeless Noon—

It will not stir for Doctor's—   10
This Pendulum of snow—
The Shopman importunes it—
While cool—concernless No—

Nods from the Gilded pointers—
Nods from the Seconds slim—   15
Decades of Arrogance between
The Dial life—
And Him—

The Soul selects her own Society

The Soul selects her own Society—
Then—shuts the Door—
To her divine Majority—
Present no more—

Unmoved—she notes the Chariots—pausing—   5
At her low Gate—
Unmoved—an Emperor be kneeling
Upon her Mat—

I've known her—from an ample nation—
Choose One—   10
Then—close the Valves of her attention—
Like Stone—

A Bird came down the Walk

A Bird came down the Walk—
He did not know I saw—
He bit an Angleworm in halves
And ate the fellow, raw,

And then he drank a Dew   5
From a convenient Grass—
And then hopped sidewise to the Wall
To let a Beetle pass—

He glanced with rapid eyes
That hurried all around—   10
They looked like frightened Beads, I thought—
He stirred his Velvet Head

Like one in danger, Cautious,
I offered him a Crumb
And he unrolled his feathers   15
And rowed him softer home—

Than Oars divide the Ocean,
Too silver for a seam—
Or Butterflies, off Banks of Noon
Leap, plashless as they swim.   20

After great pain, a formal feeling comes

After great pain, a formal feeling comes—
The Nerves sit ceremonious, like Tombs—
The stiff Heart questions was it He, that bore,
And Yesterday, or Centuries before?

The Feet, mechanical, go round—   5
Of Ground, or Air, or Ought—
A Wooden way
Regardless grown,
A Quartz contentment, like a stone—

This is the Hour of Lead—   10
Remembered, if outlived,
As Freezing persons, recollect the Snow—
First—Chill—then Stupor, then the letting go—

I had not minded—Walls

I had not minded—Walls—
Were Universe—one Rock—
And far I heard his silver Call
The other side the Block—

I'd tunnel—till my Groove   5
Pushed sudden thro' to his—
Then my face take her Recompense—
The looking in his Eyes—

But 'tis a single Hair—
A filament—a law—   10
A Cobweb—wove in Adamant—
A Battlement—of Straw—

A limit like the Vail
Unto the Lady's face—
But every Mesh—a Citadel—   15
And Dragons—in the Crease—

What Soft—Cherubic Creatures

What Soft—Cherubic Creatures—
These Gentlewomen are—
One would as soon assault a Plush—
Or violate a Star—

Such Dimity Convictions—   5
A Horror so refined
Of freckled Human Nature—
Of Deity—ashamed—

It's such a common—Glory—
A Fisherman's—Degree   10
Redemption—Brittle Lady—
Be so—ashamed of Thee—

---

3. **Plush:** a fabric softer than velvet.   5. **Dimity:** a fine, thin, corded cotton fabric.

'Twas like a Maelstrom, with a notch

'Twas like a Maelstrom, with a notch,
That nearer, every Day,
Kept narrowing it's boiling Wheel
Until the Agony

Toyed coolly with the final inch   5
Of your delirious Hem—
And you dropt, lost,
When something broke—
And let you from a Dream—

As if a Goblin with a Gauge—   10
Kept measuring the Hours—
Until you felt your Second
Weigh, helpless, in his Paws—

And not a Sinew—stirred—could help,
And sense was setting numb—   15
When God—remembered—and the Fiend
Let go, then Overcome—

As if your Sentence stood—pronounced—
And you were frozen led
From Dungeon's luxury of Doubt   20
To Gibbets, and the Dead—

And when the Film had stitched your eyes
A Creature gasped "Reprieve"!
Which Anguish was the utterest—then—
To perish, or to live?   25

I heard a Fly buzz—when I died

I heard a Fly buzz—when I died—
The Stillness in the Room
Was like the Stillness in the Air—
Between the Heaves of Storm—

The Eyes around—had wrung them dry—   5
And Breaths were gathering firm
For the last Onset—when the King
Be witnessed—in the Room—

---

1. **Maelstrom:** an ocean whirlpool.   21. **Gibbets:** gallows.

I willed my Keepsakes—Signed away
What portion of me be   10
Assignable—and then it was
There interposed a Fly—

With Blue—uncertain stumbling Buzz—
Between the light—and me—
And then the Windows failed—and then   15
I could not see to see—

It was not Death, for I stood up

It was not Death, for I stood up,
And all the Dead, lie down—
It was not Night, for all the Bells
Put out their Tongues, for Noon.

It was not Frost, for on my Flesh   5
I felt Siroccos—crawl—
Nor Fire—for just my Marble feet
Could keep a Chancel, cool—

And yet, it tasted, like them all,
The Figures I have seen   10
Set orderly, for Burial,
Reminded me, of mine—

As if my life were shaven,
And fitted to a frame,
And could not breathe without a key,   15
And 'twas like Midnight, some—

When everything that ticked—has stopped—
And Space stares all around—
Or Grisly frosts—first Autumn morns,
Repeal the Beating Ground—   20

But, most, like Chaos—Stopless—cool—
Without a Chance, or Spar—
Or even a Report of Land—
To justify—Despair.

6. **Siroccos:** a hot desert wind.   8. **Chancel:** sanctuary of a church.

Departed—to the Judgment

Departed—to the Judgment—
A Mighty Afternoon—
Great Clouds—like Ushers—leaning—
Creation—looking on—

The Flesh—Surrendered—Cancelled—   5
The Bodiless—begun—
Two Worlds—like Audiences—disperse—
And leave the Soul—alone—

I like to see it lap the Miles

I like to see it lap the Miles—
And lick the Valleys up—
And stop to feed itself at Tanks—
And then—prodigious step

Around a Pile of Mountains—   5
And supercilious peer
In Shanties—by the sides of Roads—
And then a Quarry pare

To fit its sides
And crawl between   10
Complaining all the while
In horrid—hooting stanza—
Then chase itself down Hill—

And neigh like Boanerges—
Then—prompter than a Star   15
Stop—docile and omnipotent
At it's own stable door—

Because I could not stop for Death

Because I could not stop for Death—
He kindly stopped for me—
The Carriage held but just Ourselves—
And Immortality.

14. **Boanerges:** in Mark 3: 17, the name
given by Christ to James and John, literally
"sons of thunder."

We slowly drove—He knew no haste   5
And I had put away
My labor and my leisure too,
For His Civility—

We passed the School, where Children strove
At Recess—in the Ring—   10
We passed the Fields of Gazing Grain—
We passed the Setting Sun—

Or rather—He passed Us—
The Dews drew quivering and chill—
For only Gossamer, my Gown—   15
My Tippet—only Tulle—

We paused before a House that seemed
A Swelling of the Ground—
The Roof was scarcely visible—
The Cornice—in the Ground—   20

Since then—'tis Centuries—and yet
Feels shorter than the Day
I first surmised the Horses Heads
Were toward Eternity—

She rose to His Requirement—dropt

She rose to His Requirement—dropt
The Playthings of Her Life
To take the honorable Work
Of Woman, and of Wife—

If ought She missed in Her new Day,   5
Of Amplitude, or Awe—
Or first Prospective—Or the Gold
In using, wear away,

It lay unmentioned—as the Sea
Develope Pearl, and Weed,   10
But only to Himself—be known
The Fathoms they abide—

16. **Tippet . . . Tulle:** a scarf of thin
material.

It dropped so low—in my Regard

It dropped so low—in my Regard—
I heard it hit the Ground—
And go to pieces on the Stones
At bottom of my Mind—

Yet blamed the Fate that fractured—*less*   5
Than I reviled Myself,
For entertaining Plated Wares
Upon my Silver Shelf—

Presentiment—is that long Shadow—on the Lawn

Presentiment—is that long Shadow—on the Lawn—
Indicative that Suns go down—

The Notice to the startled Grass
That Darkness—is about to pass—

Finding is the first Act

Finding is the first Act
The second, loss,
Third, Expedition for
The "Golden Fleece"

Fourth, no Discovery—   5
Fifth, no Crew—
Finally, no Golden Fleece—
Jason—sham—too.

A narrow Fellow in the Grass

A narrow Fellow in the Grass
Occasionally rides—
You may have met Him—did you not
His notice sudden is—

The Grass divides as with a Comb—   5
A spotted shaft is seen—
And then it closes at your feet
And opens further on—

4. **Golden Fleece:** To regain his kingdom
Jason and his crew, the Argonauts, brought
the magical Golden Fleece to Greece.

He likes a Boggy Acre
A Floor too cool for Corn—   10
Yet when a Boy, and Barefoot—
I more than once at Noon
Have passed, I thought, a Whip lash
Unbraiding in the Sun
When stooping to secure it   15
It wrinkled, and was gone—

Several of Nature's People
I know, and they know me—
I feel for them a transport
Of cordiality—   20

But never met this Fellow
Attended, or alone
Without a tighter breathing
And Zero at the Bone—

He preached upon "Breadth" till it argued him narrow

He preached upon "Breadth" till it argued him narrow—
The Broad are too broad to define
And of "Truth" until it proclaimed him a Liar—
The Truth never flaunted a Sign—

Simplicity fled from his counterfeit presence   5
As Gold the Pyrites would shun—
What confusion would cover the innocent Jesus
To meet so enabled a Man!

Those—dying then

Those—dying then,
Knew where they went—
They went to God's Right Hand—
That Hand is amputated now
And God cannot be found—   5

The abdication of Belief
Makes the Behavior small—
Better an ignis fatuus
Than no illume at all—

8. **ignis fatuus:** false light; will o' the wisp.

Apparently with no surprise

Apparently with no surprise
To any happy Flower
The Frost beheads it at it's play—
In accidental power—
The blonde Assassin passes on—   5
The Sun proceeds unmoved
To measure off another Day
For an Approving God.

Elysium is as far as to

Elysium is as far as to
The very nearest Room
If in that Room a Friend await
Felicity or Doom—
What fortitude the Soul contains,   5
That it can so endure
The accent of a coming Foot—
The opening of a Door—

GERARD MANLEY HOPKINS
[1844–1889]

God's Grandeur

The world is charged with the grandeur of God.
    It will flame out, like shining from shook foil;
    It gathers to a greatness, like the ooze of oil
Crushed. Why do men then now not reck his rod?
Generations have trod, have trod, have trod;   5
    And all is seared with trade; bleared, smeared with toil;
    And wears man's smudge and shares man's smell: the soil
Is bare now, nor can foot feel, being shod.

And for all this, nature is never spent;
    There lives the dearest freshness deep down things;   10
And though the last lights off the black West went
    Oh, morning, at the brown brink eastward, springs—
Because the Holy Ghost over the bent
    World broods with warm breast and with ah! bright wings.

3. **oil:** The minute contributions of each   4. **reck:** heed.
crushed olive gradually mount to a great
volume of oil.

The Windhover

To Christ Our Lord

I caught this morning morning's minion, kingdom of daylight's
    dauphin, dapple-dawn-drawn Falcon, in his riding
Of the rolling level underneath him steady air, and striding
High there, how he rung upon the rein of a wimpling wing
In his ecstasy! then off, off forth on swing,
    As a skate's heel sweeps smooth on a bow-bend; the hurl and
      gliding   5
    Rebuffed the big wind. My heart in hiding
Stirred for a bird,—the achieve of, the mastery of the thing!

Brute beauty and valor and act, oh, air, pride, plume, here
    Buckle! AND the fire that breaks from three then, a billion
Times told lovelier, more dangerous, O my chevalier!   10

No wonder of it: shéer plód makes plough down sillion
Shine, and blue-bleak embers, ah my dear,
Fall, gall themselves, and gash gold-vermilion.

Pied Beauty

    Glory be to God for dappled things—
        For skies of couple-color as a brinded cow;
            For rose-moles all in stipple upon trout that swim;
    Fresh-firecoal chestnut falls; finches' wings;
        Landscape plotted and pieced—fold, fallow, and plough;   5
        And áll trádes, their gear and tackle and trim.
    All things counter, original, spare, strange;
        Whatever is fickle, freckled (who knows how?)
        With swift, slow; sweet, sour; adazzle, dim;
    He fathers-forth whose beauty is past change: 10
            Praise him.

Windhover: hoverer in the wind: the kestrel, a small falcon.
1. minion: paramour, favorite (as in a court).
1. dauphin: heir to a throne.
3. rung . . . rein: circled by braking with one wing. **wimpling:** rippling.
9. Buckle: join together (?); grapple (?); break (?).
10. chevalier: literally, knight. Christ.

11. sillion: ridge between plowed furrows.
13. gash: The seemingly dead embers break open and show the glow within. Christ's blood.

2. brinded: brindled, streaked.
4. chestnut falls: (roasted) chestnuts fallen from the husks.
7. counter: contrary.

Inversnaid

This darksome burn, horseback brown,
His rollrock highroad roaring down,
In coop and in comb the fleece of his foam
Flutes and low to the lake falls home.

A windpuff-bonnet of fáwn-fróth　　　　　　　　　　5
Turns and twindles over the broth
Of a pool so pitchblack, féll-frówning,
It rounds and rounds Despair to drowning.

Degged with dew, dappled with dew
Are the groins of the braes that the brook treads through,　　10
Wiry heathpacks, flitches of fern,
And the beadbonny ash that sits over the burn.

What would the world be, once bereft
Of wet and of wildness? Let them be left,
O let them be left, wildness and wet;　　　　　　　　　　15
Long live the weeds and the wilderness yet.

Carrion Comfort

Not, I'll not, carrion comfort, Despair, not feast on thee;
Not untwist—slack they may be—these last strands of man
In me, or, most weary, cry *I can no more.* I can;
Can something, hope, wish day come, not choose not to be.
But ah, but O thou terrible, why wouldst thou rude on me　　5
Thy wring-world right foot rock? lay a lionlimb against me? scan
With darksome devouring eyes my bruisèd bones? and fan,
O in turns of tempest, me heaped there; me frantic to avoid thee and
　　flee?
Why? That my chaff might fly; my grain lie, sheer and clear.
Nay in all that toil, that coil, since (seems) I kissed the rod,　　10
Hand rather, my heart lo! lapped strength, stole joy, would laugh,
　　chéer.
Cheer whom though? the hero whose heaven-handling flung me, fóot
　　tród
Me? or me that fought him? O which one? is it each one? That
　　night, that year
Of now done darkness I wretch lay wrestling with (my God!) my
　　God.

Inversnaid: mountainous spot on shore of　　10. **braes:** sloping shores.
Loch Lomond.
1. **burn:** swift brook.
3. **comb:** coomb, ravine.
7. **féll:** fierce; also, a moor, barren hill.　　10. **coil:** uproar.

No worst, there is none

No worst, there is none. Pitched past pitch of grief,
More pangs will, schooled at forepangs, wilder wring.
Comforter, where, where is your comforting?
Mary, mother of us, where is your relief?
My cries heave, herds-long; huddle in a main, a chief   5
Woe, world-sorrow; on an age-old anvil wince and sing—
Then lull, then leave off. Fury had shrieked "No ling-
ering! Let me be fell: force I must be brief."

O the mind, mind has mountains; cliffs of fall
Frightful, sheer, no-man-fathomed. Hold them cheap   10
May who ne'er hung there. Nor does long our small
Durance deal with that steep or deep. Here! creep,
Wretch, under a comfort serves in a whirlwind: all
Life death does end and each day dies with sleep.

That Nature Is a Heraclitean Fire and of the Comfort of the Resurrection

Cloud-puffball, torn tufts, tossed pillows flaunt forth, then chevy
    on an air-
built thoroughfare: heaven-roysterers, in gay-gangs they throng;
    they glitter in marches.
Down roughcast, down dazzling whitewash, wherever an elm
    arches,
Shivelights and shadowtackle in long lashes lace, lance, and pair.
Delightfully the bright wind boisterous ropes, wrestles, beats earth
    bare   5
Of yestertempest's creases; in pool and rut peel parches
Squandering ooze to squeezed dough, crust, dust; stanches, starches
Squadroned masks and manmarks treadmire toil there
Footfretted in it. Million-fuelèd, nature's bonfire burns on.

---

8. **fell:** cruel and fierce. **force:** perforce,
by necessity.
12. **Durance:** endurance.

Heraclitean: Heraclitus (c. 535–c. 475
B.C.) taught that constant change and union
of opposites are characteristic of nature;
that fire is the essence of everything; and
that man's soul and mind are a fire,
partaking of a universal soul-fire.
1. **chevy:** scamper.
4. **Shivelights:** strips of light. **shadowtackle:** shadows like the complicated rope
tackle of a ship.
6. **peel:** the surface of the earth.
7. **stanches, starches:** stops the flow and
stiffens (the wet foot prints and other
marks of man "fretted" in the earth).

But quench her bonniest, dearest to her, her clearest-selvèd spark   10
Man, how fast his firedint, his mark on mind, is gone!
Both are in an unfathomable, all is in an enormous dark
Drowned. O pity and indignation! Manshape, that shone
Sheer off, disseveral, a star, death blots black out; nor mark
        Is any of him at all so stark   15
But vastness blurs and time beats level. Enough! the Resurrection,
A heart's clarion! Away grief's grasping, joyless days, dejection.
        Across my foundering desk shone
A beacon, an eternal beam. Flesh fade, and mortal trash
Fall to the residuary worm; world's wildfire, leave but ash: 20
        In a flash, at a trumpet's crash,
I am all at once what Christ is, since he was what I am, and
This Jack, joke, poor potsherd, patch, matchwood, immortal diamond,
        Is immortal diamond.

Thou art indeed just, Lord

*Justus quidem tu es, Domine, si disputem tecum: verumtamen
justa loquar ad te: Quare via impiorum prosperatur? etc.*

Thou art indeed just, Lord, if I contend
With thee; but, sir, so what I plead is just.
Why do sinners' ways prosper? and why must
Disappointment all I endeavour end?
    Wert thou my enemy, O thou my friend,   5
How wouldst thou worse, I wonder, than thou dost
Defeat, thwart me? Oh, the sots and thralls of lust
Do in spare hours more thrive than I that spend,
Sir, life upon thy cause. See, banks and brakes
Now, leavèd how thick! lacèd they are again   10
With fretty chervil, look, and fresh wind shakes
Them; birds build—but not I build; no, but strain,
Time's eunuch, and not breed one work that wakes.
Mine, O thou lord of life, send my roots rain.

14. **disseveral**: separated, each individual
to himself.
20. **residuary**: inheriting.

Justus . . . etc: opening words of Jeremiah
12, which Hopkins adapts and modifies
in the first three lines of the poem.
9. **brakes**: ferns.
11. **fretty**: with fretted edges.

WILLIAM BUTLER YEATS

[1865–1939]

Easter 1916

I have met them at close of day
Coming with vivid faces
From counter or desk among grey
Eighteenth-century houses.
I have passed with a nod of the head   5
Or polite meaningless words,
Or have lingered awhile and said
Polite meaningless words,
And thought before I had done
Of a mocking tale or a gibe   10
To please a companion
Around the fire at the club,
Being certain that they and I
But lived where motley is worn:
All changed, changed utterly: 15
A terrible beauty is born.

That woman's days were spent
In ignorant good-will,
Her nights in argument
Until her voice grew shrill.   20
What voice more sweet than hers
When, young and beautiful,
She rode to harriers?
This man had kept a school
And rode our wingèd horse;   25
This other his helper and friend
Was coming into his force;
He might have won fame in the end,
So sensitive his nature seemed,
So daring and sweet his thought.   30
This other man I had dreamed

Easter 1916: beginning of the week-long Easter Rebellion against the English. All the characters mentioned in the poem were executed.
14. motley: vari-colored costume of a court jester.

17. That woman: Constance Gore-Booth. See poem with her name in title, below. Harriers are small hawks.
24. This man: Patrick Pearse. Pegasus is the horse of the muses: Pearse was a poet. His "friend" was Thomas Mac-Donagh.

A drunken, vainglorious lout.
He had done most bitter wrong
To some who are near my heart,
Yet I number him in the song;   35
He, too, has resigned his part
In the casual comedy;
He, too, has been changed in his turn,
Transformed utterly:
A terrible beauty is born.   40

Hearts with one purpose alone
Through summer and winter seem
Enchanted to a stone
To trouble the living stream.
The horse that comes from the road,   45
The rider, the birds that range
From cloud to tumbling cloud,
Minute by minute they change;
A shadow of cloud on the stream
Changes minute by minute;   50
A horse-hoof slides on the brim,
And a horse plashes within it;
The long-legged moor-hens dive,
And hens to moor-cocks call;
Minute by minute they live;   55
The stone's in the midst of all.

Too long a sacrifice
Can make a stone of the heart.
O when may it suffice?
That is Heaven's part, our part   60
To murmur name upon name,
As a mother names her child
When sleep at last has come
On limbs that had run wild.
What is it but nightfall?   65
No, no, not night but death;
Was it needless death after all?
For England may keep faith
For all that is done and said.
We know their dream; enough   70
To know they dreamed and are dead;

32. **lout**: John MacBride, who for two
years was married to Maud Gonne, Yeats's
great love. She left MacBride.

And what if excess of love
Bewildered them till they died?
I write it out in a verse—
MacDonagh and MacBride   75
And Connolly and Pearse
Now and in time to be,
Wherever green is worn,
Are changed, changed utterly:
A terrible beauty is born.   80

An Irish Airman Foresees His Death

I know that I shall meet my fate
Somewhere among the clouds above;
Those that I fight I do not hate,
Those that I guard I do not love;
My country is Kiltartan Cross,   5
My countrymen Kiltartan's poor,
No likely end could bring them loss
Or leave them happier than before.
Nor law, nor duty bade me fight,
Nor public men, nor cheering crowds,   10
A lonely impulse of delight
Drove to this tumult in the clouds;
I balanced all, brought all to mind,
The years to come seemed waste of breath,
A waste of breath the years behind   15
In balance with this life, this death.

The Second Coming

Turning and turning in the widening gyre
The falcon cannot hear the falconer;
Things fall apart: the centre cannot hold;
Mere anarchy is loosed upon the world,
The blood-dimmed tide is loosed, and everywhere   5
The ceremony of innocence is drowned;
The best lack all conviction, while the worst
Are full of passionate intensity.

1. **gyre:** spiral.

Surely some revelation is at hand;
Surely the Second Coming is at hand.   10
The Second Coming! Hardly are those words out
When a vast image out of *Spiritus Mundi*
Troubles my sight: somewhere in sands of the desert
A shape with lion body and the head of a man,
A gaze blank and pitiless as the sun,   15
Is moving its slow thighs, while all about it
Reel shadows of the indignant desert birds.
The darkness drops again; but now I know
That twenty centuries of stony sleep
Were vexed to nightmare by a rocking cradle,   20
And what rough beast, its hour come round at last,
Slouches towards Bethlehem to be born?

A Prayer for My Daughter

Once more the storm is howling, and half hid
Under this cradle-hood and coverlid
My child sleeps on. There is no obstacle
But Gregory's wood and one bare hill
Whereby the haystack- and roof-levelling wind,   5
Bred on the Atlantic, can be stayed;
And for an hour I have walked and prayed
Because of the great gloom that is in mind.

I have walked and prayed for this young child an hour
And heard the sea-wind scream upon the tower,   10
And under the arches of the bridge, and scream
In the elms above the flooded stream;
Imagining in excited reverie
That the future years had come,
Dancing to a frenzied drum,   15
Out of the murderous innocence of the sea.

13. **Spiritus Mundi:** spirit of the universe. An originally Neo-Platonic conception of an entity which, generated by a higher power, generates everything in space and time.
20. **cradle:** Yeats believed that one cycle of history came to an end with the birth of Christ, and that another is ending today

4. **Gregory's wood:** wood near Yeats's residence, a refitted Norman tower in Galway.

May she be granted beauty and yet not
Beauty to make a stranger's eye distraught,
Or hers before a looking-glass, for such,
Being made beautiful overmuch,   20
Consider beauty a sufficient end,
Lose natural kindness and maybe
The heart-revealing intimacy
That chooses right, and never find a friend.

Helen being chosen found life flat and dull   25
And later had much trouble from a fool,
While that great Queen, that rose out of the spray,
Being fatherless could have her way
Yet chose a bandy-legged smith for man.
It's certain that fine women eat   30
A crazy salad with their meat
Whereby the Horn of Plenty is undone.

In courtesy I'd have her chiefly learned;
Hearts are not had as a gift but hearts are earned
By those that are not entirely beautiful;   35
Yet many, that have played the fool
For beauty's very self, has charm made wise,
And many a poor man that has roved,
Loved and thought himself beloved,
From a glad kindness cannot take his eyes.   40

May she become a flourishing hidden tree
That all her thoughts may like the linnet be,
And have no business but dispensing round
Their magnanimities of sound,
Nor but in merriment begin a chase,   45
Nor but in merriment a quarrel.
O may she live like some green laurel
Rooted in one dear perpetual place.

My mind, because the minds that I have loved,
The sort of beauty that I have approved,   50
Prosper but little, has dried up of late,
Yet knows that to be choked with hate
May well be of all evil chances chief.
If there's no hatred in a mind
Assault and battery of the wind   55
Can never tear the linnet from the leaf.

26. **fool:** Paris carried off Helen from her husband. His vanity and unsteadiness emerge in the *Iliad*.

29. **smith:** Vulcan, god of fire and metalwork, was the husband of Venus.

42. **linnet:** a little bird, not found in America.

An intellectual hatred is the worst,
So let her think opinions are accursed.
Have I not seen the loveliest woman born
Out of the mouth of Plenty's horn,   60
Because of her opinionated mind
Barter that horn and every good
By quiet natures understood
For an old bellows full of angry wind?

Considering that, all hatred driven hence,   65
The soul recovers radical innocence
And learns at last that it is self-delighting.
Self-appeasing, self-affrighting,
And that its own sweet will is Heaven's will;
She can, though every face should scowl   70
And every windy quarter howl
Or every bellows burst, be happy still.

And may her bridegroom bring her to a house
Where all's accustomed, ceremonious;
For arrogance and hatred are the wares   75
Peddled in the thoroughfares.
How but in custom and in ceremony
Are innocence and beauty born?
Ceremony's a name for the rich horn,
And custom for the spreading laurel tree.   80

Two Songs from a Play

I

I saw a staring virgin stand
Where holy Dionysus died,
And tear the heart out of his side,
And lay the heart upon her hand
And bear that beating heart away;   5
And then did all the Muses sing
Of Magnus Annus at the spring,
As though God's death were but a play.

64. **bellows:** Maud Gonne remained a
passionate nationalist.

1. **virgin:** The mother of Christ begins a
new cycle, ending that of ancient civilization, symbolized by Dionysus, whose
cult of physical death and rebirth was
celebrated by virgins who ritually tore
apart and ate animals, as Dionysus had
been treated. Magnus Annus is the Great,
or Platonic, Year (many thousands of
regular years) after which everything
returns to its beginning to repeat the past.
The god both dies and is reborn, so that
God's death is in one sense a symbol, "but
a play," and not final. Also Greek tragedy
originated in the rites of Dionysus. The
complexity of the "Two Songs" cannot be
done justice to in this and following notes.
The reader must look for much more than
can be explained here.

Another Troy must rise and set,
Another lineage feed the crow,   10
Another Argo's painted prow
Drive to a flashier bauble yet.
The Roman Empire stood appalled:
It dropped the reins of peace and war
When that fierce virgin and her Star   15
Out of the fabulous darkness called.

2

In pity for man's darkening thought
He walked that room and issued thence
In Galilean turbulence;
The Babylonian starlight brought   20
A fabulous, formless darkness in;
Odor of blood when Christ was slain
Made all Platonic tolerance vain
And vain all Doric discipline.

Everything that man esteems   25
Endures a moment or a day.
Love's pleasure drives his love away,
The painter's brush consumes his dreams;
The herald's cry, the soldier's tread
Exhaust his glory and his might: 30
Whatever flames upon the night
Man's own resinous heart has fed.

Leda and the Swan

A sudden blow: the great wings beating still
Above the staggering girl, her thighs caressed
By the dark webs, her nape caught in his bill,
He holds her helpless breast upon his breast.

11. **Argo:** boat which carried Jason and companions to win the Golden Fleece: one of the great mythical patterns of ancient civilization.
15. **Star:** the day-star, Christ; also the star of Bethlehem. The Virgin is called Star of the Sea. For "fabulous darkness" see line 21.
19. **Galilean:** Christ, who came to dispel the "darkness" of the earlier cycle, which began with "Babylonian starlight." Two virtues of the earlier cycle—(1) the Socratic ("Platonic") openness to all ideas and rational questioning of all tradition, and (2) the sturdy ("Doric") belief in the individual's ability to discipline himself into excellence without superhuman aid—yield before the categorical demand and mystery of Christ's suffering and death.
32. **resinous:** A pine knot used as a torch contains resin that burns with a bright, crackling flame.

Leda: Zeus visited Leda in the form of a swan. This encounter was a favored subject in classical art.

How can those terrified vague fingers push   5
The feathered glory from her loosening thighs?
And how can body, laid in that white rush,
But feel the strange heart beating where it lies?

A shudder in the loins engenders there
The broken wall, the burning roof and tower   10
And Agamemnon dead.
              Being so caught up,
So mastered by the brute blood of the air,
Did she put on his knowledge with his power
Before the indifferent beak could let her drop?

Among School Children

1

I walk through the long schoolroom questioning;
A kind old nun in a white hood replies;
The children learn to cipher and to sing,
To study reading-books and history,
To cut and sew, be neat in everything   5
In the best modern way—the children's eyes
In momentary wonder stare upon
A sixty-year-old smiling public man.

2

I dream of a Ledaean body, bent
Above a sinking fire, a tale that she   10
Told of a harsh reproof, or trivial event
That changed some childish day to tragedy—
Told, and it seemed that our two natures blent
Into a sphere from youthful sympathy,
Or else, to alter Plato's parable,   15
Into the yolk and white of the one shell.

10. **broken wall:** Zeus fathered Helen on Leda; Yeats imagined the whole tragic story of the Greeks and Trojans as generated here. When Agamemnon, the Greek leader, came home, he was murdered by his wife and her lover. Yeats implies elsewhere that he sees a parallel between the descent of the divine here to impregnate a mortal and the later descent to the Virgin Mary. For him each of these acts began a cycle of history.

9. **Ledaean:** beautiful as Leda and Helen of Troy, her daughter. Yeats means his early beloved, Maud Gonne. Helen was born from an egg (see line 16). Her father was Zeus in the figure of a swan.
14. **sphere:** the myth that humans were originally spherical, but split into two halves, which now yearn for each other, is told in Plato's *Symposium*.

3

And thinking of that fit of grief or rage
I look upon one child or t'other there
And wonder if she stood so at that age—
For even daughters of the swan can share   20
Something of every paddler's heritage—
And had that color upon cheek or hair,
And thereupon my heart is driven wild:
She stands before me as a living child.

4

Her present image floats into the mind—   25
Did Quattrocento finger fashion it
Hollow of cheek as though it drank the wind
And took a mess of shadows for its meat?
And I though never of Ledaean kind
Had pretty plumage once—enough of that,   30
Better to smile on all that smile, and show
There is a comfortable kind of scarecrow.

5

What youthful mother, a shape upon her lap
Honey of generation had betrayed,
And that must sleep, shriek, struggle to escape   35
As recollection or the drug decide,
Would think her son, did she but see that shape
With sixty or more winters on its head,
A compensation for the pang of his birth,
Or the uncertainty of his setting forth?   40

6

Plato thought nature but a spume that plays
Upon a ghostly paradigm of things;
Soldier Aristotle played the taws
Upon the bottom of a king of kings;

---

26. **Quattrocento:** (Ital.) 15th century. Some of the female figures in Botticelli's painting and children in the reliefs of Andrea della Robbia look like this.
34. **Honey:** Yeats develops a Neoplatonic doctrine that "honey of generation" tempts souls to be born from a happier otherworld into this one. He means that the soul will recollect its former happiness or be drugged by the honey to forget.

41. **spume:** the foam thrown up by the underlying spiritual pattern ("paradigm") of reality.
43. **Aristotle:** Unlike Plato, he thought that our world of time and space possessed reality, and was not just "spume" thrown up by a spiritual reality. He was the tutor of Alexander the Great ("taws": strap).

World-famous golden-thighed Pythagoras   45
Fingered upon a fiddle-stick or strings
What a star sang and careless Muses heard:
Old clothes upon old sticks to scare a bird.

7

Both nuns and mothers worship images,
But those the candles light are not as those   50
That animate a mother's reveries,
But keep a marble or a bronze repose.
And yet they too break hearts—O Presences
That passion, piety or affection knows,
And that all heavenly glory symbolize—   55
O self-born mockers of man's enterprise;

8

Labor is blossoming or dancing where
The body is not bruised to pleasure soul,
Nor beauty born out of its own despair,
Nor blear-eyed wisdom out of midnight oil.   60
O chestnut tree, great rooted blossomer,
Are you the leaf, the blossom or the bole?
O body swayed to music, O brightening glance,
How can we know the dancer from the dance?

Sailing to Byzantium

I

That is no country for old men. The young
In one another's arms, birds in the trees,
—Those dying generations—at their song,
The salmon-falls, the mackerel-crowded seas,
Fish, flesh, or fowl, commend all summer long   5
Whatever is begotten, born, and dies.
Caught in that sensual music all neglect
Monuments of unageing intellect.

II

An aged man is but a paltry thing,
A tattered coat upon a stick, unless   10
Soul clap its hands and sing, and louder sing
For every tatter in its mortal dress,

---

45. Pythagoras: Greek philosopher who reduced reality to numerical and mathematical relations, as seen in the arithmetical symmetry of musical intervals and in the symmetry and precision of the recurring movements of heavenly bodies. His later followers considered him a god with a golden thigh.
48. Old clothes: See line 32.

Nor is there singing school but studying
Monuments of its own magnificence;
And therefore I have sailed the seas and come   15
To the holy city of Byzantium.

III

O sages standing in God's holy fire
As in the gold mosaic of a wall,
Come from the holy fire, perne in a gyre,
And be the singing-masters of my soul.   20
Consume my heart away; sick with desire
And fastened to a dying animal
It knows not what it is; and gather me
Into the artifice of eternity.

IV

Once out of nature I shall never take   25
My bodily form from any natural thing,
But such a form as Grecian goldsmiths make
Of hammered gold and gold enamelling
To keep a drowsy Emperor awake;
Or set upon a golden bough to sing   30
To lords and ladies of Byzantium
Of what is past, or passing, or to come.

In Memory of Eva Gore-Booth
and Con Markiewicz

The light of evening, Lissadell,
Great windows open to the south,
Two girls in silk kimonos, both
Beautiful, one a gazelle.

16. **Byzantium:** modern Istanbul. Byzantine art, notably the mosaic work with glittering gold background covering the interior walls and inner domes of churches, is said to create a fixed world of timeless and beautiful significances, suitable to the otherworldly nature of its subject-matter.
19. **perne in a gyre:** Yeats means "revolve in a spiral." A perne is a spool or bobbin: the Fates spun a thread for each man's fate, and Yeats saw this circular motion, and the spiral motion of a gyre, as a symbol of spiritual life and transformation, and of cyclical change.

27. **form:** Yeats says that he read of a gold and silver tree, with artificial singing birds, in the Emperor's palace.

In . . . Markiewicz: two sisters, members of the Sligo county aristocracy. Constance Gore-Booth (Con Markiewicz) turned from a charming girl into an embittered nationalist.
1. **Lissadell:** the home of the Gore-Booths in County Sligo.

But a raving autumn shears   5
Blossom from the summer's wreath;
The older is condemned to death,
Pardoned, drags out lonely years
Conspiring among the ignorant.
I know not what the younger dreams—   10
Some vague Utopia—and she seems,
When withered old and skeleton-gaunt,
An image of such politics.
Many a time I think to seek
One or the other out and speak   15
Of that old Georgian mansion, mix
Pictures of the mind, recall
That table and the talk of youth,
Two girls in silk kimonos, both
Beautiful, one a gazelle.   20
Dear shadows, now you know it all,
All the folly of a fight
With a common wrong or right.
The innocent and the beautiful
Have no enemy but time;   25
Arise and bid me strike a match
And strike another till time catch;
Should the conflagration climb,
Run till all the sages know.
We the great gazebo built,   30
They convicted us of guilt;
Bid me strike a match and blow.

A Dialogue of Self and Soul

I

MY SOUL. I summon to the winding ancient stair;
Set all your mind upon the steep ascent,
Upon the broken, crumbling battlement,
Upon the breathless starlit air,
Upon the star that marks the hidden pole;   5
Fix every wandering thought upon
That quarter where all thought is done:
Who can distinguish darkness from the soul?

30. **gazebo:** literally, a tower or turret
built to view an expanse of scenery.

MY SELF. The consecrated blade upon my knees
Is Sato's ancient blade, still as it was,   10
Still razor-keen, still like a looking-glass
Unspotted by the centuries;
That flowering, silken, old embroidery, torn
From some court-lady's dress and round
The wooden scabbard bound and wound,   15
Can, tattered, still protect, faded adorn.

MY SOUL. Why should the imagination of a man
Long past his prime remember things that are
Emblematical of love and war?
Think of ancestral night that can,   20
If but imagination scorn the earth
And intellect its wandering
To this and that and t'other thing,
Deliver from the crime of death and birth.

MY SELF. Montashigi, third of his family, fashioned it   25
Five hundred years ago, about it lie
Flowers from I know not what embroidery—
Heart's purple—and all these I set
For emblems of the day against the tower
Emblematical of the night,   30
And claim as by a soldier's right
A charter to commit the crime once more.

MY SOUL. Such fullness in that quarter overflows
And falls into the basin of the mind
That man is stricken deaf and dumb and blind,   35
For intellect no longer knows
Is from the *Ought*, or *Knower* from the *Known*—
That is to say, ascends to Heaven;
Only the dead can be forgiven;
But when I think of that my tongue's a stone.   40

II

MY SELF. A living man is blind and drinks his drop.
What matter if the ditches are impure?
What matter if I live it all once more?
Endure that toil of growing up;
The ignominy of boyhood; the distress   45
Of boyhood changing into man;
The unfinished man and his pain
Brought face to face with his own clumsiness;

10. **Sato:** This Japanese, giving Yeats the sword, had said that it was a symbol of   life, and its embroidered sheath a symbol of beauty.

The finished man among his enemies?—
How in the name of Heaven can he escape   50
That defiling and disfigured shape
The mirror of malicious eyes
Casts upon his eyes until at last
He thinks that shape must be his shape?
And what's the good of an escape   55
If honor find him in the wintry blast?

I am content to live it all again
And yet again, if it be life to pitch
Into the frog-spawn of a blind man's ditch,
A blind man battering blind men;   60
Or into that most fecund ditch of all,
The folly that man does
Or must suffer, if he woos
A proud woman not kindred of his soul.

I am content to follow to its source   65
Every event in action or in thought;
Measure the lot; forgive myself the lot!
When such as I cast out remorse
So great a sweetness flows into the breast
We must laugh and we must sing,   70
We are blest by everything,
Everything we look upon is blest.

Byzantium

The unpurged images of day recede;
The Emperor's drunken soldiery are abed;
Night resonance recedes, night-walkers' song
After great cathedral gong;
A starlit or a moonlit dome disdains   5
All that man is,
All mere complexities,
The fury and the mire of human veins.

Before me floats an image, man or shade,
Shade more than man, more image than a shade;   10
For Hades' bobbin bound in mummy-cloth
May unwind the winding path;

11. **bobbin:** See "perne" line 19 in "Sailing to Byzantium." A mummy was wrapped in a long strip of cloth as a bobbin is wound. The unwinding reveals the speaker's guide into the other world.

A mouth that has no moisture and no breath
Breathless mouths may summon;
I hail the superhuman;   15
I call it death-in-life and life-in-death.

Miracle, bird or golden handiwork,
More miracle than bird or handiwork,
Planted on the star-lit golden bough,
Can like the cocks of Hades crow,   20
Or, by the moon embittered, scorn aloud
In glory of changeless metal
Common bird or petal
And all complexities of mire or blood.

At midnight on the Emperor's pavement flit   25
Flames that no faggot feeds, nor steel has lit,
Nor storm disturbs, flames begotten of flame,
Where blood-begotten spirits come
And all complexities of fury leave.
Dying into a dance,   30
An agony of trance,
An agony of flame that cannot singe a sleeve.

Astraddle on the dolphin's mire and blood,
Spirit after spirit! The smithies break the flood,
The golden smithies of the Emperor!   35
Marbles of the dancing floor
Break bitter furies of complexity,
Those images that yet
Fresh images beget,
That dolphin-torn, that gong-tormented sea.   40

Crazy Jane Talks with the Bishop

I met the Bishop on the road
And much said he and I.
"Those breasts are flat and fallen now,
Those veins must soon be dry;
Live in a heavenly mansion   5
Not in some foul sty."

20. **cocks:** Outside the world of time, they crowed to proclaim the great cycles for mortals.
26. **Flames:** purgatorial flames to cleanse the earthly spirits.
33. **dolphin:** a symbol of striving from this world to another one (as the dolphin jumps from sea into air).

Crazy Jane: appears in a series of poems as a crone whose madness is part wisdom.

"Fair and foul are near of kin,
And fair needs foul," I cried.
"My friends are gone, but that's a truth
Nor grave nor bed denied,   10
Learned in bodily lowliness
And in the heart's pride.

"A woman can be proud and stiff
When on love intent;
But Love has pitched his mansion in   15
The place of excrement;
For nothing can be sole or whole
That has not been rent."

ROBERT FROST

[1874–1963]

The Wood-Pile

Out walking in the frozen swamp one gray day,
I paused and said, "I will turn back from here.
No, I will go on farther—and we shall see."
The hard snow held me, save where now and then
One foot went through. The view was all in lines   5
Straight up and down of tall slim trees
Too much alike to mark or name a place by
So as to say for certain I was here
Or somewhere else: I was just far from home.
A small bird flew before me. He was careful   10
To put a tree between us when he lighted,
And say no word to tell me who he was
Who was so foolish as to think what *he* thought.
He thought that I was after him for a feather—
The white one in his tail; like one who takes   15
Everything said as personal to himself.
One flight out sideways would have undeceived him.
And then there was a pile of wood for which
I forgot him and let his little fear
Carry him off the way I might have gone,   20
Without so much as wishing him good-night.

He went behind it to make his last stand.
It was a cord of maple, cut and split
And piled—and measured, four by four by eight.
And not another like it could I see.   25
No runner tracks in this year's snow looped near it.
And it was older sure than this year's cutting,
Or even last year's or the year's before.
The wood was gray and the bark warping off it
And the pile somewhat sunken. Clematis   30
Had wound strings round and round it like a bundle.
What held it though on one side was a tree
Still growing, and on one a stake and prop,
These latter about to fall. I thought that only
Someone who lived in turning to fresh tasks   35
Could so forget his handiwork on which
He spent himself, the labor of his axe,
And leave it there far from a useful fireplace
To warm the frozen swamp as best it could
With the slow smokeless burning of decay.   40

The Cow in Apple Time

Something inspires the only cow of late
To make no more of a wall than an open gate,
And think no more of wall-builders than fools.
Her face is flecked with pomace and she drools
A cider syrup. Having tasted fruit,   5
She scorns a pasture withering to the root.
She runs from tree to tree where lie and sweeten
The windfalls spiked with stubble and worm-eaten.
She leaves them bitten when she has to fly.
She bellows on a knoll against the sky.   10
Her udder shrivels and the milk goes dry.

Range-Finding

The battle rent a cobweb diamond-strung
And cut a flower beside a ground bird's nest
Before it stained a single human breast.
The stricken flower bent double and so hung.
And still the bird revisited her young.   5

30. **Clematis:** a vine of the crowfoot   4. **pomace:** crushed apple pulp.
family.

A butterfly its fall had dispossessed
A moment sought in air his flower of rest,
Then lightly stooped to it and fluttering clung.
On the bare upland pasture there had spread
O'ernight 'twixt mullein stalks a wheel of thread   10
And straining cables wet with silver dew.
A sudden passing bullet shook it dry.
The indwelling spider ran to greet the fly,
But finding nothing, sullenly withdrew.

"*Out, Out—*"

The buzz-saw snarled and rattled in the yard
And made dust and dropped stove-length sticks of wood,
Sweet-scented stuff when the breeze drew across it.
And from there those that lifted eyes could count
Five mountain ranges one behind the other   5
Under the sunset far into Vermont.
And the saw snarled and rattled, snarled and rattled,
As it ran light, or had to bear a load.
And nothing happened: day was all but done.
Call it a day, I wish they might have said   10
To please the boy by giving him the half hour
That a boy counts so much when saved from work.
His sister stood beside them in her apron
To tell them "Supper." At the word, the saw,
As if to prove saws knew what supper meant,   15
Leaped out at the boy's hand, or seemed to leap—
He must have given the hand. However it was,
Neither refused the meeting. But the hand!
The boy's first outcry was a rueful laugh,
As he swung toward them holding up the hand   20
Half in appeal, but half as if to keep
The life from spilling. Then the boy saw all—
Since he was old enough to know, big boy
Doing a man's work, though a child at heart—
He saw all spoiled. "Don't let him cut my hand off— 25
The doctor, when he comes. Don't let him, sister!"
So. But the hand was gone already.

10. **mullein:** a herb of the figwort family.   "**Out, Out—**": "Out, out brief candle," *Macbeth*, V, v, 23.

The doctor put him in the dark of ether.
He lay and puffed his lips out with his breath.
And then—the watcher at his pulse took fright   30
No one believed. They listened at his heart.
Little—less—nothing!—and that ended it.
No more to build on there. And they, since they
Were not the one dead, turned to their affairs.

Fire and Ice

Some say the world will end in fire,
Some say in ice.
From what I've tasted of desire
I hold with those who favor fire.
But if it had to perish twice, .   5
I think I know enough of hate
To say that for destruction ice
Is.also great
And would suffice.

Stopping by Woods on a Snowy Evening

Whose woods these are I think I know.
His house is in the village though;
He will not see me stopping here
To watch his woods fill up with snow.

My little horse must think it queer   5
To stop without a farmhouse near
Between the woods and frozen lake
The darkest evening of the year.

He gives his harness bells a shake
To ask if there is some mistake.   10
The only other sound's the sweep
Of easy wind and downy flake.

The woods are lovely, dark and deep,
But I have promises to keep,
And miles to go before I sleep,   15
And miles to go before I sleep.

To Earthward

Love at the lips was touch
As sweet as I could bear;
And once that seemed too much;
I lived on air

That crossed me from sweet things   5
The flow of—was it musk
From hidden grapevine springs
Down hill at dusk?

I had the swirl and ache
From sprays of honeysuckle   10
That when they're gathered shake
Dew on the knuckle.

I craved strong sweets, but those
Seemed strong when I was young;
The petal of the rose   15
It was that stung.

Now no joy but lacks salt
That is not dashed with pain
And weariness and fault;
I crave the stain   20

Of tears, the aftermark
Of almost too much love,
The sweet of bitter bark
And burning clove.

When stiff and sore and scarred   25
I take away my hand
From leaning on it hard
In grass and sand,

The hurt is not enough:
I long for weight and strength   30
To feel the earth as rough
To all my length.

The Egg and the Machine

He gave the solid rail a hateful kick.
From far away there came an answering tick
And then another tick. He knew the code:
His hate had roused an engine up the road.
He wished when he had had the track alone   5
He had attacked it with a club or stone
And bent some rail wide open like a switch
So as to wreck the engine in the ditch.
Too late though, now, he had himself to thank.
Its click was rising to a nearer clank.   10
Here it came breasting like a horse in skirts.
(He stood well back for fear of scalding squirts.)
Then for a moment all there was was size
Confusion and a roar that drowned the cries
He raised against the gods in the machine.   15
Then once again the sandbank lay serene.
The traveler's eye picked up a turtle trail,
Between the dotted feet a streak of tail,
And followed it to where he made out vague
But certain signs of buried turtle's egg;   20
And probing with one finger not too rough,
He found suspicious sand, and sure enough,
The pocket of a little turtle mine.
If there was one egg in it there were nine,
Torpedo-like, with shell of gritty leather   25
All packed in sand to wait the trump together.
"You'd better not disturb me any more,"
He told the distance, "I am armed for war.
The next machine that has the power to pass
Will get this plasm in its goggle glass."   30

Desert Places

Snow falling and night falling fast, oh, fast
In a field I looked into going past,
And the ground almost covered smooth in snow,
But a few weeds and stubble showing last.

The woods around it have it—it is theirs.   5
All animals are smothered in their lairs.
I am too absent-spirited to count:
The loneliness includes me unawares.

And lonely as it is, that loneliness
Will be more lonely ere it will be less,   10
A blanker whiteness of benighted snow,
With no expression, nothing to express.

They cannot scare me with their empty spaces
Between stars—on stars where no human race is.
I have it in me so much nearer home   15
To scare myself with my own desert places.

Neither Out Far Nor In Deep

The people along the sand
All turn and look one way.
They turn their back on the land.
They look at the sea all day.

As long as it takes to pass   5
A ship keeps raising its hull;
The wetter ground like glass
Reflects a standing gull.

The land may vary more;
But wherever the truth may be—   10
The water comes ashore,
And the people look at the sea.

They cannot look out far.
They cannot look in deep.
But when was that ever a bar   15
To any watch they keep?

Design

I found a dimpled spider, fat and white,
On a white heal-all, holding up a moth
Like a white piece of rigid satin cloth—
Assorted characters of death and blight
Mixed ready to begin the morning right,   5
Like the ingredients of a witches' broth—
A snow-drop spider, a flower like froth,
And dead wings carried like a paper kite.

14. **on . . . race is:** An earlier version reads;
"on stars void of human races."

What had that flower to do with being white,
The wayside blue and innocent heal-all?   10
What brought the kindred spider to that height,
Then steered the white moth thither in the night?
What but design of darkness to appall?—
If design govern in a thing so small.

Provide, Provide

The witch that came (the withered hag)
To wash the steps with pail and rag,
Was once the beauty Abishag,

The picture pride of Hollywood.
Too many fall from great and good   5
For you to doubt the likelihood.

Die early and avoid the fate.
Or if predestined to die late,
Make up your mind to die in state.

Make the whole stock exchange your own!   10
If need be occupy a throne,
Where nobody can call *you* crone.

Some have relied on what they knew;
Others on being simply true.
What worked for them might work for you.   15

No memory of having starred
Atones for later disregard,
Or keeps the end from being hard.

Better to go down dignified
With boughten friendship at your side   20
Than none at all. Provide, provide!

The Silken Tent

She is as in a field a silken tent
At midday when a sunny summer breeze
Has dried the dew and all its ropes relent,
So that in guys it gently sways at ease,
And its supporting central cedar pole,   5

3. **Abishag:** In I Kings 1: 3–4, Abishag, a   aged and dying King David so that he may
beautiful damsel, is brought to lie with the   "get heat."

That is its pinnacle to heavenward
And signifies the sureness of the soul,
Seems to owe naught to any single cord,
But strictly held by none, is loosely bound
By countless silken ties of love and thought   10
To everything on earth the compass round,
And only by one's going slightly taut
In the capriciousness of summer air
Is of the slightest bondage made aware.

All Revelation

A head thrusts in as for the view,
But where it is it thrusts in from
Or what it is it thrusts into
By that Cyb'laean avenue,
And what can of its coming come,   5

And whither it will be withdrawn,
And what take hence or leave behind,
These things the mind has pondered on
A moment and still asking gone.
Strange apparition of the mind!   10

But the impervious geode
Was entered, and its inner crust
Of crystals with a ray cathode
At every point and facet glowed
In answer to the mental thrust.   15

Eyes seeking the response of eyes
Bring out the stars, bring out the flowers,
Thus concentrating earth and skies
So none need be afraid of size.
All revelation has been ours.   20

The Most of It

He thought he kept the universe alone;
For all the voice in answer he could wake
Was but the mocking echo of his own
From some tree-hidden cliff across the lake.
Some morning from the boulder-broken beach   5

---

4. **Cyb'laean:** from Cybele, in ancient times worshipped as the mother of nature; a goddess of fertility.

11. **geode:** a nodule of stone having a cavity lined with crystals.

He would cry out on life, that what it wants
Is not its own love back in copy speech,
But counter-love, original response.
And nothing ever came of what he cried
Unless it was the embodiment that crashed   10
In the cliff's talus on the other side,
And then in the far distant water splashed,
But after a time allowed for it to swim,
Instead of proving human when it neared
And someone else additional to him,   15
As a great buck it powerfully appeared,
Pushing the crumpled water up ahead,
And landed pouring like a waterfall,
And stumbled through the rocks with horny tread,
And forced the underbrush—and that was all.   20

Directive

Back out of all this now too much for us,
Back in a time made simple by the loss
Of detail, burned, dissolved, and broken off
Like graveyard marble sculpture in the weather,
There is a house that is no more a house   5
Upon a farm that is no more a farm
And in a town that is no more a town.
The road there, if you'll let a guide direct you
Who only has at heart your getting lost,
May seem as if it should have been a quarry—   10
Great monolithic knees the former town
Long since gave up pretense of keeping covered.
And there's a story in a book about it:
Besides the wear of iron wagon wheels
The ledges show lines ruled southeast northwest,   15
The chisel work of an enormous Glacier
That braced his feet against the Arctic Pole.
You must not mind a certain coolness from him
Still said to haunt this side of Panther Mountain.
Nor need you mind the serial ordeal   20
Of being watched from forty cellar holes
As if by eye pairs out of forty firkins.

---

11. **talus:** rock debris at the cliff's base.   22. **firkins:** small wooden casks.

As for the woods' excitement over you
That sends light rustle rushes to their leaves,
Charge that to upstart inexperience.   25
Where were they all not twenty years ago?
They think too much of having shaded out
A few old pecker-fretted apple trees.
Make yourself up a cheering song of how
Someone's road home from work this once was,   30
Who may be just ahead of you on foot
Or creaking with a buggy load of grain.
The height of the adventure is the height
Of country where two village cultures faded
Into each other. Both of them are lost.   35
And if you're lost enough to find yourself
By now, pull in your ladder road behind you
And put a sign up CLOSED to all but me.
Then make yourself at home. The only field
Now left's no bigger than a harness gall.   40
First there's the children's house of make believe,
Some shattered dishes underneath a pine,
The playthings in the playhouse of the children
Weep for what little things could make them glad.
Then for the house that is no more a house,   45
But only a belilaced cellar hole,
Now slowly closing like a dent in dough.
This was no playhouse but a house in earnest.
Your destination and your destiny's
A brook that was the water of the house,   50
Cold as a spring as yet so near its source,
Too lofty and original to rage.
(We know the valley streams that when aroused
Will leave their tatters hung on barb and thorn.)
I have kept hidden in the instep arch   55
Of an old cedar at the waterside
A broken drinking goblet like the Grail
Under a spell so the wrong ones can't find it,
So can't get saved, as Saint Mark says they mustn't.
(I stole the goblet from the children's playhouse.)   60
Here are your waters and your watering place.
Drink and be whole again beyond confusion.

---

40. **gall:** a sore on a horse caused by a rubbing harness.
57. **Grail:** The Holy Grail, the cup Christ used at the last supper. In Arthurian legend most of the knights who sought it were unworthy.
59. **Saint Mark:** possibly Mark 4: 11–12.

THOMAS STEARNS ELIOT

[*1888–*   ]

The Love Song of J. Alfred Prufrock

*S'io credesse che mia risposta fosse
A persona che mai tornasse al mondo,
Questa fiamma staria senza piu scosse.
Ma perciocche giammai di questo fondo
Non torno vivo alcum, s'i'odo il vero,
Senza tema d'infamia ti rispondo.*

Let us go then, you and I,
When the evening is spread out against the sky
Like a patient etherized upon a table;
Let us go, through certain half-deserted streets,
The muttering retreats   5
Of restless nights in one-night cheap hotels
And sawdust restaurants with oyster-shells:
Streets that follow like a tedious argument
Of insidious intent
To lead you to an overwhelming question. . . .   10
Oh, do not ask, "What is it?"
Let us go and make our visit.

In the room the women come and go
Talking of Michelangelo.

The yellow fog that rubs its back upon the window-panes,   15
The yellow smoke that rubs its muzzle on the window-panes
Licked its tongue into the corners of the evening,
Lingered upon the pools that stand in drains,
Let fall upon its back the soot that falls from chimneys,
Slipped by the terrace, made a sudden leap,   20
And seeing that it was a soft October night,
Curled once about the house, and fell asleep.

S'io . . . rispondo: "If I thought that my reply would be to one who would ever return to the world, this flame would stay without further movement; but since none has ever returned alive from this depth, if what I hear is true, I answer you without fear of infamy." Dante, *Inferno*, xxvii, 61–66. Here Guido da Montefeltro, imprisoned in the flame surrounding each false counselor, confesses his crimes to Dante.

And indeed there will be time
For the yellow smoke that slides along the street,
Rubbing its back upon the window-panes;   25
There will be time, there will be time
To prepare a face to meet the faces that you meet;
There will be time to murder and create,
And time for all the works and days of hands
That lift and drop a question on your plate;   30
Time for you and time for me,
And time yet for a hundred indecisions,
And for a hundred visions and revisions,
Before the taking of a toast and tea.   => LAST SUPPER
                                            BREAD + WINE

In the room the women come and go   35
Talking of Michelangelo.

And indeed there will be time
To wonder, "Do I dare?" and, "Do I dare?"
Time to turn back and descend the stair,
With a bald spot in the middle of my hair—   40
(They will say: "How his hair is growing thin!")
My morning coat, my collar mounting firmly to the chin,
My necktie rich and modest, but asserted by a simple pin—
(They will say: "But how his arms and legs are thin!")
Do I dare   45
Disturb the universe?
In a minute there is time
For decisions and revisions which a minute will reverse.

For I have known them all already, known them all:
Have known the evenings, mornings, afternoons,   50
I have measured out my life with coffee spoons;   TIME TO COMPARISONS
I know the voices dying with a dying fall
Beneath the music from a farther room.
    So how should I presume?

And I have known the eyes already, known them all—   55
The eyes that fix you in a formulated phrase,
And when I am formulated, sprawling on a pin,
When I am pinned and wriggling on the wall,
Then how should I begin
To spit out all the butt-ends of my days and ways?   60
    And how should I presume?

29. **works ... days:** a poem about the   52. **dying fall:** cf. Orsino's speech in
farming year by Hesiod, 8th century B.C.   *Twelfth Night*, I, i, 4.

And I have known the arms already, known them all—
Arms that are braceleted and white and bare
(But in the lamplight, downed with light brown hair!)
Is it perfume from a dress   WOMAN   65
That makes me so digress?
Arms that lie along a table, or wrap about a shawl,
   And should I then presume?
   And how should I begin?

Shall I say, I have gone at dusk through narrow streets   70
And watched the smoke that rises from the pipes
Of lonely men in shirt-sleeves, leaning out of windows? . . .

I should have been a pair of ragged claws   LOBSTER
Scuttling across the floors of silent seas.

And the afternoon, the evening, sleeps so peacefully!   75
Smoothed by long fingers,
Asleep . . . tired . . . or it malingers,
Stretched on the floor, here beside you and me.
Should I, after tea and cakes and ices,
Have the strength to force the moment to its crisis?   80
But though I have wept and fasted, wept and prayed,
Though I have seen my head (grown slightly bald) brought in upon
     a platter,
I am no prophet—and here's no great matter;
I have seen the moment of my greatness flicker,
And I have seen the eternal Footman hold my coat, and snicker,   85
And in short, I was afraid.   DEATH

And would it have been worth it, after all,
After the cups, the marmalade, the tea,
Among the porcelain, among some talk of you and me,
Would it have been worth while,   90
To have bitten off the matter with a smile,
To have squeezed the universe into a ball
To roll it toward some overwhelming question,
To say: "I am Lazarus, come from the dead,
Come back to tell you all, I shall tell you all"—   95
If one, settling a pillow by her head,
   Should say: "That is not what I meant at all;
   That is not it, at all."

82. **platter**: like John the Baptist.
92–93. **universe . . . question**: cf. Marvell's
"To His Coy Mistress," 41–42.

94. **Lazarus**: the man Christ raised from
the dead, John 12: 1–18; also the beggar
carried to Abraham's bosom, Luke 16:
19–31.

And would it have been worth it, after all,
Would it have been worth while,   100
After the sunsets and the dooryards and the sprinkled streets,
After the novels, after the teacups, after the skirts that trail along the
        floor—
And this, and so much more?—
It is impossible to say just what I mean!
But as if a magic lantern threw the nerves in patterns on a screen: 105
Would it have been worthwhile
If one, settling a pillow or throwing off a shawl,
And turning toward the window, should say:
  "That is not it at all,
    That is not what I meant, at all."   110

No! I am not Prince Hamlet, nor was meant to be;
Am an attendant lord, one that will do
To swell a progress, start a scene or two,
Advise the prince; no doubt, an easy tool,
Deferential, glad to be of use,   115
Politic, cautious, and meticulous;
Full of high sentence, but a bit obtuse;
At times, indeed, almost ridiculous—
Almost, at times, the Fool.

I grow old. . . . I grow old. . . .   120
I shall wear the bottoms of my trousers rolled.
Shall I part my hair behind? Do I dare to eat a peach?
I shall wear white flannel trousers, and walk upon the beach.
I have heard the mermaids singing, each to each.

I do not think that they will sing to me.   125

I have seen them riding seaward on the waves
Combing the white hair of the waves blown back
When the wind blows the water white and black.

We have lingered in the chambers of the sea
By sea-girls wreathed with seaweed red and brown   130
Till human voices wake us, and we drown.

Morning at the Window

    They are rattling breakfast plates in basement kitchens,
    And along the trampled edges of the street
    I am aware of the damp souls of housemaids
    Sprouting despondently at area gates.

113. **swell a progress:** join a royal pro-   117. **sentence:** judgments, opinions.
cession.

The brown waves of fog toss up to me   5
Twisted faces from the bottom of the street,
And tear from a passer-by with muddy skirts
An aimless smile that hovers in the air
And vanishes along the level of the roofs.

Gerontion

Thou hast nor youth nor age
But as it were an after dinner sleep
Dreaming of both.

Here I am, an old man in a dry month,
Being read to by a boy, waiting for rain.
I was neither at the hot gates
Nor fought in the warm rain
Nor knee deep in the salt marsh, heaving a cutlass,   5
Bitten by flies, fought.
My house is a decayed house,
And the jew squats on the window sill, the owner,
Spawned in some estaminet of Antwerp,
Blistered in Brussels, patched and peeled in London.   10
The goat coughs at night in the field overhead;
Rocks, moss, stonecrop, iron, merds.
The woman keeps the kitchen, makes tea,
Sneezes at evening, poking the peevish gutter.
                    I an old man,   15
A dull head among windy spaces.

Signs are taken for wonders. "We would see a sign!"
The word within a word, unable to speak a word,
Swaddled with darkness. In the juvescence of the year
Came Christ the tiger   20

Thou ... both: *Measure for Measure*, III,
i, 32–34. The Duke's speech to Claudio
advising him to "Be absolute for death."
3. **hot gates:** a translation of Thermopylae,
the place where 300 Spartans for a while
held off the Persian army (480 B.C.).
9. **estaminet:** a small café.
12. **merds:** dung.

17–19. **Signs ... darkness:** These phrases
come from a sermon on Christ's nativity
by Lancelot Andrewes (1555–1626). In
Matthew 12: 38 the Scribes and Pharisees
ask Christ for a sign, for which he rebukes
them.
19. **juvescence:** springtime.

DE PRIVED

In depraved May, dogwood and chestnut, flowering judas,
To be eaten, to be divided, to be drunk =? COMMUNION
Among whispers; by Mr. Silvero
With caressing hands, at Limoges
Who walked all night in the next room;   25

By Hakagawa, bowing among the Titians;
By Madame de Tornquist, in the dark room TO WO PURPOSE
Shifting the candles; Fräulein von Kulp
Who turned in the hall, one hand on the door.
                    Vacant shuttles   30
Weave the wind. I have no ghosts,
An old man in a draughty house
Under a windy knob.

After such knowledge, what forgiveness? Think now
History has many cunning passages, contrived corridors   35
And issues, deceives with whispering ambitions,
Guides us by vanities. Think now
She gives when our attention is distracted
And what she gives, gives with such supple confusions
That the giving famishes the craving. Gives too late   40
What's not believed in, or if still believed,
In memory only, reconsidered passion. Gives too soon
Into weak hands, what's thought can be dispensed with
Till the refusal propagates a fear. Think
Neither fear nor courage saves us. Unnatural vices   45
Are fathered by our heroism. Virtues
Are forced upon us by our impudent crimes.
These tears are shaken from the wrath-bearing tree.

The tiger springs in the new year. Us he devours.
                    Think at last   50
We have not reached conclusion, when I
Stiffen in a rented house. Think at last
I have not made this show purposelessly
And it is not by any concitation
Of the backward devils   55
I would meet you upon this honestly.

---

24. **Limoges:** French center for making enamels.
26. **Titians:** paintings by the Venetian master Titian (1477–1576).
27–28. **dark ... candles:** practicing spiritualism.
48. **tree:** of knowledge of good and evil; the cross.
54. **concitation:** stirring up.
55. **backward devils:** false religions preceding Christianity.

I that was near your heart was removed therefrom
To lose beauty in terror, terror in inquisition.
I have lost my passion: why should I need to keep it
Since what is kept must be adulterated?   60
I have lost my sight, hearing, taste and touch:
How should I use them for your closer contact?
These with a thousand small deliberations
Protract the profit of their chilled delirium,
Excite the membrane, when the sense has cooled,   65
With pungent sauces, multiply variety
In a wilderness of mirrors. What will the spider do,
Suspend its operations, will the weevil
Delay? De Bailhache, Fresca, Mrs. Cammel, whirled
Beyond the circuit of the shuddering Bear   70
In fractured atoms. Gull against the wind, in the windy straits
Of Belle Isle, or running on the Horn,
White feathers in the snow, the Gulf claims,
And an old man driven by the Trades
To a sleepy corner.   75

                    Tenants of the house,
Thoughts of a dry brain in a dry season.

Sweeney Among the Nightingales

ὤμοι, πέπληγμαι καιρίαν πληγὴν ἔσω.

Apeneck Sweeney spreads his knees
Letting his arms hang down to laugh,
The zebra stripes along his jaw
Swelling to maculate giraffe.

The circles of the stormy moon   5
Slide westward toward the River Plate,
Death and the Raven drift above
And Sweeney guards the hornèd gate.

---

70. **Bear:** the big dipper; Ursa Major.

Nightingales: the birds traditionally associated with song and tragedy, because of Philomela, who was turned into a nightingale after being ravished and having her tongue cut out. The Greek inscription is from Aeschylus, *Agamemnon*, 1343: "Ah me I am struck a deadly blow and deep within," Agamemnon's death cry when Clytemnestra, his wife, murders him.
4. **maculate:** spotted.
6. **Plate:** La Plata.
7. **Raven:** Corvus, a southern constellation.
8. **hornèd gate:** the gates of horn in Hades through which true dreams rise to the upper world.

Gloomy Orion and the Dog
Are veiled; and hushed the shrunken seas;   10
The person in the Spanish cape
Tries to sit on Sweeney's knees

Slips and pulls the table cloth
Overturns a coffee-cup,
Reorganized upon the floor   15
She yawns and draws a stocking up;

The silent man in mocha brown
Sprawls at the window-sill and gapes
The waiter brings in oranges
Bananas figs and hothouse grapes;   20

The silent vertebrate in brown
Contracts and concentrates, withdraws;
Rachel *née* Rabinovitch
Tears at the grapes with murderous paws;

She and the lady in the cape   25
Are suspect, thought to be in league;
Therefore the man with heavy eyes
Declines the gambit, shows fatigue,

Leaves the room and reappears
Outside the window, leaning in,   30
Branches of wisteria
Circumscribe a golden grin;

The host with someone indistinct
Converses at the door apart,
The nightingales are singing near   35
The Convent of the Sacred Heart,

And sang within the bloody wood
When Agamemnon cried aloud,
And let their liquid siftings fall
To stain the stiff dishonoured shroud.   40

9. **Orion ... Dog:** Orion, the hunter, mistakenly killed by Artemis (Diana) and transformed into a constellation. The Dog Star (Sirius) is associated with hot weather and "dog days"; it follows Orion across the heavens.

37. **bloody wood:** Agamemnon, killed in his bath, is here fused with Philomela, who was ravished in a wood; also the "bloody wood" of Nemi, where in ancient times the old priest was killed by his successor.

THOMAS STEARNS ELIOT

The Waste Land

"Nam Sibyllam quidem Cumis ego ipse
oculis meis vidi in ampulla pendere, et
cum illi pueri dicerent: Σίβυλλα τί
θέλεις; respondebat illa:
ἀποθανεῖν θέλω."

For Ezra Pound
il miglior fabbro

I. THE BURIAL OF THE DEAD

April is the cruellest month, breeding
Lilacs out of the dead land, mixing
Memory and desire, stirring
Dull roots with spring rain.
Winter kept us warm, covering   5
Earth in forgetful snow, feeding
A little life with dried tubers.

Summer surprised us, coming over the Starnbergersee
With a shower of rain; we stopped in the colonnade,
And went on in sunlight, into the Hofgarten,   10
And drank coffee, and talked for an hour.
Bin gar keine Russin, stamm' aus Litauen, echt deutsch.
And when we were children, staying at the archduke's,
My cousin's, he took me out on a sled,
And I was frightened. He said, Marie,   15
Marie, hold on tight. And down we went.
In the mountains, there you feel free.
I read, much of the night, and go south in the winter.

What are the roots that clutch, what branches grow
Out of this stony rubbish? Son of man,   20
You cannot say, or guess, for you know only
A heap of broken images, where the sun beats,
And the dead tree gives no shelter, the cricket no relief,

The Waste Land: In his own notes to the poem Eliot states: "Not only the title, but the plan and a good deal of the incidental symbolism of the poem were suggested by Miss Jessie L. Weston's book on the Grail legend: *From Ritual to Romance....* To another work of Anthropology I am indebted profoundly ... *The Golden Bough* ... especially the two volumes *Adonis, Attis, Osiris.*" The epitaph comes from *The Satyricon* of Petronius, 1st century A.D.: "For once I myself saw with my own eyes the Sybil at Cumae hanging in a jar and when the boys said to her, 'Sybil, what do you want?' she replied 'I want to die.'" The Sybil of Cumae, one of the prophetic women of ancient time, had been granted by Apollo as many years as the number of grains of sand she could hold in her hand, but she was not granted youth. Aeneas consulted with her before journeying to the underworld on his quest for the golden bough. Il ... Fabbro: "the better craftsman," praise given to the Provençal poet Arnaut Daniel, *Purgatorio,* xxvi, 117.
8. **Starnbergersee:** lake resort near Munich.
12. **Bin ... deutsch:** "I am not a Russian woman; I come from Lithuania, a true German."
20. **Son of man:** "Cf. Ezekiel II, i." [Eliot]
23. **dead ... relief:** "Cf. Ecclesiastes XII, v." [Eliot]

And the dry stone no sound of water. Only
There is shadow under this red rock,   25
(Come in under the shadow of this red rock),
And I will show you something different from either
Your shadow at morning striding behind you
Or your shadow at evening rising to meet you;
I will show you fear in a handful of dust.   30

> *Frisch weht der Wind*
> *Der Heimat zu,*
> *Mein Irisch Kind,*
> *Wo weilest du?*

"You gave me hyacinths first a year ago;   35
They called me the hyacinth girl."
—Yet when we came back, late, from the Hyacinth garden,
Your arms full, and your hair wet, I could not
Speak, and my eyes failed, I was neither
Living nor dead, and I knew nothing,   40
Looking into the heart of light, the silence.
Oed' und leer das Meer.
Madame Sosostris, famous clairvoyante,
Had a bad cold, nevertheless
Is known to be the wisest woman in Europe,   45
With a wicked pack of cards. Here, said she,
Is your card, the drowned Phoenician Sailor,
(Those are pearls that were his eyes. Look!)
Here is Belladonna, the Lady of the Rocks,
The lady of situations.   50
Here is the man with three staves, and here the Wheel,
And here is the one-eyed merchant, and this card,

---

25. rock: Isaiah 32: 2 prophesies the king who will be "as rivers of water in a dry place, as the shadow of a great rock in a weary land."

31–34. Frisch . . . du?: "Fresh blows the wind to the homeland, my Irish child (sweetheart), where are you waiting?": the sailor's melancholy song in *Tristan and Isolde*.

42. Oed' . . . Meer: "waste and empty is the sea." In *Tristan and Isolde*, III, the shepherd's report to the dying Tristan, waiting for Isolde.

46. cards: the Tarot deck of cards, used by fortune tellers. "I am not familiar with the exact constitution of the Tarot pack of cards, from which I have obviously departed to suit my own convenience. The Hanged Man, a member of the traditional pack, fits my purpose in two ways:

because he is associated in my mind with the Hanged God of Frazer, and because I associate him with the hooded figure in the passage of the disciples to Emmaus in Part V. The Phoenician Sailor and the Merchant appear later; also the 'crowds of people,' and Death by Water is executed in Part IV. The Man with Three Staves (an authentic member of the Tarot pack) I associate, quite arbitrarily, with the Fisher King himself." [Eliot]

48. Those . . . eyes: an echo of Ariel's song "Full fathom five thy father lies" in *The Tempest*, I, ii, 398, sung to young Ferdinand, who thinks his father has drowned.

49. Belladonna . . . Rocks: Belladonna is the poisonous plant "deadly nightshade"; in Italian it also means "beautiful lady." The Lady of the Rocks is one of Leonardo's paintings of the Madonna.

Which is blank, is something he carries on his back,
Which I am forbidden to see. I do not find
The Hanged Man. Fear death by water.   55
I see crowds of people, walking round in a ring.
Thank you. If you see dear Mrs. Equitone,
Tell her I bring the horoscope myself:
One must be so careful these days.
Unreal City,   60
Under the brown fog of a winter dawn,
A crowd flowed over London Bridge, so many,
I had not thought death had undone so many.
Sighs, short and infrequent, were exhaled,
And each man fixed his eyes before his feet.   65
Flowed up the hill and down King William Street,
To where Saint Mary Woolnoth kept the hours
With a dead sound on the final stroke of nine.
There I saw one I knew, and stoppped him, crying: "Stetson!
You who were with me in the ships at Mylae!   70
That corpse you planted last year in your garden,
Has it begun to sprout? Will it bloom this year?
Or has the sudden frost disturbed its bed?
Oh keep the Dog far hence, that's friend to men,
Or with his nails he'll dig it up again!   75
You! hypocrite lecteur!—mon semblable,—mon frère!"

II. A GAME OF CHESS

The Chair she sat in, like a burnished throne,
Glowed on the marble, where the glass
Held up by standards wrought with fruited vines
From which a golden Cupidon peeped out   80
(Another hid his eyes behind his wing)

60. Unreal City: "Cf. Baudelaire: 'Four-millante cité, cité pleine de rêves, / Où le spectre en plein jour raccroche le passant.'" [Eliot]; the opening lines of Poem 93, in *Fleurs du Mal:* "Swarming city, city filled with dreams, / where the ghost in full daylight hails the passerby."
63. I . . . many: an adaptation of *Inferno*, III, 55–57, where Dante expresses his surprise upon seeing the multitudes who chose neither good nor evil.
64. Sighs . . . exhaled: *Inferno*, IV, 25–27, lines describing the virtuous heathen sighing because they can never see God.
67. Saint . . . Woolnoth: the London church opposite the Bank of England and the Stock Exchange. The crowds cross London Bridge going to work in the financial center of the city.
70. Mylae: Battle in the Punic War (260 B.C.).

74–75. Dog . . . again: "Cf. the Dirge in Webster's *White Devil*." [Eliot] He has changed the "wolf" of the original to "dog" and "foe" to "friend." The song is sung by a demented mother whose son is burying the brother he slew.
76. You . . . frère: "hypocrite reader, my likeness, my brother"; the last line of Baudelaire's "Au Lecteur," the introductory poem to *Fleurs du Mal.*
A Game of Chess: Thomas Middleton (1570–1627) wrote one play called *A Game at Chess*, which satirized a royal marriage based on expedience, and another, *Women Beware Women*, in which a woman is distracted by a game of chess while her daughter-in-law is being seduced.
77. Chair . . . throne: "Cf. *Antony and Cleopatra*, II, ii, *l.* 190." [Eliot]
80. Cupidon: a winged child, a putto.

Doubled the flames of sevenbranched candelabra
Reflecting light upon the table as
The glitter of her jewels rose to meet it,
From satin cases poured in rich profusion;   85
In vials of ivory and coloured glass
Unstoppered, lurked her strange synthetic perfumes,
Unguent, powdered, or liquid—troubled, confused
And drowned the sense in odours; stirred by the air
That freshened from the window, these ascended   90
In fattening the prolonged candle-flames,
Flung their smoke into the laquearia,
Stirring the pattern on the coffered ceiling.
Huge sea-wood fed with copper
Burned green and orange, framed by the coloured stone,   95
In which sad light a carvèd dolphin swam.
Above the antique mantel was displayed
As though a window gave upon the sylvan scene
The change of Philomel, by the barbarous king
So rudely forced; yet there the nightingale   100
Filled all the desert with inviolable voice
And still she cried, and still the world pursues,
"Jug Jug" to dirty ears.
And other withered stumps of time
Were told upon the walls; staring forms   105
Leaned out, leaning, hushing the room enclosed.
Footsteps shuffled on the stair.
Under the firelight, under the brush, her hair
Spread out in fiery points
Glowed into words, then would be savagely still.   110

"My nerves are bad to-night. Yes, bad. Stay with me.
Speak to me. Why do you never speak. Speak.
    What are you thinking of? What thinking? What?
I never know what you are thinking. Think."
I think we are in rats' alley   115
Where the dead men lost their bones.
"What is that noise?"
                    The wind under the door.

92. **laquearia:** a paneled ceiling. Eliot refers to the room in the *Aeneid* where Dido celebrates the arrival of Aeneas.
98. **sylvan scene:** "V. Milton, *Paradise Lost*, IV, 140." [Eliot]
99. **Philomel:** the girl raped by her brother-in-law Tereus, who then had her tongue cut out. She was transformed into a nightingale.

103. **Jug:** conventional spelling of the sound of the nightingale.
115. **alley:** "Cf. Part III, *l*. 195." [Eliot]
118. **wind . . . door:** "Cf. Webster: 'Is the wind in that door still?'" [Eliot] The line, from *The Devil's Law Case*, III, ii, 62, is spoken by a surgeon surprised that the stabbed Duke is still alive.

What is that noise now? What is the wind doing?"
                    Nothing again nothing.   120

                                                    "Do
You know nothing? Do you see nothing? Do you remember
Nothing?"

    I remember
Those are pearls that were his eyes.   125
"Are you alive, or not? Is there nothing in your head?"
                                                    But

O O O O that Shakespeherian Rag—
It's so elegant
So intelligent   130
"What shall I do now? What shall I do?"
"I shall rush out as I am, and walk the street
With my hair down, so. What shall we do tomorrow?
What shall we ever do?"
                    The hot water at ten.   135
And if it rains, a closed car at four.
And we shall play a game of chess,
Pressing lidless eyes and waiting for a knock upon the door.

When Lil's husband got demobbed, I said—
I didn't mince my words, I said to her myself,   140
HURRY UP PLEASE ITS TIME
Now Albert's coming back, make yourself a bit smart.
He'll want to know what you done with that money he gave you
To get yourself some teeth. He did, I was there.
You have them all out, Lil, and get a nice set,   145
He said, I swear, I can't bear to look at you.
And no more can't I, I said, and think of poor Albert,
He's been in the army four years, he wants a good time,
And if you don't give it him, there's others will, I said.
Oh is there, she said. Something o' that, I said.   150
Then I'll know who to thank, she said, and give me a straight look,
HURRY UP PLEASE ITS TIME
If you don't like it you can get on with it, I said.
Others can pick and choose if you can't.
But if Albert makes off, it won't be for lack of telling. 155
You ought to be ashamed I said, to look so antique.
(And her only thirty-one.)

125. **pearls:** "Cf. Part I, *l.* 37, 48." [Eliot]   141. **Hurry . . . time:** the bartender's tradi-
139. **demobbed:** slang for demobilized.   tional call at closing time.

I can't help it, she said, pulling a long face,
It's them pills I took, to bring it off, she said.
(She's had five already, and nearly died of young George.)   160
The chemist said it would be all right, but I've never been the same.
You *are* a proper fool, I said.
Well, if Albert won't leave you alone, there it is, I said,
What you get married for if you don't want children?
HURRY UP PLEASE ITS TIME   165
Well, that Sunday Albert was home, they had a hot gammon,
And they asked me into dinner, to get the beauty of it hot—
HURRY UP PLEASE ITS TIME
HURRY UP PLEASE ITS TIME
Goonight Bill. Goonight Lou. Goonight May. Goonight.   170
Ta ta. Goonight. Goonight.
Good night, ladies, good night, sweet ladies, good night, good
    night.

III. THE FIRE SERMON

The river's tent is broken: the last fingers of leaf
Clutch and sink into the wet bank. The wind
Crosses the brown land, unheard. The nymphs are departed   175
Sweet Thames, run softly, till I end my song.
The river bears no empty bottles, sandwich papers,
Silk handkerchiefs, cardboard boxes, cigarette ends
Or other testimony of summer nights. The nymphs are departed.
And their friends, the loitering heirs of city directors;   180
Departed, have left no addresses.
By the waters of Leman I sat down and wept . . .
Sweet Thames, run softly till I end my song,
Sweet Thames, run softly, for I speak not loud or long.
But at my back in a cold blast I hear   185
The rattle of the bones, and chuckle spread from ear to ear.
A rat crept softly through the vegetation
Dragging its slimy belly on the bank
While I was fishing in the dull canal
On a winter evening round behind the gashouse   190
Musing upon the king my brother's wreck
And on the king my father's death before him.

161. **chemist:** druggist.
166. **gammon:** ham or bacon, also thigh.
172. **Good . . . night:** in *Hamlet*, IV, v, 72, mad Ophelia's parting words.
Fire Sermon: In his notes Eliot compares Buddha's "Fire Sermon" to Christ's "Sermon on the Mount." Buddha warned against surrender to the senses, which are on fire. Only when purged of passion, he said, can one become free.

176. **Sweet . . . song:** refrain of Spenser's "Prothalamion."
182. **By . . . wept:** Psalms 137: 4, the lament of a Jew exiled in Babylon. Eliot substitutes "Leman" for Babylon, perhaps referring to Lake Leman (Geneva) where he wrote the poem.
191–92. **Musing . . . him:** "Cf. *The Tempest*, I, ii." [Eliot]

White bodies naked on the low damp ground
And bones cast in a little low dry garret,
Rattled by the rat's foot only, year to year.   195
But at my back from time to time I hear
The sound of horns and motors, which shall bring
Sweeney to Mrs. Porter in the spring.
O the moon shone bright on Mrs. Porter
And on her daughter   200
They wash their feet in soda water
Et O ces voix d'enfants, chantant dans la coupole!

Twit twit twit
Jug jug jug jug jug jug
So rudely forc'd.   205
Tereu

Unreal City
Under the brown fog of a winter noon
Mr. Eugenides, the Smyrna merchant
Unshaven, with a pocket full of currants   210
C.i.f. London: documents at sight,
Asked me in demotic French
To luncheon at the Cannon Street Hotel
Followed by a weekend at the Metropole.

At the violet hour, when the eyes and back   215
Turn upward from the desk, when the human engine waits
Like a taxi throbbing waiting,

196. **But ... hear:** "Cf. Marvell, *To His Coy Mistress.*" [Eliot]
197. **sound of horns:** "Cf. Day, *Parliament of Bees;* 'When of the sudden, listening, you shall hear, / A noise of horns and hunting, which shall bring / Actaeon to Diana in the spring, / Where all shall see her naked skin ...'" [Eliot] Actaeon was changed to a stag and hunted to death after he saw Diana, the goddess of chastity, bathing. The poem is by John Day (1574?–1640).
198–99. **Mrs. Porter:** "I do not know the origin of the ballad from which these lines are taken; it was reported to me from Sydney, Australia." [Eliot] In the song Mrs. Porter is the keeper of a brothel.
202. **Et ... coupole:** "And O those children's voices singing in the dome," from Verlaine's sonnet "Parsifal." Parsifal is described as resisting sensual temptation and keeping himself pure for the Holy Grail. Wagner's Parsifal has his feet washed by a temptress.
206. **Tereu:** Tereus, the one who raped Philomela; also the conventional spelling of the nightingale's song.
209. **Smyrna:** seaport in western Turkey.
211. **C.i.f. ... sight:** "The currants were quoted at a price 'carriage and insurance free to London'; and the Bill of Lading etc. were to be handed to the buyer upon payment of the sight draft." [Eliot]
212. **demotic:** vulgar.
213. **Cannon ... Hotel:** by the station which was then chief terminus for travelers to the continent.
214. **Metropole:** resort hotel in Brighton.

I Tiresias, though blind, throbbing between two lives,
Old man with wrinkled female breasts, can see
At the violet hour, the evening hour that strives   220
Homeward, and brings the sailor home from sea,
The typist home at teatime, clears her breakfast, lights
Her stove, and lays out food in tins.
Out of the window perilously spread
Her drying combinations touched by the sun's last rays,   225
On the divan are piled (at night her bed)
Stockings, slippers, camisoles, and stays.
I Tiresias, old man with wrinkled dugs
Perceived the scene, and foretold the rest—
I too awaited the expected guest.   230
He, the young man carbuncular, arrives,
A small house agent's clerk, with one bold stare,
One of the low on whom assurance sits
As a silk hat on a Bradford millionaire.

The time is now propitious, as he guesses,   235
The meal is ended, she is bored and tired,
Endeavours to engage her in caresses
Which still are unreproved, if undesired.
Flushed and decided, he assaults at once;
Exploring hands encounter no defence;   240
His vanity requires no response,
And makes a welcome of indifference.
(And I Tiresias have forsuffered all
Enacted on this same divan or bed;
I who have sat by Thebes below the wall   245
And walked among the lowest of the dead.)
Bestows one final patronising kiss,

218. **Tiresias:** "Tiresias, although a mere spectator and not indeed a 'character,' is yet the most important personage in the poem, uniting all the rest. Just as the one-eyed merchant, seller of currants, melts into the Phoenician Sailor, and the latter is not wholly distinct from Ferdinand Prince of Naples, so all the women are one woman, and the two sexes meet in Tiresias. What Tiresias *sees*, in fact, is the substance of the poem. The whole passage from Ovid is of great anthropological interest . . ." [Eliot] Eliot then quotes *Metamorphoses*, III, 320–38, which tells that when Tiresias "struck violently with his staff two great serpents who were coupling in the forest," he was immediately transformed into a woman. Eight years later he found the same serpents and striking them again, was transformed back into a man. When Jove and Juno were arguing about who received the most pleasure from making love, men or women, they called upon Tiresias to settle the matter, as he had known the pleasures of love "on both sides." He upheld Jove's assertion that women received more pleasure, whereupon Juno condemned him to eternal blindness. To compensate Tiresias, Jove granted him the power to foretell the future.
221. **Homeward . . . sea:** "This may not appear as exact as Sappho's lines, but I had in mind the 'longshore' or 'dory' fisherman, who returns at nightfall." [Eliot] Sappho's poem addressed Hesperus, the evening star, as the star that brings every one home to evening rest.
234. **Bradford:** A Yorkshire woolen-manufacturing town, where many fortunes were made during World War I.
245–46. **I . . . dead:** Tiresias prophesied in Thebes until he died, then in Hades.

And gropes his way, finding the stairs unlit . . .
She turns and looks a moment in the glass,
Hardly aware of her departed lover;   250
Her brain allows one half-formed thought to pass:
"Well now that's done: and I'm glad it's over."
When lovely woman stoops to folly and
Paces about her room again, alone,
She smoothes her hair with automatic hand,   255
And puts a record on the gramophone.

"This music crept by me upon the waters"
And along the Strand, up Queen Victoria Street.
O City city, I can sometimes hear
Beside a public bar in Lower Thames Street,   260
The pleasant whining of a mandoline
And a clatter and a chatter from within
Where fishmen lounge at noon: where the walls
Of Magnus Martyr hold
Inexplicable splendour of Ionian white and gold.   265

    The river sweats
    Oil and tar
    The barges drift
    With the turning tide
    Red sails   270
    Wide
    To leeward, swing on the heavy spar.
    The barges wash
    Drifting logs
    Down Greenwich reach   275
    Past the Isle of Dogs.
        Weialala leia
        Wallala leialala

---

253. **When . . . folly:** a song from Gold-smith's *Vicar of Wakefield*, saying that any betrayed maiden who wished to wash away her guilt must die.
257. **"This . . . waters":** "V. *The Tempest*, as above." [Eliot]
264. **Magnus Martyr:** "The interior of St. Magnus Martyr is to my mind one of the finest among Wren's interiors." [Eliot] The church is in the neighborhood of the Billingsgate Fish Market.
265. **Ionian:** Ionic columns.

266. **The . . . sweats:** "The Song of the (three) Thames-daughters begins here. From line 292 to 306 inclusive they speak in turn, V. *Götterdämmerung*, III, i: the Rhine-daughters." [Eliot] In Wagner's opera, the Rhine-daughters lament that the gold of the Nibelungs, which they guarded, has been stolen, and with it has gone their happiness and the river's beauty. They plead with Siegfried to restore the treasure. Eliot repeats their refrain.
276. **Isle of Dogs:** peninsula opposite Greenwich.

Elizabeth and Leicester
Beating oars   280
The stern was formed
A gilded shell
Red and gold
The brisk swell

Rippled both shores   285
Southwest wind
Carried down stream
The peal of bells
White towers
      Weialala leia   290
      Wallala leialala

"Trams and dusty trees.
Highbury bore me. Richmond and Kew
Undid me. By Richmond I raised my knees
Supine on the floor of a narrow canoe."   295

"My feet at at Moorgate, and my heart
Under my feet. After the event
He wept. He promised 'a new start'.
I made no comment. What should I resent?"

"On Margate sands.   300
I can connect
Nothing with nothing.
The broken fingernails of dirty hands.
My people humble people who expect
Nothing."   305
      La la

To Carthage then I came

279. **Elizabeth . . . Leicester:** "V. Froude, *Elizabeth*, Vol. I, ch. iv., letter of De Quadra to Philip of Spain: 'In the afternoon we were in a barge, watching the games on the river. (The queen) was alone with Lord Robert and myself on the poop, when they began to talk nonsense, and went so far that Lord Robert at last said, as I was on the spot there was no reason why they should not be married if the queen pleased.'" [Eliot]
293–94. **Highbury . . . me:** *Purgatorio*, V, 133–34, goes "Remember me, who am La Pia / Siena made me, Maremma undid me." She was murdered by her husband. Highbury is a London suburb; Richmond is a London suburb a few miles up the Thames; Kew, adjoining Richmond, has the famous gardens.
296. **Moorgate:** slum area in east London.
300. **Margate:** seaside resort near the mouth of the Thames.
307. **To . . . Carthage:** "V. St. Augustine's *Confessions:* 'to Carthage then I came, where a cauldron of unholy loves sang all about mine ears.'" [Eliot]

Burning burning burning burning
O Lord Thou pluckest me out
O Lord Thou pluckest   310

burning

IV. DEATH BY WATER

Phlebas the Phoenician, a fortnight dead,
Forgot the cry of gulls, and the deep sea swell
And the profit and loss.
                          A current under sea   315
Picked his bones in whispers. As he rose and fell
He passed the stages of his age and youth
Entering the whirlpool.
                          Gentile or Jew
O you who turn the wheel and look to windward,   320
Consider Phlebas, who was once handsome and tall as you.

V. WHAT THE THUNDER SAID

After the torchlight red on sweaty faces
After the frosty silence in the gardens
After the agony in stony places
The shouting and the crying   325
Prison and palace and reverberation
Of thunder of spring over distant mountains
He who was living is now dead
We who were living are now dying
With a little patience   330

Here is no water but only rock
Rock and no water and the sandy road
The road winding above among the mountains
Which are mountains of rock without water
If there were water we should stop and drink   335
Amongst the rock one cannot stop or think
Sweat is dry and feet are in the sand
If there were only water amongst the rock

308. **Burning:** Buddha's Fire Sermon.
309. **O . . . out:** "From St. Augustine's *Confessions* again. The collocation of these two representatives of eastern and western asceticism, as the culmination of this part of the poem is not an accident." [Eliot]
What the Thunder Said: "In the first part of Part V three themes are employed; the journey to Emmaus, the approach to the Chapel Perilous (see Miss Weston's book) and the present decay of eastern Europe." [Eliot] On the journey to Emmaus, on the third day after he was crucified, Christ appeared to two of his disciples. Luke 24: 13–34. The Chapel Perilous was the place of the Christian knight's final ordeal. 322–28. **After . . . dead:** allusions to Christ's passion. The gardens are Gethsemane, scene of the final temptation, and Golgotha, site of the crucifixion.

Dead mountain mouth of carious teeth that cannot spit
Here one can neither stand nor lie nor sit   340
There is not even silence in the mountains
By dry sterile thunder without rain
There is not even solitude in the mountains
But red sullen faces sneer and snarl
From doors of mudcracked houses   345
                        If there were water

        And no rock
        If there were rock
        And also water
        And water   350
        A spring
        A pool among the rock
        If there were the sound of water only
        Not the cicada
        And dry grass singing   355
        But sound of water over a rock
        Where the hermit-thrush sings in the pine trees
        Drip drop drip drop drop drop drop
        But there is no water

Who is the third who walks always beside you?   360
When I count, there are only you and I together
But when I look ahead up the white road
There is always another one walking beside you
Gliding wrapt in a brow mantle, hooded
I do not know whether a man or a woman   365
—But who is that on the other side of you?

What is that sound high in the air
Murmur of maternal lamentation
Who are those hooded hordes swarming
Over endless plains, stumbling in cracked earth   370
Ringed by the flat horizon only
What is the city over the mountains
Cracks and reforms and bursts in the violet air

339. **carious:** decaying.
357. **hermit-thrush:** In his note Eliot says this bird's "'water-dripping song' is justly celebrated."
360. **who . . . you:** "The following lines were stimulated by the account of one of the Antarctic expeditions (I forget which, but I think one of Shackleton's): it was related that the party of explorers, at the extremity of their strength, had the constant delusion that there was *one more member* than could actually be counted." [Eliot]

368–76. **Murmur . . . London:** "Cf. Hermann Hesse, *Blick ins Chaos . . .*" [Eliot] The passage Eliot quotes is translated: "Already half of Europe, already at least half of Eastern Europe, on the way to Chaos, drives drunk in sacred infatuation along the edge of the precipice, sings drunkenly, as though hymn-singing, as Dmitri Karamazov sang. The offended bourgeois laughs at the song; the saint and the seer hear them with tears."

Falling towers
Jerusalem Athens Alexandria   375
Vienna London
Unreal
A woman drew her long black hair out tight
And fiddled whisper music on those strings
And bats with baby faces in the violet light   380
Whistled, and beat their wings
And crawled head downward down a blackened wall
And upside down in air were towers
Tolling reminiscent bells, that kept the hours
And voices singing out of empty cisterns and exhausted wells. 385

In this decayed hole among the mountains
In the faint moonlight, the grass is singing
Over the tumbled graves, about the chapel
There is the empty chapel, only the wind's home.
It has no windows, and the door swings,   390
Dry bones can harm no one.
Only a cock stood on the rooftree
Co co rico co co rico
In a flash of lightning. Then a damp gust
Bringing rain   395

Ganga was sunken, and the limp leaves
Waited for rain, while the black clouds
Gathered far distant, over Himavant.
The jungle crouched, humped in silence
Then spoke the thunder   400
DA
Datta: what have we given?
My friend, blood shaking my heart
The awful daring of a moment's surrender
Which an age of prudence can never retract   405
By this, and this only, we have existed
Which is not to be found in our obituaries
Or in memories draped by the beneficent spider
Or under seals broken by the lean solicitor
In our empty rooms   410
DA

---

388. **chapel:** The illusion of nothingness is the knight's final test.
392–93. **cock . . . rico:** a weathercock. Perhaps an allusion to Peter's denying of Christ three times before the cock crew.
396. **Ganga:** Ganges River.
398. **Himavant:** Himalayas.
401. **Da: Datta, Dayadhvam, damyata**
(give, sympathize, control). The fable of the meaning of the Thunder is found in the *Brihadaranyaka-Upanishad*, 5. 1." [Eliot]
408. **spider:** "Cf. Webster, The White Devil, V, vi: '. . . they'll remarry / Ere the worm pierce your winding-sheet, ere the spider / Make a thin curtain for your epitaphs.'" [Eliot]

Dayadhvam: I have heard the key
Turn in the door once and turn once only
We think of the key, each in his prison
Thinking of the key, each confirms a prison   415
Only at nightfall, aethereal rumours
Revive for a moment a broken Coriolanus
DA
Damyata: The boat responded
Gaily, to the hand expert with sail and oar   420
The sea was calm, your heart would have responded
Gaily, when invited, beating obedient
To controlling hands

                    I sat upon the shore
Fishing, with the arid plain behind me   425
Shall I at least set my lands in order?
London Bridge is falling down falling down falling down
Poi s'ascose nel foco che gli affina
Quando fiam uti chelidon—O swallow swallow
Le Prince d'Aquitaine à la tour abolie   430
These fragments I have shored against my ruins
Why then Ile fit you. Hieronymo's mad againe.
Datta. Dayadhvam. Damyata.
    Shantih   shantih   shantih

412–13. **key . . . only:** *Inferno*, XXXIII, 46. In this passage Ugolino recalls his imprisonment in the tower with his children, where after they starved to death, he ate them. "And I heard below the door of the horrible tower being locked up." In his note to these lines Eliot quotes from F. H. Bradley, *Appearance and Reality*, p. 346. "My external sensations are no less private to myself than are my thoughts or my feelings. In either case my experience falls within my own circle, a circle closed on the outside; and, with all its elements alike, every sphere is opaque to the others which surround it . . . In brief, regarded as an existence which appears in a soul, the whole world for each is peculiar and private to that soul."
417. **Coriolanus:** The proud general (5th century B.C.), being exiled from Rome, became the leader of the Volscians. When he spared his native city, they executed him.
425. **Fishing:** "V. Weston: From *Ritual to Romance*; chapter on the Fisher King." [Eliot]
428. **Poi . . . affina:** *Purgatorio*, XXVI, 148. In his notes Eliot quotes the two preceding lines in which Arnaut Daniel says to Dante "Now I pray you, by

that virtue which guides you to the summit of the stairway, be mindful in due time of my pain." Then follows the line in the poem: "he hid himself in the fire which refines them."
429. **Quando . . . chelidon:** "V. *Pervigilium Veneris*. Cf. Philomela in Parts II and III." [Eliot] The phrase, which comes from the "Vigil of Venus," means "When shall I be as the swallow?" The Latin poem praises Venus and describes the Spring. Its last two stanzas recollect the Philomela legend, but associate her with the swallow.
430. **Le . . . abolie:** "The Prince of Aquitaine in the ruined tower," from Gerard de Nerval's sonnet "El Desdichado."
432. **Why . . . againe:** Thomas Kyd's tragedy, *The Spanish Tragedy or Hieronymo Is Mad Again* (1594), tells of Hieronymo's revenge on the murderers of his son. Asked to write an entertainment for the court, he replies "Why, then Ile fit you" (accommodate you) and writes a play in which he, as an actor, was able to kill the villains. He then killed himself.
434. **Shantih:** "Shantih. Repeated as here, a formal ending to an Upanishad. 'The Peace which passeth understanding' is our equivalent to this word." [Eliot]

Journey of the Magi

"A cold coming we had of it,
Just the worst time of the year
For a journey, and such a long journey:
The ways deep and the weather sharp,
The very dead of winter."　　　　　　　　　　　　　　　5
And the camels galled, sore-footed, refractory,
Lying down in the melting snow.
There were times we regretted
The summer palaces of slopes, the terraces,
And the silken girls bringing sherbet.　　　　　　　　10
Then the camel men cursing and grumbling
And running away, and wanting their liquor and women,
And the night-fires going out, and the lack of shelters,
And the cities hostile and the towns unfriendly
And the villages dirty and charging high prices:　　　15
A hard time we had of it.
At the end we preferred to travel all night,
Sleeping in snatches,
With the voices singing in our ears, saying
That this was all folly.　　　　　　　　　　　　　　20

Then at dawn we came down to a temperate valley,
Wet, below the snow line, smelling of vegetation;
With a running stream and a water-mill beating the darkness.
And three trees on the low sky,
And an old white horse galloped away in the meadow.　25
Then we came to a tavern with vine-leaves over the lintel,
Six hands at an open door dicing for pieces of silver,
And feet kicking the empty wine-skins.
But there was no information, and so we continued
And arrived at evening, not a moment too soon　　　30
Finding the place; it was (you may say) satisfactory.

All this was a long time ago, I remember,
And I would do it again, but set down
This set down
This: were we led all that way for　　　　　　　　35
Birth or Death? There was a Birth, certainly,
We had evidence and no doubt. I had seen birth and death,

Magi: the wise men who came to pay
homage to the infant Jesus.

1–5. A . . . winter: adapted from a passage
in a Nativity Sermon by Lancelot
Andrewes.

But had thought they were different; this Birth was
Hard and bitter agony for us, like Death, our death.
We returned to our places, these Kingdoms,   40
But no longer at ease here, in the old dispensation,
With an alien people clutching their gods.
I should be glad of another death.

The Dry Salvages

I

I do not know much about gods; but I think that the river
Is a strong brown god—sullen, untamed and intractable,
Patient to some degree, at first recognised as a frontier;
Useful, untrustworthy, as a conveyor of commerce;
Then only a problem confronting the builder of bridges.   5
The problem once solved, the brown god is almost forgotten
By the dwellers in cities—ever, however, implacable,
Keeping his seasons and rages, destroyer, reminder
Of what men choose to forget. Unhonoured, unpropitiated
By worshippers of the machine, but waiting, watching and waiting. 10
His rhythm was present in the nursery bedroom,
In the rank ailanthus of the April dooryard,
In the smell of grapes on the autumn table,
And the evening circle in the winter gaslight.

   The river is within us, the sea is all about us;   15
The sea is the land's edge also, the granite
Into which it reaches, the beaches where it tosses
Its hints of earlier and other creation:
The starfish, the hermit crab, the whale's backbone;
The pools where it offers to our curiosity   20
The more delicate algae and the sea anemone.
It tosses up our losses, the torn seine,
The shattered lobsterpot, the broken oar
And the gear of foreign dead men. The sea has many voices,
Many gods and many voices.   25
                        The salt is on the briar rose,
The fog is in the fir trees.

                        The sea howl
And the sea yelp, are different voices
Often together heard; the whine in the rigging,   30

The Dry Salvages: "presumably *les trois sauvages* is a small group of rocks, with a beacon, off the N.E. coast of Cape Ann, Massachusetts. *Salvages* is pronounced to rhyme with *assuages*." [Eliot]

12. **ailanthus:** a common plant, "tree of heaven," which once established is difficult to root out.
22. **seine:** a large net.

The menace and caress of wave that breaks on water,
The distant rote in the granite teeth,
And the wailing warning from the approaching headland
Are all sea voices, and the heaving groaner
Rounded homewards, and the seagull: 35
And under the oppression of the silent fog
The tolling bell
Measures time not our time, rung by the unhurried
Ground swell, a time
Older than the time of chronometers, older   40
Than time counted by anxious worried women
Lying awake, calculating the future,
Trying to unweave, unwind, unravel
And piece together the past and the future,
Between midnight and dawn, when the past is all deception,   45
The future futureless, before the morning watch
When time stops and time is never ending;
And the ground swell, that is and was from the beginning,
Clangs
The bell.   50

                                II

Where is there an end of it, the soundless wailing,
The silent withering of autumn flowers
Dropping their petals and remaining motionless;
Where is there an end to the drifting wreckage,
The prayer of the bone on the beach, the unprayable   55
Prayer at the calamitous annunication?

    There is no end, but addition: the trailing
Consequence of further days and hours,
While emotion takes to itself the emotionless
Years of living among the breakage   60
Of what was believed in as the most reliable—
And therefore the fittest for renunciation.

    There is the final addition, the failing
Pride or resentment at failing powers,
The unattached devotion which might pass for devotionless,   65
In a drifting boat with a slow leakage,
The silent listening to the undeniable
Clamour of the bell of the last annunciation.

34. **groaner:** "a whistling buoy." [Eliot]

Where is the end of them, the fishermen sailing
Into the wind's tail, where the fog cowers?   70
We cannot think of a time that is oceanless
Or of an ocean not littered with wastage
Or of a future that is not liable
Like the past, to have no destination.

We have to think of them as forever bailing,   75
Setting and hauling, while the North East lowers
Over shallow banks unchanging and erosionless
Or drawing their money, drying sails at dockage;
Not as making a trip that will be unpayable
For a haul that will not bear examination.   80

There is no end of it, the voiceless wailing,
No end to the withering of withered flowers,
To the movement of pain that is painless and motionless,
To the drift of the sea and the drifting wreckage,
The bone's prayer to Death its God. Only the hardly, barely
      prayable   85
Prayer of the one Annunciation.

It seems, as one becomes older,
That the past has another pattern, and ceases to be a mere sequence—
Or even development: the latter a partial fallacy,
Encouraged by superficial notions of evolution,   90
Which becomes, in the popular mind, a means of disowning the past.
The moments of happiness—not the sense of well-being,
Fruition, fulfilment, security or affection,
Or even a very good dinner, but the sudden illumination—
We had the experience but missed the meaning,   95
And approach to the meaning restores the experience
In a different form, beyond any meaning
We can assign to happiness. I have said before
That the past experience revived in the meaning
Is not the experience of one life only   100
But of many generations—not forgetting
Something that is probably quite ineffable:
The backward look behind the assurance
Of recorded history, the backward half-look
Over the shoulder, towards the primitive terror.   105
Now, we come to discover that the moments of agony
(Whether, or not, due to misunderstanding,
Having hoped for the wrong things or dreaded the wrong things,

---

86. **Annunciation:** Mary prays: "Be it unto me according to thy word" when the angel announces she is to become the Mother of Jesus. Luke 1: 30–38.

Is not in question) are likewise permanent
With such permanence as time has. We appreciate this better   110
In the agony of others, nearly experienced,
Involving ourselves, than in our own.
For our own past is covered by the currents of action,
But the torment of others remains an experience
Unqualified, unworn by subsequent attrition.   115
People change, and smile: but the agony abides.
Time the destroyer is time the preserver,
Like the river with its cargo of dead Negroes, cows and chicken coops,
The bitter apple and the bite in the apple.
And the ragged rock in the restless waters,   120
Waves wash over it, fogs conceal it;
On a halcyon day it is merely a monument,
In navigable weather it is always a seamark
To lay a course by: but in the sombre season
Or the sudden fury, is what it always was.   125

III

I sometimes wonder if that is what Krishna meant—
Among other things—or one way of putting the same thing:
That the future is a faded song, a Royal Rose or a lavender spray
Of wistful regret for those who are not yet here to regret,
Pressed between yellow leaves of a book that has never been
          opened.   130
And the way up is the way down, the way forward is the way back.
You cannot face it steadily, but this thing is sure,
That time is no healer: the patient is no longer here.
When the train starts, and the passengers are settled
To fruit, periodicals and business letters   135
(And those who saw them off have left the platform)
Their faces relax from grief into relief,
To the sleepy rhythm of a hundred hours.
Fare forward, travellers! not escaping from the past
Into different lives, or into any future;   140
You are not the same people who left that station
Or who will arrive at any terminus,
While the narrowing rails slide together behind you;
And on the deck of the drumming liner
Watching the furrow that widens behind you,   145
You shall not think "the past is finished"
Or "the future is before us."

122. **halcyon**: peaceful.   *Bhagavad Ghita*, whose sayings are trans-
126. **Krishna**: Hindu deity, hero of the   lated in *ll.* 131–33 and *ll.* 151–68.

At nightfall, in the rigging and the aerial,
Is a voice descanting (though not to the ear,
The murmuring shell of time, and not in any language)   150
"Fare forward, you who think that you are voyaging;
You are not those who saw the harbour
Receding, or those who will disembark.
Here between the hither and the farther shore
While time is withdrawn, consider the future   155
And the past with an equal mind.
At the moment which is not of action or inaction
You can receive this: 'on whatever sphere of being
The mind of a man may be intent
At the time of death'—that is the one action   160
(And the time of death is every moment)
Which shall fructify in the lives of others:
And do not think of the fruit of action.
Fare forward.
                    O voyagers, O seamen,   165
You who come to port, and you whose bodies
Will suffer the trial and judgement of the sea,
Or whatever event, this is your real destination."
So Krishna, as when he admonished Arjuna
On the field of battle.   170
                    Not fare well,
But fare forward, voyagers.

                              IV

Lady, whose shrine stands on the promontory,
Pray for all those who are in ships, those
Whose business has to do with fish, and   175
Those concerned with every lawful traffic
And those who conduct them.

   Repeat a prayer also on behalf of
Women who have seen their sons or husbands
Setting forth, and not returning: 180
Figlia del tuo figlio,
Queen of Heaven.

   Also pray for those who were in ships, and
Ended their voyage on the sand, in the sea's lips
Or in the dark throat which will not reject them   185
Or wherever cannot reach them the sound of the sea bell's
Perpetual angelus.

---

169. **Krishna:** in the eighth lesson of the
Bhagavad Ghita.
173. **Lady:** the Virgin Mary.

181. **Figlia . . . figlio:** "the daughter of
Thy Son."
187. **angelus:** a devotion commemorating
the Incarnation.

V

To communicate with Mars, converse with spirits,
To report the behaviour of the sea monster,
Describe the horoscope, haruspicate or scry,   190
Observe disease in signatures, evoke
Biography from the wrinkles of the palm
And tragedy from fingers; release omens
By sortilege, or tea leaves, riddle the inevitable
With playing cards, fiddle with pentagrams   195
Or barbituric acids, or dissect
The recurrent image into pre-conscious terrors—
To explore the womb, or tomb, or dreams; all these are usual
Pastimes and drugs, and features of the press:
And always will be, some of them especially   200
When there is distress of nations and perplexity
Whether on the shores of Asia, or in the Edgware Road.
Men's curiosity searches past and future
And clings to that dimension. But to apprehend
The point of intersection of the timeless   205
With time, is an occupation for the saint—
No occupation either, but something given
And taken, in a lifetime's death in love,
Ardour and selflessness and self-surrender.
For most of us, there is only the unattended   210
Moment, the moment in and out of time,
The distraction fit, lost in a shaft of sunlight,
The wild thyme unseen, or the winter lightning
Or the waterfall, or music heard so deeply
That is not heard at all, but you are the music   215
While the music lasts. These are only hints and guesses,
Hints followed by guesses; and the rest
Is prayer, observance, discipline, thought and action.
The hint half guessed, the gift half understood, is Incarnation.
Here the impossible union.   220
Of spheres of existence is actual,
Here the past and future
Are conquered, and reconciled,
Where action were otherwise movement
Of that which is only moved   225
And has in it no source of movement—

---

190. **haruspicate; scry:** foresee the future by examining the entrails of sacrificed animals; crystal gazing.

194. **sortilege:** divination, enchantment.
195. **pentagrams:** symbolic five pointed stars.
202. **Edgware Road:** in London.

Driven by daemonic, chthonic
Powers. And right action is freedom
From past and future also.
For most of us, this is the aim   230
Never here to be realised;
Who are only undefeated
Because we have gone on trying;
We, content at the last
If our temporal reversion nourish   235
(Not too far from the yew-tree)
The life of significant soil.

THOMAS HARDY [1840–1928]

The Ruined Maid

"O 'Melia, my dear, this does everything crown!
Who could have supposed I should meet you in Town?
And whence such fair garments, such prosperi—ty?"—
"O didn't you know I'd been ruined?" said she.

—"You left us in tatters, without shoes or socks,   5
Tired of digging potatoes, and spudding up docks;
And now you've gay bracelets and bright feathers three!"—
"Yes: that's how we dress when we're ruined," said she.

—"At home in the barton you said 'thee' and 'thou',
And 'thik oon', and 'theäs oon', and 't 'other'; but now   10
Your talking quite fits 'ee for high compa—ny!"—
"Some polish is gained with one's ruin," said she.

—"Your hands were like paws then, your face blue and bleak
But now I'm bewitched by your delicate cheek,
And your little gloves fit as on any la—dy!"—   15
"We never do work when we're ruined," says she.

227. **chthonic:** underworld.

6. **spudding up docks:** digging out dock-
weed.
9. **barton:** farmyard.
10. **thik oon, theäs oon:** this one, that one.

—"You used to call home-life a hag-ridden dream,
And you'd sigh, and you'd sock; but at present you seem
To know not of megrims or melancho—ly!"—
"True. One's pretty lively when ruined," said she.   20

—"I wish I had feathers, a fine sweeping gown,
And a delicate face, and could strut about Town!"—
"My dear—a raw country girl, such as you be,
Cannot quite expect that. You ain't ruined," said she.

Hap

If but some vengeful god would call to me
From up the sky, and laugh: "Thou suffering thing,
Know that thy sorrow is my ecstasy,
That thy love's loss is my hate's profiting!"
Then would I bear it, clench myself, and die,   5
Steeled by the sense of ire unmerited;
Half-eased in that a Powerfuller than I
Had willed and meted me the tears I shed.

But not so. How arrives it joy lies slain,
And why unblooms the best hope ever sown?   10
—Crass Casualty obstructs the sun and rain,
And dicing Time for gladness casts a moan. . . .
These purblind Doomsters had as readily strown
Blisses about my pilgrimage as pain.

Neutral Tones

We stood by a pond that winter day,
And the sun was white, as though chidden of God,
And a few leaves lay on the starving sod;
    They had fallen from an ash, and were gray.

Your eyes on me were as eyes that rove   5
Over tedious riddles solved years ago;
And some words played between us to and fro
    On which lost the more by our love.

18. **sock:** sigh aloud.   **Hap** chance (also "Casualty," *l.* 11).
19. **megrims:** low spirits.   13. **purblind Doomsters:** blind judges.

The smile on your mouth was the deadest thing
Alive enough to have strength to die;   10
And a grin of bitterness swept thereby
   Like an ominous bird a-wing. . . .

Since then, keen lessons that love deceives,
And wrings with wrong, have shaped to me
Your face, and the God-curst sun, and a tree,   15
   And a pond edged with grayish leaves.

I look into my glass

   I look into my glass,
   And view my wasting skin,
   And say, "Would God it came to pass
   My heart had shrunk as thin!"

   For then, I, undistrest   5
   By hearts grown cold to me,
   Could lonely wait my endless rest
   With equanimity.

   But Time, to make me grieve,
   Part steals, lets part abide;   10
   And shakes this fragile frame at eve
   With throbbings of noontide.

Channel Firing

That night your great guns unawares,
Shook all our coffins as we lay,
And broke the chancel window-squares,
We thought it was the Judgment-day

Channel Firing: written four months before
World War I.

And sat upright. While drearisome   5
Arose the howl of wakened hounds:
The mouse let fall the altar-crumb,
The worms drew back into the mounds,

The glebe cow drooled. Till God called, "No;
It's gunnery practice out at sea   10
Just as before you went below;
The world is as it used to be:

"All nations striving strong to make
Red war yet redder. Mad as hatters
They do no more for Christès sake   15
Than you who are helpless in such matters.

"That this is not the judgment-hour
For some of them's a blessed thing,
For if it were they'd have to scour
Hell's floor for so much threatening . . .   20

"Ha, ha. It will be warmer when
I blow the trumpet (if indeed
I ever do; for you are men,
And rest eternal sorely need)."

So down we lay again. "I wonder,   25
Will the world ever saner be,"
Said one, "than when He sent us under
In our indifferent century!"

And many a skeleton shook his head.
"Instead of preaching forty year,"   30
My neighbor Parson Thirdly said,
"I wish I had stuck to pipes and beer."

Again the guns disturbed the hour,
Roaring their readiness to avenge,
As far inland as Stourton Tower,   35
And Camelot, and starlit Stonehenge.

9. **glebe:** land belonging to a church (here, the burial ground).
35–36. **Stourton . . . Stonehenge:** a fictional town, associated by Hardy with the River Stour in Dorset; Camelot: legendary capital of King Arthur; Stonehenge: prehistoric and mysterious circle of huge stones on Salisbury Plain.

OSCAR WILDE [1856–1900]

Impression du Matin

The Thames nocturne of blue and gold
    Changed to a harmony in gray;
    A barge with ocher-colored hay
Dropped from the wharf: and chill and cold

The yellow fog came creeping down   5
    The bridges, till the houses' walls
    Seemed changed to shadows, and St. Paul's
Loomed like a bubble o'er the town.

Then suddenly arose the clang
    Of waking life; the streets were stirred   10
    With country wagons; and a bird
Flew to the glistening roofs and sang.

But one pale woman all alone,
    The daylight kissing her wan hair,
    Loitered beneath the gas lamps' flare,   15
With lips of flame and heart of stone.

E Tenebris

Come down, O Christ, and help me! reach thy hand,
    For I am drowning in a stormier sea
    Than Simon on thy lake of Galilee:
The wine of life is spilt upon the sand,
My heart is as some famine-murdered land   5
    Whence all good things have perished utterly,
    And well I know my soul in Hell must lie
If I this night before God's throne should stand.
"He sleeps perchance, or rideth to the chase,
    Like Baal, when his prophets howled that name   10
    From morn to noon on Carmel's smitten height."
Nay, peace, I shall behold, before the night,
    The feet of brass, the robe more white than flame,
    The wounded hands, the weary human face.

Impression du Matin: "Impression of the Morning."
4. **Dropped:** dropped downstream.

E Tenebris: "Out of Darkness."
10. **Baal:** When Baal did not perform what his worshippers prayed for, Elijah ironically suggested that their god was sleeping or hunting.
13. **feet of brass:** "One like unto the Son of man" (Christ) is described as having "feet like unto fine brass" in Revelation 1: 15.

A. E. HOUSMAN [1859–1936]

To an Athlete Dying Young

The time you won your town the race
We chaired you through the market-place;
Man and boy stood cheering by,
And home we brought you shoulder-high.

To-day, the road all runners come,   5
Shoulder-high we bring you home,
And set you at your threshold down,
Townsman of a stiller town.

Smart lad, to slip betimes away
From fields where glory does not stay   10
And early though the laurel grows
It withers quicker than the rose.

Eyes the shady night has shut
Cannot see the record cut,
And silence sounds no worse than cheers   15
After earth has stopped the ears:

Now you will not swell the rout
Of lads that wore their honours out,
Runners whom renown outran
And the name died before the man.   20

So set, before its echoes fade,
The fleet foot on the sill of shade,
And hold to the low lintel up
The still-defended challenge-cup.

And round that early-laurelled head   25
Will flock to gaze the strengthless dead,
And find unwithered on its curls
The garland briefer than a girl's.

On Wenlock Edge

On Wenlock Edge the wood's in trouble;
    His forest fleece the Wrekin heaves;
The gale, it plies the saplings double,
    And thick on Severn snow the leaves.

'Twould blow like this through holt and hanger   5
    When Uricon the city stood:
'Tis the old wind in the old anger,
    But then it threshed another wood.

Then, 'twas before my time, the Roman
    At yonder heaving hill would stare: 10
The blood that warms an English yeoman,
    The thoughts that hurt him, they were there.

There, like the wind through woods in riot,
    Through him the gale of life blew high;
The tree of man was never quiet: 15
    Then 'twas the Roman, now 'tis I.

The gale, it plies the saplings double,
    It blows so hard, 'twill soon be gone:
To-day the Roman and his trouble
    Are ashes under Uricon.   20

Think no more, lad

Think no more, lad; laugh, be jolly:
    Why should men make haste to die?
Empty heads and tongues a-talking
Make the rough road easy walking,
And the feather pate of folly   5
    Bears the falling sky.

Oh, 'tis jesting, dancing, drinking
    Spins the heavy world around.
If young hearts were not so clever,
Oh, they would be young for ever: 10
Think no more; 'tis only thinking
    Lays lads underground.

1. **Wenlock Edge:** ridge in Shropshire. The Wrekin is a hill, the Severn a river, in Shropshire.
5. **holt ... hanger:** wooded hill, and wood on side of steep hill.
6. **Uricon:** ancient Roman city in Shropshire.

Terence, this is stupid stuff

"Terence, this is stupid stuff:
You eat your victuals fast enough;
There can't be much amiss, 'tis clear,
To see the rate you drink your beer.
But oh, good Lord, the verse you make,   5
It gives a chap the belly-ache.
The cow, the old cow, she is dead;
It sleeps well, the horned head:
We poor lads, 'tis our turn now
To hear such tunes as killed the cow.   10
Pretty friendship 'tis to rhyme
Your friends to death before their time
Moping melancholy mad:
Come, pipe a tune to dance to, lad."

   Why, if 'tis dancing you would be,   15
There's brisker pipes than poetry.
Say for what were hop-yards meant,
Or why was Burton built on Trent?
Oh many a peer of England brews
Livelier liquor than the Muse,   20
And malt does more than Milton can
To justify God's ways to man.
Ale, man, ale's the stuff to drink
For fellows whom it hurts to think:
Look into the pewter pot   25
To see the world as the world's not.
And faith 'tis pleasant till 'tis past:
The mischief is that 'twill not last.
Oh I have been to Ludlow fair
And left my necktie God knows where,   30
And carried halfway home, or near,
Pints and quarts of Ludlow beer:
Then the world seemed none so bad,
And I myself a sterling lad;
And down in lovely muck I've lain,   35
Happy till I woke again.

Terence: Housman had planned to call his collection *The Poems of Terence Hearsay.* 18. **Burton:** Burton-on-Trent, an impor- tant brewing center. Brewers were often raised to the peerage. 29. **Ludlow:** town in Shropshire.

Then I saw the morning sky:
Heigho, the tale was all a lie;
The world it was the old world yet,
I was I, my things were wet,   40
And nothing now remained to do
But begin the game anew.

   Therefore, since the world has still
Much good, but much less good than ill,
And while the sun and moon endure   45
Luck's a chance but trouble's sure,
I'd face it as a wise man would,
And train for ill and not for good.
'Tis true, the stuff I bring for sale
Is not so brisk a brew as ale: 50
Out of a stem that scored the hand
I wrung it in a weary land.
But take it: if the smack is sour,
The better for the embittered hour;
I should do good to heart and head   55
When your soul is in my soul's stead;
And I will friend you, if I may,
In the dark and cloudy day.

   There was a king reigned in the East:
There, when kings will sit to feast,   60
They get their fill before they think
With poisoned meat and poisoned drink.
He gathered all that springs to birth
From the many-venomed earth;
First a little, thence to more,   65
He sampled all her killing store;
And easy, smiling, seasoned sound,
Sate the king when healths went round.
They put arsenic in his meat
And stared aghast to watch him eat;   70
They poured strychnine in his cup
And shook to see him drink it up:
They shook, they stared as white's their shirt:
Them it was their poison hurt.
—I tell the tale that I heard told.   75
Mithridates, he died old.

---

51. **scored:** made many cuts on.   have immunized himself to poisons by
76. **Mithridates:** King of Pontus, said to   taking small quantities frequently.

Eight O'Clock

He stood, and heard the steeple
  Sprinkle the quarters on the morning town.
One, two, three, four, to market-place and people
  It tossed them down.

Strapped, noosed, nighing his hour,   5
  He stood and counted them and cursed his luck;
And then the clock collected in the tower
  Its strength, and struck.

Easter Hymn

If in that Syrian garden, ages slain,
You sleep, and know not you are dead in vain,
Nor even in dreams behold how dark and bright
Ascends in smoke and fire by day and night
The hate you died to quench and could but fan,   5
Sleep well and see no morning, son of man.

But if, the grave rent and the stone rolled by,
At the right hand of majesty on high
You sit, and sitting so remember yet
Your tears, your agony and bloody sweat,   10
Your cross and passion and the life you gave,
Bow hither out of heaven and see and save.

EDWIN ARLINGTON ROBINSON [1869–1935]

The Clerks

I did not think that I should find them there
When I came back again; but there they stood,
As in the days they dreamed of when young blood
Was in their cheeks and women called them fair.
Be sure, they met me with an ancient air,   5
And yes, there was a shop-worn brotherhood
About them; but the men were just as good,
And just as human as they ever were.

And you that ache so much to be sublime,
And you that feed yourselves with your descent,   10
What comes of all your visions and your fears?
Poets and kings are but the clerks of Time,
Tiering the same dull webs of discontent,
Clipping the same sad alnage of the years.

Mr. Flood's Party

Old Eben Flood, climbing alone one night
Over the hill between the town below
And the forsaken upland hermitage
That held as much as he should ever know
On earth again of home, paused warily.   5
The road was his with not a native near;
And Eben, having leisure, said aloud,
For no man else in Tilbury Town to hear:

"Well, Mr. Flood, we have the harvest moon
Again, and we may not have many more;   10
The bird is on the wing, the poet says,
And you and I have said it here before.
Drink to the bird." He raised up to the light
The jug that he had gone so far to fill,
And answered huskily: "Well, Mr. Flood,   15
Since you propose it, I believe I will."

Alone, as if enduring to the end
A valiant armor of scarred hopes outworn,
He stood there in the middle of the road
Like Roland's ghost winding a silent horn.   20
Below him, in the town among the trees,
Where friends of other days had honored him,
A phantom salutation of the dead
Rang thinly till old Eben's eyes were dim.

Then, as a mother lays her sleeping child   25
Down tenderly, fearing it may awake,
He set the jug down slowly at his feet
With trembling care, knowing that most things break;

14. **alnage:** a measurement of cloth by the ell, especially with official inspection and certification.

8. **Tilbury Town:** fictional New England town, setting of many of Robinson's poems.

20. **Roland:** legendary hero of Charlemagne's time. Though his horn could be heard at great distances, he blew it too late to save himself from an ambush and massacre.

And only when assured that on firm earth
It stood, as the uncertain lives of men   30
Assuredly did not, he paced away,
And with his hand extended paused again:

"Well, Mr. Flood, we have not met like this
In a long time; and many a change has come
To both of us, I fear, since last it was   35
We had a drop together. Welcome home!"
Convivially returning with himself,
Again he raised the jug up to the light;
And with an acquiescent quaver said:
"Well, Mr. Flood, if you insist, I might.   40

"Only a very little, Mr. Flood—
For auld lang syne. No more, sir; that will do."
So, for the time, apparently it did,
And Eben evidently thought so too;
For soon amid the silver loneliness   45
Of night he lifted up his voice and sang,
Secure, with only two moons listening,
Until the whole harmonious landscape rang—

"For auld lang syne." The weary throat gave out,
The last word wavered, and the song was done.   50
He raised again the jug regretfully
And shook his head, and was again alone.
There was not much that was ahead of him,
And there was nothing in the town below—
Where strangers would have shut the many doors   55
That many friends had opened long ago.

New England

Here where the wind is always north-north-east
And children learn to walk on frozen toes,
Wonder begets an envy of all those
Who boil elsewhere with such a lyric yeast
Of love that you will hear them at a feast   5
Where demons would appeal for some repose,
Still clamoring where the chalice overflows
And crying wildest who have drunk the least.

Passion is here a soilure of the wits,
We're told, and Love a cross for them to bear;   10
Joy shivers in the corner where she knits
And Conscience always has the rocking-chair,
Cheerful as when she tortured into fits
The first cat that was ever killed by Care.

WALLACE STEVENS [1879–1955]

The Emperor of Ice Cream

Call the roller of big cigars,
The muscular one, and bid him whip
In kitchen cups concupiscent curds.
Let the wenches dawdle in such dress
As they are used to wear, and let the boys   5
Bring flowers in last month's newspapers.
Let be be finale of seem.
The only emperor is the emperor of ice-cream.

Take from the dresser of deal,
Lacking the three glass knobs, that sheet   10
On which she embroidered fantails once
And spread it so as to cover her face.
If her horny feet protrude, they come
To show how cold she is, and dumb.
Let the lamp affix its beam.   15
The only emperor is the emperor of ice-cream.

Sunday Morning

I

Complacencies of the peignoir, and late
Coffee and oranges in a sunny chair,
And the green freedom of a cockatoo
Upon a rug mingle to dissipate
The holy hush of ancient sacrifice.   5
She dreams a little, and she feels the dark
Encroachment of that old catastrophe,
As a calm darkens among water-lights.

9. **deal:** fir or pine; cheap, plain wood.   1. **peignoir:** negligee.

The pungent oranges and bright, green wings
Seem things in some procession of the dead,   10
Winding across wide water, without sound.
The day is like wide water, without sound,
Stilled for the passing of her dreaming feet
Over the seas, to silent Palestine,
Dominion of the blood and sepulchre.   15

II

Why should she give her bounty to the dead?
What is divinity if it can come
Only in silent shadows and in dreams?
Shall she not find in comforts of the sun,
In pungent fruit and bright, green wings, or else   20
In any balm or beauty of the earth,
Things to be cherished like the thought of heaven?
Divinity must live within herself:
Passions of rain, or moods in falling snow;
Grievings in loneliness, or unsubdued   25
Elations when the forest blooms; gusty
Emotions on wet roads on autumn nights;
All pleasures and all pains, remembering
The bough of summer and the winter branch.
These are the measures destined for her soul.   30

III

Jove in the clouds had his inhuman birth.
No mother suckled him, no sweet land gave
Large-mannered motions to his mythy mind.
He moved among us, as a muttering king,
Magnificent, would move among his hinds,   35
Until our blood, commingling, virginal,
With heaven, brought such requital to desire
The very hinds discerned it, in a star.
Shall our blood fail? Or shall it come to be
The blood of paradise? And shall the earth   40
Seem all of paradise that we shall know?
The sky will be much friendlier then than now,
A part of labor and a part of pain,
And next in glory to enduring love,
Not this dividing and indifferent blue.   45

---

31. **Jove:** He was god of the sky and its
phenomena, as well as king of the gods
and men.

38. **hinds ... star:** shepherds seeing the
Star of Bethlehem ("hinds": field-
servants).

IV

She says, "I am content when wakened birds,
Before they fly, test the reality
Of misty fields, by their sweet questionings;
But when the birds are gone, and their warm fields
Return no more, where, then, is paradise?"   50
There is not any haunt of prophecy,
Nor any old chimera of the grave,
Neither the golden underground, nor isle
Melodious, where spirits gat them home,
Nor visionary south, nor cloudy palm   55
Remote on heaven's hill, that has endured
As April's green endures; or will endure
Like her remembrance of awakened birds,
Or her desire for June and evening, tipped
By the consummation of the swallow's wings.   60

V

She says, "But in contentment I still feel
The need of some imperishable bliss."
Death is the mother of beauty; hence from her,
Alone, shall come fulfillment to our dreams
And our desires. Although she strews the leaves   65
Of sure obliteration on our paths,
The path sick sorrow took, the many paths
Where triumph rang its brassy phrase, or love
Whispered a little out of tenderness,
She makes the willow shiver in the sun   70
For maidens who were wont to sit and gaze
Upon the grass, relinquished to their feet.
She causes boys to pile new plums and pears
On disregarded plate. The maidens taste
And stray impassioned in the littering leaves.   75

VI

Is there no change of death in paradise?
Does ripe fruit never fall? Or do the boughs
Hang always heavy in that perfect sky,
Unchanging, yet so like our perishing earth,
With rivers like our own that seek for seas   80
They never find, the same receding shores
That never touch with inarticulate pang?

54. **gat:** (archaic) got.

Why set the pear upon those river-banks
Or spice the shores with odors of the plum?
Alas, that they should wear our colors there,   85
The silken weavings of our afternoons,
And pick the strings of our insipid lutes!
Death is the mother of beauty, mystical,
Within whose burning bosom we devise
Our earthly mothers waiting, sleeplessly.   90

VII

Supple and turbulent, a ring of men
Shall chant in orgy on a summer morn
Their boisterous devotion to the sun,
Not as a god, but as a god might be,
Naked among them, like a savage source.   95
Their chant shall be a chant of paradise,
Out of their blood, returning to the sky;
And in their chant shall enter, voice by voice,
The windy lake wherein their lord delights,
The trees, like serafin, and echoing hills,   100
That choir among themselves long afterward.
They shall know well the heavenly fellowship
Of men that perish and of summer morn.
And whence they came and whither they shall go
The dew upon their feet shall manifest.   105

VIII

She hears, upon that water without sound,
A voice that cries, "The tomb in Palestine
Is not the porch of spirits lingering.
It is the grave of Jesus, where he lay."
We live in an old chaos of the sun,   110
Or old dependency of day and night,
Or island solitude, unsponsored, free,
Of that wide water, inescapable.
Deer walk upon our mountains, and the quail
Whistle about us their spontaneous cries;   115
Sweet berries ripen in the wilderness;
And, in the isolation of the sky,
At evening, casual flocks of pigeons make
Ambiguous undulations as they sink,
Downward to darkness, on extended wings.   120

95. **source:** one meaning is "spring" or "fountain."

100. **serafin:** Seraphim (pl.), the highest order of angels, who sing around the throne of God.

Peter Quince at the Clavier

1

Just as my fingers on these keys
Make music, so the self-same sounds
On my spirit make a music too.

Music is feeling then, not sound;
And thus it is that what I feel,   5
Here in this room, desiring you,

Thinking of your blue-shadowed silk,
Is music. It is like the strain
Waked in the elders by Susanna:

Of a green evening, clear and warm,   10
She bathed in her still garden, while
The red-eyed elders, watching, felt

The basses of their being throb
In witching chords, and their thin blood
Pulse pizzicati of Hosanna.   15

2

In the green water, clear and warm,
Susanna lay.
She searched
The touch of springs,
And found   20
Concealed imaginings.
She sighed
For so much melody.

Upon the bank, she stood
In the cool   25
Of spent emotions.
She felt, among the leaves,
The dew
Of old devotions.

9. **Susanna:** The story of Susanna and the elders is given in The History of Susanna in the Apocrypha of the Authorized Version of the Bible. In other translations, see Daniel 13.

15. **pizzicati:** sounds made by plucking a stringed instrument.

She walked upon the grass, 30
Still quavering.
The winds were like her maids,
On timid feet,
Fetching her woven scarves,
Yet wavering. 35

A breath upon her hand
Muted the night.
She turned—
A cymbal crashed,
And roaring horns. 40

3

Soon, with a noise like tambourines,
Came her attendant Byzantines.

They wondered why Susanna cried
Against the elders by her side:

And as they whispered, the refrain 45
Was like a willow swept by rain.

Anon their lamps' uplifted flame
Revealed Susanna and her shame.

And then the simpering Byzantines,
Fled, with a noise like tambourines. 50

4

Beauty is momentary in the mind—
The fitful tracing of a portal;
But in the flesh it is immortal.
The body dies; the body's beauty lives.
So evenings die, in their green going, 55
A wave, interminably flowing.
So gardens die, their meek breath scenting
The cowl of Winter, done repenting.
So maidens die to the auroral
Celebration of a maiden's choral. 60
Susanna's music touched the bawdy strings
Of those white elders; but, escaping,
Left only Death's ironic scraping.
Now in its immortality, it plays
On the clear viol of her memory, 65
And makes a constant sacrament of praise.

42. **Byzantines:** A word chosen probably for sound more than sense. A pack of fawning servitors as might be imagined in the formal atmosphere of the court of the Eastern Roman (Byzantine) Empire is probably meant.

Thirteen Ways of Looking at a Blackbird

I

Among twenty snowy mountains,
The only moving thing
Was the eye of the blackbird.

II

I was of three minds,
Like a tree   5
In which there are three blackbirds.

III

The blackbird whirled in the autumn winds.
It was a small part of the pantomime.

IV

A man and a woman
Are one.   10
A man and a woman and a blackbird
Are one.

V

I do not know which to prefer,
The beauty of inflections
Or the beauty of innuendoes,   15
The blackbird whistling
Or just after.

VI

Icicles filled the long window
With barbaric glass.
The shadow of the blackbird   20
Crossed it, to and fro.
The mood
Traced in the shadow
An indecipherable cause.

VII

O thin men of Haddam,   25
Why do you image golden birds?
Do you not see how the blackbird
Walks around the feet
Of the women about you?

VIII

I know noble accents   30
And lucid, inescapable rhythms;
But I know, too,
That the blackbird is involved
In what I know.

IX

When the blackbird flew out of sight,   35
It marked the edge
Of one of many circles.

X

At the sight of blackbirds
Flying in a green light,
Even the bawds of euphony   40
Would cry out sharply.

XI

He rode over Connecticut
In a glass coach.
Once, a fear pierced him,
In that he mistook   45
The shadow of his equipage
For blackbirds.

XII

The river is moving.
The blackbird must be flying,

XIII

It was evening all afternoon.   50
It was snowing
And it was going to snow.
The blackbird sat
In the cedar-limbs.

25. **Haddam:** town on Connecticut River,
specializing in metal products.

The Glass of Water

That the glass would melt in heat,
That the water would freeze in cold,
Shows that this object is merely a state,
One of many, between two poles. So,
In the metaphysical, there are these poles.   5

Here in the centre stands the glass. Light
Is the lion that comes down to drink. There
And in that state, the glass is a pool.
Ruddy are his eyes and ruddy are his claws
When light comes down to wet his frothy jaws   10

And in the water winding weeds move round.
And there and in another state—the refractions,
The *metaphysica*, the plastic parts of poems
Crash in the mind—But, fat Jocundus, worrying
About what stands here in the centre, not the glass,   15

But in the centre of our lives, this time, this day,
It is a state, this spring among the politicians
Playing cards. In a village of the indigenes,
One would have still to discover. Among the dogs and dung,
One would continue to contend with one's ideas.   20

Connoisseur of Chaos

I

A. A violent order is disorder; and
B. A great disorder is an order. These
Two things are one. (Pages of illustrations.)

II

If all the green of spring was blue, and it is;
If the flowers of South Africa were bright   5
On the tables of Connecticut, and they are;
If Englishmen lived without tea in Ceylon, and they do;
And if it all went on in an orderly way,
And it does; a law of inherent opposites,
Of essential unity, is as pleasant as port,   10
As pleasant as the brush-strokes of a bough,
An upper, particular bough in, say, Marchand.

13. **metaphysica:** things outside or beyond physical nature. See *l. 5.*
18. **indigenes:** (Span.) natives (South American Indians are principally implied).

12. **Marchand:** probably Jean Marchand, the French painter and lithographer, and illustrator of Paul Valéry (1883–1941).

III

After all the pretty contrast of life and death
Proves that these opposite things partake of one,
At least that was the theory, when bishops' books   15
Resolved the world. We cannot go back to that.
The squirming facts exceed the squamous mind,
If one may say so. And yet relation appears,
A small relation expanding like the shade
Of a cloud on sand, a shape on the side of a hill.   20

IV

A. Well, an old order is a violent one.
This proves nothing. Just one more truth, one more
Element in the immense disorder of truths.
B. It is April as I write. The wind
Is blowing after days of constant rain.   25
All this, of course, will come to summer soon.
But suppose the disorder of truths should ever come
To an order, most Plantagenet, most fixed . . .
A great disorder is an order. Now, A
And B are not like statuary, posed   30
For a vista in the Louvre. They are things chalked
On the sidewalk so that the pensive man may see.

V

The pensive man . . . He sees that eagle float
For which the intricate Alps are a single nest.

The Sense of the Sleight-of-Hand Man

One's grand flights, one's Sunday baths,
One's tootings at the wedding of the soul
Occur as they occur. So bluish clouds
Occurred above the empty house and the leaves
Of the rhododendrons rattled their gold,   5
As if someone lived there. Such floods of white
Came bursting from the clouds. So the wind
Threw its contorted strength around the sky.

15. **bishops' books:** theological treatises   28. **Plantagenet:** family name of medieval
to show the order and system of the world   dynasty of English kings, beginning with
under God.   Henry II. Under him a strict feudal order
                                                 was firmly established.

Could you have said the bluejay suddenly
Would swoop to earth? It is a wheel, the rays   10
Around the sun. The wheel survives the myths.
The fire eye in the clouds survives the gods.
To think of a dove with an eye of grenadine
And pines that are cornets, so it occurs,
And a little island full of geese and stars: 15
It may be that the ignorant man, alone,
Has any chance to mate his life with life
That is the sensual, pearly spouse, the life
That is fluent in even the wintriest bronze.

WILLIAM CARLOS WILLIAMS [1883–1963]

El Hombre

It's a strange courage
you give me ancient star.

Shine alone in the sunrise
toward which you lend no part!

Spring and All

By the road to the contagious hospital
under the surge of the blue
mottled clouds driven from the
northeast—a cold wind. Beyond, the
waste of broad, muddy fields   5
brown with dried weeds, standing and fallen

patches of standing water
the scattering of tall trees

All along the road the reddish
purplish, forked, upstanding, twiggy   10
stuff of bushes and small trees
with dead, brown leaves under them
leafless vines—

Lifeless in appearance, sluggish
dazed spring approaches— 15

They enter the new world naked,
cold, uncertain of all
save that they enter. All about them
the cold, familiar wind—

Now the grass, tomorrow 20
the stiff curl of wild carrot leaf
One by one objects are defined—
It quickens: clarity, outline of leaf

But now the stark dignity of
entrance—Still, the profound change 25
has come upon them: rooted they
grip down and begin to awaken

To Elsie

The pure products of America
go crazy—
mountain folk from Kentucky

or the ribbed north end of
Jersey 5
with its isolate lakes and

valleys, its deaf-mutes, thieves
old names
and promiscuity between

devil-may-care men who have taken 10
to railroading
out of sheer lust of adventure—

and young slatterns, bathed
in filth
from Monday to Saturday 15

to be tricked out that night
with gauds
from imaginations which have no

peasant traditions to give them
character   20
but flutter and flaunt

sheer rags—succumbing without
emotion
save numbed terror

under some hedge of choke-cherry   25
or viburnum—
which they cannot express—

Unless it be that marriage
perhaps
with a dash of Indian blood   30

will throw up a girl so desolate
so hemmed round
with disease or murder

that she'll be rescued by an
agent—   35
reared by the state and

sent out at fifteen to work in
some hard pressed
house in the suburbs—

some doctor's family, some Elsie—   40
voluptuous water
expressing with broken

brain the truth about us—
her great
ungainly hips and flopping breasts   45

addressed to cheap
jewelry
and rich young men with fine eyes

as if the earth under our feet
were   50
an excrement of some sky

and we degraded prisoners
destined
to hunger until we eat filth

while the imagination strains   55
after deer
going by fields of goldenrod in

the stifling heat of September
Somehow
it seems to destroy us   60

It is only in isolate flecks that
something
is given off

No one
to witness   65
and adjust, no one to drive the car

Poem

As the cat
climbed over
the top of

the jamcloset
first the right   5
forefoot

carefully
then the hind
stepped down

into the pit of   10
the empty
flowerpot

The Jungle

It is not the still weight
of the trees, the
breathless interior of the wood,
tangled with wrist-thick

vines, the flies, reptiles,   5
the forever fearful monkeys
screaming and running
in the branches—

        but

a girl waiting   10
shy, brown, soft-eyed—
to guide you
        Upstairs, sir.

E Z R A   P O U N D   [1885–   ]

The Garden

En robe de parade. Samain

Like a skein of loose silk blown against a wall
She walks by the railing of a path in Kensington Gardens,
And she is dying piece-meal
      of a sort of emotional anæmia.

And round about there is a rabble
Of the filthy, sturdy, unkillable infants of the very poor.   5
They shall inherit the earth.

In her is the end of breeding.
Her boredom is exquisite and excessive.
She would like some one to speak to her,
And is almost afraid that I
      will commit that indiscretion.   10

Portrait d'une Femme

Your mind and you are our Sargasso Sea,
London has swept about you this score years
And bright ships left you this or that in fee:
Ideas, old gossip, oddments of all things,
Strange spars of knowledge and dimmed wares of price.   5
Great minds have sought you—lacking someone else.

En ... Samain: "dressed for a walk."   **Portrait ... Femme:** Portrait of a Lady.
Albert Samain (1858–1900), French poet.   1. **Sargasso Sea:** a part of the Atlantic
2. **Kensington Gardens:** a park in London.   between the Azores and the West Indies
    named for the seaweed which accumulates
    there.

You have been second always. Tragical?
No. You preferred it to the usual thing:
One dull man, dulling and uxorious,
One average mind—with one thought less, each year.   10
Oh, you are patient, I have seen you sit
Hours, where something might have floated up.
And now you pay one. Yes, you richly pay.
You are a person of some interest, one comes to you
And takes strange gain away: 15
Trophies fished up; some curious suggestion;
Fact that leads nowhere; and a tale or two,
Pregnant with mandrakes, or with something else
That might prove useful and yet never proves,
That never fits a corner or shows use,   20
Or finds its hour upon the loom of days:
The tarnished, gaudy, wonderful old work;
Idols and ambergris and rare inlays,
These are your riches, your great store; and yet
For all this sea-hoard of deciduous things,   25
Strange woods half sodden, and new brighter stuff:
In the slow float of differing light and deep,
No! there is nothing! In the whole and all,
Nothing that's quite your own.
                Yet this is you.   30

In a Station of the Metro

The apparition of these faces in the crowd;
Petals on a wet, black bough.

The Lake Isle

O God, O Venus, O Mercury, patron of thieves,
Give me in due time, I beseech you, a little tobacco-shop,
With the little bright boxes
          piled up neatly upon the shelves
And the loose fragrant cavendish   5
          and the shag,

9. **uxorious:** doting on one's wife.
18. **mandrakes:** a plant having a forked
root, thought to promote fertility.
23. **ambergris:** a waxy substance valued in
making perfume; a morbid secretion of the
sperm whale.
25. **deciduous:** falling off at maturity, as
leaves and some antlers.

Metro: the Paris subway.

The Lake Isle: possibly an allusion to
Yeats's romantic "The Lake Isle of Innis-
free."

And the bright Virginia
      loose under the bright glass cases,
And a pair of scales not too greasy,
And the whores dropping in for a word or two in passing,   10
For a flip word, and to tidy their hair a bit.

O God, O Venus, O Mercury, patron of thieves,
Lend me a little tobacco-shop,
      or install me in any profession
Save this damned profession of writing,   15
      where one need one's brains all the time.

The River-Merchant's Wife: A Letter

While my hair was still cut straight across my forehead
Played I about the front gate, pulling flowers.
You came by on bamboo stilts, playing horse,
You walked about my seat, playing with blue plums.
And we went on living in the village of Chokan: 5
Two small people, without dislike or suspicion.

At fourteen I married My Lord you.
I never laughed, being bashful.
Lowering my head, I looked at the wall.
Called to, a thousand times, I never looked back.   10

At fifteen I stopped scowling,
I desired my dust to be mingled with yours
Forever and forever and forever.
Why should I climb the look out?

At sixteen you departed,   15
You went into far Ku-to-yen, by the river of swirling eddies,
And you have been gone five months.
The monkeys make sorrowful noise overhead.

You dragged your feet when you went out.
By the gate now, the moss is grown, the different mosses,   20
Too deep to clear them away!
The leaves fall early this autumn, in wind.

The paired butterflies are already yellow with August
Over the grass in the West garden;
They hurt me. I grow older.   25
If you are coming down through the narrows of the river Kiang,
Please let me know beforehand,
And I will come out to meet you
        As far as Cho-fu-Sa.

By Rihaku

Hugh Selwyn Mauberley

E. P. Ode Pour L'election de Son Sepulchre

I

For three years, out of key with his time,
He strove to resuscitate the dead art
Of poetry; to maintain "the sublime"
In the old sense. Wrong from the start—

No, hardly, but seeing he had been born   5
In a half-savage country, out of date;
Bent resolutely on wringing lilies from the acorn;
Capaneus; trout for factitious bait;

Ἴδμεν γάρ τοι πάνθ', ὅσ' ἐνὶ Τροίῃ
Caught in the unstopped ear;   10
Giving the rocks small lee-way
The chopped seas held him, therefore, that year.

His true Penelope was Flaubert,
He fished by obstinate isles;
Observed the elegance of Circe's hair   15
Rather than the mottoes on sun-dials.

Rihaku: an 8th-century A.D. Chinese poet.

Ode ... Sepulchre: Ode on the choice of his tomb.
8. **Capaneus:** One of the seven against Thebes. He swore he would enter the city in spite of Zeus, and on reaching the top of the wall, was struck down by a thunder-bolt.
9. *Ἴδμεν ... Τροίῃ*: a variation of the Siren's song in *The Odyssey*, meaning "For we know all the things that are in Troy." The Sirens lured mariners onto dangerous rocks.
10. **unstopped ear:** Odysseus stopped the ears of the crew so that they would not hear the sirens; he had himself tied to the mast.
13. **Penelope; Flaubert:** the faithful wife of Odysseus; Gustav Flaubert (1821–1880), the French novelist who searched for exact expression and satirized the banality of contemporary life.
15. **Circe:** the sorceress who held Odysseus captive and transformed his crew into swine.
16. **mottoes:** usually reminders that time flies.

Unaffected by "the march of events"
He passed from men's memory in *l'an trentiesme*
De son eage; the case presents
No adjunct to the Muses' diadem.   20

II

The age demanded an image
Of its accelerated grimace,
Something for the modern stage,
Not, at any rate, an Attic grace;

Not, not certainly, the obscure reveries   25
Of the inward gaze;
Better mendacities
Than the classics in paraphrase!

The "age demanded" chiefly a mould in plaster,
Made with no loss of time,   30
A prose kinema, not, not assuredly, alabaster
Or the "sculpture" of rhyme.

III

The tea-rose tea-gown, etc.
Supplants the mousseline of Cos,
The pianola "replaces"   35
Sappho's barbitos.

Christ follows Dionysus,
Phallic and ambrosial
Made way for macerations;
Caliban casts out Ariel,   40

All things are a flowing,
Sage Heracleitus says;
But a tawdry cheapness
Shall outlast our days.

18–19. l'an . . . eage: "In the thirtieth year of his life," a line from François Villon's (1431–1463?) *Grand Testament*.
24. Attic: Attica, the part of Greece surrounding Athens.
31. kinema: in Greek, motion; cinema.
34. mousseline . . . Cos: muslin of silk from Cos in Greece.
35. pianola: player piano.
36. barbitos: lyre of the Greek poetess.
37. Dionysus: god of wine and fertility.
39. macerations: wastings away, softenings, torments.
40. Caliban; Ariel: In *The Tempest* Caliban is the monster; Ariel the helpful spirit.
42. Heracleitus: 6th century B.C. Greek philosopher.

Even the Christian beauty   45
Defects—after Samothrace;
We see τὸ καλὸν
Decreed in the market place.

Faun's flesh is not to us,
Nor the saint's vision.   50
We have the press for wafer;
Franchise for circumcision.

All men, in law, are equals.
Free of Pisistratus,
We choose a knave or an eunuch   55
To rule over us.

O bright Apollo,
τίν' ἄνδρα, τίν' ἥρωα, τίνα θεὸν,
What god, man, or hero
Shall I place a tin wreath upon!   60

                            IV

These fought in any case,
and some believing,
            pro domo, in any case . . .

Some quick to arm,
some for adventure,   65
some from fear of weakness,
some from fear of censure,
some for love of slaughter, in imagination,
learning later . . .
some in fear, learning love of slaughter;   70
Died some, pro patria,
            non "dulce" non "et decor" . . .
walked eye-deep in hell
believing in old men's lies, then unbelieving
came home, home to a lie,   75

---

46. **Samothrace:** Greek isle noted for its
mystery cult; for the statue found there,
the "Winged Victory"; and for being
St. Paul's first stop on his Macedonian trip.
47. τὸ καλὸν: (Greek) the beautiful.
54. **Pisistratus:** 6th century B.C. Athenian
dictator.
58. τίν' . . θεὸν: a variation on a line

from Pindar's Second Olympian Ode,
"What God, what hero, what man shall
we praise." The first Greek word sounds
like "tin."
63. **pro domo:** "for home."
71–72. **pro . . . decor:** from Horace, *Odes*,
III, ii, 13; "It is sweet and fitting to die
for one's own country."

home to many deceits,
home to old lies and new infamy;
usury age-old and age-thick
and liars in public places.

Daring as never before, wastage as never before.   80
Young blood and high blood,
fair cheeks, and fine bodies;

fortitude as never before

frankness as never before,
disillusions as never told in the old days,   85
hysterias, trench confessions,
laughter out of dead bellies.

V

There died a myriad,
And of the best, among them,
For an old bitch gone in the teeth,   90
For a botched civilization,

Charm, smiling at the good mouth,
Quick eyes gone under earth's lid,

For two gross of broken statues,
For a few thousand battered books.   95

Yeux Glauques

Gladstone was still respected,
When John Ruskin produced
"King's Treasuries"; Swinburne
And Rossetti still abused.

Yeux Glauques: "sea green eyes," words used by Théophile Gautier (1811–1872) to describe "a mysterious woman." Pound adapted into French Gautier's Latin title "Caerulei Oculi" and imitated his "cameo-like" metrical style.
96. Gladstone: William Gladstone (1809–1898), leader of the Liberal Party, Prime Minister four times.
97. Ruskin: John Ruskin (1819–1900) art critic and essayist. "Of Kings' Treasuries" was the opening lecture of *Sesame and*

Lilies (1865) in which Ruskin advocated the reconstruction of an England grown ugly because of its commercialism and industry.
98–99. Swinburne . . . Rossetti: Algernon Charles Swinburne (1837–1909) and Dante Gabriel Rossetti (1828–1882) wrote sensual poetry. Rossetti, also a painter, was one of the leaders of the Pre-Raphaelite movement, which emphasized the beauty of art instead of its utility and didacticism.

Fœtid Buchanan lifted up his voice   100
When that faun's head of hers
Became a pastime for
Painters and adulterers.

The Burne-Jones cartons
Have preserved her eyes;   105
Still, at the Tate, they teach
Cophetua to rhapsodize;

Thin like brook-water,
With a vacant gaze.
The English Rubaiyat was still-born   110
In those days.

The thin, clear gaze, the same
Still darts out faunlike from the half-ruin'd face,
Questing and passive. . . .
"Ah, poor Jenny's case" . . .   115

Bewildered that a world
Shows no surprise
At her last maquero's
Adulteries.

        " *Siena Mi Fe' ; Disfecemi Maremma* "

Among the pickled fœtuses and bottled bones,   120
Engaged in perfecting the catalogue,
I found the last scion of the
Senatorial families of Strasbourg, Monsieur Verog.

---

100. **Buchanan:** In 1871 Robert William Buchanan wrote an article attacking "The Fleshly School of Poetry," singling out Rossetti's poem "Jenny" as an obnoxious example. (Cf. *l.* 115) This poem describes a young man's reflections while Jenny, a prostitute, rests her head on his knees.
101. **hers:** Elizabeth Siddal, Rossetti's wife, who modeled for her husband and other Pre-Raphaelites, such as Sir Edward Burne-Jones (1833–1898). She later killed herself.
104. **cartons:** cartoons, full-sized studies for frescos or stained glass windows.
106. **Tate:** the Tate Gallery in London.
107. **Cophetua:** legendary African king who fell in love with a beggar maid; the

subject of a famous Burne-Jones painting for which Elizabeth Siddal modeled.
110. **Rubaiyat:** *The Rubaiyat of Omar Khayyam* by Edward Fitzgerald (1809–1883) had gone unnoticed until 1861 when Rossetti came upon it and recommended it. **Siena . . . Maremma:** *Purgatorio,* V, 135: "Siena made me, Maremma undid me," spoken by Pia de Tolomei whose husband, to marry another woman, murdered her.
123. **Verog:** Victor Gustave Plarr, born in Strasbourg, whose family migrated to England following the Franco-Prussian War. He was librarian of the Royal College of Surgeons, a poet, author of "In the Dorian Mood," and the biographer of Ernest Dowson.

For two hours he talked of Gallifet;
Of Dowson; of the Rhymers' Club;   125
Told me how Johnson (Lionel) died
By falling from a high stool in a pub . . .

But showed no trace of alcohol
At the autopsy, privately performed—
Tissue preserved—the pure mind   130
Arose toward Newman as the whiskey warmed.

Dowson found harlots cheaper than hotels;
Headlam for uplift; Image impartially imbued
With raptures for Bacchus, Terpsichore and the Church.
So spoke the author of "The Dorian Mood,"   135

M. Verog, out of step with the decade,
Detached from his contemporaries,
Neglected by the young,
Because of these reveries.

Brennbaum

The skylike limpid eyes,   140
The circular infant's face.
The stiffness from spats to collar
Never relaxing into grace;

The heavy memories of Horeb, Sinai and the forty years,
Showed only when the daylight fell   145
Level across the face
Of Brennbaum "The Impeccable."

Mr. Nixon

In the cream gilded cabin of his steam yacht
Mr. Nixon advised me kindly, to advance with fewer
Dangers of delay. "Consider   150
        "Carefully the reviewer.

124. **Gallifet:** Gastende Gallifet, a French general who led a brilliant cavalry charge at Sedan (1870).
125. **Rhymers' Club:** the club of the most promising young poets of the 1890's. Plarr was himself a member, along with Dowson, Lionel Johnson (1867–1902), and Yeats.
126. **Johnson:** He suffered a stroke in a pub, but did not die from the fall. His autopsy revealed that he had never matured physically. Both he and Dowson were excessive drinkers. They were converts to Roman Catholicism, as were many Oxonians who came under the influence of Cardinal Newman.
133. **Headlam; Image:** The Rev. Stewart Headlam and Professor Selwyn Image were members of the artistic colony living at "Fitzroy" House in London. The group also included Dowson, Johnson, Wilde, and other "Rhymers."
Brennbaum: Possibly Pound based this portrait on Max Beerbohm, mistakenly imagining him of Jewish descent.
144. **Horeb . . . years:** the exile, mission and wandering of Moses.
Nixon: probably based on the novelist Arnold Bennett.

"I was as poor as you are;
"When I began I got, of course,
"Advance on royalties, fifty at first," said Mr. Nixon,
"Follow me, and take a column,   155
"Even if you have to work free.

"Butter reviewers. From fifty to three hundred
"I rose in eighteen months;
"The hardest nut I had to crack
"Was Dr. Dundas.   160

"I never mentioned a man but with the view
"Of selling my own works.
"The tip's a good one, as for literature
"It gives no man a sinecure.
"And no one knows, at sight, a masterpiece.   165
"And give up verse, my boy,
"There's nothing in it."

Likewise a friend of Bloughram's once advised me:
Don't kick against the pricks,
Accept opinion. The "Nineties" tried your game   170
And died, there's nothing in it.

                          X

Beneath the sagging roof
The stylist has taken shelter,
Unpaid, uncelebrated,
At last from the world's welter   175

Nature receives him;
With a placid and uneducated mistress
He exercises his talents
And the soil meets his distress.

The haven from sophistications and contentions   180
Leaks through its thatch;
He offers succulent cooking;
The door has a creaking latch.

160. **Dundas:** no one in particular, the type of the literary high priest.
168. **Bloughram:** "Bishop Bloughram's Apology" is one of Browning's ironic monologues.

173. **stylist:** perhaps Pound refers to Ford Madox Ford, who lived under these conditions.

XI

"Conservatrix of Milésien"
Habits of mind and feeling,   185
Possibly. But in Ealing
With the most bank-clerkly of Englishmen?

No, "Milesian" is an exaggeration.
No instinct has survived in her
Older than those her grandmother   190
Told her would fit her station.

XII

"Daphne with her thighs in bark
"Stretches toward me her leafy hands,"—
Subjectively. In the stuffed-satin drawing-room
I await The Lady Valentine's commands,   195

Knowing my coat has never been
Of precisely the fashion
To stimulate, in her,
A durable passion;

Doubtful, somewhat, of the value   200
Of well-gowned approbation
Of literary effort,
But never of The Lady Valentine's vocation:

Poetry, her border of ideas,
The edge, uncertain, but a means of blending   205
With other strata
Where the lower and higher have ending;

A hook to catch the Lady Jane's attention,
A modulation toward the theatre,
Also, in the case of revolution,   210
A possible friend and comforter.

184. **Conservatrix of Milésien:** a phrase taken from Remy de Gourmont (1858–1915), the French symbolist and critic, which means the preservers of sexuality. The Milesians were the inhabitants of Miletus, the Greek city in Asia Minor, at one time famous for its learning and art, also the supposed place of origin of the spicy stories known as Milesian Tales.

186. **Ealing:** a London suburb.
192–93. **Daphne ... hands:** an adaptation of lines from Gautier's "Le Château de Souvenir." Daphne is the nymph who prayed to escape the pursuit of Apollo and was turned into a laurel tree. Pound has changed the original "toujours" (always) to "toward me."
195. **Lady Valentine:** the type of the modern literary lady.

Conduct, on the other hand, the soul
"Which the highest cultures have nourished"
To Fleet St. where
Dr. Johnson flourished;   215

Beside this thoroughfare
The sale of half-hose has
Long since superseded the cultivation
Of Pierian roses.

Envoi (1919)

Go, dumb-born book,   220
Tell her that sang me once that song of Lawes:
Hadst thou but song
As thou hast subjects known,
Then were there cause in thee that should condone
Even my faults that heavy upon me lie,   225
And build her glories their longevity.

Tell her that sheds
Such treasure in the air,
Recking naught else but that her graces give
Life to the moment,   230
I would bid them live
As roses might, in magic amber laid,
Red overwrought with orange and all made
One substance and one colour
Braving time.   235

Tell her that goes
With song upon her lips
But sings not out the song, nor knows
The maker of it, some other mouth,
May be as fair as hers,   240
Might, in new ages, gain her worshippers,
When our two dusts with Waller's shall be laid,
Siftings on siftings in oblivion;
Till change hath broken down
All things save Beauty alone.   245

213. **Which . . . nourished:** an adaptation of lines from Jules Laforgue's (1860–1887) "Complainte des Pianos Qu'on Entend dans les Quartiers Aisés."
219. **Pierian:** Pieria, place sacred to the Muses. Sappho writes of an uncultured woman who will have no share of Pierian roses.
220–21. **Go . . . Lawes:** cf. Edmund Waller's "Go Lovely Rose." Henry Lawes set it to music.

Poetry

I, too, dislike it: there are things that are important beyond
  all this fiddle.
Reading it, however, with a perfect contempt for it, one
  discovers in
  it after all, a place for the genuine.   5
    Hands that can grasp, eyes
    that can dilate, hair that can rise
      if it must, these things are important not because a

high-sounding interpretation can be put upon them but
  because they are   10
useful. When they become so derivative as to become
  unintelligible,
the same thing may be said for all of us, that we
  do not admire what
    we cannot understand: the bat   15
      holding on upside down or in quest of something to

eat, elephants pushing, a wild horse taking a roll, a tireless
  wolf under
a tree, the immovable critic twitching his skin like a
  horse that feels a flea, the base-   20
ball fan, the statistician—
    nor is it valid
      to discriminate against "business documents and

school-books"; all these phenomena are important. One
  must make a distinction   25
however: when dragged into prominence by half poets,

    the result is not poetry,
nor till the poets among us can be
  "literalists of
  the imagination"—above   30
    insolence and triviality and can present

for inspection, "imaginary gardens with real toads in them,"
　　shall we have
it. In the meantime, if you demand on the one hand,
　　　　the raw material of poetry in　　　　　　　　　　35
　　all its rawness and
　　that which is on the other hand
　　　　genuine, then you are interested in poetry.

A Grave

Man looking into the sea,
taking the view from those who have as much right to it as you
　　have to it yourself,
it is human nature to stand in the middle of a thing,
but you cannot stand in the middle of this;　　　　　　　　5
the sea has nothing to give but a well excavated grave.
The firs stand in a procession, each with an emerald turkey-foot
　　at the top,
reserved as their contours, saying nothing;
repression, however, is not the most obvious characteristic of　10
　　the sea;
the sea is a collector, quick to return a rapacious look.
There are others besides you who have worn that look—
whose expression is no longer a protest; the fish no longer in-
　　vestigate them　　　　　　　　　　　　　　　　　　15
for their bones have not lasted:
men lower nets, unconscious of the fact that they are desecrating
　　a grave,
and row quickly away—the blades of the oars
moving together like the feet of water-spiders as if there were　20
　　no such thing as death.
The wrinkles progress among themselves in a phalanx-beautiful
　　under networks of foam,
and fade breathlessly while the sea rustles in and out of the
　　seaweed;　　　　　　　　　　　　　　　　　　　25
the birds swim through the air at top speed, emitting cat-calls
　　as heretofore—
the tortoise-shell scourges about the feet of the cliffs, in motion
　　beneath them;
and the ocean, under the pulsation of lighthouses and noise of　30
　　bell-buoys,
advances as usual, looking as if it were not that ocean in which
　　dropped things are bound to sink—
in which if they turn and twist, it is neither with volition or
　　consciousness.　　　　　　　　　　　　　　　　　35

ARCHIBALD MACLEISH [1892-   ]

The Silent Slain

We too, we too, descending once again
The hills of our own land, we too have heard
Far off—Ah, que ce cor a longue haleine—
The horn of Roland in the passages of Spain,
The first, the second blast, the failing third,   5
And with the third turned back and climbed once more
The steep road southward, and heard faint the sound
Of swords, of horses, the disastrous war,
And crossed the dark defile at last, and found
At Roncevaux upon the darkening plain   10
The dead against the dead and on the silent ground
The silent slain—

EDWARD ESTLIN CUMMINGS [1894-1962]

Buffalo Bill's

Buffalo Bill's
defunct
          who used to
          ride a watersmooth-silver
                              stallion   5
and break onetwothreefourfive pigeonsjustlikethat
                                        Jesus

he was a handsome man
                    and what i want to know is
how do you like your blueeyed boy   10
Mister Death

"next to of course god america i

"next to of course god america i
love you land of the pilgrims' and so forth oh
say can you see by the dawn's early my
country 'tis of centuries come and go

3. **Ah ... haleine:** "Ah, this horn has long   Roland's horn.
breath," Charlemagne's statement upon   10. **Roncevaux:** the pass in the Pyrenees
hearing the third and dying blast of   where Roland was ambushed.

and are no more what of it we should worry   5
in every language even deafanddumb
thy sons acclaim your glorious name by gorry
by jingo by gee by gosh by gum
why talk of beauty what could be more beautiful than these heroic happy dead   10
who rushed like lions to the roaring slaughter
they did not stop to think they died instead
then shall the voice of liberty be mute?"

He spoke. And drank rapidly a glass of water

my sweet old etcetera

my sweet old etcetera
aunt lucy during the recent

war could and what
is more did tell you just
what everybody was fighting   5

for,
my sister

isabel created hundreds
(and
hundreds)of socks not to   10
mention shirts fleaproof earwarmers
etcetera wristers etcetera, my
mother hoped that

i would die etcetera
bravely of course my father used   15
to become hoarse talking about how it was
a privilege and if only he
could meanwhile my

self etcetera lay quietly
in the deep mud et   20

cetera
(dreaming,
et
    cetera, of
Your smile   25
eyes knees and of your Etcetera)

anyone lived in a pretty how town

anyone lived in a pretty how town
(with up so floating many bells down)
spring summer autumn winter
he sang his didn't he danced his did.

Women and men(both little and small)   5
cared for anyone not at all
they sowed their isn't they reaped their same
sun moon stars rain

children guessed(but only a few
and down they forgot as up they grew   10
autumn winter spring summer)
that noone loved him more by more

when by now and tree by leaf
she laughed his joy she cried his grief
bird by snow and stir by still   15
anyone's any was all to her

someones married their everyones
laughed their cryings and did their dance
(sleep wake hope and then)they
said their nevers they slept their dream   20

stars rain sun moon
(and only the snow can begin to explain
how children are apt to forget to remember
with up so floating many bells down)

one day anyone died i guess   25
(and noone stooped to kiss his face)
busy folk buried them side by side
little by little and was by was

all by all and deep by deep
and more by more they dream their sleep   30
noone and anyone earth by april
wish by spirit and if by yes.

Women and men(both dong and ding)
summer autumn winter spring
reaped their sowing and went their came   35
sun moon stars rain

ROBERT GRAVES [1895-   ]

Ogres and Pygmies

Those famous men of old, the Ogres—
They had long beards and stinking arm-pits,
They were wide-mouthed, long-yarded and great-bellied
Yet of no taller stature, Sirs, than you.
They lived on Ogre-Strand, which was no place   5
But the churl's terror of their vast extent,
Where every foot was three-and-thirty inches
And every penny bought a whole hog.
Now of their company none survive, not one,
The times being, thank God, unfavourable   10
To all but nightmare shadows of their fame;
Their images stand howling on the hill
(The winds enforced against those wide mouths),
Whose granite haunches country-folk salute
With May Day kisses, and whose knobbed knees.   15

So many feats they did to admiration:
With their enormous throats they sang louder
Than ten cathedral choirs, with their grand yards
Stormed the most rare and obstinate maidenheads,
With their strong-gutted and capacious bellies   20
Digested stones and glass like ostriches.
They dug great pits and heaped huge mounds,
Deflected rivers, wrestled with the bear
And hammered judgements for posterity—
For the sweet-cupid-lipped and tassel-yarded   25
Delicate-stomached dwellers
In Pygmy Alley, where with brooding on them
A foot is shrunk to seven inches
And twelve-pence will not buy a spare rib.
And who would judge between Ogres and Pygmies—   30
The thundering text, the snivelling commentary—
Reading between such covers he will marvel
How his own members bloat and shrink again.

The Portrait

She speaks always in her own voice
Even to strangers; but those other women
Exercise their borrowed, or false, voices
Even on sons and daughters.

She can walk invisibly at noon   5
Along the high road; but those other women
Gleam phosphorescent—broad hips and gross fingers—
Down every lampless alley.

She is wild and innocent, pledged to love
Through all disaster; but those other women   10
Decry her for a witch or a common drab
And glare back when she greets them.

Here is her portrait, gazing sidelong at me,
The hair in disarray, the young eyes pleading:
"And you, love? As unlike those other men   15
As I those other women?"

ALLEN TATE [1899–   ]

Ode to the Confederate Dead

Row after row with strict impunity
The headstones yield their names to the element,
The wind whirrs without recollection;
In the riven troughs the splayed leaves
Pile up, of nature the casual sacrament   5
To the seasonal eternity of death;
Then driven by the fierce scrutiny
Of heaven to their election in the vast breath,
They sought the rumor of mortality.

Autumn is desolation in the plot   10
Of a thousand acres where these memories grow
From the inexhaustible bodies that are not
Dead, but feed the grass row after rich row.
Think of the autumns that have come and gone!—
Ambitious November with the humors of the year,   15
With a particular zeal for every slab,
Staining the uncomfortable angels that rot
On the slabs, a wing chipped here, an arm there:

7. **phosphorescent:** like some decaying
objects (e.g., wood, fish) in which bacterial
action produces a cold glow.

The brute curiosity of an angel's stare
Turns you, like them, to stone,   20
Transforms the heaving air
Till plunged to a heavier world below
You shift your sea-space blindly
Heaving, turning like the blind crab.

      Dazed by the wind, only the wind   25
      The leaves flying, plunge

You know who have waited by the wall
The twilight certainty of an animal,
Those midnight restitutions of the blood
You know—the immitigable pines, the smoky frieze   30
Of the sky, the sudden call: you know the rage,
The cold pool left by the mounting flood,
Of muted Zeno and Parmenides.
You who have waited for the angry resolution
Of those desires that should be yours tomorrow,   35
You know the unimportant shrift of death
And praise the vision
And praise the arrogant circumstance
Of those who fall
Rank upon rank, hurried beyond decision—   40
Here by the sagging gate, stopped by the wall.

      Seeing, seeing only the leaves
      Flying, plunge and expire

Turn your eyes to the immoderate past,
Turn to the inscrutable infantry rising   45
Demons out of the earth—they will not last.
Stonewall, Stonewall, and the sunken fields of hemp,
Shiloh, Antietam, Malvern Hill, Bull Run.
Lost in that orient of the thick and fast
You will curse the setting sun.   50

      Cursing only the leaves crying
      Like an old man in a storm

You hear the shout, the crazy hemlocks point
With troubled fingers to the silence which
Smothers you, a mummy, in time.   55
                  The hound bitch
Toothless and dying, in a musty cellar
Hears the wind only.

33. **Zeno ... Parmenides:** Eleatic Greek philosophers of the 6th century B.C., believers in the unreality of motion and change.

Now that the salt of their blood
Stiffens the saltier oblivion of the sea,   60
Seals the malignant purity of the flood,
What shall we who count our days and bow
Our heads with a commemorial woe
In the ribboned coats of grim felicity,
What shall we say of the bones, unclean,   65
Whose verdurous anonymity will grow?
The ragged arms, the ragged heads and eyes
Lost in these acres of the insane green?
The gray lean spiders come, they come and go;
In a tangle of willows without light   70
The singular screech-owl's tight
Invisible lyric seeds the mind
With the furious murmur of their chivalry.

We shall say only the leaves
Flying, plunge and expire   75

We shall say only the leaves whispering
In the improbable mist of nightfall
That flies on multiple wing:
Night is the beginning and the end
And in between the ends of distraction   80
Waits mute speculation, the patient curse
That stones the eyes, or like the jaguar leaps
For his own image in a jungle pool, his victim.

What shall we say who have knowledge
Carried to the heart? Shall we take the act   85
To the grave? Shall we, more hopeful, set up the grave
In the house? The ravenous grave?

Leave now
The shut gate and the decomposing wall:
The gentle serpent, green in the mulberry bush,   90
Riots with his tongue through the hush—
Sentinel of the grave who counts us all!

Mr. Pope

When Alexander Pope strolled in the city
Strict was the glint of pearl and gold sedans.
Ladies leaned out, more out of fear than pity;
For Pope's tight back was rather a goat's than man's.

One often thinks the urn should have more bones   5
Than skeletons provide for speedy dust;
The urn gets hollow, cobwebs brittle as stones
Weave to the funeral shell a frivolous rust.

And he who dribbled couplets like the snake
Coiled to a lithe precision in the sun,   10
Is missing. The jar is empty; you may break
It only to find that Mr. Pope is gone.

What requisitions of a verity
Prompted the wit and rage between his teeth
One cannot say: around a crooked tree   15
A mortal climbs whose name should be a wreath.

HART CRANE [1899–1932]

from The Bridge: *To Brooklyn Bridge*

How many dawns, chill from his rippling rest
The seagull's wings shall dip and pivot him,
Shedding white rings of tumult, building high
Over the chained bay waters Liberty—

Then, with inviolate curve, forsake our eyes   5
As apparitional as sails that cross
Some page of figures to be filed away;
—Till elevators drop us from our day . . .

I think of cinemas, panoramic sleights
With multitudes bent toward some flashing scene   10
Never disclosed, but hastened to again,
Foretold to other eyes on the same screen;

And Thee, across the harbor, silver-paced
As though the sun took step of thee, yet left
Some motion even unspent in thy stride,—   15
Implicitly thy freedom staying thee!

Out of some subway scuttle, cell or loft
A bedlamite speeds to thy parapets,
Tilting there momently, shrill shirt ballooning,
A jest falls from the speechless caravan.   20

Down Wall, from girder into street noon leaks,
A rip-tooth of the sky's acetylene;
All afternoon the cloud-flown derricks turn . . .
Thy cables breathe the North Atlantic still.

And obscure as that heaven of the Jews,   25
Thy guerdon . . . Accolade thou dost bestow
Of anonymity time cannot raise:
Vibrant reprieve and pardon thou dost show.

O harp and altar, of the fury fused,
(How could mere toil align thy choiring strings!)   30
Terrific threshold of the prophet's pledge,
Prayer of pariah, and the lover's cry,—

Again the traffic lights that skim thy swift
Unfractioned idiom, immaculate sigh of stars,
Beading thy path—condense eternity: 35
And we have seen night lifted in thine arms.

Under thy shadow by the piers I waited;
Only in darkness is thy shadow clear.
The City's fiery parcels all undone,
Already snow submerges an iron year . . .   40

O Sleepless as the river under thee,
Vaulting the sea, the prairies' dreaming sod,
Unto us lowliest sometimes sweep, descend
And of the curveship lend a myth to God.

Legend

As silent as a mirror is believed
Realities plunge in silence by . . .

I am not ready for repentance;
Nor to match regrets. For the moth
Bends no more than the still   5
Imploring flame. And tremorous
In the white falling flakes
Kisses are,—
The only worth all granting.

It is to be learned—   10
This cleaving and this burning,
But only by the one who
Spends out himself again.

Twice and twice
(Again the smoking souvenir,   15
Bleeding eidolon!) and yet again.
Until the bright logic is won
Unwhispering as a mirror
Is believed.

Then, drop by caustic drop, a perfect cry   20
Shall string some constant harmony,—
Relentless caper for all those who step
The legend of their youth into the noon.

Voyages: I

Above the fresh ruffles of the surf
Bright striped urchins flay each other with sand.
They have contrived a conquest for shell shucks,
And their fingers crumble fragments of baked weed
Gaily digging and scattering.   5

And in answer to their treble interjections
The sun beats lightning on the waves,
The waves fold thunder on the sand;
And could they hear me I would tell them:

O brilliant kids, frisk with your dog,   10
Fondle your shells and sticks, bleached
By time and the elements; but there is a line
You must not cross nor ever trust beyond it
Spry cordage of your bodies to caresses
Too lichen-faithful from too wide a breast.   15
The bottom of the sea is cruel.

Voyages: VI

Where icy and bright dungeons lift
Of swimmers their lost morning eyes,
And ocean rivers, churning, shift
Green borders under stranger skies,

16. **eidolon**: an unsubstantial image.

Steadily as a shell secretes   5
Its beating leagues of monotone,
Or as many waters trough the sun's
Red kelson past the cape's wet stone;

O rivers mingling toward the sky
And harbor of the phoenix' breast—   10
My eyes pressed black against the prow,
—Thy derelict and blinded guest

Waiting, afire, what name, unspoke,
I cannot claim: let thy waves rear
More savage than the death of kings,   15
Some splintered garland for the seer.

Beyond siroccos harvesting
The solstice thunders, crept away,
Like a cliff swinging or a sail
Flung into April's inmost day—   20

Creation's blithe and petalled word
To the lounged goddess when she rose
Conceding dialogue with eyes
That smile unsearchable repose—

Still fervid covenant, Belle Isle,   25
—Unfolded floating dais before
Which rainbows twine continual hair—
Belle Isle, white echo of the oar!

The imaged Word, it is, that holds
Hushed willows anchored in its glow.   30
It is the unbetrayable reply
Whose accent no farewell can know.

RICHARD EBERHART [1904-   ]

The Groundhog

In June, amid the golden fields,
I saw a groundhog lying dead.
Dead lay he; my senses shook,
And mind outshot our naked frailty.

There lowly in the vigorous summer   5
His form began its senseless change,
And made my senses waver dim
Seeing nature ferocious in him.
Inspecting close his maggots' might
And seething cauldron of his being,   10
Half with loathing, half with a strange love,
I poked him with an angry stick.
The fever arose, became a flame
And Vigour circumscribed the skies,
Immense energy in the sun,   15
And through my frame a sunless trembling.
My stick had done nor good nor harm.
Then stood I silent in the day
Watching the object, as before;
And kept my reverence for knowledge   20
Trying for control, to be still,
To quell the passion of the blood;
Until I had bent down on my knees
Praying for joy in the sight of decay.
And so I left; and I returned   25
In Autumn strict of eye, to see
The sap gone out of the groundhog,

But the bony sodden hulk remained.
But the year had lost its meaning,
And in intellectual chains   30
I lost both love and loathing,
Mured up in the wall of wisdom.
Another summer took the fields again
Massive and burning, full of life,
But when I chanced upon the spot   35
There was only a little hair left,
And bones bleaching in the sunlight
Beautiful as architecture;
I watched them like a geometer,
And cut a walking stick from a birch.   40
It has been three years, now.
There is no sign of the groundhog.
I stood there in the whirling summer,
My hand capped a withered heart,
And thought of China and of Greece,   45
Of Alexander in his tent;
Of Montaigne in his tower,
Of Saint Theresa in her wild lament.

WYSTAN HUGH AUDEN [1907–   ]

Musée des Beaux Arts

About suffering they were never wrong,
The Old Masters: how well they understood
Its human position; how it takes place
While someone else is eating or opening a window or just walking
    dully along;
How, when the aged are reverently, passionately waiting   5
For the miraculous birth, there always must be
Children who did not specially want it to happen, skating
On a pond at the edge of the wood:
They never forgot
That even the dreadful martyrdom must run its course   10
Anyhow in a corner, some untidy spot
Where the dogs go on with their doggy life and the torturer's horse
Scratches its innocent behind on a tree.
In Brueghel's *Icarus*, for instance: how everything turns away
Quite leisurely from the disaster; the ploughman may   15
Have heard the splash, the forsaken cry,
But for him it was not an important failure; the sun shone
As it had to on the white legs disappearing into the green
Water; and the expensive delicate ship that must have seen
Something amazing, a boy falling out of the sky,   20
Had somewhere to get to and sailed calmly on.

Who's Who

A shilling life will give you all the facts:
How Father beat him, how he ran away,
What were the struggles of his youth, what acts
Made him the greatest figure of his day:
Of how he fought, fished, hunted, worked all night,   5
Though giddy, climbed new mountains; named a sea:
Some of the last researchers even write
Love made him weep his pints like you and me.

Musée ... Arts: Museum of Fine Arts.
14. Brueghel's Icarus: a painting by Pieter
Brueghel (1525?–1569) in the Royal
Museum in Brussels. Icarus, the son of
Daedalus, flew too near the sun, whereupon the wax holding on his wings
melted, and he plunged into the sea.

1. shilling life: inexpensive biography,
costing one shilling.

With all his honours on, he sighed for one
Who, say astonished critics, lived at home;   10
Did little jobs about the house with skill
And nothing else; could whistle; would sit still
Or potter round the garden; answered some
Of his long marvellous letters but kept none.

The Cultural Presupposition

Happy the hare at morning, for she cannot read
The Hunter's waking thoughts, lucky the leaf
Unable to predict the fall, lucky indeed
The rampant suffering suffocating jelly
Burgeoning in pools, lapping the grits of the desert,   5

But what shall man do, who can whistle tunes by heart,
Knows to the bar when death shall cut him short like the cry of the
    shearwater,
What can he do but defend himself from his knowledge?

How comely are his places of refuge and the tabernacles of his peace,
The new books upon the morning table, the lawns and the afternoon
    terraces!   10
Here are the playing-fields where he may forget his ignorance
To operate within a gentleman's agreement: twenty-two sins have
    here a certain licence.
Here are the thickets where accosted lovers combatant
May warm each other with their wicked hands,
Here are the avenues for incantation and workshops for the cunning
    engravers.   15
The galleries are full of music, the pianist is storming the keys, the
    great cellist is crucified over his instrument,
That none may hear the ejaculations of the sentinels
Nor the sigh of the most numerous and the most poor; the thud of
    their falling bodies
Who with their lives have banished hence the serpent and the
    faceless insect.

4. **jelly:** slimy animalculous matter.   9. **How . . . peace:** Auden here echoes
5. **grits:** sands.   biblical passages. Cf. Psalms 84: 1.
7. **shearwater:** a sea bird.

In Memory of W. B. Yeats

(*d. Jan. 1939*)

I

He disappeared in the dead of winter:
The brooks were frozen, the air-ports almost deserted,
And snow disfigured the public statues;
The mercury sank in the mouth of the dying day.
O all the instruments agree   5
The day of his death was a dark cold day.

Far from his illness
The wolves ran on through the evergreen forests,
The peasant river was untempted by the fashionable quays;
By mourning tongues   10
The death of the poet was kept from his poems.

But for him it was his last afternoon as himself,
An afternoon of nurses and rumours;
The provinces of his body revolted,
The squares of his mind were empty,   15
Silence invaded the suburbs,
The current of his feeling failed: he became his admirers.

Now he is scattered among a hundred cities
And wholly given over to unfamiliar affections;
To find his happiness in another kind of wood   20
And be punished under a foreign code of conscience.
The words of a dead man
Are modified in the guts of the living.

But in the importance and noise of to-morrow
When the brokers are roaring like beasts on the floor of the   25
     Bourse,
And the poor have the sufferings to which they are fairly
     accustomed,
And each in the cell of himself is almost convinced of his
     freedom;
A few thousand will think of this day
As one thinks of a day when one did something slightly unusual.
O all the instruments agree   30
The day of his death was a dark cold day.

---

9. **quays:** docks.   25. **Bourse:** the Paris Stock Exchange.

II

You were silly like us: your gift survived it all;
The parish of rich women, physical decay,
Yourself; mad Ireland hurt you into poetry.
Now Ireland has her madness and her weather still,   35
For poetry makes nothing happen: it survives
In the valley of its saying where executives
Would never want to tamper; it flows south
From ranches of isolation and the busy griefs,
Raw towns that we believe and die in; it survives,   40
A way of happening, a mouth.

III

Earth, receive an honoured guest;
William Yeats is laid to rest:
Let the Irish vessel lie
Emptied of its poetry.   45

Time that is intolerant
Of the brave and innocent,
And indifferent in a week
To a beautiful physique,

Worships language and forgives   50
Everyone by whom it lives;
Pardons cowardice, conceit,
Lays its honours at their feet.

Time that with this strange excuse
Pardoned Kipling and his views,   55
And will pardon Paul Claudel,
Pardons him for writing well.

In the nightmare of the dark
All the dogs of Europe bark,
And the living nations wait,   60
Each sequestered in its hate;

Intellectual disgrace
Stares from every human face,
And the seas of pity lie
Locked and frozen in each eye.   65

55. **views:** Kipling was an apologist for imperialism.

56. **Claudel:** Paul Claudel (1868–1955), French dramatist, a Roman Catholic and extreme right-winger.

Follow, poet, follow right
To the bottom of the night,
With your unconstraining voice
Still persuade us to rejoice;

With the farming of a verse   70
Make a vineyard of the curse,
Sing of human unsuccess
In a rapture of distress;

In the deserts of the heart
Let the healing fountain start,   75
In the prison of his days
Teach the free man how to praise.

The Unknown Citizen

*(To JS/07/M/378
This Marble Monument
Is Erected by the State)*

He was found by the Bureau of Statistics to be
One against whom there was no official complaint,
And all the reports on his conduct agree
That, in the modern sense of an old-fashioned word, he was a saint,
For in everything he did he served the Greater Community.   5
Except for the War till the day he retired
He worked in a factory and never got fired,
But satisfied his employers, Fudge Motors Inc.
Yet he wasn't a scab or odd in his views,
For his Union reports that he paid his dues,   10
(Our report on his Union shows it was sound)
And our Social Psychology workers found
That he was popular with his mates and liked a drink.
The Press are convinced that he bought a paper every day
And that his reactions to advertisements were normal in every way. 15
Policies taken out in his name prove that he was fully insured,
And his Health-card shows he was once in hospital but left it cured.
Both Producers Research and High-Grade Living declare
He was fully sensible to the advantages of the Instalment Plan
And had everything necessary to the Modern Man,   20
A phonograph, a radio, a car and a frigidaire.

9. **scab:** a worker who crosses the picket lines to replace a striker; one disloyal to the union.

Our researchers into Public Opinion are content
That he held the proper opinions for the time of year;
When there was peace, he was for peace; when there was war, he
    went.
He was married and added five children to the population,   25
Which our Eugenist says was the right number for a parent of his
    generation,
And our teachers report that he never interfered with their education.
Was he free? Was he happy? The question is absurd:
Had anything been wrong, we should certainly have heard.

In Praise of Limestone

If it form the one landscape that we the inconstant ones
    Are consistently homesick for, this is chiefly
Because it dissolves in water. Mark these rounded slopes
    With their surface fragrance of thyme and beneath
A secret system of caves and conduits; hear these springs   5
    That spurt out everywhere with a chuckle
Each filling a private pool for its fish and carving
    Its own little ravine whose cliffs entertain
The butterfly and the lizard; examine this region
    Of short distances and definite places: 10
What could be more like Mother or a fitter background
    For her son, for the nude young male who lounges
Against a rock displaying his dildo, never doubting
    That for all his faults he is loved, whose works are but
Extensions of his power to charm? From weathered outcrop   15
    To hill-top temple, from appearing waters to
Conspicuous fountains, from a wild to a formal vineyard,
    Are ingenious but short steps that a child's wish
To receive more attention than his brothers, whether
    By pleasing or teasing, can easily take.   20

Watch, then, the band of rivals as they climb up and down
    Their steep stone gennels in twos and threes, sometimes
Arm in arm, but never, thank God, in step; or engaged
    On the shady side of a square at midday in
Voluble discourse, knowing each other too well to think   25
    There are any important secrets, unable
To conceive a god whose temper-tantrums are moral
    And not to be pacified by a clever line

22. **gennels:** narrow passageways.

Or a good lay: for, accustomed to a stone that responds,
   They have never had to veil their faces in awe   30
Of a crater whose blazing fury could not be fixed;
   Adjusted to the local needs of valleys
Where everything can be touched or reached by walking,
   Their eyes have never looked into infinite space
Through the lattice-work of a nomad's comb; born lucky,   35
   Their legs have never encountered the fungi
And insects of the jungle, the monstrous forms and lives
   With which we have nothing, we like to hope, in common.

THEODORE ROETHKE [1908–1963]

Dolor

I have known the inexorable sadness of pencils,
Neat in their boxes, dolor of pad and paper-weight,
All the misery of manila folders and mucilage,
Desolation in immaculate public places,
Lonely reception room, lavatory, switchboard,   5
The unalterable pathos of basin and pitcher.
Ritual of multigraph, paper-clip, comma,
Endless duplication of lives and objects.
And I have seen dust from the walls of institutions,
Finer than flour, alive, more dangerous than silica,   10
Sift, almost invisible, through long afternoons of tedium,
Dropping a fine film on nails and delicate eyebrows,
Glazing the pale hair, the duplicate gray standard faces.

I knew a woman

I knew a woman, lovely in her bones,
When small birds sighed, she would sigh back at them;
Ah, when she moved, she moved more ways than one:
The shapes a bright container can contain!
Of her choice virtues only gods should speak,   5
Or English poets who grew up on Greek
(I'd have them sing in chorus, cheek to cheek).

How well her wishes went! She stroked my chin,
She taught me Turn, and Counter-turn, and Stand;
She taught me Touch, that undulant white skin;   10
I nibbled meekly from her proffered hand;
She was the sickle; I, poor I, the rake,
Coming behind her for her pretty sake
(But what prodigious mowing we did make).

Love likes a gander, and adores a goose: 15
Her full lips pursed, the errant note to seize;
She played it quick, she played it light and loose;
My eyes, they dazzled at her flowing knees;
Her several parts could keep a pure repose,
Or one hip quiver with a mobile nose   20
(She moved in circles, and those circles moved).

Let seed be grass, and grass turn into hay:
I'm martyr to a motion not my own;
What's freedom for? To know eternity.
I swear she cast a shadow white as stone.   25
But who would count eternity in days?
These old bones live to learn her wanton ways:
(I measure time by how a body sways).

DYLAN THOMAS [1914–1953]

The force that through the green fuse drives the flower

The force that through the green fuse drives the flower
Drives my green age; that blasts the roots of trees
Is my destroyer.
And I am dumb to tell the crooked rose
My youth is bent by the same wintry fever.   5

The force that drives the water through the rocks
Drives my red blood; that dries the mouthing streams
Turns mine to wax.
And I am dumb to mouth unto my veins
How at the mountain spring the same mouth sucks.   10

The hand that whirls the water in the pool
Stirs the quicksand; that ropes the blowing wind
Hauls my shroud sail.
And I am dumb to tell the hanging man
How of my clay is made the hangman's lime.   15

The lips of time leech to the fountain head;
Love drips and gathers, but the fallen blood
Shall calm her sores.
And I am dumb to tell a weather's wind
How time has ticked a heaven round the stars.   20

And I am dumb to tell the lover's tomb
How at my sheet goes the same crooked worm.

Especially when the October wind

Especially when the October wind
With frosty fingers punishes my hair,
Caught by the crabbing sun I walk on fire
And cast a shadow crab upon the land,
By the sea's side, hearing the noise of birds,   5
Hearing the raven cough in winter sticks,
My busy heart who shudders as she talks
Sheds the syllabic blood and drains her words.

Shut, too, in a tower of words, I mark
On the horizon walking like the trees   10
The wordy shapes of women, and the rows
Of the star-gestured children in the park.
Some let me make you of the vowelled beeches,
Some of the oaken voices, from the roots
Of many a thorny shire tell you notes,   15
Some let me make you of the water's speeches.

Behind a pot of ferns the wagging clock
Tells me the hour's word, the neural meaning
Flies on the shafted disk, declaims the morning
And tells the windy weather in the cock.   20
Some let me make you of the meadow's signs;
The signal grass that tells me all I know
Breaks with the wormy winter through the eye.
Some let me tell you of the raven's sins.

Especially when the October wind   25
(Some let me make you of autumnal spells,
The spider-tongued, and the loud hill of Wales)
With fists of turnips punishes the land,
Some let me make you of the heartless words.
The heart is drained that, spelling in the scurry   30
Of chemic blood, warned of the coming fury.
By the sea's side hear the dark-vowelled birds.

A Refusal to Mourn the Death, by Fire, of a Child in London

Never until the mankind making
Bird beast and flower
Fathering and all humbling darkness
Tells with silence the last light breaking
And the still hour   5
Is come of the sea tumbling in harness

And I must enter again the round
Zion of the water bead
And the synagogue of the ear of corn
Shall I let pray the shadow of a sound   10
Or sow my salt seed
In the least valley of sackcloth to mourn

The majesty and burning of the child's death.
I shall not murder
The mankind of her going with a grave truth   15
Nor blaspheme down the stations of the breath
With any further
Elegy of innocence and youth.

Deep with the first dead lies London's daughter.
Robed in the long friends,   20
The grains beyond age, the dark veins of her mother,
Secret by the unmourning water
Of the riding Thames.
After the first death, there is no other.

Fern Hill

Now as I was young and easy under the apple boughs
About the lilting house and happy as the grass was green,
     The night above the dingle starry,
       Time let me hail and climb
     Golden in the heydays of his eyes,   5
And honoured among wagons I was prince of the apple towns
And once below a time I lordly had the trees and leaves
     Trail with daisies and barley
     Down the rivers of the windfall light.

And as I was green and carefree, famous among the barns   10
About the happy yard and singing as the farm was home,
     In the sun that is young once only,

Time let me play and be
Golden in the mercy of his means,
And green and golden I was huntsman and herdsman, the calves   15
Sang to my horn, the foxes on the hills barked clear and cold,
   And the sabbath rang slowly
  In the pebbles of the holy streams.

All the sun long it was running, it was lovely, the hay
Fields high as the house, the tunes from the chimneys, it was air   20
   And playing, lovely and watery
   And fire green as grass.
  And nightly under the simple stars
As I rode to sleep the owls were bearing the farm away,
All the moon long I heard, blessed among stables, the nightjars   25
   Flying with the ricks, and the horses
   Flashing into the dark.

And then to awake, and the farm, like a wanderer white
With the dew, come back, the cock on his shoulder: it was all
   Shining, it was Adam and maiden,   30
   The sky gathered again
  And the sun grew round that very day.
So it must have been after the birth of the simple light
In the first, spinning place, the spellbound horses walking warm
   Out of the whinnying green stable   35
   On to the fields of praise.

And honoured among foxes and pheasants by the gay house
Under the new made clouds and happy as the heart was long,
  In the sun born over and over,
   I ran my heedless ways,   40
  My wishes raced through the house high hay
And nothing I cared, at my sky blue trades, that time allows
In all his tuneful turning so few and such morning songs
   Before the children green and golden
   Follow him out of grace,   45

Nothing I cared, in the lamb white days, that time would take
   me
Up to the swallow thronged loft by the shadow of my hand,
  In the moon that is always rising,
   Nor that riding to sleep
I should hear him fly with the high fields   50
And wake to the farm forever fled from the childless land.
Oh as I was young and easy in the mercy of his means,
   Time held me green and dying
  Though I sang in my chains like the sea.

Do not go gentle into that good night

Do not go gentle into that good night,
Old age should burn and rave at close of day;
Rage, rage against the dying of the light.
Though wise men at their end know dark is right,
Because their words had forked no lightning they   5
Do not go gentle into that good night.

Good men, the last wave by, crying how bright
Their frail deeds might have danced in a green bay,
Rage, rage against the dying of the light.

Wild men who caught and sang the sun in flight,   10
And learn, too late, they grieved it on its way,
Do not go gentle into that good night.

Grave men, near death, who see with blinding sight
Blind eyes could blaze like meteors and be gay,
Rage, rage against the dying of the light.   15

And you, my father, there on the sad height,
Curse, bless, me now with your fierce tears, I pray.
Do not go gentle into that good night.
Rage, rage against the dying of the light.

R O B E R T   L O W E L L [1917–   ]

New Year's Day

Again and then again . . . the year is born
To ice and death, and it will never do
To skulk behind storm-windows by the stove
To hear the postgirl sounding her French horn
When the thin tidal ice is wearing through.   5
Here is the understanding not to love
Our neighbor, or tomorrow that will sieve
Our resolutions. While we live, we live

To snuff the smoke of victims. In the snow
The kitten heaved its hindlegs, as if fouled,   10
And died. We bent it in a Christmas box
And scattered blazing weeds to scare the crow

Until the snake-tailed sea-winds coughed and howled
For alms outside the church whose double locks
Wait for St. Peter, the distorted key.   15
Under St. Peter's bell the parish sea

Swells with its smelt into the burlap shack
Where Joseph plucks his hand-lines like a harp,
And hears the fearful *Puer natus est*
Of Circumcision, and relives the wrack   20
And howls of Jesus whom he holds. How sharp
The burden of the Law before the beast:
Time and the grindstone and the knife of God.
The Child is born in blood, O child of blood.

Salem

In Salem seasick spindrift drifts or skips
To the canvas flapping on the seaward panes
Until the knitting sailor stabs at ships
Nosing like sheep of Morpheus through his brain's
Asylum. Seaman, seaman, how the draft   5
Lashes the oily slick about your head,
Beating up whitecaps! Seaman, Charon's raft
Dumps its damned goods into the harbor-bed,—
There sewage sickens the rebellious seas.
Remember, seaman, Salem fishermen   10
Once hung their nimble fleets on the Great Banks.
Where was it that New England bred the men
Who quartered the Leviathan's fat flanks
And fought the British Lion to his knees?

Mr. Edwards and the Spider

I saw the spiders marching through the air,
Swimming from tree to tree that mildewed day
In latter August when the hay
Came creaking to the barn. But where
The wind is westerly,   5

19. **Puer ... est:** "The Child is Born."

4. **Morpheus:** god of sleep.
7. **Charon:** ferryman who takes souls to Hades.

Mr. Edwards: Jonathan Edwards (1703–1758), American theologian and preacher, who as a boy of eleven or twelve wrote an exacting account of the habits of the balloon spider.

Where gnarled November makes the spiders fly
Into the apparitions of the sky,
They purpose nothing but their ease and die
Urgently beating east to sunrise and the sea;
    What are we in the hands of the great God?   10
    It was in vain you set up thorn and briar
      In battle array against the fire
      And treason crackling in your blood;
        For the wild thorns grow tame
    And will do nothing to oppose the flame;   15
    Your lacerations tell the losing game
    You play against a sickness past your cure.
How will the hands be strong? How will the heart endure?

    A very little thing, a little worm,
    Or hourglass-blazoned spider, it is said,   20
      Can kill a tiger. Will the dead
      Hold up his mirror and affirm
        To the four winds the smell
    And flash of his authority? It's well
    If God who holds you to the pit of hell,   25
    Much as one holds a spider, will destroy,
Baffle and dissipate your soul. As a small boy

    On Windsor Marsh, I saw the spider die
    When thrown into the bowels of fierce fire:
      There's no long struggle, no desire   30
      To get up on its feet and fly—
        It stretches out its feet
    And dies. This is the sinner's last retreat;
    Yes, and no strength exerted on the heat
    Then sinews the abolished will, when sick   35
And full of burning, it will whistle on a brick.

    But who can plumb the sinking of that soul?
    Josiah Hawley, picture yourself cast
      Into a brick-kiln where the blast
      Fans your quick vitals to a coal—   40
        If measured by a glass,
    How long would it seem burning! Let there pass
    A minute, ten, ten trillion; but the blaze
    Is infinite, eternal: this is death.
To die and know it. This is the Black Widow, death.   45

38. **Josiah Hawley:** Joseph Hawley Sr., Edwards's uncle, depressed by one of Edwards's sermons, cut his own throat.

39. **brick-kiln:** This and the following images are taken from Edwards's sermon "Future Punishment of the Wicked Unavoidable and Intolerable."

After the Surprising Conversions

September twenty-second, Sir: today
I answer. In the latter part of May,
Hard on our Lord's Ascension, it began
To be more sensible. A gentleman
Of more than common understanding, strict   5
In morals, pious in behavior, kicked
Against our goad. A man of some renown,
An useful, honored person in the town,
He came of melancholy parents; prone
To secret spells, for years they kept alone—   10
His uncle, I believe, was killed of it:
Good people, but of too much or little wit.
I preached one Sabbath on a text from Kings;
He showed concernment for his soul. Some things
In his experience were hopeful. He   15
Would sit and watch the wind knocking a tree
And praise this countryside our Lord has made.
Once when a poor man's heifer died, he laid
A shilling on the doorsill; though a thirst
For loving shook him like a snake, he durst   20
Not entertain much hope of his estate
In heaven. Once we saw him sitting late
Behind his attic window by a light
That guttered on his Bible; through that night
He meditated terror, and he seemed   25
Beyond advice or reason, for he dreamed
That he was called to trumpet Judgment Day
To Concord. In the latter part of May
He cut his throat. And though the coroner
Judged him delirious, soon a noisome stir   30
Palsied our village. At Jehovah's nod
Satan seemed more let loose amongst us: God
Abandoned us to Satan, and he pressed
Us hard, until we thought we could not rest
Till we had done with life. Content was gone.   35
All the good work was quashed. We were undone.

Surprising Conversions: This poem is based on a letter ("a Narrative of the Surprising Conversions") Edwards wrote to a Boston clergyman who had asked about the "Great Awakening," the revival which Edwards had inspired in Western Massachusetts. Edwards's letter is dated May 30, 1735. It is followed by a note in which Edwards tells of the suicide of his uncle Hawley. 4. sensible: evident. "... it began to be very sensible that the spirit of God was gradually withdrawing from us." This statement comes from Edwards's full account of the Surprising Conversions, published two years afterward, *A Faithful Narrative of the Surprising Work of God in the Conversions of Many Hundred Souls . . .* 7. man: Joseph Hawley, Edwards's uncle, was a leading merchant.

The breath of God had carried out a planned
And sensible withdrawal from this land;
The multitude, once unconcerned with doubt,
Once neither callous, curious nor devout,   40
Jumped at broad noon, as though some peddler groaned
At it in its familiar twang: "My friend,
Cut your own throat. Cut your own throat. Now! Now!"
September twenty-second, Sir, the bough
Cracks with the unpicked apples, and at dawn   45
The small-mouth bass breaks water, gorged with spawn.

Words for Hart Crane

"When the Pulitzers showered on some dope
or screw who flushed our dry mouths out with soap,
few people would consider why I took
to stalking sailors, and scattered Uncle Sam's
phoney gold-plated laurels to the birds.   5
Because I knew my Whitman like a book,
stranger in America, tell my country: I,
Catullus redivivus, once the rage
of the Village and Paris, used to play my role
of homosexual, wolfing the stray lambs   10
who hungered by the Place de la Concorde.
My profit was a pocket with a hole.
Who asks for me, the Shelley of my age,
must lay his heart out for my bed and board."

RICHARD WILBUR [1921–   ]

Bell Speech

The selfsame toothless voice for death or bridal:
It has been long since men would give the time
To tell each someone's-change with a special chime,
And a toll for every year the dead walked through.
And mostly now, above this urgent idle   5
Town, the bells mark time, as they can do.

42–43. **My . . . Now:** a quote from Edwards's *Faithful Narrative*. After the suicide the people of Northampton reported hearing voices which seemed to tell them to cut their throats.

1. **Pulitzers:** referring to the Pulitzer Prize.
8. **Catullus redivivus:** Catullus reborn. Catullus (84?- 54? B.C.) was perhaps the greatest of Roman lyric poets.
11. **Place . . . Concorde:** square in the center of Paris.

This bavardage of early and of late
It what is wanted, and yet the bells beseech
By some excess that's in their stricken speech
Less meanly to be heard. Were this not so,   10
Why should Great Paul shake every window plate
To warn me that my pocket watch is slow?

Whether or not attended, bells will chant
With a clear dumb sound, and wide of any word
Expound our hours, clear as the waves are heard   15
Crashing at Mount Desert, from far at sea,
And dumbly joining, as the night's descent
Makes deltas into dark of every tree.

Great Paul, great pail of sound, still dip and draw
Dark speech from the deep and quiet steeple well,   20
Bring dark for doctrine, do but dim and quell
All voice in yours, while earth will give you breath.
Still gather to a language without flaw
Our loves, and all the hours of our death.

The Death of a Toad

A toad the power mower caught,
Chewed and clipped of a leg, with a hobbling hop has got
To the garden verge, and sanctuaried him
Under the cineraria leaves, in the shade
Of the ashen heartshaped leaves, in a dim,   5
Low, and a final glade.

The rare original heartsblood goes,
Spends on the earthen hide, in the folds and wizenings, flows
In the gutters of the banked and staring eyes. He lies
As still as if he would return to stone,   10
And soundlessly attending, dies
Toward some deep monotone,

Toward misted and ebullient seas
And cooling shores, toward lost Amphibia's emperies.
Day dwindles, drowning, and at length is gone   15
In the wide and antique eyes, which still appear
To watch, across the castrate lawn,
The haggard daylight steer.

7. **bavardage:** prattle.   14. **emperies:** absolute dominions.

PHILIP LARKIN [1922–   ]

Deceptions

*"Of course I was drugged, and so heavily I did not regain my consciousness till the next morning. I was horrified to discover that I had been ruined, and for some days I was inconsolable, and cried like a child to be killed or sent back to my aunt."—*Mayhew, London Labour and the London Poor.

Even so distant, I can taste the grief,
Bitter and sharp with stalks, he made you gulp.
The sun's occasional print, the brisk brief
Worry of wheels along the street outside
Where bridal London bows the other way,   5
And light, unanswerable and tall and wide,
Forbids the scar to heal, and drives
Shame out of hiding. All the unhurried day
Your mind lay open like a drawer of knives.

Slums, years, have buried you. I would not dare   10
Console you if I could. What can be said,
Except that suffering is exact, but where
Desire takes charge, readings will grow erratic?
For you would hardly care
That you were less deceived, out on that bed,   15
Than he was, stumbling up the breathless stair
To burst into fulfilment's desolate attic.

WILLIAM DEWITT SNODGRASS [1926–   ]

Orpheus

Stone lips to the unspoken cave;
Fingering the nervous strings, alone,
I crossed that gray sill, raised my head
To lift my song into the grave
Meanders of unfolding stone,   5
Following where the echo led
Down blind alleys of our dead.

Orpheus: legendary Greek whose power of song enabled him to enter the underworld in an attempt to bring back to life his beloved Eurydice.

Down the forbidden, backward street
To the lower town, condemned, asleep
In blank remembering mazes where   10
Smoke rose, the ashes hid my feet
And slow walls crumpled, settling deep
In rubble of the central square.
All ruin I could sound was there.

At the charred rail and windowsill,   15
Widows hunched in fusty shawls,
This only once the Furies wept;
The watchdog turned to hear me till
Head by head forgot its howls,
Loosed the torn images it kept,   20
Let sag its sore jaws and slept.

Then to my singing's radius
Seethed faces like a pauper's crowd
Or flies of an old injury.
The piteous dead who lived on us   25
Whined in my air, anarchic, loud
Till my soft voice that set them free,
Lost in this grievous enemy,

Rose up and laid them in low slumbers;
I meant to see in them what dark   30
Powers be, what eminent plotters.
Midmost those hushed, downcast numbers
Starved Tantalus stood upright, stark,
Waistdeep where the declining waters
Swelled their tides, where Danaus' daughters   35

Dropped in full surf their unfilled tub;
Now leaned against his rolling stone
Slept Sisyphus beneath the hill;
That screaming half-beast, strapped at the hub,
Whom Juno's animal mist had known,   40
Ixion's wheel creaked and was still.
I held all hell to hear my will.

18. **watchdog:** Cerberus, the three-headed dog.
33. **Tantalus:** a disloyal son of Zeus, punished by being placed up to his neck in a lake which receded when he tried to drink.
35. **Danaus' daughters:** for killing their husbands, they were condemned to pour water eternally into a broken cistern.
38. **Sisyphus:** for his avarice, he had to roll a huge stone incessantly to the top of a hill.
41. **Ixion:** for aspiring to Juno's love, Ixion was strapped to a perpetually turning wheel.

"Powers of the Underworld, who rule
All higher powers by graft or debt,
Within whose mortgage all men live: 45
No spy, no shining power's fool,
I think in the unthought worlds to get
The light you only freely give
Who are all bright worlds' negative

You gave wink in an undue crime   50
To love—strong even here, they say.
I sing, as the blind beggars sing,
To ask of you this little time
—All lives foreclose in their due day—
That flowered bride cut down in Spring,   55
Struck by the snake, your underling."

In one long avenue she was
Wandering toward me, vague, uncertain,
Limping a little still, the hair
And garments tenuous as gauze   60
And drifting loose like a white curtain
Vacillating in black night air
That holds white lilacs, God knows where.

"Close your eyes," said the inner ear;
"As night lookouts learn not to see   65
Ahead but only off one side,
As the eye's sight is never clear
But blind, dead center, you must be
Content; look not upon your bride
Till day's light lifts her eyelids wide."   70

I turned my back to her, set out
My own way back and let her follow
Like some curious albino beast
That prowls in areas of drought,
Lured past the town's slack doors, the hollow 75
Walls, the stream-bed lost in mist,
That breathless long climb, with no least

Doubt she must track me close behind;
As the actual scent of flesh, she must
Trail my voice unquestioning where.   80
Yet where the dawn first edged my mind
In one white flashing of mistrust
I turned and she, she was not there.
My hands closed on the high, thin air.

It was the nature of the thing: 85
No moon outlives its leaving night,
No sun its day. And I went on
Rich in the loss of all I sing
To the threshold of waking light,
To larksong and the live, gray dawn.   90
So night by night, my life has gone.

April Inventory

The green catalpa tree has turned
All white, the cherry blooms once more.
In one whole year I haven't learned
A blessed thing they pay you for.
The blossoms snow down in my hair;   5
The trees and I will soon be bare.

The trees have more than I to spare.
The sleek, expensive girls I teach,
Younger and pinker every year,
Bloom gradually out of reach.   10
The pear tree lets its petals drop
Like dandruff on a tabletop.

The girls have grown so young by now
I have to nudge myself to stare.
This year they smile and mind me how   15
My teeth are falling with my hair.
In thirty years I may not get
Younger, shrewder, or out of debt.

The tenth time, just a year ago,
I made myself a little list   20
Of all the things I'd ought to know;
Then told my parents, analyst,
And everyone who's trusted me
I'd be substantial, presently.

I haven't read one book about   25
A book or memorized one plot.
Or found a mind I did not doubt.
I learned one date. And then forgot.
And one by one the solid scholars
Get the degrees, the jobs, the dollars.   30

And smile above their starchy collars.
I taught my classes Whitehead's notions;
One lovely girl, a song of Mahler's.
Lacking a source-book or promotions,
I showed one child the colors of   35
A luna moth and how to love.

I taught myself to name my name,
To bark back, loosen love and crying;
To ease my woman so she came,
To ease an old man who was dying.   40
I have not learned how often I
Can win, can love, but choose to die.

I have not learned there is a lie
Love shall be blonder, slimmer, younger;
That my equivocating eye   45
Loves only by my body's hunger;
That I have poems, true to feel,
Or that the lovely world is real.

While scholars speak authority
And wear their ulcers on their sleeves,   50
My eyes in spectacles shall see
These trees procure and spend their leaves.
There is a value underneath
The gold and silver in my teeth.

Though trees turn bare and girls turn wives,   55
We shall afford our costly seasons;
There is a gentleness survives
That will outspeak and has its reasons.
There is a loveliness exists,
Preserves us, not for specialists.   60

JAMES WRIGHT [1927–   ]

At the Slackening of the Tide

Today I saw a woman wrapped in rags
Leaping along the beach to curse the sea.
Her child lay floating in the oil, away
From oarlock, gunwale, and the blades of oars.
The skinny lifeguard, raging at the sky,   5
Vomited sea, and fainted on the sand.

The cold simplicity of evening falls
Dead on my mind.
And underneath the piles the water
Leaps up, leaps up, and sags down slowly, farther   10
Than seagulls disembodied in the drag
Of oil and foam.

Plucking among the oyster shells a man
Stares at the sea, that stretches on its side.
Now far along the beach, a hungry dog   15
Announces everything I knew before:
Obliterate naiads weeping underground,
Where Homer's tongue thickens with human howls.

I would do anything to drag myself
Out of this place: 20
Root up a seaweed from the water,
To stuff it in my mouth, or deafen me,
Free me from all the force of human speech;
Go drown, almost.

Warm in the pleasure of the dawn I came   25
To sing my song
And look for mollusks in the shallows,
The whorl and coil that pretty up the earth,
While far below us, flaring in the dark,
The stars go out.   30

What did I do to kill my time today,
After the woman ranted in the cold,
The mellow sea, the sound blown dark as wine?
After the lifeguard rose up from the waves
Like a sea-lizard with the scales washed off?   35
Sit there, admiring sunlight on a shell?

Abstract with terror of the shell, I stared
Over the waters where
God brooded for the living all one day.
Lonely for weeping, starved for a sound of mourning,   40
I bowed my head, and heard the sea far off
Washing its hands.

17. **naiads:** sea nymphs.

ANNE SEXTON [1928–   ]

For God While Sleeping

Sleeping in fever, I am unfit
to know just who you are:
hung up like a pig on exhibit,
the delicate wrists,
the beard drooling blood and vinegar;   5
hooked to your own weight,
jolting toward death under your nameplate.

Everyone in this crowd needs a bath.
I am dressed in rags.
The mother wears blue. You grind your teeth   10
and with each new breath
your jaws gape and your diaper sags.
I am not to blame
for all this. I do not know your name.

Skinny man, you are somebody's fault.   15
You ride on dark poles—
a wooden bird that a trader built
for some fool who felt
that he could make the flight. Now you roll
in your sleep, seasick   20
on your own breathing, poor old convict.

JOHN MORRIS [1931–   ]

Shh! The Professor is Sleeping

He is a man who thinks
He sits in a tiny corner of the rain.

He is what he is not thinking of.
He is a large part of Japan.

He is closed, like a small business.   5
An illustration of the snow.

A Letter from a Friend

Let the robed kings march in the mind
As in the opulent eye of God,
But do not speak of them. Now is a time
For plain words and good order.

Nothing succeeds like winter.   5
Do not set up as an alarming
Eloquent boy of vivid habits.
Here even the good prosper.

Emulate the model poor,
For whom tact is the fine art.   10
The dead and the serious old
Do not expect the main things from us.

GREGORY CORSO [1934–   ]

Marriage

Should I get married? Should I be good?
Astound the girl next door
with my velvet suit and faustus hood?
Don't take her to movies but to cemeteries
tell all about werewolf bathtubs and forked clarinets   5
then desire her and kiss her and all the preliminaries
and she going just so far and I understanding why
not getting angry saying You must feel! It's beautiful to feel!
Instead take her in my arms lean against an old crooked tombstone
and woo her the entire night the constellations in the sky—   10

When she introduces me to her parents
back straightened, hair finally combed, strangled by a tie,
should I sit knees together on their 3rd-degree sofa
and not ask Where's the bathroom?
How else to feel other than I am,   15
often thinking Flash Gordon soap—
O how terrible it must be for a young man
seated before a family and the family thinking
We never saw him before! He wants our Mary Lou!
After tea and homemade cookies they ask What do you do for a
living?   20
Should I tell them? Would they like me then?
Say All right get married, we're losing a daughter
but we're gaining a son—
And should I then ask Where's the bathroom?

O God, and the wedding! All her family and her friends   25
and only a handful of mine all scroungy and bearded
just waiting to get at the drinks and food—
And the priest! he looking at me as if I masturbated
asking me Do you take this woman for your lawful wedded wife?
And I, trembling what to say say Pie Glue!   30

I kiss the bride all those corny men slapping me on the back:
She's all yours, boy! Ha-ha-ha!
And in their eyes you could see some obscene honeymoon going on—
Then all that absurd rice and clanky cans and shoes
Niagara Falls! Hordes of us! Husbands! Wives! Flowers! Chocolates!   35
All streaming into cozy hotels
All going to do the same thing tonight
The indifferent clerk he knowing what was going to happen
The lobby zombies they knowing what
The whistling elevator man he knowing   40
The winking bellboy knowing
Everybody knows! I'd be almost inclined not to do anything!
Stay up all night! Stare that hotel clerk in the eye!
Screaming: I deny honeymoon! I deny honeymoon!
running rampant into those almost climactic suites   45
yelling Radio belly! Cat shovel!
O I'd live in Niagara forever! in a dark cave beneath the Falls
I'd sit there the Mad Honeymooner
devising ways to break marriages, a scourge of bigamy
a saint of divorce—   50

But I should get married I should be good
How nice it'd be to come home to her
and sit by the fireplace and she in the kitchen
aproned young and lovely wanting my baby
and so happy about me she burns the roast beef   55
and comes crying to me and I get up from my big papa chair
saying Christmas teeth! Radiant brains! Apple deaf!
God what a husband I'd make! Yes, I should get married!
So much to do! like sneaking into Mr. Jones' house late at night
and cover his golf clubs with 1920 Norwegian books   60
Like hanging a picture of Rimbaud on the lawnmower
Like pasting Tannu Tuva postage stamps all over the picket fence
Like when Mrs. Kindhead comes to collect for the Community Chest
grab her and tell her There are unfavorable omens in the sky!
And when the mayor comes to get my vote tell him   65
When are you going to stop people killing whales!
And when the milkman comes leave him a note in the bottle
Penguin dust, bring me penguin dust, I want penguin dust—

Yet if I should get married and it's Connecticut and snow
and she gives birth to a child and I am sleepless, worn,   70
up for nights, head bowed against a quiet window, the past behind me
finding myself in the most common of situations a trembling man

61. **Rimbaud:** *avant-garde* French poet
(1854–1891).

knowledged with responsibility not twig-smear nor Roman coin soup
O what would that be like!
Surely I'd give it for a nipple a rubber Tacitus   75
For a rattle a bag of broken Bach records
Tack Della Francesca all over its crib
Sew the Greek alphabet on its bib
And build for its playpen a roofless Parthenon

No, I doubt I'd be that kind of father   80
not rural not snow no quiet window
but hot smelly tight New York City
seven flights up, roaches and rats in the walls
a fat Reichian wife screeching over potatoes Get a job!
And five nose-running brats in love with Batman   85
And the neighbors all toothless and dry haired
like those hag masses of the 18th century
all wanting to come in and watch TV
The landlord wants his rent

Grocery store Blue Cross Gas & Electric Knights of Columbus   90
Impossible to lie back and dream Telephone snow, ghost parking—
No! I should not get married I should never get married!
But—imagine if I were married to a beautiful sophisticated woman
tall and pale wearing an elegant black dress and long black gloves
holding a cigarette holder in one hand and a highball in the other   95
and we live high up in a penthouse with a huge window
from which we could see all of New York and even further on clearer
days
No, can't imagine myself married to that pleasant prison dream—

O but what about love? I forget love
not that I am incapable of love   100
it's just that I see love as odd as wearing shoes—
I never wanted to marry a girl who was like my mother
And Ingrid Bergman was always impossible
And there's maybe a girl now but she's already married
And I don't like men and—   105
but there's got to be somebody!
Because what if I'm 60 years old and not married,
all alone in a furnished room with pee stains on my underwear
and everybody else is married! All the universe married but me!

Ah, yet well I know that were a woman possible as I am possible   110
then marriage would be possible—
Like SHE in her lonely alien gaud waiting her Egyptian lover
so I wait—bereft of 2,000 years and the bath of life.

75. **Tacitus**: Roman historian (55–120).

ROBERT MEZEY [1935–   ]

A Coffee-House Lecture

Come now, you who carry
   Your passions on your back,
Will insolence and envy
   Get you the skill you lack?
Scorning the lonely hours   5
   That other men have spent,
How can you hope to fathom
   What made them eloquent?

Blake tells you in his notebooks,
   If you could understand,   10
That Style and Execution
   Are Feeling's only friend,
That all Poetic Wisdom
   Begins in the minute,
And Vision sees most clearly   15
   While fingering a lute.

Robert Burns in Ayreshire
   With meter and with gauge
Studied the strict exactitudes
   That luminate his page,   20
Ignored the vulgar grandeur
   That you and yours revere,
And labored with his body
   And his perfected ear.

Paul Valery gripped a scalpel   25
   And sweated at his task,
Bent over bleeding Chaos
   In spotless gown and mask;
And in reluctant lectures
   Spoke of the cruel art   30
And cold precise transactions
   That warm the human heart.

25. **Paul Valéry:** French poet (1871–1945).

How many that have toiled
  At the hard craft of verse
Had nothing more than music   35
  To fill their empty purse,
But found it was sufficient,
  In making out a will,
To pay for their mortality,
  And they are living still.   40

The Lovemaker

I see you in her bed,
Dark, rootless epicene,
Where a lone ghost is laid
And other ghosts convene;

And hear you moan at last   5
Your pleasure in the deep
Haven of her who kissed
Your blind mouth into sleep.

But the body, once enthralled,
Wakes in the chains it wore,   10
Dishevelled, stupid, cold,
And famished as before—

And hears its paragon
Breathe in the ghostly air,
Anonymous carrion,   15
Ravished by despair.

Lovemaker, I have felt
Desire taking my part,
But lacked your constant fault
And something of your art,   20

Unwilling to bend my knees
To such unmantled pride
As left you in that place,
Restless, unsatisfied.

Versification

THERE is no generally accepted scientific description of the sound-patterns of poetry, but there is a useful traditional way of talking about them. The main point to remember is that in most verse there is a theoretical, felt, regular rhythm, as in music, from which background the actual behavior of the spoken sounds varies considerably, line by line.

Theoretically, verse rhythm (*meter*), which is an alternating arrangement of spoken sounds, depends in English on various combinations of accented (*stressed*) and unaccented (*unstressed*) syllables.[1] The fundamental unit of these combinations in a line is the *foot*. There are four main varieties of feet, all illustrated in the Table below, in which stressed syllables are marked ´, unstressed syllables are marked ˘, and divisions between feet are marked /.

In the *iambic foot*, or *iamb* (the most common in English), one unstressed syllable precedes a stressed syllable. In the *trochaic foot*, or *trochee*, one unstressed syllable follows a stressed syllable. In the *dactylic foot*, or *dactyl*, two unstressed syllables follow a stressed syllable. In the *anapestic foot*, or *anapest*, two unstressed syllables precede a stressed syllable. In addition, two stressed syllables together form a *spondaic foot*, or *spondee* (as in the words *wave-like, heartbreak*); and two unstressed syllables together form a *Pyrrhic foot*, or *Pyrrhus*.

Each line of verse has a definite number of feet (see the examples in the Table). Two feet make a *dimeter* line, three a *trimeter*, four a *tetrameter*, five a *pentameter*, six a *hexameter*.

TABLE

Iambic Pentameter:

˘ ´ ˘ ´ ˘ ´ ˘ ´ ˘
But tar/ries yet/ the Cause/ for which/ He died.

Iambic Trimeter:

˘ ´ ˘ ´ ˘ ´
Let all/ the rest/ be thine.

[1] Theoretically, any phonetic qualities of a language may be organized metrically. In ancient Greek and Latin poetry, not stress or the degree of energy in utterance, but length of time of utterance, in terms of long and short syllables, was considered to form the pattern. The Greek terms to describe such patterns are the ones we use in English, but for us, of course, they are made to apply to stress phenomena.

[*621*]

Trochaic Tetrameter:

Thús the/ Bírch Cán/oe wás buíldéd.

Anapestic Dimeter:

With their skíts/ on the tíme.

Dactylic Hexameter, with last foot Trochaic:

Thís is the/ fórest prím/evál. The/ múrmuring/ pínes and the/ hémlocks . . .

In actuality no line achieves the exact regularity within each foot that the theoretical background rhythm calls for. For one thing, there are degrees of stress in English rather than an absolute distinction between the stressed and the unstressed syllable. An American speaker stresses the first and third syllables of *Pennsylvania*, but he stresses the third syllable more than the first. If he says *Pennsylvania Railroad*, he stresses *Rail-* more strongly than he does the other two stressed syllables, and if he says *The Pennsylvania Railroad is the main Pennsylvania railroad*, he is likely to stress *main* even more strongly. Similar phenomena appear in a line of poetry:

$$\text{I} \qquad 2 \qquad 3 \qquad 4 \qquad 5$$

Amíd/ the cír/cle, ón/ the gíld/ed mást.

Stresses 2, 4, and 5 should be strongest, Stress 1 should be weaker, and Stress 3 should be weakest (some would classify Stress 3 as unstressed, in which case the foot in which it occurs would be called a Pyrrhus). Reading the line so that each foot receives equal stress produces a monotonous, sing-song effect, and should be avoided. The variations referred to appear most strongly in iambic pentameter (as in the above example), the most frequent line in English; other kinds of verse may demand a more even stress and are more difficult to vary, as in this well-known nonsense:

> The boy stood on the burning deck,
> Eating peanuts by the peck.

This kind of line, the iambic tetrameter, invites monotonous delivery and is fatally easy to write. To a less degree the same is true, in English, of the dactylic hexameter, although there are a few obvious differentiations of stress in the example in the Table.

Besides the differences in degree of stress, another source of variation is the introduction into the fundamental beat of extra syllables or different kinds of feet:

Whére is/ it nów,/ the glór/y and/ the dréam?

Here, in a fundamentally iambic pentameter line, the first foot becomes a trochee (a very frequent device) and the fourth foot a Pyrrhus (alternatively, *and* may be explained as very lightly stressed). In another theoretically iambic pentameter example, the third foot becomes an anapest and an extra syllable is added to the last foot:

And so/ farewell/ to the lit/tle good/ you bear me.

A famous extreme example is Milton's theoretically iambic pentameter line in which the first three feet become spondees:

Rocks, caves,/ lakes, fens,/ bogs, dens,/ and shades/ of death.

Yet another source of variation is the *caesura*, or apparent pause, within the line. The example "Amid the circle,// on the gilded mast" exemplifies this device, as does "Where is it now,// the glory and the dream?" An opposite device is the *run-on line*, or *enjambment*, in which there is no pause between lines, as in these iambic pentameters with caesura within the lines:

> Feel we these things?—that moment we have stepped
> Into a sort of oneness, and our state
> Is like a floating spirit's. But there are
> Richer entanglements . . .

Lines at the end of which there is a strong pause, signified by a punctuation-mark, are called *end-stopped lines*.

Two modern departures from the orthodoxly defined stress pattern also need to be noted. In the verse of Gerard Manley Hopkins allowance is made for an indefinitely varying number of unstressed syllables associated with each stressed syllable (this is similar to the situation in Old English, or Anglo-Saxon, verse). Hopkins himself also distinguished two degrees of stress. The stronger is indicated here thus // :

> I caught this morning morning's minion, kingdom of daylight's
> dauphin dapple-dawn-drawn Falcon, in his riding
> Of the rolling level underneath him steady air, and striding . . .

In *free verse*, poets like Walt Whitman have liberated themselves from even the theoretical underlying regular stress pattern and have composed, in lines of irregular length, free cadences of stressed and unstressed syllables according to expressive need.

Although all the variations mentioned above are found in some of the greatest English poetry, it must not be thought that approximate regularity or a limited spectrum of variation is always or necessarily monotonous: the effect in context is what counts. The neoclassic verse of Pope, the incantatory tetrameters of Ben Jonson (as in "Queen and huntress," p. 109) or of W. H. Auden in the third part of "In Memory of W. B. Yeats" (p. 594), or the tetrameters and trimeters of the popular ballad achieve their special effect through a considerable degree of regularity.

Apart from rhythm and rhythmical variations other qualities of sound are important in poetry. Harsh and soft sounds, and monosyllabic and polysyllabic words, for instance, create quite different effects, depending on context. Traditional names have been given to the patterns resulting from resemblance among vowel sounds and among consonantal sounds. The repetition of the same sounds in the first syllables, or the first accented syllables, of words is called *alliteration:*

> Looking and *l*oving, our behaviors pass
> The *st*ones, the *st*eels, and the polished glass.

The repetition of the same vowel sounds is called *assonance:* "The *a*rmy of un*a*lterable l*aw*"; "Br*ea*thing like one that hath a w*ea*ry dr*ea*m." The repetition of consonantal sounds is called *consonance:* "And fee*d* dee*p*, dee*p* u*p*on her *p*eerless eyes."

The most obvious of the devices which use resemblance of sounds is the repetition of both vowel and consonantal sounds together, which is called *rhyme.* In the usual *end-rhyme* (at the end of lines), a repetition of sound in the last syllable (*return, unlearn*) is called *masculine rhyme*; if an unstressed syllable follows the stressed syllable (*returning, unlearning*), the rhyme is called *feminine.* Rhymes of three syllables, or more, generally have a comic effect (*uniform, cuneiform*). Rhymes within a line are *internal:*

> We are the first that ever burst
> Into that silent sea.

Many poets in the past and most poets today use *imperfect* (or *slant,* or *off*) rhymes, in which the vowel or consonantal agreement is not exact (*love, remove; soul, oil*), in order to avoid monotony or for some other purpose. In older poetry what seems to us an imperfect rhyme may have been pronounced as a perfect rhyme by the writer:

> Yet from my lord shall not my foot remove:
> Sweet is the death that taketh end by love.

In the sixteenth century, when this was written, *love* was pronounced to rhyme perfectly with *remove.*

End-rhyme is not used in the most popular verse form in English, *blank verse,* which is unrhymed iambic pentameter, as used in Shakespearean drama, Milton's *Paradise Lost,* or Wordsworth's "Yew Trees" (p. 294). Also, end-rhyme is not used in free verse.

On the other hand, end-rhyme is used, for instance, to establish a two-line unit called the iambic *couplet,* which appears in Chaucer's *Canterbury Tales* and in Ben Jonson's "To Penshurst" (p. 102). In its developed form—end-stopped, with exactly ten syllables per line and with marked caesura—it is the *heroic couplet* of Alexander Pope and others:

> Know then thyself, presume not God to scan;
> The proper study of mankind is man.

Iambic tetrameter (or, loosely, octosyllabic) couplets have also been popular: as noted above, the line is difficult to vary, but Andrew Marvell varies it expertly in "To His Coy Mistress" (p. 170, *ll.* 5–10, for example).

Rhyme is of course used in more complicated patterns, or *rhyme-schemes*. These may conveniently be indicated by a series of letters in which each of the recurring rhymes is designated by one letter. *Terza rima* has the scheme aba bcb cdc ded, and so on (see Shelley's "Ode to the West Wind," p. 334); this scheme is borrowed from Italian verse.

The group of lines through which a rhyme-scheme extends is called a *stanza*; and in poems of more than one stanza the rhyme-scheme is generally repeated without variation in each succeeding stanza, although a poet may modify the resulting sense of recurrence by introducing a new pattern. Another determinant of stanza pattern in addition to rhyme-scheme may be an alternation of longer and shorter lines.

A stanza of four lines is a *quatrain*. If it rhymes abab and alternates tetrameter and trimeter lines, it is a *ballad stanza* (see "Barbara Allan," p. 11). A stanza of seven iambic pentameter lines rhyming ababbcc was used by Chaucer and has been much imitated. It is called *rime royal*. *Ottava rima* is an eight-line stanza rhyming abababcc (see the last eight lines of Milton's "Lycidas," p. 142). It is the stanza of Byron's *Don Juan*. The *Spenserian Stanza*, developed by Spenser for *The Faerie Queene*, has eight lines of iambic pentameter and a ninth line of iambic hexameter, rhyming ababbcbcc. In spite of the difficulty of composing nine lines with only three rhyme-sounds, it has been much imitated (see Keats' "The Eve of St. Agnes," p. 354).

The *sonnet* is a poem of one stanza usually containing 14 lines, although in the Renaissance the term might be used for any short lyric. The *Shakespearean*, or *English*, *Sonnet* is made up of three quatrains and a couplet of iambic pentameter lines, rhyming abab cdcd efef gg (see Shakespeare's *Sonnets*, pp. 57–64). The *Petrarchan*, or *Italian*, *Sonnet*, a form borrowed from the sonnets of the Italian Petrarch (1304–74) and his followers, is composed of an eight-line unit, called the *octave*, rhyming abba abba, plus a concluding six-line unit, called the *sestet*, which may be rhymed in a variety of ways, often ending in English examples with a couplet (see Wyatt's "My galley charged with Forgetfulness," p. 18).

A *refrain* is a line or series of lines which reappear from stanza to stanza throughout a poem, as in many popular ballads, in Chaucer's (?) "A Ballade Against Woman Inconstant," and in Spenser's "Prothalamion."

Poetic Meaning

JUST as there is a traditional terminology for discussing how sound is used in poetry, so there is another terminology to discuss the poetic use of meaning. We cannot describe here the complex and necessary ways in which meanings in poetry are indirect or interrelated, but it is useful to understand the terms with which these matters have most usually been talked about. Modern criticism has shown that most or all of these terms need refinement if we are to come to grips with how poetry means; but no new terminology is in general use, and each of the older terms stands for a distinction which has some significance.

If something is said to be or act like something else, the resulting expression is *simile*: "As flies to boys, so are we to the gods:/ They kill us for their sport." If we mean that something is like something else, but speak as though the two things were the same, the result is *metaphor*: "The wolf at the door has eaten my lamb, for I have lost my daughter to pay my mortgage"; "In me thou see'st the twilight of such day/ As after sunset fadeth in the West." An object, event, or situation which exists in itself in a poem but also by its qualities evokes or stands for another meaning is a *symbol*; it is a concrete entity, but through its concrete qualities summons up a nexus of ideas and associations, not by metaphorical comparison, but through a kind of equivalency, although in practice the distinction between the metaphorical and the symbolic is fluctuating: the sun is often used as a symbol of God or majesty, because of its qualities; the Byzantium which Yeats creates in "Sailing to Byzantium" is a symbol of eternal ideas and enduring artistic creations outside the realm of nature, as opposed to the ever-changing round of birth and death in nature, partly because of the fixed, changeless "gold mosaic" and golden bird which Yeats associates with Byzantium, but also because of our own ideas of Byzantium as a fixed, changeless society (even though the Byzantine Empire was not really like that at all). Alternatively, the mosaic and the bird are symbols of much the same meaning: a single word or a whole poem may function symbolically.

Another term for an ancient and widely used indirect meaning is *personification*, which is the attribution of human qualities to something inanimate or to a concept: "The cruel sea"; "When I have seen by Time's fell hand defaced . . ." A narrative in which personifications are the actors is an *allegory*.

Irony is a term which has extended its meaning for modern critics: it may be used to describe almost any literary procedure in which two contrasting or greatly differing attitudes are implied. Special poetic modes for approaching one matter in terms of another, or two matters simultaneously, are numerous (some may be described as ironic, others not). One such mode known to everyone is the *Aesopic fable*, in which the behavior of beasts is made to refer to that of men. Another less familiar one, which is more important for poetry, is the *pastoral mode*, in which the speech and actions of simple, humble people in a traditional, rural environment are made to contrast with, or parallel, or comment in some fashion on, another, generally contrasting environment. The oldest form of this mode, going back to very ancient Greek poetry, has to do with shepherds (*pastoral* means "pertaining to shepherds"). Milton uses the convention in its original form in "Lycidas," and his implied comparison of the duties, pleasures, and milieu of the shepherds of ancient poetry with the contemporary concerns of his poem are one of the most perfect specimens of the indirection by which a poem may say what it has to say.

OTHER TERMS:

Emblem is an entity which arbitrarily (not by reason of its own qualities) is made to stand for something else. Thus the cross stands for Christianity; blue, in Chaucer's (?) "A Ballade Against Woman Inconstant," stands for faithful love contrasted to fickleness (green). Sometimes emblem is considered a kind of symbol; sometimes it is thought of as opposed to the symbol, in which case it is often called a *sign*.

Synecdoche substitutes a part for the whole ("Nay, if you read this line, remember not/ The *hand* that writ it") or the whole for the part ("I put the package in my *coat*").

Metonymy, a more general term, is the use of one word for another which it suggests ("a statement from the *White House*").

Oxymoron is a contradiction ("And then there crept/ A little *noiseless noise* among the leaves,/ Born of the very *sigh which silence heaves*").

Hyperbole is willful exaggeration, for humorous or serious purposes ("Blind with thine hair the eyes of day"). Its opposite is *understatement*, or (loosely) *litotes* ("*not a few* people dislike ice cream in salads").

Apostrophe is direct address to a person or thing absent or present ("With how sad steps, O moon, thou climb'st the skies!").

Antithesis parallels opposing ideas ("With mirth in funeral, and with dirge in marriage").

Paradox states a truth in what seem absurd terms ("Man is born to die"; "The pen is mightier than the sword"), or contradictory terms ("O Grave, where is thy victory?").

General Bibliography

General History and Reference

R. D. Altick and A. Wright, *Selective Bibliography for the Study of English and American Literature* (1960).

George Arms and J. M. Kuntz (eds.), *Poetry Explication* (1950).

F. W. Bateson (ed.), *The Cambridge Bibliography of English Literature* (4 vols., 1941); Supplement ed. by George Watson to 1955.

A. C. Baugh and others, *A Literary History of England* (1948).

Carl Beckson and A. Ganz, *A Reader's Guide to Literary Terms* (1960).

Hardin Craig and others, *A History of English Literature* (1950).

Arthur G. Kennedy, *A Concise Bibliography for Students of English* (1954).

R. E. Spiller and others, *Literary History of the United States* (1948) (Vol. III, Bibliography, edited by Thomas H. Johnson).

W. F. Thrall and A. Hibbard, *A Handbook to Literature*, revised by H. Holman, (1960).

Influential Literary Criticism

Maud Bodkin, *Archetypal Patterns in Poetry* (1934).

Cleanth Brooks, *The Well Wrought Urn* (1947).

Ronald Crane, *The Language of Criticism and the Structure of Poetry* (1953).

T. S. Eliot, *Selected Essays* (1951); *On Poetry and Poets* (1957).

William Empson, *Seven Types of Ambiguity* (3rd edition, 1953).

Northrop Frye, *Anatomy of Criticism* (1957).

F. R. Leavis, *Revaluation* (1936).

J. L. Lowes, *The Road to Xanadu* (rev. 1930).

I. A. Richards, *Principles of Literary Criticism* (5th edition, 1934); *Practical Criticism* (1930).

Lionel Trilling, *The Liberal Imagination* (1948).

René Wellek and Austin Warren, *Theory of Literature* (1942).

Special Periods

The Middle Ages

H. S. Bennett, *Chaucer and the Fifteenth Century* (1947).

W. L. Renwick and H. Orton, *The Beginnings of English Literature to Skelton* (rev. 1952).

D. M. Zesmer, *Guide to English Literature from Beowulf through Chaucer . . .* (1961).

[*629*]

The Sixteenth Century

Douglas Bush, *Mythology and the Renaissance Tradition in English Poetry.* (1932)
C. S. Lewis, *English Literature in the Sixteenth Century* . . . (1954).
V. de Sola Pinto, *The English Renaissance* (1938).
Hallett Smith, *Elizabethan Poetry* (1952).

The Seventeenth Century in England

Douglas Bush, *English Literature in the Earlier Seventeenth Century* (1945).
Rosemond Tuve, *Elizabethan and Metaphysical Imagery* (1947).
Ruth Wallerstein, *Studies in 17th Century Poetic* (1950).
C. V. Wedgwood, *Seventeenth Century English Literature* (1950).

The Eighteenth Century in England

Bonamy Dobrée, *English Literature in the Early Eighteenth Century, 1700–1740* (1959).
Ian Jack, *Augustan Satire* . . . , *1660–1750* (1952).
A. D. McKillop, *English Literature from Dryden to Burns* (1948).
J. M. Sutherland, *A Preface to Eighteenth-Century Poetry* (1948).
J. M. Sutherland, *English Satire* (1955).

The Romantic Period in England

M. H. Abrams, *The Mirror and the Lamp: Romantic Theory and the Critical Tradition* (1953).
Ernest Bernbaum, *Guide Through the Romantic Movement* (2nd edition, 1949).
Harold Bloom, *The Visionary Company: A Reading of English Romantic Poetry* (1961).
Douglas Bush, *Mythology and the Romantic Tradition in English Poetry* (1937).
C. W. Houchens and L. H. Houchens, *The English Romantic Poets and Essayists* (1957).
Graham Hough, *The Romantic Poets* (1953).
Mario Praz, *The Romantic Agony* (1933).
T. M. Raysor (ed.), *The English Romantic Poets, a Review of Research* (rev. 1956).

The Victorian Period in England

F. E. Faverty (ed.), *The Victorian Poets, A Guide to Research* (1956).
Graham Hough, *The Last Romantics* (1949).
E. D. H. Johnson, *The Alien Vision of Victorian Poetry* (1952).
R. Langbaum, *The Poetry of Experience* (1957).
F. L. Lucas, *Ten Victorian Poets* (1940).

The Moderns in England

D. Daiches, *The Present Age in British Literature* (1958).
G. S. Fraser, *The Modern Writer and His World* (1953).
F. R. Leavis, *New Bearings in English Poetry* (2nd edition, 1950).
F. B. Millett, *Contemporary British Literature* (1935).
W. Y. Tindall, *Forces in Modern British Literature* (1956).

American Literature

R. P. Blackmur, *Language as Gesture* (1952); (also includes essays on modern British poetry).
Louise Bogan, *Achievement in American Poetry* (*1900–1950*), (1951).
Horace Gregory and Marya Zaturenska, *A History of American Poetry* (*1900–1940*), (1946).
F. O. Matthiessen, *American Renaissance* (1941).

Index

INDEX

vi